5-28-04

6/04

4 WEEKS

P9-CNH-722

The Guermantes
Way

Marcel Proust

The Guermantes Way

Translated with an Introduction
and Notes by Mark Treharne

GENERAL EDITOR:
CHRISTOPHER PRENDERGAST

VIKING

VIKING
Published by the Penguin Group
Penguin Group (USA) Inc., 375 Hudson Street,
New York, New York 10014, U.S.A.
Penguin Books Ltd, 80 Strand, London WC2R 0RL, England
Penguin Books Australia Ltd, 250 Camberwell Road, Camberwell,
Victoria 3124, Australia
Penguin Books Canada Ltd, 10 Alcorn Avenue, Toronto, Ontario, Canada M4V 3B2
Penguin Books India (P) Ltd, 11 Community Centre, Panchsheel Park,
New Delhi–110 017, India
Penguin Books (N.Z.) Ltd, Cnr Rosedale and Airborne Roads, Albany,
Auckland, New Zealand
Penguin Books (South Africa) (Pty) Ltd, 24 Sturdee Avenue,
Rosebank, Johannesburg 2196,
South Africa

Penguin Books Ltd, Registered Offices: 80 Strand, London WC2R 0RL, England

First American edition
Published in 2004 by Viking Penguin, a member of Penguin Group (USA) Inc.

1 3 5 7 9 10 8 6 4 2

Translation, introduction, and notes copyright © Mark Treharne, 2002
Note on the translation copyright © Lydia Davis, 2002
All rights reserved

LIBRARY OF CONGRESS CATALOGING-IN-PUBLICATION DATA
Proust, Marcel, 1871–1922.
[Côté de Guermantes. English]
The Guermantes way / Marcel Proust ; translated with an introduction
by Mark Treharne ; general editor Christopher Prendergast.
p.   cm.
Includes bibliographical references.
ISBN 0-670-03317-0
1. France–Social life and customs–Fiction. I. Treharne, Mark.
II. Prendergast, Christopher. III. Title.
PQ2631.R63C7413 2004   2003066571

This book is printed on acid-free paper. ∞

Printed in the United States of America
Set in Berthold Garamond
Designed by Francesca Belanger

Contents

Introduction

The Guermantes Way was published by Gallimard in two parts, in 1920 and 1921 respectively. The two parts corresponded to the present bipartite division of the book, but the second volume of the original edition, emphasizing the temporal and thematic link between *Guermantes* and the ensuing part of the sequence, included the opening section of *Sodom and Gomorrah*, which was subsequently annexed to its appropriate place at the beginning of that volume.

If the various parts of *In Search of Lost Time* were published in the sequence now familiar to us, it is well known that the genesis of that sequence was complex. *The Guermantes Way* was originally the title of the second part of a tripartite work. Following the publication of the first part (*Swann's Way*) by Grasset in 1913, *Guermantes* had been scheduled to appear (with the same publisher) the following year, as the second part. However, the 1914–18 war interrupted preparations for publication of this original version of *Guermantes* and was cause for major alterations and additions to the project of a tripartite work. The principal addition was the introduction of Albertine, which was to lead Proust to reconceive his whole cycle in seven parts. The introduction of Albertine into the narrative necessitated a rearrangement of the expanded material, which resulted in the creation of the volume *In the Shadow of Young Girls in Flower* as the second part of the cycle and a shift in the *Guermantes* material to its present place as the third part and alteration of its original content. The war also brought about a change of publisher: in 1916, Proust transferred his work to Gallimard.

The first sketches of the material we now recognize as *The Guer-*

mantes Way date back as far as 1909. A notebook of that year contains early drafts of the grandmother's death. A series of notebooks from 1910 and 1911 contain the early versions of material reflecting the principal social episodes of *Guermantes* as we now know it: the move to a new apartment in Paris; the narrator's fantasies about the name Guermantes; the Villeparisis afternoon party and evening reception; the narrator's various attempts to draw close to the Duchesse de Guermantes; a gala evening at the theater; attending the theater with Montargis (the original name given to Saint-Loup) and his mistress; a period in a garrison town, including dinner with the Guermantes; an invitation from the Princesse de Guermantes. Worked into continuous narrative, the original version of *Guermantes* was sent to Grasset, and proofs had begun to reach Proust by 1914. He seems to have returned to these proofs only in 1916, after his change of publisher, and his lengthy additions to them made new proofs necessary; the new proofs in turn were subject to additions and changes. The main decision about the *Guermantes* material during the war, apart from the introduction of episodes concerning Albertine, was the one made to place the episode of the grandmother's illness and death in this part of the cycle, and to place it centrally. This has important implications for the reading of *Guermantes*, and I shall return to them shortly. Other important additions were the encounters between the narrator and Charlus; symmetrically placed in each part of *Guermantes* after a lengthy society scene, they hark back to and develop upon previous encounters with Charlus in *In the Shadow of Young Girls in Flower* and anticipate the overt revelations of what Proust called "sexual inversion" in *Sodom and Gomorrah*.

It is not entirely clear whether *Guermantes* was published in two parts for reasons of expediency or by deliberate intention, but one of the most striking features of its bipartite structure is the distribution of the material dealing with the grandmother's illness and death. Proust seems to have made a conscious decision to present that material as a divided episode. Part I ends with the stroke that anticipates the grandmother's death in the first short chapter of Part II, so the two parts of the book are "hinged" on this centrally placed material. Interestingly, Part II itself concludes with a parallel anticipation, the death of Swann, in an episode in which the compulsive charade of social obligations is used to mask the penury of ethical responsibility toward a dying friend. This itself contrasts ironically with the grandmother's compassionate attempts, in the concluding episode of Part I, to mask her stroke from her grandson. The terms in which she does so (the parallel she draws between the genteel posturing of a public lavatory attendant–the "Marquise"–and the conduct of society people) carry their own implicit condemnation of the social world into which the narrator is now being drawn. In a late addition to the opening passage of *Guermantes*, Proust had inserted a further anticipatory reminder of this kind by presenting the poor state of the grandmother's health as the reason for the move to a new apartment. There seems to be a deliberate strategy to frame *The Guermantes Way* in black, to emphasize that its world of social activity unfolds amid death and loss (actual or anticipated). The impression is reinforced by details in other episodes in the text: for instance, the narrator's anxiety in the telephone conversation with his grandmother from Doncières, where he casts himself as Orpheus "repeating the name of his dead wife," and his return to Paris to discover a "ghostly image" of her as "a crushed old woman whom I did not know"; similarly, the material at the end of Part II dealing with the dying Marquis d'Osmond accentuates the episode of the Duchesse's red shoes and heightens the sense of mortality which the social world of the book would seek to deny.

If death and loss are presences in *Guermantes*, they are held at bay by the focus on a social world obsessed with appearances, whose peculiar ethics is unable to respond adequately to them. Interesting in this respect is the fact that the narrator himself refrains, in these volumes, from any account of the immediate effect of his grandmother's death upon him. The affective impact is to be treated later, in *Sodom and Gomorrah*, although Proust had at one stage planned the two episodes in sequence. All this is sufficiently in keeping with the narrator's social infatuations and aspirations in *Guermantes*, and it is further emphasized by the preoccupation of Proust's reworkings and additions to the episode of the grandmother's death with presenting it in a "society" context–practitioners favored by society people (it is the Duc de Guermantes who recommends Dieulafoy as he might recommend a "top-quality caterer"), the emphasis on visits to a dying woman as part of a social ritual, and, not least, Françoise's inclination to see death in terms of a spectacle demanding the appropriate sort of staging and costume: "She had ordered herself a mourning outfit. . . . In most women's lives, everything, even the greatest sorrow, comes down to a question of 'I haven't got a thing to wear.' " The final generalization here resonates with another passage, early in the first part of *Guermantes*, where the narrator glimpses Mme de Guermantes playing out the role of a "fashionable woman" and envying the style of smartly dressed actresses.

Playing out a role: notations of theatricality—and they abound—are an important feature of the way the society world is presented by Proust. In fact, the narrator's access to this world is carefully prefaced in *Guermantes* by theater scenes. They function rather differently but contribute to the presentation of social life as an addictive theatrical performance which helps both to pass the time and to anesthetize awareness of the fact that time in the end runs out, that death and loss are inevitable. The first of these theater episodes, the gala evening at the Opéra, cleverly dramatizes a deflection of the narrator's interest from the art of La Berma (which he has so far failed to appreciate and now finally manages to grasp), toward the illusory magic of the main theatrical event of his evening, the glittering spectacle of the Princesse de Guermantes's theater box, presented in an extended metaphor of a world of mythical marine deities. The metaphor is a vivid translation of the narrator's absorption, and its elaboration is so engaging that it is easy to neglect the nature of that absorption—he is being drowned in an illusion. At the beginning of the book, his fantasies about the name Guermantes (familiar to the reader of "Combray") seem to be partly dispelled by various prosaic details conveyed to him by Saint-Loup, but fantasy assumes a new lease on life when, learning that the Duchesse de Guermantes reigns supreme over the Faubourg Saint-Germain, he begins to invest her name with further images of a glamorous and inaccessible world. So, when in the course of this evening at the Opéra the Duchesse de Guermantes enters her cousin's box—a deliberately staged late entrance, with far more impact upon the narrator than La Berma's stage entrance—and unexpectedly acknowledges his presence with a smile (conveyed in a sentence that surely reads as ironical hyperbole), he is won over into illusion and propelled upon the quest for access to this woman and her world. That world is presented to us as a series of performances, and its salons and dinner parties are characterized by an insistence on setting, entries and exits, ritualized codes and gestures, the pageantry of aristocratic titles, the need to adopt roles and to impress an audience, fastidious consciousness of dress and fashion. This is perhaps slightly less true of the mixed and uneven society entertained by Mme de Villeparisis, a woman of some accomplishment whose aspirations are partly motivated by the kinds of cultural values the tutelary grandmother (her old school friend) tries to instill in the narrator. But she is also motivated by social aspirations and rivalries, and her salon, frequented not only by intellectuals but by her Guermantes relations, is a confused dumb-show in which her intellectual acquaintances are at a loss how to conduct themselves adequately with her more aristocratic callers. The comic charade with hats that runs as a theme throughout the narrator's afternoon visit to her salon underlines the disparity of mind and attitude among her various guests, whose conversations reflect a fragmented medley of evasiveness, ignorant assertion, rivalry, prejudice, sheer malice, and, famously in the case of Norpois on Dreyfus, the art of saying nothing.

Proust chooses to preface the Villeparisis afternoon reception with another theater episode, which dramatizes a whole series of disconcerting behavioral and sexual conundrums (Rachel's exchanges with the ambivalent dancer, her sadistic provocation of Saint-Loup; violent physical exchanges between Saint-Loup and a journalist and, slightly later, with a man who accosts him in the street). Here the narrator speculates on the real motivations of actors under their greasepaint masks, on the way in which the stage uses distance and disguise convincingly, whereas in close-up and unmasked, actors can lose their glamour (Rachel is the particular case in point here), though their offstage behavior is not necessarily any less of a disguise, any the less illusive and enigmatic. If I stress this episode, it is because it sets the scene for the kind of activity the narrator is to observe with some bafflement in the salons and dinner parties he is to attend. The point is emphasized in the predilection of society people for the theatricals, recitations, and fancy-dress balls that are frequently referred to. The second of the two long set-pieces in the book (the Guermantes dinner party), if we compare it with the salon of Mme de Villeparisis, is a deliberately staged event. The whole theatrical performance centers upon the parade of "wit" from the star performer, Mme de Guermantes, with her husband acting out the role of her impresario. This wit is a variously deployed mask and involves the ability to make puns, to undermine a range of standard assumptions, to ridicule the vulnerable points of other people (particularly if they offer any threat of rivalry or competition) in ironical or purely malicious anecdote, to trivialize serious issues (the Dreyfus Affair, for instance, becomes a convenient pretext for witty repartee; a Maeterlinck play, the opportunity for a vicious attack on Rachel). Of course it demands a willing audience, but to be invited to her house is already to have submitted to snobbish captivation, and her guests are unquestioning of the power she holds over them, and also fearful of her. Her abilities as an actress are to do with holding people at the distance that suits her and thereby maintaining a safe distance between herself and issues that could demand serious ethical or intellectual commitment. Maintaining a glittering social position demands the ironic touch of an Offenbach operetta, not the capacity to confront pain and loss. Mme de Guermantes's theatrical masquerades will ultimately result not in power over others but in loss of social status: in *Finding Time Again*, we are told that one of the reasons her social position has declined is precisely that she consorts too much with actresses. In a neat reversal of fortunes, she has sought out the actress she had previously so bitchily denigrated, Rachel, and Rachel herself, in the final party of the whole book, has eclipsed Mme de Guermantes and become the darling of society receptions.

In *Guermantes*, the narrator, admitted to the Duchesse's society after he has been cured of his infatuation with her, tends to record what he sees and hears, to note the disparity between glamour seen from a distance and the triviality it masks when encountered at close quarters. His reflections in the cab taking him on to the Baron de Charlus after the

Guermantes dinner party hint, but only hint, at the possible use his observations might have. His ultimate reflections on this society world will await the postwar presentation of it in *Finding Time Again* and the grimmest piece of social theater in the whole work, the dance of death represented by the afternoon reception of a Princesse de Guermantes very different from the one he is to encounter at the peak of his social accession in *Sodom and Gomorrah*. By that point in the cycle, of course, the narrator will be able to offer a concerted account of his creative intentions. In *Guermantes*, he is still an apprentice, and although he reminds us here that his narrative is the history of an "invisible vocation," what he is essentially recording is a world of dispersion and dissimulation, and the way that his creative energies were distracted by social life.

I should, finally, like to acknowledge my debt to the Moncrieff/Kilmartin edition revised by D. J. Enright. I have worked very much in the shadow of these previous translators and with much gratitude toward them.

Mark Treharne

A Note on the Translation

The present translation came into being in the following way. A project was conceived by the Penguin UK Modern Classics series in which the whole of *In Search of Lost Time* would be translated freshly on the basis of the latest and most authoritative French text, *À la recherche du temps perdu,* edited by Jean-Yves Tadié (Paris: Pléiade, Gallimard, 1987–89). The translation would be done by a group of translators, each of whom would take on one of the seven volumes. The project was directed first by Paul Keegan, then by Simon Winder, and was overseen by general editor Christopher Prendergast. I was contacted early in the selection process, in the fall of 1995, and I chose to translate the first volume, *Swann's Way.* The other translators are James Grieve, for *In the Shadow of Young Girls in Flower;* Mark Treharne, for *The Guermantes Way;* John Sturrock, for *Sodom and Gomorrah;* Carol Clark, for *The Prisoner;* Peter Collier, for *The Fugitive;* and Ian Patterson, for *Finding Time Again.*

Between 1996 and the delivery of our manuscripts, the tardiest in mid-2001, we worked at different rates in our different parts of the world—one in Australia, one in the United States, the rest in various parts of England. After a single face-to-face meeting in early 1998, which most of the translators attended, we communicated with one another and with Christopher Prendergast by letter and e-mail. We agreed, often after lively debate, on certain practices that needed to be consistent from one volume to the next, such as retaining French titles like Duchesse de Guermantes, and leaving the quotations that occur within the text—from Racine, most notably—in the original French, with translations in the notes.

At the initial meeting of the Penguin Classics project, those present had acknowledged that a degree of heterogeneity across the volumes was inevitable and perhaps even desirable, and that philosophical differences would exist among the translators. As they proceeded, therefore, the translators worked fairly independently and decided for themselves how close their translations should be to the original—how many liberties, for instance, might be taken with the sanctity of Proust's long sentences. And Christopher Prendergast, as he reviewed all the translations, kept his editorial hand relatively light. The Penguin UK translation appeared in October 2002, in six hardcover volumes and as a boxed set.

Some changes may be noted in this American edition, besides the adoption of American spelling conventions. One is that the UK decision concerning quotations within the text has been reversed, and all the French has been translated into English, with the original quotations in the notes. We have also replaced the French punctuation of dialogue, which uses dashes and omits certain opening and closing quotation marks, with standard American dialogue punctuation, though we have respected Proust's paragraphing decisions—sometimes long exchanges take place within a single paragraph, while in other cases each speech begins a new paragraph.

Lydia Davis

Suggestions for Further Reading

Beckett, Samuel. *Proust.* New York: Grove Press, 1931.

Carter, William C. *Marcel Proust: A Life.* New Haven and London: Yale University Press, 2000.

Milly, Jean. *La Phrase de Proust.* Paris: Éditions Champion, 1983.

Painter, George D. *Proust: The Later Years.* Boston: Atlantic–Little, Brown, 1965.

Proust, Marcel. *Remembrance of Things Past,* vol. 3: *The Guermantes Way,* tr. C. K. Scott Moncrieff. New York: Modern Library, 1933.

——. *À la recherche du temps perdu,* ed. Jean-Yves Tadié, vol. 2: *À l'ombre de jeunes filles en fleurs* (second part) and *Le Côté de Guermantes.* Paris: Pléiade, Gallimard, 1988.

——. *In Search of Lost Time,* vol. 3: *The Guermantes Way,* tr. C. K. Scott Moncrieff and Terence Kilmartin, rev. D. J. Enright. New York: Random House, 1992.

Shattuck, Roger. *Proust's Binoculars: A Study of Memory, Time and Recognition in* À la recherche du temps perdu. New York: Random House, 1963.

——. *Proust's Way: A Field Guide to* In Search of Lost Time. New York: W. W. Norton & Co., 2000.

Tadié, Jean-Yves. *Marcel Proust: A Life,* tr. Euan Cameron. New York: Viking, 2000.

White, Edmund. *Marcel Proust.* New York: Viking, 1999.

For Léon Daudet.[1]
Author of
Le Voyage de Shakespeare,
Le Partage de l'enfant,
L'Astre noir,
Fantômes et vivants,
Le Monde des images,
and so many masterpieces.

To the perfect friend,
as a token of
gratitude and admiration.

M.P.

PART I

THE EARLY-MORNING TWITTER of the birds sounded tame to Françoise. Every word from the maids' quarters made her jump; their every footstep bothered her, and she was constantly wondering what they were doing. All this was because we had moved. It is true that the servants in our former home had made quite as much stir in their quarters on the top floor, but they were servants she knew, and their comings and goings had become friendly presences to her. Now she even made silence the object of her painful scrutiny. And since the district to which we had moved appeared to be as quiet as the boulevard we had previously looked out upon was noisy, the sound of a man singing in the street as he passed (as feeble perhaps as an orchestral motif, yet quite clear even from a distance) brought tears to the eyes of the exiled Françoise. And if I had made fun of her when she had been distressed at leaving an apartment building where we had been "so well thought of by everybody," weeping as she packed her trunks in accordance with the rituals of Combray and declaring that our former home was superior to any other imaginable, I, who found it as difficult to assimilate new surroundings as I found it easy to abandon old ones, nonetheless felt a close sympathy with our old servant when I realized that the move to a building where the concierge, who had not yet made our acquaintance, had not shown her the tokens of respect necessary to the nourishment of her good spirits had driven her to a state close to total decline. She alone could understand my feelings; this was certainly not the case with her young footman; for him, a person as remote from the Combray world as it was possible to be, moving into a

new district was like taking a holiday in which the novelty of the surroundings provided the same sense of relaxation as an actual journey;
he felt he was in the country, and a headcold gave him the delightful
sensation, as if he had been a victim of a draft from the ill-fitting window of a railway carriage, of having seen something of the world; every
time he sneezed, he rejoiced that he had found such a select position,
having always wanted to work for people who traveled a great deal. And
so it was not to him I went, but straight to Françoise; and because I had
laughed at her tears over a departure that had not affected me in the
least, she now showed a frosty indifference to my misery, because she
shared it. The so-called sensitivity of neurotics develops along with their
egotism; they cannot bear it when other people flaunt the sufferings
with which they are increasingly preoccupied themselves. Françoise,
who would not allow the least of her own troubles to pass unobserved,
would turn her head away if I was suffering, so that I should not have
the satisfaction of seeing my suffering pitied, let alone noticed. This is
what happened when I tried to talk to her about our move. What is
more, she was obliged, two days later, to return to our former home to
collect some clothes that had been forgotten in the move, while I, as a
result of the same move, was still running a temperature and, like a boa
constrictor that has just swallowed an ox, was feeling painfully swollen
by the sight of a long sideboard that my eyes needed to "digest"; and
Françoise, with a woman's inconstancy, returned home saying that she
thought she was going to choke to death on our old boulevard, that she
had gone "all around the houses" to get there, that never had she seen
such awkward stairs, that she would not go back there to live for all the
world, not if you were to offer her a fortune—unlikely hypotheses—and
that *everything* (meaning everything to do with the kitchen and the hall-
ways) was far better appointed in our new home. And this new home, it
is time to explain—and to add that we had moved into it because my
grandmother was far from well (though we kept this reason from her)
and needed cleaner air—was an apartment that formed part of the Hôtel
de Guermantes.

At an age when Names, offering us the image of the unknowable
that we have invested in them and simultaneously designating a real

place for us, force us accordingly to identify the one with the other, to a point where we go off to a city to seek out a soul that it cannot contain but which we no longer have the power to expel from its name, it is not only to cities and ruins that they give an individuality, as do allegorical paintings, nor is it only the physical world that they spangle with differences and people with marvels, it is the social world as well: so every historic house, every famous residence or palace, has its lady or its fairy, as forests have their spirits and rivers their deities. Sometimes, hidden deep in her name, the fairy is transformed by the needs of our imaginative activity through which she lives; this is how the atmosphere surrounding Mme de Guermantes, after existing for years in my mind only as the reflection of a magic-lantern slide and of a stained-glass window, began to lose its colors when quite different dreams impregnated it with the bubbling water of fast-flowing streams.

However, the fairy wastes away when we come into contact with the actual person to whom her name corresponds, for the name then begins to reflect that person, who contains nothing of the fairy; the fairy can reappear if we absent ourselves from the person, but if we stay in the person's presence the fairy dies forever, and with her the name, as with the Lusignan family,[1] which was fated to become extinct on the day when the fairy Mélusine should die. So the Name, beneath the successive retouchings that might eventually lead us to discover the original handsome portrait of an unknown woman we have never met, becomes no more than the mere photograph on an identity card to which we refer when we need to decide whether we know, whether or not we should acknowledge a person we encounter. But should a sensation from the distant past—like those musical instruments that record and preserve the sound and style of the various artists who played them[2]—enable our memory to make us hear that name with the particular tone it then had for our ears, even if the name seems not to have changed, we can still feel the distance between the various dreams which its unchanging syllables evoked for us in turn. For a second, rehearing the warbling from some distant springtime, we can extract from it, as from the little tubes of color used in painting, the precise tint—forgotten, mysterious, and fresh—of the days we thought we remembered when, like bad painters, we were in fact spreading our whole past on a single canvas and painting it with the conventional monochrome of voluntary memory. Yet, on the contrary, each of the moments that composed it, in order to create something original, a unique blend, was using those colors from the past that now elude us, colors that, for instance, are still able to fill me with sudden delight, should the name Guermantes—assuming for a second after so many years the ring it had for me, so different from its present resonance, on the day of Mlle Percepied's marriage—chance to restore to me the mauve color, so soft, too bright and new, that lent the smoothness of velvet to the billowing scarf of the young Duchesse, and made her eyes like inaccessible and everflowering periwinkles lit by the blue sun of her smile. And the name Guermantes, belonging to that period of my life, is also like one of those little balloons that have been filled with oxygen or some other gas: when I manage to puncture it and free what it contains, I can breathe the Combray air from that year, that day, mingled with the scent of hawthorns gusted from the corner of the square by the wind, announcing rain, and at times driving the sunlight away, at others letting it spread out on the red wool carpet of the sacristy and tingeing it brightly to an almost geranium pink with that "Wagnerian" softness of brio, which preserves the nobility of a festive occasion. Yet, even apart from rare moments such as this one, when we can suddenly feel the original entity give a stir and resume its shape, chisel itself out of syllables that have become lifeless, if in the dizzy whirl of daily life, where they serve merely the most practical purposes, names have lost all their color, like a prismatic top that revolves too fast and seems only gray, when, on the other hand, we reflect upon the past in our daydreams and seek to grasp it by slowing down and suspending the perpetual motion in which we are carried along, we can see the gradual reappearance, side by side but utterly distinct from one another, of the successive tints that a single name assumed for us in the course of our existence.

Of course, what shape this name Guermantes projected for me when my nurse—knowing no more, probably, than I today, in whose honor it had been composed—rocked me to sleep with that old song "Gloire à la Marquise de Guermantes," or when, several years later, the veteran

Maréchal de Guermantes filled my nursemaid with pride by stopping in the Champs-Élysées and exclaiming, "A fine child you have there!," giving me a chocolate drop from his pocket bonbonnière, I cannot now say. Those years of my earliest childhood are no longer with me; they are external to me; all I can know about them, as with what we can know about events that took place before we were born, comes from other people's accounts. But after these earliest years, I can find a succession of seven or eight different figures spanning the time this name inhabited me; the first ones were the finest: gradually my dream, forced by reality to abandon a position that was no longer tenable, took up its position afresh, a little further back, until it was obliged to retreat even further. And as Mme de Guermantes changed, so did her dwelling place, itself born from that name fertilized from year to year by hearing some word or other that modified my dreams of it; the dwelling place itself mirrored them in its very masonry, which had become as much a mirror as the surface of a cloud or of a lake. A two-dimensional castle keep which was really no more than a strip of orange light where the lord and his lady, high up, decided upon life or death for their vassals, had been replaced—right at the end of the "Guermantes way," along which I used to follow the course of the Vivonne with my parents on all those sunny afternoons—by the land of bubbling streams where the Duchesse taught me to fish for trout and to recognize the names of the flowers whose purple-and-reddish clusters adorned the low walls of the neighboring garden plots; then it had become the hereditary property, the poetic domain from which the proud race of the Guermantes, like a mellowing, crenellated tower spanning the ages, was rising already over France, at a time when the sky was still empty in those places where Notre-Dame de Paris and Notre-Dame de Chartres were later to rise; a time when on the summit of the hill in Laon the cathedral nave had not been placed like the Ark of the Flood on the summit of Mount Ararat,³ full of patriarchs and judges anxiously leaning from its windows to see whether the wrath of God has been appeased, carrying with it the species of plants that will multiply on earth, brimming over with animals spilling out even from the towers, where oxen, moving calmly around on the roofs, gaze down over the plains of Champagne; a time when the traveler who left Beauvais at close of day did not yet see, following him and turning with the bends in the road, the black branching wings of the cathedral spread out against the golden screen of sunset. It was, this "Guermantes," like the setting of a novel, an imaginary landscape I could picture to myself only with difficulty and thereby longed all the more to discover, set amid real lands and roads that would suddenly become immersed in heraldic details, a few miles from a railway station; I recalled the names of the places around it as if they had been situated at the foot of Parnassus or of Helicon, and they seemed precious to me as the physical conditions necessary—in topographical science—for the production of an inexplicable phenomenon. I remembered the coats of arms painted beneath the windows of the church in Combray, their quarters filled, century after century, with all the lordly domains that this illustrious house had appropriated by marriage or gain from all the corners of Germany, Italy, and France: vast territories in the North, powerful cities in the South, assembled together to compose the name Guermantes and, losing their material form, to inscribe allegorically their sinople keep or castle triple-towered argent upon its azure field. I had heard of the famous Guermantes tapestries and could see them, medieval and blue, somewhat coarse, standing out like a cloud against the amaranth, legendary name beneath the ancient forest where Childebert so often went hunting,4 and it seemed to me that, without making a journey to see them, I might just as easily penetrate the secrets of the mysterious corners of these lands, this remoteness of the centuries, simply by coming into contact for a moment, in Paris, with Mme de Guermantes, the suzerain of the place and lady of the lake, as if her face and her words must possess the local charm of forests and streams and the same age-old characteristics as those recorded in the book of ancient customs in her archives. But then I had met Saint-Loup; he had told me that the house had borne the name Guermantes only since the seventeenth century, when his family had acquired it. They had lived, until then, in the neighborhood, and their title did not belong to the area. The village of Guermantes had taken its name from the château and had been built after it, and, so that the village should not destroy the view from it, building regulations that were still in force dictated the lines of its streets and set limits on the height of its houses. As for the tapestries, they were by Boucher,⁵ acquired in the nineteenth century by a Guermantes with artistic tastes and hung, along with mediocre hunting scenes that he had painted himself, in a particularly ugly drawing room done out in adrinople and plush. By revealing these things to me, Saint-Loup had introduced into the château elements that were foreign to the name Guermantes, and they no longer made it possible for me to go on extracting from its syllables alone the style in which it was built. Then the château reflected in its lake had disappeared from the depths of this name, and what had appeared to me around Mme de Guermantes as her dwelling had been her Paris house, the Hôtel de Guermantes, as limpid as its name, for no physical and opaque element intervened to disrupt and darken its transparency. Just as the word "church" signifies not merely the building but also the company of the faithful, the Hôtel de Guermantes included all those who shared in the life of the Duchesse, but these close friends I had never seen were for me merely famous and poetic names, and, knowing only persons who were themselves merely names as well, they only enlarged and protected the mystery surrounding the Duchesse by extending around her a vast halo, which at best grew dimmer as it increased in size.

In the parties she gave, since I could not imagine the guests as having bodies, mustaches, boots, as making any remark that was banal, or even original in a human and rational manner, this whirl of names, introducing less physical presence than a banquet of ghosts or a ball of specters around the statuette in Dresden china known as Mme de Guermantes, maintained a showcase transparency around her glass mansion. Then, when Saint-Loup had told me various anecdotes about his cousin's chaplain and her gardeners, the Hôtel de Guermantes had become—as some Louvre might have become in the past—a kind of castle surrounded, in the very center of Paris, by its lands, acquired by inheritance, by virtue of an ancient right that had oddly survived, and over which she still enjoyed feudal privileges. But this last dwelling had itself faded away by the time we had come to live right next to Mme de Villeparisis, in one of the apartments adjoining the one occupied by

Mme de Guermantes in a wing of the Hôtel. It was one of those old houses, some of which may still exist, in which the main courtyard was often flanked—alluvial deposits washed up by the rising tide of democracy or the legacy of bygone days when the various trades were grouped around the seigneurial dwelling—by the backs of shops, premises like a bootmaker's or a tailor's, for instance (like those you see clustered around cathedrals when restorers have not had the aesthetic sense to remove them), together with a concierge who was also a cobbler, kept chickens, and grew flowers—and, at the far end, in the main house, lived an aristocratic lady who, when she drove out in her old carriage and pair, her hat sporting a few nasturtiums that seemed to have escaped from the concierge's garden (with a footman at her coachman's side who got down to leave cards at every aristocratic mansion in the neighborhood), dispensed smiles and little waves of the hand indiscriminately to the porter's children and to any middle-class tenants who happened to be passing, and between whom her disdainful affability and her egalitarian hauteur could not distinguish.

In the house to which we had moved, the aristocratic lady at the end of the courtyard was a duchesse, elegant and still young. Her name was Mme de Guermantes, and, thanks to Françoise, it was not long before I came to know something about her household. For the Guermantes (often referred to by Françoise as the people "below" or "downstairs") constantly occupied her thoughts from the morning, when, as she did Mama's hair, unable to resist casting a forbidden, furtive glance into the courtyard, she would remark: "Oh, there go two Holy Sisters: they'll be for downstairs," or "Oh! Just look at those pheasants in the kitchen window. No need to ask where they've come from. The Duc will have been out hunting"—to the evening, when, handing me my nightclothes, she might chance to hear the sound of a piano or a snatch of song and would conclude: "Gay goings-on below, they've got company"; and in the steady set of her face, beneath her now whitened hair, a smile from her younger days, lively and demure, would for a second set each one of her features in its place and match them together in a carefully ordered readiness, as if to dance a quadrille.

But the moment in the Guermantes' day that most aroused Françoise's curiosity, that gave her the most satisfaction and also the most annoyance, was the moment when the doors of the carriage entrance opened and the Duchesse stepped into her barouche. This usually happened shortly after our servants had finished celebrating the solemn Passover feast that none might disturb, otherwise known as their midday meal, during which they were so "taboo" that not even my father would have dared to ring for them, in the full knowledge that not a single one of them would have stirred even if the bell had rung five times, and that he would have committed this breach of etiquette to no effect whatsoever, but not without detriment to himself. For Françoise (who, in her old age, lost no opportunity to assume "a suitable expression") would not have failed to present him, for the rest of the day, with a face covered with little red cuneiform markings, which was her way, indecipherable though it was, of displaying to the outside world the long record of her grievances and the underlying causes of her displeasure. She would enlarge upon these by addressing herself to no one in particular, but not in a way that made what she said at all clear. And this is what she meant—in the belief that for us it was exasperating, "mortifying," "vexing" as she put it—when she talked about saying "low mass" for us the whole blessed day.

The last rites completed, Françoise, who was at once, as in the early church, both celebrant and a member of the faithful, poured herself a final glass of wine, removed the napkin from her neck, and, wiping the traces of red liquid and coffee from her lips, folded it up and slipped it into its ring; she directed a doleful look of thanks to "her" young footman, who was ingratiating himself with her with a "Come, madame, a few more grapes, they're 'eavenly," then went straight to open the window on the pretext that it was too hot "in this wretched kitchen." As she turned the window knob and let in the air, she managed, at the same time, to steal a skillfully indifferent glance toward the back of the courtyard; from this she gained the stealthy assurance that the Duchesse was not yet ready to leave, and gazed longingly for a moment, with scornful and impassioned eyes, at the waiting carriage; once this second of attention had been paid to the things of this earth, she raised her eyes to heaven, whose purity she had already anticipated as she felt the mildness of the air and the warmth of the sun; at the corner of the roof, her gaze rested on the place where, each spring, there came to nest, immediately above my bedroom chimney, two pigeons like the ones that used to coo in her kitchen in Combray.

"Ah! Combray, Combray!" she would cry. (And the almost singing tone in which she declaimed this invocation, just as much as the Arlésienne purity of her features, could have made one suspect that Françoise was of southern origin, and that the lost homeland she was bewailing was simply a land of adoption. But one might have been wrong here, for it seems that no province is without its "south"; are there not any number of Bretons or Savoyards we come across whose speech has all the delightful transpositions of longs and shorts characteristic of the south?) "Ah! Combray, when will I see you again, my poor old home? When will I be able to spend every blessed hour of the day among your hawthorns, under our poor old lilacs, listening to the finches and the Vivonne murmuring away like someone whispering, instead of that wretched bell from the young master, who has me running up and down that dratted corridor every half-hour. And even then he thinks I don't come quick enough; but you'd need to hear the bell before he'd rung it, and if you're a minute late he 'takes on' something dreadful. My poor old Combray! I dare say I'll be dead before I see you again, when they throw me like a stone into a hole in the ground. And I'll never smell your lovely white hawthorns again. It seems to me that what I'll be hearing in my final rest are those three rings of the bell, which put a curse on me when I was still alive."

But she was interrupted by the voice of the waistcoat-maker in the courtyard below, the one whom my grandmother had found so agreeable in the past, when she had gone to pay a call on Mme de Villeparisis, and who now ranked no less highly in the affections of Françoise. The sound of our window opening had made him look up, and he had already spent some time trying to attract his neighbor's attention so that he could bid her good day. At this point, the flirtatiousness of the young girl Françoise had once been softened, for M. Jupien's benefit, the grumpy face of our old cook, weighed down by age, bad temper, and the heat of the stove, and it was with a charming blend of reserve, familiarity, and demureness that she gracefully acknowledged the waistcoat-maker, but without a word to him; if she was infringing Mama's instructions by looking into the courtyard, she would not have dared to challenge them to the point of talking from the window, which would have entailed, as Françoise saw it, a "whole lecture" on the subject from her mistress. She pointed out the waiting carriage to Jupien with a gesture that seemed to convey, "A fine pair of horses there all right!" But what she actually muttered was, "What an old crate!," and she did this mainly because she knew what his response was going to be: he would put his hand to his lips so that he would be audible without having to shout: "*You* could have one, too, if you wanted, more than just one perhaps, but you're not interested in that sort of thing."

And Françoise, after a modest, furtive, and delighted gesture that conveyed something like, "Each to his own; but simplicity's the thing in this house," closed the window in case Mama should enter the room. The "you" who might have owned more horses than the Guermantes meant us, but Jupien was right to use "you" in this way, because, apart from a few strictly personal indulgences (like pretending with an irritating giggle that she did not have a cold when she was coughing all the time and the whole household lived in fear of catching it), Françoise, like those plants that are completely attached to a particular animal and nourished by that animal with food it catches, eats, and digests for them, offering it to them in its final and easily assimilable residue, lived with us symbiotically; we were the ones who, with our virtues, our wealth, our style of living, our position, had to take it upon ourselves to devise little ways of humoring her, which constituted—along with the recognized right freely to practice the ritual of the midday meal according to ancient custom, including a breath of air at the window afterward, a certain amount of lingering when she went out to shop, and a Sunday visit to her niece—the portion of contentment without which her life could not be lived. So one can understand why Françoise had pined away during the first days of our move, a prey to a sickness—in a house where my father's claims to distinction were not yet known—which she herself called "ennui," in the strong sense in which the word is used by Corneille, or in the letters of soldiers who end up by committing suicide because they "pine" too much for their fiancées or for their native villages. Françoise's ennui had been quickly remedied, in fact, by Jupien, because his attitude procured her an immediate sense of pleasure, no less keenly felt and more refined than it would have been had we decided to keep a carriage. "A good class of people, these Juliens"—Françoise was always ready to assimilate new names into the ones she already knew—"decent souls; it's written all over their faces." Indeed, Jupien was able to understand the situation and to let it be known that if we had no carriage it was because we had no wish for one. This friend of Françoise's had obtained a post in a government office and was seldom to be found at home. He had initially been a waistcoat-maker with the "slip of a girl" my grandmother had assumed to be his daughter, but it was no longer worthwhile for him to go on doing the job after the girl, who could already repair a torn skirt with great skill when she was little more than a child (at the time my grandmother paid her call on Mme de Villeparisis), had turned to ladies' dressmaking and become a skirt-maker. After a period as apprentice seamstress with a dressmaker, employed to stitch, to sew up a flounce, to secure a button or a press stud, and to fix a waistband with fasteners, she had quickly risen to become second, then chief assistant, and after creating her own clientele of ladies from the best circles, she now worked at home (to wit, in our courtyard), generally with one or two of her young friends from the dressmaker's workshop, whom she engaged as apprentices. So Jupien's presence was not really needed there any more. No doubt the little girl, now a grown woman, was often required to make waistcoats. But with her friends to help her, she no longer needed anyone else. And so Jupien, her uncle, had looked for a job elsewhere. At first his work had allowed him to get home for midday, but he then permanently replaced the man whose assistant he had been and could not return home until the evening meal. Fortunately, he was appointed to this "tenured position" several weeks after we had moved in, so that his kind attention lasted sufficiently long for Françoise to get through the dif-ficulties of these early days without undue discomfort. At the same time, without underrating Jupien's value as an "interim palliative" for Françoise, I have to say that I did not initially take to him. From a few feet away, completely destroying the effect that his plump cheeks and florid complexion would have otherwise produced, his eyes, brimming with dreamy, woeful sympathy, created the impression that he either was very ill or had just suffered a major bereavement. Not only was this not the case, but as soon as he spoke—perfectly well, in fact—he tended to be cold and mocking. The disparity between his gaze and his speech produced an uncomfortable sense of falsity, and it seemed to embarrass him in the way that a guest wearing ordinary clothes at a party where everyone else is in evening dress is embarrassed, or, likewise, someone who has to speak to a member of royalty without knowing exactly how, and whose reaction to the dilemma is to use as few words as possible. There the comparison ends, because Jupien's way of speaking was, by contrast, charming. Indeed, in the same way that his face was inundated by his eyes (and this passed unnoticed once you knew him), I soon discovered that he was a man of rare intelligence, one of the most spontaneously literary men who have come my way, in the sense that, although he was probably uneducated, he possessed, or had acquired, with the sole help of a few hastily scanned books, the most ingenious turns of phrase. The most gifted people I had known had died very young. And I was convinced that Jupien's life would be a short one. He had kindness, sympathy, and the most sensitive and generous feelings. His role in Françoise's life had soon ceased to be indispensable. She had learned the role for herself.

Even when a tradesman or a servant delivered a parcel to our door, while seeming to pay no attention to him and merely pointing him absently to a chair as she continued with her work, Françoise took such shrewd advantage of the few moments he spent in the kitchen awaiting Mama's instructions that only rarely did he depart without the certain knowledge ineradicably engraved in his mind that, "if we did not have one, it was because we had no wish for it." And if it was so important to her that other people should know we "had money" (for she knew nothing about the use of what Saint-Loup called partitive articles and would say "have money," "fetch water"[6]), that we were rich, it was not because wealth alone, wealth without virtue, was the supreme good for Françoise; but virtue without wealth was not her ideal, either. For her, wealth was like a necessary condition without which virtue would lack both merit and charm. She made so little distinction between the two that she came to see their qualities as interchangeable, expecting material comfort from virtue and moral edification from wealth.

Once she had closed the window, fairly quickly (otherwise, it seemed, Mama would have given her "a real piece of her mind"), Françoise began with a sigh to clear the kitchen table.

"There are some Guermantes on the rue de la Chaise," said our valet. "I had a friend who worked there. He was their second coachman. And I know someone, not my pal but his brother-in-law, who did his time in the army with one of the Baron de Guermantes's grooms. 'So how's your father?' " added the valet, who had a habit of sprinkling his conversation with the latest witticisms, just as he liked to hum the latest popular tunes.

Françoise, with the weary look in her eyes of an aging woman, and viewing the world entirely from Combray, in a distant blur, grasped not the witticism in these words but the fact that they must be witty, since they were unrelated to the rest of the valet's remarks and had been uttered with strong emphasis by someone she knew to be a joker. So she smiled with dazzled benevolence, as if to say, "He doesn't change, our Victor!" Besides, she was pleased, because she knew that listening to wit of this kind was connected—remotely—to those reputable social pleasures for which, in all classes of society, people are eager to dress up and risk catching cold. In fact, she regarded the valet as a good friend for her to have, since he was always angrily denouncing the dreadful measures the Republic was about to take against the clergy. Françoise had not yet grasped that our cruelest adversaries are not those who contradict and try to convince us, but those who exaggerate or invent things that are likely to distress us, taking care not to present them in any justifiable light, which would diminish our distress and perhaps lead us to entertain some slight respect for an attitude they are anxious to display to us, to complete our torment, as being both hideous and unassailable.

"The Duchesse must be connected to all that," said Françoise, resuming the remarks made about the Guermantes on the rue de la Chaise, as one takes up a piece of music again at the andante. "I can't remember who it was told me that one of them married a cousin of the Duc. But they all belong to the same 'bracket.' A great family, those Guermantes!" she added with respect, attributing the greatness of the family both to the number of its members and to the brilliance of its reputation, as Pascal attributes the truth of religion to reason and the authority of the Scriptures. With the single word "great" as her only means of expressing both ideas, it seemed to her that these were one and the same, her vocabulary, like certain gemstones, thus presenting a flaw in places that projected darkness into the depths of her mind.

"I wonder if they're the ones with a château in Guermantes, ten miles from Combray? If they are, they've got to be related to their cousin in Algiers, too." My mother and I were kept wondering for a long time who this cousin in Algiers might be, but we finally realized that by "Algiers" Françoise meant the city of Angers. The remote can be more familiar to us than the near. Françoise, who knew the name Algiers from some very nasty dates we were customarily sent at New Year's, had never heard of Angers. Her language, like the French language itself, particularly its toponymy, was strewn with errors. "I meant to ask their butler about it. . . . What is it they call him?" She broke off, as if she were consulting herself on a matter of protocol, then came out with the answer: "Oh yes! They call him Antoine," as if "Antoine" had been some sort of title. "He's the one could tell me, but he's a real dandy that one, a great pedant; you'd think they'd cut off his tongue or that he'd forgotten to learn to speak. He makes no reply when you talk to him," added Françoise, who used the expression "make reply" like Mme de Sévigné.⁷ "But," she went on, untruthfully, "as long as I know what's cooking in my own pot, I don't bother about what's in other people's. Anyway, it's not Catholic. And he's not a courageous man, either." (You would have thought from this estimation of the man that Françoise had revised her ideas about physical courage, which when she was in Combray she saw as reducing men to the level of wild beasts. But this was not the case. "Courageous" simply meant "hardworking.") "They say he's as thievish as a magpie as well, but you can't always believe what you hear. Their staff are always leaving because of the concierge. He's jealous, and he sets the Duchesse against them. But that

Antoine is a real idler, that's for sure, and his Antoinesse is no better," continued Françoise, whose need to find a feminine form of the name "Antoine" for the butler's wife was no doubt unconsciously motivated in this grammatical invention by the memory of the words *chanoine* and *chanoinesse*. She was not entirely wrong in this. There is still a street called rue Chanoinesse, near Notre-Dame, a name given it (since it was only occupied by canons) by those Frenchmen in the past whose contemporary Françoise in fact was. She went on immediately to provide another example of this way of forming feminines, with the remark: "It's got to be the Duchesse who owns the Guermantes château. And she's the one who's mayoress down there. That's quite something."

"I should think it *is*," said the footman with conviction, having failed to detect the irony.

"You think so, do you, my boy? For people like them, being mayor or mayoress is not worth two cents. Now, if I had the Guermantes château, you wouldn't see me setting foot in Paris. Why on earth do important folk, well-off people like Monsieur and Madame, get it into their heads to stay in this wretched city when they could be going off to Combray the minute they're free and there's no one to stop them? What's stopping them from retiring? They're not short of anything. Why wait till they're dead? All I'd need would be a bit of plain food and enough wood to keep me warm in winter, and I'd have been off home to my brother's poor old place in Combray a long time ago. At least you feel alive there, without all these houses around you. It's so quiet you can hear the frogs singing at night for miles around."

"That must be wonderful, madame," the young footman broke out enthusiastically, as if this last detail had been as much a part of Combray as gondolas are of Venice.

A more recent arrival in the household than the valet, he would talk with Françoise about things that might be of interest not so much to himself as to her. And Françoise, who grimaced with resentment when she was treated as the cook, was particularly well disposed toward this footman (who referred to her as "the housekeeper"), in the same way that princes of the second rank are toward the well-meaning young men who treat them like royalty.

"At least you know what you're supposed to be doing there and what time of the year it is. Not like this place, where seeing one measly buttercup at holy Easter is like looking for one at Christmas. I can't even hear the tiniest bit of an angelus ring when I shift my old bones out of bed in the morning. Down there you can hear every hour strike. It's a only a poor old bell but you think, 'My brother's on his way back from the fields now.' You can see the daylight fading, they ring the bells to bless the fruits of the earth, there's time to turn round before you light the lamp. In this place it's day, then it's night, and off you go to bed, with no more idea of what you've been doing than a dumb animal."

"I hear that Méséglise is really pretty, too," broke in the young footman, for whom the conversation was taking rather too abstract a turn, and who happened to remember hearing us talk at table about Méséglise.

"Oh! Méséglise," said Françoise with the broad smile that always came to her lips whenever she heard the names Méséglise, Combray, or Tansonville. They were so much part of her that whenever she encountered them outside herself, heard them in a conversation, she felt a similar sort of glee to that which a professor provokes among his students by alluding to some contemporary figure whose name they would never have expected to have fall upon their ears from the rostrum. Her pleasure also arose from the feeling that these places meant something to her that they did not for other people, old friends with whom one has experienced much; and she smiled at them as if she found something witty about them, because they contained a great deal of herself.

"You're right, my boy, Méséglise *is* quite a pretty place," she went on with a gentle laugh, "but how have *you* heard of Méséglise?"

"How have I heard of Méséglise? But it's well known. People have told me about it many a time," he replied with that criminal inexactitude of the informant who, whenever we try to assess objectively the possible importance for someone else of a thing that matters to us, makes it impossible for us to do so.

"Ah! It's better down there, under the cherry trees, than it is in front of this stove, I can tell you."

She even spoke to the servants of Eulalie as a good person. For, since Eulalie's death, Françoise had completely forgotten that she had liked her as little when she was alive as she liked anyone who had nothing to eat in the house, who was "starving to death" and who then, like a good-for-nothing and thanks to the bounty of the rich, started to "put on airs." It no longer galled her that Eulalie had so skillfully managed, week after week, to ensure that she received her "tip" from my aunt. As for the latter, Françoise never stopped singing her praises.

"So it was at Combray itself that you were with Madame's cousin, then?" asked the young footman.

"That's right, with Mme Octave, a real saint, my dears, and a house where there was always more than enough, the very best—a good woman she was, I can tell you, she didn't begrudge the partridges or the pheasants, or anything; five or six people to dinner and plenty of meat to go round, best-quality meat, too, white wine, red wine, the works." (Françoise used the verb "begrudge" in the same way as La Bruyère.)[8] "She always paid the damages, even if the family stayed for months, for donkey's years." (There was nothing offensive intended toward us in this remark; Françoise belonged to an era when the word "damages" was not restricted to legal use and simply meant "expenses.") "People didn't go away with empty stomachs, I can tell you! M. le Curé was always coming out with it: if there was ever a woman who could count on going straight to our good Lord, it was her. Poor Madame, I can hear that tiny voice of hers now: 'Françoise, I eat nothing myself, as you know, but I want the food to be as nice for everyone else as if I did.' The food wasn't for her, of course not. You should have seen her, she weighed no more than a bag of cherries; there wasn't much of her. She'd never listen to a thing I said, she'd never see the doctor. Ah! You didn't gobble down your food in that house. She wanted her servants to be fed properly. And look at us, we hardly had time for a bite to eat this morning. It's all one big rush in this place."

What exasperated her most were the slices of toast my father was in the habit of eating. She was convinced that he ate them out of affectation and to keep her "dancing attention." "I have to admit," the young footman assured her, "that I never saw the likes of it." He said this as if he had seen everything there was to see, and as if his range of experience included all countries and customs, among which the custom of eating toast was completely unknown. "Yes, yes," muttered the butler, "but all that could come to an end, the workers are supposed to be going on strike in Canada, and the minister told Monsieur the other night that he'd got two hundred thousand francs out of it." There was no note of blame attached to the butler's remarks; not that he himself was not perfectly honest, but, because he thought that all politicians were dubious, the criminal misappropriation of public money seemed to him less serious than the pettiest case of larceny. It did not even occur to him that he might have misheard this historic remark, nor was he struck by the unlikelihood that the guilty party would have said it to my father without being asked to leave the house. But Combray philosophy did not allow Françoise to entertain the hope that strikes in Canada would have any effect on the consumption of toast. "Ah well, as long as the world is the way it is, there'll be masters to keep us on the trot, and servants to pander to their whims." Notwithstanding this theory of perpetually trotting about, for the last quarter of an hour my mother, who probably did not have the same sense of time as Françoise in regard to the duration of the servants' midday meal, had been saying: "What on earth can they be up to? They've been at table for more than two hours." And she rang timidly three or four times. Françoise, her footman, and the butler heard the bell ring, not as a summons and with no thought of answering it, but, rather, as the first sounds of instruments tuning up for the next part of a concert, when it is clear that there are only a few more minutes of the interval left to go. And so, when the bell rang again, more insistently, our servants began to take notice, and, judging that there was not much time left before they must take up their duties, when the bell rang once again, even more loudly this time, they each heaved a sigh and went their separate ways: the footman going down to smoke a cigarette outside; Françoise, after various remarks about us such as "They've really got the fidgets today," up to the top floor to tidy her room; and the butler, after supplying himself with notepaper from my bedroom, to deal hurriedly with his private correspondence.

Despite the apparent haughtiness of their butler, Françoise had been

able, from very early on, to inform me that the Guermantes did not occupy their *hôtel* because of some immemorial right, but were fairly recent tenants, and that the garden they overlooked on the side that was
unknown to me was quite small and no different from all the other
neighboring gardens; so I discovered at last that it contained no feudal
gallows or fortified mill, no fishpond or pillared dovecote, no commu-
nal bakehouse, tithe barn, or fortress, no fixed bridges or drawbridges,
not even flying bridges or toll bridges, no pointed towers, wall charters,
or commemorative mounds. But just as Elstir, when the bay at Balbec
lost its mystery for me and became a nondescript part, interchangeable
with any other, of the quantity of salt water spread over the globe, had
suddenly restored it to something distinctive by revealing that it was
the opal gulf Whistler painted in his *Harmonies in Blue and Silver*,[9] so
the name Guermantes had seen the last of the dwellings it evoked destroyed by Françoise's blows, when, one day, an old friend of my father's said to us, speaking of the Duchesse: "She has the highest status
in the Faubourg Saint-Germain. Hers is the leading house in the Faubourg." No doubt the leading house in the Faubourg Saint-Germain
counted as next to nothing beside all the other dwellings dreamed up in
turn by my imagination. Yet this one, too—and it was to be the last—
however humble it was, possessed something that exceeded its material
substance, some hidden quality of its own.

And it became all the more vital for me to be able to seek out in
Mme de Guermantes's salon, among her friends, the mystery of her
name, since I did not discover it in her person when I saw her leave the
house in the morning on foot, or in the afternoon in her carriage. It is
true that she had once appeared to me, in the church at Combray, in a
momentary flash of transfiguration, with cheeks that were irreducible
to, impervious to, the color of the name Guermantes and of afternoons
on the banks of the Vivonne, dislocating my shattered dream, like a
god or a nymph changed into a swan or a willow and henceforth subjected to natural laws, gliding over the water or shaken by the wind. Yet
scarcely had I left her presence when these vanished glints had come together again like the pink-and-green reflections of sunset behind the oar
that has disturbed them, and in the solitude of my thoughts the name

had been quick to appropriate my memory of the face. But now I often saw her at her window, in the courtyard, in the street; and if I did not manage to match the name Guermantes with her person, to think of her as Mme de Guermantes, I could at least put the blame on the failure of my mind to carry out completely the act I demanded of it; but she, too, our neighbor, seemed to be committing the same error, and committing it without a qualm, without any of my misgivings, without even suspecting that it was an error. Thus, in the way she dressed, Mme de Guermantes showed the same concern to follow fashion as if, in the belief that she had become a woman like any other, she had aspired to the sort of elegance in which ordinary women might equal or perhaps surpass her; I had seen her in the street look admiringly at a well-dressed actress; and in the morning, just as she was about to leave the house on foot, as if the opinion of people in the street, whose vulgarity she accentuated by parading her inaccessible life familiarly among them, might be there to pass judgment on her, I would see her in front of her mirror, where, with a conviction devoid of all pretense and irony, with passion, with ill-humor, with conceit, like a queen accepting the part of a servant girl in a comedy staged at court, she played out the role, so unworthy of her, of a fashionable woman; and in this mythological obliviousness of her native grandeur, she checked the position of her veil, smoothed her cuffs, arranged her cape, as the divine swan goes through all the movements of his animal species, keeps his painted eyes on either side of his beak without any sign of movement in them, and then darts suddenly after a button or an umbrella, behaving like a swan and forgetting that he is a god. But, like a traveler who is disappointed by his first impression of a city and who tells himself that he might perhaps penetrate its charm by visiting its museums, getting to know its inhabitants, and working in its libraries, I assured myself that, had I been a regular visitor to Mme de Guermantes's house, were I one of her circle, were I to enter into her life, I should then know what was really enclosed within the brilliant orange-colored envelope of her name, know it objectively, through the eyes of others, since, after all, my father's friend had said that the Guermantes were an exclusive set in the Faubourg Saint-Germain.

The life I supposed them to be living stemmed from a source so different from anything I knew, and must, it seemed to me, be so special, that I could not have imagined the presence at the Duchesse's parties of the sort of people I had frequented so far, of people who really existed. For, incapable of suddenly changing their nature, they would have conducted conversations there in a way that was familiar to me; their partners would perhaps have stooped to answer them in the same human speech; and, in the course of an evening spent in the leading salon of the Faubourg Saint-Germain, there would have been moments identical to moments I had already experienced; but this was impossible. It is true that my mind was hampered by certain difficulties, and the presence of the body of Jesus Christ in the sacrament seemed to me no more obscure a mystery than that this leading salon of the Faubourg Saint-Germain was situated on the Right Bank and the fact that, every morning, from my bedroom, I could hear its carpets being beaten. But the line of demarcation that separated me from the Faubourg Saint-Germain seemed to me all the more real because it was purely ideal; I had a strong sense of its already being the Faubourg when I saw, spread out on the other side of this equator, the Guermantes doormat, of which my mother had been bold enough to say, having, like myself, caught sight of it one day when their door was open, that it was in a dreadful state. Besides, how could their dining room, their dim gallery with its red plush furniture, which I could sometimes see from our kitchen window, have failed to possess for me the mysterious spell of the Faubourg Saint-Germain, to form an essential part of it, to be geographically located within it, when to be invited into that dining room was to have gone into the Faubourg Saint-Germain, to have breathed its air, since the people who sat down beside Mme de Guermantes on the leather sofa in the gallery before proceeding to table all belonged to the Faubourg Saint-Germain? No doubt, outside the Faubourg, at certain parties, majestically enthroned amid the vulgar herd of fashionable people, one might occasionally see one of those men who are no more than names, and who, when one tries to picture them, assume in turn the aspect of a tournament or of a royal forest. But here, in the leading salon of the Faubourg Saint-Germain, in the dim gallery, they were the only company. They were the columns, built with precious material, that upheld the temple. Even for intimate gatherings, it was from among them alone that Mme de Guermantes could select her guests, and in the dinner parties for twelve, assembled around the lavishly set table, they were like the golden statues of the apostles in the Sainte-Chapelle, symbolic and sanctifying pillars before the Lord's Table. As for the tiny patch of garden that lay behind high walls at the back of the house, where in summer Mme de Guermantes had liqueurs and orangeade served to her guests after dinner, how could I have failed to feel that to sit there between nine and eleven at night on its wrought iron chairs—they had the same magic power as the leather sofa—and not to breathe in the air peculiar to the Faubourg Saint-Germain, was as impossible as to take a siesta in the oasis of Figuig and not to be in Africa? Only imagination and belief can differentiate certain objects and people from the rest, and create a particular atmosphere. Alas, those picturesque sites, those natural features, those local curiosities and works of art of the Faubourg Saint-Germain would doubtless remain forbidden territory to me. So I made do with a twitch of excitement as I sighted from the open sea (without the least hope of ever landing), like a prominent minaret, like the first palm tree, like the first signs of exotic industry and vegetation, the well-trodden doormat of its shore.

But if for me the Hôtel de Guermantes began at the door to its entrance hall, its dependencies must have extended much farther in the estimation of the Duc de Guermantes, who—regarding all the tenants as farmers, villeins, acquisitors of national assets, whose views were of no importance—stood shaving himself at his window in his nightshirt every morning, then came down into the courtyard, dressed, depending on the temperature, in his shirtsleeves, in pajamas, in a plaid jacket of unusual colors and a shaggy nap, in little light-colored waistcoats shorter than his jacket, and had one of his grooms lead past him at a trot some horse he had just purchased. On more than one occasion, the horse damaged Jupien's shopfront, and Jupien, to the Duc's indignation, demanded compensation. "If it were only out of respect for all the good work that Mme la Duchesse does here and in the parish," said M. de Guermantes, "it's outrageous that this fellow should claim anything at all from us."

But Jupien had held his ground and appeared to be completely un-aware of what "good" the Duchesse had ever done. And yet she did do good, but, since we cannot do good to everyone at once, the memory of the help heaped on one person becomes a reason for not helping an-other, whose discontent is then all the more aroused. From other points of view that had nothing to do with good works, the neighborhood seemed to the Duc—and this over a considerable area—to be little more than an extension of his own courtyard, a longer track for his horses. After seeing how a newly purchased horse trotted on its own, he would have it harnessed and taken through all the streets in the area, the groom running alongside the carriage holding the reins, making it pass to and fro before the Duc, who stood there on the pavement, a giant, enormous in his light-colored clothes, a cigar between his teeth, his head in the air, his monocle alert, until the moment came when he jumped up onto the box, tried out the horse for himself, then set off with his new equipage to meet up with his mistress in the Champs-Élysées. M. de Guermantes would bid good day in the courtyard to two couples who belonged more or less to his world: some cousins of his who, like working-class couples, were never at home to look after their children, since every morning the wife went off to study counterpoint and fugue at the Schola Cantorum, and the husband to carve wood and tool leather in his workshop; and then the Baron and the Baronne de Norpois, who were always dressed in black, she like a pew attendant and he like an undertaker, and who appeared several times a day on their way to church. They were the nephew and niece of the former ambas-sador we knew, whom my father had in fact met at the foot of the stair-case without realizing where he was coming from; for, to my father's mind, such an important figure, who had consorted with the most emi-nent men in Europe and was probably quite indifferent to empty dis-tinctions of social rank, was hardly likely to keep company with these obscure, clerical, and narrow-minded nobles. They were newcomers to the place; Jupien, who had come out into the courtyard to say some-thing to the husband, who was in the process of greeting M. de Guer-mantes, called him "M. Norpois," uncertain of his real title.

"So it's M. Norpois, is it? How very original! Just wait and see!

This individual will be calling you Citizen Norpois next!" exclaimed M. de Guermantes, turning to the Baron. He had finally found the opportunity to give vent to his rancor against Jupien, who addressed him as "Monsieur" and not as "M. le Duc."

One day, when M. de Guermantes needed some advice that my father was professionally qualified to give, he had introduced himself with great courtesy. After that, he had often some neighborly service to ask of my father, and as soon as he saw him coming downstairs, his mind occupied by work and anxious to avoid meeting anyone, the Duc would leave his stable boys and come up to him in the courtyard, straighten the collar of his greatcoat with the obliging attentiveness he had inherited from a line of royal valets, take his hand and hold it in his own, stroking it even, to prove to him, with the shamelessness of a courtesan, that he did not begrudge him the honor of contact with his noble flesh, and then lead him off, extremely disgruntled, and bent only on escape, to the carriage entrance and out into the street. He had run into us and greeted us effusively one day, as he was setting out in the carriage with his wife; he must have told her my name, but what chance was there of her remembering either my name or my face? And, besides, what a feeble recommendation, to be pointed out merely as one of her tenants! It would have been more effective to meet the Duchesse at the house of Mme de Villeparisis, who had, as it happened, sent a message through my grandmother that I was to pay her a visit and, knowing that I had been intending to pursue a literary career, had added that I would meet various writers at her house. But my father felt that I was still rather young to go into society, and since the state of my health was a continuing cause of concern to him, he was not keen to provide me with fresh opportunities for leaving the house when I did not have to.

Since one of Mme de Guermantes's footmen spent a lot of time gossiping with Françoise, I heard the names of several of the salons she frequented, but was unable to picture any of them: once they were part of her life, the life I could see only through the screen of her name, were they not inconceivable?

"There's a big shadow-theater party tonight at the Princess of

Parma's," said the footman, "but we won't be going, because Madame is taking the five o'clock train to Chantilly and spending a couple of days with the Duc d'Aumale. But it's her maid and the valet who are going with her. I'm to stay here. She won't be at all pleased, will the Princess of Parma? She's written to Mme la Duchesse four times or more."

"Then you're not off to the Guermantes château this year?"

"It's the first time we're not going. Because of M. le Duc's rheumatism; the doctor says he's not to go there again until they get a heating boiler installed, but we've been there every year so far, right through to January. If the boiler's not ready, Madame will probably go to Cannes for a few days, to the Duchesse de Guise's, but that's still to be decided."

"And do you ever get to the theater?"

"We sometimes go to the Opéra. Sometimes when the Princess of Parma has her box. That's once a week. They do really good things there by all accounts—plays, operas, everything. Mme la Duchesse didn't want to take out a subscription herself, but that doesn't stop us from going to the boxes of one or another of Madame's friends. It's often the Princesse de Guermantes, the wife of M. le Duc's cousin. She's sister to the Duc de Bavière. . . . So you're off again upstairs, are you?" said the footman. Although he was identified with the Guermantes, he regarded "masters" in general in a political light that allowed him to treat Françoise with as much respect as if she, too, were in service with a duchess. "I see you're in good health, madame."

"Oh, if it weren't for these blasted legs of mine! I'm all right on the plain" ("on the plain" meant in the courtyard or in the street, where Françoise was not averse to walking—in other words, on the flat) "but it's these dratted stairs. Goodbye, monsieur. Perhaps I'll see you again this evening."

She was all the more eager to continue her conversations with the footman after he told her that the sons of dukes often bore a princely title, which they retained until the fathers were dead. Clearly the cult of nobility, accommodatingly mingled with a certain spirit of revolt against it, and springing hereditarily from the soil of France, must be strongly ingrained in her people. For Françoise, to whom you might speak of Napoleon's genius or of wireless telegraphy without managing to attract her attention and without her pausing for a moment in her work as she cleared the grate or set the table, at the least hint of such details as learning that the younger son of the Duc de Guermantes was generally called the Prince d'Oléron, would burst out with, "Isn't that lovely!" and stand there in wonder, as though in front of a stained-glass window.

Françoise had also learned from the Prince d'Agrigente's valet, who had become friendly with her because he often called round to deliver letters to the Duchesse, that there had been a great deal of talk in society about the marriage of the Marquis de Saint-Loup to Mlle d'Ambresac, and that it was virtually settled.

The particular villa, the particular opera box into which Mme de Guermantes decanted her life were places I saw as no less magical than her home. The names Guise, Parma, Guermantes-Bavière differentiated from all others the holiday places to which the Duchesse went, the daily festivities that the track of her carriage wheels linked to her mansion. If they told me that the life of Mme de Guermantes consisted of a succession of such holidays and festivities, they enlightened me no further on the subject. Each name gave a different determination to the Duchesse's life, yet merely added a change of mystery without allowing any of its own mystery to escape, so that it simply moved about, protected by an impenetrable barrier, enclosed in a vase, amid the waves of other people's lives. The Duchesse could have lunch beside the Mediterranean at Carnival time, but in the villa of Mme de Guise, where the queen of Parisian society was no more, in her white piqué dress, and amid numerous princesses, than a guest like any other, yet on that account more moving still to me, more herself by being made new, like a prima ballerina who, in an elaborate dance figure, takes the place of each of her sister ballerinas in turn; she could look at shadow-theater performances, but at a party given by the Princess of Parma; she could listen to tragedy or opera, but from the Princesse de Guermantes's box.

Since we localize in a person's body all the potentialities of that person's life, the memory of the people they know and have just left or are

on their way to meet, if, after discovering through Françoise that Mme
de Guermantes was going on foot to luncheon with the Princess of
Parma, I saw her coming down around midday in her flesh-colored
satin dress, above which her face was of the same shade, like a cloud at
sunset, what I saw before me were all the pleasures of the Faubourg
Saint-Germain, contained in that small volume, as though between the
lustrous pearl-pink valves of a shell.

My father had a friend at the ministry, a certain A.-J. Moreau, who,
to distinguish himself from other people named Moreau, always took
care to prefix his name with his two initials, and so became known as
"A.-J." for short. For some reason or other, this A.-J. found himself in
possession of an orchestra ticket for a gala night at the Opéra; he sent
the ticket to my father, and since La Berma, whom I had not seen onstage since my first disappointing experience, was to appear in an act of
Phèdre, my grandmother saw to it that my father gave the ticket to me.

To tell the truth, I set no great store by this opportunity of seeing La
Berma perform, which a few years earlier had thrown me into such a
state of overexcitement. And it was not without a feeling of melancholy
that I registered my indifference to something I had previously put before my health and peace of mind. My need to be able to contemplate
closely the precious particles of reality glimpsed by my imagination had
not diminished; it was not that. But I no longer imagined them to be
found in the diction of a great actress; since my visits to Elstir, it was to
certain tapestries, to certain modern paintings that I had transferred the
inner allegiance I had formerly given to the acting and the tragic art of
La Berma; since my allegiance and my enthusiasm no longer came to
pay incessant worship to the diction and the stage presence of La Berma,
the "double" I possessed of them in my heart had gradually shriveled
away like those other "doubles" of the deceased in ancient Egypt, which
needed to be nourished constantly in order to ensure the life of their
souls. La Berma's art had become pathetically thin. It was no longer inhabited by a profundity of soul.

As I ascended the grand staircase of the Opéra, armed with the ticket
my father had been given, I saw in front of me a man whom I took at
first to be M. de Charlus, whose bearing he had; when he turned to ask

something of an attendant, I saw that I had been mistaken, but I had no hesitation in placing the stranger in the same social class, not only from the way in which he was dressed but also from his manner of speaking to the ticket attendant and to the usherettes who were keeping him waiting. For, quite apart from individual characteristics, there was still at this time a very marked difference between a rich and dressy man from this section of the aristocracy and a rich and dressy man from the world of finance or high industry. Whereas one of the latter would have thought he was asserting his elegance by adopting a cutting and haughty tone in speaking to an inferior, the aristocrat, mild and affable, would convey the impression of respect, of practicing an affectation of humility and patience, the pretense of being any ordinary member of the audience, as the prerogative of his good breeding. It is likely that, seeing him thus dissemble behind such a good-natured smile the uncrossable threshold of the exclusive little world he carried inside him, more than one wealthy banker's son, entering the theater at that moment, would have taken this nobleman for a man of little importance, had he not been struck by the astonishing resemblance to a portrait that had recently appeared in the illustrated papers of a nephew of the Emperor of Austria, the Prince de Saxe, who happened to be in Paris at that moment. I knew him to be a great friend of the Guermantes. And as I reached the ticket attendant myself, I heard the Prince de Saxe (if this is who he really was) say with a smile: "I don't know which number. My cousin told me I need only ask for her box."

He may well have been the Prince de Saxe; perhaps it was the Duchesse de Guermantes (and if it was, I would be able to see her living out one of the moments of her unimaginable life in her cousin's box) that he saw in his mind's eye when he used the words "my cousin told me I need only ask for her box," and this feeling was so strong that his distinctive smiling gaze and the utter simplicity of his words caressed my heart (far more than any abstract reverie would have done) with the alternate intuitions of a possible happiness and a vague glamour. At least, by uttering these words to the ticket attendant, he opened up an ordinary evening in my everyday life to the possibility of entry into a new world: the corridor to which he was directed after he had mentioned the word "box" and into which he now turned was damp and cracked and seemed to lead to marine grottoes, to the mythological realm of the water nymphs. Ahead of me there was simply a gentleman in evening dress walking away from me; but around him, as if I were playing with a clumsy reflector which I was unable to focus accurately upon him, I projected the idea that he was the Prince de Saxe on his way to join the Duchesse de Guermantes. And although he was alone, this idea, external to him, impalpable, immense, and as unsteady as a searchlight, seemed to go before him as a guide, like the deity who stands beside Greek warriors in battle but is invisible to others.

I took my seat, trying to recall a line from *Phèdre* that I could not quite remember. There was not the right number of feet in the form in which I repeated it to myself, but I was not trying to count them, and it simply seemed to me that the imbalance of my line had nothing in common with a line of classical verse. It would not have surprised me to discover that I needed to subtract at least six syllables from my monstrous phrase to make it into an alexandrine. But it suddenly came back to me, and the insurmountable harshness of an inhuman world vanished as if by magic; the syllables of the line immediately matched the required length of an alexandrine, and the excess moved off with the fluid ease of a bubble rising to break on the surface of the water. And as it happened, the monstrosity with which I had struggled turned out to be only a single foot.

A certain number of the front orchestra seats on sale at the box office had been bought by those who wished, out of snobbishness or curiosity, to study the appearance of people whom they would have not otherwise been able to see at close quarters. And it was true that something of their actual society life, normally concealed, could be examined here in public; since the Princess of Parma had distributed her friends in the dress circle, in balcony and parterre boxes, the auditorium was like a drawing room where everyone moved around and went to sit here or there, next to friends.

I was sitting next to some vulgar people who did not know who the regular seat-holders were but were anxious to show that they were capable of identifying them and were naming them loudly. They went on to remark that these regulars behaved as if they were in their own drawing rooms, which implied that they were paying no attention to what was being performed. In fact, it was quite the opposite. The inspired student who has taken an orchestra seat in order to see La Berma thinks only of keeping his gloves clean, of not disturbing, of ingratiating himself with the neighbor whom chance has placed in the next seat, of pursuing with an intermittent smile the fleeting glance, or avoiding with apparent bad manners the intercepted glance, of someone he knows and has seen in the audience; after endless indecision, he decides to go and pay his respects just as the three knocks from the stage, sounding before he has had time to reach his acquaintance, force him to flee back to his seat, like the Hebrews in the Red Sea, through the heaving swell of men and women in the audience whom he has made to get up from their seats, and whose dresses he tears and whose boots he crushes on the way. By contrast, it was because society people sat in their boxes (behind the tiered circle) as in so many little suspended drawing rooms with the fourth wall removed, or little cafés where refreshment can be taken, unintimidated by the gilt-framed mirrors and the red plush seats of this Neapolitan establishment; it was because they rested an indifferent hand on the gilded shafts of the columns supporting this temple of lyric art, and because they remained unmoved by the excessive honors they seemed to receive from the two sculpted figures that held out palm and laurel branches toward each box, that they alone would have had the clarity of mind to attend to the play, if only they had had minds.

At first there were only vague shadows in which one suddenly encountered, like the gleam of an unseen jewel, the phosphorescence of a pair of famous eyes or, like a medallion of Henri IV against a dark background, the bent profile of the Duc d'Aumale, to whom an invisible lady was exclaiming, "Your Highness must allow me to take his coat," and who responded with, "Oh, come, now, Mme d'Ambresac, there's really no need." She went ahead, despite this vague demurral, and became the envy of all for being thus honored.

But in almost all the other boxes, the white deities who inhabited these dark abodes had taken refuge against their shadowy walls and remained invisible. Yet, as the performance proceeded, their vaguely human forms began to emerge in languid succession from the depths of the darkness they embroidered, and, rising toward the light, they allowed their half-naked bodies to emerge as far as the vertical surface of half-light where their gleaming faces appeared behind the gently playful foam of their fluttering feather fans, and beneath their purple, pearl-threaded coiffures, which seemed to have been bent by the motion of incoming waves; beyond lay the front orchestra, the abode of mortals forever separated from the somber transparent realm to which the limpid and reflecting eyes of the water goddesses, dotted about on the smooth liquid surface, served as a frontier. For the folding seats on the shore and the forms of the monsters in the stalls were figured in their eyes in simple accordance with the laws of optics and their angle of incidence, as is the case with those two elements of external reality to which, in the knowledge that they are without any soul, however rudimentary, analogous to our own, we would consider it insane to address a smile or a glance: namely, mineral substances and people to whom we have not been introduced. But within the limits of their domain, by contrast, these radiant daughters of the sea were constantly turning round to smile at the bearded tritons who hung from the anfractuous rocks of the ocean depths, or at some aquatic demigod, whose skull was a polished stone, around which the tide had washed up a smooth deposit of seaweed, and whose gaze was a disc of rock crystal. They leaned toward these creatures and offered them bonbons; occasionally the waters parted to reveal a new Nereid who had just blossomed out of the shadowy depths, a late arrival who smiled apologetically; then, at the end of the act, with no further hope of hearing the melodious sounds of the earth that had drawn them to the surface, the divine sisters plunged back together and disappeared into darkness. But of all these retreats to whose thresholds their idle curiosity to behold the works of man brought the inquisitive goddesses who let no one approach them, the most celebrated was the block of semidarkness known as the parterre box of the Princesse de Guermantes.

Like a great goddess who presides from afar over the sport of lesser deities, the Princesse had deliberately remained somewhat to the back of her box, on a side-facing sofa, red as a coral rock, beside a wide, vitreous reflection that was probably a mirror, and which suggested a section, perpendicular, dark, and liquid, cut by a ray of sunlight in the dazzled crystal of the sea. At once a feather and a corolla, like certain marine plants, a great white flower, as downy as a bird's wing, hung down from the Princesse's forehead along one of her cheeks, following its curve with flirtatious suppleness, lovingly attentive, as if half enclosing it, like a pink egg in the down of a halcyon's nest. Over her hair, reaching down to her eyebrows and continuing lower down at her throat, hung a net made up of little white shells that are fished from certain Southern seas, mingled with pearls, a marine mosaic barely emerging from the waves and every so often plunged back into darkness, in which, even then, a human presence was revealed by the glittering motility of the Princesse's eyes. The beauty that set her far above the other mythical daughters of the semidarkness was not altogether materially and inclusively inscribed in the nape of her neck, in her shoulders, in her arms, or in her waist. But the exquisite, unfinished line of this last was the exact starting point, the inevitable origin of invisible lines into which the eye could not help extending them, marvelous lines, engendered around the woman like the specter of an ideal figure projected against the darkness.

"That's the Princesse de Guermantes," said my neighbor to the gentleman who was with her, taking care to preface the word "Princesse" with a whole string of "P"s to show that the title was ludicrous. "She's not short of a pearl or two. I'm sure if I had as many as that I wouldn't be making such a show of them. It's rather common, to my way of thinking."

And yet, as their eyes caught sight of the Princesse, all those who were looking round to see who was in the audience felt in their hearts that the rightful prize for beauty went to her. The truth was that, with the Duchess of Luxembourg, with Mme de Morienval, Mme de Saint-Euverte, and any number of others, the features that made their faces distinctive were a big red nose next to a harelip, or two wrinkled cheeks and a faint mustache. Such features cast their own spell well enough, since, as a merely conventional form of handwriting, they enabled one to read a famous and impressive name; but ultimately they also gave rise to the notion that ugliness was somehow aristocratic, that it was a matter of indifference that the face of a grand lady should be beautiful, provided it was distinguished. But, like certain painters who sign the bottom of their canvases not with the letters of their names but with some figure that is beautiful in itself, a butterfly, a lizard, a flower, it was the figure of her exquisite body and face that the Princesse affixed to the corner of her box, thus proving that beauty can be the noblest of signatures; for the presence of the Princesse de Guermantes, who brought to the theater only those who were permanent members of her intimate circle, was in the eyes of connoisseurs of the aristocracy the best possible guarantee of authenticity for the painting represented by her box, a sort of scene from the familiar round of her exclusive life in her palaces in Munich and in Paris.

The imagination being like a barrel organ that does not work properly and always plays a different tune from the one it should, every time I had heard anyone mention the Princesse de Guermantes-Bavière, a recollection of certain sixteenth-century masterpieces began to sing in my head. I was forced to rid myself of the association now that I saw her there before me, offering crystallized fruit to a stout gentleman in tails. In no way did this lead me to conclude that she and her guests were mere mortals like the rest of us. I was very conscious of the fact that what they were doing was only a game, and that as a prelude to the acts of their real life (the important part of which they presumably did not conduct here) it was appropriate, in accordance with rituals of which I knew nothing, that they should pretend to offer and decline bonbons, a gesture stripped of its normal significance and decided beforehand, like the steps of a ballerina who alternately dances on point or circles around a scarf. For all I knew, perhaps as she offered him bonbons, the goddess was saying, with that irony in her voice (for I saw her smile), "Will you have a bonbon?" What did it matter to me? I should have found a delicious refinement in the deliberate dryness, in the style of Mérimée[10] or Meilhac,[11] of these words addressed by a goddess to a demigod who knew what sublime thoughts they both held in their minds, reserved no doubt for the moment when they would resume their real life, and who played along with the game by answering her with the same mysterious roguish connivance: "Thank you. I should rather like a cherry bonbon." And I would have listened to this exchange as eagerly as to a scene from *Le Mari de la débutante*, in which the absence of poetry and lofty thought, elements that Meilhac would have been perfectly capable of introducing, seemed to me in itself a refinement, conventional enough and therefore all the more mysterious and instructive.

"The fat fellow over there is the Marquis de Garançay," said the man next to me in a knowing voice. He had not quite caught the name that had been whispered in the row behind.

The Marquis de Palancy, his head turned sideways on his craning neck, his great round eye glued to the glass of his monocle, moved slowly around in the transparent gloom and appeared no more to see the public in the orchestra than a fish that drifts by, unaware of the crowd of curious visitors, behind the glass wall of an aquarium. Occasionally he paused, venerable, wheezy, and moss-covered, and the onlooker could not have told whether he was unwell, asleep, swimming, spawning, or simply taking breath. No one aroused my envy more, because of his apparent familiarity with this box and the indifference with which he allowed the Princesse to offer him her box of bonbons; as she did so, she threw him a glance from her lovely eyes, cut from a diamond that intelligence and friendliness seemed to turn liquid at such moments, whereas when they were still, reduced to their purely material beauty, to their merely mineral brilliance, if the least thing caused them to move, even slightly, they set the depths of the orchestra seats ablaze with the horizontal splendor of their inhuman fire. But now, because the act from *Phèdre* to be performed by La Berma was about to begin, the Princesse moved to the front of her box; and, as if she herself were a theatrical apparition, as she crossed through a different zone of light, I saw not only the color but the fabric of her ornate costume change. There in the box, now drained dry, emergent and no longer part of the kingdom of the sea, the Princesse, ceasing to be a Nereid, appeared turbaned in white and blue, like some marvelous tragic actress dressed for the part of Zaïre or possibly Orosmane;[12] then, when she had taken her seat in the front row, I saw that the downy halcyon's nest which lovingly shielded the pearly pink of her cheeks was an immense bird of paradise, soft, glittering, and velvety.

But my eyes were diverted from the Princesse de Guermantes's box by a badly dressed, ugly little woman, her eyes aflame with anger, accompanied by two young people, who came and sat a few seats away from me. Then the curtain rose. I could not help being saddened by the fact that there was now nothing left of my former frame of mind, when, in order to miss nothing of the extraordinary phenomenon I would have gone to the ends of the earth to see, I used to keep my mind prepared, like the sensitive plates astronomers take to Africa or the West Indies for the scrupulous observation of a comet or an eclipse; when I sat there in fear that a cloud (a bad mood on the performer's part, an incident in the auditorium) might prevent the spectacle from taking place with maximum intensity; when I should not have believed I was seeing it in the best conditions unless I went to the very theater that had been consecrated to her like an altar, where it still felt that an integral (though ancillary) part of her appearance from behind the little red curtain was played by the ticket attendants with their white carnations whom she had appointed, by the vaulted gallery over a pit crowded with badly dressed people, by the women selling programs with her photograph, by the chestnut trees in the square outside, by all these companions, these confidants of my impressions at that time and, to my mind, inseparable from them. *Phèdre*, the "declaration scene," La Berma had had for me then a sort of absolute existence. Placed at a remove from the world of daily experience, they existed in their own right; I had to move toward them, penetrate what I could of them; and even if I opened my eyes and my soul wide to them, I would still absorb very little. But how pleasant life seemed to me then: the insignificance of my daily life did not matter, any more than the time we spend dressing, getting ready to go out, since beyond it there existed, in absolute form, rewarding yet difficult to approach, impossible to possess in their entirety, the more substantial realities of *Phèdre* and the way La Berma spoke her lines. Steeped in these daydreams of the perfection possible in dramatic art, from which a strong dose of drama could have been extracted had anyone chosen to analyze my mind at the time, at whatever hour of the day or even of the night, I was like a battery charging itself with electricity. And things had reached such a point that, ill as I was, even if I had thought I would die from it, I needed at all costs to go and hear La Berma. But now all this, like a hill that seems to be sky-blue when seen from a distance but from close up reverts to our common-place vision of things, had left the world of the absolute and was no more than a thing like other things; I took notice of it because I was there; actors were no different in substance from the people I knew, try-ing to deliver as best they could these lines from *Phèdre*, which them-selves no longer formed some sublime and distinct essence, existing in isolation, but were lines that were more or less effective, ready to rejoin the vast corpus of French verse, to which they belonged. This made me feel a sense of despondency all the more profound in that, if the object of my stubbornly persistent desire had ceased to exist, by contrast, the same tendency to get stuck in daydreams, which varied from year to year but still led to sudden, heedless impulses, refused to go away. A day on which I left my sickbed to go and see one of Elstir's paintings or a medieval tapestry in some country house was so like the day on which I ought to have left for Venice, the day I went to see La Berma, the day I departed for Balbec, that I felt in advance that the immediate object of my sacrifice would leave me indifferent in no time at all, that I might therefore pass very close to the place without actually going to see the painting or the tapestries for which I was prepared at this time to face any number of sleepless nights and bouts of pain. The shifting nature of its object made me sense the vanity of my effort and at the same time its immensity, which I had not really acknowledged, like one of those neurasthenics whose exhaustion is doubled when it is pointed out to them that they are exhausted. In the meantime, my daydreams lent glamour to anything that came their way. And even in my most carnal desires, oriented always in a particular direction, concentrated around a single dream, I could have recognized as their primary motive an idea, one for which I would have laid down my life, at the very heart of which lay, as in my daydreams when I used to sit reading in the after-noon in the garden at Combray, the notion of perfection.

I no longer felt the same indulgence as before for the painstaking endeavors to convey feelings of love or anger that I had then observed in the delivery and gestures of Aricie, Ismène, and Hippolyte. It was not that the actors—they were the same—did not still seek as intelligently as they had before to introduce a caressing inflexion or a calculated ambiguity into their voices, a tragic breadth or an appealing sense of supplication into their gestures. Their intonations commanded the voice—"Be gentle, sing like a nightingale, be soothing," or, conversely, "Make yourself furious"—and then fell upon it in an attempt to carry it along with them in their frenzy. But their voices, rebellious and independent of their diction, refused to be anything but their natural voices with their material defects or charms, their everyday ordinariness or affectation, and so presented a set of acoustic and social phenomena which the emotive power of the lines they were delivering could do nothing to alter.

Similarly, the actors' gestures said to their arms, to their robes, "Be majestic." But their unsubmissive limbs allowed a biceps that knew nothing of the part they were playing to flaunt itself between shoulder and elbow; their bodies continued to express the triviality of everyday life and to emphasize not the subtlety of Racine but the related functions of their muscles; and the hanging robes that they held up fell back into a vertical drop in which the laws governing falling bodies were challenged solely by the tame movement of textiles. At this point the little woman sitting near me exclaimed: "Not a jot of applause! Just look at her getup! She's too old for it, she can't do it any more. She really ought to give it up."

Amid protests of "Hush!" from the people near them, the two young people who were with her attempted to quiet her down, and her fury became confined to her eyes alone. In any case, such fury could have been relevant only to success and fame, and La Berma, who had earned so much money in the past, had nothing now but her debts. Since she was forever making business or social appointments she was unable to keep, she had messengers running all over the place with her apologies, hotel suites booked in advance which she would never use, oceans of perfume for her dogs, penalties to be paid for breaches of contract with all her managers. Failing any more serious expenses, and being less voluptuous than Cleopatra, she would have found the means to squander provinces and kingdoms on telegrams and hired carriages. But the little woman near me was an actress whose career had not been successful, and who had vowed a deadly hatred toward La Berma. The latter had just come onstage. And then, miraculously, like the lessons that we have vainly spent an exhausting evening trying to learn, and which we find we know by heart after a night's sleep, and like the faces of dead friends which the intense efforts of our memory pursue without success and which then appear right there before our eyes, lifelike, when we are no longer thinking of them, the talent of La Berma, which had escaped me when I had struggled hard to grasp its essence, now, after these years of oblivion, in this hour of indifference, imposed itself forcefully upon my admiration as something self-evident. Previously, in my attempts to distinguish this talent, I had somehow deducted the part of Phèdre itself from what I was hearing, a part that was the common property of all the actresses who played the role, and which I had studied in advance so that I could subtract it and, from what was left, glean the talent of Mme Berma in isolation. But this talent, which I was trying to perceive outside the role, was inseparable from it. The same is true of a great musician (it seems that this was the case with Vinteuil when he played the piano): his playing is that of so great a pianist that you forget completely that the performer is a pianist; by avoiding the whole apparatus of strenuous muscularity, which achieves sporadically brilliant effects like the whole splatter of notes in which the undiscerning listener at least sees evidence of talent in its material, tangible form, his playing has become so transparent, so full of what he is interpreting, that he himself disappears and becomes simply a window opening onto a masterpiece. The reasons that dictated the diction and the gestures of Aricie, Ismène, and Hippolyte and seemed to frame them like an imposing or an unobtrusive border, were obvious to me; but Phèdre had interiorized her own, and my mind had not managed to wrest from her diction or her moods, to apprehend in the spare simplicity of their flawless surfaces, the strokes of inspiration, the effects, which remained unobtrusive, so completely had they been absorbed. La Berma's voice, which retained no scrap of inert matter refractory to the mind, betrayed no sign of the excessive tears which, because they had been unable to soak into it, could be seen trickling down the marble of the voices of Aricie or Ismène; it had been rendered supple and sensitive down to its smallest cells, like the instrument of a great violinist in whom, when one says that he produces a beautiful sound, one means to praise not a physical property but a superiority of soul; and as in a classical landscape where in the place of a vanished nymph there is an inanimate spring, discernible and conscious intention had become a strangely limpid quality of tone, apt and cold. La Berma's arms, which the lines of verse themselves, with the same force that they used to project her voice from her lips, seemed to raise to her breast like branches displaced by rushing water; her stage presence, which she had gradually developed, which she was to modify still further, and which was based upon motivations that were anchored in something quite different from those that could be glimpsed in the gestures of her fellow actors, but motivations that had lost their initial self-consciousness, melted into a kind of radiance, and set throbbing around the character of Phèdre rich and complex elements which the fascinated spectator took not for accomplished acting but for real life; those white veils themselves, exhausted and faithful, which seemed to be made of a living substance and to have been spun by the half-pagan, half-Jansenist suffering around which they clung like a frail and shrinking cocoon—all these, voice, stage presence, gestures, veils, around that embodiment of an idea represented by a line of poetry (an embodiment that, unlike human bodies, does not stand in the way of the soul like an opaque obstacle that prevents us from seeing it, but is there like a purified, vitalized garment in which the soul is diffused and can be discovered), were merely additional coverings that, instead of concealing, revealed the greater splendor of the soul that had assimilated and spread itself through them, like lava flows of different substances, turned translucent, superimposed upon each other only to refract the more richly the imprisoned, central ray of light that shines through them, and to render more far-reaching, more precious, and more beautiful the flame-drenched matter in which it is sheathed. So La Berma's interpretation was, around Racine's work, a second work, it, too, enlivened by genius.

My impression, to tell the truth, though more agreeable than before, was not really different. Only, I no longer pitted it against a preconceived, abstract, and false notion of dramatic genius, and I understood now that dramatic genius was precisely this. I had been thinking earlier that if I had not enjoyed my first experience of La Berma it was because, as with my earlier encounters with Gilberte in the Champs-Élysées, I had approached it with too strong a desire. Between these two disappointments there was perhaps not only this resemblance, but another, deeper one. The impression made upon us by a person or a work of strong character (or its interpretation) is intrinsic to them. We have brought along with us the ideas of "beauty," "breadth of style," "pathos," which we might just possibly think we recognize in the banality of a passable talent or face, but our critical mind is confronted in fact with the nagging presence of a form for which it possesses no intellectual equivalent, the unknown part of which it needs to extricate. It hears a high-pitched sound, an oddly questioning intonation. It asks: "Is that good? Is it admiration I am feeling? Is this what is meant by richness of color, nobility, power?" And what answers back is a high-pitched voice, an oddly questioning tone, the despotic impression, wholly material, caused by a person we do not know, in which no scope is left for "breadth of interpretation." And for this reason, really fine works of art, if they are given genuine attention, are the ones that disappoint us most, because in the sum total of our ideas there is none that responds to an individual impression.

This was exactly what La Berma's acting made clear to me. This was indeed what was meant by nobility, by sensitivity of diction. Now I could appreciate the merits of a wide-ranging, poetic, and powerful interpretation; or, rather, it was upon this that these words are conventionally conferred, but only in the way that we give the names Mars, Venus, Saturn to planets that have nothing mythological about them. Our feelings belong to one world, our ability to name things and our thoughts belong to another; we can establish a concordance between the two, but not bridge the gap. And it was something like this gap, this fault, that I had to cross when, the first time I went to see La Berma act, and after straining to catch her every word, I had found some difficulty in connecting my ideas of "nobility of interpretation" and "originality" and had broken into applause only after a moment's blankness, and as if my applause did not spring from my actual impression but was somehow linked to my preconceived ideas and to the pleasure I felt in saying to myself, "At last I am listening to La Berma." And the difference that exists between a person or a work of art of strongly individual character and the idea of beauty exists just as much between what it makes us feel and the idea of love or admiration. Listening to La Berma had given me no pleasure (any more than seeing Gilberte). I had said to myself, "So I *don't* admire her." Yet all the while I was thinking only about deepening my understanding of her acting, I was preoccupied with that alone, and I was trying to open my mind as wide as possible to grasp everything that was involved in her acting; I now understood that this was exactly what admiration was.

Was this genius, which La Berma's interpretation was there only to reveal, the genius of Racine alone?

This is what I thought at first. I was soon to think differently, once the act from *Phèdre* was over, and after the curtain calls, during which my furious old neighbor, drawing her tiny body up to its full height, turning sideways in her seat, sat there poker-faced with her arms folded across her breast to show that she was not joining in the general applause and to draw attention to a protest which to her seemed sensational but which nobody noticed. The play that followed was one of those novelties which at one time I would have expected, since they were not famous, to be slight and restricted in scope, given that they had no existence outside their current performance. But I did not feel, as I did with a classic play, the disappointment of seeing the eternity of a masterpiece reduced to the dimensions of the footlights and to the duration of a performance that dealt with it just like some minor piece of theater. Also, at each set speech that I sensed the audience liked and that would one day be famous, in the absence of any past fame that could be attributed to it, I added the fame it would enjoy in the future, through a mental effort that is the reverse of that which consists of imagining masterpieces on the day of their first frail appearance, when it seemed utterly unlikely that a title that no one had ever heard before would one day be placed beside those of the author's other works and bathed in the same light. And this role would one day figure in the list of her finest interpretations, next to that of Phèdre. Not that the role in itself was devoid of all literary merit; but La Berma played it as sublimely as she did Phèdre. I understood then that the work of the writer was for the actress no more than the raw material, of no particular distinction in itself, for the creation of her masterly interpretation, just as the great painter I had met in Balbec, Elstir, had found the inspiration for two equally good paintings in the drabness of a school building and in a cathedral that is itself a masterpiece. And in the same way that a painter dissolves houses, carts, people in some broad effect of light that makes them homogeneous, La Berma spread great sheets of terror or tenderness over the words, which were equally blended, all smoothed down or heightened, and which a mediocre performer would have painstakingly detached from one another. Of course, each word had its own inflection, and La Berma's diction did not blur the distinction between the lines of verse. Is it not already a first element of ordered complexity, of beauty, to hear a rhyme—that is to say, something that is at once similar to and distinct from the preceding rhyme-word, something that is prompted by it, yet which introduces the variation of a new idea—and to have the sense of two systems superimposed, one intellectual, the other metrical? But La Berma also integrated the words, the lines, and even whole speeches into ensembles that were vaster than themselves, at the margins of which it was magical to see them obliged to stop, to break off; in the same way, a poet will delight in momentarily delaying at the rhyme break the next word to come, and a composer in merging the various words of the libretto into a single rhythm which both runs counter to them and carries them along. Thus, into the prose of the modern playwright as into the verse of Racine, La Berma had the ability to introduce those vast images of suffering, nobility, and passion that were her personal masterpieces, and which bore her hallmark in the same way as the portraits a painter has made of different sitters.

I would not have wanted, as I once did, to be able to retain a fixed image of the poses adopted by La Berma, or of the fine sense of color she presented for a mere second in a lighting effect that immediately faded, never to reappear, or to have her repeat the same line over and over again. I realized that my former desire had been more exacting than the requirements of the poet, the actress, and the great decorative artist who had staged the production, and that the magic surrounding a line as it was delivered, the shifting gestures perpetually transformed into others, the successive tableaux were the fleeting result, the momentary objective, the mobile masterpiece which the art of the theater meant itself to be, and which the attentiveness of an overcaptivated spectator would destroy by trying to hold it in a fixed image. I was not even anxious to come back and hear La Berma again another day; I had been completely gratified; it was when I was too full of admiration not to be disappointed by the object of my admiration, whether it was Gilberte or La Berma, that I was already asking tomorrow's impression to provide me with the pleasure yesterday's had denied me. Without seeking to question more deeply the elation that I had just felt, and which I could have perhaps turned to more profitable use, I said to myself, as some of my school friends used to say, "La Berma tops them all for me," but with the confused feeling that La Berma's genius was not perhaps very accurately expressed by the way I was stating my preference and my award of "top place," however much peace of mind this brought me.

Just as the second play began, I looked over to Mme de Guermantes's box. The Princesse, with a movement that generated an exquisite contour which my mind pursued into the void, had just turned her head toward the back of the box; her guests were standing and looking in the same direction, and between the double hedge they formed, with the self-assured grandeur of a goddess, but with an uncharacteristic mildness of manner that was due to her feigned and smiling embarrassment at arriving so late and forcing everyone to get up in the middle of the performance, the Duchesse de Guermantes entered the box, smothered in white chiffon. She went straight up to her cousin, made a deep curtsy to a young man with fair hair seated in the front row, and, turning toward the idolized sea monsters floating in the depths of the cavern, greeted these demigods of the Jockey Club—and at that moment I would have given anything to be one of them, particularly M. de Palancy—with the familiarity of an old friend, an allusion to her day-to-day relations with them over the last fifteen years. I could feel the mystery but could not decipher the secret of the smiling glance she addressed to her friends, of its azure brilliance as she gave her hand to them in turn, and had I been able to break down its prism and analyze its crystallizations, it might have revealed to me the essence of the unknown life inhabiting it at that moment. The Duc de Guermantes came in behind his wife, the flash of his monocle, the smiling gleam of his teeth, the whiteness of his carnation or of his pleated shirtfront casting their own light and relegating his eyebrows, lips, and tailcoat to the shadows; with a gesture of his outstretched hand, which he let fall on their shoulders, standing bolt upright with his head motionless, he commanded the inferior monsters who were making way for him to resume their seats, and made a deep bow to the fair-haired young man. It was as if the Duchesse had guessed that her cousin, of whom, rumor had it, she was prone to make fun for what she called her "exaggerations" (a word that from her own point of view, so wittily French and restrained, lent itself readily to Germanic poetry and enthusiasm), would be dressed this evening in a manner that the Duchesse thought of as "theatrical," and that she had decided to give her a lesson in good taste. Instead of the wonderful soft plumage that hung from the Princesse's head down to her neck, instead of the net of shells and pearls, the Duchesse wore only a simple aigrette in her hair, and because it surmounted her arched nose and prominent eyes, it looked like the crest of a bird. Her neck and shoulders emerged from a snowy drift of chiffon against which fluttered a fan of swan's feathers, but below this her gown, the bodice of which was adorned simply with innumerable sequins (either tiny metal sticks or beads, or brilliants), clung to her figure with a positively British precision. But, however differently they were dressed, after the Princesse had given her cousin the seat she had previously occupied, the two women could be seen turning to eye each other in mutual admiration.

Perhaps Mme de Guermantes would smile next day as she mentioned the Princesse's slightly overelaborate coiffure, but this would not prevent her from declaring that her cousin had looked nonetheless ravishing and wonderfully dressed; and the Princesse, for whose taste there was something a little cold, a little severe and "tailored" in the way her cousin dressed, would discern an exquisite refinement in such strict sobriety. Furthermore, the harmony that existed between the two women, the universal and preordained gravitational force of their upbringing, neutralized the contrasts not only in their ways of dressing but in their attitudes. At the invisible magnetic boundary lines that the elegance of their manners drew between them, the expansiveness natural to the Princesse became more subdued, while the formal correctness of the Duchesse allowed itself to be drawn toward them, to become more flexible, to turn to sweetness and charm. As in the play that was now being performed, to understand how much personal poetry La Berma drew from it, one had only to transfer her role, the role she alone knew how to play, to any other actress, so the spectator who looked up toward the balcony would have seen, in two of the boxes there, how an "arrangement" that was supposed to resemble that of the Princesse de Guermantes's box merely made the Baronne de Morienval appear eccentric, pretentious, and ill bred, and how an attempt, both painstaking and costly, to imitate the dress and style of the Duchesse de Guermantes merely made Mme de Cambremer look like some provincial schoolgirl mounted on wires, rigid, desiccated, and crabby, with a plume of feathers from some funeral procession stuck vertically in her hair. Perhaps the latter had no place in a theater where only the most distinguished women of that season filled the boxes (even those on the highest tier, which, seen from below, seemed like huge hampers dotted with human flowers, attached to the circle of the auditorium by the red cords of their plush-covered partitions) and presented an ephemeral panorama which deaths, scandals, illnesses, quarrels would soon alter, but which was for the moment held motionless by attentiveness, heat, dizziness, dust, elegance, and boredom, in the sort of eternally tragic instant of unconscious expectancy and calm torpor which, in retrospect, seems to have preceded the explosion of a bomb or the first flames of a great fire.

The reason for Mme de Cambremer's presence was that the Princess of Parma—who, like most other aristocratic people, was utterly without snobbery and, by contrast, eaten up with a proud and passionate sense of charity as strong as her taste for what she believed to be the Arts—had ceded a few boxes here and there to women like Mme de Cambremer, who did not belong to the highest ranks of aristocratic society, but whom she knew through her charity work. Mme de Cambremer kept her eyes on the Duchesse and the Princesse de Guermantes, which was easy enough for her to do, because she was not really acquainted with either and so could not be suspected of fishing for some sign of recognition. To be received into the society of these two great ladies was nonetheless what she had been striving toward with untiring patience over the last ten years. She had calculated that it would possibly take her another five years. But since she had succumbed to an incurable disease, the inexorable nature of which she thought she knew, for she was a woman who prided herself on her medical knowledge, she was afraid that she might not live to see her aim achieved. She was happy enough this evening with the thought that all these women she scarcely knew would be able to see a person from their own set seated beside her, the young Marquis de Beausergent, the brother of Mme d'Argencourt, who moved between both social worlds, and whom the women of the second were delighted to parade before the eyes of those in the first. He was seated beside Mme de Cambremer, on a chair placed at an angle so that he could inspect who was in the other boxes. He knew everyone in them, and to acknowledge his friends, with the exquisite elegance of his attractively arched figure, his delicate features and fair hair, with a smile in his blue eyes, he half raised his upright body in a gesture of nonchalant deference, thus cutting a precise image into the rectangle of the oblique plane in which he was placed, like one of those old prints depicting the proud bearing of a noble courtier. He often accepted Mme de Cambremer's invitations to the theater; in the auditorium and the lobby as they were leaving, he stayed loyally at her side amid the press of more brilliant women friends around him, to whom he refrained from speaking, to avoid any embarrassment, as if he had been in doubtful company. If the Princesse de Guermantes happened to pass by on such an occasion, like some beautiful light-footed Diana, trailing her incomparable cloak, with everyone's head and eyes turning to follow her (Mme de Cambremer's in particular), M. de Beausergent would become engrossed in conversation with his companion and respond to the Princesse's dazzling smile only with constraint and with the well-bred reserve and well-intentioned aloofness of a person whose friendly attention might have caused a momentarily awkward situation.

Had Mme de Cambremer not already known that the box belonged to the Princesse, she could still have told that the Duchesse was a guest from the semblance of greater interest which the latter was devoting to the spectacle of stage and auditorium, out of politeness toward her hostess. But, concurrently with this centrifugal force, another, opposite force, generated by the same desire to be agreeable, drew the Duchesse's attention back to her own dress, her aigrette, her necklace, her bodice, and to that of the Princesse herself, whose subject, whose slave her cousin seemed to proclaim herself to be, present with the sole purpose of seeing her, ready to follow her elsewhere had the titular holder of the box taken it into her head to leave, and regarding the rest of the audience merely as a collection of strangers who were interesting as curiosities, although she had any number of friends among them in whose boxes she was to be found on other occasions, when she never failed to give them proof of the same loyalty, exclusive, relativistic, and lasting exactly one week. Mme de Cambremer was surprised to see her there that evening. She knew that the Duchesse stayed on very late at Guermantes and had supposed that she was still there. But she had been told that sometimes, when there was some entertainment in Paris that caught her interest, Mme de Guermantes would order one of her carriages to be waiting for her as soon as she had taken tea with the hunt party and, as the sun was going down, set off at full trot through the half-light of the forest, then along the road, to catch the train at Combray to be in Paris the same evening. "Perhaps she has come from Guermantes specially to see La Berma," thought Mme de Cambremer admiringly. And she remembered Swann saying, in the ambiguous jargon he shared with M. de Charlus, "The Duchesse is one of the noblest creatures in Paris, the cream of the choicest, most refined society." And I, who derived from the names Guermantes, Bavière, and Condé my notions of the life and thoughts of the two cousins (something I could no longer do from their faces, now that I had seen them), would rather have had their opinion of *Phèdre* than that of the greatest critic in the world. For in the critic's opinion I would have found merely intelligence, intelligence superior to my own but of the same kind. But the opinion of the Duchesse and Princesse de Guermantes, which would have furnished me with invaluable facts about the nature of these two poetic creatures, was something I imagined through the power of their names and credited with an irrational charm, and, with the thirst and longing of a man in a fever, what I demanded that their opinion of *Phèdre* should restore to me was the charm of the summer afternoons I had spent on walks along the Guermantes way.

Mme de Cambremer was trying to distinguish how the two cousins were dressed. Personally, I had no doubt that their manner of dressing was peculiar to themselves, not merely in the sense that livery with red collar or blue lapels had once been peculiar to the houses of Guermantes and Condé, but, rather, as for a bird, whose plumage is not some added adornment of its beauty but an extension of its body. The way the two women dressed seemed to me like the snow-white or the many-colored materialization of their inner worlds and, like the gestures I had seen the Princesse de Guermantes make, and which, I assumed, corresponded to some hidden motivation, the feathers that hung down from her forehead and the dazzling, sequined bodice of her cousin seemed to have a particular significance and to represent for each of the women an attribute which was hers alone, the meaning of which I should have liked to know; the bird of paradise seemed to be as inseparable from one of them as the peacock is from Juno; I did not believe that any other woman could usurp the sequined bodice of the other any more than the fringed and shining shield of Minerva. And when I looked over toward their box, far more than on the ceiling of the theater, which was painted with lifeless allegories, it was like seeing, thanks to some miraculous break in the customary clouds, the assembly of the Gods contemplating the spectacle of mortals, beneath a red canopy, in a clear patch of light, between two pillars of heaven. My eyes studied this momentary apotheosis with a disquiet that was partly attenuated by the feeling that I was unknown to the Immortals; the Duchesse had certainly seen me once, with her husband, but could surely have retained no memory of that, and it did not disturb me that she should find herself so placed in her box that she could gaze down at the anonymous collection of madrepores in the orchestra, for I was happy to be dissolved in their midst; and then, at the moment in which, by virtue of the laws of refraction, the blurred outline of the protozoan with no individual existence which I was must have been reflected in the impassive current of her two blue eyes, I saw them light up: the Duchesse, goddess turned woman, and for that moment a thousand times more beautiful, raised in my direction the white-gloved hand that had been resting on the edge of the box and waved it as a sign of friendship; my eyes were met by the spontaneous incandescence and the flashing eyes of the Princesse, who had unwittingly set them ablaze merely by the movement of looking to see whom her cousin had just greeted, and the latter, who had recognized me, showered upon me the sparkling and celestial rain of her smile.

Now, every morning, well before the time she left the house, I made a long detour and went to post myself at the corner of the street she normally took, and when I thought she was about to appear, I would walk back along the street as if I were absorbed in my thoughts, looking in the opposite direction, and then raising my eyes toward her the moment I drew level with her, as if she were the last person I expected to see. Indeed, for the first few mornings, to be sure of not missing her, I even waited in front of the house. And every time the carriage gate opened (to let out a succession of people who were not the one I was waiting for), its shuddering clatter would go on vibrating in my heart and take a long time to die down. For never did a devotee of a famous actress whom he does not know, hanging around at the stage door, never did an angry or idolatrous crowd, gathered to insult or to carry in triumph through the streets the condemned man or the hero it believes to be about to emerge every time any sound is heard from inside the prison or the palace—never did either feel the emotion I felt as I awaited the departure of the aristocratic lady, who, in her ordinary dress, had the power, in the grace of her deportment (quite different from the manner she adopted when she entered a drawing room or a theater box), to transform her morning walk—and for me she was the only one in the world out walking—into a whole poem of elegance, into the most refined adornment, the rarest flower under the sun. But after three days of this, so that the concierge should not realize what I was up to, I went much farther afield, to some point along the route usually taken by the Duchesse. Before the evening at the theater, I had often made similar outings before lunch when the weather was fine; if it had been raining, I would go down to take a short walk as soon as there was a bright spell, and suddenly, coming toward me on the still-wet pavement that the sunshine had transformed into a surface of lacquered gold, in the apotheosis of a crossroads powdery with a mist tanned and bleached by the sun, I caught sight of a schoolgirl followed by her teacher, or a dairymaid with her white sleeves, and I would stand there motionless, my hand against my heart, which was already leaping forward toward an unknown life; I would try to remember the name of the street, the time of day, the doorway into which the young girl (I sometimes followed her) had disappeared and from which she had not re-emerged. Fortunately, the fleeting nature of these pet images, which I promised myself I would seek out again, meant that they did not remain very vividly in my memory. No matter, I felt less unhappy now about my poor health and the fact that I had never mustered enough conviction to begin work, to start writing a book; the world seemed a better place to live in, life more interesting to experience, now that I could see that the streets of Paris, like the roads in Balbec, blossomed with those unknown beauties I had so often tried to spirit up from the woods of Méséglise, each one of whom aroused a voluptuous desire that she alone seemed capable of satisfying.

After returning home from the Opéra, I had added for the following morning another image to the ones I had been hoping to encounter again for the last few days, the image of Mme de Guermantes, tall, with her fine, fair hair piled high, with the affection promised by the smile she had sent me from her cousin's box. I intended to follow the route that Françoise had told me the Duchesse took, and I would try at the same time to cross paths with the two girls I had seen two days earlier by not missing anyone emerging from a class or a catechism. But, meanwhile, from time to time, the glittering smile of Mme de Guermantes and the feeling of warmth it had created came back to me. And without knowing quite what I was doing, I tried to place these (in the way that a woman who has just been given a certain kind of jeweled buttons examines their effect against a dress) against the romantic notions that I had long held, and which had been set free by Albertine's coldness, Gisèle's premature departure, and, before that, by my deliberate and overlong separation from Gilberte (the idea, for instance, of being loved by a woman, of having a life in common with her); then it was the image of one or the other of the two girls seen in the street that I matched against these ideas, and immediately after came my memory of the Duchesse, which I tried to adapt to them. Compared with these romantic ideas of mine, the image of Mme de Guermantes at the Opéra was very insignificant, a tiny star beside the long tail of a blazing comet; moreover, I had been very familiar with these ideas long before I knew Mme de Guermantes; by contrast, the memory of her was something I possessed imperfectly; it was during the hours when, instead of floating around in my mind like images of other pretty women, it gradually developed into a unique and definitive association—utterly distinct from every other feminine image—with the romantic ideas I had held for so long before it appeared, it was during those few hours when I remembered it best that I ought to have decided to discover exactly what it was; but at that point I was still unaware of the importance it was to assume for me; I cherished it simply as a first encounter with Mme de Guermantes inside myself, the first, the only true sketch, the only one taken from life, the only one that was really Mme de Guermantes; yet, during the few hours when I was fortunate enough to be able to hold it there without conscious attention, this memory must have been really charming, since it was always to it, still freely then, unhurriedly and untiring, with no trace of compulsion or anxiety, that my ideas of love returned; then, as these ideas came to fix it more securely, it acquired greater strength from them but became less clear itself; soon I could no longer recapture it; and in my dreams I no doubt distorted it completely, because, each time I saw Mme de Guermantes, I realized that there was a gap, always a different sort of gap, between what I had imagined and what I saw. It is true that, every morning now, at the moment when Mme de Guermantes appeared at the top of the street, I went on seeing her tall figure, the face with its bright eyes beneath the fine hair, all the things for which I stood waiting; but by contrast, a few minutes later, when I directed my gaze elsewhere so as to seem not to be expecting the encounter I had come to seek, and raised my eyes to the Duchesse the moment we drew level in the street, what my eyes then encountered were red patches (it was not clear whether they were caused by the fresh air or by a blotchy complexion) on a sullen face that gave a distinctly curt nod, far removed from the friendly gesture of the *Phèdre* evening, in response to the greeting that I addressed to her daily with an air of surprise, and which did not seem to please her. Yet, after a few days, during which the memory of the two girls fought against heavy odds with that of Mme de Guermantes for the mastery of my amorous feelings, it was generally the latter that in the end emerged unscathed, as if of its own accord, while its challengers withdrew; it was to it, in the end, voluntarily still and as if from choice and with pleasure, that I had transferred all my thoughts of love. The girls from catechism class and a certain dairymaid left my mind forever; and yet I had given up hope of encountering in the street what I had come there to seek, the affection promised to me at the theater in a smile, the figure of a woman, and the bright face beneath her fair hair, which were only real when seen from a distance. Now I could not even have said what Mme de Guermantes was like, what I recognized her by, for every day, in the picture she presented as a whole, the face was as different as the dress and the hat.

Why was it, on any given day, as I saw coming toward me beneath a mauve hood a sweet, smooth face whose charms were symmetrically distributed around a pair of blue eyes, and into which the curve of the nose seemed to be absorbed, that a delighted sense of shock informed me that I would not return home without having caught a glimpse of Mme de Guermantes? Why did I feel the same stir of emotion, affect the same indifference, look away with the same air of abstraction as the day before, when, in some side street, I caught sight of the profile, be-neath a navy-blue toque, of a beaklike nose against a red cheek, barred across by a piercing eye, like some Egyptian deity? On one occasion it was not merely a woman with a bird's beak that I saw, but almost the bird itself: Mme de Guermantes was dressed in fur to the tip of her toque, and since no other material was visible, she seemed to be natu-rally furred, like certain vultures, whose thick, soft, tawny plumage looks like the coat of an animal. Amid this natural plumage, her tiny head curved out its beak, and the prominent eyes were piercing and blue.

On such-and-such a day, after I had been pacing up and down the street for hours on end without catching sight of Mme de Guermantes, suddenly, inside a dairy shop hidden away between two town houses in this district both aristocratic and working-class, the vague and unfamil-iar face of a smartly dressed woman who was asking to see some *petits suisses* would emerge, and before I had time to see who it was, I would be struck, as by a flash of lightning reaching me sooner than the rest of the image, by the glance of the Duchesse; on another occasion, having failed to see her and hearing midday strike, I realized that it was point-less to wait any longer, and I was making my mournful way home; deep in my disappointment, staring blindly at a disappearing carriage, I sud-denly realized that the nod a lady had given from the carriage window was intended for me, and that the lady, whose features, relaxed and pale or, conversely, tense and vivid, beneath a round hat with a tall feather, constituted the face of a person whom I had assumed to be an unknown stranger, but who was in fact Mme de Guermantes, whose greeting I had let pass without so much as an acknowledgment. And sometimes I encountered her as I entered the house, standing by the lodge where the detestable concierge, whose prying eyes I loathed, would be bowing and scraping to her, and also no doubt supplying her with "reports" of what was going on. For the entire staff of the Guermantes household, hidden behind the window nets, would tremble with fear as they spied upon this conversation, which they were unable to hear, and which would surely result in the Duchesse's depriving one or another of them of his days off after the concierge had sneaked on him. Because of this whole succession of different faces offered in turn by Mme de Guermantes, faces that occupied a relative and changing space, sometimes narrow, sometimes vast, in her style of dress as a whole, my love was not attached to any particular part of flesh and fabric, different with each day, which she could modify or renew almost completely without affecting my state of agitation, because beneath them, the new cape and the unfamiliar cheek, I felt that it was still Mme de Guermantes. What I loved was the invisible person who set all this in motion, the woman whose hostility caused me distress, whose approaching presence threw me into turmoil, whose life I should have liked to exclude from her friends and hold as my own. Whether she wore a blue feather or displayed an inflamed complexion, her actions would lose none of their importance for me.

I should not myself have felt that Mme de Guermantes was irritated at meeting me every single day had I not gathered it indirectly from the coldness, disapproval, and pity that filled Françoise's face when she helped me get ready for these morning excursions. The moment I asked for my things, I felt a contrary wind arise in her worn and shrunken features. I made no attempt to gain her confidence, knowing that I should not succeed. She had a knack, the nature of which has always been a mystery to me, of sensing immediately anything bad that might happen to my parents or myself. This was not a supernatural power perhaps, but could be explained by sources of information best known to herself–rather like the news that reaches certain primitive tribes several days before the mail has brought it to the European colony, transmitted not by telepathy but from hilltop to hilltop by beacon fires. So, in the particular instance of my morning excursions, it was possible that Mme de Guermantes's servants had heard their mistress say how tired she was of inevitably running into me when she went out, and had repeated her remarks to Françoise. It is true that my parents could have placed someone other than Françoise at my service, but that would not have improved matters. Françoise was in a sense less of a servant than the others. Her way of feeling, of being kind and commiserative, harsh and disdainful, shrewd and narrow-minded, her white skin and red hands made her very much the village girl whose parents "went back a long way" but had now fallen on hard times and been forced to put her into service. Her presence in our household was the country air and the social life of a farm of fifty years ago transported into our midst by a kind of inverse journey in which the holiday destination travels toward the traveler. Like the glass cases of a local museum with their exhibits of curious handiwork, still crafted or embroidered by peasant women in certain parts of the country, our Paris apartment was decorated with Françoise's words, inspired by a traditional local sentiment and governed by very ancient laws. And she knew how to trace her way back through them, as if with lengths of colored thread, to the cherry trees and birds of her childhood, to the bed where her mother had died, which she could still see. But in spite of all this, once she had come to Paris and entered our service, she had adopted—as anyone else would have done in her place, and with better reason to do so—the ideas, the agreed codes of procedure used by the servants on the other floors, compensating for the respect she was obliged to show us by repeating the bad language the cook on the fourth floor had used to her mistress, and with a satisfaction so typical of a servant that, for the first time in our lives, feeling a sort of solidarity with the detestable tenant on the fourth floor, we told ourselves that perhaps we, too, were employers like any others. This change in Françoise's character was perhaps inevitable. Some ways of life are so abnormal that they are bound to produce their characteristic defects, like the life led by the King among his courtiers at Versailles, a life as strange as that of a pharaoh or a doge, and stranger still for his courtiers themselves. The life led by servants is perhaps even more strange and abnormal, and it is only familiarity that conceals the fact from us. But it was for even more peculiar matters of detail that I should have been compelled, even if I had dismissed Françoise, to stick to the same servant. For various others were to enter my service later; already possessing the defects common to all servants, they nonetheless underwent a rapid transformation with me. As the laws of attack govern those of riposte, to avoid being harmed by the asperities of my character, they all adopted in their own the same withdrawal tactics, and always at the same point; in compensation for this, they took advantage of the gaps in my defenses to gain ground there. Of these gaps I knew nothing, any more than of the ground gained in the spaces they left, precisely because they were gaps. But my servants, as their faults became gradually more apparent, taught me of their existence. It was in the defects that they invariably acquired that I learned of my own natural, invariable defects, and their character presented me with a sort of negative proof of my own. In the past we used to laugh, my mother and I, at Mme Sazerat, for referring to servants as "that race," "that species." But I have to admit that the reason why I had no grounds for wishing to replace Françoise by anyone else was that her replacement would have inevitably belonged just as much to the race of servants in general and to my own species of servant in particular.

To return to Françoise, I have never once experienced a humiliation without having seen beforehand on her face the signs of condolences held there in readiness; and when, in my anger at the thought of being pitied by her, I tried to pretend that I had in fact done something successful, my lies broke pointlessly against her respectful but quite obvious disbelief and her awareness of her own infallibility. For she knew the truth; she kept it back and confined herself merely to a slight movement of the lips, as if she still had her mouth full and were finishing some tasty morsel. She kept it back? At least this is what I believed for a long time, for in those days I supposed that it was through words that the truth was communicated to other people. Even the words that people addressed to me impressed their meaning so unalterably on my sensitive mind that I could not believe it possible that someone who said she loved me did not, any more than Françoise herself could have doubted it when she read in the paper that a priest or some gentleman or other was able, on receipt of a stamped envelope, to send us free of charge an infallible remedy for every illness in the book or the means of hugely increasing our income. (By contrast, if our doctor prescribed for her the simplest ointment for a headcold, she, so hardy in the face of the harshest pain, would groan about what she had been made to sniff, insisting that it tickled her nose and that life had become a torture.) But Françoise was the first person to demonstrate to me by her example (which I was to understand only much later, when it was repeated more painfully, as the final volumes of this work will show, by a person who was much dearer to me) that the truth does not have to be spoken to be made apparent, and that it may perhaps be gathered with more certainty, without waiting for words and without even taking them into account, from countless external signs, even from certain unseen phenomena, analogous in the world of human character to atmospheric changes in the physical world. I might perhaps have suspected this, since it often occurred to me at that time to say things myself that contained no ounce of truth, while I made the real truth plain through all kinds of involuntary confidences expressed by my body and my actions (and these were all too easy for Françoise to interpret); I should have suspected as much, but to do so I would have had to be conscious of the fact that I was on occasion lying and deceitful. Now, my lies and deceitfulness, like everyone else's, arose in such an immediate and contingent fashion, in defense of a particular interest, that my mind, fixed on some high ideal, allowed my character to fulfill these pressing, paltry needs in the dark and did not bother to observe them. When, in the evening, Françoise was nice to me and asked if she could come and sit in my room, it seemed to me that her face became transparent and that I could see her kindness and honesty revealed. But Jupien, whose lapses into indiscretion were unfamiliar to me at the time, revealed afterward that she had told him that I was not worth the price of the rope it would take to hang me, and that I had tried to do her all the harm I could. Jupien's words immediately set before me, in unfamiliar colors, a print of my relations with Françoise so different from the one I often took pleasure in contemplating, and in which, beyond any shadow of doubt, Françoise adored me and lost no opportunity of singing my praises, that I realized that it is not only the physical world that differs from the particular way we see it; that all reality is perhaps equally dissimilar from what we believe ourselves to be directly perceiving, which we compose with the help of ideas that do not reveal themselves but are functioning all the same, just as trees, the sun, and the sky would not be the way we see them if they were perceived by creatures with eyes differently constituted from our own, or with organs other than eyes, which fulfilled the same purpose and conveyed equivalents of trees and sky and sun, but not visual ones. Whatever it was, this sudden glimpse of the real world that Jupien had opened up to me filled me with horror.

Yet it concerned only Françoise, about whom I cared little. Was it the same with all social relations? And to what depths of despair would it lead me if it were the same with love? That was the future's secret. For the moment it only concerned Françoise. Did she genuinely believe what she had told Jupien? Had she said it simply to put Jupien on bad terms with me, so that there might be less risk of our appointing Jupien's niece as her successor? At all events, I realized the impossibility of obtaining any direct and certain knowledge of whether Françoise loved me or hated me. And thus it was she who first gave me the idea that people do not, as I had imagined, present themselves to us clearly and in fixity with their merits, their defects, their plans, their intentions in regard to ourselves (like a garden viewed through railings with all its flower beds on display), but, rather, as a shadow we can never penetrate, of which there can be no direct knowledge, about which we form countless beliefs based upon words and even actions, neither of which give us more than insufficient and in fact contradictory information, a shadow that we can alternately imagine, with equal justification, as masking the burning flames of hatred and of love.

I really was in love with Mme de Guermantes. The greatest boon I could have asked of God would have been that He should bring down upon her every possible calamity, and that—ruined, discredited, stripped of all the privileges that separated me from her, with no home of her own or people who would consent to speak to her—she would come to me for asylum. In my imagination, I would picture her doing this. And even on those evenings when a change in the atmosphere or in my own state of health led to my awareness of some forgotten scroll on which impressions of earlier days were inscribed, instead of taking advantage of the forces of renewal they generated, instead of using them to unravel the thoughts that usually eluded me, instead of finally setting myself to work, I could find nothing better to do than to recite out loud and at length, following a bustling, external train of thought that added up to no more than a useless and florid exposition, a mere adventure novel, sterile and unreal, in which the Duchesse, fallen upon misfortune, came to beg help from me, who had become, by a converse set of circumstances, rich and powerful. And when I had spent hours in this way, imagining circumstances, uttering the words with which I would welcome the Duchesse beneath my roof, the situation remained unaltered; I had, alas, in the real world, chosen to love the very woman whose person possibly combined the greatest number of different advantages there are, in whose eyes I therefore could not hope to cut any sort of figure; for she was richer than the richest people outside the nobility, not to mention the personal charm that placed her in the eye of fashion and made her into a sort of queen among all others.

I felt that I displeased her by my deliberate encounters with her each morning; but even if I had had the will to forgo them for two or three days, Mme de Guermantes might not have noticed such an abstention, which would have represented a great sacrifice on my part, or might have put it down to some hitch beyond my control. As it happens, I could not have brought myself to stop dogging her except by making sure that it was impossible for me to do so, because the constantly recurring need to meet her, to be for a second the object of her attention, the person to whom her greeting was addressed, was a need far stronger than the pain of arousing her displeasure. I should have needed to go away for a period; I did not have the heart for it. I did think of it several times. I then told Françoise to pack for me, and immediately afterward to unpack. And as the mania for imitation, for being seen to be keeping up with the times, alters the most natural and most reliable version of oneself, Françoise, borrowing the expression from her daughter's vocabulary, remarked that I was "crazy." She did not like my indecision and told me I was always "balancing": when she was not trying to rival the moderns, she used the language of Saint-Simon. It is true that she liked it even less when I spoke to her as her employer. She knew that this did not come naturally to me and did not suit me, something she expressed in the phrase "If there's no will, there's no way." I would not have had the heart to leave Paris except to go somewhere that would bring me closer to Mme de Guermantes. This was not an impossibility. Would I not find myself nearer to her than I was every morning in the street—solitary, humiliated, with the feeling that not one of the thoughts I should like to convey would ever reach her, forever marking time on those walks, which might continue indefinitely without my getting anywhere—if I were to go miles away from Mme de Guermantes, but to someone she knew, someone whom she knew to be particular in his choice of friends and who valued my acquaintance, who might speak to her about me and, if not obtain from her what I wanted, then at least make her aware of it, someone, at all events, in whose company, simply because we would discuss together whether it would be possible for him to convey this or that message to her, I would give a new form to my solitary and silent daydreams, a spoken, active form, which would seem to me like a move forward, almost a realization? What she did during the mysterious life of the "Guermantes" that she was, this was the constant object of my thoughts, and to be able to break into that life, even indirectly, as with a lever, by employing the services of someone who was not excluded from the Duchesse's house, from her evening reception, and from extended conversations with her, would that not be a more distant yet more effective contact than my contemplation of her every morning in the street?

The friendship and admiration that Saint-Loup had shown me seemed to me to be undeserved and had been a matter of indifference to me up to this point. Suddenly they seemed important to me; I should have liked him to disclose them to Mme de Guermantes; I was quite prepared even to ask him to do this. For, when we are in love, we long to divulge to the woman we love all the secret little privileges we enjoy, as bores and underprivileged people do as a matter of course. It causes us pain that she is unaware of them, and we try to console ourselves with the thought that, precisely because they are never visible, she has perhaps added to her present opinion of us this possibility of undisclosed advantages.

For a long time now, Saint-Loup had been unable to come to Paris, either—as he put it, because of his military duties, or, as was more likely, because of the painful relationship he was having with his mistress, with whom he had twice now been on the point of breaking off. He had often told me how much pleasure it would give him if I came to see him in his garrison town, the name of which, two days after his departure from Balbec, had caused me so much joy when I read it on the envelope of the first letter I had received from my friend. This town, not so far from Balbec as its wholly landlocked surroundings would have suggested, was one of those small fortified towns, aristocratic and military, set in a broad expanse of countryside over which, on fine days, there so often floats a sort of distant mist of intermittent sound—which, like the curving line of a screen of poplar trees indicating the course of an unseen river, reveals the movements of a regiment on maneuvers—that the very atmosphere of its streets, avenues, and squares has ended up contracting a sort of perpetual vibrancy, musical and martial, and the most humdrum sound of a cart or tram is prolonged in vague trumpet-calls, indefinitely repeated, to the hallucinated ear, by the silence. It was not too far away from Paris for me to be able to step off the express, go back home to my mother and grandmother, and sleep in my own bed. As soon as I realized this, troubled by a painful longing, I had too little willpower to decide not to return to Paris and to stay on in the town; but also too little to prevent a porter from carrying my case to a cab and to follow behind him without assuming the destitute soul of a traveler looking after his belongings with no grandmother in attendance, or not to get into the cab with the indifference of a person who, having ceased to think of what he wants, appears to know what he wants, and not to give the driver the address of the cavalry barracks. I thought that Saint-Loup might come and sleep that night at the hotel where I was staying, so that I should find my first contact with this strange town less harrowing. One of the men on guard went to fetch him, and I waited at the barracks gate, in front of that huge hulk, booming with the November wind, out of which at every moment—for it was six in the evening—men emerged into the street in pairs, staggering unsteadily, as if they were coming ashore in some exotic port where they were temporarily stationed.

Saint-Loup arrived, bustling about all over the place, his monocle flying in front of him: I had not given my name, and I could not wait to enjoy his surprise and delight.

"Oh, what a bore!" he exclaimed, suddenly catching sight of me and blushing to the tips of his ears. "I've just taken a week's leave, and I won't be off duty for another week!"

And, preoccupied with the thought that I should have to spend this first night on my own, for he knew better than anyone my bedtime anxieties, which he had often noticed and soothed at Balbec, he broke off his complaint to turn and look at me, to give me little smiles, tender but lopsided glances, some of them coming directly from his eye and the rest through his monocle, but all of them indicative of the emotion he felt on seeing me again, and also indicative of that important matter which I still did not understand but which now vitally concerned me, our friendship.

"Dear me, where are you going to sleep? I really don't recommend the hotel where we mess: it's next to the exhibition grounds, and there's a show about to start there. Far too crowded for you. No, the Hôtel de Flandre would be better. It's a little eighteenth-century palace with old tapestries. 'Old historic dwelling' sort of place."

Saint-Loup was always using turns of phrase like the last, because the spoken language, like the written, feels the need for these alterations of usage, these refinements of expression. And just as journalists are often quite ignorant of the schools of literature from which they derive their "fine turns of phrase," so Saint-Loup's vocabulary, even his diction, was formed in imitation of three different aesthetes, none of whom he knew, but whose modes of speech had been indirectly inculcated into him. "Besides," he concluded, "the hotel I mean is more or less adapted to your oversensitive ears. You won't have any neighbors. That's a slight enough advantage, I can see that, and with the possibility of another guest arriving tomorrow it would not be worth choosing that particular hotel on such precarious grounds. No, it's for its appearance that I'm recommending it. The rooms are rather attractive: all the furniture is old and comfortable. There's something reassuring about it." But to me, less artistically inclined than Saint-Loup, the pleasure that an attractive dwelling might give was superficial, almost nonexistent, and incapable of soothing my incipient anxiety, which was as painful as the anguish that I used to feel at Combray in the past, when my mother failed to come upstairs to say good night to me, or that I experienced on the evening of my arrival at Balbec, in the bedroom with the unnaturally high ceiling, which smelled of vetiver. Saint-Loup understood all this from my staring gaze.

"A lot you care, though, about this charming palace, my poor fellow. You're quite pale. Here I go, great brute that I am, talking to you about tapestries that you won't even have the heart to look at. I know the room they'll give you. Personally, I find it most cheerful, but I can quite understand that for you, with your sensitive nature, it won't be the same. You mustn't think I don't understand. It's not the same for me, but I can see just how you feel."

At this point, an officer who was putting a horse through its paces in the yard, intent on making it jump, disregarding the salutes of passing soldiers but hurling torrents of abuse at those who got in his way, turned with a smile to Saint-Loup and, seeing that he had a friend with him, saluted. But his horse suddenly reared up, frothing. Saint-Loup flung himself at its head, managed to calm it down, and returned to my side.

"Yes," he continued, "I assure you that I do understand what you go through, and I sympathize. I feel bad," he added, laying his hand affectionately on my shoulder, "when I think that if I could have stayed with you we could have talked together into the small hours, and I might have been able to make you feel a bit better. I could lend you some books, but you won't want to read them if you're feeling like you do. I don't have a chance of getting someone to stand in for me here; I've done it twice already, when my girl came to see me."

And he frowned with annoyance in his effort to decide, like a doctor, what remedy he could prescribe for me.

"Run along and light a fire in my quarters," he called to a passing soldier. "Hurry up, get a move on!"

Then, once more, he turned toward me, and both monocle and myopic gaze bore witness to our great friendship.

"I can't believe it! You, here, in these barracks, where I've so often thought of you. I can't believe my eyes—I feel I must be dreaming. But tell me, how's your health? Are you any better? You can tell me all about it later. We'll go up to my room. We mustn't stay out here too long, there's a devil of a wind. I don't feel it any more, but you're not used to it. I don't want you to catch cold. What about your work? Have you settled down to it? No? You're an odd fellow! If I had your gifts,

I'm sure I'd be writing all day long. It amuses you more to do nothing. What a pity it's the second-rate people like me who are always ready to work, and the ones who could don't want to! And I've not even asked you how your grandmother is. I'm never without the Proudhon[13] she gave me."

An officer, tall, majestic, and handsome, emerged from one of the staircases with slow and solemn steps. Saint-Loup saluted him and stilled the perpetual restlessness of his body long enough to hold his hand at the level of his cap. But he had made this gesture with such force, straightened himself up with so brusque a movement, and, once the salute had been made, brought his hand down with so abrupt a release, changing all the positions of his shoulders, leg, and monocle, that this moment was less a moment of immobility than of vibrant tension, in which the excessive movements he had just made and the ones he was about to make canceled one another out. Meanwhile, the officer, without approaching, calm, benevolent, dignified, imperial—in fact, the direct opposite of Saint-Loup—also raised his hand, but unhurriedly, to his cap.

"I must just have a word with the captain," whispered Saint-Loup. "Would you mind going to wait for me in my room? It's the second on the right, on the third floor. I'll be with you in a minute."

And, setting off on the double, preceded by his monocle flying all over the place, he went straight up to the dignified and unhurried captain, whose horse was being brought round, and who, before getting ready to mount, was giving orders with a studied nobility of gesture that belonged to some historical painting, and as though he were setting off to some battle of the First Empire, when in fact he was simply about to ride home, to the house that he had rented for the period of his service at Doncières, which stood in a square that was named, as if in ironic anticipation of the presence of this child of Napoleon, Place de la République. I started to climb the staircase, just avoiding slipping on each of its nail-studded steps, catching glimpses of bare-walled barrack rooms with their double rows of beds and kits. I was shown Saint-Loup's room. I stopped for a moment outside the closed door, for I could hear movement: something was being moved, something else was being dropped; I could feel that the room was not empty, that there was someone in it. But it was merely the recently lighted fire burning away. It could not keep quiet; it was shifting the logs about, and very clumsily. I went in. It sent one log rolling and another smoking. And even when it was still, as common people do, it made constant noises, which, from the moment I saw the flames rising, revealed themselves as the noises that come from a fire, whereas if I had been on the other side of the wall I should have thought that they came from someone who was blowing his nose and walking about. I finally sat down. Liberty hangings and old eighteenth-century German fabrics preserved the room from the smell that exuded from the rest of the building, a coarse, sickly, corruptible smell like that of brown bread. It was here, in this charming room, that I could have dined and slept with calm and contentment. It was almost as if Saint-Loup were in the room, because his textbooks were there on the table, beside his photographs, among which I was able to recognize my own and that of Mme de Guermantes, now that there was light from the fire, which had finally settled itself in the grate and, like an animal crouched in ardent watchfulness, noiseless and faithful, merely let fall an occasional log, which crumbled into sparks or licked the sides of the chimney with a tongue of flame. I could hear the tick of Saint-Loup's watch, which must have been somewhere near at hand. The tick changed place all the time, for I could not see the watch; it seemed to be coming from behind me, from in front, from my right, from my left, sometimes to die away as though it were coming from a long way off. Suddenly I caught sight of the watch on a table. So now I heard the tick in a fixed place, from which it did not move again. Or I thought I did; in fact, I did not hear it in this place, I saw it there, for sounds have no fixed point in space. We connect sounds with movements, and in that way they serve to alert us to those movements, appearing to make them necessary and natural. And indeed it does sometimes happen that a sick man whose ears have been plugged ceases to hear the noises of a fire like the one that was crackling away at that moment in Saint-Loup's fireplace, as it worked to produce embers and cinders, which it then dropped into the grate; nor would he hear the passing tram cars, whose music rose at regular intervals over the main square of Doncières. Then, if the sick man is reading, the pages will turn silently, as if they are being moved by the fingers of a god. The heavy rumble of a running bath becomes faint, light, and remote, like a celestial babbling. The withdrawal of sound, its dilution, robs it of any aggressive power it may have over us; thrown into a panic a moment ago by the sound of hammer blows that seemed to be making the ceiling shudder over our heads, we now find it possible to enjoy them, light, caressing, distant, like the rustle of leaves playing along the roadside with the passing breeze. We play games of patience with cards we cannot hear, so much so that we imagine we have not shuffled them, that they are moving of their own accord and, anticipating our desire to play with them, have begun to play with us. And in this connection we may wonder whether, in the case of Love (to which we may even add the love of life, the love of fame, since there are people, it appears, who are acquainted with these two), we should not behave like those who, when noise disturbs them, rather than praying for it to stop, block their ears against it; and, following their example, bring our attention, our defenses, to bear upon ourselves, give them as an object to subdue not the external being whom we love, but our capacity to suffer on account of the loved one.

To return to the question of sound, we have merely to use thicker earplugs to close the aural passages and the girl who has been playing a boisterous tune overhead is reduced to pianissimo; and if we grease our cotton plugs, then the whole household immediately obeys their despotism, and their sway extends even beyond the house. Pianissimo is no longer enough; the earplug instantly shuts the keyboard, and the music lesson comes to an abrupt end; the gentleman who was pacing the room above us stops at once; the movement of carriages and trams is interrupted as though a state procession were about to take place. And this attenuation of sounds can sometimes disturb our sleep instead of protecting it. Only yesterday, the incessant sounds we heard, by continuously describing to us everything that was going on in the street and in the house, eventually managed to send us to sleep like a boring book; today, on the surface of silence spread over our sleep, a burst of sound louder than the rest manages to make itself heard, gentle as a sigh, unrelated to any other sound, mysterious; and the need for explanation it exhales is enough to wake us up. On the other hand, remove for a moment from the sick man the cotton plugs placed in his ears and in an instant the light, the full sunlight of sound, appears afresh, blindingly, and is born again in the universe; the host of exiled sounds comes rushing back; we witness, as if it were chanted by singing angels, the resurrection of the voice. The empty streets are filled for a moment with the rapid succession of whirring wings of the singing tram cars. In the bedroom itself, the sick man has this moment created, not, like Prometheus, fire, but the sound of fire. And when we increase or reduce the thickness of cotton in our ears, it is like working alternately one or the other of the two pedals we have added to the sonority of the external world.

Only there are some suppressions of sound that are not temporary. Someone who has become completely deaf cannot even heat a pan of milk at his bedside without having constantly to keep his eyes open for the hyperborean reflection, on the lifted lid, like that of a snowstorm, the premonitory sign it is wise to obey by stopping, as the Lord stilled the waves, the electric current; for already the unevenly rising egg of the boiling milk is peaking in a series of sidelong undulations, swelling and filling out a few drooping sails puckered by the cream, sending one of them billowing out gleaming into the tempest, until the cutting off of the current, if the electric storm is exorcised in time, will make them all swirl round on themselves and scatter, transformed into magnolia petals. Should the sick man not have been quick enough to take the necessary precautions, he will soon see his drowned books and watch barely emerging from the white sea left by this tidal wave of milk and be obliged to call for his old nurse, who, whether he be an eminent statesman or a famous writer, will tell him that he has no more sense than a five-year-old. At other times in the magic room, standing in front of the closed door, someone who was not there a moment ago has appeared, a visitor who has entered unheard and who merely gesticulates, like a character from one of those little puppet shows that are so restful for those who have developed a distaste for the spoken language. And for this stone-deaf man, since the loss of one of the senses brings as much beauty to the world as its acquisition did, to walk about on this earth is close to tasting the delights of an Eden in which sound has not yet been created. The highest waterfalls unfold their sheets of crystal for the eye alone, stiller than the still sea, pure as cascades in paradise. Since sound was for him, before his deafness, the perceptible form the cause of movement assumed, objects that are moved now without sound seem to be moved without cause; stripped of all qualities of sound, they display a spontaneous activity, they seem to be alive; they move, remain static, burst into flames of their own accord. Of their own accord they fly off into the air like the winged monsters of prehistory. In the solitary, neighborless house of the deaf man, the servants' duties, which were already being carried out with more discretion and in silence before the onset of total deafness, are now performed almost surreptitiously by mutes, as for a king in a fairy tale. And as in the theater, the building the deaf man sees from his window—a barracks, a church, a town hall—is merely part of the stage set. If one day it falls to the ground, it may send up a cloud of dust and leave rubble; but, with less substance than a palace onstage, though not in fact as flimsy, it will fall to the ground in the magic universe without letting the crash of its heavy blocks of stone blemish the chastity of the silence with anything so vulgar as a noise.

The silence, altogether more relative, that dominated the little barrack room where I had been waiting was suddenly broken. The door opened, and Saint-Loup rushed in, dropping his monocle.

"Ah, Robert, how pleasant it is here," I said. "It would be so good to be allowed to dine and sleep here."

And indeed, had it not been against the regulations, what untroubled sleep I could have enjoyed there, protected by the atmosphere of tranquillity, vigilance, and gaiety that was maintained by a thousand ordered and unruffled wills, a thousand carefree minds, in that great community known as a barracks, where, with time transformed into action, the gloomy bell that usually tolls the hours was replaced by the same joyous fanfare of the bugle calls, which constantly hovered as a sonorous memory over the paved streets of the town like a scattered dust haze— a voice certain of being heard, and a harmonious one, since it represented the command not only of authority to obedience but of wisdom to happiness.

"So you'd rather stay with me and sleep here than go to the hotel by yourself, would you?" said Saint-Loup with a smile.

"Oh, Robert, it's cruel of you to be so ironic about it," I answered, "when you know that it's out of the question, and you know how miserable I'll be over there."

"Well, you flatter me!" he replied. "Because it actually occurred to me that you'd prefer to stay here tonight, and that is precisely what I went to talk to the captain about."

"And he has given his permission?" I cried.

"He has no objection at all."

"Oh! I adore him!"

"No, that would be going too far. Look, let me just go and find my orderly and tell him to see about our dinner," he added, while I turned away to hide my tears.

At several points, one or another of Saint-Loup's comrades came into the room. He drove them all out.

"Come on, clear off."

I asked him to let them stay.

"No, it's not worth it, they would bore you silly. They're so uncouth. They can talk about nothing but racing and grooming horses. I don't really want them here anyway: they'd spoil these precious moments I've been looking forward to so much. Mind you, when I say these fellows are not very interesting, I don't mean that everything to do with the army is mindless. Far from it. We have a major here who's an admirable man. He's given a course in which military history is treated like a demonstration, a bit like an algebraic equation. Even from the aesthetic point of view, there's a beauty about it, inductive and deductive in turn. It wouldn't leave you unmoved."

"Are we talking about the officer who's allowed me to stay here tonight?"

"No, thank God! The man you 'adore' for that tiny privilege is the biggest fool who's ever walked the earth. He's the perfect man for looking after messing and uniform inspection. He spends hours with the squadron sergeant major and the master tailor. That just about sums him up. Besides, like everyone here, he has nothing but contempt for the admirable major I'm talking about. They all avoid him, because he's a Freemason and doesn't go to confession. The Prince de Borodino would never have such a petit-bourgeois in his house. Which is some nerve when you think about it, coming from a man whose great-grandfather was a small farmer, and who'd probably be one himself if the Napoleonic Wars hadn't happened. Not that he isn't just that little bit conscious of his own ambiguous position in society, neither fish nor fowl. He scarcely shows his face at the Jockey, this so-called Prince; it makes him feel so awkward," added Robert, who, having been led, through a similar spirit of imitation, to adopt the social theories of his teachers and the worldly prejudices of his relatives, unwittingly combined a democratic love of humanity with a contempt for the nobility created by the Empire.

I studied the photograph of his aunt, and the thought that Saint-Loup, as the owner of this photograph, might perhaps give it to me, made me value him all the more dearly and long to do a thousand things for him—a small enough exchange for it, it seemed to me. For this photograph was like a further encounter with Mme de Guermantes, added to all the others I had already had; better still, it was a prolonged encounter, as if, through some sudden stride forward in our relations, she had stopped beside me, in a garden hat, and allowed me for the first time to gaze at leisure at the fullness of her cheek, the curve of her neck, the kink of her eyebrows (so far veiled from me by the rapidity of her passage, the dizzy nature of my impressions, the unreliability of memory); and to be able to study all these, as well as the throat and arms of a woman I had only ever seen in a high-necked dress, was to me a voluptuous discovery, a special favor. Those forms, which I had thought of as an almost forbidden spectacle, were now there for me to study as in a textbook of the only geometry that had any value for me. Later on, looking at Robert, I could see that he, too, was a little like a photograph of his aunt, through some mysterious process that I found almost as moving, since, if his face had not been directly produced by hers, the two nonetheless shared a common origin. The features of the Duchesse de Guermantes that were pinned to the way I had seen her at Combray—the nose like a falcon's beak, the piercing eyes—seemed to have served for the cutting out—in another copy, analogous and slender, with too delicate a skin—of Robert's face, which could almost be superimposed on his aunt's. I looked longingly at the characteristic features he shared with the Guermantes, a race that retains its individuality in a world by which it is not submerged, and in which it remains isolated in its divinely ornithological glory, for it seems to have sprung, in the age of mythology, from the union of a goddess and a bird.

Robert, unaware of what provoked it, was touched by my affectionate mood. This was increased by the sense of well-being induced in me by the heat of the fire and the champagne, which simultaneously brought beads of sweat to my forehead and tears to my eyes; the wine accompanied some partridges; I ate them with the unexpected surprise of any uninitiated person when he discovers in a way of life that was unfamiliar to him what he supposed it to exclude (the surprise, for instance, of the unbeliever who is given an exquisite dinner in a presbytery). And when I woke up the following morning, I went over to Saint-Loup's window, which was high enough to offer a view over the whole countryside, curious to make the acquaintance of my new neighbor, the landscape, which I had been unable to see the day before, arriving too late and at an hour when it was already asleep in the darkness. But, however early it had awoken, when I opened the window I could only see it, as I might have done from the window of a country house beside a lake, still muffled in its soft white morning robe of mist, which prevented me from seeing scarcely anything distinctly. But I knew that, before the soldiers who were busy with their horses in the courtyard had finished grooming them, the robe of mist would be cast aside. In the meantime, I could see only a bare hill, raising its lanky, rugged hump, already stripped clean of shadow, over the barracks. Through the open screenwork of hoarfrost, I could not take my eyes off this stranger who was looking at me for the first time. But once I had got into the habit of coming to the barracks, the awareness that the hill was there, and thus more real, even when I could not see it, than the hotel at Balbec, than our house in Paris, which I thought of as absent or dead friends—that is to say, scarcely believing in their continued existence—meant that its reflected form never stopped silhouetting itself, even without my realizing it, against the slightest impressions I experienced at Doncières, and among them, to start with this first morning, the agreeable impression of warmth conveyed by the cup of chocolate, prepared by Saint-Loup's orderly in this comfortable room, which seemed like a sort of optical center from which to look out at the hill (the idea of being able to do anything other than gaze at it, the idea of actually climbing it, being rendered impossible by the presence of the mist). Absorbed into the shape of the hill, and associated with the taste of the chocolate and the whole web of my current thoughts, this mist, without my having given it the least thought, came to soak into all my thoughts of that time, just as something golden, massive, and unchanging had remained allied to my impressions of Balbec, or as the close presence of the darkened sandstone steps outside gave a grayish tinge to my impressions of Combray. Yet it did not linger on into the morning; the sun first threw a few vain darts at it, studding it with brilliants, then got the better of it. The hill could now expose its gray rump to the sunlight, which, an hour later, when I went into the town, poured onto the red leaves of the trees, onto the reds and blues of the election posters on the walls, in an exaltation that put me in high spirits myself and made me sing and stamp on the paving stones as I went, only just refraining from jumping for joy.

But after that first night, I had to sleep at the hotel. And I knew beforehand that I was doomed to find it miserable. The sadness was like an unbreathable aroma, which every unfamiliar bedroom—that is to say, every bedroom—had exhaled for me for as long as I could remember: in my usual bedroom I was not really there; my mind stayed behind somewhere else and sent mere Habit to take its place. But I could not expect this less mindful servant to look after my needs in a new place, where I had arrived in advance of him, alone, and where I had to face the world with a "self" that I encountered only after years of absence, but which was always the same, the self that had never grown up since Combray, since my first arrival at Balbec, weeping inconsolably as it sat on the corner of an unpacked trunk.

But as it happened, I was wrong. I had no time to be miserable, because I was never alone. The fact was that there remained of the old palace a surplus of luxurious features that were inappropriate to a modern hotel, and, released from any practical use, their very uselessness had acquired a sort of life: passages winding back on themselves, which one was constantly crossing in their aimless wanderings; lobbies as long as corridors and as ornate as drawing rooms, which gave the impression not so much of forming part of the dwelling as of simply being there, which could not be induced to enter any of the rooms, but which roamed about outside my own and came at once to offer me their company—neighbors, if you like, idle but never noisy, subservient ghosts of the past who had been allowed to stay quietly by the doors of the rooms rented to guests, and who behaved toward me with silent deference whenever I came across them. In short, the idea of a lodging as a mere container for our existence of the moment, simply protecting us from the cold and from the sight of other people, was totally inapplicable to this dwelling, an assembly of rooms that were as real as a colony of people, which lived in silence, it is true, but which you were obliged to encounter, to avoid, to greet when you returned. You tried not to disturb, and were forced to look with respect upon the main drawing room, which since the eighteenth century had formed the habit of reclining comfortably between its armrests of old gold beneath the clouds of its painted ceiling. And you were drawn by a more familiar sense of curiosity in regard to the smaller rooms, which, without the least concern for symmetry, ran around it in vast numbers, in amazement, fleeing in disorder to the garden, easily accessible by the three broken steps that led down to it.

If I wished to go out or come in without taking the elevator or being seen on the main staircase, a smaller, private staircase, no longer in use, offered me its steps, so skillfully arranged, one close above the next, that their gradation seemed perfectly proportioned and similar in kind to that which in colors, scents, and tastes often arouses a special sensuous pleasure. But the pleasure of going up- and downstairs was one that I had had to come here to learn, as I had once learned in an alpine resort that the act of breathing, to which we habitually pay no attention, can be a constant source of pleasure. I was exempted from effort, an exemption usually granted to us only by the things with which long use has made us familiar, the first time I set my feet on those steps, familiar before I even knew them, as if they possessed something that had possibly been left and incorporated in them by former masters whom they used to welcome every day, the prospective charm of habits I had not yet contracted, which could only pale once they had become my own. I went into a room, the double doors closed behind me, the hangings ushered in a silence over which I felt myself to exert a sort of intoxicating regal authority; a marble fireplace with ornamental brass chasing, which it would have been wrong to see placed there solely as a statement of the art of the Directory, provided me with a fire, and a small, low armchair helped me to warm myself as comfortably as if I had been sitting on the hearth rug. The walls clasped the room in a tight embrace, separating it from the rest of the world, and to let into it, to enclose inside it, the things that made it complete, they stood aside to make way for the bookcase, reserved a recess for the bed, on either side of which columns provided light support for the unusually high ceiling of the alcove. And the room was extended in depth by two closets as wide as itself, the farther one of which had hanging from its wall, to scent the withdrawal for which it was intended, a voluptuous rosary of orrisroot; the doors, if I left them open when I withdrew into this last retreat, were not only content to triple its dimensions without altering the harmony of its proportions, and not only allowed my eyes to enjoy the pleasures of extension after those of concentration, but also added to the pleasure of my solitude, which remained inviolable but no longer shut in, the sense of freedom. This closet looked out onto a courtyard, a lone beauty whom I was glad to have as a neighbor when, next morning, I discovered her there, a captive between her high walls, in which no other window opened, with only two yellowing trees to give a mauve softness to the clear sky.

Before going to bed, I felt the need to leave my room and explore the whole of my enchanted domain. I walked down a long gallery, which successively honored me with all it had to offer if I could not sleep, an armchair, in a corner, a spinet, a blue porcelain vase filled with cinerarias on a console table, and, in an old frame, the ghost of a lady of long ago, her powdered hair threaded with blue flowers, holding a bunch of pinks. When I came to the end, the bare wall in which no door opened said to me simply, "Now you must go back, but you know you are at home here," while the soft carpet, not to be outdone, added that if I could not sleep that night I could perfectly well come along in bare feet, and the unshuttered windows looking out over the countryside assured me that they would spend a night without sleep and that, at whatever hour I wished to come, I need not be afraid of waking anyone. And behind a hanging curtain I discovered nothing more than a small closet whose escape had been blocked by the outer wall, hiding there rather sheepishly, staring at me in fright from its little round window, turned blue by the moonlight. I went to bed, but the presence of the eiderdown, the small columns, the tiny fireplace, heightening my attention beyond its usual pitch in Paris, prevented me from giving myself up to the normal routine of my idle thoughts. And since it is this particular state of attention that enfolds our sleeping hours, acts upon them, modifies them, puts them into contact with one or another of our various strands of memory, the images that filled my dreams that first night were borrowed from a memory quite distinct from the one that my sleeping hours normally drew upon. If, while I slept, I had been tempted to let myself be dragged back toward my usual patterns of memory, then the unfamiliar bed, and the pleasurable attention I needed to pay to the position of my body when I turned over, were sufficient to regulate or to maintain the new thread of my dreams. The same is true of sleep as of our perception of the external world. It needs only some modification in our habits to make it poetic; we need only to have dozed off involuntarily on top of the bed while undressing for the dimensions of sleep to be altered and its beauty felt. We wake up, consult our watch, and see it is four o'clock; it is only four in the morning, but we think that the whole day has gone by, so ready are we to regard this unsolicited few minutes' sleep as heaven-sent, issued by some divine right, as huge and weighty as an emperor's golden orb. In the morning, worried by the thought that my grandfather was ready and they were waiting for me for our Méséglise walk, I was woken by the blare of a military band that passed beneath my windows every day. But once or twice—and I am saying this because it is not possible to describe human life without bathing it in the sleep into which it plunges, and which, night after night, encircles it like the sea around a promontory—the intervening barrier of sleep was resistant enough to withstand the impact of the blare, and I heard nothing. On other mornings, its resistance relaxed for a moment; but my consciousness, still smoothed over by sleep—like organs that, after a preliminary anesthetic, react to a cauterization first as something unfelt, then, at the very end, as something like a faint smarting—was touched only gently by the shrillest notes of the fifes, which caressed it distantly with a cool early-morning warble; and after this minimal intrusion, in which the silence had turned to music, it joined my sleep again, even before the dragoons had gone by, depriving me of the last blossoming sprays of the bouquet of surging sound. And the zone of my consciousness that had been brushed by its springing stems was so narrow, so hemmed in by sleep, that later on, when Saint-Loup asked me if I had heard the band, I was not certain that the sound of the brass had not been as imaginary as what I heard during the day rising up, after the slightest noise, above the paved streets of the town. Perhaps I had heard it only in a dream, out of fear of being awakened, or else of not being awakened and thus not seeing the dragoons march past. For, often when I remained asleep at the very moment when I had supposed that the noise would have awakened me, for the next hour I would imagine I was awake, while in fact I was still dozing, and I played out to myself in frail shadows on the screen of my sleeping consciousness the various scenes of which it deprived me but which I had the illusion of witnessing.

In fact, it happens that things one meant to do during the day are only accomplished, when sleep intervenes, in one's dreams—that is, after they have been diverted by drowsiness onto a different path from the one they would have followed in waking life. The same story turns off toward a different destination. In the end, the world in which we live when we are asleep is so different that the foremost concern of people who have difficulty in going to sleep is to escape from the waking world. After they have closed their eyes and desperately mulled over, for hours on end, the same sort of thoughts that they would have had with their eyes open, they take heart again when they notice that the

preceding minute has been dulled by a pattern of thought in strict contradiction to the laws of logic and present reality, this short "absence"
indicating that there is now an open door through which, in a while,
they may perhaps be able to escape the perception of the real, reach a
resting place more or less distant from it, which will mean that they
have a more or less "good" night's sleep. But it is already a great step
forward when we turn our backs on the real, when we reach the outer
caves in which "autosuggestions," like witches, stir up the hell-broth of
imaginary illnesses or a new wave of nervous disorders, and watch for
the hour when the convulsions that have been building up during the
unconsciousness of sleep break out with enough force to bring sleep to
an end.

Not far from this point is the private garden in which various kinds
of sleep, so different from one another, grow like unknown flowers:
sleep induced by datura, by Indian hemp, by the multiple extracts of
ether, the sleep of belladonna, of opium, of valerian, flowers that remain closed until the day when the predestined stranger comes to
touch them open and to let loose for long hours the aroma of their special dreams upon an amazed and unsuspecting being. At the end of the
garden stands the convent with open windows through which we hear
voices repeating the lessons learned before we went to sleep, which we
shall know only when we wake up; while, as a prediction of that moment, our inner alarm clock ticks on, so well regulated by our preoccupation that when our housekeeper comes in to tell us it is seven o'clock
she will find us already awake. On the dark walls of the chamber that
opens upon our dreams, and within which that oblivion of the sorrows
of love works away incessantly, its task sometimes interrupted and destroyed by a nightmare crowded with reminiscences but soon resumed,
the memories of our dreams are hung, even after we are awake; but they
are so shrouded in darkness that often they become apparent to us for
the first time only in the middle of the afternoon, when the ray of a
similar idea happens to strike them by chance; some of them, harmonious and clear while we slept, are already so distorted that, having
failed to recognize them, we can only hasten to lay them to earth, like
corpses that have decomposed too soon, or objects so seriously dam-

aged and crumbling to dust that the most skillful restorer would be unable to reshape them or do anything with them.

Near to the railings is the quarry where deep sleep comes in search of substances that coat the brain with such a hard surface that, for the sleeper to awaken, his own will is obliged, even on a golden morning, to deliver mighty blows of the ax, like a young Siegfried. Beyond this are the nightmares, which doctors stupidly claim to be more exhausting than insomnia itself, whereas what they in fact do is to enable the thinker to escape from concentrated thought: nightmares, with their fanciful picture-albums in which our dead relatives are seen to be meeting with serious accidents, and in which, at the same time, their speedy recovery is not ruled out. In the meantime, we keep them in a little rat-cage, in which they are smaller than white mice, and, covered with big red spots, each sprouting a feather, they harangue us with Ciceronian oratory. Next to this picture-album is the revolving disc of awakening, thanks to which we submit for a second to the annoyance of having to return in a while to a house that was demolished fifty years ago, the image of which is gradually effaced by several other images as sleep recedes, until we reach the one that only appears when the disc has ceased to spin, and which coincides with what we shall see when we have opened our eyes.

Sometimes I heard nothing, having been immersed in the sort of sleep into which we fall as into a pit from which we are more than glad to be dragged a little later, heavy, overfed, digesting all that has been brought to us, like the food brought by the nymphs to the infant Hercules, by those agile vegetative powers whose activity is doubled while we sleep.

We call that a leaden sleep, and it seems as if, during the few minutes after such a sleep has ended, we have ourselves turned into mere figures of lead. Identity has vanished. So how, then, searching for our thoughts, our identities, as we search for lost objects, do we eventually recover our own self rather than any other? Why, when we regain consciousness, is it not an identity other than the one we had previously that is embodied in us? It is not clear what dictates the choice, or why, among the millions of human beings we might be, it is the being we were the day before that we unerringly grasp. What is it that guides us when there has been a genuine interruption (whether it be that we have been totally taken over by sleep, or that our dreams have been utterly different from ourselves)? What has happened really is a death, as when the heart has ceased to beat and a rhythmical traction of the tongue revives us. No doubt the room, even if we have seen it only once before, awakens memories to which older memories cling; or possibly some of them have been lying dormant inside us and we now become conscious of them. The resurrection that takes place when we wake up—after that beneficent attack of mental derangement we call sleep—must in the end be similar to what happens when we recall a name, a line of poetry, or a refrain we had forgotten. And perhaps the resurrection of the soul after death is to be thought of as a phenomenon of memory.

When I had finished sleeping, drawn by the sunny sky but held back by the chill of those last autumn mornings, so bright and sharp, which usher in the winter, in order to see the trees, on which the only remaining sign of leaves was to be found in the few strokes of gold or pink that seemed to have been left in the air, on an invisible web, I raised my head and stretched out my neck, keeping my body half hidden beneath the bedclothes; like a chrysalis in the process of metamorphosis, I was a dual creature whose various parts were not at home in the same environment; for my eyes, color was enough, without warmth; my chest, on the other hand, was concerned with warmth and not color. I got out of bed only when the fire had been lit and gazed at the picture, so transparent and soothing, of the mauve-golden morning to which I had just artificially added the elements of warmth that it lacked, poking away at the fire, which was burning and smoking like a good pipe and giving me, as the pipe would have done, a pleasure at once gross, because it was based upon physical comfort, and delicate, because behind it were the blurred outlines of a pure vision. My bathroom was papered in a violent red dotted with black-and-white flowers, which suggested that they would take some getting used to. But they affected me merely as something novel, forcing me to enter not into conflict but into contact with them, slightly changing my gaiety and my singing when I got up in the morning, imprisoning me in the heart of a sort of poppy from which I viewed the world, quite otherwise than in Paris, from behind the gay screen represented by this new abode, differently disposed from my parents' house, and with pure air flowing through it. On certain days, I was disturbed by the desire to see my grandmother again or by the fear that she might be ill; or by the memory of some unfinished business in Paris that was getting nowhere; or sometimes by some difficulty in which, even here, I had managed to become caught up. One or another of these worries could prevent me from sleeping, and I was powerless in the face of such anxiety, which could overshadow my existence in a mere second. If this happened, I would send someone from the hotel to the barracks with a message for Saint-Loup saying that if it was physically possible—and I knew it was extremely difficult for him— would he be good enough to stop by for a minute. An hour later he would appear; and hearing him ring at the door would set me free from my worries. I knew that, if they were stronger than I, he was stronger then they, and my attention would be diverted from them toward him, who was the one to settle them. He had only to enter the room to surround me with the fresh air in which he had been busying himself so actively since the early morning, a vital atmosphere very different from that of my room, and to which I responded immediately with appropriate reactions.

"I hope you don't mind too much my disturbing you like this. Something's bothering me. You probably guessed."

"Not really. I just thought you wanted to see me; and I thought that was very nice. I was delighted you sent for me. But what's wrong? Things not good? What can I do to help?"

He would listen to my explanation and respond pertinently; but before he had uttered a word he had transformed me into his own likeness; compared with the important duties that kept him so busy, so alert, so happy, the worries that a moment ago I had been unable to endure a second longer seemed to me as negligible as they did to him; I was like a man who, after being unable to open his eyes for days, sends for the doctor, who gently and adroitly raises his eyelid, removes a grain of sand, and shows it to him; the patient is healed and reassured. All my worries resolved themselves in a telegram that Saint-Loup undertook to send for me. Life seemed so different, so wonderful, I was flooded with such an excess of strength that I needed action.

"What are you doing now?" I asked Saint-Loup.

"I shall have to leave you. We're going on a route march in three-quarters of an hour, and I have to be there."

"Then it's been awkward for you to come here?"

"Not awkward at all. The captain was very understanding. He told me that if it was for you I must go at once. But I don't want to be seen to be abusing his kindness."

"But if I got up quickly and made my way to the place where you'll be training, it would interest me a lot, and perhaps I could talk to you during the breaks."

"I wouldn't if I were you. You've been lying awake worrying yourself silly over something that I can assure you is not of the slightest importance, and now that you have stopped worrying about it you'd better turn over and go to sleep. It would do your demineralized nerve cells no end of good. But don't fall asleep too soon, because our blasted band will be coming along under your windows. Once they've gone I think you'll be left in peace, and we shall see each other at dinner this evening."

But shortly after this I often went to see the regiment doing field maneuvers, as I started to get interested in the military theories expounded by Saint-Loup's friends over the dinner table, and my chief interest became to see their various leaders at closer quarters, just as someone who makes music his main area of study and spends his whole time in concert halls finds pleasure in frequenting the cafés where he can be surrounded by the life of the members of the orchestra. I had to walk a long way to reach the training ground. In the evening, after dinner, the need for sleep would make my head droop from time to time, as in a spell of dizziness. Next morning I would realize that I had not heard the band passing, just as, at Balbec, after the evenings when Saint-Loup had taken me to dinner at Rivebelle, I had not heard the concert on the beach. And when I wanted to get up, I felt deliciously incapable of doing so; it was as if I were anchored in deep, invisible soil by the articulations of muscular and nourishing roots, of which my tiredness made me conscious. I felt full of strength, life seemed to stretch out more fully before me; I had in fact reverted to the healthy exhaustion of my childhood in Combray on the mornings after those walks along the Guermantes way the day before. Poets claim that we recapture for a moment the self we once were when we revisit some house or garden in which we lived when young. Such pilgrimages are extremely hazardous, and they end as often in disappointment as in success. Those fixed places, which exist along with the changing years, are best discovered in ourselves. Great tiredness followed by a good night's rest can in part help us in this. To make us descend into the most subterranean galleries of sleep, where no reflection of the previous day, no flicker of memory, is present to light up the interior monologue, if such monologue itself has not ceased, tiredness followed by rest turns over the soil and subsoil of our bodies so thoroughly that they enable us to rediscover, in a place where our muscles plunge down and twist around in their ramifications and breathe in new life, the garden where we lived as children. There is no need to travel to be able to see it again; we need to go deep into ourselves to find it. What once covered the earth is no longer above but beneath it, and it takes more than an excursion to visit the dead city: excavation is necessary. But we shall see how certain fugitive and fortuitous impressions can carry us more successfully back to the past, with sharper precision, in a flight more light-winged, immaterial, dizzy, unerring, and timeless than such organic displacement.

At times my exhaustion was greater still: I had followed the maneuvers for several days in a row, without being able to go to bed. What a blessing it was to return to the hotel! As I got into bed, I seemed to have escaped at last from enchanters, from sorcerers, like those who inhabit the "romances" seventeenth-century readers liked so much. My sleep and the long lie-in that followed it the next morning became a charming fairy tale. Charming—but perhaps beneficial as well. I reminded myself that the worst hardships have their place of sanctuary, that when all else fails rest can be found. These thoughts carried me far.

On off-duty days when Saint-Loup had nonetheless to stay in the barracks, I would often go and visit him there. It was a long way; I had to leave the town and cross the viaduct, with its immense views on either side. There was nearly always a strong wind over this high ground, and it swept through the buildings that stood on three sides of the barracks square, which was always howling like a cavern of the winds. Robert would be occupied with some duty or other, and while I waited for him outside his door or in the mess, talking to friends of his to whom he had introduced me and whom I came to see from time to time, even when he was not going to be there, looking down from the window at the countryside three hundred feet below, bare but for a few recently sown fields, often still soaked with rain and lit by the sun, which added an occasional strip of green to it, brilliant green with the translucent limpidity of enamel, I would often hear him spoken of by others; and I soon learned how much he was liked and how popular he was. Among many of the volunteers from other squadrons, the sons of rich middle-class families who viewed aristocratic high society only from the outside and without access to it, the attraction that they spontaneously felt toward what they knew of Saint-Loup's character was reinforced by the glamour that attached in their eyes to this young man, whom, when they went on leave to Paris, they had often seen on Saturday nights dining in the Café de la Paix with the Duc d'Uzès and the Prince d'Orléans. And this was why they now associated his handsome face, his gangling way of walking and saluting, his perpetually dancing monocle, the jaunty overstatement of his high caps, and the trousers that were of too fine a cloth and too pink a shade, with a notion of stylishness they certainly did not find among the best-turned-out officers in the regiment, not even the majestic captain to whom I owed the privilege of sleeping in the barracks, who seemed, in comparison, too imposing and too obviously stylish.

One of them mentioned that the captain had bought a new horse. "He can buy as many horses as he likes. I saw Saint-Loup on Sunday morning on the Allée des Acacias. Now, *there's* a horseman with some style!" replied his companion; he knew what he was talking about, for these young men belonged to a class that, without frequenting the same elevated milieu, thanks to its money and leisure does not differ from the aristocracy in its experience of all the refinements of life that money can procure. At most their own elegance—in the matter of dress, for instance—had something more contrived, more immaculate about it than the casual and careless elegance of Saint-Loup, which my grandmother found so appealing. It gave quite a thrill to these sons of important bankers and stockbrokers, as they sat eating their oysters after the theater, to see Sergeant Saint-Loup at a nearby table. And what a tale there was to tell in the barracks on Monday, after a weekend leave, by one of them who was from Robert's squadron, and whom he had acknowledged "really pleasantly," or by another, who was not in the same squadron but was positive that in spite of this Saint-Loup had recognized him, since he had set his monocled eye in his direction two or three times.

"Yes, my brother saw him at the Café de la Paix," said another, who had been spending the day with his mistress. "Apparently his jacket was cut too loose and hung badly."

"What about his waistcoat?"

"It wasn't a white one. He was wearing a mauve one with sort of palms on it—stunning!"

To the older soldiers (men of the people who had never heard of the Jockey Club and who simply placed Saint-Loup in the category of exceedingly rich noncommissioned officers, in which they ranked all those who, whether bankrupt or not, lived in a certain style, whose incomes or debts ran into several figures, and who were generous toward their men), Saint-Loup's gait, his monocle, his pants and caps, even if they saw nothing particularly aristocratic about them, held just as much interest and significance. They recognized in these details the character, the style that they had assigned once and for all to this most popular of the officers in the regiment, manners like no one else's, scorn for the opinion of his superior officers, which seemed to them to be the natural upshot of his kindness to his subordinates. The morning cup of coffee taken in the barrack room, the afternoon rest seemed more enjoyable when an old soldier served up to the greedy ears of the idle squad some savory detail about one of Saint-Loup's caps.

"It was as high as my pack."

"Come off it, you're kidding us. It couldn't have been as high as your pack," broke in an arts graduate, who used these slang terms to avoid being taken for a raw recruit, and who had dared to make this contradiction so that he could hear confirmation of a detail that enchanted him.

"Oh, not as high as my pack, wasn't it? You measured it, did you? I can tell you this, the CO just stood there looking at him as if he'd have liked to clap him in clink. And you needn't think that made any impression on our great Saint-Loup—oh no! He just walked about the place, looked up, looked down, with that monocle of his doing its usual thing. We'll have to see what the captain's got to say about it. Probably nothing, but he's not going to be pleased about it, that's for sure. But there's nothing so special about that cap. They say he's got thirty of them or more at home in Paris."

"And how come you know that, pal? Through that damned corporal of ours?" asked the young graduate, pedantically flaunting the new grammatical forms he had only recently acquired, and proud to let them adorn his conversation.

"How come I know? From his orderly—who else d'you think?"

"Now, there's a bloke who knows when he's well off!"

"You don't have to tell me! He's got more money than I have, I can tell you! And he gives him all his own things and everything. He wasn't getting enough to eat in the canteen, according to him. So along comes old de Saint-Loup and gives cookie a piece of his mind: 'I want him properly fed, and to hell with the cost.' " And the old soldier made up for the nondescript words by his spirited tone, in a pale imitation of Saint-Loup that scored an enormous success.

When I left the barracks I would take a stroll, then, to pass the time before I went, as I did every day, to dine with Saint-Loup at the hotel where he and his friends took their meals, I went back to my own, as soon as the sun had gone down, so that I could rest and read for a couple of hours. In the square, the evening sky set little pink clouds on the pear-shaped turrets of the castle, matching the color of the bricks, and the harmonious effect was completed by the softening reflection of the light upon them. So strong a current of vitality coursed through my veins that no amount of movement on my part could exhaust it; every step I took, as I walked on the paving stones in the square, had a re-

bounding spring about it, and the wings of Mercury seemed to be attached to my heels. One of the fountains was filled with a red glow, and
in the other the moonlight was already turning the water opal in color.
Between them were children at play, shouting shrilly and wheeling
about in circles, obeying some inescapable impulse of the hour, like
swifts or bats. Next to the hotel, the former law courts and the Louis XVI
orangery, which now housed the savings bank and the army-corps offices, were lit from within by the pale-golden globes of their gas jets, already aglow, and their light, although it was still daylight outside, suited
the huge, tall eighteenth-century windows, from which the gleam of the
setting sun had not yet disappeared, as a yellow tortoiseshell ornament
would have suited a complexion heightened with rouge, and persuaded
me to get back to my fireside and to the lamp that, standing there alone
in the façade of my hotel, was struggling with the oncoming darkness,
and for whose sake I was returning before it was completely dark, for
pleasure, like going home for tea. Inside my hotel, I retained the same
fullness of sensation I had experienced out of doors. It gave such a full
and rounded appearance to the suface of things that normally seem flat
and lifeless—the yellow flame of the fire, the crude blue paper of the
sky on which the evening light, like a schoolboy, had scrawled wiggly
pink chalkmarks, the oddly patterned cloth of the round table where a
ream of essay paper and an inkpot awaited me in company with one of
Bergotte's novels—that, ever since that moment, these things have continued to seem laden with a particularly rich form of existence, which I
feel I could extract from them if I were given the chance to set eyes
upon them again. I thought delightedly about the barracks I had just
left and their weathervane blown in all directions. Like a diver breathing through a tube that rises above the surface of the water, I felt I was
somehow in contact with healthy, open-air life through my connection
with these barracks, this high observatory dominating countryside furrowed with canals of green enamel, into whose various buildings I regarded it as a priceless privilege, one I hoped would last, to be free to go
whenever I chose, always certain of a welcome.

At seven o'clock, I dressed and went out again to dine with Saint-
Loup at the hotel where he took his meals. I liked to go there on foot. It

was now pitch-dark, and after the third day of my stay, as soon as night fell, an icy wind began to blow, like a sign that it was going to snow. As I walked, I ought, it would seem, to have kept Mme de Guermantes constantly in my mind; it was only an attempt to draw nearer to her that had brought me to Robert's garrison. But memories, griefs are unstable things. There are days when they become so remote that we are scarcely aware of them, we think they have disappeared. And so we give our attention to other things. And the streets of this town had not yet become for me what streets are in our usual whereabouts, merely a means of getting from one place to another. The life led by the inhabitants of this unfamiliar world must be something wondrous, it seemed to me, and often the lighted windows of a building would keep me standing for a long time in the dark, motionless, laying before my eyes the genuine and mysterious scenes of lives I might not enter. Here the genie of fire showed me in a crimson tableau the booth of a chestnut-vendor where a pair of noncommissioned officers, their belts abandoned on chairs, were playing cards, without suspecting that they had been conjured out of the darkness by a magician, like a stage apparition, and presented as they actually were at that very moment to the eyes of a stopping passerby who was invisible to them. In a little junk shop, a half-spent candle projected its red glow onto an engraving and turned it the color of blood, while the light cast by a big lamp, struggling with the darkness, bronzed a fragment of leather, nielloed a dagger with glittering spangles, spread a sheen of precious gold like the patina of the past or the varnish of a master over pictures that were only bad copies, and turned this whole hovel, in which there was nothing but cheap imitations and cast-off rubbish, into a marvelous Rembrandt painting. Occasionally I looked up toward some vast old apartment with its shutters still open, where amphibious men and women, adapting themselves each evening to living in an element different from their daytime one, swam about slowly in the dense liquid that at nightfall rises incessantly from the wells of lamps and fills the rooms to the brink of their walls of stone and glass, and as they moved about in it, their bodies sent forth unctuous golden ripples. I walked on, and often, in the dark alley that runs past the cathedral, as, in the past, on the road to Méséglise, the force of my desire made me pause; I felt that a woman must be about to appear and to satisfy it; if I suddenly felt a skirt brush past me in the darkness, the very intensity of the pleasure I experienced made it impossible for me to believe that the contact was unintentional, and I would attempt to put my arms round a terrified stranger. There was something so real to me about this Gothic alley that, if I had managed to pick up and enjoy a woman there, I would have found it difficult not to believe it was the ancient voluptuous charm of the place that was bringing us together, even if she were no more than a streetwalker, stationed there every evening, but invested with mystery by the wintry night, the strange place, the darkness, and the medieval ambience. I began to think about what lay ahead: to try to put Mme de Guermantes out of my mind seemed really painful, but sensible, and for the first time possible, perhaps even easy. In the total quiet of this part of the town, I could hear ahead of me words and laughter that must have been coming from people returning home half drunk. I waited to see them and stood peering in the direction from which I had heard these sounds. But I had to wait for a long time, because the surrounding silence was so deep that it had enabled sounds that were still a long way off to reach me with enormous clarity and force. Finally, they did appear, but not from in front, as I had supposed, but a long way behind me. Either the intersection of the streets and the position of the houses in between had created this acoustic error by refracting the sound, or, because it is very difficult to locate sound when its source is unknown, I had been as mistaken about distance as about direction.

The wind was blowing harder. It was grainy, spiked with coming snow; I returned to the main street and jumped onto the little tram, from the platform of which an officer was blindly returning the salutes of the blundering soldiers passing on the pavement, their faces painted bright with cold, reminding me, in this little town that the sudden leap from autumn into early winter seemed to have transported farther north, of the rubicund faces Brueghel gives to his joyful, carousing, frostbitten peasants.

And indeed, at the hotel where I was to meet Saint-Loup and his friends, the beginning of the festive season was attracting a great many people from near and far; as I hastened across the courtyard, with its glimpses of glowing kitchens in which chickens were turning on spits, pigs were roasting, and lobsters were being flung alive into what the landlord called the "everlasting fire," I discovered an influx of new arrivals (worthy of some *Census of the People at Bethlehem* such as the old Flemish masters painted), gathering there in groups, asking the landlord or one of his staff (who, if they did not like the look of them, would recommend accommodations elsewhere in the town) for board and lodging, while a kitchen boy passed by holding a struggling fowl by its neck. Similarly, in the big dining room, which I had passed through on my first day here on my way to the small room where my friend awaited me, one was again reminded of some Biblical feast, portrayed with the naïveté of former times and with Flemish exaggeration, because of the quantity of fish, chickens, grouse, woodcock, pigeons, brought in garnished and piping hot by breathless waiters who slid along the floor in their haste to set them down on the huge sideboard where they were carved immediately, but where—for many of the diners were finishing their meal as I arrived—they piled up untouched; it was as if their profusion and the haste of those who carried them in were prompted far less by the demands of those eating than by respect for the sacred text, scrupulously followed to the letter but naïvely illustrated by real details taken from local custom, and by a concern, both aesthetic and devotional, to make visible the splendor of the feast through the profusion of its victuals and the bustling attentiveness of those who served it. One of them stood lost in thought by a sideboard at the end of the room; and in order to find out from him, who alone appeared calm enough to give me an answer, where our table had been set, I made my way forward among the various chafing dishes that had been lit to keep warm the plates of latecomers (which did not prevent the desserts, in the center of the room, from being displayed in the hands of a huge mannequin, sometimes supported on the wings of a duck, apparently made of crystal but actually of ice, carved each day with a hot iron by a sculptorcook, in a truly Flemish manner), and, at the risk of being knocked down by the other waiters, went straight toward the calm one, in whom I seemed to recognize a character traditionally present in these sacred subjects, since he reproduced with scrupulous accuracy the snub-nosed features, simple and badly drawn, and the dreamy expression of such a figure, already dimly aware of the miracle of a divine presence which the others have not yet begun to suspect. In addition, and doubtless in view of the approaching festive season, the tableau was reinforced by a celestial element recruited entirely from a personnel of cherubim and seraphim. A young angel musician, his fair hair framing a fourteen-year-old face, was not playing any instrument, it is true, but stood dreaming in front of a gong or a stack of plates, while less infantile angels were dancing attendance through the boundless expanse of the room, beating the air with the ceaseless flutter of the napkins, which hung from their bodies like the wings in primitive paintings, with pointed ends. Taking flight from these ill-defined regions, screened by a curtain of palms, from which the angelic waiters looked, from a distance, as if they had descended from the empyrean, I squeezed my way through to the small dining room and to Saint-Loup's table. There I found several of his friends who dined with him regularly, nobles except for one or two commoners in whom the nobles had detected likely friends as early as their school days, and with whom they had readily formed friendships, thus proving that they were not in principle hostile to the middle classes, even if they were Republican, provided they had clean hands and attended mass. On the very first of these evenings, before we sat down to dinner, I drew Saint-Loup into a corner, and, with the others present but out of earshot, said this to him:

"Robert, this is hardly the time or place to ask you, but it won't take a second. I keep forgetting to ask you when I'm at the barracks, but isn't it Mme de Guermantes's photograph that you have on your table?"

"Why, yes, she's my darling aunt."

"But of course. How silly of me. I had known that, but I'd never really thought about it. Oh dear, your friends will be getting impatient. Let's be quick, they're looking at us. Another time will do, it's not important."

"That's all right, take your time. They can wait."

"No, no, I don't want to offend them; they're so nice. It really doesn't matter, I assure you."

"You know the splendid Oriane, then?"

"The splendid Oriane," as he might have said "the good Oriane," did not imply that Saint-Loup regarded Mme de Guermantes as particularly good. In this case the words "good," "excellent," "splendid" are no more than a means of emphasizing the definite article indicating someone who is known to both parties and whom the speaker is at a loss to discuss with someone outside the family. The word "good" serves as a stopgap and allows the speaker time to hit upon "Do you see much of her?" or "I haven't seen her for months" or "I'll be seeing her on Tuesday" or "She's no longer as young as she used to be, I imagine."

"I can't tell you how funny it is that it should be her photograph, because we're living in her house now, and I've been hearing the most astonishing things about her." I would have been hard pressed to say what. "That has made me enormously interested in her, from a literary point of view, you understand, from a—how shall I put it?—from a Balzacian point of view. But I didn't need to spell that out to someone as clever as you—you already understood. But I must stop. Whatever will your friends think of my manners?"

"They'll think nothing at all. I've told them you're a very special person, and they're far more nervous than you are."

"You're too kind. But listen, what I really wanted to ask you was this: I suppose Mme de Guermantes hasn't any idea I know you, does she?"

"I really have no idea. I haven't seen her since last summer, because I haven't been on leave when she's been in Paris."

"The fact is that I've been told that she regards me as an absolute idiot."

"I really can't believe that. Oriane is no genius, but, all the same, she's far from stupid."

"You know that as a rule I'm not at all keen for you to broadcast your good opinion of me. I'm not conceited. Which is why I'm sorry you've said flattering things about me to your friends here—we'll join them in two seconds. But Mme de Guermantes is different. If you could let her know what you think of me, even exaggerate it a little, I can't tell you how much pleasure it would give me."

"Why, of course I can. If that's all you're asking me to do, it's really not very difficult. But what difference can it make to you what she thinks of you? I suppose you couldn't really care less. Anyway, if that's all you wanted to say, we can talk about it in front of the others or when we're on our own. I'm afraid you're going to tire yourself, standing up talking and in such an awkward situation. We'll have plenty of opportunities to be alone together."

It was precisely this awkward situtaion that had given me the courage to speak to Robert: the presence of the others was a pretext for me to be able to say what I needed to in a brief and disjointed manner, which enabled me to disguise more easily the falsehood of telling my friend that I had forgotten his connection with the Duchesse, and also to prevent him from having the time to ask questions about my reasons for wanting Mme de Guermantes to know I was his friend, that I was intelligent, and so on, questions that would have been all the more disturbing to me in that I could not have answered them.

"Robert, I'm surprised that a man of your intelligence should fail to understand that one doesn't talk about the things that will please one's friends, one just does them. You could ask anything of me, and indeed I really wish you would ask me to do something for you, and I would demand no explanations, I assure you. I've gone further than I really intended; I have no desire to know Mme de Guermantes, but, just to test you, I should have told you that I wanted to dine with Mme de Guermantes, and I'm sure you would never have arranged it."

"Not only would I have arranged it, but I will."

"When?"

"As soon as I get back to Paris, in three weeks, I expect."

"We shall see. I'm sure she won't want it anyway. But I can't tell you how grateful I am."

"Don't mention it. It's nothing."

"Please don't say that. It's a great deal, because now I can see what a friend you are to me. Whether what I ask of you is important or not, disagreeable or not, whether I am being serious or simply testing you, it makes no difference. You say you will do it, and by saying that, you show the sensitivity of your mind and heart. A stupid friend would have argued."

This is precisely what he had just been doing, but perhaps I wanted to sway him by flattery; perhaps, again, I was being sincere, the only touchstone of merit seeming to me to be the way someone could be useful in connection with the one thing that seemed important—my love. Then, perhaps out of duplicity, or in a genuine surge of affection inspired by gratitude, by self-interest, and by all the physical features of Mme de Guermantes that nature had replicated in her nephew, I went on to add:

"But it really is time to join the others, and I've mentioned only one of the two things that I meant to ask you, the least important one. The other is more important to me, but I'm afraid you will say no. Would you mind if we were to call each other *tu*?"

"Mind? I'd be delighted. 'Joy! Tears of joy! Undreamed-of happiness!' "14

"Oh, thank you ... thank you ... After you! It's such a pleasure to me that you needn't bother about Mme de Guermantes if you'd prefer—calling each other *tu* is enough."

"I can do both."

"Really, Robert! Listen to me a minute," I said to him later, over dinner. "It's really so silly, this erratic conversation we're having. I can't think why. . . . But you remember the lady I was talking about just now?"

"Yes."

"You're quite sure?"

"Of course I am. What do you take me for? The village idiot? A half-wit?"

"I suppose I couldn't ask you to give me her photograph, could I?"

I had meant to ask him only for the loan of it. But as I spoke I suddenly became shy, feeling that my request was indiscreet, and in order to conceal my embarrassment, I formulated it more bluntly and overstated it, as if it had been quite natural.

"No. I would have to ask her permission first," came his reply.

He blushed as he said this. I could see that he had a reservation in his mind, that he suspected me of an ulterior motive, that he would serve the cause of my love only partially, subject to certain moral principles, and I hated him for it.

And yet I was touched to see how differently Saint-Loup treated me now that I was no longer alone with him and his friends were part of the company. His increased affability would have left me cold had I thought that it was deliberate; but I felt it was spontaneous and simply consisted of all the things that he was used to saying about me in my absence and not when I was alone with him. True, in our private conversations I could sense the pleasure he derived from talking to me, but that pleasure almost always remained unexpressed. Now, when I made the sort of remark that ordinarily he enjoyed without showing it, he watched from the corner of his eye to see if I produced on his friends the effect on which he had counted and which clearly corresponded to what he had led them to expect. The mother of a debutante could not have been more attentive to her daughter's repartee and its effect upon her listeners. When I made a remark at which, alone in my company, he would have merely smiled, but which he was presently afraid the others might not grasp, he kept saying, "What? What?" to make me repeat it, to attract their attention, and, turning to them immediately with a hearty laugh, transforming himself inadvertently into the ringleader of their laughter, he presented me for the first time with the opinion that he had of me, and which he must often have expressed to them. So I suddenly caught sight of myself from the outside, like someone who reads his name in the newspaper or sees himself in a mirror.

On one of these evenings, it occurred to me to tell a mildly amusing story about Mme Blandais, but I stopped myself immediately when I remembered that Saint-Loup knew it already, and that when I had started to tell it to him the day after my arrival he had interrupted me with, "You told it to me before, at Balbec." So I was surprised to find him begging me to continue, assuring me that he did not know the story and that it would amuse him immensely. "You've forgotten it for the moment," I said, "but you'll soon remember." "No, really, I swear, you're mistaken. You've never told it to me. Do go on." And throughout the story he kept his excited and enraptured gaze fixed upon myself, and upon his friends. It was only when I had finished, amid general laughter, that I realized that it had occurred to him that this story would give his comrades an excellent impression of my wit, and this was why he had feigned ignorance. Such is friendship.

On the third evening, one of his friends, to whom I had not had the opportunity to speak on the previous occasions, talked with me at great length; and I then overheard him telling Saint-Loup how much he was enjoying himself. And in fact we sat talking together for most of the evening, in front of our neglected glasses of Sauternes, separated, protected from the others by the magnificent veils of one of those instinctive likings between men that, when they are not based on physical attraction, are the only ones that are altogether mysterious. That had seemed to me to be the feeling, enigmatic in nature, that Saint-Loup had for me at Balbec, a feeling not to be confused with the interest of our conversations, free from any physical attachment, invisible, intangible, and yet experienced by him as the inner presence of a sort of phlogiston, or gas, sufficient to bring a smile to his lips when he referred to it. And perhaps there was something more surprising still in the mutual sympathy that had arisen here in a single evening, like a flower that had opened within minutes in the warmth of this small room. I could not refrain from asking Robert when he spoke to me about Balbec whether it was really settled that he was to marry Mlle d'Ambresac. He made it quite clear that, not only was it not settled, but there had never been any question of such a thing, that he had never set eyes on her, that he did not know who she was. If any of the society people who had told me of this forthcoming marriage had happened to be there at that moment, they would have simply announced the engagement of Mlle d'Ambresac to someone who was not Saint-Loup, and that of Saint-Loup to someone who was not Mlle d'Ambresac. I would have surprised them greatly had I reminded them of the discrepant predictions they had so recently made. So that this little game should continue multiplying its false reports and attaching the greatest possible number of them to every name in turn, nature has endowed those who play it with a memory as short as their gullibility is profound.

Saint-Loup had spoken to me about another of his comrades, also of the party, with whom he was on particularly good terms, since they were the only two in the place to champion the reopening of the Dreyfus case.[15]

"Oh, him!" said my new friend. "He's not like Saint-Loup. He's got the devil in him! He's not even sincere. At first he used to say: 'You wait and see. There's a man I know well, a shrewd fellow, kindhearted,

Général de Boisdeffre. You can believe what he has to say beyond a doubt.' But as soon as he heard that Boisdeffre had pronounced Dreyfus guilty, that was the end of Boisdeffre. Clericalism, the prejudices of the General Staff prevented him from forming a genuine opinion, although there is—or rather, was—before this Dreyfus business no one as clerical as our friend here. The next thing he told us was that, whatever happened, we would get the truth, because the case was being put in the hands of Saussier, and he, Saussier, as a Republican soldier—I might add that our friend here comes from an ultra-monarchist family—was a man of steel with an unflinching conscience. But when Saussier pronounced Esterhazy innocent, he found fresh reasons to account for the verdict, ones that were damaging not to Dreyfus but to Général Saussier. Saussier was blinded by the militarist spirit—and note that our friend is as militarist as he is clerical, or at least was. I don't know what to make of him anymore. His family is really distressed to see him mixed up in such ideas."

"You know, it seems to me," I said, half turning toward Saint-Loup so as not to appear to be excluding him from my conversation with his comrade, "that the influence we attribute to environment is particularly true of an intellectual environment. We are men conditioned by ideas. There are far fewer ideas than men, so men with similar ideas are alike. Since there is nothing material in an idea, those who are only materially linked to a man with an idea in no way modify it."

At this point I was interrupted by Saint-Loup because one of the young soldiers had smiled across to him and pointed to me with the words, "Duroc! Duroc to a tee!" I had no idea what this meant, but I sensed that the expression on the shy face of this young soldier was more than friendly. Saint-Loup was not satisfied with the comparison. In an outburst of delight that was no doubt intensified by the delight he took in showing me off to his friends, with extreme volubility he kept saying, as he patted me like a horse that has just come in first, "You really are the cleverest man I know." He corrected himself and added: "Along with Elstir, that is. I hope you're not offended. I'm only being scrupulously accurate. It's like saying to Balzac, 'You're the greatest novelist of the century . . . along with Stendhal.' I couldn't be more scrupulous, could I? But, all the same, immense admiration. No? you don't agree about Stendhal?" he went on, with a naïve confidence in my judgment that was expressed by a charming look of smiling interrogation, almost childish, from his green eyes. "Oh, good! I can see you share my view. Bloch can't stand Stendhal. Idiotic of him. After all, the *Chartreuse* is a stunning book, don't you think? I'm so glad you agree. What do you like best about the *Chartreuse*? Come on, tell me," he said with boyish enthusiasm. And his physical strength, present like a threat, made his question feel almost terrifying. "Is it Mosca? Fabrice?" I answered timidly that there was something of M. de Norpois about Mosca. This provoked a storm of laughter from young Siegfried Saint-Loup. And no sooner had I added, "But Mosca is far more intelligent, far less of a pedant," than I heard Robert shout "Bravo," actually clap his hands in helpless laughter, and exclaim, "That's perfect! Wonderful! You're extraordinary!" While I was speaking, even the approval of the others seemed superfluous to Saint-Loup. He demanded silence. And just as a conductor stops the orchestra with a rap from his baton because someone has made a noise, so he would reprimand the person responsible for any disturbance: "Gibergue, you must be quiet when someone else is speaking. You can say what you have to say afterward." And to me: "Do go on."

I breathed a sigh of relief, for I had been afraid that he would make me go back and begin all over.

"And since an idea," I went on, "is something separate from human interests and could not enjoy any of their advantages, men devoted to an idea are not affected by self-interest."

"That really leaves you floored, doesn't it, lads," said Saint-Loup when I had finished; he had been following me with his eyes with the same nervous anxiety as if I had been walking a tightrope. "What were you trying to say, Gibergue?"

"I was saying that your friend reminded me a lot of Major Duroc. It was like hearing his voice."

"Why, I've often thought the same," replied Saint-Loup. "They have several things in common, but you'll find that my friend here has a great many qualities Duroc hasn't."

In the same way that a brother of this friend of Saint-Loup's, a student at the Schola Cantorum, formed an opinion of every new work of music that differed entirely from the opinion of his father, his mother, his cousins, his club associates, but followed to the letter the views of all the other students at the Schola, likewise this noncommissioned nobleman (of whom Bloch formed an extraordinary opinion when I mentioned him, because, touched to hear that he was on the same side as himself, he nonetheless imagined him, on account of his aristocratic origins and his religious and military upbringing, as utterly different, endowed with the same sort of magic as a native of some distant country) had a "mentality," as it was becoming fashionable to say, analogous to that of Dreyfusards in general and of Bloch in particular, upon which the traditions of his family and the interests of his career could exert no hold of any kind. As a similar instance of this sort of thing, one of Saint-Loup's cousins had married a young Eastern princess who was reputed to write poetry as fine as that of Victor Hugo or Alfred de Vigny, but who, in spite of this, was presumed to have a different type of mind from anything that could normally be conceived, the mind of an Eastern princess shut away in a palace out of the *Arabian Nights*. It was left to the writers who were privileged to meet her to taste the disappointment—or, rather, the delight—of listening to conversation that was reminiscent not of Scheherazade but of a person of genius like Alfred de Vigny or Victor Hugo.

It gave me particular pleasure to talk to this young man, as it did to Robert's other friends and to Robert himself, about the barracks, the garrison officers, and the army in general. Thanks to the enormously exaggerated scale on which we see even the things, however trifling they may be, in the midst of which we take our meals, talk, and lead our real lives, thanks to the formidable enlargement that they undergo, which means that the rest of the world, in its absence, cannot compete with them and assumes in comparison the flimsiness of a dream, I had started to take an interest in the various personalities of the barracks, in the officers I saw in the courtyard when I went to visit Saint-Loup, or, if I was awake at the time, when the regiment passed beneath my windows. I should have liked to know more about the major Saint-Loup admired so much, and the course in military history that would have fascinated me "even from the aesthetic point of view." I knew that Robert was all too often given to rather hollow wordiness, but this occasionally indicated the assimilation of profound ideas, which he was perfectly capable of grasping. Unfortunately, as far as army matters were concerned, Robert was chiefly preoccupied at this time by the Dreyfus case. He said very little about it, because he alone of the party at table was a Dreyfusard; the others were violently opposed to a fresh trial, apart from my neighbor at table, the new friend, whose opinions seemed less fixed. A firm admirer of the colonel, who was regarded as an exceptional officer and had castigated the tide of unrest against the army in several of his regimental orders, thereby earning himself a reputation as an anti-Dreyfusard, my neighbor had heard that his commanding officer had been known to make certain remarks that suggested he had his doubts as to the guilt of Dreyfus and retained his admiration for Picquart. On this last point, at any rate, the rumor of the colonel's relative Dreyfusism was ill grounded, like all rumors that arise out of thin air and come to surround any great scandal. For, shortly afterward, this colonel, after being detailed to interrogate the former chief of the Intelligence Branch, treated him with a previously unparalleled brutality and contempt. Whatever the truth of the matter, and although he had not taken the liberty of questioning the colonel about it directly, my neighbor had been kind enough to inform Saint-Loup—in the tone in which a Catholic lady might inform a Jewish one that her parish priest denounced the pogrom in Russia and admired the generosity of certain Jews—that the colonel was not, in regard to Dreyfusism—to a certain kind of Dreyfusism, at least—the fanatical, narrow-minded opponent he had been taken to be.

"That doesn't surprise me," said Saint-Loup. "He's an intelligent man. But he's still blinded by the prejudices of his class, and even more by his clericalism." He turned to me: "Ah yes, Major Duroc, the man I was telling you about who lectures to us on military history. He's someone who, from all accounts, is deeply in support of our views. I'd have been surprised to learn that he wasn't, because he's not only supremely intelligent but a Radical Socialist and a Freemason as well."

Out of respect for his friends, who found Saint-Loup's Dreyfusard declarations painful, but also because the subject was of more interest to me, I asked my neighbor if it was true that the major really did manage to present military history in a way that was aesthetically pleasing.

"It's absolutely true."

"But in what way?"

"Well, it's something like this. All that you read, for example, in the narrative of a military historian—the smallest facts, the most insignificant events—are merely the indications of an idea that has to be extracted, and which often conceals other ideas, like a palimpsest. So that you have a body of material that is as intellectual as any science or any art, and one that is mentally satisfying."

"Would you be good enough to give me some examples?"

"It's not that easy to explain," Saint-Loup broke in. "You read, for instance, that such and such a corps has attempted . . . But before we go any further, the name of that corps, the way it is constituted, is not without its importance. If it isn't the first time the operation has been attempted, and if for the same operation we find a different corps being deployed, this could indicate that the previous corps has been wiped out or suffered serious casualties in the said operation, that it's no longer equipped to see the operation through successfully. So we need to ask ourselves what this corps that has been wiped out consisted of; if it was made up of shock troops, held in reserve for major attacks, then a fresh corps of lesser efficiency will have little chance of succeeding where those troops have failed. And also, if we are not at the start of a campaign, the fresh corps may itself be made up of any old odds and ends, and this could provide an indication of the forces still available to the belligerent and the proximity of the moment when its forces will be inferior to the enemy's, which places the operation on which this corps is about to embark in a different focus, because, if it is no longer in a position to make good its losses, its successes themselves will, by simple arithmetic, drag it toward its ultimate destruction. Moreover, the serial number of the opposing corps is of no less significance. If, for instance, it is a much weaker unit and has already exhausted several important units of the attacking force, the nature of the operation is completely changed, since, even if it culminates in the loss of the position held by the defending force, the very fact of holding it for any length of time can be a great success if a very small defending force has been sufficient to destroy considerable numbers on the other side. You can see that if, in the analysis of the corps engaged in this operation, there are all these important points, then the study of the position itself, of the roads and railways it commands, of the supply lines it protects, is of even greater importance. What you might call the whole geographical context needs to be thoroughly examined," he added with a laugh. (In fact, he was so taken with this expression that every time he used it, even months later, he laughed in the same way.) "While the operation is being set up by one of the belligerents, if you read that one of its patrols has been wiped out in the area around the position by the other belligerent, one of the conclusions you are entitled to draw is that one side was attempting to reconnoiter the defenses with which the other was attempting to counter the attack. Particularly violent action at any given point may indicate the desire to capture that point, but equally the desire to keep the enemy from moving off from there, not to retaliate at the point at which you have been attacked; or it may simply indicate a dummy move in which intensified activity is a way of covering the withdrawal of troops in the area. (This was a classic feint in the Napoleonic Wars.) On the other hand, to gauge the significance of a maneuver, its probable objective, and, as a consequence, the further maneuvers that will accompany or follow it, it is not irrelevant to consult, not so much the announcements coming from the High Command, which may be intended to deceive the enemy or to mask a possible setback, as the field regulations of the country in question. One can always assume that the maneuver that an army has attempted to carry out is the one prescribed by the rules in force for analogous circumstances. If, for instance, the rules establish that a frontal attack must be accompanied by a flank attack, and if, in the event that this flank attack has failed, the High Command claims that it had no connection with the main attack and was merely a diversion, then there is every likelihood that the truth will be found by consulting the field regulations rather than the statements made by Headquarters. And we need to consider not just the regulations that operate for each army, but their traditions, their habits, their doctrines. The study of diplomatic activity, which is constantly acting on or reacting to military activity, is another important factor. Apparently insignificant incidents, misinterpreted at the time, will explain to you how the enemy, counting on support that these incidents reveal to have been unforthcoming, was in fact able to carry out only a part of his strategic plan. So that, if you know how to interpret military history, what is a jumbled account for the ordinary reader becomes a logical sequence, which is as rational as a painting is for a lover of pictures who knows how to look at what a person is wearing in a portrait, what he is holding in his hands, whereas the ordinary visitor to an art gallery is bewildered and develops a headache amid the dizzying blur of color. But just as with certain paintings in which it isn't enough to notice that the figure is holding a chalice, and you need to know why the painter put a chalice in his hands, what it's meant to symbolize, it's the same with these military operations: quite apart from their immediate objective, they're habitually modeled, in the mind of the general who is directing the campaign, on earlier battles, which constitute, if I can put it like this, the past, the library holdings, the learning, the etymology, the aristocracy of the battles that are to come. And notice that I'm not talking for the moment about the local, the . . . how shall I say? . . . spatial identity of battles. That's a further factor. A battlefield has never been, and never will be throughout the centuries, simply the particular ground upon which a battle has been fought. If it has been a battlefield, it was because it featured certain conditions of geographical position, of geological formation, even of certain defects that could be used to hinder the enemy (for instance, a river dividing it), which made it a good battlefield. It was a good location, and it will continue to be. You don't create an artist's studio out of any old room, and you don't make a battlefield out of any old piece of ground. There are predestined sites. But I've strayed off the subject again. What I was really talking about was the type of battle that is taken as a model, a sort of strategic carbon copy, a pastiche of former tactics, if you like, of battles like Ulm, Lodi, Leipzig, Cannae. I don't know whether there'll be another war in the future, or what nations will be involved, but if there is, you can be certain that it will contain (and deliberately, on the commander's part) another Cannae, an Austerlitz, a Rossbach, a Waterloo, and so on and so forth. Some people are quite outspoken on the subject. Marshal von Schlieffen and General von Falkenhausen have made advance plans for a Battle of Cannae against France, in the style of Hannibal, pinning down the enemy along the whole front and advancing on both flanks, especially on the right, through Belgium, whereas Bernhardi prefers the oblique tactics of Frederick the Great, Leuthen rather than Cannae. Others air their views less crudely, but I can tell you one thing, my friend, and that's that Beauconseil, the squadron leader I introduced you to the other day, who's an officer with a great future in front of him, has studied his own little Pratzen attack; he knows it inside out, and he's saving it up for the day when he has the opportunity to put it into practice; when that day comes, he's not going to botch his chances, and we'll get it good and proper. And that breakthrough in the center at Rivoli—the same thing will happen if there's another war. It's no more obsolete than the *Iliad*. I can tell you, too, that we're more or less condemned to frontal attacks now, because we can't afford to repeat the mistake we made in '70. We have to assume the offensive, nothing but the offensive. The only thing that worries me is that, although I can see that the only resistance to this splendid doctrine comes from minds that are not quick on the uptake, there is one of the youngest of my masters, Mangin, a genius, who feels there ought to be a place—a provisional one, of course—for the defensive. It's really not very easy to come back at him when he cites the example of Austerlitz, where the defensive was simply a prelude to attack and victory."

Saint-Loup's theories put me in a cheerful mood. They encouraged me to believe that perhaps I was not falling prey, in my time at Doncières, with regard to these officers whom I heard being discussed as I sat drinking a Sauternes that cast the charm of its glimmering light upon them, to the same power of exaggeration that had affected me at Balbec and caused people to seem larger than life: the king and queen of the South Seas, the little group of the four gastronomes, the young gambler, Legrandin's brother-in-law, all of them now so reduced in my mind as to appear nonexistent. What gave me pleasure today would not perhaps leave me indifferent tomorrow, as had always been the case so far; the person I still was at this moment was not perhaps fated to future destruction, since to the fierce and fugitive passion which I felt on these few evenings for everything to do with military life Saint-Loup, by what he had just been telling me about the art of war, added an intellectual foundation, of a permanent nature, capable of absorbing me sufficiently for me to believe, without any attempt at self-deception, that once I had left Doncières I should continue to take an interest in the work of my friends there, and should visit them again before long. But in order to be quite sure that this art of war was really an art in the meaningful sense of the word, I said to Saint-Loup:

"What you say is interesting. Sorry, I should say it interests me enormously. But tell me, there's one thing that puzzles me. I feel that I could become fascinated by the art of war, but first I should need to be sure that it wasn't so very different from the other arts, that there was more involved in it than knowing the rules. You say that battles are modeled on former ones. I do find something aesthetic, as you put it, in seeing beneath a modern battle the plan of an older one. I can't tell you how pleasing that idea is to me. But does the genius of the commander really count for nothing? Does he really do no more than apply the rules? Or, given parity of knowledge, are there great generals as there are great surgeons, who, when the symptoms shown in two cases of illness are outwardly identical, nonetheless feel, for some merest hint of a reason, based perhaps on their experience but newly scrutinized, that in one case they need to do this, in another case that, that in one case they should operate, in another not?"

"But of course! You find Napoleon not attacking when all the rules said he should, but some vague intuition warned him not to. Look at Austerlitz, for instance, or his instructions to Lannes in 1806. But you'll find generals slavishly imitating one of Napoleon's maneuvers and achieving a diametrically opposite result. I could give you ten examples of that in 1870. But even on the question of trying to interpret what the enemy *may* do, what he actually does is no more than a symptom that may point to any number of different things. Any one of them may turn out to be the right one, if you confine yourself to a rational, scientific approach, just as in certain difficult cases all the medical knowledge in the world will be powerless to decide whether an invisible tumor is fibrous or not, whether or not an operation ought to be performed. It's his flair for these things, his crystal-gazing, Mme la Clairvoyante side (you know what I mean), that's the deciding factor, for the great general as for the great doctor. To take a single example, I explained to you what a reconnaissance before a battle might mean. But it may mean a dozen other things as well, such as making the enemy think you're going to attack him at one point when you want to attack him at another, putting up a screen to prevent him from seeing the preparations for the real operation, forcing him to muster fresh troops, to position them there, to immobilize them in a different place from where they are needed, estimating the forces at his disposal, sounding him out, forcing him to show his hand. Sometimes, even, the fact that you deploy large numbers of troops in an operation doesn't mean that the operation is really your main concern; you could actually carry it out in earnest, even though it is only a feint, and so have a better chance of deceiving the enemy. If I had the time to describe all the Napoleonic Wars from this point of view, I can assure you that the simple, classic movements that we are studying, and that you'll see us practicing in the field, just for the pleasure of getting out a bit, you young cad (I'm sorry—I *know* you're not well!), well, in a war, when you feel backed by the vigilance, the judgment, and the thorough knowledge of the High Command, the whole thing moves you as directly as the beams coming from a lighthouse, a purely physical light but at the same time an emanation of the mind, scouring through space to warn ships of danger. But perhaps I'm wrong to talk to you only about the literature of war. In effect, as the formation of the soil, the direction of the wind and light tell us which way a tree will grow, so the conditions in which a campaign is conducted, the features of the terrain on which you maneuver, partially dictate and limit the various options that present themselves to the general. This means that, along a mountain range, through a system of valleys, over certain plains, it's almost with the inevitability and grandiose beauty of an avalanche that you can predict the route an army will take."

"So now you're denying the commander's freedom of choice, the enemy's instinct to gauge the intentions of the other side, things that you granted me a moment ago."

"Not in the least! You remember that philosophy book we read together in Balbec, the richness of the world of possibility compared with the real world. Well, it's just the same with the art of war. In a given situation there will be four options available from which the general has had to choose, like the doctor who has to be prepared for the various courses taken by a disease. And here, too, human weakness and human greatness are further causes for uncertainty. For, of these four options, let us assume that contingent factors (such as the attainment of minor objectives, or lack of time, or inferior numbers and inadequate supplies) persuade the general to adopt the first, which is less perfect but less costly, less time-consuming, and involving as its terrain richer country for feeding his troops. After starting with this first plan, which the enemy, uncertain at first, will soon detect, he may not be able to carry it through, because of the many obstacles involved—this is what I call the unpredictable element of human weakness—and so abandon it and attempt the second, third, or fourth option. But it may be that he has tried the first plan—and this is what I call human greatness—merely as a feint to pin down the enemy and surprise him, at a point where he had not expected an attack. This is how Mack, at Ulm, expecting the enemy to attack from the west, was surrounded from the north, where he thought he was under no threat. But in fact this isn't a very good example. Ulm is better as an example of the battle of encirclement, and it's something we shall see repeated in the future, for it's not just a classic example from which generals will derive inspiration, but also a form of battle that has something inevitable about it (not exclusively so; there is some choice and variety), like a type of crystallization. But all that doesn't much matter, because these situations are ultimately artificial ones. To go back to our philosophy book, it's like the principles of logic or scientific laws. Reality conforms to them more or less, but remember the great mathematician Poincaré: he's by no means certain that mathematics is a rigorously exact discipline. As to the rules themselves, which I mentioned to you, in the end they're of secondary importance, and, besides, they are changed from time to time. For instance, we cavalrymen live by the 1895 *Field Service*, a book that can be said to be out of date, given that it's based on the old and obsolete doctrine that maintains that cavalry action has little more than a psychological effect by creating panic in the enemy ranks. Now, the most intelligent of our teachers, all the best minds in the cavalry, and particularly the major I was speaking about, take the contrary view, that the issue will be decided by a real free-for-all with saber and lance, and that the side that can hold out longer will be the victor, not just in psychological terms by creating panic, but physically."

"Saint-Loup is right, and it's likely that the next edition of *Field Service* will bear the stamp of these new ideas," my neighbor remarked.

"I'm glad to have your approval, since your opinions seem to impress my friend more than mine do," said Saint-Loup with a smile, either because he was slightly miffed by the growing bond between his comrade and myself, or because he thought it obliging to stamp it with his official recognition. "Perhaps I've underestimated the importance of the rules. They do change, I admit. But in the meantime, they do control the military situation, the plans of campaign and troop positioning. If they reflect a false conception of strategy, they may be the initial cause of defeat. This is all a bit too technical for you," he said to me. "Always remember that, in the end, what does most to accelerate the development of the art of war is wars themselves. In the course of a campaign, if it is at all prolonged, you find one belligerent benefiting from the lessons that emerge from the enemy's successes and mistakes, perfecting the methods of the opposing side, and the enemy in turn will go on improving these. But all that is past history. With the amazing advances in artillery, the wars of the future, if there are any, will be so short that peace will have been declared before there is time to put our lessons into practice."

"There is no need to be so touchy," I told Saint-Loup, reverting to what he had said before this. "I've been listening to you with a great deal of interest!"

"Please don't go into a huff," said his comrade, "but allow me to add this to what you've been saying. If battles reproduce themselves in exactly the same form, it isn't merely because of the attitude of the commander. It can happen that a mistake on his part (his failure to appreciate the strength of the enemy, for instance) will lead him to demand excessive sacrifices from his troops, the sort of sacrifices that some units will make with such sublime self-denial that the part they play will parallel the role of some other unit in some other battle, and they'll be presented as interchangeable examples in history. If we stick to 1870, we have the Prussian Guard at Saint-Privat and the Turcos at Froeschviller and Wissembourg."

"Ah, interchangeable—exactly so! That's excellent! How very perceptive you are," returned Saint-Loup.

I was not unimpressed by these last examples, as always when, beneath the particular detail, I was shown evidence of the general law. Yet what really interested me was the genius of the commander, and I was keen to discover in what it consisted, how, in a given instance, when the uninspired commander was unable to resist the enemy, the commander of genius would set about redeeming his jeopardized situation, something that, in Saint-Loup's view, was quite feasible and had been achieved several times by Napoleon. And to understand what military excellence was, I asked for comparisons between the various generals whose names were familiar to me, which of them had the most obvious marks of a leader, the most striking tactical gifts, even if this meant boring my new friends, who in fact betrayed no signs of boredom and went on answering my questions with unstinting goodwill.

I felt myself isolated—not only from the great icy expanse of darkness that spread out into the distance, and in which we would occasionally hear the whistle of a train, which only intensified the pleasure of being where we were, or the chimes of an hour that was happily distant from the one at which these young men would have to take up their sabers and leave—but also from all external preoccupations, and almost from the memory of Mme de Guermantes, thanks to the kindness of Saint-Loup, to which the kindness of his friends seemed to add greater solidity, and also because of the warmth of that little dining room, and the tastiness of the excellent food we were served. This gave as much pleasure to my imagination as to my liking for good food; occasionally the small fragment of nature from which the food had been extracted, the scaly-surfaced stoup of the oyster with its few remaining drops of sea water, or the gnarled stem and yellowed branches of a bunch of grapes, still enveloped it, inedible, poetic, and distant as a landscape, evoking in the course of our meal the successive images of a siesta beneath a vine trellis and a boat trip on the sea; on other evenings it was the chef alone who brought out these original properties of each dish, presenting it in its natural setting like a work of art: a fish cooked in a court bouillon was brought in on a long earthenware dish, and because it was presented in relief on a bed of bluish herbs, intact but still contorted after being dropped alive into boiling water, surrounded by a ring of shellfish, satellite animalcules, crabs, shrimps, and mussels, it seemed to belong to one of Bernard Palissy's ceramics.[16]

"I'm furiously jealous," Saint-Loup said to me, half joking, half in earnest, alluding to the huge amount of time I had devoted exclusively to talking with his friend. "Is it because you find him more intelligent than me? Do you like him better? If that's the way things are, I suppose no one else will get a look-in?" (Men who are enormously in love with a woman, who live in a society of woman-lovers, permit themselves to joke in a way that others, less easily deceived by harmless pleasantry, would never dare to do.)

The moment the conversation became general, the subject of Dreyfus was avoided for fear of offending Saint-Loup. Yet, a week later, two of his comrades remarked how odd it was that, for someone who lived in such a military environment, he was so enthusiastic a Dreyfusard, almost an antimilitarist. Not wanting to enter into details, I said that it was because the influence of environment is less important than people think. I intended, of course, to stop at that and not to reiterate the views I had presented to Saint-Loup a few days earlier. Yet, since I had already said the same thing to him almost word for word, I was about to excuse myself by adding, "Just as I was saying the other day . . ." But I had not reckoned with the other side of Robert's genial admiration for myself and certain other people. His admiration went hand in hand with so total an assimilation of their ideas that, after a couple of days, he would have completely forgotten that those ideas were not his own. And so, in the matter of my modest thesis, Saint-Loup, for all the world as if it had always been part of his own mental property, and as though I were poaching his territory, felt duty-bound to greet my discovery with warm approval.

"But of course, environment is of no importance!"

And this was said with such emphasis it seemed he was afraid I might interrupt him or misunderstand what he said:

"The real influence comes from the intellectual environment! One is conditioned by ideas!"

He paused for a moment and smiled like someone who has just finished a good meal, dropped his monocle, and, fixing me with a piercing look, said challengingly:

"All men with similar ideas are alike." No doubt he had completely forgotten that I was the one who had said these words to him a few days earlier; the words themselves he remembered very well.

I did not turn up at Saint-Loup's restaurant in the same frame of mind every evening. If a memory or a particular sadness we feel is capable of disappearing, to the point where we no longer notice it, it can also return and sometimes remain there for a long time. There were evenings when, as I crossed the town on my way to the restaurant, I felt so great a pang of longing for Mme de Guermantes that it took my breath away: it was as if part of my breast had been cut out by a skilled anatomist and replaced by an equal part of immaterial suffering, by an equivalent degree of nostalgia and love. And, however neat the surgeon's stitches are, life is rather painful when longing for another person is substituted for the intestines; it seems to occupy more space than they do; it is a constantly felt presence; and then how utterly unsettling it is to be obliged to *think* with part of the body! Yet it does somehow make us feel more authentic. The whisper of a breeze makes us sigh with oppression, but also with languor. I would look up at the sky. If it was cloudless, I would think: "Perhaps she has gone to the country; she's looking at the same stars, and perhaps when I arrive at the restaurant Robert will say to me: 'Good news. I've just heard from my aunt. She wants to see you. She's coming down here.'" My thoughts of Mme de Guermantes were not confined just to the sky above. A passing breath of air, sweeter than the rest, seemed to be bringing a message from her, as it once had from Gilberte in the cornfields of Méséglise: we do not change; we bring to the feeling we associate with a person the many dormant elements that that person awakens in us but which are foreign to the person in question. And then there is always something in us that tries hard to make these strange sentiments more real—that is, to assimilate them to a more general feeling, shared by the whole of humanity, with which individuals and the pain they cause us are merely a means to allow us to communicate: what brought an element of pleasure with my pain was that I knew it to be a tiny measure of universal love. Because I seemed to recognize the same sorts of sadness I had experienced in connection with Gilberte—or on those occasions in Combray when Mama had not stayed in my room, and also when I recalled certain pages of Bergotte—in the pain I now felt, and to which Mme de Guermantes, her coldness, her absence, were not clearly linked as cause is to effect in the mind of a scientist, I did not therefore conclude, it is true, that she was not the cause of my suffering. Is there not such a thing as diffused bodily pain, radiating out into parts outside the affected area, but leaving them and disappearing completely the moment the practitioner lays his finger on the precise spot from which it springs? And yet, until that moment, the way it was diffused made it seem so vague and threatening that, powerless to explain or even locate it, we imagined it to be incurable. As I made my way to the restaurant, I was thinking: "It's already a fortnight since I last saw Mme de Guermantes." A fortnight: it seemed so little except to me, who, where Mme de Guermantes was concerned, counted every minute. It was no longer just the stars and the breeze that assumed a painful and poetic aura, but the arithmetical divisions of time itself. Each day became like the crest of a hazy hill: on one side I felt I could descend toward forgetfulness, on the other I was carried along by the need to see the Duchesse again. And I was continually swayed toward one of these slopes, with no stable equilibrium. One day I thought, "Perhaps there'll be a letter tonight," and as I arrived for dinner I plucked up my courage and asked Saint-Loup:

"You don't happen to have had any news from Paris, do you?"

"Yes, I do," he replied gloomily, "bad news."

I breathed a sigh of relief when I understood that it was only he who had cause for unhappiness, and that the news was from his mistress. But I soon realized that one of the consequences of this bad news would be to prevent Robert from taking me to see his aunt for some time to come.

I learned that there had been a fierce quarrel between him and his mistress, either by letter or on some morning when she had come down by train on a flying visit. And the quarrels that had previously occurred between them, even less serious ones, had always seemed as though they were insoluble. She had a bad temper and would stamp her foot and burst into tears for reasons as incomprehensible as those that make children shut themselves up in dark closets, absent themselves from dinner, refuse to give any explanation, and only cry the more when our patience is exhausted and we give them a slap. To say that Saint-Loup suffered dreadfully from this falling-out with his mistress would be an oversimplification and would give a false idea of the pain involved. When he found himself alone, with nothing else to think about except his mistress's leaving him, impressed by the forceful energy she had seen in him, the anxieties he had suffered for the first few hours ceased in the face of the irretrievable situation, and the cessation of anxiety is such a welcome relief that the rupture, once it was a fact, assumed something of the same charm as a reconciliation. What he began to suffer from a little later was a secondary, unpredictable sort of grief, surging incessantly from inside himself, at the idea that perhaps she would have liked to make up, that it was not inconceivable that she was waiting to hear from him, that in the meantime, by way of revenge, she would perhaps, on a certain evening, in a certain place, do a certain thing, and that he had only to telegraph his arrival to keep it from happening, that others might be taking advantage of the time he was letting slip, and that in a few days it would be too late to get her back, because she would already be with someone else. All these possibilities told him nothing; his mistress preserved a silence that eventually put him into such a frenzy of grief that he began to wonder whether she might not be in hiding in Doncières, or have disappeared to the Indies.

It has been said that silence is a powerful weapon; in a quite different sense, it has a terrible power when wielded by those who are loved.

It increases the anxiety of the one who waits. Nothing so tempts us to approach another person as the thing that is keeping us apart, and what greater barrier is there than silence? It has been said, too, that silence is torture, capable of driving the man condemned to it in a prison cell to madness. But what an even greater torture it is, greater than having to keep silent, to endure the silence of the person one loves! Robert asked himself: "What can she be doing, to stay silent like this? Is it that she's being unfaithful to me?" And again: "What have I done to make her keep so silent? Perhaps she hates me, and will go on hating me forever." And he blamed himself for it. So silence was in fact driving him mad, with jealousy and remorse. More cruel than the silence of the prison cell, the silence he endured was its own kind of prison. An intangible kind of enclosure, perhaps, but an impenetrable one, this segment of empty atmosphere between them, through which the visual rays of the abandoned lover cannot pass. Is there a more terrible form of illumination than silence, which casts its light on not one absent love but a thousand, each one involved in some new act of betrayal? Occasionally, in sudden moments of diminished stress, Robert would imagine that this silence was about to be broken, that a letter from her was on its way. He saw it, it had arrived, he was alert to every sound, he was already appeased, he murmured, "The letter! The letter!" After this glimpse of a mirage oasis of tender affection, he would find himself trudging once more across the real desert of uninterrupted silence.

He suffered in anticipation every single painful detail of a rupture that at other times he saw as something it was in his power to avoid, like people who set their affairs in order before an expatriation that will never take place, and whose minds, no longer certain where they will find themselves living the next day, throb on momentarily, no longer part of them, like a heart removed from a sick man and continuing to beat though no longer part of his body. At all events, the hope that his mistress would return gave him the strength to persevere with the separation, as the belief in returning alive from battle helps to brave death. And since Habit, among all the plants that grow in human beings, is the one that has least need of nutritious soil in order to live, the first to appear on the most apparently arid rock, had he begun by treating the rupture as a pretense, he might eventually have become genuinely accustomed to it. But his uncertainty kept him in a state that, linked with the memory of the woman in question, was close to love. He nonetheless forced himself not to write to her, thinking perhaps that it was less agonizing to live without his mistress than with her in certain circumstances, or that, after the way in which they had parted, he needed to receive her apologies if she was to preserve what he thought she felt for him in terms, if not of love, then of esteem and regard. He went no further than to go to the telephone, recently installed in Doncières, to ask for news from, or to give instructions to, the maid he had placed in the service of his mistress. These calls were complicated and time-consuming, because Robert's mistress, swayed by the views of her literary friends about the ugliness of the capital, but primarily concerned with the well-being of her pets—her dogs, her monkey, her canaries, and her parrot—after her Paris landlord would no longer tolerate their incessant din, had just taken a little house in the neighborhood of Versailles. Meanwhile, he, in Doncières, could no longer sleep a wink all night. Once, when he was with me at the hotel, overcome by exhaustion, he did doze off for a while. But suddenly he began to speak, wanting to rush off and stop something from happening: "I can hear her, you're not going to . . . you shan' . . ." were his words. He awoke. He told me that he had been dreaming he was in the country with the squadron sergeant major. The latter had tried to keep him away from a certain part of the house. Saint-Loup had worked out that there was a lieutenant staying there, an extremely wealthy and lecherous man, whom he knew to harbor a violent passion for his mistress. And suddenly in his dream he had distinctly heard the intermittently regular cries that his mistress was apt to make at moments of orgasm. He had tried to force the sergeant major to take him to her room. The man had held on to him to prevent him from going, with an expression of annoyance at such indiscretion, which Robert said he would never be able to forget.

"What a stupid dream," he added, still quite choked.

But I was well aware, in the hour that followed, that he was several times on the point of telephoning his mistress to seek an end to their quarrel. My father now had a telephone, but I doubt whether that would have been of much use to Saint-Loup. Besides, it hardly seemed to be quite proper to make my parents, or even an appliance installed in their house, play the role of intermediary between Saint-Loup and his mistress, however refined and high-minded the latter might be. The bad dream gradually began to fade from his memory. With a fixed and absent stare, he came to see me on every single one of those dreadful days, and as one day followed another, they came to represent in my mind the magnificent sweep of a painfully forged staircase where Robert stood wondering what decision his mistress was going to make.

She finally asked him whether he would agree to forgive her. As soon as he realized that a rupture had been avoided, he saw all the disadvantages of a reconciliation. Besides, he was already suffering less, and had almost come to accept a pain whose sharp stab he would have to experience again, in a few months perhaps, if their liaison were to be resumed. And perhaps he hesitated only because he was now certain of being able to recover his mistress, of being able to do so and therefore of doing it. The only thing she asked of him, in the interests of regaining her composure, was not to come to Paris until January 1. And he did not have the heart to go to Paris without seeing her. On the other hand, she had made it clear that she was quite willing to go abroad with him, but for that he would need formal leave, which Captain de Borodino was unwilling to grant.

"I'm really sorry about it, because it will mean putting off our visit to my aunt. I imagine I'll be back in Paris at Easter."

"We can't visit Mme de Guermantes then, because I shall have already gone to Balbec. But it doesn't matter in the least."

"Balbec? But you didn't go there till August."

"I know. But this year I'm being sent there earlier, for health reasons."

His main fear was that I might form a bad impression of his mistress after what he had told me. "She seems violent only because she's too frank, too monopolized by her feelings. But she's a sublime creature. You can't imagine the poetic finesse she has. Every year she goes to spend All Souls' Day in Bruges. Rather fine, don't you think? If you ever meet her, you'll see what I mean; there's something noble about her. . . ." And since he was steeped in certain of the mannerisms current in the literary circles in which the lady moved: "She has an astral quality, even something quite vatic. You grasp my meaning—the poet veering toward the status of priest."

All through dinner, I hunted for a pretext that would enable Saint-Loup to ask his aunt to receive me without my having to wait until he was in Paris. And what finally furnished me with this pretext was my desire to see more paintings by Elstir, the famous painter whom Saint-Loup and I had met in Balbec. There was, moreover, an element of genuine interest involved, for if, on my visits to Elstir, what I had asked of his painting was that it should lead me to the understanding and love of things better than itself, a real thaw, an authentic provincial square, live women on the beach (at most I would have commissioned him to paint realities I had been unable to fathom, such as a hedge of hawthorns, not as a means of preserving their beauty but of revealing it to me), now, on the contrary, it was the originality, the attraction of the paintings themselves that aroused my desire, and what I most wanted to see were further examples of Elstir's work.

It seemed to me also that the least of his paintings represented something quite different from the masterpieces of painters even greater than himself. His work was like a world of its own whose frontiers could not be crossed, unique in substance. By eagerly tracking down the handful of periodicals that contained articles on his work, I had learned that landscapes and still lifes were only a recent feature of his painting, and that he had started with mythological subjects (I had seen photographs of two of these in his studio) and had then passed through a long period of being influenced by Japanese art.

Some of the works most characteristic of his various styles were housed in provincial collections. A certain house in Les Andelys, where one of his finest landscapes was to be found, seemed to me as precious, made me as keen to go there, as a village in the Chartres area with a glorious stained-glass window set into one of its millstone walls would have done; and toward the possessor of this masterpiece, toward the man who, inside the rough stone walls of his house, on the main street, sat closeted like an astrologer as he studied one of those mirrors of the world which Elstir's paintings are, and who had perhaps paid many thousands of francs for it, I felt myself drawn by the closeness of feeling that unites the very hearts, the inmost natures, of those who think alike upon some vital subject. Now, three important works by my favorite painter were described in one of these periodicals as belonging to Mme de Guermantes. So, on the evening Saint-Loup told me about his mistress going to Bruges, it was possible, without being completely insincere, for me to say to him casually at dinner, in front of his friends, as if it had just occurred to me:

"Oh, by the way, if you don't mind, one final word on the subject of the lady we've talked about. You remember Elstir, the painter I met in Balbec?"

"Yes, of course I do."

"You remember how much I admired his work?"

"I do indeed. And the letter we sent him."

"Well, one of the reasons—not the main reason, it's a secondary one, really—why I should like to meet the lady in question . . . You do know who I mean, don't you?"

"Of course I do! Why all this circumlocution?"

"Well, she has at least one very fine painting by Elstir in her house."

"Really? I never knew that."

"Elstir is likely to be in Balbec at Easter. You know that he now spends almost the entire year on that coast. I would really like to see that picture before I leave Paris. I don't know whether you're on close enough terms with your aunt, but do you think you could somehow contrive to give her the kind of impression of me that will make it difficult for her to refuse, and ask her to let me go and see the picture without you, since you won't be there?"

"Certainly. I'll answer for her. Leave the matter in my hands."

"Oh, Robert, what a wonderful friend you are."

"It's very nice of you to say that, but it would be even nicer if you could carry on as you started and call me *tu*, as you promised."

"I hope you two are not plotting your departure," one of Robert's friends said to me. "You know, if Saint-Loup does go off on leave, it needn't make any difference to you—we shall still be here. It might not be so much fun, but we'll do our very best to make you forget he's not with us!"

As it happened, just when it had been assumed that Robert's mistress would be going to Bruges on her own, the news went round that Captain de Borodino, who had so far refused his permission, had authorized Sergeant Saint-Loup to go to Bruges on extended leave. This is what had happened: The Prince, who was extremely proud of his abundant head of hair, was a devoted customer of the best barber in town, a former apprentice of the man who had been barber to Napoleon III. Captain de Borodino was on the best of terms with this barber, for, in spite of his airs and graces, he had the common touch. But his account was five years in arrears, with expenses like bottles of Eau de Portugal and Eau des Souverains, curling tongs, razors, and strops, on top of the usual charges for shampooings, haircutting, and so forth, and the barber had a greater regard for Saint-Loup, who always paid on the nail, and who kept several carriages and saddle horses. Learning of Saint-Loup's problem of not being able to go with his mistress, he had mentioned it heatedly to the Prince just as the latter, trussed up in a white surplice, was having his head held back and his throat menaced by the barber's razor. This account of a young man's amatory adventures wrested a smile of Bonapartist indulgence from our captain-prince. It is unlikely that he had his unpaid bill in mind, but the barber's recommendation inclined him toward indulgence in the way that a duke's would have inclined him to be ill disposed. With his chin still smothered in soap lather, he promised leave there and then, and the warrant was signed that evening. As for the barber, who was in the habit of boasting all the time and sustained his boasting by laying claim, with an extraordinary capacity for lying, to exploits that were entirely fictitious, having for once rendered a remarkable service to Saint-Loup, not only did he not claim public credit for it, but, as if vanity depended on lying and gives way to modesty when lies are unnecessary, he never mentioned the matter to Robert again.

All of Robert's friends made it clear to me that, for as long as I stayed in Doncières, or if I should come back there at any time, even in Robert's absence, their carriages, their horses, their quarters, their free time would be at my disposal, and I could feel how kindheartedly these young men were offering to put their wealthy circumstances, youth, and vigor at the service of my poor state of health.

"But why," they went on, after insisting that I stay, "don't you come here every year? You can see how much you like this simple life of ours! You're quite the old soldier, the way you take an interest in all that goes on in the regiment."

For I continued to ask them eagerly to rank the various officers whose names I knew in terms of the degree of admiration they felt to be appropriate, just as I once used to make my school friends rank the actors of the Théâtre-Français. If, instead of one of the generals I was always hearing placed at the top of the list, like Gallifet or Négrier, one of Saint-Loup's friends happened to say, "But Négrier is one of the most humdrum of our general officers," and then put forward the new, clean, appetizing name of Pau or Geslin de Bourgogne, I experienced the same happy sense of surprise as I did in the past when the outworn names of Thiron and Febvre were squashed by the sudden burgeoning of the unfamiliar name Amaury. "Even better than Négrier? How? Give me an example." I would have liked to see the existence of deep differences even between the junior officers of the regiment, and I hoped, in the reason for these differences, to grasp the essence of what constituted military superiority. One of the men I would have been most interested to hear discussed, because he was the one I had seen most often, was the Prince de Borodino. But neither Saint-Loup nor his friends, though recognizing him as a fine officer who maintained impeccably high standards in his squadron, liked him as a man. Although they obviously did not speak about him in the same tone as they used for certain other officers, rankers and Freemasons, who kept themselves to themselves and treated others with a brash, barrack-room manner, they still seemed not to rank M. de Borodino with the other officers of noble birth, from whom, indeed, he differed considerably in his attitude, even toward Saint-Loup. The noble officers themselves, taking advantage of the fact that Robert was only a noncommissioned officer and that his influential relatives might be happy to see him invited by superior officers whom they might otherwise have snubbed, lost no opportunity of having him to dine when they were entertaining any bigwig who might be of some use to a young cavalry sergeant. It was only Captain de Borodino whose relations with Robert—and they were excellent ones—were purely official. The fact was that the Prince, whose grandfather had been made a maréchal and a prince-duc by the Emperor, into whose family he had subsequently married, and whose father had then married a cousin of Napoleon III and had twice been a minister after the coup d'état, felt that all of this meant very little to Saint-Loup and the Guermantes set, who in turn, since his outlook was very different from theirs, meant very little to him. He suspected that for Saint-Loup he represented, through his connection with the Hohenzollerns, someone who was not a true noble but the grandson of a farmer, but at the same time he saw Saint-Loup himself as the son of a man whose countship had been confirmed by the Emperor—one of those "patched-up" counts, as they were known in the Faubourg Saint-Germain—from whom he had sought first a prefecture and then some other post placed very low on the list of subordinates to His Highness the Prince de Borodino, Minister of State, who was to be addressed as "Monseigneur" and was a nephew of the sovereign.

More than a nephew, perhaps. The first Princesse de Borodino was thought to have bestowed her favors on Napoleon I, whom she followed to the isle of Elba, and the second hers on Napoleon III. And if, in the captain's features, there was something of Napoleon I—if not in his natural expression, then at least in the studied majesty he adopted— the officer somehow reminded one, too, particularly in his kindly, melancholic gaze and with his drooping mustache, of Napoleon III; this was so striking that, when he asked permission to join the Emperor after Sedan[17] and was summarily dismissed by Bismarck, into whose presence he had been ushered, the latter, happening to look up at the young man, who was preparing to leave the room, was instantly struck by the likeness and, reconsidering the matter, called him back and granted the request, which, like everyone else, he had just been refused.

If the Prince de Borodino was disinclined to make overtures either to Saint-Loup or to the other representatives of the Faubourg Saint-Germain in the regiment (whereas he often invited two lieutenants of humble origin whose company he found agreeable), it was because, judging them both from the heights of his imperial grandeur, he drew the following distinction between these two species of inferiors: the first species were inferiors who were aware of the fact, and with these he was delighted to associate, since beneath his majestic airs he was a man of simple, jovial nature; the second were inferiors who thought of themselves as superior, and this he could not tolerate. And so, whereas all the other officers in the regiment behaved warmly toward him, the Prince de Borodino, to whom Saint-Loup had been recommended by Marshal X, confined himself to being helpful toward him in professional matters, where Saint-Loup was in fact exemplary, but never invited him to his house, apart from one exceptional occasion when he was practically forced to do so, and since this occurred during my visit, he asked him to bring me, too. On the evening in question, as I sat watching Saint-Loup at his captain's dinner table, I found it easy to distinguish, even in the details of their respective manners and refinements, the difference between the two aristocracies: the old nobility and that of the Empire. As the product of a caste whose faults, even if he repudiated them with every ounce of his intellect, had passed into his blood, a caste that, after ceasing to exert any real authority for at least a century, no longer sees the patronizing affability inherent in its upbringing as anything more than an exercise, like horsemanship or fencing, cultivated without any serious purpose, as a diversion, Saint-Loup, unlike those members of the bourgeoisie that the old nobility despises enough to believe they are flattered by its intimacy with them or would be honored by its lack of formality, would take the hand of any bourgeois to whom he was introduced and whose name he had probably failed to catch, and in the course of their conversation (continually crossing and uncrossing his legs, lounging back in his seat in an unbuttoned manner with one foot in the palm of his hand) he would address him as "my dear fellow." Conversely, as a product of a nobility whose titles were still meaningful, endowed as they still were with the fat emoluments given in reward for glorious services and recalling the high offices involving command of numerous men and a knowledge of how to deal with them, the Prince de Borodino—if not distinctly and as a matter of his own conscious awareness, but certainly in the revelatory attitudes and manners of his body—regarded his rank as a prerogative that carried weight; the same commoners whom Saint-Loup would have slapped on the shoulder and taken by the arm, were treated by him with a majestic affability, in which a reserve weighed down by grandeur tempered his naturally friendly disposition, and addressed in a tone marked at once by a genuine sense of kindness and a deliberate standoffishness. No doubt this was due to his relative familiarity with the great embassies and with the court, at which his father had held the highest posts, and where the manners of Saint-Loup, with his elbow on the table and his foot in his hand, would have been frowned upon, but it was primarily due to the fact that he was less inclined to look down on the bourgeoisie, since it was the great reservoir from which the first Emperor had drawn his marshals and his nobles, in which the second had found a Fould or a Rouher.[18]

Whether or not he was the son or grandson of an emperor, and with nothing more to do than to command a squadron, the preoccupations of his father and grandfather could not in fact, with no object on which to focus, be described as surviving in the mind of M. de Borodino. But as the spirit of an artist continues, many years after his death, to shape the statue he sculpted, so those preoccupations had become embodied in him in material, incarnate form, and it was they his face reflected. It was with the brusqueness of voice of the first Emperor that he reprimanded a corporal, with the pensive melancholy of the second that he exhaled a puff of cigarette smoke. When he walked through the streets of Doncières in civilian clothes, a special glint in his eye, beneath his bowler hat, created an aura of royal incognito about him; people trembled when he entered the squadron sergeant major's office, followed by the warrant officer and the quartermaster, as though they were Berthier or Masséna.[19] When he chose the cloth for his squadron's breeches, the stare that he kept aimed at the master tailor was capable of baffling Talleyrand and deceiving Alexander; and at times, in the middle of a kit inspection, he would pause, with a dreamy look in his striking blue eyes, and twist his mustache like a man intent on building up a new Prussia or a new Italy. But the next minute, reverting from Napoleon III to Napoleon I, he would be pointing out that the equipment was not properly polished, and asking to sample the men's rations. And at home, in his private life, it was for the wives of middle-class officers (provided they were not Freemasons) that he would bring out not only crockery in royal-blue Sèvres, fit for an ambassador (given to his father by Napoleon and looking even more precious than they actually were in the rather humdrum house he inhabited on the mall, like those rare porcelains that tourists admire with particular pleasure in the rustic china-cabinet of some old manor that has been converted into a comfortable, prosperous farmhouse), but other gifts from the Emperor as well: the noble and charming manners—and they would also have gone down brilliantly in a diplomatic post abroad, if for some the mere fact of having a "name" did not entail lifelong condemnation to the most unjust forms of ostracism—the easy gestures, the kindness, the graciousness, and, enclosing images of glory in an enamel that was also royal-blue, the reliquary of his gaze, that mysterious, illuminated survival. And since we have mentioned the Prince's relations with the bourgeoisie of Doncières, we ought to add the following. The lieutenant colonel was a wonderful pianist, the wife of the senior medical officer sang like a prize student from the Conservatoire. The latter couple, as well as the lieutenant colonel and his wife, used to dine every week with M. de Borodino. They were undoubtedly flattered by this, in the knowledge that when the Prince went on leave to Paris he dined with Mme de Pourtalès, the Murats, and the like. "But," they said to themselves, "he's just a captain, after all, and he's only too happy to have us as his guests. All the same, he's a very good friend to us." But when M. de Borodino, who had long been taking steps to secure himself an appointment nearer to Paris, was posted to Beauvais, he packed up and went, and forgot all about the two musical couples, in the same way that he forgot the Doncières theater and the little restaurant to which he used to send out for his lunch, and, to their great indignation, neither the lieutenant colonel nor the senior medical officer, who had so often dined at his table, ever heard from him again for the rest of their lives.

One morning, Saint-Loup confessed that he had written to my grandmother to give her news of me and to suggest that, since there was a telephone service between Doncières and Paris, she might like to speak to me. In short, she was going to give me a call, and he advised me to be at the post office at about a quarter to four. The telephone was not so commonly used then as it is today. And yet habit is so quick to demystify the sacred forces with which we are in contact that, because I was not connected immediately, my only reaction was to see it as all very time-consuming and inconvenient, and to be on the point of lodging a complaint: like everybody nowadays, I found it too slow for my liking, with its abrupt transformations, this admirable magic that needs only a few seconds to bring before us, unseen but present, the person to whom we wish to speak, and who, seated at his table, in the town he inhabits (in my grandmother's case, Paris), under another sky than our own, in weather that is not necessarily the same, amid circumstances and preoccupations that are unknown to us and which he is about to reveal, finds himself suddenly transported hundreds of miles (he and all the surroundings in which he remains immersed) to within reach of our hearing, at a particular moment dictated by our whim. And we are like the character in the fairy tale at whose wish an enchantress conjures up, in a supernatural light, his grandmother or his betrothed as they turn the pages of a book, shed tears, gather flowers, very close to the spectator and yet very far away, in the place where they really are. For this miracle to happen, all we need to do is approach our lips to the magic panel and address our call—often with too much delay, I agree—to the Vigilant Virgins whose voices we hear every day but whose faces we never get to know, and who are the guardian angels of the dizzy darkness whose portals they jealously guard; the All-Powerful Ones who conjure absent beings to our presence without our being permitted to see them; the Danaids[20] of the unseen, who constantly empty and refill and transmit to one another the urns of sound; the ironic Furies, who, just as we are murmuring private words to a loved one in the hope we are not overheard, call out with brutal invasiveness, "This is the operator speaking"; the forever fractious servants of the Mysteries, the shadowy priestesses of the Invisible, so quick to take offense, the Young Ladies of the Telephone!

And as soon as our call has rung out, in the darkness peopled with apparitions to which our ears alone are opened, a shred of sound—an abstract sound–the sound of distance suppressed–and the voice of the dear one speaks to us.

The dear ones, the voices of the dear ones speaking, are with us. But how far away they are! How often I have been unable to listen without anguish, as if, in the face of this impossibility of seeing, without long hours of travel, the woman whose voice was so close to my ear, I could feel more acutely how illusory the effect of such intimate proximity was, and at what a distance we can be from those we love at a moment when it seems we have only to stretch out our hands to retain them. A real presence, the voice that seems so close–but is in fact miles away! But it is also a foreglimpse of an eternal separation! Many times, as I listened in this way without seeing the woman who spoke to me from so far, I have felt that the voice was crying out to me from depths from which it would never emerge again, and I have experienced the anxiety that was one day to take hold of me when a voice would return like this (alone and no longer part of a body I was never to see again) to murmur in my ear words I would dearly like to have kissed as they passed from lips forever turned to dust.

Alas, that afternoon in Doncières the miracle did not take place. When I arrived at the post office, my grandmother had already put in her call; I stepped into the booth, the line was engaged, somebody was speaking who probably did not realize that there was nobody there to answer him, for as I took the receiver, the dead piece of wood began to speak like Punchinello; I silenced it, as I would a puppet, by putting it back on its hook, but, like Punchinello, as soon as I picked it up again it went on with its chatter. I eventually gave up in despair, hung up the receiver for good to stifle the convulsions of this vociferous stump that kept up its chatter to the very end, and went off in search of the telephonist, who advised me to wait awhile; then I spoke, and after a few seconds of silence, I suddenly heard the voice I mistakenly thought I knew so well, for until then, whenever my grandmother had talked with me, I had always followed what she was saying on the open score of her face, in which her eyes were so predominant; but today what I was hearing for the first time was her actual voice. And because the proportions of that voice seemed different the minute it was isolated, reaching me on its own in this way, unaccompanied by the facial features, I was aware for the first time how affectionate that voice was; and perhaps it had never been so affectionate, because my grandmother, sensing me to be far away and unhappy, felt that she could allow herself unrestrained expression of the affection that, in accordance with her "principles" of upbringing, she normally contained and kept hidden. Her voice was sweet, but how sad it was, primarily because of its sweetness, and it was, more than all but a few human voices can ever have been, almost drained of every element of harshness, of resistance to others, of selfishness; frail by reason of its delicacy, it seemed constantly likely to become choked, to expire into an unbroken flood of tears, and with it alone beside me, experienced without the mask of her face, I noticed for the first time how pain had cracked it in the course of a lifetime.

But was it solely the voice, heard in isolation, that created the new impression that tore at my heart? Not at all; it was, rather, that the isolation of the voice was like a symbol, an evocation, a direct consequence of another isolation, that of my grandmother, separated from me for the first time. The orders and interdictions she constantly addressed to me in the normal course of life, the tedium of obeying her, or the fire of rebelling, which neutralized my affection for her, were at this moment absent and might go on being absent (since my grandmother no longer insisted on having me with her, under her control, and was in fact in the process of expressing her hope that I would see out my stay in Doncières, or would at least extend it for as long as possible, for the benefit it was likely to give to my health and my work); thus what the little bell I held to my ear contained was our mutual affection, unencumbered by the conflicting pressures that had daily counteracted it, an irresistible fact from this moment on, utterly uplifting. By telling me to stay, my grandmother filled me with an anxious, desperate desire to return home. The freedom she was now granting me, and to which I had never suspected she would consent, suddenly seemed as painful as the sort of freedom I might experience after her death (when I would still love her and she would have abandoned me forever). I cried out, "Grandmother! Grandmother!," and I wanted to kiss her; but all that I had beside me was her voice, a ghost as bodiless as the one that would perhaps come back and visit me when my grandmother was dead. "Speak to me"; then, suddenly, I ceased to hear the voice, and was left even more alone. My grandmother could no longer hear me, was no longer in communication with me; we had ceased to be in contact, to be audible to each other; I continued to call her, groping in the darkness, with the feeling that calls from her must also be going astray. I was throbbing with the same anguish I had felt before, in the distant past, when, as a small child, I lost her one day in a crowd, an anguish that was less connected to not finding her than to the thought that she was searching for me and telling herself that I was searching for her, an anguish not unlike the feeling I was to have later, on the day when we speak to those who are no longer able to reply, and when we are anxious for them at least to hear all the things we have left unsaid to them, and our assurance that we are not unhappy. I felt as though it were already a beloved ghost that I had just allowed to disappear into the world of shadows, and, standing there alone in front of the telephone, I went on vainly calling, "Grandmother! Grandmother!" like the abandoned Orpheus repeating the name of his dead wife. I decided to leave the post office, go and find Robert in his restaurant, and tell him that, as I was half expecting a telegram recalling me to Paris, I needed to know the times of the trains, just in case that happened. And yet, before deciding upon this course of action, I felt I must make one last attempt to invoke the Daughters of the Night, the Messengers of the Word, the faceless divinities; but the fickle Guardians had been unwilling to open the miraculous Portals, or perhaps powerless to do so; untiringly though they invoked, as was their custom, the venerable inventor of printing and the young prince who championed Impressionist painting and motorcars (a nephew of Captain de Borodino), Gutenberg and Wagram[21] left their supplications unanswered, and I went away, feeling that the Invisible would continue to turn a deaf ear.

When I joined Robert and his friends, I made no confession that my heart was no longer with them, that my departure was already irrevocably settled. Saint-Loup appeared to believe what I said, but I learned later that he had immediately realized that my uncertainty was a pretense and that he would not see me again the next day. While he and his friends, letting their food grow cold, consulted the timetable for a train that would take me back to Paris, and while the whistling of the locomotives sounded in the cold, starry night, I certainly no longer felt the same peaceful contentment that I had derived on so many evenings in this place from the friendship of the company and the trains passing in the distance. Yet neither of these failed, this evening, to provide the same service, but in a different form. My departure weighed less heavily upon my mind when I was no longer obliged to think about it alone, when I felt that the more normal and healthier efforts of my energetic friends, Robert's comrades, were being applied to the matter in hand, and when I thought of those other strong creatures, the trains, whose comings and goings, morning and night, between Doncières and Paris, broke up in retrospect what had been too compacted and unendurable about my long separation from my grandmother into daily possibilities of rejoining her.

"I quite believe what you say, and that you aren't thinking of leaving just yet," said Saint-Loup with a smile, "but let's pretend you are going. Come and say goodbye to me tomorrow morning, early; otherwise there's a risk I might not see you. I'm going out to lunch, in fact. I've got leave from the captain. I shall have to be back in barracks by two, because we're off on a march for the rest of the day. I imagine the noble friend at whose house I'm lunching—it's three kilometers from here—will bring me back in time for two o'clock."

Scarcely had he said this when a messenger came for me from my hotel: the post office had asked for me on the telephone. I rushed there, because it was about to close. The words "trunk call" cropped up incessantly as the staff answered my questions. My anxiety was at fever pitch, for it was my grandmother who was trying to contact me. The post office was on the point of closing. I was finally put through. "Is that you, Grandmother?" A woman's voice with a strong English accent replied, "Yes, it's me, but I don't recognize your voice." Neither did I recognize the voice that was speaking to me—and my grandmother certainly did not address me as *vous*. And then all was explained. The young man to whom his grandmother had put through a call had a name almost identical with mine and was staying in an annex of my hotel. Since this call had come on the very day I had been wanting to telephone my grand-mother, I had never for a moment doubted that it was she who was ask-ing for me. It was pure coincidence that both the post office and the hotel had been jointly mistaken.

The following morning, I managed to be late and failed to see Saint-Loup, who had already gone off to lunch in the nearby country house. Toward half past one, I was thinking of going to the barracks on the off chance of being there when he returned; as I was crossing one of the avenues on my way there, I saw a tilbury coming up in the same direc-tion as myself, and as it passed I was obliged to jump out of the way; it was being driven by an NCO with a monocle—Saint-Loup! By his side was the friend with whom he had lunched, whom I had met once be-fore, at the hotel where Robert dined. Since he was not alone, I did not dare to shout to Robert, but in the hope that he would stop and give me a lift, I attracted his attention by a sweeping gesture of greeting, sup-posedly motivated by the presence of a stranger. I knew that Robert was shortsighted, but I imagined that if he saw me at all he could not fail to recognize me; he did see my gesture of greeting and returned it, but he did not stop; driving on at high speed, without a smile, without moving a muscle of his face, he made no response except to keep his hand raised for a moment to the peak of his cap, as though he were acknowl-edging a trooper who was unknown to him. I rushed on to the barracks, but it was still a long way; when I arrived, the regiment was forming up in the courtyard, where I was not allowed to remain, and I was heart-broken at not being able to say good-bye to Saint-Loup; I went up to his room and found it empty; I managed to inquire after him to a group of sick soldiers, recruits who had been excused from route marches, the young graduate, and one of the "old soldiers," who were all watching the regiment gather.

"You haven't seen Sergeant Saint-Loup, have you?" I asked.

"He's already gone down, monsieur," said the old soldier.

"I didn't see him," said the graduate.

"You didn't see him!" said the old soldier, losing all interest in me. "You didn't see old Saint-Loup parading about the place in his new pants! Wait till our captain sees it—it's officer's cloth!"

"Officer's cloth, is it? Tell us another one!" said the young graduate who lay sick in his room and was not going on the route march; he was trying, not without some misgivings, to take a bold tone with the veterans. "It's not officer's cloth. Just ordinary old stuff."

"*What* did you say?" asked the old soldier angrily.

He was the one who had mentioned the pants, and he was indignant that the young graduate should query the business of officer's cloth, but, being a Breton, born in a village that went by the name of Penguern-Stereden, and having learned French with as much difficulty as if it had been English or German, whenever he felt deeply upset he would repeat, "*What* did you say?" several times, in order to give himself the opportunity to find his words; then, after this preparatory move, he would launch into his own brand of eloquence, confining himself to the repetition of the few words he knew better than others, but without haste, taking care to play down his unfamiliarity with the pronunciation.

"So it's just ordinary old stuff, is it?" he exclaimed with a rage that increased in direct proportion to the dragging intensity of the way he spoke. "Just ordinary old stuff, eh? When I tell you it's officer's cloth, when-I-tell-you, because-I'm-telling-you, it's because I know what I'm talking about, don't you think? Don't come to me with your cock-and-bull stories."

"Oh well, if you say so," said the young graduate, overcome by the force of this argument.

"Look, there's our captain now. No, but just think of Saint-Loup, the way he flings his legs, and that head of his. What sort of NCO is that? And that monocle—all over the ruddy place."

I asked this group of soldiers, who were quite undisturbed by my presence, if I might also have a look out of the window. They made no objection, but neither did they bother to move out of the way. I saw Captain de Borodino pass majestically by with his horse at a trot, as if he fancied himself taking part in the Battle of Austerlitz. A few passersby had gathered at the gate to see the regiment file out. Sitting rigid on his horse, his face slightly chubby, his cheeks of an imperial fullness, his gaze clearsighted, the Prince must have been the victim of some hallucination, as I was myself whenever a tram had passed and the silence that followed its rumble seemed crossed and striped by some sort of musical palpitation. I was heartbroken not to have said good-bye to

Saint-Loup, but I left nevertheless, for my sole concern was to return to my grandmother; up to this day, in this small town, whenever I thought of what my grandmother was doing on her own, I pictured her as she was when I was with her, but eliminating my own presence and not taking into account the effect upon her of this elimination; now I had to free myself as quickly as possible, in her arms, from the ghostly image, unsuspected until now but suddenly evoked by her voice, of a grandmother who was really separated from me, resigned, getting on in years (something that had never occurred to me before), and who had just received a letter from me in the empty apartment in which I had already imagined Mama when I had left for Balbec.

Alas, it was this ghostly image that I saw when I entered the drawing room, before my grandmother had been informed of my return, and found her there reading. I was there in the room, but in another way I was not there, because she was ignorant of the fact, and, like a woman who has been caught unawares at some piece of handiwork that she will hide away if anyone comes in, she was absorbed in thoughts she had always kept hidden in my presence. The only part of myself that was present—in that privileged moment which does not last, and in which, during the brief space of a return, we suddenly find ourselves able to perceive our own absence—was the witness, the observer, in traveling coat and hat, the stranger to the house, the photographer who has called to take a photograph of places that will never be seen again. What my eyes did, automatically, in the moment I caught sight of my grandmother, was to take a photograph. We never see those who are dear to us except in the animated workings, the perpetual motion of our incessant love for them, which, before allowing the images their faces represent to reach us, draws them into its vortex, flings them back onto the idea of them we have always had, makes them adhere to it, coincide with it. How, since I had interpreted all that was most subtle and permanent in my grandmother's mind from her forehead and her cheeks; how, since every habitual glance is necromancy, and every face we love a mirror of the past—how could I have done otherwise than to neglect what had become dulled and changed about her, given that, in the most indifferent spectacles of daily life, our eyes, burdened with thought, pay no attention, as classical tragedy pays no attention, to any image that does not contribute to the action of the play, and limits itself to those that have the power to make its purpose meaningful? But if, instead of our eyes, it should happen to be a purely material lens, a photographic plate, that has been watching things, then what we see—in the courtyard of the Institut, for example—instead of an Academician emerging into the street to hail a cab, will be his tottering attempts to avoid falling on his back, the parabola of his fall, as though he were drunk or the ground covered in ice. Similarly, some cruel trick of chance may prevent the intelligent devotion of our affection from rushing forward in time to hide from our eyes what they ought never to linger upon, and, outstripped by chance, they get there first, with the field to themselves, and start to function mechanically like photographic film, showing us, not the beloved figure who has long ceased to exist, and whose death our affection has never wanted to reveal, but the new person it has clothed, hundreds of times each day, in a lovingly deceptive likeness. And, like a sick man who has not looked in a mirror for a long time and who constantly composes the set of the features he never sees in accordance with the ideal image of his face he carries in his mind, then recoils when he catches sight in a mirror of a monumental red nose, slanting out of the arid desert of his face like an Egyptian pyramid, I, for whom my grandmother was still myself—I who had only ever seen her with my soul, always at the same point of the past, through the transparency of contiguous and overlapping memories—suddenly, in our drawing room, which had now become part of a new world, the world of Time, inhabited by the strangers we describe as "aging well," for the first time and for a mere second, since she vanished almost immediately, I saw, sitting there on the sofa beneath the lamp, red-faced, heavy, and vulgar, ill, her mind in a daze, the slightly crazed eyes wandering over a book, a crushed old woman whom I did not know.

My request to gain access to Mme de Guermantes's collection of Elstir paintings had been met by Saint-Loup with, "I'll answer for her." And, unfortunately, it was he and he alone who did the answering. We find it easy enough to answer for other people when we set little images of them in our mind and manipulate them to suit our needs. No doubt even then we are mindful of the difficulties that arise from other people's natures being different from our own, and are ready enough to resort to whatever means are powerful enough to influence them—self-interest, persuasion, emotion—and will cancel out any inclination to oppose our wishes. But these differences in other people's natures are still conceived by our own nature; the difficulties are raised by us; the compelling motives are measured by our own standards. So, when we want to see the other person actually perform the actions we have made him rehearse in our mind's eye, things are quite different, we encounter unforeseen resistances that may be insuperable. Perhaps one of the strongest of these is the resistance that can grow, in a woman who is not in love, from the unconquerable and fetid repulsion she feels for the man who loves her: during the long weeks when Saint-Loup still did not come to Paris, his aunt, to whom I was certain he had written begging her to do so, did not once invite me to call and see her Elstirs.

I encountered signs of coldness on the part of another occupant of the building. This was Jupien. Did he feel that I ought to have gone in to greet him when I got back from Doncières, even before I went up to our own apartment? My mother told me not to worry, that it was nothing unusual. Françoise had told her that he was like that, suddenly given to bad moods, for no reason at all. They always wore off after a while.

Meanwhile, the winter was nearly over. One morning, after several weeks of showers and storms, I heard in my chimney, not the formless, elastic, sullen wind that made me restless for the sea, but the cooing of the pigeons nesting in the outside wall: iridescent and unexpected, like a first hyacinth gently tearing open its nourishing heart to release its mauve and satined flower of sound, and, like an open window, letting into my still-shuttered, darkened bedroom the warmth, the brightness, the fatigue of a first day of fine weather. That morning, I caught myself humming a *café-concert* tune, forgotten since the year I was supposed to go to Florence and Venice. So profoundly, and so unpredictably, does the atmosphere work upon our organism and draw from the hidden reserves where they lie forgotten the melodies inscribed there which our memory has left unsung. A more conscious dreamer was soon to accompany this musician I could hear inside myself, even without any immediate recognition of what he was playing.

I was well aware that it was not for any reason peculiar to Balbec that on my arrival there I had no longer found its church as magical as it had been before I saw it; that in Florence or Parma or Venice, too, my imagination could not substitute itself for my eyes when I looked at things. I realized this. Similarly, on a January 1 evening at nightfall, standing before a column of playbills, I had discovered how illusory it is to think that certain feast days are essentially different from the ordinary run of days. And yet I could not prevent my memory of the time during which I had expected to spend Holy Week in Florence from continuing to transform that festival into something like the special atmosphere of the City of Flowers, attributing something Florentine to Easter Day and, at the same time, something paschal to Florence itself. Easter Week was still a long way off; but in the run of days that stretched out before me, the days of Holy Week stood out more vividly than those that came between. Seen in a shaft of sunlight, like certain houses in a distant village caught in the effects of light and shade, they had retained all that brightness for themselves.

The weather had become milder. And this time it was my parents who, by urging me to take the fresh air, gave me the excuse for continuing my morning walks. I had wanted to stop taking them, because they meant meeting Mme de Guermantes. But for that very reason they were constantly in my mind, and this made me go on finding further excuses for taking them, excuses that had nothing to do with Mme de Guermantes, and which readily convinced me that, had she not existed, I should still have gone for a walk at the same time of day.

Alas, if for me meeting anyone other than herself would have been a matter of indifference, I felt that, for her, meeting anyone other than myself would have been perfectly tolerable. As it happened, in the course of her morning walks she was greeted by any number of idiots, whom she saw for what they were. But the fact that they crossed her path seemed to her to be, if not something to look forward to, then at least something purely accidental. And she occasionally stopped them, for there are moments when there is a need to escape self, to accept the hospitality of another person's soul, provided that soul, however modest and mean, belongs to someone else, whereas in mine she had the exasperating feeling that she would have found only herself. And so, even when my reason for taking the same route was nothing to do with seeing her, I would tremble with guilt as she came by; and sometimes, in order to play down anything that might seem excessive in my overtures, I would barely acknowledge her greeting, or stare at her mutely, managing only to irritate her even more, and to set off the impression that I was rude and ill bred.

She was now wearing lighter, or at least lighter-colored, dresses, and she would come down the street, on which already, as if spring had come—in front of the narrow shops between the broad fronts of the old aristocratic mansions—awnings hung down over the booth of the butterwoman and over fruit-and-vegetable stalls, to protect them from the sun. I told myself that the woman I could see walking in the distance, opening her parasol, crossing the street, was, in the eyes of those who knew how to judge, the greatest living exponent of the art of performing such actions and transforming them into something exquisite. Meanwhile, she was drawing nearer: unaware of this far-reaching celebrity of hers, her narrow, refractory body, which had gleaned nothing of it, was arched forward beneath a violet surah scarf; her sullen, bright eyes looked ahead absently and had perhaps caught sight of me; she was biting the corner of her lip; I watched her adjust her muff, give some money to a beggar, buy a bunch of violets from a flower-woman, with the same sort of interest I should have shown in the brush strokes of a great painter at work. And as she passed me, she acknowledged me, sometimes with a faint smile, as if she had painted me a watercolor that was a masterpiece and added a personal dedication to it. Each of her dresses seemed like a natural setting, inevitable, like the projection of a particular aspect of her soul. On one of these mornings, in Lent, as she was setting out for a lunch appointment, I ran into her wearing a dress of light-red velvet, cut slightly low at the neck. Her face seemed pensive beneath the fair hair. I felt less unhappy than usual, because her melancholy expression, the way the vivid color of her dress almost cut her off from the rest of the world, made her seem somehow lonely and unhappy, and I found this reassuring. I felt the dress to be the material form around her of the scarlet rays of emotions that I did not know she felt, and which I might have been able to console; seeking asylum in the mystical light of the garment's soft folds, she reminded me of some early Christian saint. So I felt ashamed of inflicting my presence on this holy martyr. "But, after all, the street belongs to everyone."

"The street belongs to everyone." I took up the words again, giving them a different meaning, and marveled at the thought that in the crowded street, often drenched with rain and made precious like the streets of some old Italian towns, the Duchesse de Guermantes did indeed mingle the moments of her own secret life with the public world, on view to everybody, a mysterious presence jostled by everybody, with the splendid wantonness of the greatest works of art. Since I tended to go out in the morning after staying awake all night, in the afternoon my parents would tell me to go to bed for a while and try to get some sleep. It takes no great thought to know how to go to sleep, but habit is very useful, and even the absence of thought. But during these afternoons I lacked both. Before going to sleep, I spent so much time thinking that I would be unable to do so that even after I had gone to sleep a little of my thought remained. It was no more than a glimmer in almost total darkness, but it was enough to cast its reflection into my sleep–first the idea that I could not sleep; then, as a reflection of this reflection, that it was in my sleep that I sensed I was not asleep; then, by a further refraction, my awakening . . . to a new state of drowsiness, in which I was trying to tell some friends who had entered the room that a moment ago, when I was asleep, I had thought I was awake. These shadows were barely distinguishable: it would have required a great deal of subtlety, wasted subtlety, to perceive them clearly. Similarly, later in my life, in Venice, long after the sun had set, thanks to the imperceptible echo of a last note of light held indefinitely over the canals as though sustained by some optical pedal, I saw the reflections of the palaces unfurled as if for eternity in an even darker velvet over the twilight grayness of the water. One of my dreams was the synthesis of what my imagination had often tried to envisage, during my waking hours, of a particular landscape by the sea and its medieval past. In my sleep I saw a Gothic citadel rising from a sea whose waves were frozen still, as in a stained-glass window. An inlet of the sea divided the town in two; the green water came right up to my feet; on the opposite shore it lapped around an Oriental church, and around houses that already existed in the fourteenth century, so that to move across to them would have been to go backward through the centuries. This dream in which nature had taken lessons from art, in which the sea had become Gothic, this dream in which I longed to reach, and believed I was reaching, the impossible, was one I felt I had often dreamed before. But since it is the nature of what we imagine in sleep to multiply itself in the past and to appear familiar even when it is new, I supposed I was mistaken. What I did notice, though, was that I frequently had this dream.

Those compressions that characterize sleep were reflected in mine, but symbolically: the darkness made it impossible for me to distinguish the faces of the friends who were in the room, for we sleep with our eyes shut; I, who carried on endless verbal arguments with myself while I dreamed, as soon as I tried to speak to these friends felt the words stick in my throat, for we do not speak distinctly in our sleep; I wanted to go to them and could not move my legs, for we do not walk when we are asleep, either; then, suddenly, I felt ashamed to be seen by them, for we sleep without our clothes. And so, with blind eyes, sealed lips, legs held captive, naked body, the image of sleep projected by my own sleep was like the great allegorical figures of Giotto, once given me by Swann, among which Envy is depicted with a serpent in her mouth.

Saint-Loup did come to Paris, but only for a few hours. And he assured me that he had not yet been able to speak to his cousin: "Oriane's not at all nice," he told me, without realizing he was going back on his previous words. "She's not the Oriane she was, they've gone and changed her. It's not worth your bothering with her, I promise you. You overestimate her qualities. Why don't you let me introduce you to my cousin Poictiers?" he added, unconscious of the fact that this could not possibly give me any pleasure. "Now, *she's* an intelligent young woman you'd like. She's married to my cousin the Duc de Poictiers. He's a good fellow, but not quite bright enough for her. I've told her about you. She's asked me to invite you. She's pretty, but not in the same way as Oriane, and she's younger. She's a really nice person—you know, a really fine person." There were expressions newly—and all the more enthusiastically—adopted by Robert to indicate that the person in question was finely discriminating: "I'm not saying she's a Dreyfusard. You only have to remember her background. But I did hear her say, 'If he was innocent, how perfectly dreadful for him to have been imprisoned on Devil's Island!' You see what I mean, don't you? And, then, she's someone who does an awful lot for her old governesses. She's insisted that they are never to be made to use the servants' entrance. She's a really fine person, believe me. Oriane doesn't really like her, because she can feel that she's more intelligent."

Although she was much preoccupied by the pity she felt for one of the Guermantes footmen—who could not go and see his fiancée, even when the Duchesse was out, because it would immediately have been reported by the concierge—Françoise was upset to have been out when Saint-Loup had called, but the reason for this was that she was now in the habit of going out to call on people herself. She was certain to go out on the days when I most needed her. It was always to see her brother, her niece, and most often her own daughter, who had recently come to live in Paris. The family nature of these visits was an additional element in the irritation I felt at being deprived of her services, for I foresaw that she would talk about them as duties that could not be shirked, according to the laws laid down at Saint-André-des-Champs. And so I never listened to her excuses without a grumpy attitude, which was not at all fair to her, and which was pushed to its peak by Françoise's way of saying, not, "I've been to see my brother," or "I've been to see my niece," but: "I've been to see the brother," "I just popped in to say hello to the niece" (or "to my niece the butcheress"). As for her daughter, Françoise would have liked to see her return to Combray. But the latter, now transformed into a Parisienne with a fashionable woman's taste for abbreviations, though her own were vulgar ones, had been heard to say that the week she was due to spend in Combray would seem more than long enough to be away from the columns of the *"Intran."* [22] She was even less inclined to go to Françoise's sister, who lived in a mountain region, for, according to this daughter of Françoise, mountains were not really *interesting*, and she gave the word a new and dreadful meaning. She could not bring herself to go back to Méséglise, where "everyone is so stupid," where the market gossips would claim cousinhood with her and say, "Why, it's not poor dead Bazireau's daughter?" She would sooner die than go back and settle down there, "now that she had tasted Parisian life," yet Françoise, for all her traditionalism, smiled complacently at the spirit of innovation embodied in this new "Parisienne" saying to her, "Well, Mother, if you don't get your day off, you can always send me a wire."

The weather had turned cold again. "Go out? What for? To catch your death?" said Françoise, who preferred to remain at home during the week her daughter, brother, and butcher-niece had gone to spend in Combray. As the last disciple in whom my aunt Léonie's doctrine of natural philosophy dimly lived on, Françoise would add, in reference to this unseasonable weather, "It's the leftovers of God's wrath!" My only response to her complaints was a languid smile; I was all the more indifferent to these predictions because, whatever happened, it would be fine for me; I could already see the morning sun shining on the slope of Fiesole, warming me in its rays; they were so strong that, smiling, I had to half open, half shut my eyelids, which, like alabaster lamps, were filled with a pink glow. It was not only the bells that came back to me from Italy, but Italy itself. My devoted hands would not be empty of flowers to honor the anniversary of the journey I ought to have made long ago, for, since the weather had turned cold again in Paris, as it had in another year when we were getting ready to go away at the end of Lent, in the liquid, icy air that bathed the chestnuts and planes on the boulevards and the tree in the courtyard of our house, the narcissi, the daffodils, the anemones of the Ponte Vecchio were already beginning to open as in a bowl of clear water.

My father had told us that, through A.-J., he now knew where M. de Norpois was off to when he ran into him in our building.

"He goes to see Mme de Villeparisis. They're great friends. I had no idea. It seems she's a delightful person, an exceptional woman. You ought to go and call on her," he said to me. And I was very surprised by the way he spoke of M. de Guermantes as a man of the highest distinction; I always thought him a boor myself. "It seems that he is enormously well informed and has perfect taste, only he's very proud of his name and his connections. But according to Norpois, he does command enormous respect, not only here but all over Europe. Apparently the Emperor of Austria and the Tsar treat him like a good friend. Old Norpois told me that Mme de Villeparisis was very fond of you, and that you would be able to meet interesting people at her gatherings. He was full of praise for you. You'll meet him there, too, and he may have good advice to give you even if you are going to be a writer. I can see your mind is set on it. It's a fine career in some people's eyes, but it's not the one I should have chosen for you myself. Anyway, you'll soon be a man now, we won't always be here to look after you, and it's not for us to prevent you from following your vocation."

If only I had been able to start writing! But, however I set about it (all too similarly, alas, to the resolve to give up alcohol, to go to bed early, to get enough sleep, and to keep fit), whether it was in a spurt of activity, with method, with pleasure, in depriving myself of a walk, or postponing it and reserving it as a reward, taking advantage of an hour of feeling well, making use of the inaction forced upon me by a day's illness, the inevitable result of my efforts was a blank page, untouched by writing, as predestined as the forced card that you inevitably end up drawing in certain tricks, however thoroughly you have first shuffled the pack. I was merely the instrument of habits of not working, of not going to bed, of not sleeping, which had to fulfill themselves at any cost; if I offered no resistance, if I made do with the pretext they drew from the first opportunity that arose for them to act as they chose, I escaped without serious harm, I still slept for a few hours toward morning, I managed to read a little, I did not overexert myself; but if I tried to resist them, by deciding to go to bed early, to drink only water, to work, they became annoyed, they resorted to strong measures, they made me really ill, I was obliged to double my dose of alcohol, I did not go to bed for two days, I could not even read, and I would vow to be more reasonable in future—that is to say, less wise—like the victim who allows himself to be robbed for fear of being murdered if he puts up resistance.

In the meantime, my father had run into M. de Guermantes once or twice, and now that M. de Norpois had told him that the Duc was a remarkable man, he had started to pay more attention to what he said. In fact, they had met in the courtyard and discussed Mme de Villeparisis. "He told me she's his aunt. He pronounces the name 'Vilparisi.' She's an extraordinarily intelligent woman, he tells me. He went as far as to say that she keeps a Bureau of Wit," my father added, impressed by the vagueness of this expression, which he had in fact come across once or twice in volumes of memoirs but without attaching any precise meaning to it. My mother had so much respect for him that, when she saw that he did not simply dismiss this Bureau of Wit of Mme de Villeparisis, she decided that it must be something of consequence. Although she had always known of the Marquise's worth through my grandmother's detailed accounts, she immediately rated it even higher. My grandmother, who was in rather poor health at this time, was not at first in favor of the proposed visit, and subsequently lost interest in the matter. Since we had moved into our new apartment, Mme de Villeparisis had asked her to call on several occasions. And my grandmother had always written back to say that she was not calling on people at present, in one of the letters that, through some new habit of hers we did not understand, she no longer sealed herself but left Françoise to deal with. As for myself, lacking any very clear picture of this Bureau of Wit, it would not have come as any great surprise to find the old lady from Balbec installed behind a bureau, as in fact I eventually did.

My father would also very much have liked to know whether the ambassador's support would gain him many votes at the Institut,[23] for which he was thinking of standing as an independent candidate. The fact was that, though he did not go as far as to doubt that he would have M. de Norpois's support, he was not entirely certain of it. He had thought it to be simply malicious gossip when he had been told at the ministry that M. de Norpois, wishing to be the sole representative of the Institut there, would put every possible obstacle in the way of a candidature that would cause him particular embarrassment at the moment, since he was supporting another candidate. Yet, when M. Leroy-Beaulieu had advised him to stand and calculated his chances, my father had been struck by the fact that, among the colleagues upon whom he could count for support, the eminent economist had not mentioned M. de Norpois. He dared not ask the former ambassador to his face, but hoped that I would return from my visit to Mme de Villeparisis with his election as good as assured. This visit was about to take place. Propaganda from M. de Norpois, capable of ensuring him the votes of at least two-thirds of the Academy, seemed all the more probable to my father since the ambassador's willingness to oblige was proverbial, those who liked him least admitting that there was no one who took so much pleasure in being of service. And, further, at the ministry, his patronage extended itself to my father far more markedly than to any other official.

My father had another encounter, too, but one that caused him not only a great deal of surprise, but also extreme indignation. He ran into Mme Sazerat, whose comparative poverty meant that her Parisian life was restricted to occasional visits to a friend. There was no one who irritated my father more than Mme Sazerat, so much so that Mama found it necessary to adopt a sweet and suppliant tone of voice when she made her yearly announcement to him: "My dear, I really must invite Mme Sazerat here, just once. She won't stay long"; or even, "Listen, dear, I have a very special request to ask of you. Please go and pay Mme Sazerat a little visit. You know how I hate bothering you, but it would be so nice of you." He would laugh, slightly irritated by it all, then go and pay the visit. So, when he ran into her this time, despite the fact that she left him cold, he went up to her and doffed his hat; but, to his astonishment, Mme Sazerat confined herself to the sort of stiff acknowledgment that is dictated by politeness toward someone who has done something disgraceful or who has been condemned to live in another hemisphere. My father arrived home speechless with anger. The following day, my mother met Mme Sazerat in someone's house. She did not offer her hand, but smiled at my mother with vague melancholy, as one smiles at a playmate from one's childhood with whom all connection has been severed because she has lived a debauched life, married a jailbird or, worse still, a divorced man. Now, from time immemorial my parents had accorded to Mme Sazerat, and she to them, the profoundest respect. But what my mother did not know was that Mme Sazerat, alone of her kind in Combray, was a Dreyfusard. My father, a friend of M. Méline,[24] was convinced that Dreyfus was guilty. When some of his colleagues had asked him to sign a petition for a retrial, he had sharply sent them packing. He refused to speak to me for a week when he discovered that my own view did not coincide with his. His opinions were common knowledge. He came very near to being thought of as a Nationalist. As for my grandmother, the sole member of the family who seemed likely to be stirred by generous doubt, whenever anyone spoke to her of the possible innocence of Dreyfus she would shake her head in a way that we did not understand at the time, but which was like the gesture of someone who has been interrupted when she has more serious things to think about. My mother, torn between her love for my father and the hope that I would develop into someone clever, remained unable to make up her mind, and conveyed as much by her silence. And then my grandfather, who adored the army (although his duties with the National Guard had been the bugbear of his adulthood), could never see a regiment march past the garden railings in Combray without baring his head as the colonel and the colors passed. All this was enough for Mme Sazerat, who was perfectly aware of the disinterestedness and probity of my father and grandfather, to regard them as pillars of Injustice. We forgive the crimes of individuals, but not their participation in a collective crime. As soon as she knew my father was an anti-Dreyfusard, she put continents and centuries between herself and him. And this explains why, at such a distance of time and space, her greeting had appeared imperceptible to my father, and why it had not occurred to her to shake hands or to speak, since neither gesture could have crossed the worlds that stretched between them.

Saint-Loup, who was expected in Paris, had promised to take me to visit Mme de Villeparisis, and although I had not mentioned it to him, I hoped that we might meet Mme de Guermantes there. He invited me to lunch in a restaurant with his mistress, whom we were then to accompany to a rehearsal. We were to call for her in the morning at her house on the outskirts of Paris.

I had asked Saint-Loup whether it would be at all possible to lunch at a particular restaurant (in the lives of moneyed young noblemen, the restaurant plays as important a part as the chests of rich fabric in Arabian tales), the one to which Aimé had told me he was going as headwaiter until the start of the Balbec season. It held great charm for me, who dreamed of so many journeys and made so few, to be able to re-encounter someone who formed part not only of my memories of Balbec but of Balbec itself, who went there year after year and, when fatigue and my studies forced me to remain in Paris, would still be there during the long late afternoons of July, waiting for guests to come in to dinner, watching the sun descend and set in the sea, through the glass panels of the main dining room, behind which, when the light had gone, the motionless wings of distant bluish vessels looked like exotic moths in a display case. Magnetized himself by his contact with the powerful magnet of Balbec, this headwaiter became in turn a magnet for me. I hoped by talking to him to experience something of Balbec before the event, to have realized here in Paris something of the magic of travel.

I left the house first thing, leaving Françoise to bewail the footman-fiancé who had once again been prevented, the evening before, from going to see his wife-to-be. Françoise had found him in tears; he had been itching to go and hit the concierge, but had held back because it would have cost him his job.

Before reaching Saint-Loup's, where we had arranged for him to meet me at his door, I ran into Legrandin, of whom we had lost sight since Combray, and who, though now quite gray, still preserved his look of youthful candor. He stopped.

"So it's you!" he exclaimed. "A man of fashion, and in a frock coat, too! Too uncomfortable a uniform for a man of my independent spirit. But you are a man of the world, I suppose, so you're always calling on people! To go and meditate, as I do, beside some half-ruined tomb, my floppy necktie and the jacket I wear are not inappropriate. You know how I admire the charming quality of your soul, which is my way of saying how deeply I regret that you should go forth and betray it among the Gentiles. Your ability to stay for a single moment in the nauseating atmosphere of the salons—it would suffocate me—is its own condemnation, its own damnation of your future in the eyes of the Prophet. I can see it all: you frequent the frivolous-minded society of gracious livers; it's the vice of the present bourgeoisie. Ah, those aristocrats! The Terror has a lot to answer for; it should have guillotined every one of them. They're a repulsive crowd even when they're not just dreary fools. Still, poor boy, if you like that sort of thing! While you're off to some society tea party, your old friend will be out there on his own in some remote suburb watching the pink moon rise in a violet sky, a happier man than you. The truth is that I scarcely belong to this earth, where I feel myself to be such an exile; it takes the full force of the law of gravity to keep me here and stop me from escaping into another sphere. I belong to a different planet. Farewell. Don't take offense at the traditional frankness of the Vivonne peasant, who has also remained a peasant of the Danube.[25] In token of my sincere regard, I shall send you a copy of my latest novel. You will not care for it; it is not deliquescent enough, not *fin-de-siècle* enough for you; it is too frank, too honest. What you need is Bergotte—you've admitted it—gamy fare for the jaded palates of refined voluptuaries. Your set must see me as very old hat; I have the misfortune to put my heart into what I write, and that's no longer the done thing; and the life of ordinary people isn't distinguished enough to interest your little bunch of snobs. Anyway, try to recall occasionally what Christ said: 'This do, and thou shalt live.' Farewell, my friend."

I left Legrandin without any particular ill-feeling toward him. Some memories are like friends in common, they can bring about reconciliations; set there, amid fields of buttercups and the mounds of feudal ruins, the little wooden bridge still joined us, Legrandin and myself, as it joined the two banks of the Vivonne.

After we left Paris, where, despite the onset of spring, the trees on the boulevards were barely in leaf, Saint-Loup and I were amazed, when the circle train set us down in the suburban village where his mistress was living, to see each small garden decked with the huge white altars of the flowering fruit trees. It was like one of those special local festivals, poetic, ephemeral, which people come a long way to see on set occasions, but this one was the spontaneous gift of nature. The cherry blossom clings so closely to the branches, like a white sheath, that from a distance, among other trees that were scarcely in flower or leaf, one might have thought, on this sunny day that was still so cold, that it was snow, melted everywhere else, but still clinging there. But the tall pear trees enveloped each house, each humble courtyard, in a more extensive, more uniform, and dazzling whiteness, as if all the dwellings, all the gardens in the village were making their first communion on the same day.

These villages around Paris are still gateways to seventeenth- and eighteenth-century parks that were the "follies" of royal stewards and favorites. A horticulturist had used one of these, set on low ground beside the road, to grow fruit trees (or had perhaps simply preserved the plan of an immense orchard that dated back to the past). Laid out in quincunxes, these pear trees, more spaciously planted and less advanced than those I had seen, formed huge quadrilaterals—divided by low walls—of white blossom, with the light falling differently on each side, so that all these airy, roofless chambers seemed to belong to some Palace of the Sun, such as might have been found somewhere like Crete; and they also reminded one of the various ponds of a reservoir, or of those parts of the sea that have been subdivided by man for fisheries or oyster beds, when one saw, depending on their exposure to it, the light playing upon the espaliers as it does on the waters in spring, and in places unfurling, amid the openings of the sky-studded trellis of the branches, the dazzling foamy whiteness of a creamy, sunlit flower.

It was an old village with its ancient *mairie* baked golden by the sun; in front of this, pretending they were Maypoles and streamers, stood three tall pear trees, elegantly decked with white satin flags as if for some local civic festival.

Never had Robert spoken to me more lovingly of his mistress than during this journey. She was the only woman to have taken root in his heart; his future career in the army, his position in society, his family, all these were not, of course, matters of indifference to him, but they counted as nothing beside the least thing that had to do with her. This was all that mattered to him, infinitely more than the Guermantes and all the kings of the earth put together. I do not know whether he invented the notion that she was of a superior essence to the rest of the world, but I do know that he was exclusively preoccupied and concerned with what affected her. Through her he was capable of suffering, of being happy, perhaps of killing. There was really nothing that interested or excited him except what his mistress wanted, what she was going to do, what was going on, discernible at best in fleeting changes of expression, in the narrow expanse of her face and behind her privileged brow. However scrupulous he was in everything else, he looked forward to the prospect of a brilliant marriage solely in order to be able to continue maintaining and keeping her. If one had asked oneself what value he set on her, I doubt whether one could have imagined a high enough figure. If he did not marry her, it was because his practical instincts warned him that as soon as she had nothing more to expect from him she would leave him, or would at least live as she pleased, and that he must retain his hold on her by playing on her expectations. The possibility that she did not love him had crossed his mind. No doubt the general ailment we call love must have forced him—as it forces all men— to believe at times that she did. But his sense of reality made him feel that her love for him did not exclude her remaining with him only for his money, and that, the day she had nothing more to expect from him, the first thing she would do (as the dupe of her literary friends' theories, though still loving him, he thought) would be to leave him.

"Today, if she's nice," he told me, "I'm going to give her a present she'll really like. It's a necklace she saw at Boucheron."[26] I can't really afford it at present—thirty thousand francs. But she doesn't have much pleasure in life, poor love. She'll be really pleased with it, I think. She mentioned it to me, and told me she knew somebody who might give it to her. I don't think that's true, but, just in case, I came to an arrangement with Boucheron—he's our family jeweler—and he reserved it for me. I'm so pleased to think that you're going to meet her. She's no stunning beauty, you know." I could see he thought just the opposite and was only saying this to increase my admiration. "But what she does have is a marvelous sense of judgment. She might not bring herself to say much while you're there, but it already makes me delighted to think what she'll say about you when you've gone. She comes out with things, you know, that keep you pondering for hours. There's really something quite Pythian about her!"

On our way to her house we passed a row of gardens, and I had to stop and look, for they were full of pear and cherry blossoms; yesterday, no doubt, they were as empty and unlived in as an unlet house, but now they were suddenly inhabited and embellished by these newcomers, who had arrived the evening before, and whose lovely white dresses could be seen through the railings along the garden paths.

"I'll tell you what—you stay here," said Robert. "I can see you want to look at all this and play the poet. My friend's house is quite near; I'll go and fetch her."

As I waited, I walked up and down the road, past these modest gardens. If I looked up, from time to time I could see groups of girls at the windows, but also outside in the open air, at the level of one of the small stories, hanging there in the foliage, light and supple in their fresh mauve dresses, clusters of young lilacs swaying in the breeze without a thought for the passerby who was looking up at their leafy mezzanine. I recognized in them the violet platoons posted beyond the little white gate at the entrance to the grounds of M. Swann's house on warm spring afternoons, forming an enchanting rustic tapestry. I followed a path that led into a field. It was swept by a cool breeze, as lively as the breeze in Combray; but in the middle of this rich, moist, rural plot, which might have been on the banks of the Vivonne, there had nevertheless sprung up, as punctually as the whole group of its companions, a great white pear tree, its blossoms waving a smile in the face of the sun, like a curtain of light made material to the touch, convulsed by the wind yet smoothed with a silver glaze by the rays of sunlight.

Suddenly Saint-Loup appeared, accompanied by his mistress, and, in this woman, who was for him the essence of love, of all the sweet possibilities of life, whose personality, mysteriously enshrined in a body as in a tabernacle, was the constant focus of my friend's imaginative attention, something he felt he would never really know as he went on asking himself what her inner self could be, behind the veil of eyes and flesh—in this woman I recognized at once "Rachel, when of the Lord,"[27] the woman who, a few years ago (women change their status so rapidly in that world, when they do change), used to say to the procuress, "Tomorrow evening, then, if you need me for someone, you'll send for me, won't you?"

And when she had been "sent for" and she found herself alone in the room with this "someone," she knew so well what she was expected to do that, after locking the door, as the precaution of a prudent woman or a ritual gesture, she would start to remove all her clothes, as you do for the doctor who is going to examine you, and would only stop doing so if the "someone," not caring for nudity, told her she could keep on her chemise, as some doctors do when they have expert hearing and are concerned about their patient's catching cold, and are happy to listen to the breathing or the heartbeat through the undergarments. I sensed that this woman, whose whole life, whose every thought, whose entire past and all the men by whom she must have been possessed, were so indifferent to me that, had she told me about them, I should have listened only out of politeness and with one ear, this woman was so much the focus of Saint-Loup's anxiety, his torment, his love, that she—for me a clockwork toy—had become for him the cause of endless suffering, an object of life-consuming cost. With these two disparate elements in mind (because I had known "Rachel, when of the Lord" in a brothel), I realized that many women to whom men devote everything, for whom they suffer and take their own lives, may be in themselves, or for others, what Rachel was for me. The idea that anyone could be painfully consumed with curiosity in regard to her life dumbfounded me. I could have told Robert a great deal about her promiscuity, which seemed to me to be the least interesting thing in the world. And how painful this would have been for him. And what had he not given to know about it, and to no end.

I realized how much a human imagination can put behind a tiny scrap of a face, such as this woman's, if it is the imagination that has been the first to know it; and, conversely, into what miserable, worthless material elements something that was once the target of countless dreams might be decomposed if, on the contrary, it had been perceived in a quite different manner, by the coarsest sort of acquaintance. I saw that what had seemed to me to be not worth twenty francs when it had been offered to me for twenty francs in a brothel, where I had simply seen it as a woman wanting to earn twenty francs, might be worth more than a million, more than family, more than the most coveted position, if I had started to imagine her as an intriguing being, interesting to know, difficult to seize and to hold. Undoubtedly Robert and I saw the same thin and narrow face. But we had come to it by two opposite paths that could never converge, and we would never see the same face. I had known this face from the outside, with its looks, its smiles, the movements of its mouth, as the face of some woman who would do anything I asked for twenty francs. And so for me her looks, her smiles, the movements of her mouth, had seemed meaningful merely as generalized actions with nothing individual about them, and beneath them I should not have had the curiosity to look for a person. But what to me had in a sense been offered from the outset, a consenting face, had been for Robert a goal toward which he had been struggling through endless hopes and doubts, suspicions and dreams. Now he was giving more than a million francs to possess, in order that others should not be offered it, what had been offered to me, and to the rest of the world, for twenty. The reason he had not had her at that price might have been the chance of a moment, the moment in which she who seemed ready to give herself withdraws, with another assignment perhaps, or some reason for being difficult on that particular day. If she is involved with a highly emotional man, even if she has not noticed it, and even more if she has, a really horrible game begins. Unable to swallow his disappointment, to forget about the woman, he chases after her again, she does everything to avoid him, to the point where a mere smile, for which he no longer dared to hope, is bought at a thousand times what total intimacy with her should have cost. It sometimes even happens in such a case, when a man has been mad enough, through a mixture of naïve judgment and cowardice in the face of pain, to make an inaccessible idol out of a whore, that he will never obtain total intimacy, or even the first kiss, and no longer even ventures to ask for them, for fear of compromising his assurances of Platonic love. And it then becomes horribly painful to leave the world without ever having experienced the embrace of the woman he has loved most. Luckily for Saint-Loup, he had managed to enjoy all Rachel's favors. True, had he known that they had been offered to all and sundry for a louis,[28] he would have suffered dreadfully, but would still have given a million francs to keep them, for nothing he had learned could have deflected him—what is beyond a man's power can only happen in spite of him, as the effect of some great natural law—from the path he had taken, and from which that face could appear to him only through the dream world he had created. The immobility of that thin face, like that of a sheet of paper subjected to the colossal pressure of two atmospheres, seemed to me to be held in balance by two infinities which converged on her without meeting, for she held them apart. And indeed, as we looked at her, Robert and I, neither of us saw her from the same side of the mystery.

It was not so much that I found "Rachel, when of the Lord" of little consequence, but that I found the power of the human imagination, the illusion that fostered the pains of love, so momentous. Robert noticed that I seemed moved. I looked away toward the pear and cherry trees in the garden opposite to make him think that it was their beauty I was moved by. And it did move me in somewhat the same way, by bringing close to me things we not only see with our eyes but also feel in our hearts. By likening the trees I had seen in the garden to strange gods, had I not made the same mistake as Mary Magdalene when, in another garden, on a day whose anniversary was fast approaching, she saw a human form, "supposing him to be the gardener"? Guardians of the memories of the golden age, keepers of the promise that reality is not what we suppose, that the splendor of poetry, the magical light of innocence may shine in it and may be the reward we strive to deserve— were they not, these great white creatures so magnificently stooped over the shade that invites us to rest, to fish, to read, were they not more like angels? I exchanged a few words with Saint-Loup's mistress. We cut across the village. The houses were sordid. But beside the most dilapidated of them, the ones that looked as if they had been scorched by a shower of brimstone, a mysterious traveler, making a day's stay in the cursed city, a resplendent angel, stood over it, stretching the dazzling protection of his widespread wings of innocence in blossom: a pear tree. Saint-Loup walked ahead with me a little way:

"I would have liked it to be just the two of us. In fact, I'd much rather have had lunch just with you and stayed together until it was time to go to my aunt's. But it gives her so much pleasure, this dear girl of mine, and she's being so nice to me that I couldn't say no. Anyway, you'll like her; she's literary, so responsive, and it's such fun to lunch with her in a restaurant; she's so pleasant to be with, so simple, always so delighted with everything."

Yet I seem to remember that it was on this very morning, probably the only time it happened, that Robert was able to stand aside for a second from the woman he had gradually created out of layer upon layer of affection, and suddenly distance himself enough to glimpse another Rachel, identical yet entirely different, whose behavior was clearly that of a little tart. We had left the lovely fruit blossoms and were on our way to catch the train back to Paris when, at the station, Rachel, who was walking on her own, was recognized and hailed by a pair of common little tarts like herself; thinking at first that she was alone, they called out: "Hey there, Rachel, why don't you come with us? Lucienne and Germaine are on the train, and there's room for you as well. Come on, we'll all go to the skating rink together." They were about to introduce her to the two shop assistants who were with them, their lovers, when they noticed Rachel's slightly embarrassed manner, looked inquiringly beyond her, caught sight of us, and bade her an apologetic goodbye, to which she responded somewhat uneasily but in a friendly enough tone. They were two poor little tarts with imitation–otter-skin collars, looking more or less the way Rachel must have looked when Saint-Loup first met her. He did not know them or their names, and, seeing that they appeared to be on the friendliest terms with his mistress, it occurred to him that she might have had, and perhaps still had, a place in an unsuspected life, very different from the life she led with him, a life in which women were available for a louis, whereas Rachel cost him more than a hundred thousand francs a year. He not only glimpsed this life, but saw there in the midst of it a Rachel quite different from the one he knew, a Rachel like those two little tarts, Rachel at twenty francs a time. In short, Rachel had for a second become double for him; he had seen, at some distance from his own Rachel, Rachel the little tart, the real Rachel, if it is true that Rachel the tart was more real than the other. And it might have occurred to Robert that from the hell in which he was living, with the prospect and the necessity of a wealthy marriage, of the sale of his name, to enable him to go on giving Rachel a hundred thousand francs a year, he might easily have escaped and enjoyed the favors of his mistress, like those shop assistants with their girls, for a mere song. But how? She had done nothing reprehensible. With less lavished upon her, she would be less nice to him, she would no longer say or write the things that moved him so much, and which he would quote to his comrades with shy pride, taking care to emphasize how nice it was of her to say them, but omitting to point out that he was keeping her in luxury, or even that he gave her anything at all, that the declarations inscribed on photographs or the tender words at the end of telegrams represented the most meager, yet the most precious, transmutation of a hundred thousand francs. If he refrained from mentioning that these rare kindnesses on Rachel's part were all paid for, it would be wrong to say—and yet this oversimplification is directed, without any justification, at every lover who has to fork out the money, and at a great number of husbands—that he did so out of pride, out of vanity. Saint-Loup was intelligent enough to realize that all the pleasures of vanity were easily available to him in society, where they would have cost him nothing, thanks to his distinguished name and handsome face, and that his liaison with Rachel had in fact tended to cut him off from society, made him less sought after. No, the pride that seeks to create the impression that the apparent signs of affection from the woman one loves are freely given, is simply a by-product of love, the need to see oneself, and to be seen by others, as being loved by the person whom one loves so much. Rachel rejoined us, leaving the two tarts to get into their compartment; but, no less than their imitation otter skins and the self-conscious unease of their shop boys, the names Lucienne and Germaine meant that the new image of Rachel lingered for a second in Robert's mind. For a moment he imagined a life of haunting the Place Pigalle with anonymous friends, sordid pickups, afternoons of mindless pleasure, walks and outings, in a Paris where the sunny streets that run down from the Boulevard de Clichy seemed quite different from the solar brightness in which he strolled with his mistress, and inevitably so, for love, and the pain that is inseparable from it, have the power, like intoxication, to differentiate things for us. It was almost like an unknown Paris in the heart of Paris itself that he glimpsed;

his relationship seemed like the exploration of a strange life, for if when she was with him Rachel was somewhat similar to himself, it was nonetheless a part of her real life that she lived with him, the most precious part even, given the reckless amount of money he spent on her, the part that made her so much the envy of her friends and would one day allow her to retire to the country or to make her name in the leading theaters, when she had feathered her nest. Robert would have liked to ask her who Lucienne and Germaine were, what they would have said to her if she had joined them on the train, how they would have all spent the day together, a day that would perhaps have ended, as a supreme treat, after the pleasures of the skating rink, at the Taverne de l'Olympia,[29] if Robert and I not been there. For a second the area around the Olympia, which until then had seemed to him deadly dull, stirred his curiosity, and his anguish, and the thought of this spring day's sunshine falling on the rue Caumartin, where, if she had not known Robert, she might have gone later to earn a louis, filled him with a vague longing to be there. But what use was it to question Rachel when he knew in advance that she would answer him with mere silence, or a lie, or with something extremely painful for him to hear that would explain nothing? The porters were shutting the doors; we climbed hurriedly into a first-class carriage; Rachel's magnificent pearls reminded Robert that she was a woman of great price; he embraced her, restored her to the place in his heart where he could contemplate her, from within, as he had always done up until now—apart from the brief moment when he had envisaged her in some Impressionist painter's Place Pigalle—and the train moved away.

It was true that she was "literary." She never stopped talking to me about books, Art Nouveau, Tolstoyism, except to criticize Robert for drinking too much wine.

"A year with me would do you the world of good! I'd make you drink water, and you'd be much better for it."

"All right. Let's go away."

"But you know how much work I've got to do." (She took her dramatic training very seriously.) "And what would your family have to say about it?"

And she began to criticize his family to me in terms that seemed completely to the point, and which Saint-Loup, who was all the while disobeying Rachel on the matter of champagne, endorsed. Since I was so concerned about the effect of wine on him and could feel the good influence of his mistress, I found myself quite prepared to tell him to let his family get off his back. And when I was rash enough to mention Dreyfus, tears sprang to the young woman's eyes.

"The poor man's a martyr," she almost sobbed. "It will be the death of him, where they've put him."

"Calm down, Zézette. He'll come back. He'll be acquitted. They'll admit they made a mistake."

"But he'll be dead before they do! At least his children's name won't be blemished. But what he must be going through, I can't bear to think about it! And can you believe that Robert's mother, a religious woman, says that he ought to be left on Devil's Island even if he's innocent? Isn't that ghastly?"

"Yes, it's absolutely true, she does say that," Robert confirmed. "She's my mother, I can't go against her, but it's obvious that she's far less sensitive than Zézette."

The truth of the matter was that these luncheons, which were supposed to be "such a pleasure," were always an uncomfortable experience. For, as soon as Saint-Loup found himself in public with his mistress, he got it into his head that she was eyeing all the men around her, and turned sullen; she would notice his bad mood and perhaps took pleasure in aggravating it, but more probably, out of a foolish sense of pride, feeling wounded by his tone, she did not wish to appear to be trying to diffuse it; she would pretend that she could not take her eyes off some man or other, and indeed this was not always just a pretense. In fact, if the man sitting next to them in a theater or a café, or even their cab-driver, happened to be remotely attractive, Robert, his attention heightened by jealousy, would notice it before his mistress; he immediately saw the man in question as one of those foul creatures he had spoken to me about in Balbec, who derive amusement from corrupting and dishonoring women, and he would beg his mistress to avert her eyes from the man, which was all that was needed to draw her attention to him.

And sometimes she found that Robert had shown such good taste in his suspicions that she would eventually go so far as to stop teasing him, so that he would calm down and consent to go off alone on some errand, which would give her time to enter into conversation with the stranger, often to make an assignation, sometimes even to have her way with him on the spot. I could see as soon as we entered the restaurant that Robert was looking troubled. For the first thing he noticed—and it had escaped our attention in Balbec—was that among his more ordinary colleagues Aimé had a certain distinction and exuded, quite unconsciously, the romantic appeal that stems, for a few years at least, from a head of fine hair and a Grecian nose, which is what made him stand out among the crowd of other waiters. These, most of them quite old, presented the typical features—extraordinarily ugly and exaggerated—of hypocritical priests, smarmy confessors, and particularly of comic actors of the old school, whose sugar-loaf foreheads are scarcely to be seen today outside the collections of portraits displayed in the humbly historic greenrooms of antiquated little theaters, where they are represented in the roles of valets or grand pontiffs, though this restaurant, through selected recruiting and possibly through some system of hereditary appointment, seemed to preserve their solemn characteristics in something like a School of Augurs. It was our ill luck to be recognized by Aimé, and it was he who came across to take our order, while the cortège of high priests from light opera moved past us to other tables. Aimé inquired after my grandmother's health; I asked for news of his wife and children. He provided it with feeling, being a family man. His manner was intelligent and spirited, but respectful. Robert's mistress started to eye him with unusual attention. But Aimé's sunken eyes, to which his slight shortsightedness gave a sort of hidden depth, betrayed no awareness of this in his motionless face. In the provincial hotel where he had worked for many years before he came to Balbec, the handsome picture of his face, now a touch discolored and faded, which had been visible for years, always in the same place, like some engraved portrait of Prince Eugène,[30] at the far end of an almost empty dining room, cannot have attracted many curious looks. And so, for a long time—for want of connoisseurs, no doubt—he had remained unaware of the artistic value of his face, and as a man of cold character, he was disinclined to draw attention to it. At most some passing Parisienne, who happened to be stopping in the town, had cast her eyes upon him and asked him to serve her in her room before she caught her next train and, in the translucent, deeply humdrum void of the existence of this caring husband and provincial hotel waiter, had buried the secret of a one-night whim that no one would ever reveal. And yet Aimé must have been conscious of the insistent gaze the young actress was directing at him now. It certainly did not escape Robert's attention, and I saw a flush begin to spread beneath his skin, not the purplish flush of sudden emotion, but something faint and fitful.

"Is there anything particularly interesting about the waiter, Zézette?" he asked his mistress when he had dismissed Aimé somewhat abruptly. "You seem to be making quite a study of him."

"Here we go again. I knew it!"

"You knew what, my love? If I've said something wrong, I take it all back, of course. But it's my right to warn you against that flunky. I know him from Balbec, otherwise I wouldn't give a damn. He's one of the world's biggest scoundrels."

She seemed concerned to concur with Robert and began to engage me in a literary conversation in which he joined. I was not bored by her conversation, because she was well acquainted with the works I admired and shared more or less the same opinion of them; but since I had heard Mme de Villeparisis describe her as untalented, I attached little importance to her knowledge. She had witty things to say about a great many subjects and would have been genuinely entertaining had she not affected the irritating jargon of literary cliques and artists' studios. And she extended it to everything she talked about: for instance, having adopted the habit of saying of a painting, if it was Impressionist, or an opera, if it was Wagnerian, "Oh, that's *good!,*" one day, when a young man kissed her on the ear and, as a reaction to her pretense of the thrill it gave her, affected modesty, she said, "Yes, the sensation it gives me is decidedly *good.*" But what really did take me aback was that the expressions peculiar to Robert (who had probably derived them anyway from the literary men she knew) were used by her to him and by him to her as an inevitable form of language, without any sense of the sort of pointless originality that anyone can command.

She was so clumsy with her hands when she ate that one got the impression that she must appear extremely awkward onstage. She recovered her dexterity only when she was making love, with the touchingly intuitive foresight of women who are so in love with men's bodies that they immediately sense what will give most pleasure to those bodies, which are yet so different from their own.

I ceased to take part in the conversation when it turned to the theater, because of Rachel's excessive maliciousness on the subject. She did, it is true, come to the defense of La Berma, but in a commiserative tone—meant for Saint-Loup, and evidence that he was used to hearing Rachel attack the actress: "Oh, she's a remarkable woman, really. Of course, her way of doing things no longer appeals to us, it's not in keeping with what we're trying to do, but one needs to see her in the context of her early career; we owe her a great deal. She has done some good things, you know. Besides, she's such a wonderful person, so kindhearted. I know she doesn't care for the things that interest us now, but in her day her face was quite impressive, and there was something pleasingly intelligent about her." (Our fingers do not play the same accompaniment to all our aesthetic judgments. If we want to describe a painting as a fine, densely textured piece of work, we have only to stick out our thumb. But "something pleasingly intelligent" demands more. It requires two fingers, or, rather, two fingernails, as if we needed to flick away a speck of dust.) But with this one exception, Saint-Loup's mistress spoke about all acting celebrities in a tone of ironic superiority, which irritated me because I believed—quite wrongly, as it happened—that it was she who was inferior to them. She was plainly aware that I must regard her as a mediocre actress and, conversely, hold in high esteem the ones she despised. But she showed no resentment, because in all great talent that is not yet recognized, as hers was not at the time, however self-confident it may be, there is an element of humility, and because we calculate the amount of esteem we expect from others in terms not of our latent potential but of our present achievements. (An hour later, at the theater, I was to see Saint-Loup's mistress show great deference toward the very artists she now judged so harshly.) And so, whatever misgivings my silence must have conveyed to her, she nevertheless insisted on our dining together that evening, assuring me that never had anyone's conversation given her so much pleasure as mine. Although we were not yet in the theater, to which we were to go after lunch, it felt as if we were in a greenroom hung with the portraits of former members of the Palais-Royal company, so much did the waiters' faces resemble the kind of faces that seem to have disappeared along with a whole generation of outstanding actors. They bore a resemblance to Academicians, too: one of them, standing in front of a sideboard, was examining a bowl of pears with an expression of detached curiosity that might have belonged to M. de Jussieu.[31] Others, standing beside him, cast their eyes about the room with the same cold scrutiny that those members of the Institut who have arrived in advance direct at the public, while they mutter inaudibly among themselves. To the regular customers, they were well-known faces. However, one of them was being pointed out, a priest-like newcomer with a furrowed nose and sanctimonious lips, who was a novice to the job, and everyone gazed with interest at this recently elected candidate. But after a while, perhaps to drive Robert away and be alone with Aimé, Rachel began making eyes at a young student who was lunching with a friend at one of the next tables.

"Zézette, would you mind not looking at that young man like that," said Saint-Loup, on whose face the hesitant flush of a moment ago had by this time intensified into a blood-red cloud, which dilated and darkened his strained features. "If you have to make an exhibition of us like this, I'd rather go off and lunch elsewhere and wait for you at the theater afterward."

At this point someone came to inform Aimé that there was a gentleman requesting him for a word at the door of his carriage. Saint-Loup, still uneasy, and fearing that it was some amorous message intended for his mistress, looked out of the window to be greeted by the sight of M. de Charlus, sitting there in the back of his brougham, wearing tight white gloves with black stripes, and a flower in his buttonhole.

"There, you see!" Robert said to me, lowering his voice. "My family track me down everywhere. Please, could you—I can't really do it myself— but since you know the headwaiter so well, ask him not to go to the carriage. He's sure to give us away. Ask him to send some other waiter who doesn't know me. I know my uncle; if they tell him they don't know me, he won't come inside to look for me, he hates this sort of place. But it's pretty disgusting, isn't it? An old womanizer like him, and still at it, preaching at me and coming here to spy on me!"

Aimé, after receiving my instructions, sent one of his assistants to say that he was too busy to come and, should the gentleman ask for the Marquis de Saint-Loup, that they did not know anyone of that name. The carriage departed soon after. But Saint-Loup's mistress, who had failed to catch our whispered remarks and thought they were about the young man Robert had reproached her for ogling, unleashed a torrent of abuse.

"So—what is it now? It's that young man, isn't it? Thank you for warning me. It's just what I need to really enjoy my meal! Don't pay any attention to him," she added, turning to me, "he's a bit crazy today. He just says these things to be smart. He thinks it's aristocratic to behave as if he's jealous."

And her hands and feet started to betray signs of irritation.

"But, Zézette, I'm the one who finds it unpleasant. You're making us look ridiculous in the eyes of that man. He's going to think that you're making advances, and he looks like a cad to me."

"Not to me; I think he's very attractive. For one thing, he's got the most lovely eyes, and a way of looking at women. You can feel he must really like them."

"You must be out of your mind! But you can at least keep quiet until I've left the room," Robert shouted. "Waiter! My things."

I did not know whether he expected me to follow him.

"No, I need to be on my own," he told me in the same tone in which he had just spoken to his mistress, and as if he were quite as furious with me. His anger was like a single musical phrase in an opera to which several lines of dialogue are sung, each of completely different character and meaning in the libretto, yet fused into an overall mood by the music. When Robert had gone, his mistress summoned Aimé and asked him various questions. She then wanted to know what I thought of him.

"He has an amusing expression, hasn't he? You know, it would intrigue me to discover what he really thinks. I'd like to have him wait on me often, to take him traveling. But that's as far as it goes. If we were obliged to love all the people we find attractive, things would be pretty ghastly, don't you think? It's wrong of Robert to get such ideas. None of these things have any reality outside my head. Robert really has no need to get so upset." She still had her gaze fixed on Aimé. "Do look at those dark eyes of his. I'd love to know what goes on behind them."

After a while, someone came to inform her that Robert was waiting for her in a private room where he had gone to finish his lunch, using another entrance to avoid passing through the restaurant again. So I remained alone until I, too, was summoned by Robert. I found his mistress lying on a sofa, laughing beneath the kisses and caresses he was showering upon her. They were drinking champagne. "Hello, you!" she kept saying to him, using an expression that she had recently picked up, which seemed to her to be the last word in witty affection. I had not enjoyed my lunch, I felt ill at ease, and although Legrandin's words had not really affected me, I was sorry to think that I was beginning this first afternoon of spring in the back room of a restaurant and would end it in the wings of a theater. After checking the time to make sure that she would not make herself late, Rachel offered me some champagne, passed me one of her Turkish cigarettes, and unpinned a rose from her bodice for me. At which point I thought, "I needn't feel I've spent the day too badly; the time spent in the company of this young woman has not been wasted, since I have had from her—gracious things that cannot be bought too dear—a rose, a scented cigarette, a glass of champagne." I thought this because it seemed to me that such thoughts would lend an aesthetic flavor to these hours of boredom, and so justify and redeem them. I ought perhaps to have been aware that the very need of a justification to make my boredom bearable was sufficient proof that my feelings were anything but aesthetic. Robert and his mistress, for their part, seemed to have utterly forgotten their quarrel of a few minutes earlier, and my presence at it. They made no allusion to it, offered no excuse for it, any more than for the contrast with it that their present behavior indicated. As I drank champagne with them, I began to feel something of the intoxication I had experienced at Rivebelle, though probably not quite the same. Not only every kind of intoxication, from that which we get from the sun or travel to that which is brought on by exhaustion or wine, but every degree of intoxication—and each should have a different grading mark, like sea depths on a map—lays bare in us, at the exact level affected, a particular sort of man. Saint-Loup's private dining room was small, but the single mirror that hung in it was such that it seemed to reflect some thirty others, in an endless progression; and when it was lit at night and followed by the procession of thirty or more reflections of itself, the lightbulb placed at the top of the mirror frame must have given the drinker, even when alone, the impression that the surrounding space was multiplying itself along with his own sensations, heightened by drink, and that, shut up by himself in this tiny room, he was nevertheless reigning over something far more extensive in its indefinite, luminous curve than a walkway in the Jardin de Paris.³² And at that moment, I *was* the drinker in question: suddenly, as I looked for him in the mirror, I saw him, a hideous stranger, staring back at me. The joy of intoxication was stronger than my disgust; out of gaiety or bravado, I smiled at him and found that my smile was simultaneously returned. And I felt myself to be so much under the ephemeral and powerful sway of this minute's intense sensation that it is not clear to me whether the only disquieting element of the experience was not the thought that the hideous self I had just glimpsed was perhaps about to breathe his last, and that I should never meet this stranger again in my lifetime.

Robert was annoyed only because I showed no inclination to shine more in the eyes of his mistress.

"Come on, what about that gentleman you met this morning who's a mixture of snobbery and astronomy? Do tell her about him. I can't quite remember the story." He was watching her out of the corner of his eye.

"But, my dear fellow, there's nothing to tell. Apart from what you've just said."

"Don't be such a bore. Then tell her about Françoise in the Champs-Élysées. She'll love that."

"Please do! Bobby's told me so much about Françoise." And, taking

Saint-Loup by the chin, she said once again, for lack of anything more original, as she drew this chin into the light, "Hello, you!"

Ever since I had ceased to see actors solely as the depositories, in their diction and acting ability, of an artistic truth, they had begun to interest me in their own right; with the feeling that I was watching the characters from some old comic novel, I was amused to see the naïve heroine of a play, her attention drawn to the new face of some young duke who had just taken his seat in the theater, listen abstractedly to the declaration of love the juvenile lead was addressing to her, while he, through the rolling passion of this declaration, was in turn directing an enamored eye at an old lady seated in a stage box, whose magnificent pearls had caught his interest; and in this way, largely owing to what Saint-Loup had told me about the private lives of actors, I saw another drama, silent but telling, being played out beneath the words of the play that was being performed, yet the play itself, however uninspired, was still something that interested me, too; for within it I could feel germinating and blossoming for an hour in the glare of the footlights—created out of the agglutination on the face of an actor of another face of greasepaint and pasteboard, and on his individual soul the words of a part—the ephemeral and spirited personalities, captivating, too, who form the cast of a play, whom one loves, admires, pities, whom one would like to meet again after the play is over, but who by that time have already disintegrated into the actors, who are no longer what they were in their roles, into a script that no longer shows the actors' faces, into a colored powder that can be wiped off by a handkerchief, who have reverted, in a word, to elements that contain nothing of them, because their dissolution is complete as soon as the play has ended, and this, like the dissolution of a loved one, causes one to doubt the reality of the self and to meditate on the mystery of death.

I found one part of the program extremely painful. A young woman whom Rachel and several of her friends detested was to make her debut in a recital of old songs, and she had based all her hopes for her future and her family on its success. This young woman had an unduly, almost absurdly prominent rump and a voice that was pretty but not full enough, a marked contrast to her muscular development and further enfeebled by her nerves. Rachel had placed a number of her friends, male and female, among the audience and instructed them to make sarcastic comments and disconcert the novice, who was known to be timid, to make her lose her head so that her performance would be a complete fiasco, with the result that the manager would refuse to give her a contract. Hardly had the poor woman sung a few notes when several of the male spectators, recruited for the purpose, began pointing at her backside and giggling, while certain women who were also involved in the plot laughed out loud, and with every fluty note that was sung the willful hilarity increased, until it verged on the scandalous. The unfortunate woman, sweating with discomfort under her greasepaint, struggled for a moment to ignore it all but then started to throw miserably angry looks among the audience, which served only to make them boo the louder. The instinct to do what others were doing, the desire to show off their own wit and audacity, caused several pretty actresses who knew nothing of the situation to join in, and they now exchanged with the others glances of malicious complicity, creased themselves into violent outbursts of laughter, so that by the end of the second song (and there were still five more on the program) the stage manager rang down the curtain. I did my utmost not to dwell on this incident any more than I had dwelt on my grandmother's misery when my great-uncle used to tease her by making my grandfather drink brandy, finding the idea of intentional unkindness too painful to bear. And yet, in the same way that our pity for misfortune perhaps misses the point, since in our imagination we re-create an inflated idea of the pain that the sufferer is too busy combating to think of succumbing to self-pity, so unkindness in the minds of the unkind is probably devoid of the thrill of outright cruelty, which we, at such painful cost to ourselves, imagine. Unkindness is inspired by hatred, anger fuels it into action in which there is no great joy; it would take sadism to turn it into something pleasurable; unkind people imagine themselves to be inflicting pain on someone equally unkind. Rachel certainly believed that the actress she was tormenting was far from talented, and that, by having her booed, she was at least defending good taste and teaching a poor colleague a lesson. However, I chose not to speak of this incident, since I had had neither

the courage nor the power to prevent it; I would have found it too difficult to say anything good about the victim without making the feelings that incited the tormentors of the novice look like gratifications of
cruelty.

But the beginning of this performance interested me for quite different reasons. It made me realize something about the nature of the illusion of which Saint-Loup was a victim in regard to Rachel, and which
had set a gulf between the images we both had of his mistress when we
saw her that very morning, beneath the blossoming pear trees. Rachel
had little more than a walk-on part in the short play. But, seen thus, she
was another woman. Rachel had one of those faces that distance—and
not necessarily that between the auditorium and the stage, the world itself in this respect being merely a larger theater—throws into sharp outline, and which, seen close up, crumble to dust. Close beside her, all
you saw was a nebula, a Milky Way of freckles, of tiny spots, nothing
more. At a respectable distance, all this ceased to be visible, and from
the cheeks, now erased and reabsorbed into her features, there rose, like
a crescent moon, so fine and pure a nose that it made you want to be
the object of Rachel's attention, to see her whenever you liked, to keep
her near, provided you had not seen her differently and at close range.
This was not the case for me, but it had been for Saint-Loup when he
first saw her onstage. At that point he had asked himself how he might
approach her, get to know her; a whole magical world had opened up
inside him—the world in which she lived, and from which came exquisite radiance, but into which he could not find a way. He left the theater
telling himself that it would be madness to write to her, that she would
not reply, quite prepared to give his fortune and his name for the creature who now lived within him, in a world so distinctly superior to such
humdrum realities, a world enriched by desire and dream; and at that
very moment he saw emerging from the stage door of the theater, itself
a small old building that seemed to have stepped out of a stage set, the
gay and charmingly hatted band of actresses who had just been playing.
Young people who knew them stood there waiting for them. The number of pawns on the human chessboard being less than the number of
positions they are capable of occupying, in a theater where all the people we might know are absent, there turns out to be one whom we

thought we would never chance to meet again, and whose arrival on the scene is so exactly what we need that it seems a providential coincidence, although no doubt some other, equally providential coincidence would have occurred had we not been in that place but in some other, where other desires would have arisen and another old acquaintance been there to support them. The golden portals of the world of dreams had closed upon Rachel before Saint-Loup saw her step out of the theater, so that the freckles and spots did not really matter. Yet he did not like them, especially because he was no longer alone with the same power to dream he had experienced in the theater. But she, although he could no longer see it, continued to dictate his actions, like the stars that govern us by their attraction even at the times when they are not visible to us. And so his desire for the actress with the delicate features, which were now not even present in Robert's memory, caused him to foist himself upon the old friend who just happened to be on the spot and get himself introduced to the person with no features at all and with freckles into the bargain, since she was the same person, telling himself that in due course he would see to it that he found out which of the two this same lady really was. She was in a hurry, and addressed not a single word to Saint-Loup on this occasion; it was not until some days later that he finally managed to get her to leave her companions and to walk her home. He was already in love with her. The need for dreams, the desire to be made happy by the woman one has dreamed of, means that it can take no time at all to settle all one's chances of happiness on someone who a few days earlier was no more than a fortuitous, unknown, commonplace apparition on the boards of a theater.

When the curtain had fallen and we had moved on to the stage, my shyness at being there drove me to try to enter into a spirited conversation with Saint-Loup: in this way my conduct, since I did not know what sort of attitude to adopt in this unfamiliar setting, would be entirely dominated by our conversation, and people would think that I was so absorbed in it, so distracted, that it was quite natural for my face to express nothing of what was expected in such surroundings, which, deep in talk, I scarcely registered; acting quickly, I seized upon the first topic of conversation that entered my head:

"You know," I said to Robert, "I did come to say goodbye the day I left Doncières. I've never had the opportunity to mention it. I waved to you in the street."

"Don't talk about it," Robert replied. "I was so upset. I ran into you just by the barracks, but I couldn't stop because I was already so late. I felt really bad about it, believe me."

So he had seen me! I could still see the utterly impersonal salute he had given me, with his hand raised to his cap and no sign of recognition in his eyes, no gesture to indicate that he was sorry he could not stop. Clearly the pretense of not recognizing me he had adopted at the time must have simplified matters for him greatly. But I was amazed that he had been able to adopt it so swiftly, and before some instinctive response had betrayed his initial reaction. I had already observed in Balbec that, compared with the spontaneous sincerity of his face, with that transparent skin which revealed the sudden surge of his emotions, his body had been admirably trained to perform a number of the dissimulations demanded by etiquette, and that, like a truly skilled actor, he had the ability, in his regimental and in his society life, to play a succession of different roles. In one of his roles he loved me deeply and behaved toward me almost like a brother; my brother he had been, and was now again, but for a moment that day he had been another person, who did not know me, and who, with the reins in his hand and his monocle stuck in his eye, without a look or a smile, had raised his other hand to the peak of his cap to give me the regulation military salute!

I moved around among the stage sets, which had not yet been dismantled; seen at close quarters, without the effects of distance and lighting that the eminent artist who had painted them had included in his plan, they were a sorry sight, and Rachel, when I moved close to her, was subject to a no less destructive perspective. The curves of her charming nostrils, seen from the auditorium when she was onstage, had, like the scenery, stood out distinctly. Now she was no longer the same person: I recognized her only by her eyes, in which her identity had taken refuge. The form and radiance of this young star, so brilliant a moment ago, had disappeared. By contrast, as if we were to look more closely at the moon and to find that it was no longer pink and gold, on this face that had seemed so smooth before I could distinguish only protuberances, blemishes, hollows. Despite the incoherence into which both this woman's face and the painted backdrops melted when seen from close up, I was happy to be where I was, to stroll among the sets, in surroundings that my love of nature would have once led me to regard as tiresome and artificial, although Goethe's depiction of them in *Wilhelm Meister*33 had given them a certain beauty for me; and to my delight, I had already singled out, among the journalists or fashionable people, admirers of the actresses, who were exchanging greetings, talking, smoking, as if this were some gathering in town, a young man in a black velvet toque and Hortense-colored skirt, his cheeks chalked red like a page from a Watteau album,34 who, with a smile on his lips and his eyes fixed aloft, tracing graceful patterns with the palms of his hands and springing lightly about, seemed so entirely of another species from the sensible people in conventional dress among whom he was pursuing his ecstatic trance like a madman, so removed from the preoccupations of their lives, so anterior to the customs of their civilization, so emancipated from the laws of nature, that it was as restful and refreshing as watching a butterfly fluttering through a crowd to let one's eyes follow, between the various border hangings, the natural arabesques he capriciously traced in his winged, greasepainted frolics. But in the same moment, Saint-Loup got it into his head that his mistress was directing her attention to this dancer, who was now running through a dance figure one last time before his ballet performance, and his face darkened.

"You could look the other way," he said to her darkly. "You know that these dancers aren't worth the rope they'd do well to trip over and break their necks. The sort who go about bragging they've been noticed. Anyway, you've heard them tell you to go to your dressing room and get changed. You'll miss your call again."

Three men—journalists—noticing how furious Saint-Loup was looking, drew nearer with amusement on their faces to listen in to the conversation. And since some scenery was being set in place on the other side of us, we were pushed into close contact with them.

"Oh, but I know him! He's a friend of mine," cried Saint-Loup's mistress, with her eyes fixed on the dancer. "Now, there's a beautifully made man for you. Just look at those little hands dancing away like the rest of him!"

The dancer turned his head toward her, and the human being

appeared beneath the sylph he was practicing to be, the clear gray jelly of his eyes trembled brightly between the stiffened, painted eyelashes, and a smile stretched the corners of his mouth in a face that was plastered in rouge; then, to amuse the young woman, like a singer who obligingly hums the tune of the song of hers we have told her we admire, he began to repeat the movement of his hands, mimicking himself in a clever pastiche with the good humor of a child.

"Oh, isn't it sweet, the way he mimics himself!" cried Rachel, clapping her hands.

"Sweetheart, *please* . . ." said Saint-Loup, with utter misery in his voice, "don't make an exhibition of yourself like this. I can't stand it. Another word, and I swear I won't go with you to your dressing room. I'll leave. Come on, don't be difficult. . . . Don't stand around in this cigar smoke, it'll make you ill," he added, turning to me with the solicitude he had shown for me since we met in Balbec.

"Oh! I'd be more than happy if you did leave!"

"I'm warning you. I won't come back."

"I couldn't wish for anything better."

"Now, look here, I promised you that necklace if you behaved nicely, but given the way you're treating me . . ."

"Ah! That doesn't surprise me in the least, coming from you. You make me a promise, and I should have known you wouldn't keep it. You just want the world to know you're made of money. I set less store by it myself. You can keep your damned necklace. I know someone else who'll give it to me."

"No one else *can* give it to you. I've told Boucheron to keep it for me, and he's promised not to sell it to anyone else."

"So that's it! You were out to blackmail me, so you set it all up in advance. It's true what they say: Marsantes, Mater Semita, it smells of the race," retorted Rachel, repeating an etymology that is based on a gross misinterpretation, for *Semita* means "path," not "Semite," but one which the Nationalists applied to Saint-Loup on account of his Dreyfusard views, which, ironically enough, he had borrowed from the actress. (She had less cause than anyone to attribute Jewish origin to Mme de Marsantes, in whom the social ethnographers could manage to find no trace of Jewishness other than her kinship with the Lévy-Mirepoix family.) "But you haven't heard the last of it, believe me. A promise like that is meaningless. You've gone behind my back. Boucheron will be told about it, and he'll be paid twice as much for his necklace. We'll soon see who's right, don't you worry."

Robert was in the right a hundred times over. But circumstances are always so muddled that the man who is so much in the right might have been in the wrong for once in his life. And I could not help recalling the unpleasant and yet quite innocent remark he had made in Balbec: "That is how I keep a hold over her."

"You've got it wrong about the necklace. I made no binding promise to you about it. Once you start doing everything you can to make me leave you, of course I'm not going to give it to you; surely that's obvious. I don't know what you mean about me going behind your back, or setting store by money. No one can say I go about bragging that I'm made of money. I'm always telling you what an impoverished fellow I am. You're taking it all the wrong way, sweetest. You know very well what I set store by. One thing only, and that's you."

"Yes, yes . . . carry on, do," she countered ironically, with a cutthroat gesture that suggested she was bored to tears. She turned toward the dancer:

"Oh, look! He's just wonderful with his hands. I couldn't do what he's doing there, even though I'm a woman." She went up to the dancer and pointed to the torture written all over Robert's face: "Look, he can't bear it," she murmured, in a momentary burst of sadistic cruelty that had nothing at all to do with her genuine feelings of affection for Saint-Loup.

"Listen to me. I'm telling you for the last time. I promise you that you can try as hard as you like, but in a week you can be as sorry as you like and I won't come back. I've had as much as I can take, do you hear? Enough is enough. You'll be sorry one day, when it's too late."

Perhaps his words were sincere, and the torture of breaking with his mistress seemed less cruel than that of remaining with her in certain circumstances.

"But, my dear man," he added, addressing himself to me, "you really oughtn't to stay here, you know, it'll make you start coughing."

I pointed to the scenery that blocked my way. He touched his hat lightly and said to one of the journalists:

"Excuse me, would you mind throwing away your cigar? The smoke is bad for my friend."

His mistress, not bothering to wait for him, was on her way to her dressing room. She turned and addressed the dancer from backstage: "Is that what they do with women, too, those little hands of yours?" she called, in an artificially melodious tone of girlish innocence. "You look like a woman yourself. I'm sure I could have a really exciting time with you and a girl I know."

"I'm not aware of any rule against smoking. If people are ill, they should stay at home," said the journalist.

The dancer smiled mysteriously at the actress.

"Oh! Stop it! You're driving me crazy," she cried. "The things we could do together!"

"All the same, sir, you are not being very civil about it," said Saint-Loup to the journalist, still in a mild and courteous tone, and with the matter-of-factness of someone retrospectively appraising the rights and wrongs of an incident that is now closed.

At that moment I saw Saint-Loup raise his arm vertically above his head, as if he were signaling to someone I could not see, or like an orchestra conductor, and indeed—without any greater transition than when, in a symphony or a ballet, at the mere movement of a bow, violent rhythms take over from a graceful andante—after the courteous words he had just uttered, he brought down his hand and delivered a resounding smack on the journalist's cheek.

Now that the measured exchanges of the diplomats, the smiling arts of peace, had been followed by the furious onslaught of war, since blows lead to further blows, I should not have been surprised to see the combatants bathed in one another's blood. But what I could not comprehend (like people who feel that the rules are being broken if a war breaks out between two countries over something that has so far been seen merely as a matter of adjusting a frontier, or if a sick man dies when there was supposedly nothing more to worry about than a swelling of the liver) was how Saint-Loup had been able to follow up his words, which carried a hint of affability, with a gesture that in no way arose out of them, which they had done nothing to anticipate, the gesture of an arm raised in defiance not only of people's rights but of the principle of causality, in a spontaneous generation of anger, a gesture created *ex nihilo*. Fortunately, the journalist, who had turned pale and hesitated for a moment as he staggered from the violence of the blow, did not retaliate. As for his friends, one of them had immediately turned away and stared intently into the wings at some nonexistent person; the second pretended there was a speck of dust in his eye and began to squeeze his eyelid and screw his face up with pain; the third had rushed away, exclaiming: "Heavens, I think the curtain's about to go up. We'll never get back to our seats."

I should have liked to say something to Saint-Loup, but he was so full of his indignation at the dancer that it was pasted all over his very eyes; it distended his cheeks as if they were stretched on an inner framework, so that the agitation within expressed itself in an outward and utter immobility, and he had not even the elasticity, the "play," necessary to take in a word I might say and answer it. The journalist's friends, seeing that the incident was over, returned to his side, still trembling. But, ashamed of having deserted him, they were absolutely determined he should be under the impression that they had noticed nothing. And so they talked at length, one about the dust in his eye, one about his false alarm that the curtain was going up, the third about the astonishing resemblance between someone who had walked by him and his own brother. And they even went so far as to show some disgruntlement that their colleague had not shared these emotional experiences.

"You mean you really didn't notice? Haven't you got eyes in your head?"

"You're a bunch of cowards, the lot of you," growled the journalist who had been struck.

Heedless of the pretense they had adopted, for to be consistent with it they ought—but they did not think of it—to have made it seem that they did not understand what he meant, they resorted to the kinds of expression traditionally used in such circumstances: "What's got into you? Keep your hair on. You seem a bit worked up."

I had realized that morning, beneath the pear blossom, that Robert's love for "Rachel, when of the Lord" was based on an illusion. Yet I was no less aware how real the pain arising from that love was. Gradually the relentless pain he had been suffering for the last hour diminished and withdrew inside him, and a zone of accessibility appeared in his eyes. The two of us left the theater and walked for a while. I had lingered for a moment at a corner of the Avenue Gabriel from which I had often seen Gilberte appear in the past. I tried for a few seconds to recall those distant impressions; then, as I moved on at a jog to catch up with Saint-Loup, I saw that a somewhat shabbily dressed gentleman appeared to be talking to him in a fairly confidential manner. I came to the conclusion that this was a personal friend of Robert's; meanwhile, they seemed to be drawing even closer to each other; suddenly, like some astral phenomenon appearing in the sky, I saw ovoid bodies assuming with dizzying speed all the positions they needed to form an unstable constellation in front of Saint-Loup. Hurled out like missiles from a catapult, there seemed to me to be at least seven of them. They were merely, however, Saint-Loup's two fists, multiplied by the speed with which they were changing place in this apparently ideal and decorative pattern. But this deceptive display was merely a series of punches Saint-Loup was delivering, with nothing aesthetic about it, and its aggressive nature first became obvious to me when I saw the state of the shabbily dressed gentleman, who seemed to be losing his self-possession, his jaw, and a great deal of blood. He gave false explanations to the people who came up to question him, turned his head to see Saint-Loup finally taking off in my direction, stood gazing after him with an offended, crushed, but by no means furious expression on his face. It was Saint-Loup who was furious, although he had received no blow, and his eyes were still blazing with fury when he rejoined me. The incident was in no way connected, as I had supposed, with the assault in the theater. The man had been loitering about with intent and, seeing Saint-Loup as the handsome soldier he was, had propositioned him. My friend could not get over the effrontery of this "clique" who no longer even waited for the shades of night before they ventured out, and he spoke of the proposition that had been made with the same indignation that can be found in newspaper reports of armed assault and robbery in broad daylight in the center of Paris. Yet the victim of Saint-Loup's blows was excusable in one respect: the downward slope brings desire quickly enough to the point of fulfillment for beauty alone to be seen as consent. That Saint-Loup was beautiful was beyond question. Beatings like the one he had just given have this value for men of the type that had accosted him: they make them reflect seriously on their behavior, though never for long enough to enable them to mend their ways and escape punishment at the hands of the law. And so, although Saint-Loup had thrashed the man without much preliminary thought, thrashings of this sort, even when they reinforce the law, do nothing to bring uniformity to morals.

These incidents, and particularly the one that most preoccupied him, seemed to have made Robert want to be on his own for a while. After a time, he asked me to leave him and go by myself to call on Mme de Villeparisis; he would join me there, but preferred that we should not go in together, in order to give the impression that he had only just arrived in Paris, rather than that he had already spent part of the afternoon in my company.

As I had imagined before making the acquaintance of Mme de Villeparisis in Balbec, there was a considerable difference between the world in which she lived and that of Mme de Guermantes. Mme de Villeparisis was one of those women who, born of an illustrious family and marrying into another no less illustrious, do not for all that enjoy any great position in the social world, and, apart from a number of duchesses who are their nieces or sisters-in-law, even a crowned head or two, old family connections, entertain in their salons only third-rate guests drawn from the bourgeoisie and from a nobility that is either provincial or tainted, whose presence has long since distanced those of the fashionable and snobbish world who are not constrained to be there through ties of blood or through friendship too old to be slighted. Indeed, it had taken me no more than a few minutes to understand, in Balbec, how Mme de Villeparisis had come to be so well informed—better informed than ourselves, in fact—about the smallest details of the Spanish tour my father was making at the time with M. de Norpois. But even if one knew this, it was impossible to limit oneself to the notion that the intimacy—of more than twenty years' standing—between Mme de Villeparisis and the ambassador might have been the reason behind the Marquise's loss of status in a world where the most dazzling women made no secret of lovers far less respectable than him, quite apart from the fact that it was probably years since he had been anything more to the Marquise than an old friend. Was it that Mme de Villeparisis had had other affairs in the past? Being then of a more passionate disposition than now, in the appeasement of a pious old age which nevertheless owed something of its coloring to those ardent, vanished years, had she found it impossible, living in the provinces for so long, to avoid certain scandals unknown to a younger generation, which merely noted their effect in the mixed and defective company to be found in her salon, which would otherwise have been among those least contaminated by any base alloy? Had the "sharp tongue" her nephew attributed to her made her enemies in those early days? Had it driven her to use certain successes with men as a means to avenge herself on women? All this was possible. Nor did the exquisitely sensitive way in which—with such delicate shading of both her words and her tone—Mme de Villeparisis spoke of modesty and kindness do anything to invalidate such speculation about her; for those who speak approvingly of certain virtues, and even feel their charm with perfect understanding (and will be able to paint a creditable picture of them in their memoirs), often come from, but do not themselves form part of, the silent, uncultivated, artless generation that practiced them. They reflect their generation without continuing its ways. In place of the character it possessed, they display a sensibility, an intelligence divorced from their actual behavior. And whether or not there had been scandals in the life of Mme de Villeparisis that had been effaced by the glory of her name, it was her intelligence, the intelligence of a secondary writer far more than that of a woman of rank, that was the real reason for her social decline.

It is true that the qualities Mme de Villeparisis especially favored, such as levelheadedness and moderation, had nothing very inspiring about them; but, to be able to talk about moderation in an entirely convincing way, moderation itself is not enough, and certain of a writer's qualities that entail a somewhat immoderate sense of inspiration are needed; I had noticed in Balbec that the genius of various great artists eluded Mme de Villeparisis, and that all she could do was to scoff genteelly at them and to disguise her incomprehension in graceful witticisms. The wit and the grace, to the extent to which they were developed in her, became themselves—on a different level, and despite the fact that they were used to discredit works of high art—genuinely artistic qualities. Now, the effect of such qualities on any social position is, in medical parlance, an elective morbid activity, and it is so unsettling that the most firmly established positions are very quickly affected by it. What artists call intelligence seems pure pretension to the fashionable world, which, incapable of adopting the sole perspective from which artists judge things, and failing to understand the particular attraction that leads them to choose an expression or to draw a parallel, feels their company to be overdemanding and irritating to the point of rapidly developing antipathy. Yet, in her conversation, and the same is true of the memoirs that she published later, the kind of gracefulness that Mme de Villeparisis displayed was nothing if not eminently social. Passing over great works without considering them in detail, or sometimes without even noticing them, she retained from the period in which she had lived, and which she depicted with great accuracy and charm, scarcely more than its most frivolous aspects. But a piece of writing, even if it directs itself exclusively to subjects that are not intellectual, is still a work of the intelligence, and to achieve a perfect impression of frivolity in a book, or in a talk that is not dissimilar, requires a measure of seriousness that a purely frivolous person would not be able to muster. In some memoirs written by women and regarded as masterpieces, the sort of sentences people quote as models of unlabored grace have always made me suspect that, in order to achieve such lightness of touch, the writer must once have possessed a rather weighty learning, a daunting culture, and that as a girl she probably seemed to her friends an insufferable bluestocking. And between certain literary qualities and lack of social success the connection is so inevitable that, in reading Mme de Villeparisis's memoirs today, any apposite epithet, any sustained metaphor will be enough for the reader to reconstruct the deep but icy bow that must have been given to the old Marquise on some embassy staircase by a snob like Mme Leroi, who may have left her card when she went to call on the Guermantes, but never set foot in her salon, for fear of losing status by frequenting the wives of doctors and solicitors. A bluestocking Mme de Villeparisis may have been in her earliest youth, and, heady with her learning at the time, she had perhaps been unable to resist directing at society people, less intelligent and less educated than herself, the sort of barbed remarks that the victim never forgets.

Again, talent is not a separate appendage that can be artificially attached to the other qualities that lead to social success to create the overall picture of what society people call a "complete woman." It is the living product of a particular mold of character, which generally lacks a great many qualities and is dominated by a sensibility whose manifestations are not evident in a book but may make a fairly vivid impact in the course of a life: certain curious traits, for instance, certain whims, the desire to go to this place or that for one's own pleasure and not with a view to the broadening, the maintenance, or the mere exercise of social relations. In Balbec I had seen Mme de Villeparisis locked in her own circle and not even glancing at the people sitting in the hotel foyer. But I had the feeling that this abstention did not point to indifference on her part, and it seems that she had not always confined herself to it. She would suddenly get it into her head to make the acquaintance of some individual who had no claim to her society, sometimes because she thought him good-looking, or simply because she had been told he was amusing, or because he had seemed different from the people she knew, and they at the time, when she had not yet begun to appreciate them because she thought they would never abandon her, all belonged to the cream of the Faubourg Saint-Germain. To the bohemian or petit-bourgeois she had singled out with her favor she was obliged to address invitations, whose value he was unable to appreciate, with an insistence that gradually lowered her status in the eyes of snobs who were in the habit of rating a salon by the people its mistress excluded rather than by those she received. Indeed, if at some stage in her youth Mme de Villeparisis, in blasé smugness at belonging to the flower of the aristocracy, had somehow amused herself by scandalizing the people of her world, and deliberately undermining her social status, she had begun to attach importance to that status once she had lost it. She had wanted to show the duchesses that she surpassed them all, by saying and doing all the things they dared not say or do. But now that they had ceased to call, apart from those who were closely related to her, she felt herself diminished and was anxious to regain her sovereignty, but by other means than her wit. She would have liked to attract all those whom she had taken such pains to distance from her. How many women's lives, lives so little known in fact (for we all know a different aspect of them, according to our age, and the discretion of their elders prevents the young from having any real idea of the past and grasping a whole life-cycle), have been divided in this way into contrasting periods, the last entirely devoted to recuperating what in the second had been so blithely cast to the winds! Cast to the winds in what way? The young are less capable of imagining it because what they see before them is an elderly and respectable Mme de Villeparisis, and they cannot conceive that the solemn memorialist of today, so dignified beneath her wig of white hair, might once have been the toast of supper parties, who was perhaps the delight, who perhaps devoured the fortunes, of men long since in their graves. That she should have also worked, with the perseverance and the ingenuity that came naturally to her, to undo the social status she owed to her high birth does not in any way imply that, even in that remote period of her youth, Mme de Villeparisis did not attach great importance to her position. In the same way, the neurasthenic can contrive the web of isolation and inactivity in which he lives from morning to night without its seeming any more bearable, and as he hastens to add another mesh to the net that holds him captive, it is possible that he is dreaming only of dancing, sport, and travel. We constantly strive to give our life its form, but by copying, in spite of ourselves, like a drawing, the features of the person we are, not the person we should like to be. Mme Leroi's disdainful acknowledgments might somehow indicate the true nature of Mme de Villeparisis; they in no way matched up to what she really wanted.

No doubt, at the very moment when Mme Leroi was *cutting* her–to borrow an expression dear to Mme Swann—the Marquise could seek consolation by remembering how Queen Marie-Amélie had once said to her, "You are like a daughter to me." But royal favors of this kind, secret and undisclosed, existed for the Marquise alone, as dusty as the diploma of some former star pupil at the Conservatoire. The only real social advantages are those that create something living, and these can disappear without the person who has benefited by them needing to try to cling to them or make them known, because in the same day a hundred more will take their place. Mme de Villeparisis might well remember the words of the Queen, but she would have traded them gladly for Mme Leroi's permanent ability to be invited everywhere, just as, in a restaurant, a talented but unknown artist whose genius is written neither in the features of his diffident face nor in the outmoded cut of his threadbare jacket would readily change places with the young broker from the lowest ranks of society who is dining with two actresses at a neighboring table, and upon whom, in an obsequious and incessant bustle, owner, manager, waiters, pages dance attention; even the kitchen staff file out of the kitchen to salute him, as in fairy tales, while the sommelier comes forward, as dusty as his bottles, hobbling and dazed, as if, coming up from the cellar, he had twisted his foot before emerging into the light of day.

Yet it must be said that, if Mme Leroi's absence from Mme de Villeparisis's salon distressed the mistress of the house herself, it went unnoticed by a large number of her guests. They were completely ignorant of Mme Leroi's peculiar social position, which was known only to the fashionable world, and they never doubted that Mme de Villeparisis's receptions were, as the readers of her memoirs today are convinced that they must have been, the most brilliant in Paris.

On this first visit, which, following the advice M. de Norpois had given to my father, I went to pay Mme de Villeparisis after leaving Saint-Loup, I found her in a drawing room hung with yellow silk, against which the sofas and the admirable armchairs upholstered in Beauvais tapestry stood out with the almost violet pink of ripe raspberries. Side by side with portraits of the Guermantes and the Villeparisis were others—gifts from the sitters themselves—of Queen Marie-Amélie, the

Queen of the Belgians, the Prince de Joinville, and the Empress of Austria. Mme de Villeparisis, in an old-fashioned bonnet of black lace (which she insisted on wearing with the same shrewd instinct for local or historical color as a Breton hotelier who, however Parisian his clientele may have become, sees it as more astute to keep his maids in coifs and wide sleeves), was seated at a little desk on which, along with her brushes, her palette, and the beginnings of a watercolor of flowers, were a number of glasses, saucers, and cups containing moss roses, zinnias, maidenhair ferns, which she had stopped painting because of the present influx of visitors, and which looked like a display on a florist's counter from some eighteenth-century print. In this drawing room—which had been deliberately heated a bit, because the Marquise had caught cold on the way back from her country residence—among those present when I arrived were an archivist with whom Mme de Villeparisis had spent the morning sorting the autograph letters addressed to her by various historical figures, which were to be presented in facsimile as documentary evidence in the memoirs she was preparing for publication, and a solemn, overawed historian who had heard that there was an inherited portrait of the Duchesse de Montmorency in her possession and had come to ask her permission to reproduce it as a plate in his work on the Fronde, these two guests being joined by my old school friend Bloch, now an up-and-coming dramatist upon whom she counted to secure free performances from actors and actresses for her future afternoon receptions. It is true that the social kaleidoscope was in the process of shifting, and that the Dreyfus case was about to hurl Jews to the lowest rung of the social ladder. But, for one thing, however fiercely the Dreyfus cyclone was raging, it is not at the onset of a storm that the waves are at their most violent. And, then, Mme de Villeparisis, leaving a whole part of her family to thunder against the Jews, had so far kept utterly aloof from the Affair, and never gave it a second thought. Finally, a young man like Bloch, who was unknown to the world, could pass unnoticed, whereas important Jews representative of their side were already threatened. Bloch's chin was now punctuated by a goatee, he wore a pince-nez and a long frock coat, and in his hand he carried a glove like a roll of papyrus. The Romanians, the Egyptians, the Turks may hate the Jews. But in a French salon the differences between those peoples are not so evident, and a Jew making his entry as though he were coming in from some remote part of the desert, his body bent forward like a hyena, his neck sloped forward, offering effusive "salaams," satisfies in every way a taste for things Oriental. The only requirement necessary is that the Jew in question should not "belong" in social terms; otherwise he will quickly assume the demeanor of a lord, and his manners will become so Gallicized that his recalcitrant nose, growing like a nasturtium in unpredictable directions, will be more reminiscent of Mascarille[35] than of Solomon. But, for a lover of the exotic, Bloch, who had not been limbered up by the gymnastics of the Faubourg Saint-Germain or ennobled by cross-blood from England or Spain, remained, in spite of his European dress, as strange and savory a spectacle as a Jew in a painting by Decamps.[36] How admirable the power of the race that from the depths of time thrusts forward right into modern Paris, into the corridors of our theaters, behind the counters of our public offices, at a funeral, in the street, an inviolate phalanx, setting its mark on the styles of modern hairdressing, absorbing, making us forget, disciplining the frock coat, which in the end has remained identical to the garment of the Assyrian scribes as they are depicted in their ceremonial robes on the frieze of a monument at Susa in front of the gates of the palace of Darius.[37] (An hour later, Bloch was to read anti-Semitic malice into M. de Charlus's asking him whether his first name was Jewish, whereas it was simply from aesthetic interest and love of local color.) But in any case, to speak of racial continuity is to give an inaccurate picture of the impression we receive from the Jews, the Greeks, the Persians, from all those races we would do better to leave to their variousness. We know the faces of the ancient Greeks from classical paintings, we have seen Assyrians on the pediment of the palace at Susa. And so, when we actually meet Orientals belonging to a particular group, we feel that we are in the presence of creatures spirited before our eyes by necromancy. Our image of them so far has been a superficial one; now it has acquired depth, it has become three-dimensional, it moves. The young Greek banker's daughter who is such a society favorite at present, seems like one of those dancers in a ballet, at once historical and aesthetic, who symbolize Hellenic art in flesh and blood; yet the theater setting makes these images seem banal; by contrast, the spectacle before us when a Turkish lady or a Jewish gentleman enters a drawing room and her or his features are set in motion is stranger still, as if they really were creatures evoked by the efforts of a medium. It is the soul (or, rather, the tiny shred to which the soul is reduced, up until now at least, in this sort of materialization), it is the soul we have so far glimpsed only in museums, the soul of the ancient Greeks, the ancient Hebrews, torn from a life at once insignificant and transcendental, which seems to be performing this disconcerting pantomime in our presence. What we seek in vain to embrace in this elusive young Greek woman is the figure we admired long ago on the side of a vase. I felt that, if I had taken some photographs of Bloch against the background of Mme de Villeparisis's salon, they would have produced an image of Israel like the images in spirit photographs—so disturbing because they do not appear to emanate from humanity, so disappointing because they nonetheless resemble humanity too closely. And, more generally, there is nothing, not even the insignificance of the remarks made by the people among whom we spend our lives, that does not offer a sense of the supernatural, in our poor everyday world where even a man of genius from whom, as we gather around him like a séance table, we wait to hear the secret of the infinite, simply utters the words—words that had just escaped from Bloch—"Take care of my top hat."

"Good gracious, ministers, my dear sir," Mme de Villeparisis was saying, directing her remarks at my old school friend as she resumed the thread of a conversation that my arrival had interrupted, "nobody wanted to see ministers. I was only a child at the time, but I can still remember the King begging my grandfather to invite M. Decazes[38] to a rout at which my father was to dance with the Duchesse de Berry. 'It will give me pleasure, Florimond,' said the King. My grandfather, who was a little deaf, thought he had said M. de Castries, and so found nothing unusual about the request. When he understood it was M. Decazes, he bridled at first, then complied, and wrote the same evening to M. Decazes, begging him to favor him with the honor of his presence at the ball he was giving the following week. For we had manners in those days, sir, and no hostess would have dreamed of merely sending her card and writing on it 'Tea' or 'Tea dance' or 'Music.' But if we knew about manners, impertinence was not unknown to us, either. M. Decazes accepted, but the day before the ball people were informed that my grandfather was indisposed and had canceled the rout. He had obeyed the King, but he had not had M. Decazes at his ball. . . . Yes, I remember M. Molé[39] very well indeed. He was a man of wit, as he showed when he received M. de Vigny at the Académie, but he stood too much on ceremony. I can see him now, coming down to dinner in his own house with his top hat in his hand."

"Ah! It all evokes a rather pernicious, philistine period. It was undoubtedly a universal habit to carry one's hat in one's own house," said Bloch, who was keen to make the most of this rare opportunity to acquaint himself with the details of former aristocratic life from an eyewitness, while the archivist, in his capacity as a sort of occasional secretary to the Marquise, threw tender glances in her direction, as if to convey to us, "There, you can see what she's like, she knows everything, she's known everybody, you can ask her about anything, she's an extraordinary woman."

"It was certainly not," replied Mme de Villeparisis as she drew toward her the glass containing the maidenhair fern, which she would continue painting presently. "It was just something particular to M. de Molé. I never saw my father carrying his hat in the house, except of course when the King came, because the King is at home wherever he is, and the master of a house then becomes a mere visitor to his own drawing room."

"Aristotle tells us in chapter two of . . ." ventured M. Pierre, the Fronde historian, but so timidly that no one paid any attention. He had been suffering for some weeks from a nervous insomnia that resisted every kind of treatment, had given up going to bed, and, crippled with exhaustion, went out only when his work made it necessary. Incapable of repeating too often the expeditions that others find so simple but which cost him as much effort as if he had to come down from the moon, he was frequently surprised by the fact that other people's lives were not organized in some permanent way to provide maximum utility to his own sudden bursts of activity. Sometimes he would find a library closed after setting out to visit it, something he achieved only by planting himself artificially on his feet and into a frock coat like a character from a story by Wells.[40] Luckily, he had found Mme de Villeparisis at home and was to be shown the portrait.

Bloch cut him short.

"Really," he interrupted, responding to Mme de Villeparisis's remarks about the etiquette observed for royal visits, "I never knew that"— as though it were strange for him not to know.

"Since we're on the subject of royal visits, do you know the stupid joke my nephew Basin played on me yesterday morning?" Mme de Villeparisis asked the archivist. "Instead of announcing his arrival, he sent word to say that the Queen of Sweden had called to see me."

"What? Just like that, with a straight face! What a joker!" exclaimed Bloch, guffawing with laughter, while the historian confined himself shyly to a stately smile.

"I was rather surprised, because I had only been back from the country for a few days. I wanted to be left in peace for a while, and I had given instructions that no one was to be told I was in Paris. So I wondered how the Queen of Sweden could know of my presence so soon," continued Mme de Villeparisis, leaving her visitors startled with the intelligence that a visit from the Queen of Sweden was nothing out of the ordinary for their hostess.

If Mme de Villeparisis had spent the morning sifting through the documentation of her memoirs, she was now unconsciously gauging the sort of spell they might cast on an average audience, typical of the public from whom she would one day draw her readers. Her salon might be different from a truly fashionable one, which would not be frequented by many of the bourgeois ladies she entertained, and in which one would have encountered instead the sort of brilliant women that Mme Leroi had finally managed to attract, but nothing of this is perceptible in her memoirs, where certain dull acquaintances of the author's have disappeared because there is no reason for them to be included; and the visitors who did not frequent her salon leave no gap in her work, because, in the necessarily restricted space available, there is room for only a few figures, and if they happen to be royal personages, historic personalities, then the utmost impression of elegance that any memoir can present to the public has been achieved. In Mme Leroi's opinion, Mme de Villeparisis's salon was third-rate; and Mme de Villeparisis was stung by that opinion. But hardly anyone today knows who Mme Leroi was, her opinions have completely vanished, and it is the salon of Mme de Villeparisis, frequented by the Queen of Sweden, and before her by the Duc d'Aumale, the Duc de Broglie, Thiers,[41] Montalambert, Monseigneur Dupanloup, that will be regarded as one of the most brilliant of the nineteenth century by posterity, which has not changed since the days of Homer and Pindar, and in whose eyes the enviable signs of status are high birth, royal or quasi-royal, the friendship of kings, of leaders of the people, and of renowned men generally.

Now, of all these Mme de Villeparisis had a smattering in her present salon and in her memories—sometimes slightly embellished ones—by means of which she extended it into the past. And then there was M. de Norpois, who was not able to restore his friend to any genuine position in society, but who nevertheless provided her with foreign or French statesmen who were in need of his support and who knew that the only effective way of gaining it was to court him by frequenting Mme de Villeparisis. Perhaps Mme Leroi also knew these European celebrities. But as an amiable woman who avoided any hint of bluestocking behavior, she would no more have allowed herself to mention the Eastern question to a prime minister than she would have discussed love with a novelist or a philosopher. "Love?" she had once replied to a pretentious lady who had asked for her views on the subject. "I make love often, but I never discuss it." Like the Duchesse de Guermantes, when she received literary or political celebrities she limited herself to having them play poker. They often preferred this to the serious conversations on general ideas Mme de Villeparisis forced upon them. But conversations of this kind, however ridiculous in society gatherings, have provided the "Souvenirs" of Mme de Villeparisis with excellent passages, political dissertations that read as well in memoirs as they do in the tragedies of Corneille. And, again, the salons of the Mmes de Villeparisis of this world are the only ones that are destined for posterity, because the Mmes Leroi of this world are not writers, and if they were they would not have the time for it. And if the literary disposition of Mme de Villeparisis and her kind is the cause of the disdain of the Mmes Leroi, in its turn the disdain of the Mmes Leroi performs a singular service to the literary disposition of the Mmes de Villeparisis, by creating the leisure that bluestocking ladies require for the pursuit of their literary careers. Thus God, whose will it is that a few well-written books should exist, breathes disdain into the hearts of the Mmes Leroi, for He knows that, should they invite the Mmes de Villeparisis to dinner, then these would immediately leave their writing desks and order their carriages for eight o'clock.

Shortly afterward, an old lady entered with slow and solemn steps; she was tall in stature, and beneath the raised brim of her straw hat she revealed a monumental pile of white hair, dressed in the style of Marie-Antoinette. I did not know at the time that she was one of three women still to be seen in Parisian society, who, like Mme de Villeparisis, though of noble birth, had been reduced, for reasons now lost in the mists of time and known only to some old beaux of their generation, to receiving only the dregs of society, who were not welcome elsewhere. Each of these ladies had her "Duchesse de Guermantes," the brilliant niece who dutifully paid her respects, but none of them could have managed to attract to her house the "Duchesse de Guermantes" of either of the others. Mme de Villeparisis saw much of these three ladies, but she did not like them. Perhaps the similarity between their position and her own created a disagreeable impression for her. There was also the fact that they were soured bluestockings who sought, through the number of theatrical entertainments they hosted, to delude themselves that they kept a salon, and there was a rivalry between them, which the considerable erosion of their fortunes in the course of their rather unruly lives, by obliging them to watch their purse strings and to rely on the charity of the actors they used, transformed into a sort of life struggle. And, again, the lady with the Marie-Antoinette coiffure, whenever she set eyes on Mme de Villeparisis, could not help being reminded of the fact that the Duchesse de Guermantes did not come to her own Friday receptions. She was consoled by the unfailing presence at these

Fridays of hers of her dutiful relation, the Princesse de Poix, her own special Guermantes, who never went near Mme de Villeparisis, despite the fact that she was an intimate friend of the Duchesse.

Nevertheless, from the mansion on the Quai Malaquais to the salons of the rue de Tournon, the rue de la Chaise, and the Faubourg Saint-Honoré, a bond as strong as it was hateful united these three fallen divinities, and I would have been keen to learn, from the pages of some dictionary of society mythology, what amorous adventure, what sacrilegious presumption, had brought about their punishment. The same distinguished origins, the same present fall from favor were no doubt largely responsible for the sort of compunction that drove them, though hating one another, to seek one another's society. And, indeed, each one found in the others a convenient way of flattering her guests. How could such guests fail to imagine that they had entered the innermost circle of the Faubourg when they were presented to a lady with a whole string of titles whose sister was married to a Duc de Sagan or a Prince de Ligne? Especially since there was infinitely more newspaper coverage of these bogus salons than of the genuine ones. Even the upper-crust nephews of these ladies—with Saint-Loup first and foremost—when asked by a friend to introduce him into society, would say: "I'll take you to my aunt Villeparisis's, or to my aunt X's. You meet interesting people in their salon." They were only too well aware that this would give them less trouble than getting their friends invited by the fashionable nieces or sisters-in-law of these ladies. I was told by old men whose memories went back a long way, and by young women who had heard it from these old men, that if these ladies were now socially excluded it was because of their extraordinarily dissolute past, and when I objected that dissolute conduct was no obstacle to social success, they painted a picture of it as something utterly in excess of anything to be met with today. On the lips of those who told the tale, the misconduct of these solemn, poker-backed ladies became something I was incapable of imagining, something on a prehistoric scale belonging to the age of the mammoth. In a word, these three Fates, with their white or blue or pink hair, had spun the ruin of innumerable gentlemen. It occurred to me that men of today exaggerated the vices of the fabled past, like the

Greeks who created Icarus, Theseus, Hercules out of men who were not so different from those who turned them into gods long after. But the list of a person's vices is compiled only when he has almost ceased to be able to indulge them, when, from the extent of his social punishment, which is nearing its end and which is the only available evidence, we measure, we imagine, we exaggerate the magnitude of the crime that has been committed. In the gallery of symbolic figures that constitutes "society," the really dissolute women, the dedicated Messalinas,[42] always appear as a lady of at least seventy, solemn and haughty, who receives everyone she can but not everyone she would like to, her society shunned by women whose own conduct is not above reproach, a regular recipient of the papal "Golden Rose,"[43] and as often as not the author of a book on Lamartine's early years that has been crowned by the Académie Française. "Alix, how are you?" said Mme de Villeparisis, greeting the lady with the Marie-Antoinette hair; the lady scoured the assembled company in search of some item in this salon that might be of value to her own, in which case she would have to discover it for herself, for Mme de Villeparisis, she had no doubt, would be cunning enough to try to hide it from her. This is why Mme de Villeparisis took good care not to introduce Bloch to the old lady, in case she asked him for the same theatricals he was producing here, for her own salon, on the Quai Malaquais. Besides, it was a mere matter of giving as good as she got. For, the evening before, the old lady had had Mme Ristori[44] reciting poetry and made sure that Mme de Villeparisis, from whom she had filched the Italian artist, remained in ignorance of the event until it was over. So that she should not read about it in the papers and feel offended, the old lady had come along to tell her about it, as if there were no question of guilt involved. Judging that to introduce me to her would not entail the same drawbacks as the introduction of Bloch, Mme de Villeparisis made me known to the Marie-Antoinette of the Quai Malaquais. This lady, who sought, by making the fewest possible movements, to preserve in her old age the goddesslike contour of a Coysevox[45] sculpture that had cast its spell on the fashionable youth of years ago and was still celebrated in rhyming verse by literary hacks— and who had acquired the habit of that haughty, compensatory stiffness shared by all those whose ill-favored looks oblige them to be the ones who are continually making advances—almost imperceptibly bowed her head with icy majesty, turned away, and took no more notice of me than if I had not existed. This dual attitude seemed to be a way of conveying to Mme de Villeparisis, "You see, I'm not *that* short of acquaintances, and young men don't interest me—in any sense, you mean old bat." But fifteen minutes later, when she took her leave, she took advantage of the hubbub of voices and slipped into my ear an invitation to join her box on the following Friday with the other of the three, whose illustrious name—she had been born a Choiseul, in fact—made a prodigious impression on me.

"I do believe, m'sieur, that you want to write somethin' on Mme la Duchesse de Montmorency," said Mme de Villeparisis to the Fronde historian, in the gruff manner in which her enormous kindness was unwittingly scrunched up by the shriveled sulkiness and physiological frustration of old age, as well as by her foible for imitating the almost rustic parlance of the old aristocracy. "I'll show you her portrait, the original of the copy in the Louvre."

She put her brushes down beside the flowers and rose to her feet, revealing the little apron at her waist, which she used to keep the paint from her dress, and which heightened still further the almost rustic impression created by her bonnet and her big spectacles, in sharp contrast to the luxury of her household, the butler who had brought in the tea and cakes, the liveried footman for whom she rang to light up the portrait of the Duchesse de Montmorency, abbess of one of the most famous chapters in eastern France.[46] All had risen to their feet. "It's amusin' to think," she said, "that these chapters where our great aunts were often abbesses would not have admitted the daughters of the King of France. They were very exclusive." "Not admitted the King's daughters!" exclaimed Bloch in amazement. "Why ever not?" "Why, because the House of France had insufficient quarterings after that misalliance." Bloch's amazement increased. "A misalliance in the House of France? But when?" "When they married into the Medicis, of course," replied Mme de Villeparisis in the most natural tone in the world. "It's a fine portrait, don't you think? and perfectly preserved," she added.

"My dear," said the lady with the Marie-Antoinette hair, "don't you remember when I brought Liszt to see you? He said that this one was the copy."

"I bow to Liszt's judgment of music, but not to his judgment of painting! Besides, he was already gaga at the time, and I don't remember him saying any such thing. But it wasn't you who brought him here. I had dined with him a dozen times before, at the Princesse de Sayn-Wittgenstein's."

Alix's jibe had backfired. She said no more and stood there motionless. Her face was plastered with layers of powder and looked like a face of stone. And with her noble profile, she seemed, on the triangular, moss-covered pedestal hidden by her cape, like a crumbling goddess in a park.

"Ah! I can see another fine portrait," said the historian.

The door opened, and the Duchesse de Guermantes entered the room.

"Oh, good evening," said Mme de Villeparisis, greeting her without so much as a nod of the head and taking from her apron pocket a hand, which she held out to the new guest; then, ceasing at once to pay further attention to her, she turned back to the historian. "That is the portrait of the Duchesse de La Rochefoucauld. . . ."

A young servant with a bold manner and a charming face (but so finely pared down in its perfection that the nose was a little red and the skin slightly inflamed, as if they were still smarting from the recent effects of the sculptor's chisel) came in with a card on a salver.

"It's the gentleman who has already called several times to see Mme la Marquise."

"Did you tell him I was at home?"

"He heard the voices."

"Oh, very well, then, show him in. It's a gentleman who was introduced to me," said Mme de Villeparisis. "He told me he would very much like to be allowed to call on me. I certainly didn't say he might do so. But he's taken the trouble to call five times now, and one shouldn't hurt people's feelings. Monsieur," she said to me, "and you, monsieur," to the Fronde historian, "let me introduce my niece, the Duchesse de Guermantes."

The historian joined me in making a low bow, and, apparently thinking that some sort of friendly form of words ought to follow, he allowed his eyes to liven and was just about to speak when his spirit was dampened by the demeanor of Mme de Guermantes, who had taken advantage of the independence of her torso to thrust it forward with exaggerated politeness and bring it back exactly into position without letting her face or eyes give any indication that anyone was there before them; after a little sigh, the only other sign she gave of the nonentity of the impression made on her by the sight of the historian and myself was to perform various movements of her nostrils with a precision that was clear enough proof of the total inertia of her attention: it had nothing better to do.

The importunate visitor came into the room and made straight for Mme de Villeparisis in an artless, fervent manner: it was Legrandin.

"It is so very kind of you to allow me to call, madame," he said, with great emphasis on the word "very." "The pleasure it gives to an old solitary like myself is of a rare and subtle quality. You may be sure that its repercussion . . ."

He stopped short as he caught sight of me.

"I was just showing this gentleman my fine portrait of the Duchesse de La Rochefoucauld, the wife of the author of the *Maximes*. It's a family heirloom."

Meanwhile, Mme de Guermantes greeted Alix and presented her apologies for having been prevented, that year as in every previous year, from calling on her. "I hear all about you from Madeleine," she added.

"She lunched with me at home today," said the Marquise of the Quai Malaquais, basking in the thought that Mme de Villeparisis could never say the same.

Meanwhile, I had been talking to Bloch, and, fearing, from what I had been told of his father's change of attitude toward him, that he might be envying my life, I said to him how much happier his own must be. My remark was simply an attempt to be friendly. But people who have a high opinion of themselves are quick to respond to such friendliness as a confirmation of their own good fortune, or feel the need to convince others of it. "Yes, I do live a charmed life," Bloch responded smugly. "I've three really good friends—quite enough for me—

and an adorable mistress. I couldn't be happier. Rare is the mortal to whom Father Zeus grants so much felicity." I think his main intention was to congratulate himself and make me envious. But there was perhaps some desire to be original in his optimism. It was obvious that he did not want to trot out the same banalities as everyone else—"Oh, it was nothing, really," and so forth—when I asked him, "Was it nice?" in relation to an afternoon dance at his house that I had been unable to attend, and he replied with studied indifference, as if it were someone else's dance: "Why, yes, it was very nice, couldn't have been more successful. Enchanting, now I think about it."

"What you are telling us interests me enormously," said Legrandin to Mme de Villeparisis. "In fact, I was saying to myself only the other day that you bore a strong resemblance to him in the clarity and alertness of your turn of phrase, in something I will express in two contradictory terms: succinct rapidity and immortal instantaneousness. I should like to have noted down all the things you have said this afternoon; but I shall remember them. As Joubert[47] puts it—I think it's Joubert—they are conducive to the memory. You've never read Joubert? Oh, he would have been such an admirer of yours! I shall take the liberty of sending you his works this very evening. It will be an honor to introduce you to his mind. He lacked your vigor. But, like you, he had great elegance of expression."

I had wanted to go and greet Legrandin at once, but he kept himself as far away from me as he could, no doubt in the hope that I might not hear the highly refined flatteries he kept lavishing on Mme de Villeparisis at every turn of their exchange.

She shrugged her shoulders with a smile, as though he had been making fun of her, and turned to the historian.

"And this is the famous Marie de Rohan, Duchesse de Chevreuse, whose first husband was M. de Luynes."

"My dear, Mme de Luynes reminds me of Yolande; she was with me yesterday. If I'd known you weren't engaged yesterday evening, I'd have sent word for you to come. Mme Ristori was there, as it happened, and recited some poems by Queen Carmen Sylva[48] in the author's presence. Too, too beautiful!"

"Treacherous woman! *That's* what she was whispering about the other day with Mme de Beaulaincourt and Mme de Chaponay," thought Mme de Villeparisis. She replied: "I was free, in fact, but I would not have come anyway. I heard Mme Ristori in her great days, before she was the wreck she is now. And I hate Carmen Sylva's poetry. Ristori came here once—the Duchesse d'Aoste brought her—to recite a canto of Dante's *Inferno*. In that sort of poetry she's incomparable."

Alix bore the blow without flinching. A block of marble. Her gaze was piercing and blank, her nose nobly arched. But one cheek was flaking. A hint of strange green-and-pink vegetation was invading her chin. Another winter perhaps would lay her low.

"If you're fond of painting, monsieur, then do take a look at the portrait of Mme de Montmorency," said Mme de Villeparisis to Legrandin in an attempt to stave off a renewed flurry of compliments.

Taking advantage of his moving away, Mme de Guermantes indicated him to her aunt with an ironical, questioning movement of her eyes.

"It's M. Legrandin," murmured Mme de Villeparisis. "He has a sister named Mme de Cambremer, not that it will mean any more to you than it does to me."

"What! But it does. I know her very well!" exclaimed Mme de Guermantes, clapping her hand to her mouth. "Or, rather, I don't know her, but Basin, who for some reason or other meets the husband heaven knows where, took it into his head to tell the vile woman to call on me. Call she did. I can't begin to tell you. She told me she had been to London and gave me an endless catalogue of every picture in the British Museum. And just as you see me now, the moment I leave here, I'm going to drop my card on the monster. And she's no easy monster to deal with, believe me, because, on the pretext that she's at death's door, she's always at home. You can call at seven at night or nine in the morning and there she is, ready for you with her strawberry tarts. No, but I mean what I say, she really is a monster," said Mme de Guermantes as she met her aunt's questioning glance. "She's an impossible woman. She uses words like 'pen-pushing,' that sort of thing." "What does 'pen-pushing' mean?" Mme de Villeparisis asked her niece. "I haven't the faintest idea!" exclaimed the Duchesse in mock indignation. "I don't want to know. I don't speak that sort of language." And, seeing that her aunt really did not know what the word meant, to give herself the satisfaction of showing off her learning as well as her purism, and to make fun of her aunt after making fun of Mme de Cambremer, she said, with a stifled laugh that was controlled by the last traces of her mock ill-humor: "But of course I know, everyone knows: a pen-pusher is a writer, someone who wields a pen. But it's a horrible term. It's enough to make you lose your wisdom teeth. I'll never be persuaded to use words like that. . . . So that's her brother, is it? I still can't get the idea into my head. But, then, it's not utterly beyond belief, I suppose. They both have that doormat humility and the mental resources of a circulating library. She's just as sycophantic and just as annoying as he is. I think I begin to see the family likeness."

"Sit down and have some tea," said Mme de Villeparisis to Mme de Guermantes. "Help yourself. You don't want to spend your time looking at the portraits of your great-grandmothers. You know them as well as I do."

After a while, Mme de Villeparisis went back to sit down at her painting. Everyone gathered round her, and I took this opportunity to go up to Legrandin, without any sense that there was anything reprehensible about his presence in Mme de Villeparisis's salon, I said, never dreaming how much my words would both hurt him and cause him to believe that this was my intention, "Well, monsieur, I feel almost excused from being in a salon, now that I find you in one, too." Legrandin drew the conclusion from this (at least this is what he accused me of a few days later) that I was a thoroughly spiteful young person who delighted only in being nasty.

"You might at least have the manners to say good day to me first," he replied, without offering me his hand, and in a coarse and angry voice I did not know he possessed, which, though it bore no rational connection with his normal manner of speaking, conveyed something more immediately striking about what he was feeling. It is true that, since we are always concerned to hide our feelings, we never think about the manner in which we express them. Then, suddenly, there is this obscene and unfamiliar animal inside us making itself heard, in a voice that can sometimes even manage to frighten the recipient of the involuntary, elliptical, and almost irresistible disclosure of our defect or vice, as much as the sudden avowal indirectly and weirdly blurted by a criminal, who cannot refrain from confessing to a murder of which no one had ever thought him guilty. I knew of course that idealism, even subjective idealism, did not prevent great philosophers from remaining gourmands or from endless attempts to be elected to the Académie. But Legrandin really had no need to remind people so often that he belonged to another planet when all his violent impulses of anger or affability were governed by his desire for social status on this one.

"Naturally, when people pester me time and time again for my company," he went on in hushed tones, "although I'm perfectly free to do what I choose, I can't really behave like a boor."

Mme de Guermantes had sat down. Her name, accompanied as it was by her title, gave to her physical person the added projection of her duchy, which brought the shaded, golden freshness of the Guermantes woods to dominate this drawing room, all around the pouffe on which she was sitting. I was surprised only that the likeness of these woods was not more evident on the face of the Duchesse, which had nothing suggestive of vegetation, and on which only her blotchy cheeks—they ought, one felt, to have been emblazoned with the name Guermantes— gave any sign of the effect, not the reflection, of long gallops in the open air. Later, when I had become indifferent to her, I was to know many of the Duchesse's distinctive features, notably (to keep for the moment to what already charmed me at the time without my being able to recognize it) her eyes, which captured like a picture the blue sky of an afternoon in the French countryside, broad and expansive, drenched in light even when there was no sun; and a voice that one would have thought, from its first hoarse sounds, to be almost common, in which there lingered, as on the steps of the Combray church or the pâtisserie on the square there, the lazy, rich gold of provincial sunlight. But on this first occasion I recognized nothing; my impassioned attention immediately dispelled the little I might have been able to take in to help me try to grasp something of the name Guermantes. What I did manage to tell myself was that this was the person designated for the whole world by the title Duchesse de Guermantes: the inconceivable life behind that name was indeed contained by this body, which had just introduced that life into a gathering of various different people, in this salon, which enclosed it on every side, and on which it produced so vivid an effect that I felt I could see, at the point at which this life ceased to radiate, a fringe of effervescence outlining its frontiers—within the circumference of the circle marked out on the carpet by her ballooning skirt of painted blue silk, and in the bright eyes of the Duchesse at the intersection point of the preoccupations, the memories, the incomprehensible, scornful, amused, and curious thoughts that filled them, and the external images reflected on their surface. It is possible that I should not have been quite so deeply stirred had I met her at one of Mme de Villeparisis's evening parties, instead of seeing her like this at one of the Marquise's "at homes," one of those tea parties that for women represent no more than a brief pause in their outings, during which they keep on the hats in which they have been doing their shopping and bring the flavor of the air outside into a whole succession of salons, offering a better view of Paris in the late afternoon than the tall open windows through which the rumble of victorias can be heard—Mme de Guermantes wore a straw hat trimmed with cornflowers—and what they evoked for me was not the sunlight of distant years falling on the tilled fields of Combray, where I had so often gathered them on the slope along the Tansonville hedge, but the scent and dust of twilight as they had been a little earlier, when Mme de Guermantes walked through them down the rue de la Paix. With a smiling, disdainful, abstracted air, and a pout on her pursed lips, she was tracing circles on the carpet with the tip of her sunshade, as with the extreme point of an antenna of her mysterious life; then, with the indifferent attention that begins by obliterating every point of contact between what one is gazing at and oneself, her eyes fastened upon each of us in turn, then inspected the sofas and chairs, but softened now by the human sympathy that is aroused by the presence, however insignificant, of a familiar object, an object that is almost a person; the furniture was not like us, it belonged vaguely to her world, it was associated with the life of her aunt; then, from a Beauvais chair, her eyes were brought back to the person sitting on it, and assumed once more the same perspicacious gaze of a disapproval that the respect Mme de Guermantes felt for her aunt would have prevented her from voicing, but which she would have felt had she noticed on the chairs, not our presence, but that of a spot of grease or a layer of dust.

The excellent writer G— entered the room; he had come to pay a call on Mme de Villeparisis, something he regarded as an irksome duty. The Duchesse, who was delighted to see him again, gave no hint of greeting, but he instinctively made his way toward her, since her charm and tact singled her out for him as a woman of intelligence. In any case, common politeness demanded that he should go and talk to her, for, since he was a pleasant and celebrated character, Mme de Guermantes often had him to lunch even when she and her husband were alone, or would take advantage of her intimacy with him to invite him to dine occasionally, when she was at Guermantes in the autumn, with members of royalty who were curious to meet him. For the Duchesse liked to entertain certain distinguished men, but only if they were bachelors, a role they always adopted for her even when they were married, for, since their wives, who were invariably more or less humdrum, would have cast a slur on a salon graced only by the most fashionable beauties in Paris, their husbands were always invited on their own; and the Duc, to avert any hurt feelings, would explain to these reluctant widowers that the Duchesse never received women, could not endure feminine company, almost as if he were repeating doctor's orders on the matter, and as he might have said that she could not stay in a room where there were smells, take too much salt in her food, travel with her back to the engine, or wear a corset. It is true that at the Guermantes' these distinguished men would see the Princess of Parma, the Princesse de Sagan (whom Françoise, hearing the name so frequently mentioned, had taken to calling "La Sagante" in the belief that grammar demanded a feminine ending), and many more besides, but were told that the presence of these women was justified by the fact that they were relations, or such very old friends that it was impossible to exclude them. Whether or not they were convinced by the explanations given by the Duc de Guermantes about the Duchesse's singular phobia toward the company of women, the great men duly transmitted them to their wives. Some of these wives were of the opinion that the phobia was nothing more than an excuse to conceal her jealousy, because the Duchesse wanted to reign unrivaled over a court of worshippers. Others, who were even more simple-minded, thought that perhaps the Duchesse was so peculiar, or even had so scandalous a past, that women were loath to visit her, and that what she called caprice was in fact some failing she could do nothing to change. The more astute among them, hearing their husbands recount marvels about the Duchesse's wit, came to the conclusion that she must be so superior to other women that she was bored in their company, because they were incapable of intelligent conversation. And it was true that the Duchesse was bored by other women, unless their princely status aroused her particular interest. But the excluded wives were wrong to imagine that she chose to entertain men only in order to discuss literature, science, and philosophy with them. For she never spoke about such subjects, at least not in the company of great intellectuals. If, by virtue of the same sort of family tradition that makes the daughters of great soldiers preserve a respect for military matters even when they are at their most frivolous, she felt, as the granddaughter of women who had been on good terms with Thiers, Mérimée, and Augier,[49] that there must always be a place in her salon for men of intellect, she had at the same time retained, from the manner, both condescending and familiar, in which those famous men had been received at Guermantes, the habit of treating men of talent as family friends whose talent does not blind one to them, to whom one does not speak of their work, and who would be bored if one did. Again, the type of mind that is characteristic of Mérimée and Meilhac and Halévy, and was also hers, led her, in contrast to the verbal sentimentality of an earlier generation, to adopt a style of conversation that rejects everything to do with grandiloquence and the expression of lofty feeling, so that when she was with a musician or a poet she made it seem somehow stylish to talk only of the food they were eating or the card game that was to follow. For a stranger not really familiar with her manner, this abstention had a disturbing, even mystifying effect. If Mme de Guermantes asked him whether he would like to be invited with some famous poet, he would arrive at the appointed hour, devoured by curiosity. The Duchesse would talk to the poet about the weather. They would then pass to the table. "Do you like eggs cooked in this way?" she would ask the poet. If he approved—and it was an approval she shared, for everything in her house seemed exquisite to her, even the dreadful cider she had sent from Guermantes—"Give Monsieur some more eggs," she would tell the butler, while the anxious third party sat waiting for what surely must have been what she and the poet had met to discuss, since they had squeezed in this meeting with great difficulty before the latter's departure from Paris. But the meal would go on, the courses cleared away one after another, providing Mme de Guermantes with plentiful opportunities for witty humor or telling anecdotes. Meanwhile, the poet would go on eating without either the Duc or the Duchesse showing any sign of remembering that he was a poet. Eventually the lunch would be over and farewells exchanged, without a word having been said about poetry, which they nevertheless all admired, but to which, out of a reserve similar to that of which Swann had given me a foretaste, no one referred. The reserve was simply a matter of good form. But to an outsider, if he gave any thought to it, there was something deeply depressing about it, and these meals with the Guermantes would then seem rather like the hours diffident lovers often spend together discussing trivialities until it is time to part, without—whether from shyness, modesty, or awkwardness—allowing the great secret they would have been happier to disclose ever to pass from their hearts to their lips. Yet it must be said that this silence on deep matters that one was always waiting in vain to hear addressed, even if it could be seen as characteristic of the Duchesse, was not an unbending rule with her. Mme de Guermantes had spent her girlhood in a somewhat different environment, equally aristocratic, but less glittering and above all less futile than her present one, and highly cultured. This meant that her present frivolity was grounded in a sort of firmer bedrock, an invisible nourishment to which the Duchesse had recourse (very rarely, in fact, for she loathed pedantry) when she needed a quotation from Victor Hugo or Lamartine; the quotation was always perfectly to the point, uttered with a look of conviction from her lovely eyes, and it never failed to surprise and charm people. On occasion, unassumingly and with pertinent directness, she would even give some dramatist and Academician a piece of shrewd advice, make him modify an element of his plot or change the ending of his play.

If, in the salon of Mme de Villeparisis, as in the Combray church on the day of Mlle Percepied's wedding, I had difficulty rediscovering in the lovely, all-too-human face of Mme de Guermantes the enigma of her name, I thought at least that, when she spoke, her conversation would be profound and mysterious, strange as a medieval tapestry or a Gothic window. For me to avoid being disappointed by the words I heard uttered by someone who called herself Mme de Guermantes, even if I had not been in love with her, those words would have had to be more than subtle, beautiful, and profound, they would have had to reflect the amaranth coloring of the last syllable of her name, the color that, since I first set eyes upon her, I had been amazed not to find in her person and had then relegated to her mind. True, I had heard Mme de Villeparisis and Saint-Loup, people of quite ordinary intelligence, pronounce the name Guermantes unguardedly, simply as the name of someone who was coming to visit them or with whom they were to dine, without seeming to feel that the name carried with it wooded slopes of yellowing leaves and a whole mysterious corner of the country. But this must have been an affectation on their part, as when classical poets give us no warning of the profound intention they nevertheless had, an affectation I tried hard to imitate by saying as naturally as I could "the Duchesse de Guermantes," as though it were a name like any other. Besides, other people asserted that she was a very intelligent woman, a witty conversationalist, living in a small coterie of highly interesting people: words that came to collude with my dream. For, when they spoke of a coterie of intelligent people, of witty exchange, it was in no way intelligence as I knew it that I imagined, not even the intelligence of the greatest minds; it was not at all people like Bergotte that I imagined in this coterie. No, intelligence in this context meant for me an ineffable, golden faculty, impregnated with the cool of the forest. And had she made the most intelligent remarks (in the sense I gave the word when it was applied to philosophers or critics), Mme de Guermantes would perhaps have dashed my expectation of so special a faculty even more keenly than if, in the course of a casual conversation, she had confined herself to talking about cooking recipes or the furnishings of a country house, to listing the names of her neighbors or relatives, in an attempt to give me a picture of her life.

"I thought Basin would be here. He was meaning to come and see you," said Mme de Guermantes to her aunt.

"I haven't seen your husband for several days," replied Mme de Villeparisis in a hurt and angry voice. "Indeed, I haven't seen him—or perhaps I have once—since that charming joke of having himself announced as the Queen of Sweden."

By way of a smile, Mme de Guermantes pinched up the corners of her lips as though she were biting her veil.

"We had dinner with her last night at Blanche Leroi's. You wouldn't have recognized her. She's put on an enormous amount of weight. I'm sure she must be ill."

"I was just telling these gentlemen that you thought she looked like a frog."

Mme de Guermantes made some kind of hoarse sound which indicated that she was laughing for form's sake.

"I don't remember making such a charming comparison, but if I likened her to a frog, then she's now a frog that has managed to swell to the size of an ox.⁵⁰ But that's not very well put, because all the swelling is concentrated on her stomach. So let's call her a frog in an interesting condition."

"Oh. I do find the comparison funny," said Mme de Villeparisis, secretly proud that her guests should be sampling her niece's wit.

"It is purely *arbitrary*, all the same," replied Mme de Guermantes, ironically emphasizing her choice of adjective as Swann would have done, "for I have to say that I've never seen a frog about to give birth. Be that as it may, the frog in question has no need of a king. I've never seen her so frisky as she's been since her husband died, and she's coming to dine with us one day next week. I said I'd let you know, just in case."

Mme de Villeparisis let out something like a muffled groan and said:

"I know she was dining the night before last at Mme de Mecklenburg's. Hannibal de Bréauté was there. He came and told me about it. I have to say, his account was quite amusing."

"There was someone there who is far wittier than Babal," said Mme de Guermantes, who, close friend though she was of M. de Bréauté-Consalvi's, felt the need to advertise the fact by using this pet name. "I mean M. Bergotte."

It had never occurred to me that Bergotte could be regarded as witty; what is more, I thought of him as one of the world's intellects, by which I mean infinitely removed from the mysterious realm I had glimpsed beneath the purple hangings of a theater box in which M. de Bréauté had been making the Duchesse laugh and holding with her, in the language of the gods, that unimaginable thing: a conversation between people of the Faubourg Saint-Germain. I was distressed to see the balance upset and Bergotte ranking above M. de Bréauté. But above all I was devastated to think that I had avoided Bergotte on the evening of *Phèdre*, that I had not gone to speak with him, when I heard Mme de Guermantes, in whom one could always, as in the turn of a mental tide, see the flow of curiosity about famous intellectuals sweep past the ebb of her aristocratic snobbery, go on to say to Mme de Villeparisis:

"He's the one person I would really like to know. It would be such a pleasure."

With Bergotte at my side—and his presence would have been easy to secure, had I not imagined that it would give Mme de Guermantes a bad impression of me—I would no doubt have ended up being invited to join her in her box and asked to bring the great writer along to lunch one day.

"I gather he behaved rather badly. He was presented to M. de Cobourg and didn't address a word to him," Mme de Guermantes continued, stressing this peculiar fact as she might have recounted that a Chinese had blown his nose on a piece of paper. "He never once called him 'Your Highness,'" she added, apparently amused at this detail, as significant to her as the refusal of a Protestant, in the course of an audience with the Pope, to go down on his knees before His Holiness.

Although she stressed these peculiarities of Bergotte's, she did not appear to find them reprehensible, but seemed, rather, to find merit in them, though quite why, she would have found it hard to say. Despite her odd way of appreciating Bergotte's eccentricity, the fact that, greatly to the surprise of many people, Mme de Guermantes found Bergotte wittier than M. de Bréauté, was to strike me later as not entirely negligible. It so happens that such subversive judgments, infrequent but—contrary to expectation—right, are made in the world of society by those rare people who are superior to the rest. And they provide the first rough outlines for the hierarchy of values as the next generation will establish it, instead of holding on eternally to the old.

The Comte d'Argencourt, the chargé d'affaires at the Belgian Embassy and a second cousin by marriage of Mme de Villeparisis, came limping into the room, followed shortly after by two young men, the Baron de Guermantes and His Highness the Duc de Châtellerault, whom Mme de Guermantes greeted with a "Good evening, my dear Châtellerault"; this was uttered in an abstracted manner and without moving from her pouffe, for she was a great friend of the young man's mother, and so, since his childhood, he had had the deepest respect for her. Tall, slim, with golden hair and skin, utterly Guermantes in type, these two young men seemed to condense in their persons the light of the spring evening, which was flooding the large drawing room. Following a fashionable quirk of the time, they set their top hats on the floor beside them. The Fronde historian saw this as a sign of embarrassment, as if they were peasants entering the mayor's chambers without knowing what to do with their hats. Feeling that he ought out of charity to come to the rescue of what he saw as their awkwardness and diffidence, he protested: "No, no, don't leave them on the floor, they'll be trodden on."

A glance from the Baron de Guermantes, tilting the plane of his pupils, shot from them a sudden flash of unadulterated, piercing blue which froze the well-intentioned historian.

"What is that gentleman's name?" the Baron asked me (Mme de Villeparisis had just introduced us).

"M. Pierre," I whispered.

"Pierre what?"

"Pierre is his surname. He's a highly rated historian."

"Really? Is that so?"

"No, it's a new fashion with these gentlemen to put their hats on the floor," Mme de Villeparisis explained. "I'm like you, I can't get used to it. But it's better than my nephew Robert, who always leaves his in the hall. When he comes in hatless, I tell him he looks like a clockmaker and ask him if he's come to wind the clocks."

"You were speaking earlier, Mme la Marquise, of M. Molé's hat. We shall soon be able, like Aristotle, to write a whole chapter on the subject," said the Fronde historian, now somewhat reassured by Mme de Villeparisis's remarks, but in so faint a voice that no one heard him except me.

"Our little Duchesse is really astonishing," said M. d'Argencourt, pointing to Mme de Guermantes talking to G—. "The minute there's a prominent man in the room, you'll always find him talking to her. That obviously has to be today's pundit there with her now. It can't always be M. de Borelli, or M. Schlumberger or M. d'Avenel. And if it's not, it's got to be M. Pierre Loti or M. Edmond Rostand.[51] Yesterday evening, at the Doudeauvilles'—she was looking splendid by the way, in her emerald tiara and a pink dress with a long train—she had M. Deschanel[52] on one side and the German ambassador on the other. She was proving their equal in a discussion about China. Lesser minds, at a respectful distance where they couldn't hear the conversation, were wondering whether there wasn't going to be a war. She really was like a queen enthralling the circle around her."

People had gathered around Mme de Villeparisis to watch her paint.

"Those flowers are a really celestial pink," said Legrandin, "or, rather, sky-pink. Sky-pink does exist, you know, like sky-blue. But," he added in a murmur, in the hope that only the Marquise would hear, "I think I am even more in favor of the silkiness, the living, rosy tints of your way of painting them. Ah, you leave those overdetailed, lifeless plant depictions of Pisanello and van Huysum[53] far behind."

An artist, however ordinary, is always ready to be set above his rivals, but does try to ensure that they get the appreciation they deserve.

"Your impression of them stems from the fact that they painted flowers of their time that are no longer familiar to us, but they did it with enormous skill."

"Ah, flowers of their time!" exclaimed Legrandin. "What an ingenious idea!"

"I see you're painting some lovely cherry blossoms . . . or are they mayflowers?" said the Fronde historian, in some doubt about which flower, but with a note of confidence in his voice, now that the business of the hats was beginning to fade from his mind.

"No, they're apple blossoms," said the Duchesse de Guermantes, addressing her aunt.

"Ah, I can see you're a good countrywoman like me. You know your flowers."

"Why, yes, of course they are! But I thought the apple-blossom season was already over," hazarded the Fronde historian, to cover his blunder.

"Quite the contrary, in fact. The trees aren't in bloom yet. It will take another fortnight, even three weeks," said the archivist, who had some slight connection with the management of Mme de Villeparisis's estates and was better informed on country matters.

"Yes, and even around Paris they are very early," said the Duchesse. "In Normandy, you know, at his father's place," she added, pointing to the Duc de Châtellerault, "there are some magnificent apple trees near the sea, like a Japanese screen. They never turn really pink until after the twentieth of May."

"I never get to see them," said the young Duc. "Can you believe it, they give me hay fever."

"Hay fever? I haven't heard of that before," said the historian.

"It's the fashionable complaint at the moment," said the archivist.

"It all depends—you're unlikely to get it if it's a good year for apples. You know what they say in Normandy, 'when it's a good year for apples,' " said M. d'Argencourt, who, not being French, was always trying to behave like a Parisian.

"You're quite right," Mme de Villeparisis replied to her niece, "these blossoms are from the south. They were sent by a florist who asked me to accept them as a present. You're surprised, M. Vallenères," she said, turning to the archivist, "that a florist should send me branches of apple blossom? I may be an old woman, but I do still have a few friends in the world," she added with a smile that many people might have taken as a sign of her simplicity, though it seemed to me that it arose from the fact that she found it titillating to pride herself on friendship with a mere florist when she had such grand connections.

Bloch got up and came across in his turn to admire the flowers that Mme de Villeparisis was painting.

"Never mind, Marquise," said the historian, sitting down again, "even if we were to have another of those revolutions that have stained so much of our history with blood—and, heaven help us, these days one can never tell—" he added, looking circumspectly around the room, as if to make sure that there were no "heretics" in the company, though he was sure that there were not, "with a talent like yours and the five languages you speak, no harm could ever come to you." The Fronde historian was feeling somewhat at ease, his insomnia forgotten. But he suddenly remembered that he had not slept for six days, at which juncture a deep weariness, mentally induced, took hold of his legs and bowed his shoulders, while his distressed face drooped like an old man's.

Bloch was anxious to express his admiration with some suitable gesture, but managed only to knock over the vase containing the spray of blossom with his elbow, and all the water was spilled on the carpet.

"You really have a magic touch," the historian said to the Marquise, turning his back as he spoke, and not noticing Bloch's clumsy gaffe.

But Bloch thought the remark had been addressed to himself, and, to cover his shame, retorted insolently, "There's not the least cause for alarm. The water didn't touch me."

Mme de Villeparisis rang, and a footman appeared to wipe the carpet and pick up the pieces of glass. She invited the two young men to an afternoon party she was giving, and also Mme de Guermantes, whom she instructed as follows:

"Don't forget to tell Gisèle and Berthe"—the Duchesse d'Auberjon and the Duchesse de Portefin—"to be there a little before two o'clock so that they can help me," as she might have instructed hired waiters to come early and do the fruit arrangements.

She behaved toward her princely relatives, as she behaved toward

M. de Norpois, with none of the tokens of affability she showed to the historian, Cottard, Bloch, and me, and seemed to regard them merely as useful fodder for our curiosity. This was because she knew that she need not put herself out for people who regarded her not as a more or less brilliant woman, but as the sister of their father or uncle, a touchy woman who required careful handling. It would have been pointless for her to try to shine in their presence; there was no way of deceiving them about the strength or weakness of her social position, for they knew her whole story all too well and respected her illustrious origins. But, above all, she had come to regard them as dead stock which would never bear fruit again; they would never introduce her to their new friends or share their pleasures with her. All they could give her was their presence or the possibility of speaking about them at her five o'clock receptions, as she did later on in the pages of her memoirs, for which these receptions were only a sort of rehearsal, a preliminary reading aloud of the material before a select audience. And the group of people that all these noble relations enabled her to interest, to dazzle, to en-slave, the Cottards, the Blochs, the well-known dramatists, the histori-ans of the Fronde, and so forth, these were the people who, for Mme de Villeparisis—in the absence of the section of fashionable society that did not go to her house—created movement, novelty, entertainment, and life; these were the people from whom she was able to derive social ad-vantages (which made it worth her while to let them meet the Duchesse de Guermantes every now and then, yet without ever getting to know her): dinners with distinguished men whose work had interested her, a light opera or a pantomime staged complete by its author in her salon, boxes for entertainments of special interest. Bloch got up to go. He had said aloud that the business of the broken vase did not matter in the least, but what he said under his breath was different, and more differ-ent still what he thought: "If people can't train their servants to put vases where they won't risk soaking or even injuring their guests, then they oughtn't to surround themselves with such luxuries," he muttered crossly. He was one of those touchy, high-strung people who cannot bear to have made a blunder, will not admit it to themselves, and whose whole day is ruined by it. He was in a black rage that was dissuading him from ever going into society again. Some distraction was crucial at that moment. Fortunately, Mme de Villeparisis was about to press him to stay. Either because she was aware of the views of her friends and the rising tide of anti-Semitism, or simply out of absentmindedness, she had not introduced him to anyone in the room. But he, with his relative lack of social experience, felt that it was the done thing to take his leave of them, out of politeness, but without warmth; he bowed his head several times, thrusting his bearded chin into his stiff collar, and eyed everyone there in turn through his pince-nez with cold dissatisfaction. But Mme de Villeparisis detained him; she still needed to discuss the little play that was to be performed in her house, and she did not want him to leave before she had given him the satisfaction of meeting M. de Norpois (whose failure to appear surprised her); this introduction to Norpois was in fact an unnecessary inducement, for Bloch had already made up his mind to persuade the two actresses he had mentioned to come and sing at the Marquise's for free, in the interest of boosting their careers at one of those receptions frequented by the elite of European society. He had even proposed, as an additional attraction, a tragic actress "with blue-green eyes, beautiful as Hera," who would recite lyrical prose with a feeling for "plastic beauty." But when she heard the actress's name, Mme de Villeparisis declined. It was the name of Saint-Loup's mistress.

She whispered in my ear: "I have better news. I think that the whole thing is on its last legs and that it won't be long before they break with each other. In spite of the officer who has played such an abominable part in the whole affair," she added. (For Robert's family were beginning to resent M. de Borodino with a vengeance; he had given Robert leave, at the hairdresser's entreaty, to go to Bruges, and they accused him of furthering a scandalous liaison.) "He's a very wicked man," said Mme de Villeparisis in that virtuous tone of voice common to all the Guermantes, even the most depraved. "Very, very wicked," she repeated, rolling her "r"s emphatically. It seemed to imply that she had no doubt that the man was present at all their orgies. But since her overriding quality was kindness, the Marquise's expression of frowning severity toward the dreadful captain, whose name she uttered with an ironical emphasis,

"The Prince de Borodino!," as a woman for whom the Empire carried no weight, melted into a gentle smile toward me, and a mechanical twitch of the eyelid indicating a vague complicity between us.

"I used to have a lot of time for de Saint-Loup-en-Bray," said Bloch, "dirty rascal that he is, because he's extremely well bred. Now I don't. But I do like well-bred people very much, they're so rare," he went on, without realizing, with his own distinctive lack of breeding, how offensive his words were. "I'll give you an example, a very striking one in my view, of his perfect breeding. I once met him with a young man just as he was about to leap into his wheelèd chariot, after he himself had buckled the splendid harness on two steeds nourished with oats and barley, who had no need of the flashing whip to urge them on. He introduced us, but I didn't catch the young man's name. In fact, you never catch people's names when they are introduced," he added with a laugh, this being one of his father's witty remarks. De Saint-Loup-en-Bray didn't stand on ceremony, made no fuss about the young man, seemed absolutely at ease. And by pure chance I found out a few days later that the young man was the son of Sir Rufus Israels!"

The end of this story sounded less shocking than its beginning, since it remained incomprehensible to everyone in the room. The fact was that Sir Rufus Israels, whom Bloch and his father regarded as an almost royal figure, one to be trembled at by the likes of Saint-Loup, was in the eyes of the Guermantes world merely a foreign upstart, socially tolerated, but not a man whose friendship was anything to boast about—quite the contrary!

"I found out," said Bloch, "from Sir Rufus Israels's representative, a friend of my father's and a quite remarkable man. An outstanding individual, in fact," he added with the assertive force and enthusiastic tone we bring only to convictions that are not our own. "But tell me," he asked me, lowering his voice, "how much money do you think Saint-Loup has? Not that it matters to me a hoot, you understand. I'm only asking from a Balzacian point of view. You don't happen to know what it's in, do you? French stocks? Foreign ones? Land, or what?"

I could give him no information whatsoever. Returning to his normal voice, Bloch asked very loudly if he might open the windows, and, without waiting for an answer, went to do so. Mme de Villeparisis said that it was out of the question because of her cold. "Oh, well, if it's bad for you!" said Bloch dispiritedly. "But it's like a hothouse in here!" And, breaking into a laugh, he cast his eyes about the room in an appeal for support against Mme de Villeparisis. He found none from these well-bred people. His blazing eyes, after failing to seduce the other guests, reverted in resignation to their previously grave expression; he acknowledged defeat with: "The temperature's at least twenty-two. Twenty-five even? I'm not surprised. I'm practically dripping all over. And, unlike the sage Antenor, son of the river Alpheus, I do not have the power to bathe my sweat in the paternal wave, then lay my body in a bath of polished marble and anoint myself with fragrant oils." And, with the need that people feel to outline for the benefit of others medical theories that might be suitably applied to their own state of health: "Well, if you think it's good for you! I really can't see it myself—quite the opposite, in fact. It's exactly what is giving you your cold."

Bloch had expressed delight at the idea of being introduced to M. de Norpois. He would like, he said, to get him to talk about the Dreyfus case.

"I find his way of thinking rather difficult to understand, and it would be stimulating to have an interview with such an important diplomat," he said with sarcasm, to avoid any suggestion that he might consider himself inferior to the ambassador.

Mme de Villeparisis was embarrassed that he had said this so loud but forgot her embarrassment when she saw that the archivist, whose Nationalist views kept her, so to speak, on a leash, was standing too far off to have overheard. But what offended her more was to hear Bloch, led on by the demon of his ill-breeding, which made him blind to the effect of what he said, asking her, with a laugh, as he mimicked his father's jesting manner:

"Haven't I read some learned work of his in which he gives a string of irrefutable arguments to prove that the Russo-Japanese War was bound to end in a Russian victory and a Japanese defeat? And isn't he getting a bit past it? I'm sure he's the one I saw taking aim at his chair before sliding his way over to it as if he were on casters."

"Most certainly not! Just wait a minute," said the Marquise, "I can't think what he can be doing."

She rang, and when the servant appeared, since she made no secret of the fact—indeed, liked to broadcast it—that her old friend spent most of his time in her house, she gave him an order:

"Go and tell M. de Norpois to come. He's sorting some papers in my study, and he said it would take twenty minutes. I've been waiting for an hour and three-quarters. He'll talk to you about the Dreyfus case or about anything you care to discuss," she said to Bloch in an offended voice. "He doesn't really approve of what's happening."

For M. de Norpois was not on good terms with the ministry of the time, and Mme de Villeparisis, although he had never taken the liberty of bringing government figures to her house (as a great lady of the aristocracy, she still remained aloof, outside and above the relations he was obliged to cultivate in his work), was kept informed by him of what was going on. Likewise, these politicians of the present regime would not have dared to ask M. de Norpois to introduce them to Mme de Villeparisis. But several of them had gone to see him at her country house when they needed his advice at points of crisis. They knew the address. They went to the house. They did not see the house's mistress. But at dinner she would say, "I hear they've been here bothering you. Are things any better?"

"You're not too pressed for time?" Mme de Villeparisis asked Bloch.

"Not at all. I was thinking of leaving because I'm not very well. In fact, I may well have to take a cure at Vichy for my gall bladder," he replied, articulating these words with wicked irony.

"Why, that's just where my great-nephew Châtellerault has to go. You ought to fix it up together. Is he still here? He's such a nice young man, you know," said Mme de Villeparisis, sincerely perhaps, thinking that two people she knew had no reason not to be friends with each other.

"Oh, I don't know that he would care for that, I don't . . . I hardly know him. He's over there," said Bloch, not knowing where to turn in his delight.

The butler must not have carried out the orders he had been given about M. de Norpois correctly. For the diplomat, to give the impression that he had just come in from the street and had not yet seen his hostess, had picked up the first hat he saw in the vestibule and came up to kiss Mme de Villeparisis's hand with much ado, inquiring after her health as attentively as people do after a long separation. He had no idea that the Marquise had completely undermined the plausibility of this charade prior to his appearance, and she now put an end to it by leading M. de Norpois and Bloch into an adjoining room. Bloch, who had noticed all the polite attention that was being paid to a man he did not yet know to be M. de Norpois, and the formal, gracious, deep bows with which the ambassador responded, was feeling inferior to all this ceremonial and vexed to think that it would never be addressed to him; as a way of appearing to be at ease, he had said to me, "Who is that old fool?" It was also possible that all this deference to M. de Norpois had really shocked the better part of Bloch's nature, the freer and more spontaneous manner of the modern generation, and that he was partly sincere in scoffing at it. Be that as it may, his ridicule turned to delight the moment he himself became the object of such attention.

"M. l'Ambassadeur," said Mme de Villeparisis, "I should like you to meet this gentleman. M. Bloch, M. le Marquis de Norpois." She always made a point, despite the way she bullied M. de Norpois, of addressing him as "M. l'Ambassadeur" as a point of etiquette, out of an exaggerated respect for his position as ambassador, a respect the Marquis had inculcated in her, and also with the intention of treating one particular man with the less familiar, more ceremonious marks of respect that, in the salon of a distinguished woman, in contrast to the freedom with which she treats her other regular guests, mark out that man immediately as her lover.

M. de Norpois sank his blue gaze into his white beard, bent his tall body down deeply as if he were bowing before all the renowned and imposing resonances of the name Bloch, and murmured, "I'm honored," while his young interlocutor, moved, but feeling that the distinguished diplomat was going too far, hastened to correct him: "But no! On the contrary, it is I who am honored!" But this ceremony, which M. de Norpois, out of friendship for Mme de Villeparisis, repeated for the benefit of every unfamiliar face his old friend introduced to him, seemed to her to be insufficiently cordial for someone like Bloch, to whom she said:

"Now, just ask him anything you want to know. Take him aside if it suits you better. He'll be delighted to talk to you. Didn't you want to talk to him about the Dreyfus case?" she added, no more considering whether this would be agreeable to M. de Norpois than she would have thought of seeking the consent of the Duchesse de Montmorency's portrait before having it lighted up for the historian, or of the tea before she offered a cup of it to someone.

"You'll need to speak up," she said to Bloch, "he's a little deaf, but he'll tell you all you want to know. He knew Bismarck very well, and Cavour. It's true, is it not?" she said, raising her voice. "You knew Bismarck well."

"Are you busy writing something at the moment?" M. de Norpois asked me knowingly as he shook my hand warmly. I took advantage of this to relieve him of the hat he had felt obliged to bring with him as a sign of formality; I had just noticed that it was my own that he had picked up at random. "You once showed me a rather overwritten little piece, a bit too finicky in manner. I gave you my frank opinion: what you had done was not worth the paper it was written on. But perhaps you are preparing something for us now? You're very taken with Bergotte, if I remember rightly." "I won't hear a bad word against Bergotte!" exclaimed the Duchesse. "I don't deny his painterly gifts, Duchesse. Who would? He knows all about engraving and etching, even brushwork on a large scale, like M. Cherbuliez.54 But in my view there is a confusion about genre these days; a novelist's business is to weave a plot and inspire his readers' emotions, not to fuss about the detail of a frontispiece or a tailpiece in drypoint. I shall be seeing your father on Sunday at our good friend A.-J.'s," he added, turning to me.

I had hoped for a moment, when I saw him talking to Mme de Guermantes, that he would perhaps help me to get myself invited by her in the way he had not done in regard to Mme Swann. "Elstir is another of my great favorites," I said to him. "I gather that the Duchesse de Guermantes has some wonderful paintings by him, particularly that one of a bunch of radishes I saw at the exhibition. I'd love to see it again. What a masterpiece it is!" And, indeed, had I been a prominent figure and asked to say which was my favorite painting, I would have said Elstir's bunch of radishes.

"A masterpiece!" exclaimed M. de Norpois in astonished disapproval. "It can't even claim to be a picture. It's a mere sketch." (He was right.) "If you call an eye-catching trifle like that a masterpiece, what will you have to say about Hébert's *Virgin* or Dagnan-Bouveret?"⁵⁵

"I heard you refusing to receive Robert's lady friend," said Mme de Guermantes to her aunt, after Bloch had taken the ambassador aside. "I don't think you'll be missing much. A perfect horror, you know. Not an ounce of talent, and grotesque to look at."

"Are you telling us that you know her, Duchesse?" said M. d'Argencourt.

"Indeed I am. Haven't you heard that she performed at my house before anyone else's? Not that that's anything to be proud of," replied the Duchesse with a laugh, happy nonetheless, since the actress was the subject of conversation, to let it be known that she had been the first to sample her absurdities. "Oh well, I suppose I'd better be going," she added, without moving.

She had just seen her husband enter the room, and her last words were an allusion to the comic aspect of their appearing to be paying a call together like a newly married couple, and not to the often strained relations that existed between her and this strapping pleasure-seeker, who was getting on in years, but who still led the life of a young bachelor. Scanning the considerable crowd of people gathered around the tea table with the affable, roguish gaze—slightly dazzled by the rays of the setting sun—of the small round pupils lodged right in the center of his eyes, like the bull's-eye targets which, in his expertise as a marksman, he never failed to hit to perfection, the Duc picked his way slowly through the room with caution and wonderment, as though, intimidated by such a brilliant gathering, he was afraid of treading on ladies' skirts and interrupting conversations. The fixed smile on his face, suggestive of a slightly tipsy Good King Wenceslas, and the half-open hand floating like a shark's fin at his side, which he allowed to be clasped indiscriminately by his old friends and by the strangers who were introduced to him, enabled him, without having to make a single movement or to interrupt the genial leisureliness of his royal progress, to respond more than adequately to the pressing attentions of all by simply murmuring, "Evening, old boy; evening, my dear fellow; delighted, M. Bloch; evening, Argencourt"; and when he got to me and heard my name, I was the most favored of all: "Good evening, my young neighbor, is your father well? Such an admirable man!" He became effusive only for Mme de Villeparisis, who greeted him with a nod of the head, taking her hand from the pocket of her little apron.

As a man who was formidably wealthy in a world where people were becoming less so, and having long accustomed himself to the idea of his enormous fortune, he had the vanity both of the great nobleman and of the man of means, the refined breeding of the former only just managing to hold in check the smug assurance of the latter. But it was also possible to see that his success with women, which caused such grief to his wife, was not due simply to his name and his fortune, for he was still a very handsome man with a profile that retained the purity, the firmness of outline of a Greek god's.

"So she actually performed at your house?" M. d'Argencourt asked the Duchesse.

"Well, how can I put it? She came to recite with a bunch of lilies in her hand, and more lilies awn 'er dress." (Mme de Guermantes, like Mme de Villeparisis, affected an extremely rustic pronunciation for certain words but, unlike her aunt, she never rolled her "r"s.)

Before M. de Norpois, forced to comply with his hostess's wishes, took Bloch into the small recess where they could talk together, I went up to the old diplomat for a moment and put in a word about my father's academic chair. His first reaction was to try to postpone the conversation to some future occasion. I made the point that I would soon be leaving for Balbec. "What? Off to Balbec again? What a globetrotter you are!" He then gave me his attention. At the name Leroy-Beaulieu, M. de Norpois shot me a suspicious look. It crossed my mind that he had said something disparaging about my father to M. Leroy-Beaulieu and feared that the economist had repeated it to him. All at once, he seemed to be stirred by a genuine affection for my father. And after one of those lulls in speech out of which a word suddenly explodes, apparently in spite of the speaker, whose irresistible conviction overrides his stuttering efforts at silence: "No, no," he said to me with some feeling, "your father *must not* stand. In his own interest he must not, for his own sake, out of respect for his merits, which are great, and would be compromised by such a perilous undertaking. He is worth more than that. Were he elected, he would have everything to lose and nothing to gain. He is not an orator, thank heaven. And that is the one thing that counts with my beloved colleagues, even if it means an endless rehash of the same thing. Your father has an important goal in life; he should march straight toward it and not beat about the bush, even the bushes of the groves of Academe, which are more thorny than flowery. Besides, he would not get many votes. The Academy likes to keep its postulants waiting before admitting them to its bosom. For the moment, there is nothing to be done. Later on, I can't say. But it has to be the society itself that comes to seek him out. It observes that *Farà da sé*[56] of our neighbors across the Alps with more fetishism than success. Leroy-Beaulieu spoke to me about it all in a way I found distasteful. I should have said at a guess that he was hand in glove with your father. . . . I made it plain to him, a little sharply perhaps, that, as a man accustomed to dealing with textiles and metals, he could not be expected to understand the part played by imponderables, as Bismarck used to say. What must be avoided at all costs is your father putting himself forward as a candidate: *Principiis obsta.*[57] His friends would find themselves in a delicate position if he presented them with a fait accompli. Listen," he said with a sudden frankness of manner, fixing his blue eyes upon me, "I am going to tell you something that will surprise you coming from me, such a devoted friend of your father's. Well, precisely because I am such a devoted friend—the two of us are inseparable, *Arcades ambo*[58]— precisely because I know what he can give to his country, the wreckage he can avoid by remaining at the helm, I would not vote for him, out of affection, high regard for him, and out of patriotism. And I also think I've given him to understand as much." (And here I fancied that I could see in his eyes the stern, Assyrian profile of Leroy-Beaulieu.) "So to

give him my vote now would be a sort of recantation on my part."
M. de Norpois very frequently treated his colleagues as fossils. Other
reasons apart, every member of a club or academy likes to attribute to
his fellow members the type of character most opposed to his own, less
for the benefit of being able to say, "Ah, if the matter only rested with
me!" than for the satisfaction of making whatever honor he himself has
received seem harder to obtain and thus more flattering. "I must tell
you," he concluded, "that, in the best interests of you all, I should prefer to see your father triumphantly elected in ten or fifteen years."
Words that I took as being dictated, if not by jealousy, then by a total
lack of willingness to oblige, and which were later, in the actual event,
to acquire a different meaning.

"Have you ever thought of giving the Institut a paper on the price
of bread during the Fronde?" the historian of the movement timidly
inquired of M. de Norpois. "It would be highly successful, I think"–
which meant "bolster my own reputation enormously." He added this
while timorously risking a tender smile at the ambassador, which made
him raise his eyelids and disclose eyes as wide as the sky. I seemed to
have seen this look before, yet I had met the historian for the first time
today. It came to me suddenly: I had seen this same expression in the
eyes of a Brazilian doctor who claimed to be able to cure bouts of
breathlessness of the kind from which I suffered by means of ridiculous
inhalations of plant essences. In the hope that he would pay more attention to my case, I had told him that I knew Professor Cottard, and
he had replied, ostensibly speaking in Cottard's interest, "Were you to
tell him about this treatment of mine, it would provide him with material for the most sensational paper at the Academy of Medicine!" He
had not gone so far as to labor the point, but had gazed at me with the
same questioning look, timid, self-seeking, and urgent, that had just
startled me on the face of the Fronde historian. It is true that the two
men were not acquainted and had little or nothing in common, but
psychological laws, like physical laws, have a more or less general rele-
vance. And if the appropriate conditions are the same, the same expression lights up the eyes of different human animals, just as the same
morning sky lights up places that are remote from one another and

have no connection. I did not hear what the ambassador said in reply, because of the general hubbub of people who were making their way toward Mme de Villeparisis to see her painting.

"Do you know who we're talking about, Basin?" the Duchesse asked her husband.

"I can make a good guess," said the Duc. "I'm afraid she's not an actress of what we would call the great tradition."

"You can't imagine just how ridiculous it was," Mme de Guermantes continued, addressing herself to M. d'Argencourt.

"One might even call it burlesque," broke in M. de Guermantes, whose odd vocabulary allowed society people to declare that he was no fool and literary people to regard him as a complete imbecile.

"I really can't understand how Robert ever came to fall in love with her," the Duchesse went on. "Oh, I know one must never discuss that sort of thing!" she added, with the charming philosophical pout of a sentimentalist who had no illusions left. "I know that anybody can fall in love with anybody else. And," she added, for, if she still made fun of modern literature, it had still insinuated itself into her mind to a degree, possibly through newspaper popularization or though certain conversations she had had, "that is the beautiful thing about love, because it's what makes it so 'mysterious.' "

"Mysterious? Well, cousin, I have to admit that's a bit beyond me," said the Comte d'Argencourt.

"But it is, it's a very mysterious thing, love is," the Duchesse continued, with the sweet smile of a good-natured woman of the world, but also with the unshakable conviction of a Wagnerian assuring a friend that there is more than just noise in the *Walküre*. "And in the end, one never does know why somebody falls in love with somebody else. It may not be at all for the reasons we infer," she added with a smile, her words thus suddenly rejecting the idea she had just put forward. "After all, one never knows anything, really," she concluded with a look of weary skepticism. "So it's wiser, don't you think, never to discuss people's choices in love."

But immediately after she had laid down this principle, she ignored it by criticizing Saint-Loup's choice.

"All the same, I have to say I find it extraordinary that people can find attraction in a ridiculous person."

Hearing Saint-Loup's name mentioned, and gathering that he was in Paris, Bloch began to slander him so violently that everyone was appalled. He was beginning to nurture hatreds, and one felt he would stop at nothing to gratify them. After establishing the principle that he himself was a person of great moral integrity and that the sort of people who frequented La Boulie (a sporting club he took to be fashionable) deserved to do hard labor, he regarded any harm he could do them as commendable. He once reached the point of threatening to bring a lawsuit against one of his La Boulie friends. In the course of the trial he proposed to give false evidence that the defendant would be unable to discredit. In this way Bloch, who never in fact put his plan into action, thought he could drive his friend even further to despair and panic. What harm could there be in it, since the man he sought to harm in this way was a La Boulie man devoted only to fashion, and against people of that sort any weapon was justified, particularly one wielded by a saint such as Bloch himself?

"And yet what about Swann?" objected M. d'Argencourt, who had finally managed to grasp the point of his cousin's remarks and, impressed by how acute they were, was now combing his memory for examples of people falling in love with others whom he himself would not have found attractive.

"Oh, but things were quite different in Swann's case," the Duchesse protested. "It was extraordinary, I know, because she was something of an idiot, but she was never ridiculous, and at one time she was pretty."

"Pooh-pooh!" muttered Mme de Villeparisis.

"You didn't think so? I did. She had some charming features, very fine eyes, lovely hair, and she dressed wonderfully. She still does. She's become loathsome, I agree, but she was a ravishing woman in her time. Not that I was any less sorry when Charles married her, because it was so unnecessary." The Duchesse was not aware of having said anything remarkable, but since M. d'Argencourt began to laugh she repeated her last phrase—either because she found it amusing or because she found it nice of him to laugh—and turned a caressing gaze in his direction, to add soft enchantment to that of her wit. She went on: "It wasn't worth the trouble, was it? Still, she was not without charm, and I can quite understand why people might fall for her, whereas Robert's lady ... Well, let me tell you, you'd just die laughing. Oh, I know somebody's going to quote that thing of Augier's at me—'Does the bottle matter, if it gets one drunk?'59 Well, Robert may have got drunk all right, but he hasn't shown much taste in his choice of bottle! The first thing she wanted me to do, can you believe, was to rig up a staircase bang in the middle of my drawing room. A trifling inconvenience, wouldn't you say! Then she announced that she was going to lie flat on her stomach on the steps. And if you could have heard the thing she recited! I can only remember one scene, but I'm sure nobody could imagine anything like it. It was called *The Seven Princesses*."60

"*Seven* of them! Dear me, what a snob she must be!" cried M. d'Argencourt. "But, just a minute, I know the whole thing. The author sent a copy to the King, who couldn't follow a word of it and asked me to explain it to him."

"It's not something by Sar Péladan,61 by any chance?" asked the Fronde historian, in an attempt to convey that he was intimately in touch with the latest literary developments, but so softly that his question went unnoticed.

"So you know *The Seven Princesses*, then?" the Duchesse replied to M. d'Argencourt. "My congratulations! I only know one myself, and one's quite enough. I have no wish to make the acquaintance of the six others. Especially if they're anything like the one I've seen!"

"What a bird-brained woman!" I thought to myself, still smarting from the icy greeting she had given me. I found a sort of grim satisfaction in this evidence of her total incomprehension of Maeterlinck. "So this is the woman I walk miles to see every morning, and out of the kindness of my heart! Well, now it's my turn to turn the cold shoulder." This is what I said to myself, but my words had nothing to do with what I really thought; they were purely conversational, like the words we utter to ourselves when we are too agitated to remain on our own and feel the need, in the absence of a listener, to talk to ourselves idly, as we would to a stranger.

"I can't tell you what it was like," the Duchesse continued. "I thought I'd die laughing. Most people did, rather too much, and young Madame was not at all pleased. Robert has never really forgiven me. But I can't honestly say I'm sorry, because if the whole thing had been a success Madame would perhaps have returned, and I don't think Marie-Aynard would have been exactly enchanted."

Marie-Aynard was the name the family gave to Robert's mother, Mme de Marsantes, the widow of Aynard de Saint-Loup, to distinguish her from her cousin the Princesse de Guermantes-Bavière, also a Marie, to whose first name her nephews, cousins, and brothers-in-law added, to avoid confusion, either the first name of her husband or another of her own, which made her Marie-Gilbert or Marie-Hedwige.

"To begin with, there was a sort of rehearsal the night before, a quite amazing business!" Mme de Guermantes went on ironically. "Can you imagine, she uttered a sentence—no, not even a sentence, a quarter of one—then she stopped; and for the next five minutes—I'm not exaggerating—she stood there without a word."

"Oh dear, oh dear!" exclaimed M. d'Argencourt.

"I took the liberty of suggesting to her, as politely as possible, that this might take people somewhat aback. And she said—I quote verbatim—'One ought always to recite a thing as if one were in the process of composing it oneself.' What a monumental thing to say, when you come to think of it!"

"But I understood she was quite good at reciting poetry," said one of the two young men.

"She hasn't the least idea what poetry is," replied Mme de Guermantes. "I didn't need to listen to her to tell that. It was quite enough to see her arriving with those lilies! I knew at once that she had no talent when I saw those lilies!"

Everybody laughed.

"Aunt, I do hope my little joke the other day about the Queen of Sweden didn't offend you. I've come to beg forgiveness."

"No, I'm not offended. You're even allowed to have some tea, if you're hungry."

"Come along, M. Vallenères, you're the daughter of the house," said Mme de Villeparisis to the archivist, repeating a long-established joke.

M. de Guermantes sat up in the armchair he had sunk into, his hat on the carpet by his side, and examined with satisfaction the plate of petits fours he was offered.

"Why, certainly, now that I'm beginning to feel at home in this distinguished company. I'll have a sponge cake, they look excellent."

"The gentleman makes an admirable daughter of the house," said M. d'Argencourt, imitating Mme de Villeparisis and pursuing her little joke.

The archivist handed the plate of cakes to the Fronde historian.

"You perform your functions admirably," said the latter timidly, in an attempt to win the sympathy of the gathering.

And he cast a covert glance of complicity at those who had already pursued the joke.

"Tell me, dear Aunt," M. de Guermantes asked Mme de Villeparisis, "who was that rather impressive gentleman who was leaving as I came in? I must know him, because he gave me a great bow, but I couldn't place him. You know I have no memory for names. It's a great nuisance," he said complacently.

"M. Legrandin."

"Oh, but Oriane has a cousin whose mother, if I'm not mistaken, was born a Grandin. Yes indeed, a Grandin de l'Éprevier."

"No," replied Mme de Villeparisis, "there's no connection. These are plain Grandins. Grandins of nothing at all. But they'd like nothing better than to be Grandins of anything you'd care to name. This one has a sister named Mme de Cambremer."

"Come now, Basin, you know quite well who my aunt means," exclaimed the Duchesse indignantly. "He's the brother of that great ruminant you took it into your head to get to call on me the other day. She stayed a whole hour, and I thought I'd go mad. But I'd begun by thinking that she was the one who was mad when I saw a complete stranger come trundling into the room looking just like a cow."

"Listen, Oriane, she asked me what day you were at home, and I couldn't very well be rude to her. And, anyway, you're exaggerating: she's not in the least like a cow," he added dolefully, but taking care to smile furtively at his audience.

He knew that his wife's witty eloquence needed the stimulus of contradiction, the contradiction of common sense that protests, for instance, that a woman cannot be mistaken for a cow (and it was this that provoked Mme de Guermantes to exploit her initial image and produce some of her best witticisms). The Duc would be there with this literal-minded approach secretly to ensure the success of her witticisms, like the unacknowledged partner of a three-card trickster in a railway compartment.

"You're right, she doesn't look like a cow. She looks like a whole herd of them," exclaimed Mme de Guermantes. "Believe me, I was hard put to it to know what to do when I saw those cows come lumbering into my drawing room in a hat asking me how I was. I had half a mind to say: 'Please, cows, there must be some mistake. How can we possibly be acquainted? You're a herd of cows.' But after racking my brains I came to the conclusion that your Cambremer woman was the Infanta Dorothea. She said she was coming to see me one day and she looks rather *bovine* herself. So I was about to address her as 'Your Royal Highness' and use the third person to a herd of cows. And she's got a girth on her like the Queen of Sweden. In fact, this mass attack had been prepared by long-range artillery fire. She knows all the rules of war. I don't know how long I was bombarded with calling cards. They were everywhere, on tables, on chairs, like publicity leaflets. I couldn't imagine what such advertisement was for. The house was drowned in 'Marquis and Marquise de Cambremer' with an address I've forgotten, but you can be sure I shall never use it."

"But it's very flattering to be taken for a queen," said the Fronde historian.

"My dear sir, kings and queens don't add up to much these days!" said M. de Guermantes, wanting to be thought broad-minded and modern, but also attempting not to be seen attaching any importance to his own royal connections, which he valued immensely.

Bloch and M. de Norpois had left their seats and were now standing within earshot.

"So, monsieur," said Mme de Villeparisis, "have you been talking to him about the Dreyfus case?"

M. de Norpois raised his eyes to the ceiling, but with a smile, as though he were inviting heaven to witness the extravagant whims imposed upon him by his Dulcinea. Nevertheless, he spoke to Bloch very graciously about the dreadful, even fatal period through which France was passing. Since this presumably meant that M. de Norpois (to whom Bloch had confessed his belief in Dreyfus's innocence) was a convinced anti-Dreyfusard, the ambassador's genial manner, his way of suggesting that his interlocutor was in the right, of never doubting that they were both of the same opinion, of joining forces with him to denigrate the government, flattered Bloch's vanity and aroused his curiosity. What were the important points that M. de Norpois left unspecified, but on which he seemed implicitly to be saying that he and Bloch were in agreement? And what opinion did he hold of the case that the two of them could share? Bloch was all the more astonished at the mysterious sympathy that seemed to exist between the two of them in that it was not confined to politics, Mme de Villeparisis having spoken at some length to M. de Norpois about Bloch's literary activity.

"You don't belong to your age," the former ambassador told him, "and I congratulate you upon the fact. You don't belong to an age in which disinterested study no longer exists, in which the public is offered nothing but obscenity or inept rubbish. Efforts such as yours ought to be encouraged. They would be, with the right government."

Bloch was flattered to think of himself as swimming alone amid universal shipwreck. But once again he would have liked more details, more about the inept rubbish mentioned by M. de Norpois. Bloch had the feeling that he was working along the same lines as a good many others; he had never thought of himself as being so exceptional. He reverted to the Dreyfus case, but did not manage to disentangle M. de Norpois's real views. He tried to get him to talk about the officers whose names were constantly appearing in the newspapers at that time; they aroused more curiosity than the politicians involved in the case, because, unlike the former, they were not already established figures; in their special uniform, emerging from the depths of an unfamiliar life and a religiously guarded silence, they had only just come forward to speak, like Lohengrin stepping onto land from his swan-drawn bark.[62] Thanks to a Nationalist lawyer he knew, Bloch had been able to attend several hearings of the Zola trial.[63] He would arrive there in the morning and stay all day, with a supply of sandwiches and a flask of coffee, as though at a day-long examination session; this change of routine stimulated a nervous excitement which was exacerbated by the coffee and the turbulence of the trial, and he would come away in such a passionate state about the day's proceedings that when he returned home in the evening he longed to immerse himself again in the thrill of it all; so he would hurry out to a restaurant frequented by both parties in search of friends with whom he could rehearse the day's events for hours on end and compensate, by a supper ordered in an imperious tone that gave him the illusion of power, for the hunger and exhaustion of a day begun so early and spent with no lunch. Perpetually hovering between the two planes of experience and imagination, the human mind seeks to sound out the ideal life of the people it knows and to know the people whose life it has had to imagine. To Bloch's questions M. de Norpois replied:

"There are two officers involved in the present case whom I once heard mentioned by a man whose judgment inspired me with the greatest confidence. I mean M. de Miribel.[64] He had a high opinion of them both. They are Lieutenant Colonel Henry[65] and Lieutenant Colonel Picquart."

"But," exclaimed Bloch, "the divine Athena, daughter of Zeus, has put in the mind of each the opposite of what is in the mind of the other. And they are fighting each other like two lions. Colonel Picquart had a high position in the army, but his Moira[66] has led him to the wrong side. The sword of the Nationalists will carve his tender flesh and serve it up as food for beasts of prey and birds that feed on the fat of dead men."

M. de Norpois made no reply.

"What are those two waffling about over there?" M. de Guermantes asked Mme de Villeparisis, pointing to M. de Norpois and Bloch.

"The Dreyfus case."

"Damn! You're right. By the way, do you know who is a rabid supporter of Dreyfus? I give you a thousand guesses. My nephew Robert! When the Jockey Club heard of the stand he was taking, they were really up in arms. There was a regular outcry, I can tell you. And he's coming up for election next week. . . ."

"Of course," the Duchesse broke in, "if they're all like Gilbert, who's always maintained that all Jews ought to be sent back to Jerusalem . . ."

"Ah, then, the Prince de Guermantes is a man after my own heart," M. d'Argencourt interjected.

The Duc used his wife as a decoration, but he did not love her. His inflated self-importance made him hate to be interrupted, and he was in the habit of being brutally curt with her in private. Quivering with the twofold rage of a bad husband who is not to be spoken to and a gifted talker whose words go unnoticed, he stopped short and glared at the Duchesse in a manner that made everyone feel uncomfortable.

"What makes you think we want to hear about Gilbert and Jerusalem?" he said at last. "That's got nothing to do with it. But," he went on in a gentler tone, "you'd be the first to admit that, if one of our family were to be refused membership in the Jockey—especially Robert, whose father was president for ten years—it would be an outrage. What do you expect, my dear? It's made them all stop in their tracks and take a good look around them. I don't blame them, either. Personally, I have no racial prejudice, you know that. That sort of thing is all very out of date to me, and I like to be thought of as moving with the times. But Goddamn it! With a name like 'the Marquis de Saint-Loup,' one isn't a Dreyfusard. And that's all there is to it."

M. de Guermantes uttered the words "with a name like 'the Marquis de Saint-Loup' " with particular emphasis. He was well aware that it was far more important to have a name like "the Duc de Guermantes." But if his self-esteem was apt, if anything, to exaggerate the superiority of his own title, in this case it was perhaps not so much the rules of good taste as the laws of the imagination that prompted him to draw no attention to it. Everyone sees in a brighter light what he sees at a distance, what he sees in others. For the general laws that govern the perspective of the imagination apply just as much to dukes as to other men. And not only the laws of imagination, but those of speech. Now, one or the other of two laws of speech might apply here. One of them demands that we should express ourselves like others in our mental category and not of our caste. By this token, M. de Guermantes might, in his choice of expression, even when he wished to talk about the nobility, be indebted to the humblest class of tradesmen, who would have said "with

a name like 'the Duc de Guermantes,' " whereas an educated man like
Swann or Legrandin would not have said it. A duke may write novels in
the language of a grocer, even about life in high society, without the
help of titles and pedigrees, and a plebeian may write things that
deserve to be called "aristocratic." So from what inferior person had
M. de Guermantes borrowed the expression "with a name like"? He
probably had no idea. But another law of speech is that, from time to
time, just as certain diseases appear, vanish, and are never heard of again,
there somehow arise (either spontaneously or by some accident, like the
one that brought into France that American weed the seeds of which,
caught in the wool of a traveling rug, fell on a railway embankment)
modes of expression that one hears in the same decade on the lips of
people who have in no way concerted their efforts to use them. So, just
as one year I heard Bloch speak about himself in the following terms,
"The most charming, brilliant, well-placed, and discerning people had
discovered that there was only one man whom they felt to be intelligent
and agreeable, whom they could not do without—namely, Bloch," and
heard the same formulation repeated by countless other young people
who did not know him and who simply replaced his name with their
own, so I was often to come across this "with a name like."

"If that's his attitude," the Duc went on, "what do you expect? It's
quite understandable."

"It does have its funny side," the Duchesse replied, "when you think
of his mother's ideas, the way she bores us to tears with her Patrie
Française,[67] morning, noon, and night."

"But it's not only his mother. You mustn't palm us off with that.
There's that dreadful bed-hopping young miss of his. She has more in-
fluence over him. *And* she just happens to be a compatriot of our
M. Dreyfus. She's infected Robert with her way of thinking."

"You may not have heard, M. le Duc, but there's a new word to describe that sort of attitude," said the archivist, who acted as secretary to
various antirevisionist committees. "It's 'mentality.' It means exactly the
same thing, but it's useful in that nobody knows what you're talking
about. It's the last word in sophistication—the 'latest thing,' as they say."

Meanwhile, having heard Bloch's name, he watched him question

M. de Norpois with a disquiet that itself aroused strong misgiving, but for other reasons, in the Marquise. Trembling before the archivist as she played the anti-Dreyfusard in his presence, she dreaded what he would say were he to discover that she had invited to her house a Jew who was more or less affiliated with the "Syndicate."[68]

"So that's the word, 'mentality,' " said the Duc. "I must make a note of it and keep it for the right moment." (This was literally true. The Duc had a little notebook filled with "quotations" that he would consult before dinner parties.) "I like 'mentality.' There are quite a few new words like that, which become fashionable but never last. I read recently that a writer was 'talentuous.' Whatever that's supposed to mean. I haven't seen the word since."

"But 'mentality' " is more widely used than 'talentuous,' " said the Fronde historian, anxious to be part of the conversation. "I'm on a committee at the Ministry of Education where I've heard it on several occasions, and also at my club, the Volney, and even at dinner at M. Émile Ollivier's."[69]

"As someone who does not have the honor of belonging to the Ministry of Education," the Duc replied with false humility but with a vanity so deep-seated that his lips could not refrain from a smile, nor his eyes from embracing his audience with expressions of sparkling glee, the ironical impact of which made the poor historian blush, "as someone who does not have the honor of belonging to the Ministry of Education," he repeated, reveling in the sound of his own voice, "or to the Volney Club—my only clubs are the Union and the Jockey—I don't believe you belong to the Jockey, monsieur?" he asked the historian, who, blushing deeper red, sensing the insult but not understanding it, began to tremble from head to foot, "—as someone who has not even been invited to dine with M. Émile Ollivier, I confess I haven't come across the word 'mentality.' I feel sure you're in the same position, too, Argencourt. . . . You know why they can't publicize the proofs of Dreyfus's guilt, don't you? Apparently it's because he's the lover of the war minister's wife, or so it's mooted."

"Oh! I thought it was the prime minister's wife," said M. d'Argencourt.

"I find you all equally deadly boring about the entire thing," said the Duchesse de Guermantes, who, in social terms, was always anxious to demonstrate that she did not allow herself to be led by anyone. "The case can't make any difference to me so far as the Jews are concerned, for the very good reason that I don't know any and I intend to remain in that state of blissful ignorance. But I do find it intolerable to have Marie-Aynard or Victurnienne thrusting a whole host of Durands and Dubois upon us, women we should otherwise never have known, just because they're supposed to be right-minded and don't use Jewish tradesmen, or have 'Death to Jews' written on their parasols. I went to see Marie-Aynard the day before yesterday. It used to be a pleasure. Now she entertains all the people one has spent one's life trying to avoid, with the excuse that they're anti-Dreyfusard, and there are others of whom you have no idea who they are."

"No, it's the wife of the war minister. At least, that's one of the rumors at court," continued the Duc, who favored turns of phrase that seemed to him old-fashioned. "Anyway, as everyone knows, I personally take just the opposite view as my cousin Gilbert. There's nothing of the feudal overlord about me. I'd be happy to be seen with a Negro if he was a friend of mine, and I wouldn't give two hoots what anyone thought. But all the same, you must agree with me that, with a name like 'Saint-Loup,' it's not done to fly in the face of public opinion. The public has more sense than Voltaire, and certainly more than my nephew. And one certainly doesn't indulge in—how shall I put it?—contortions of conscience a week before one's membership in a club is to be decided. It's a bit stiff! No, it's that little tart of his who's put ideas into his head. She's probably persuaded him that he would be classed as an 'intellectual.' An 'intellectual' is *the* catchword among those people. I've got a rather good pun from that quarter, but it's very wicked."

And, lowering his voice for the benefit of his wife and M. d'Argencourt, he told them about Mater Semita, which was already going the rounds of the Jockey Club, for, of all the seeds that fly about the world, the one with the most solid wings, enabling it to be scattered at the greatest distance from its point of origin, is still a joke.

"We might ask this gentleman to explain it to us. He looks so e-erudite," he said, pointing to the historian. "But it's better not to repeat it, especially since the facts are completely untrue. I'm less ambitious than my cousin Mirepoix, who claims that she can trace her family back before Christ to the tribe of Levi, and I am quite capable of proving that there's never been a drop of Jewish blood in our family. Still, don't let's fool ourselves; the charming views of my nephew are going to land him in Queer Street. Particularly with Fezensac ill at the moment. That means Duras will be running the election, and you know how he likes to bluff," said the Duc, who had never managed to learn the precise meaning of certain words and thought that "bluffing" meant, not shooting a line, but creating complications.

"I must say, if this Dreyfus is innocent," the Duchesse broke in, "he isn't doing much to prove it. Those idiotic, heavy-handed letters he writes from his island! I don't know whether M. Esterhazy is any better, but at least there is more style about the way he writes, more of a sense of tone. M. Dreyfus's supporters can't be very pleased about it. What a pity they can't just exchange their innocent victim for one with more style." Everyone burst out laughing. "Did you hear what Oriane just said?" the Duc de Guermantes asked Mme de Villeparisis in an eager voice. "Yes, most amusing." This was not enough for the Duc: "Well, I can't say I thought it very amusing myself. What I mean is that it doesn't make an ounce of difference to me whether a thing is amusing or not. Wit means nothing to me." M. d'Argencourt protested. "He doesn't mean a word he says," murmured the Duchesse. "It's probably because I've been a member of Parliament and listened to brilliant speeches that meant nothing. It principally taught me to value logic in such matters. That's probably why I wasn't re-elected. Wit leaves me cold." "Basin, stop playing the humbug, my dear, you know quite well that no one appreciates wit more than you do." "Please, let me finish. It's precisely because a certain type of trivial humor leaves me unmoved that I very often find it possible to value my wife's wit. It is usually based upon sound observation. She reasons like a man and expresses herself like a writer."

Meanwhile, Bloch was trying to press M. de Norpois on Colonel Picquart.

"There can be no question," replied M. de Norpois, "that his evidence was necessary. I am well aware that my opinion in this matter set more than one of my colleagues squawking, but, as I saw it, the government had a duty to let the colonel speak. One can't break out of that sort of deadlock by some evasive turn—otherwise one risks falling into a quagmire. As for the officer himself, his statement made the most favorable impression at the first hearing. When one saw him come into court in that well-fitting chasseur uniform, heard him relate in a perfectly simple and direct manner what he had seen and deduced, and then say, 'On my honor as a soldier' "—here M. de Norpois's voice quavered with a faint patriotic throb—" 'this is what I truly believe,' it is impossible to deny that he made a deep impression."

"So he's a Dreyfusard, beyond a shadow of a doubt," thought Bloch.

"But it was his confrontation with the registrar, Gribelin, that alienated all the initial sympathy he had managed to attract. When one heard that old public servant, a man of his word if there ever was one"—and M. de Norpois began stressing his words with the energy of sincere conviction—"when one saw him look his superior officer in the face, not afraid to make him pay dearly, and say to him in a tone that wouldn't take no for an answer, 'Come now, Colonel, you know that I have never told a lie, and you're well aware at this moment that I am telling the truth,' then the wind changed. M. Picquart did his utmost to move heaven and earth in the subsequent hearings, but it turned out to be a complete fiasco for him."

"No, he's definitely an anti-Dreyfusard, it's obvious," said Bloch to himself. "But if he thinks Picquart is a lying traitor, how can he give credit to his revelations, and quote them as if he found them charming and believed them to be sincere? And if, on the other hand, he sees him as an honest man unburdening his conscience, how can he suppose that he was lying in his exchange with Gribelin?"

Perhaps the reason M. de Norpois spoke to Bloch in this way, as if the two of them were in agreement, arose from the fact that he himself was such a fierce anti-Dreyfusard that, finding the government insufficiently so, he was its enemy as much as the Dreyfusards were. Perhaps it was because his cherished aim in politics was something deeper, situated on another plane, from which Dreyfusism appeared as an unimportant issue unworthy of the attention of a patriot concerned with weighty matters of foreign policy. Or perhaps rather it was because the maxims of his political wisdom were applicable only to questions of form, of procedure, of expediency, and not powerful enough to solve fundamental issues, as, in philosophy, pure logic is not enough to tackle the problems of existence; or because his very wisdom made it seem dangerous to him to deal with such matters and so, in his caution, he preferred to talk only about side issues. But Bloch was wrong to assume that M. de Norpois, even had he been less cautious by nature and of a less rigidly formal cast of mind, could, had he wished, have told him the truth about the part played by Henry, Picquart, or Paty de Clam,[70] or about any of the aspects of the case. For Bloch was in no doubt that M. de Norpois knew the truth about all these matters. How could he fail to know it, given that he was a friend of all the ministers? Indeed, Bloch was of the opinion that political reality could be approximately reconstructed by the most lucid minds, but he also imagined, like the man in the street, that it resided, beyond dispute and in material form, in the secret files of the president of the Republic and the prime minister, who divulged it to the Cabinet. But in reality, even when a political truth is recorded in documents, these seldom have any more value than a radiographic plate on which the layman imagines that the patient's disease is inscribed in some obvious way, whereas the plate simply provides a single element for inspection that needs to be combined with many others, all to be submitted to the doctor's analysis before he can reach a diagnosis. And so political reality, even when one goes to well-informed men and seems about to grasp it, is elusive. Even the later events of the Dreyfus case, if we confine ourselves to that, like the startling confession of Henry and his subsequent suicide, were immediately interpreted in opposite ways by Dreyfusard ministers and by Cavaignac and Cuignet,[71] who had themselves discovered the forgery and conducted the interrogation; and even among the Dreyfusard ministers themselves, men of the same shade of opinion, who were judging not only from the same documents but in the same spirit, the part played by Henry was explained in two entirely different ways, some ministers seeing him as an accomplice of Esterhazy, others assigning that role to Paty de Clam, thus rallying to the view of their opponent Cuignet in complete opposition to their supporter Reinach.[72] The only information Bloch could draw from M. de Norpois was that, if it was true that the chief of the General Staff, M. de Boisdeffre, had had a secret communication sent to M. Rochefort, it was clear that something singularly regrettable had occurred.

"You can take it from me that the war minister must, *in petto*[73] at least, have wished his chief of staff to burn in hell. To my mind, an official disclaimer would not have come amiss. But the war minister expresses himself very bluntly on the matter *inter pocula*.[74] And there are certain matters about which it is highly imprudent to stir up trouble and then lose control of them."

"But those documents are obviously false," said Bloch.

Instead of replying to this, M. de Norpois declared that he did not approve of the public demonstrations of Prince Henri d'Orléans:[75]

"They can only disturb the objective judgment of the praetorian and encourage upheavals of a deplorable kind, whichever way you look at it. Certainly we need to put a stop to the antimilitarist machinations, but neither do we want a rumpus encouraged by those elements on the right who do a disservice to the patriotic ideal by thinking only about how it can serve their own ends. France, thank God, is not some replica of South America, and no one has yet felt the need for a military pronunciamento."

Bloch could not get him to say anything about the question of Dreyfus's guilt, or about the likely judgment in the civil trial then under way. On the other hand, M. de Norpois seemed only too pleased to speculate upon the consequences of the verdict.

"If it's a conviction," he said, "it will probably be quashed. In a case with so many witnesses, it is rare not to find some flaw in the procedure that counsel can raise on appeal. But, to come back to that angry explosion from Prince Henri d'Orléans, I very much doubt that it met with his father's approval."

"You think Chartres[76] is on Dreyfus's side?" the Duchesse inquired with a smile, her eyes wide open, a flush on her cheeks, her nose buried in her plate of petits fours, and a scandalized air about her.

"Not at all. I simply meant that the whole family, on that side, has a political sense of which we have seen the *ne plus ultra* in the admirable Princesse Clémentine,77 and which her son, Prince Ferdinand, has kept as a treasured heritage. You would never have found the Prince de Bulgarie hugging Major Esterhazy."

"He would have preferred a private soldier," murmured Mme de Guermantes, who often met the Bulgarian at the Prince de Joinville's dinner parties and had once said to him, when he asked if she was not jealous, "Yes, Your Highness, of your bracelets."

"You're not going to Mme de Sagan's ball this evening?" M. de Norpois asked Mme de Villeparisis, to cut short his conversation with Bloch. The latter had made a not unpleasing impression on the ambassador, who told us afterward, somewhat naïvely, remembering perhaps the few surviving traces in Bloch's speech of the neo-Homeric manner he had largely outgrown: "He is rather amusing, with that slightly outmoded, solemn manner of speaking he has. You expect him to start saying things like 'the Learned Sisters,' like Lamartine or Jean-Baptiste Rousseau. It's rare enough in our present youth, as indeed it was in the generation before them. We ourselves were somewhat given to Romanticism." But, however novel his interlocutor may have seemed, M. de Norpois felt that the conversation had gone on for far too long.

"No, I don't go to balls any more," she replied with an old lady's winning smile. "Are the rest of you going? You're the right age for balls," she added, her eyes embracing M. de Châtellerault, his friend, and Bloch. "I was asked, too," she continued, coyly pretending to be flattered by the invitation. "They even made a point of coming round to invite me." ("They" being the Princesse de Sagan.)

"I haven't had a printed invitation," said Bloch, thinking that Mme de Villeparisis would procure him one, and that Mme de Sagan would be happy to welcome the friend of a woman on whom she had called in person to invite.

The Marquise made no answer, and Bloch did not press the matter, for he had something more serious to discuss with her and, with this in mind, had already asked her whether he might call again in a couple of days. After hearing the two young men say that they had resigned from the Rue Royale Club now that it was admitting just anyone off the streets, he wanted to ask Mme de Villeparisis if she could get him elected to it.

"Aren't they rather pretentious, and rather snobbish with it, these Sagans?" he said sarcastically.

"Not at all. They're the best we can do for you in that line," replied M. d'Argencourt, who had adopted all the witty quips of Parisian society.

"So I can assume that it's one of the *solemnities,* one of the big *social events* of the season!" said Bloch half ironically.

Mme de Villeparisis turned smilingly to Mme de Guermantes:

"Tell us, is it a great social solemnity, Mme de Sagan's ball?"

"I'm not the one you should be asking," came the Duchesse's ironical reply. "I've never managed to discover what a social solemnity is. Society is not exactly my forte."

"Oh, I thought it was quite the opposite," said Bloch, who had taken her at her word.

He continued to ply M. de Norpois with questions about the Dreyfus case, much to the latter's frustration. M. de Norpois declared that his "broad impression" of Colonel du Paty de Clam was of someone with a woolly mind, perhaps not the happiest choice of person to conduct such a delicate matter as a judicial inquiry, which requires so much levelheadedness and discernment.

"I know that the Socialist Party are clamoring for his head, and for the immediate release of the Devil's Island prisoner. But I don't think we are at the stage where our only option is to pass through the Caudine Forks of MM. Gérault-Richard and company.[78] The case so far is about as clear as mud. I'm not saying that there isn't some pretty dirty business to be hushed up on both sides. That certain of your client's more or less disinterested protectors may be well intentioned, I don't seek to deny, but you know that hell is paved with good intentions," he added with a shrewd look. "It is imperative that the government should make it apparent that it is no more in the hands of the factions of the left than it is forced to surrender, bound hand and foot, to the demands of some praetorian guard or other, which, mark my words, is not the same thing as the army. It goes without saying that, should any fresh evidence come to light, there would be further proceedings. It's as clear as daylight; to demand it is to labor the obvious. When that day comes, the government will say what it has to say; otherwise it would be turning what is its essential prerogative to woman's work. Beating about the bush is no longer enough. We need judges to try Dreyfus. And that will be an easy matter, because—although we have become accustomed in our beloved country, where we are fond of maligning ourselves, to thinking or letting it be thought that, in order to hear the words 'Truth' and 'Justice' we need to cross the Channel, which is often merely a roundabout way of reaching the Spree, there are judges to be found outside Berlin. But once the machinery of government has been set in motion, will you actually listen to what the government has to say? When it calls upon you to perform your duty as a citizen, will you rally to it? When it makes its patriotic appeal, instead of turning a deaf ear, will you be able to answer 'Present!'?"

M. de Norpois put these questions to my friend Bloch with a vehemence that both alarmed and flattered him, for the ambassador seemed to be addressing Bloch as if he represented a whole party, to be interrogating him as though he might have been in the confidence of that party and capable of assuming responsibility for the decisions it would adopt. "Should you fail to disarm," M. de Norpois continued without waiting for Bloch's collective answer, "should you fail to do so, even before the ink has dried on the decree ordering the retrial, in obedience to I know not what insidious word of command, and group yourselves in the fruitless opposition that for some is the *ultima ratio* of politics, should you retire to your tents and burn your boats, it would be to your own detriment. Are you a prisoner of those who preach disorder? Have you pledged yourself to them?" Bloch was at a loss for an answer. M. de Norpois gave him no time for one. "If the opposite is true, as I'd like to think it was, and if you have a little of what seems to me to be sorely lacking in some of your leaders and friends—namely, political sense—then, on the day when the Criminal Court has the facts before it, if you do not allow yourselves to be recruited by the fishers in troubled waters, the day will be yours. I am not saying that the whole of the General Staff is going to come out of it unscathed, but if some of them at least can save their faces without setting the bonfire alight, it will be all to the good. And it goes without saying that it is the government's business to pronounce judgment and to close the long list of unpunished crimes. And without responding to pressure from socialist agitators or any old army rabble, either," he added, looking Bloch straight in the eye, perhaps with the instinct that leads all conservatives to seek support in the enemy's camp. Government action must not be dictated by outbidding tactics, wherever the bids may come from. The government is not distracted, thank God, by Colonel Driant, or, at the opposite end of the scale, by M. Clemenceau. We need to bring professional agitators to heel and prevent them from raising their heads again. The vast majority of French people want to be able to work in orderly conditions. For me, that is an article of faith. But we must not be afraid to enlighten public opinion; and if a few sheep, of the kind that Rabelais knew so well, should rush headlong into the water, it would be appropriate to point out to them that they are rushing into troubled water, deliberately troubled by an alien mob of people, in order to conceal the dangers lurking in its depths. And the government must not give the impression that it is emerging from its passivity with the greatest reluctance when it exercises a right that is essentially its own—I mean, the setting in motion of the wheels of justice. The government will listen to all your suggestions. If a judicial error is recognized, it is certain that an overwhelming consensus would ensure it a fair hearing."

"You, monsieur," said Bloch, turning to M. d'Argencourt, to whom he had been introduced with the rest of the party, "are a Dreyfusard, of course. Everyone is, abroad."

"It is a question that concerns only the French themselves, don't you think?" replied M. d'Argencourt with that particular brand of insolence that consists in attributing to the other speaker an opinion one knows full well he does not share, since he has just expressed the contrary view.

Bloch colored; M. d'Argencourt smiled and looked round the room, and if his smile, as he directed it at the other guests, had a malicious intention in regard to Bloch, when it finally came to rest on the face of my friend he tempered it with cordiality, so that there should be no excuse for annoyance at the words just uttered, though the words remained no less cruel. Mme de Guermantes whispered something in M. d'Argencourt's ear that I could not catch, but which must have been something to do with Bloch's religion, because there flitted over the Duchesse's face at that moment the sort of expression to which the fear of being noticed by the person one is talking about gives a certain hesitancy and falseness, combined with the inquisitive, malicious amusement inspired by a category of people experienced as fundamentally different from oneself. In an attempt to save face, Bloch turned to the Duc de Châtellerault: "As a Frenchman, monsieur, you must be aware that people abroad are all Dreyfusards, although we're always pretending in France that we never know what is going on abroad. I know that I can say this sort of thing to you. Saint-Loup told me so." But the young Duc, who could feel that everyone was turning against Bloch, and who, like many society people, was a coward, replied with an affected and mordant form of wit he seemed to have inherited somewhere along the line from M. de Charlus: "Do forgive me, monsieur, if I don't discuss Dreyfus with you. I make a point of discussing it only with Japhetics." Everyone smiled except Bloch—not that he was not himself in the habit of referring ironically to his Jewish origin, to the side of his family that came from somewhere near Sinai. But instead of an ironical remark of this sort (doubtless he did not have one to hand), something clicked in Bloch's inner mechanism and triggered a rather different response. All that was intelligible was, "But *how* did you know? Who told you?," as though he had been the son of a convict. Yet, given his name, which was not exactly Christian in flavor, and his face, there was something rather naïve in his startled words.

Not entirely satisfied by what M. de Norpois had said, he went up to the archivist and asked him whether M. Paty de Clam or M. Joseph Reinach was not sometimes to be seen at Mme de Villeparisis's. The archivist said nothing; he was a Nationalist and was constantly feeding Mme de Villeparisis with the line that the social revolution might break out at any moment and that she should be more circumspect in her choice of acquaintances. He wondered whether Bloch might not be a secret emissary of the Syndicate, come to gather information, and went off at once to Mme de Villeparisis to repeat what Bloch had said. She came to the conclusion that Bloch's sense of good breeding left much to be desired, and that he could be a compromising person for M. de Norpois to know. She also wanted to humor the archivist, the only person she was somewhat afraid of, and by whom she was being indoctrinated, though without much success (every morning he read her M. Judet's article in *Le Petit Journal*[80]). So she decided to make it clear to Bloch that he need not come to the house again, and had no difficulty in selecting from her social repertory the scene in which the great lady shows someone the door, a scene that in no way involves the raised finger and the blazing eyes people imagine. As Bloch came up to her to take his leave, sunk deep in her large armchair, she seemed only half awakened from a vague drowsiness. Her misted eyes had the faint and charming gleam of pearls. Bloch's farewells drew the merest hint of a languid smile from the wrinkles of the Marquise's face, but no word, and she did not offer him her hand. The scene left Bloch utterly astonished, but since he was surrounded by a circle of onlookers he saw no way of prolonging it without embarrassment to himself, so, to force the Marquise, he thrust out the hand she had refused to shake. Mme de Villeparisis was shocked. But doubtless, though she was still concerned to humor the archivist and the anti-Dreyfus clan, she also wished to think to the future, so she merely let her eyelids droop over her half-closed eyes.

"I think she's asleep," said Bloch to the archivist, who, feeling that he had the support of the Marquise, adopted an indignant attitude. "Goodbye, madame," Bloch shouted.

The Marquise moved her lips slightly, like a dying woman who wants to open her mouth but whose eyes show no sign of recognition. Then she turned, brimming with renewed vitality, to the Marquis d'Argencourt, while Bloch left the room convinced that she must be soft in the head. He came to see her a few days later, burning with curiosity, and intent on unearthing the reason for her strange behavior toward him. She received him with great friendliness, because she was a good-natured woman, because the archivist was absent, because she very much wanted Bloch to put on his little play for her, and because she had now played out the act of great lady which she had felt that the circumstances required; it had been admired and commented upon the very same evening in various salons, but in a version that had already ceased to bear any relation to the truth.

"You were talking about *The Seven Princesses*, Duchesse. This is nothing to be proud of, but did you know that the author of that—what shall I call it?—that contrivance is one of my fellow countrymen?" said M. d'Argencourt with an irony that was mingled with the satisfaction of knowing more than anyone else present about the author of a work that had been a talking point. "Yes, he's of Belgian nationality," he added.

"Is that so? No, we are not accusing you of being remotely responsible for *The Seven Princesses*. Fortunately for yourself and your compatriots, you bear no resemblance to the author of that nonsense. I know some charming Belgians, yourself, your King—he's rather shy but very witty—my Ligne cousins, and many others, and I'm glad to say that none of you speaks the same language as the author of *The Seven Princesses*. If you really want my opinion, we shouldn't waste words on it, because there's nothing in it to waste words on. Authors like that love to cultivate a reputation for obscurity, even if it means making themselves ridiculous in order to conceal the fact that there's not a single idea in their heads. If there was anything behind it all, then I would be in a position to say that I am not averse to bold innovation," she added in a serious tone, "but there has to be some thought content. I don't know whether you've seen Borelli's play. It shocked some people. Personally, even if I am stoned for saying it," she went on, heedless of the fact that she ran no such risk, "I found it immensely intriguing. But *The Seven Princesses*! One of those princesses may be well disposed toward my nephew, but my sense of family feeling won't extend to . . ."

The Duchesse broke off abruptly, for the lady who had just come into the room was the Vicomtesse de Marsantes, Robert's mother. Mme de Marsantes was thought of in the Faubourg Saint-Germain as a superior being endowed with the kindness and tolerance of a saint. I had been told as much and had no particular reason to be surprised by the fact, since I was unaware at the time that she was actually the sister of the Duc de Guermantes. Later, I found myself constantly surprised to discover that the melancholy, pure, self-renouncing women of that social world, venerated like ideal saints in stained-glass windows, had flowered from the same genealogical stock as brothers who were brutal, debauched, and vile. It seemed to me that brothers and sisters like the Duc de Guermantes and Mme de Marsantes, who share identical features, ought to have a single intellect in common, the same emotions, like a person who may have good or bad moments, but in whom nevertheless one cannot expect to find wide-ranging views if he is narrow-minded, or supreme self-denial if he is hardhearted.

Mme de Marsantes was following Brunetière's course of lectures.[81] She inspired the Faubourg Saint-Germain with enthusiasm and, by her saintly life, edified it as well. But the morphological connection of handsome nose and penetrating gaze led me to classify Mme de Marsantes in the same intellectual and moral family as her brother the Duc. I could not believe that the mere fact of being a woman, and perhaps of having had an unhappy life and winning everyone's estimation, could make a person so different from the rest of her family, as in the medieval epics where all the virtues and graces are embodied in the sister of brutish brothers. It seemed to me that nature, with less license than the old poets, must restrict herself almost exclusively to elements common to the family, and I was not able to credit her with enough power of invention to produce, out of materials like those that produced a fool and a lout, a great mind without a hint of foolishness, a saint without a stain of brutality. Mme de Marsantes was wearing a dress of white Indian silk with a motif of large palms, to which were attached black flowers in another material. The black was for her cousin M. de Montmorency, whom she had lost three weeks earlier, and although her bereavement did not prevent her from paying calls or going to small dinner parties, she went in mourning. She was a great lady. Her lineage filled her soul with the frivolity of generations of life at court, with all that implies about superficiality and punctiliousness. Mme de Marsantes had not had the strength to mourn her father and mother for any extended period, but nothing would have induced her to wear colors in the month following the death of a cousin. She was especially friendly to me because I was Robert's friend, and also because I did not move in the same world as Robert. The friendliness was accompanied by a pretense of shyness, by a sort of sporadic withdrawal of the voice, the eyes, the attention, as though she were gathering up the folds of a troublesome skirt so as not to take up too much room, to remain poised even when she relaxed, as good breeding demands. And this good breeding must not be taken too literally, since many such ladies lapse very quickly into loose living without ever losing the almost childlike correctness of their manners. Mme de Marsantes was somewhat irritating to talk to, because, whenever a commoner like Bergotte or Elstir was mentioned, she would say, isolating the word emphatically, intoning it on two different notes with a modulation peculiar to the Guermantes, "I have had the *honor,* the great *hon-*or, of meeting M. Bergotte, of making the acquaintance of M. Elstir," either to impress people with her humility, or from the same tendency that M. de Guermantes had to revert to obsolete forms in protest at the slipshod usages of the present day, in which people failed to assert sufficiently how "honored" they were. Whichever of these was the true reason, whenever Mme de Marsantes said, "I have the *honor,* the great *hon-*or," one had the impression that she felt herself to be playing out a grand role and showing that she could accommodate the names of important men as she would have welcomed the men themselves at her country estate, had they happened to be in the neighborhood. On the other hand, since she was devoted to her extensive family, and since, being slow of speech and fond of explaining things at length, she was always trying to make clear the various degrees of kinship involved, she found herself (without any desire to impress, and while genuinely happy to talk only about the sweetness of country folk or the sublimity of gamekeepers) alluding incessantly to all the families of Europe under allegiance to the Holy Roman Empire, which people of less illustrious origin could not forgive her and, if they were at all intellectual, scorned as a sign of stupidity.

In the country, Mme de Marsantes was adored for her good works, but primarily because the purity of blood that for several generations

had flowed only with what was greatest in the history of France had di-
vested her manner of anything ordinary people call "airs and graces"
and had endowed her with perfect simplicity. She did not shrink from
embracing a poor woman who was in trouble, and would tell her to
come up to the house for a cartload of wood. She was, as people said,
the perfect Christian. She was anxious to find Robert an immensely rich
wife. Being a great lady means playing the great lady, which in turn
means, partly at least, playing at simplicity. It is an extremely costly
game, all the more so because simplicity delights people only on condition that they know you are capable of its opposite—namely, that you
are very rich. Someone said to me later, when I mentioned that I had
met her, "You must have realized how lovely she was as a young
woman." But real beauty is so individual, so unfamiliar at first sight,
that it is not recognized as beauty. All I noticed that afternoon was that
she had a tiny nose, very blue eyes, a long neck, and a sad expression.

"I must just mention something to you," said Mme de Villeparisis to
the Duchesse de Guermantes. "I'm expecting someone whom you've
no desire to know. I thought I'd better warn you, to avoid any awkwardness. But you can rest assured, you won't find her here in the future. I
couldn't avoid having her today. It's Swann's wife."

Mme Swann, who had realized the growing impact of the Dreyfus
case and become fearful that her husband's origins might turn to her
disadvantage, had begged him never again to mention the condemned
man's innocence. When he was not present, she went a step further and
professed the most ardent Nationalism; and here she was merely following the example of Mme Verdurin, in whom a latent bourgeois anti-
Semitism had awakened and grown to a positive frenzy. Mme Swann's
attitude had won her the right of entry to several of the anti-Semitic
leagues of society women that were being formed, and she had established relations with several members of the aristocracy. It may seem
strange that the Duchesse de Guermantes, such a great friend of Swann,
had not followed suit, and had in fact always resisted his unconcealed
desire to introduce his wife to her. But it will be clear in due course that
this attitude arose from the peculiar character of the Duchesse, from her
conviction that she was not "bound to" do this or that, and from the

despotic manner in which she imposed what had been decided by her social "free will," highly arbitrary though that was.

"Thank you for warning me," replied the Duchesse. "It would certainly be most disagreeable. But since I know her by sight, I'll be able to leave at the right moment."

"Believe me, Oriane, she's very nice. She's an excellent woman," said Mme de Marsantes.

"I dare say she is, but I feel no need to convince myself of the fact in person."

"Have you been invited to Lady Israels'?" Mme de Villeparisis asked the Duchesse, to change the subject.

"Mercifully, I don't know her," replied Mme de Guermantes. "It's Marie-Aynard you ought to be asking. She knows her. I've always wondered why."

"In fact, I did use to know her, for my sins," said Mme de Marsantes. "But I decided to break off relations. It seems she's one of the very worst of them and makes no secret of the fact. Besides, we've all been too trusting, too hospitable. I shall never go near anyone of that race again. While we closed our doors to old country cousins, our own flesh and blood, we opened them to Jews. Now we can see what thanks we get for it. Dear me! I'm not supposed to open my mouth with that adorable son of mine, who goes round talking the most impossible nonsense, young fool that he is," she added, after catching M. d'Argencourt saying something about Robert. "But, talking of Robert, have you not seen him?" she asked Mme de Villeparisis. "It's Saturday, and I thought he might have come to Paris for the day, in which case he would have been sure to pay you a visit."

In reality, Mme de Marsantes thought that her son would not be on leave; but knowing that, even if he was, he would not have come to call on Mme de Villeparisis, she hoped, by this pretense of expecting to find him there, to make his sticklish aunt forgive him for all the visits he had failed to make.

"Robert come here! I haven't had as much as a word from him. I don't think I've seen him since Balbec."

"He is so busy. He has so much to do," said Mme de Marsantes.

The hint of a smile made Mme de Guermantes's eyelashes quiver as she studied the circle she was tracing on the carpet with the tip of her parasol. Whenever the Duc had been too obviously unfaithful to his wife, Mme de Marsantes had always made a great point of siding with her sister-in-law against her own brother. Her sister-in-law retained a grudgingly grateful memory of this support, and was not inclined to find Robert's pranks seriously offensive. At this point the door opened again and Robert himself entered the room.

"Well, speak of the devil! And here is the Saint-Loup himself,"[82] said Mme de Guermantes.

Mme de Marsantes, who had her back to the door, had not seen her son come in. When she did see him, all her motherly feelings fluttered with joy, her body half rose from her seat, her face quivered, and she fastened on Robert eyes that were spellbound:

"You've actually come! What a delight! What a surprise!"

"Ah! The *devil* . . . *the Saint-Loup*. Oh yes, I see!" said the Belgian diplomat in an explosion of laughter.

"Delightful, isn't it?" the Duchesse retorted dryly. She detested wordplay and had only indulged in it as a self-mocking gesture. "Hello, Robert," she said. "So this is how we forget our aunt."

They talked for a moment, doubtless about me, for, as Saint-Loup went to join his mother, Mme de Guermantes turned to me.

"Good evening, how are you?" she said.

She let all the light of her blue eyes fall upon me, hesitated for a second, unfolded the stem of her arm toward me, and leaned her body forward; then it sprang back with the rapidity of a flattened bush, released to its natural position. Her behavior was dictated by the fire in Saint-Loup's eyes, watching her from a distance and making frantic efforts to get his aunt to be more accommodating. Fearing that our conversation might come to nothing, he came over to fuel it and answered for me:

"He's not very well, he gets rather tired. And it would do him a great deal of good if he saw you more often. I won't hide the fact that he enjoys seeing you very much."

"Oh, how very sweet of him," said Mme de Guermantes in a tone of voice that was deliberately humdrum, as if I had brought her coat. "I'm most flattered."

"I must go and talk to my mother for a minute, so take my chair," said Saint-Loup, thus obliging me to sit down next to his aunt.

We were both silent.

"I sometimes see you in the morning," she said, as though she were telling me something new and as though I myself never saw her. "It's so good for one's health to take a walk."

"Oriane," said Mme de Marsantes in a low voice, "you said you were on your way to see Mme de Saint-Ferréol. Would you be so kind as to tell her not to expect me for dinner? I shall stay at home, now that Robert's here. And while I think of it, could I possibly ask you to see that someone sends out at once for those cigars Robert likes? 'Coronas,' they're called. There are none in the house."

Robert came up to us. He had caught only the name of Mme de Saint-Ferréol.

"And who on earth is Mme de Saint-Ferréol?" he asked with calculated surprise, for he affected ignorance of everything to do with society.

"But you know perfectly well who she is, darling," said his mother. "She's Vermandois's sister, the one who gave you those lovely billiards you liked so much."

"So she's Vermandois's sister. I had no idea. Really, my family are extraordinary," he said, half turning to me and unconsciously adopting Bloch's intonation, just as he borrowed his ideas. "They know the most unlikely people, people with names like 'Saint-Ferréol' "–emphasizing the final consonant of each word–"they go to balls, they drive out in victorias, they lead a fabulous existence. It's prodigious."

Mme de Guermantes made the slight, short, harsh sound in her throat of something like forced laughter choked back, which was her way of showing that she acknowledged her nephew's wit to the degree that kinship demanded. A servant came in to announce that the Prince de Faffenheim-Munsterburg-Weinigen was sending word of his arrival to M. de Norpois.

"Go and fetch him, monsieur," said Mme de Villeparisis to the ex-ambassador, who set off to greet the German prime minister.

But the Marquise called him back:

"Just a moment, monsieur. Should I show him the miniature of the Empress Charlotte?"

"Why, I think he'd be delighted," said the ambassador in a tone of deep conviction, as though he envied the fortunate minister the favor in store for him.

"Oh, I know he's very *sound*," said Mme de Marsantes, "and that is so rare among foreigners. But I've taken the trouble to find out. He's anti-Semitism personified."

The Prince's name, with the bold attack—in musical terms—of its opening syllables, and the stammering repetition that marked them, preserved the vigor, the mannered simplicity, the heavy-handed "refinements" of the Germanic race, projected like greenish boughs over the "-heim" of dark-blue enamel, which shed the mystic gleam of a Rhenish stained-glass window behind the pale and finely chiseled gildings of the German eighteenth century. The name included, among the several names of which it was composed, that of a little German spa-town I had visited with my grandmother as a child, beneath a mountain distinguished by the fact that Goethe had walked there; from its vineyards we used to drink at the *Kurhof* the illustrious vintages with their compound and sonorous names, like the epithets that Homer gives to his heroes. And so, the instant I heard it uttered, and before I had recalled the spa town, the Prince's name seemed to shrink, to become charged with humanity, to accommodate itself comfortably in a small corner in my memory, where it stayed, familiar, earthbound, picturesque, appetizing, light, somehow authorized and prescribed. And in addition to this, M. de Guermantes, in explaining who the Prince was, referred at length to a number of his titles, and I recognized the name of the village with the river running through it on which, at the end of a day's treatment, I used to go boating amid the mosquitoes, and the name of a forest far enough away for the doctor not to allow me to make the journey. And in effect it was understandable that the suzerainty of this nobleman should extend to the surrounding places, and that the enumeration of his titles should associate afresh the various names that could be read side by side on a map. Thus, beneath the visor of a prince of the Holy Roman Empire and a knight of Franconia, what I saw was the face of a beloved land, where the light of the evening sun had often lingered for me, at least before the Prince, Rhinegrave, and Elector Palatine had en-

tered the room. For I speedily learned that the revenues he drew from
the forest and the river inhabited by gnomes and water sprites, from the
magic mountain on which rose the ancient *Burg* that still held memories of Luther and Louis the German, were spent on running five Char-
ron motorcars, on a house in Paris and another in London, a Monday-
night box at the Opéra, and another for the Tuesday-night performances
at the Théâtre-Français. He did not seem to me, nor did he seem to
think himself, any different from other men of similar wealth and age
with less poetic origins. He had the same culture, the same ideals; he
was proud of his rank, but purely because of the advantages it brought
him; and he had only one remaining ambition in life, to be elected
a corresponding member of the Academy of Moral and Political Sciences, which was why he had come to call on Mme de Villeparisis.
If the Prince, whose wife reigned over the most exclusive set in Berlin,
had solicited an introduction to the Marquise, his principal reason had
nothing to do with his desire to make her acquaintance. For years now,
he had been consumed by his ambition to be elected to the Institut, but
unfortunately he had never had more than five Academicians prepared
to vote for him. He knew that M. de Norpois could by himself command ten or more votes and was capable, by skillful negotiation, of increasing the number. And so the Prince, who had known him in Russia
when they had both been there as ambassadors, had been to see him
and done everything possible to win him over. But, try as he might to
ply the Marquis with friendly gestures, to secure Russian decorations
for him, to quote him in articles on foreign policy, he had been faced
with the response of an ungrateful man, for whom these kindnesses
seemed to count as nothing, who had not furthered his cause as a candidate one inch, had not even assured him of his own vote. It is true
that M. de Norpois had received him extremely courteously, to the
point of not wanting him to put himself out and "take the trouble to
come so far out of his way to see him"; he went himself to the Prince's
mansion, and when the Teutonic knight came straight out with, "I
should very much like to be your colleague," he had replied with deep
emotion, "Ah! I should be most happy!" And no doubt a simple-
minded person like Dr. Cottard would have thought: "Well, here he is

in my house. He was the one who insisted on coming, because he regards me as a more important person than himself. He tells me he'd be happy to see me in the Academy. He can't be saying it for nothing, damn it! If he's not offering to vote for me, then perhaps it just hasn't occurred to him. He has so much to say about my powerful influence that he must think that everything just falls into my lap, that I have all the votes I need. That's why he doesn't offer me his. So what I need to do is to corner him now, while there are just the two of us, say to him, 'Right, vote for me,' and he'll have no alternative."

But the Prince was not simple-minded. He was what Dr. Cottard would have called "a shrewd diplomat," and he knew that M. de Norpois was a no less shrewd one, a man who did not need to be told that he could do a favor to a candidate by voting for him. In his ambassadorial functions and as foreign minister, the Prince had conducted conversations, not on his own behalf, as now, but on behalf of his country, in which one knows beforehand how far one is prepared to go and the extent to which one is willing to commit oneself. He was well aware that in the language of diplomacy to talk means to offer. And this was why he had arranged for M. de Norpois to receive the Order of Saint Andrew. But, had he been obliged to report to his government the conversation with M. de Norpois that followed, he would have stated in his dispatch, "I realized I had used the wrong approach." For, as soon as he had returned to the subject of the Institut, M. de Norpois had repeated:

"It would give a great deal of pleasure to me, and a great deal of pleasure to my colleagues. They must, I think, feel deeply honored that you should have thought of them. It's a really interesting candidacy, somewhat outside our normal practice. The Academy is very set in its ways, you know, and it takes fright at anything with an unfamiliar ring to it. Personally, I find this deplorable. I don't know how many times I've implied as much to my colleagues. I'm not even sure, God forgive me, that I didn't once let the term 'stick-in-the-mud' pass from my lips," he had added with a scandalized smile, and in an undertone, almost a theatrical aside, as he shot the Prince a sidelong glance from his blue eyes, like an experienced actor judging the effect he has made. "You will understand, Prince, that I should not care to allow such an eminent personality as yourself to embark on a venture that was fated from the start. As long as my colleagues' thinking remains so far behind the times, it would seem to me wiser to abstain. But you may rest assured that, if I ever sense a slightly more modern, a slightly more adventurous spirit in that learned body, which is tending to turn into a mausoleum, if I felt you had a real chance of success, I would be the first to let you know."

"The Order of Saint Andrew was a mistake," thought the Prince. "The negotiations have not moved forward one step. That's not what he wanted. I haven't yet laid my hand on the right key."

This was the sort of reasoning of which M. de Norpois, trained in the same school as the Prince, would himself have been capable. It is easy to laugh at the silly pedantry that makes diplomats like Norpois go into ecstasies over some more or less trivial piece of official wording. But there is another side to this childish enjoyment: diplomats know that on the scales that ensure that balance—European or otherwise—we call peace, good feeling, fine speeches, urgent entreaty count for very little; the heavier side of the balance, the real determinant, is something else, the scope the opponent has (if he is strong enough), or does not have, to satisfy a desire in exchange for something else. This was the order of truths, which an entirely disinterested person, such as my grandmother, for instance, would not have understood, with which M. de Norpois and the Prince von —— had frequently had to wrestle. As chargé d'affaires in countries with which we had been within an inch of going to war, M. de Norpois, in his anxiety as to the possible turn of events, knew that it was not by the word "peace," or by the word "war," that it would be revealed to him, but by some other, ostensibly commonplace word, a word of terror or blessing, which the diplomats' code of language would immediately know how to interpret, and to which, in order to safeguard the dignity of France, he would respond with another, equally commonplace word, which the minister of the enemy nation would immediately decipher as "war." Furthermore, in accordance with a long-established custom, similar to the one that gave to the first meeting of two people promised to each other in marriage the form of a chance encounter at a performance at the Théâtre du Gymnase, the dialogue fated to dictate the word "war" or "peace" took place, as a rule, not in the ministerial office, but on a bench in a *Kurgarten* where the minister and M. de Norpois went independently to a thermal spring to drink their little glasses of curative water straight from the source. By a sort of unspoken agreement, they met at the hour appointed for the cure, and began taking a walk together, which, though it looked harmless enough, the two interlocutors knew to be as tragic as an order for mobilization. And so, in a private matter like this nomination to the Institut, the Prince had employed the same system of inference as he had used in his diplomatic career, the same method of reading beneath superimposed symbols.

And it certainly cannot be said that my grandmother and the few people like her would have been alone in their failure to understand this sort of calculated maneuver. For one thing, the average run of people who follow professions with long-established codes of procedure are, with their lack of intuition, very like my grandmother in the ignorance she owed to her principled disinterestedness. You usually have to descend to the category of "kept" persons, male or female, to find ulterior motives behind actions or words that are ostensibly innocent, for purposes of self-interest or survival. What man is ignorant of the fact that, when a woman he is going to pay says to him, "Let's not talk about money," the words need to be taken as a "silent bar," as they say in music, and that if, later on, she declares, "You make me too unhappy, you're always keeping things from me; I can't stand it anymore," he needs to understand it as, "Someone else is offering her more"? And this is only the language of a kept woman, not so far removed from society women. Criminal types offer more striking examples. But M. de Norpois and the German Prince, even if criminal types were unknown to them, had grown accustomed to living on the same plane as nations, and nations, too, for all their greatness, are creatures of selfishness and cunning, tamed only by force, by consideration for their interests, which may drive them to murder, and often symbolic murder, since the mere hesitation or refusal to fight may mean for a nation, "Perish." But since none of this is set out in the various documents of official policy or elsewhere, nations tend to be peace-loving; if they are warlike, it is through instinct, from hatred, from a sense of grievance, and not for the reasons that determine their leaders on the advice of someone like Norpois.

The following winter, the Prince fell seriously ill. He recovered, but his heart was permanently affected.

"Curse it!" he said to himself. "I can't afford to lose any more time over the Institut. If I take too long, I may be dead before they elect me. That's the last thing I want."

He wrote a piece for the *Revue des deux mondes* on politics over the past twenty years with several extremely flattering references to M. de Norpois. The latter called to thank him. He added that he did not know how to express his gratitude. The Prince said to himself, like a man who had just tried to fit another key into a difficult lock, "Still not the right one," and, feeling a little out of breath as he showed M. de Norpois out, thought, "Good God! These fellows will see me dead before they let me in. Time to speed things up."

That very evening, he ran into M. de Norpois again, at the Opéra:

"My dear Ambassador," he said to him, "you said this morning you didn't know how to express your gratitude. It's quite unnecessary, you owe me none. But I'm going to make bold enough to take you at your word."

M. de Norpois had no less esteem for the Prince's tactfulness than the Prince had for his. He understood at once that it was not a request that the Prince de Faffenheim was about to put to him, but an offer, and he prepared himself for it by breaking into an affable smile.

"You're going to think me very indiscreet. But there are two people to whom I am greatly attached—in quite different ways, as you will see in a moment. They have both recently come to live in Paris, which is where they intend to stay from now on. I'm talking about my wife and the Grand Duchess John. They are to give a few dinners, notably in honor of the King and Queen of England, and their dream would have been to provide their two guests with the company of someone whom they greatly admire but whom neither has met. I have to say that I had no idea how to gratify their wish until I learned just now, by pure chance, that you knew just such a person. I know that she lives a very retired life and sees only a very few people—a *happy few*—but if you, with the kindness you have always shown me, were to give me your support, I feel sure that she would allow you to present me to her so that I might convey the wish of the Grand Duchess and the Princess. She might even consent to dine with the Queen of England, and then—who knows?—if we don't bore her too much, to come and spend the Easter vacation with us at Beaulieu, at the Grand Duchess John's. I'm talking about the Marquise de Villeparisis. I admit that the hope of becoming a habitué of such a Bureau of Wit would console me, make it less difficult for me to face abandoning my candidacy for the Institut. Her salon, too, is a center of intellectual intercourse and intelligent discussion."

With an inexpressible sense of pleasure, the Prince felt that the lock was no longer resistant, and that he had at last found the right key.

"Such an alternative is completely unnecessary, my dear Prince," replied M. de Norpois. "Nothing could be more of a match for the Institut than the salon you mention. It's a positive breeding ground of Academicians. I shall convey your request to Mme la Marquise de Villeparisis. She will most certainly be flattered. As to your dinner, she goes out very little, and it will perhaps be more difficult to arrange. But I shall introduce you to her, and you can then plead your cause in person. But on no account must you give up the Academy. It just so happens that, a fortnight from tomorrow, I am lunching with Leroy-Beaulieu, before the two of us go on to an important meeting, and without his help nobody can be elected. I have already mentioned your name to him in this connection, and, naturally, it's a name that is perfectly familiar to him. He did raise certain objections. But, as it happens, he needs the support of my group at the next election, and so I intend to press him further. I shall tell him frankly of the warm bonds that unite us, and I shall make no secret of the fact that, if you were to stand, I should ask all my friends to vote for you"—the Prince heaved a deep sigh of relief at this point—"and he knows that I have friends. If I could manage to obtain his cooperation, then I think that your chances would be very real. Meet me at six that evening at Mme de Villeparisis's. I'll introduce you to her, and I'll also be able to give you an account of my morning meeting."

And this is how the Prince de Faffenheim came to find himself call-ing on Mme de Villeparisis. Deep disillusion set in for me when he started to speak. It had never occurred to me that, if a given period has features, both localized and general, that are more accentuated than those of nationality, so that, in the sort of illustrated dictionary that even includes an authentic portrait of Minerva, Leibniz in his wig and fraise looks very much the same as Marivaux or Samuel Bernard,[83] then a nationality has particular features more accentuated than those of a caste. In the present instance, these were made apparent to me not in a discourse in which I had expected to hear the rustling of elves and the dance of the kobolds, but in a transposition that bore the imprint of that poetic origin no less markedly: the fact that, as he made his bow to Mme de Villeparisis, this short, red-faced, pot-bellied Rhinegrave said to her, "Gut-tay, Matame la Marquise," in the accent of a concierge from Alsace.

"Can't I tempt you to a cup of tea or a little of this tart? It's very good," Mme de Guermantes asked me, anxious to have behaved in as friendly a manner as possible. "I do the honors here as if I were in my own home," she explained in an ironical tone that made her voice slightly guttural, as though she were stifling a hoarse laugh.

"Monsieur," said Mme de Villeparisis to M. de Norpois, "you won't forget you have something to say to the Prince about the Academy?"

Mme de Guermantes lowered her eyes and half turned her wrist to look at the time.

"Good gracious! It's time I said goodbye to my aunt if I'm to get to Mme de Saint-Ferréol's, and I'm dining with Mme Leroi."

She rose without bidding me goodbye. She had just caught sight of Mme Swann, who seemed somewhat embarrassed by my presence. Doubtless she remembered that she had been the first to assure me that she was convinced of Dreyfus's innocence.

"I don't want my mother to introduce me to Mme Swann," Saint-Loup said to me. "She's an ex-prostitute. Her husband's a Jew, and she comes here to parade as a Nationalist. Hello, there's my uncle Palamède."

I was particularly interested to see Mme Swann there on account of something that had occurred a few days earlier, and which it is necessary to relate because of the consequences it was to have much later, the details of which will follow in due course. A few days before my present visit to Mme de Villeparisis, I had myself received a visitor, one whom I barely expected, Charles Morel, the son—unknown to me—of my great-uncle's former valet. The great-uncle in question (the one in whose house I had met the lady in pink) had died the year before. His valet had more than once expressed his intention of coming to see me; I had no idea why, but I welcomed the idea of seeing him, for I had learned from Françoise that he held my uncle's memory in genuine veneration and made a regular pilgrimage to his grave. But he had been obliged to retire to his home in the country for reasons of health, and since he expected to remain there for some time, he had sent his son in his stead. I was surprised to see a handsome young man of eighteen come into the room, dressed expensively rather than with taste, yet looking, for all that, like anything but a servant. And he made a point, from the very start, of distancing himself from his menial origins by informing me with a complacent smile that he had won a first prize at the Conservatoire. The reason he had come was this: his father had found various mementoes among the effects of my uncle Adolphe which he considered it inappropriate to send to my parents, and had set them aside as something that might interest a young man of my age. These were photographs of the famous actresses, the great courtesans my uncle had known, the last images of the rakish proclivities he kept hermetically sealed from his family life. While the young Morel was showing them to me, I became aware that he affected to speak to me as an equal. The pleasure he derived from addressing me as "you" and using "monsieur" as little as possible was that of a man whose father had only ever used the third person to address my parents. Almost all the photographs bore inscriptions like "To my dearest friend." One actress, less grateful and more shrewd than the others, had written, "To the best of friends," which enabled her (so I have been assured) to say that my uncle was far from being her best friend in any sense, but that he had been the friend who had done the most to oblige her in all sorts of small ways, the friend she made use of, a really kind man, a big silly almost. However much the young Morel tried to escape his background, one felt that the ghost of my uncle Adolphe, who had been so venerable and loomed so large in the eyes of his old valet, had never ceased to hover like something sacred over the childhood and youth of the son. While I was examining the photographs, Charles Morel was taking stock of my room. And as I was looking for somewhere to put them, "How is it," he asked me (in a tone in which the reproach had no need to be stressed, so implicit was it in the words themselves), "that I don't see a single photograph of your uncle in the room?" I felt the blood rise to my cheeks and stammered, "Why, I don't even think I have one." "What? You don't have a single photograph of the uncle who was so fond of you! I'll send you one of the old man's—he's got loads. I hope you'll give it the place of honor above the chest of drawers there, which just so happens to have come to you from your uncle." It is true that, since there was not even a photograph of my mother or father in my room, there was nothing so very shocking about my not having one of my uncle Adolphe. But it was easy enough to see that for old Morel, who had brought up his son to his own way of thinking, my uncle was the important person in the family, and my parents only dull reflections of his glorious figure. I was more privileged, because my uncle was always saying to his valet that I would turn out to be another Racine or Vaulabelle,[84] and Morel regarded me, as a favorite child of my uncle, as something like an adopted son. It did not take me long to realize that Morel's son was very much a "go-getter." In fact, on this particular occasion he asked me, being something of a composer as well and capable of setting the odd poem to music, whether I knew of any poet who was well in with "aristo" society. I named one. He had not read this poet, nor had he ever heard of him, and he noted down the name. I discovered shortly afterward that he had written to the poet as a fanatical admirer of his work to tell him that he had set one of his sonnets to music and that he would be very grateful if the author would arrange to have it performed at the home of the Comtesse ——. Such undue haste exposed his real intentions. The poet took offense and made no reply.

Together with his ambition, Charles Morel seemed to have a marked leaning toward more concrete realities. Coming through the courtyard, he had noticed Jupien's niece at work upon a waistcoat, and although he told me nothing more than that he just happened to need a fancy waistcoat at that moment, I felt that the young woman had made a vivid impression on him. He had no scruples about asking me to come downstairs and introduce him to her, "but not in connection with your family, if you see what I mean. I rely on your discretion not to mention my father. Just say that I'm a distinguished artist friend of yours. You know how important it is to make a good impression on tradespeople." He managed to convey that he quite understood I did not know him well enough to address him as "dear friend" but that I might refer to him in front of the young woman in some such terms as "not my dear maestro, of course . . . although . . . well, dear virtuoso, if you like"; but when we were in the shop, I avoided "qualifying" him, as Saint-Simon would have said, and restricted myself to a purely formal style of address between us. From the various samples of velvet presented, he went for one that was so bright-red and so loud that, for all his bad taste, he was never able to bring himself to wear the waistcoat that was made up from it. The young woman settled down to work again with her two "apprentices," but it seemed to me that the interest had been mutual, and that Charles Morel, whom she regarded as of my "station" (only smarter and richer), had struck her as singularly attractive. Since I had been greatly surprised to find among the photographs his father had sent one of Elstir's portrait of Miss Sacripant (namely, Odette), I said to Charles Morel as I accompanied him to the courtyard entrance, "I don't suppose you can help me, but did my uncle know this lady well? I'm not clear what stage of his life she belongs to, and it interests me because of M. Swann. . . ." "But, oh yes, I nearly forget to tell you that my father particularly asked me to draw your attention to that one. She's the very demimondaine who was lunching with him on the last occasion you saw him. My father was not at all sure about letting you in. It seems that you made a great impression on that loose lady, and she hoped to see you again. But it all coincided with some family quarrel, from what my father tells me, and you never set eyes on your uncle again." He broke off at this point to give Jupien's niece a smile of farewell from where he was standing. She was gazing after him, doubtless admiring his thin but regular features, his fine hair, and his sparkling eyes. And I, as I shook his hand, was thinking of Mme Swann, realizing with amazement, so far apart, so different were they in my memory, that I should now have to identify her with the "lady in pink."

M. de Charlus was soon seated next to Mme Swann. At every social gathering he attended, he scorned the men, was courted by the women, and promptly attached himself to the most elegant woman he could find, with the feeling that her stylishness somehow embellished him. The Baron's frock coat or tails recalled some great colorist's portrait of a man dressed in black but with a brilliantly colored cloak thrown over a chair beside him, which he is about to wear to a fancy-dress ball. M. de Charlus's tête-à-têtes, usually with some royal lady, secured him a number of valued privileges. For instance, one of the consequences of them was that when his hostesses put on some special entertainment he was the only man allowed to have a front seat in a row of ladies, while the other men were crowded into the back of the room. Again, when he was—to all intents and purposes—deeply absorbed in telling amusing stories to some enraptured lady at the top of his voice, M. de Charlus was exempted from having to pay his respects to any of the others, and thus free of any social duties. Behind the scented screen that the chosen beauty provided for him, he was as protected in the middle of a social gathering as he would have been in a box at the theater, and whenever anyone came up to greet him, through the screen, as it were, of his beautiful companion, it was permissible for him to reply in the curtest manner, without interrupting his conversation with the lady in question. Mme Swann, it is true, was scarcely to be classed among the people with whom he liked to flaunt himself in this way. But he professed admiration for her and friendship for Swann, knew that she would be flattered by his attentions, and was himself flattered at being compromised by the prettiest woman in the room.

Mme de Villeparisis was none too pleased to be receiving a visit from M. de Charlus. He himself, though he saw great defects in his aunt's character, was extremely fond of her. But every now and then, in a fit of anger or imaginary grievance, without any attempt to resist his impulses, he would send her letters full of violent abuse, in which he made mountains out of the most trivial incidents, which seemed to have completely escaped his attention until then. Among other examples of this, I mention the following one, which was brought to my attention during my stay in Balbec: Mme de Villeparisis, worried that she had not brought enough money to Balbec to extend her holiday there, and, as a thrifty woman who avoided spending more than she had to, reluctant to have money sent from Paris, had borrowed three thousand francs from M. de Charlus. A month later, annoyed with his aunt for some trivial reason, he had asked her to pay the money back and wire it to him. He received a money order for two thousand nine hundred and ninety-odd francs. A few days later, he ran into his aunt in Paris, and in the course of a friendly conversation he drew her attention very discreetly to the mistake made by the bank responsible for the transaction. "But there was no mistake," said Mme de Villeparisis, "the money order costs six francs seventy-five." "Ah well, if it was intentional, that's fine," replied M. de Charlus. "I simply mentioned it in case you didn't know, because in that case, had they done the same thing to someone who didn't know you as well as I do, it could have been upsetting for you." "No, no, there was no mistake." "Actually, you were quite right," M. de Charlus concluded gaily, tenderly kissing his aunt's hand. In fact, there was absolutely no grudge on his part, only amusement at her petty stinginess. But some time later, convinced that his aunt had been trying to cheat him in some family matter and had "mounted a whole conspiracy against him," and since she was foolish enough to take shelter behind the professional advisers with whom he suspected her of plotting against him, he had written her a letter seething with insolence and rage. The postscript read: "I shall not be satisfied with having my revenge. I shall make you a laughingstock. Tomorrow I shall tell everyone about the money order and the six francs seventy-five you kept back out of the three thousand I lent you. You won't be able to hold your face up in public." He had done nothing of the sort and had gone to his aunt Villeparisis the next day to apologize for the dreadful language he had used in the letter. And, anyway, to whom could he have told the story of the money order at this point? Since he wanted, not vengeance, but genuine reconciliation, this would have been the time for him to say nothing about it. But he had already told the story everywhere anyway, while still on good terms with his aunt, told it without spite, as a joke, and because he was the soul of indiscretion, he had told it without Mme de Villeparisis's knowledge. So that, when she read in his letter that he planned to disgrace her by divulging a transaction in which he had assured her personally that she had acted quite rightly, she had concluded that he had been insincere with her at the time and had lied when he pretended to be fond of her. All this had now died down, but neither of them knew exactly where he or she stood with the other. This was, of course, one of those rather unusual quarrels that happen from time to time. The quarrels of Bloch and his friends were of a different order. And of a different order again were those of M. de Charlus with people quite unlike Mme de Villeparisis, as we shall see. In spite of this, we need to bear in mind that our opinion of other people, our ties with friends or family, have only the semblance of fixity and are, in fact, as eternally fluid as the sea. Whence all the rumors of divorce between couples who have always seemed so perfectly united, and who soon afterward speak of each other with affection; all the slander uttered by one friend of another from whom he seemed inseparable, and with whom we shall find him reconciled before we have time to recover from our surprise, all the sudden reversals of alliances between nations.

"You know, things are heating up between my uncle and Mme Swann," Saint-Loup observed to me. "And here comes my innocent mama to disturb them. To the pure all things are pure!"

I turned my attention to M. de Charlus. The tuft of his gray hair, the twinkling eye beneath the eyebrow pushed up by his monocle, the red flowers in his buttonhole were like three mobile apexes in a convulsive and striking triangle. I had not been bold enough to greet him, since he had given me no sign of recognition. Yet, though he was not facing in my direction, I was convinced that he had seen me; while he sat there recounting some anecdote to Mme Swann, whose magnificent pansy-colored cape drifted over his knee, the Baron's roving eyes, like those of a street hawker constantly on the lookout for the "cops" to appear, had certainly explored every corner of the room and taken in everybody there. M. de Châtellerault came over to say good evening without

M. de Charlus's face showing any sign of recognition until the young Duc was standing in front of him. In this way, in fairly large receptions like the present one, M. de Charlus adopted an almost permanent smile, directed at nothing or no one in particular, which, by presaging the greetings of newcomers, could not be interpreted as a sign of friendliness toward them as they entered its orbit. Nevertheless, I felt obliged to go across and say good evening to Mme Swann. But since she was not certain whether I knew Mme de Marsantes or M. de Charlus, she was distinctly cold, fearing no doubt that I might ask her to introduce them to me. I then went up to M. de Charlus and immediately regretted it, because, though he could not have helped seeing me, he showed no sign at all of having done so. As I bowed, I discovered, at a distance from his body, which it prevented me from approaching by the full length of his outstretched arm, a finger that seemed only to lack the Episcopal ring he appeared to be offering as the consecrated site for a kiss, and I was made to look as if I had penetrated, without the Baron's leave and through some act of trespass for which he left me responsible, the permanence, the anonymous, vacant dispersion of his smile. This coldness was hardly calculated to urge Mme Swann out of hers.

"You're looking tired and upset," said Mme de Marsantes to her son, who had come over to say good evening to M. de Charlus.

And it was true that every now and then the expression in Robert's eyes seemed to reach down into the depths and then rise again, like a diver who has touched bottom. These depths, which were so painful for Robert to visit that he left them the moment he entered them and then returned to them a moment later, were his thoughts about the rift with his mistress.

"Never mind," his mother continued, stroking his cheek, "never mind, it's good to see my little boy again."

But since her affection seemed to irritate Robert, Mme de Marsantes took her son off to the other end of the room, into an alcove hung with yellow silk, where a group of Beauvais armchairs clustered their purplish upholstery like mauve irises in a field of buttercups. Mme Swann, finding herself alone and having realized that I was a friend of Saint-Loup, beckoned me to come and sit beside her. It was so long since I had seen her that I was at a loss for what to talk to her about. I kept my eye on my hat among all those that were there on the carpet, wondering with interest to whom one of them could belong: its lining bore a "G," surmounted by a ducal coronet, but it was not the Duc de Guermantes's. I knew who everyone there was and could not think of anyone whose hat this might be.

"What a nice person M. de Norpois is," I remarked to Mme Swann as I pointed him out to her. "I know that Robert de Saint-Loup thinks he's a pest, but . . ."

"And he's quite right there," she replied.

Seeing from her look that she was keeping something from me, I plied her with questions. Pleased, perhaps, to appear to be deeply absorbed in conversation with someone in a room where she hardly knew a soul, she drew me into a corner.

"I'm sure this is what M. de Saint-Loup meant," she said in answer to my questions, "but you mustn't tell him I said so. He would think me indiscreet, and I value his esteem a great deal. I like to observe the proprieties, you know. The other day, Charlus was dining at the Princesse de Guermantes's, and for some reason or other your name came into the conversation. M. de Norpois seems to have told them—it's all too silly, so don't get yourself into a state about it, no one paid any attention, they knew exactly the sort of person who would say such a thing— that you were a hysterical little flatterer."

I mentioned a long way back how stupefied I was to discover that a friend of my father's like M. de Norpois could have said such things about me. I was even more stupefied to learn that my feelings on that occasion long ago, when I had spoken about Mme Swann and Gilberte, were known to the Princesse de Guermantes, whom I took to be unaware of my existence. Each of our actions, our words, our attitudes is cut off from the "world," from the people who have not directly perceived them, by an ambience whose permeability is infinitely variable and unknown to us; when we learn from experience that some important remark we dearly hoped would be spread about (like the enthusiastic things I used to say at one time to everyone and at every opportunity about Mme Swann, thinking that among so many scattered seeds at least one would germinate) has at once, often because we hoped too hard, been consigned to darkness, then we are hardly likely to start believing that some tiny remark we have forgotten, which we may not even have uttered ourselves but which was formed in the course of events by the imperfect refraction of different words, could be transported, unhindered, infinite distances away—in the present case, to the Princesse de Guermantes—to divert at our expense the banquet of the gods. What we remember of our conduct remains unknown to our nearest neighbor; the things we had forgotten we had said, or even those we never did say, travel far off to provoke hilarity on another planet, and the image other people form of our actions and exploits no more corresponds to our own than an inaccurate tracing does to the original drawing, with empty spaces where there were black lines and inexplicable shapes where there were blank spaces. But it can happen that what has not been transcribed was nonexistent anyway, something we conjured up purely out of self-esteem, or, conversely, that the elements that seem to us to have been added are in fact very much a part of us, but so ingrained that they escape us. So this strange tracing, which seems to bear so little resemblance to us, has the same sort of truth about it—unflattering, certainly, but also profound and useful—as an X-ray photograph. Not that this is any reason why we should recognize ourselves in it. A man who is used to smiling in the mirror at his handsome face and figure will, if he is shown an X-ray of them, entertain the same suspicion of error at the sight of the rosary of bones presented as an image of himself as the visitor to an exhibition looking at the portrait of a young woman and reading in the catalogue, *"Camel Resting."* I was later to realize that this discrepancy between our own image of ourselves and the image others draw of us was felt not only by myself; there were people who lived unruffled amid the photographs they had taken of themselves, while round about them grinned the most fearful faces, invisible to them as a rule, but stunning them with amazement the moment the chance words "It's you" revealed them for what they were.

A few years earlier, I would have been only too glad to tell Mme Swann in what connection I had poured my heart out to M. de Norpois, since it had had to do with my desire to get to know her. But this was something I no longer felt; I was no longer in love with Gilberte. There was also the fact that I found it hard to identify Mme Swann with the lady in pink of my childhood. So I spoke to her about the woman who occupied my thoughts at the moment.

"Did you see the Duchesse de Guermantes just now?" I asked Mme Swann.

But since the Duchesse was not in the habit of acknowledging her, Mme Swann adopted the pretense of regarding her as a person of no interest, whose presence one did not even notice.

"I don't know. I didn't *realize* she was here," she replied peevishly, using the verb in its English sense.

But I was anxious for information with regard not only to Mme de Guermantes but to all the people in her entourage, and, just like Bloch, with the tactlessness of those who seek in their conversation not to give pleasure to others but selfishly to elucidate what interests them personally, in my attempt to form an exact picture of the life of Mme de Guermantes, I questioned Mme de Villeparisis about Mme Leroi.

"Yes, I know the woman you mean," she replied with affected disdain, "the daughter of those wealthy timber merchants. I know she's much in demand lately, but I must say I'm rather old now to start making new acquaintances. I've known such interesting, such delightful people in my time that I can't really think that Mme Leroi could add anything further to that."

Mme de Marsantes, who was playing lady-in-waiting to the Marquise, presented me to the Prince, and scarcely had she done so when M. de Norpois presented me as well, in the most glowing terms. Perhaps he found it easy to pay me a compliment that could not discredit him in the least, since I had just been introduced anyway; perhaps he thought that a foreigner, even a distinguished one, was less familiar with French salon life and might think he was being introduced to a young man from high society; perhaps he was exercising one of his prerogatives, that of adding the weight of his personal recommendation as an ambassador; or perhaps, in his taste for the archaic, to revive in the Prince's honor the old custom, flattering to his royal station, that entailed the necessity of two sponsors if one was to be presented.

Mme de Villeparisis called across to M. de Norpois, feeling it important that I should have it from him that she had nothing to regret in not knowing Mme Leroi.

"Isn't it true, M. l'Ambassadeur, that Mme Leroi is someone of no interest, very inferior to all the people who come here, and that I'm quite right not to have cultivated her?"

Whether he was keeping his own counsel or because he was tired, M. de Norpois replied merely with a bow that was full of respect but devoid of meaning.

"Monsieur," said Mme de Villeparisis with a laugh, "there are some absurd people about. Would you believe that I was visited this afternoon by a gentleman who tried to persuade me that he found more pleasure in kissing my hand than a young woman's?"

I guessed immediately that this must have been Legrandin. M. de Norpois smiled with a slight tremor of the eyelid, as if he felt that the remark arose from a concupiscence so natural that the person who felt it could be forgiven, almost as though it were the beginning of a romance that he was prepared to dismiss, or even encourage, with the perverse indulgence of a Voisenon or a Crébillon *fils*.[85]

"Many young women's hands would be incapable of doing what I see there," said the Prince, pointing to Mme de Villeparisis's unfinished watercolors.

And he asked her whether she had seen the recent exhibition of flower paintings by Fantin-Latour.

"They are first-class, the work, as they say nowadays, of a fine painter, one of the masters of the palette," declared M. de Norpois. "But in my view, they do not stand comparison with those of Mme de Villeparisis, which capture the coloring of a flower more successfully."

Even supposing that the partiality of an old lover, the habit of flattery, the views acceptable to a given social circle had dictated the ex-ambassador's remarks, they were nonetheless proof of the extent to which the artistic judgment of society people is based on a total absence of real taste, and so arbitrary that the merest trifle can push it into arrant nonsense, unchecked by any genuinely felt impression.

"I claim no credit for my knowledge of flowers; I've always lived among them," replied Mme de Villeparisis modestly. "But," she added graciously to the Prince, "if, when I was very young, I regarded them slightly more seriously than other country children, I owe it to a distinguished compatriot of yours, M. de Schlegel.[86] I met him at Broglie, where I was taken by my aunt Cordélia, the Maréchale de Castellane. I have a very clear memory of M. Lebrun, M. de Salvandy, M. Daudan getting him to talk about flowers. I was only a small girl, and I couldn't understand everything he said. But he liked playing with me, and when he went back to your country he sent me a lovely botany book as a reminder of the drive we took in a phaeton to the Val Richer, when I fell asleep on his knees. I've always kept the book, and it has taught me to observe a lot of things about flowers that I should not have noticed otherwise. When de Barante published some of Mme de Broglie's letters, charming and affected, as she was herself, I hoped to find among them some record of those conversations with M. de Schlegel. But she was a woman who looked to nature only for arguments in support of religion."

Robert called me away to the other end of the room, where he and his mother were.

"How very kind you've been," I said. "I don't know how to thank you. Can we dine together tomorrow?"

"Yes, tomorrow, if you like, but it will have to be with Bloch. I met him on his way out. He was rather cold with me for a moment. I'd somehow forgotten to answer his last two letters—he didn't say that was why he was put out, but I guessed. But he behaved so warmly with me subsequently that I can't say no to him. I think it's friendship for life between us, on his part at least."

I do not think that Robert was altogether mistaken. To fulminate against someone was often Bloch's way of showing a keen sympathy that he had supposed was not reciprocal. And as he had little imagination about other people's lives, and never dreamed that one might have been ill, away from home, and so forth, he was quick to interpret a week's silence as a deliberate rebuff. For this reason I never believed that his most violent outbursts as a friend, or later as a writer, went very deep. They were exacerbated if one responded to them with frosty decorum, or with the sort of platitude that encouraged him to redouble his onslaughts, but often they melted into the warmth of friendship. "As for my kindness to you," Saint-Loup went on, "I haven't really been kind at all. My aunt says that it's you who avoid her, that you never even speak to her. She wonders whether you have anything against her."

Fortunately for myself, if I had been taken in by these words, my sense of our imminent departure for Balbec would have stopped me from making any attempt to see Mme de Guermantes again, to assure her that I had nothing against her and thereby put her under the obligation to show that it was she who had something against me. But I needed only to remind myself that she had not even offered to let me see her Elstirs. None of this came as a real disappointment: I had never expected her to talk to me about the paintings; I knew I had no appeal for her, and no chance of ever making her like me; the most I had been able to hope for was that, since I would not be seeing her again before leaving Paris, her kindness would leave me with a deeply soothing impression of her, which I could take with me to Balbec as something of indefinitely lasting value, intact, and not as a memory mixed with anxiety and dejection.

Mme de Marsantes kept interrupting her conversation with Robert to tell me how often he had spoken to her about me, how fond he was of me; her solicitous behavior made me feel quite uncomfortable, because I felt it to be dictated by the fear of falling out with her son because of me, the son she had not seen all day, with whom she was anxious to be alone, and over whom she must have supposed that she had less influence than I did, and therefore needed to humor me. Having heard me earlier asking Bloch for news of his uncle M. Nissim Bernard, Mme de Marsantes inquired whether it was he who had once lived in Nice.

"In which case he would have known M. de Marsantes there before our marriage," Mme de Marsantes told me. "My husband often mentioned him to me as an excellent man, with such a discerning, generous nature."

"To think that for once in his life he wasn't lying! Amazing!" Bloch would have thought.

All this time, I would have liked to tell Mme de Marsantes that Robert was far, far fonder of her than he was of me, and that, even if she had shown hostility toward me, it was not in my nature to try to set him against her or to take him away from her. But now that Mme de Guermantes had gone, I had more time to observe Robert, and it was only then I noticed that he seemed once more possessed by a sort of anger, which had risen to the surface of his hardened, somber face. My fear was that the memory of the scene earlier in the afternoon, when he had allowed himself to be treated so harshly by his mistress without any retaliation on his part, had made him feel humiliated in my presence.

He suddenly broke away from his mother, who had put her arm around his neck, and, coming toward me, took me off behind the little desk with the flowers at which Mme de Villeparisis had now sat down again, and beckoned me to follow him into the small drawing room. As I was hurrying after him, M. de Charlus, perhaps under the impression that I was leaving, brought his conversation with M. de Faffenheim to an abrupt end and wheeled around rapidly to face me. I was alarmed to see that he had taken the hat with the "G" and the ducal coronet in the lining. In the doorway to the small drawing room, he said without looking at me:

"Now that I see you have taken to going into society, you must give me the pleasure of a visit. But it's all rather complicated," he added with casual purposefulness, as if this pleasure was something he feared he might not encounter again once he had let slip the opportunity to arrange with me the means of securing it. "I am rarely at home. You will have to write to me. But I'd prefer to explain it all to you in quieter surroundings. I'm leaving soon. Will you walk a little way with me? I shall only keep you for a moment."

"Do take care, monsieur," I said. "You've picked up the wrong hat by mistake."

"You want to stop me from taking my own hat?"

I assumed, since the same mishap had recently happened to me, that someone else had gone away with his hat, and his instinctive reaction had been to pick up one at random so as not to go home bareheaded, and that my remark had embarrassed him by exposing his ruse. So I did not pursue the matter. I told him that I needed to say a few words to Saint-Loup before I left. "He's talking to that stupid Duc de Guermantes," I added. "What a charming thing to say. I shall tell my brother." "Oh, you think that would interest M. de Charlus?" I simply supposed that, if he had a brother, the brother must be called M. de Charlus, too. Saint-Loup had in fact explained the family connections to me in Balbec, but I had forgotten them. "What do you mean, M. de Charlus?" replied the Baron contemptuously. "Go and speak to Robert. I know you were there this morning, at one of those orgiastic lunches he has with a woman who is disgracing him. You would do well to use your influence with him and get him to see how much pain he is causing his poor mother and all of us by dragging our name in the mud."

I should have liked to reply that this degrading lunch party had been entirely given over to a discussion of Emerson, Ibsen, and Tolstoy, and that the young woman in question had lectured Robert about not drinking alcohol. In the hope of soothing Robert, whose pride I thought had been wounded, I sought to excuse his mistress. I did not know as I did so that, in spite of his anger with her, it was he himself that he was reproaching. It always happens—even in quarrels between a good man and a spiteful woman, when the right is all on one side—that some trifle crops up that enables the woman to appear not to have been in the wrong on one particular matter. And since she ignores all the other points of the argument, if the man feels he needs her, if he is upset by the rift between them, his weakness will make him scrupulous, he will remember the absurd reproaches that have been leveled against him and ask himself whether they are not somehow justified.

"I think I was wrong about that business of the necklace," said Robert. "I know I didn't do it with any nasty motive, but other people don't see things in the same way. I'm well aware of that. She had a very hard childhood. I'm bound to seem to her like the rich man who can buy anything with money, against whom a poor man can't compete, whether it's persuading Boucheron or winning a lawsuit. I know she's been horribly unkind to me, when I've never thought of anything but her good. But I can see that she really thought I wanted to make her feel that I could keep a hold on her with money, and it's not true. She's so fond of me—what must she be thinking? The poor darling, if you only knew how kind and thoughtful she is; I can't tell you what adorable things she's done for me. She must be feeling really wretched! Anyway, whatever happens, I don't want her to think I'm a cad. I'm going to dash off to Boucheron's and get that necklace. Who knows? Perhaps, when she sees what I've done, she'll admit it was partly her fault. It's the idea that she's suffering at this moment that I can't bear, can you see that? What one suffers oneself one knows, and it's nothing. But the thought that *she's* suffering, without being able to imagine what she feels, is enough to drive one mad. I'd rather not see her ever again than let her suffer. All I ask is that she be happy—without me, if need be. You know, for me everything that concerns her is immensely important, it becomes something cosmic. I shall rush off to the jeweler's and then go and ask her to forgive me. Until I get to her, what can she be thinking of me? If only she knew I was on my way! Perhaps it would be a good idea for you to come, too. Perhaps everything will be all right. Perhaps," he said with a smile, as if he hardly dared to believe such a thing possible, "the three of us can go and dine in the country. But I can't really tell. I'm so bad at treating her properly. Poor sweet, I may hurt her feelings again. Besides, she may already have made up her mind for good."

Robert swept me back to his mother.

"Goodbye," he said to her. "I have to go now. I don't know when my next leave will be. Probably not for a month. I'll write as soon as I know."

Certainly Robert was not at all the sort of son who, when he accompanies his mother into society, feels it necessary to adopt an exasperated attitude toward her as a counterbalance to the smiles and greetings he addresses to strangers. Nothing is more common than this hateful form of vengeance on the part of those who appear to believe that rudeness to family is the natural complement to formal behavior. Whatever the wretched mother may say, the son, as though he had been brought along against his will and wished her to pay dearly for it, immediately counters any timidly ventured assertion with some sarcastic contradiction, which cruelly hits home; the mother at once conforms to the opinion of this superior being, though this does nothing to make him relent, and she will go on vaunting his delightful nature to the whole world in his absence, while he continues to wound her with his most barbed remarks. Saint-Loup was not at all like this, but the anguish provoked by Rachel's absence caused him, for different reasons, to be no less harsh with his mother than the sort of son I have described. And as she listened to him, I saw the same tremor, like the beating of a wing, that Mme de Marsantes had been unable to repress when her son first entered the room, run through her whole body once more; but this time it was an anxious face and distressed gaze that she fastened on him.

"You're not leaving, Robert? Not seriously? Darling! On the one day I might have seen something of you!"

And then, quite softly, in the most natural voice, from which she tried hard to banish any hint of sadness so as not to make her son feel any sense of pity, which would perhaps have been painful to him, or else useless and simply sent to irritate him, she added, as a merely common-sense proposition:

"You know that it's not very nice of you."

But in this simple remark there was so much timidity, to reassure him that she was not trespassing on his freedom, and so much affection, so that he should not reproach her with interfering with his pleasures, that Saint-Loup could not help feeling that he might himself succumb to an affectionate response, in other words to an obstacle to his spending the evening with his mistress. So he responded angrily:

"It's unfortunate, but, nice or not nice, that's the way it is."

And he heaped on his mother the reproaches he no doubt felt he perhaps deserved himself; thus it is that egotists always have the last word; starting from the premise that their resolution is unshakable, the more susceptible the feeling to which one appeals in them to make them abandon their resolve, the more objectionable they find, not themselves and their resistance to that appeal, but those who put them under pressure to resist, so that their own unbending behavior may be carried to extremes of cruelty without their seeing the matter as anything more than the aggravated culpability of the person who is so indelicate as to feel hurt, to be in the right, and who thus lets them down by making them feel the pain of acting against their natural sense of compassion. But Mme de Marsantes let the matter drop of her own accord, for she sensed that she would be unable to dissuade him.

"I'm off," he said to me, "but, Mama, please don't keep him long. He's got to pay another call in a while."

I felt certain that Mme de Marsantes would not derive any pleasure from my company, but I was glad not to give her the impression by leaving with Robert that I was involved in the pleasures that deprived her of him. I would have liked to find some excuse for her son's behavior, less from affection for him than from sympathy with her. But it was she who spoke first:

"Poor boy," she said, "I'm sure I must have hurt his feelings. You see, monsieur, mothers are such selfish creatures. And he doesn't have many pleasures in life—he comes so seldom to Paris. Oh dear, if he hadn't left already, I should have liked to catch him for a minute—not to keep him with me, of course, but just to tell him that I'm not cross, that I think he was quite right. Would you mind if I go look over the staircase?"

We went together.

"Robert! Robert!" she called. "No, he's left. I've missed him."

At that moment I would have undertaken a mission to make Robert break with his mistress as readily as I had been to make him go and live with her permanently a few hours earlier. In the one case, Saint-Loup would have regarded me as a false friend; in the other, his family would have called me his evil genius. Yet, in that interval of a few hours, I was the same man.

We returned to the drawing room. Seeing that Saint-Loup had not returned with us, Mme de Villeparisis exchanged with M. de Norpois one of those skeptical, wry, and barely sympathetic glances reserved for overjealous wives and overfond mothers (stock targets of amusement), as much as to say, "Well, well, there's been trouble there all right."

Robert went to his mistress, taking with him the splendid piece of jewelry, which, in terms of the rules they had set each other, he ought not to have given her. But it came to the same thing, for she would have nothing to do with it, and even subsequently he could never persuade her to accept it. Some of Robert's friends thought that such shows of disinterestedness on her part were deliberately calculated to bind him to her. But in fact she was not really interested in money, except perhaps in order to be able to spend it without counting every penny. I have known her to lavish wild amounts of money on people she thought were in need. "At this moment," Robert's friends would say to him, in an attempt to counter with their malicious words some disinterested deed of Rachel's, "at this moment she'll be haunting the promenade gallery of the Folies-Bergère. She's an enigma, that Rachel, a real sphinx." And yet one sees any number of mercenary women, women kept by men, taking it upon themselves to set limits on the generosity of their lovers in countless small ways, out of a consideration for others that flowers in the midst of their dubious style of life!

Robert was unaware of almost all the infidelities of his mistress, and tormented himself over what were mere nothings compared with the reality of Rachel's life, a life that began every day only after he had left her. He was unaware of almost all these infidelities. One could have told him about them without shaking his confidence in Rachel; for it is a charming law of nature, and one that is evident in the heart of the most complex societies, that we live in perfect ignorance of those we love. On one side of the glass, the lover says to himself, "She is an angel, she will never give herself to me, I may as well die. And yet she loves me; she loves me so much that perhaps . . . But no, it can never happen!" And in the rapture of his desire, in the anguish of his expectation, what jewels he flings at the feet of this woman, how he runs to borrow money to save her from financial embarrassment! Meanwhile, on the other side of the glass partition, through which these words will no more carry than those exchanged by visitors in front of an aquarium, people are saying: "You don't know her? Then you're lucky. She has robbed and ruined I don't know how many men. As such women go, she's the dregs. Nothing but a swindler. And crafty about it!" And perhaps this last epithet is not absolutely wrong, for even the skeptical man who is not really in love with the woman, who merely finds her attractive, says to his friends: "No, no, my dear fellow, she's certainly no cocotte. I'm not saying she hasn't had an adventure or two in her time, but she's not a woman who takes money, and if she did it would be a pricy business. With her it's fifty thousand francs or nothing." The reality is that he himself has spent fifty thousand francs to have her once, but she, finding a willing accomplice in the man himself, in his own self-regard, has managed to persuade him that he is one of the men who have had her for nothing. Such is society, where every being is double, and where the most transparent person, the most notorious, will be known to others only from within a protective shell, a sweet cocoon, as a charming natural curiosity. There were in Paris two utterly decent men whom Saint-Loup would no longer acknowledge, and whom he never mentioned without a tremor in his voice, referring to them as exploiters of women: this was because they had both been ruined by Rachel.

"There is one thing I reproach myself for," Mme de Marsantes said to me in a subdued voice. "I wish I hadn't told him it wasn't nice of him. He's such an adorable son, so special, there's no one like him in the world. To have told him, the one time I see him, that he wasn't being nice to me! I'd rather have been given a beating, because I'm sure that, however much he enjoys this evening, and he doesn't have much time to enjoy himself, it will be spoiled for him by what I said. It was uncalled for. But I mustn't keep you, monsieur, you're in a hurry."

Mme de Marsantes bade me an anxious goodbye. Her feelings concerned Robert, and they were sincere. But the sincerity ceased as she became a grand lady again:

"I have been so *interested*, so *happy*, so *honored* to have had this little chat with you. Thank you so very much!"

And with an air of humility she gazed at me in ecstatic gratitude, as though my conversation had been one of the greatest pleasures of her life. Her gaze admirably matched the black flowers on her leaf-patterned white dress; it came from a *grande dame* who knew exactly how to conduct herself.

"I'm really in no hurry, madame," I replied. "In fact, I'm waiting for M. de Charlus. We're leaving together."

Mme de Villeparisis overheard these last words. She seemed put out by them. If it hadn't been something that could not have involved such a reaction, I would have thought that Mme de Villeparisis's apparent alarm at that moment had to do with her sense of decency. But this hypothesis never even entered my mind. I was feeling delighted with Mme de Guermantes, with Saint-Loup, with Mme de Marsantes, with

M. de Charlus, with Mme de Villeparisis; I did not stop to think, and I spoke lightheartedly, saying whatever came into my head.

"You're leaving with my nephew Palamède?" she asked me.

Thinking that it might make a highly favorable impression on Mme de Villeparisis to think that I was on friendly terms with a nephew she esteemed so greatly, I replied gaily: "He has asked me to walk home with him. I'm delighted. And we're better friends than you think, madame. In fact, I've made up my mind that we shall be still better friends."

Mme de Villeparisis's displeasure now seemed to turn to anxiety: "Don't bother to wait for him," she said as if she had something on her mind. "He's talking to M. de Faffenheim. He's already forgotten what he said to you. Why don't you slip away while his back is turned?"

In different circumstances, this initial reaction of Mme de Villeparisis would have seemed to arise from a sense of what was decent. To judge by the expression on her face, her insistent objection could have been dictated by probity. I was not myself in any great hurry to join Robert and his mistress. But Mme de Villeparisis seemed so anxious for me to leave that, under the impression that she had some important business to discuss with her nephew, I bade her farewell. The hefty figure of M. de Guermantes was seated beside her, proud and Olympian. One got the impression that the notion of his vast riches was omnipresent in all his limbs, giving him an extraordinary density, as though they had been smelted in a crucible into a single human ingot to create this man who was worth so much. When I said goodbye to him, he rose politely to his feet, and I could sense the inert mass of thirty million being activated and raised up by old-fashioned French breeding until it stood before me. I seemed to be looking at the statue of Olympian Zeus that Phidias is said to have cast in solid gold. Such was the power a Jesuit education exercised over M. de Guermantes, or at least over his body, for it did not extend to mastery of the ducal mind. M. de Guermantes laughed at his own jokes, but did not blink an eyelid at other people's.

On my way downstairs, I heard someone calling out to me from behind:

"So this is what you call waiting for me, is it?"

It was M. de Charlus.

"You don't mind if we go a little way on foot?" he asked dryly, when we reached the courtyard. "We'll walk until I find a cab that is to my liking."

"You wished to speak to me, monsieur?"

"Ah yes, there were indeed several things I wanted to say to you, but I'm no longer sure that I shall. For you, I feel they could be the beginning of inestimable benefits. But I can also see that they would bring into my existence, at an age when one starts to value a quiet life, a great deal of wasted time, all kinds of inconvenience. I ask myself whether you are worth all the trouble I should need to take in your case, and I don't have the pleasure of knowing you well enough to be able to decide. And it may be that you are insufficiently interested in what I could do for you for me to put myself to so much trouble. So let me say again, quite frankly, monsieur, that for me it can mean nothing but trouble."

I protested that, in that case, he must not dream of it. Such a brusque end to negotiations did not seem to be to his liking.

"That sort of politeness means nothing," he said harshly. "There is nothing more agreeable than putting oneself out for someone who deserves it. For the best of us, the study of the arts, an appreciation for old things, collections, gardens, are merely ersatz, surrogates, alibis. From the depths of our tub, like Diogenes,[87] we are looking for a man. We grow begonias, we trim yew trees, for lack of anything better to do, because yews and begonias submit to it. But we should prefer to give our time to a human plant, were we sure it was worth the trouble. That is the whole question. You must know yourself a little. Are you worth the trouble or not?"

"The last thing I'd want, monsieur, would be to be a cause of anxiety to you," I told him, "but, as far as I'm concerned, you may be sure that everything that comes to me from you will give me very great pleasure. I'm deeply touched that you should take such a kind interest in me in this way and want to help me."

To my great surprise, he thanked me for these words almost effusively.

Slipping his arm through mine with the same sporadic familiarity that had already struck me in Balbec, and which was in such contrast with the harshness of his tone, he said:

"With the lack of consideration typical of your years, you are liable to say things at times that could create an unbridgeable gap between us. But what you have just said is precisely the sort of thing that is capable of touching me, and persuading me to do a great deal for you."

As he walked arm in arm with me, uttering these words, which, though tinged with condescension, were so affectionate, M. de Charlus at times fastened his gaze on me with the intense stare, the piercing scrutiny, that had struck me the first morning I saw him outside the casino in Balbec—and in fact many years before that, as he stood beside Mme Swann, whom I took to be his mistress, near the pink hawthorn bush in the Tansonville park—and at others let it stray around him and examine the considerable number of cabs passing at this busy hour, staring at them so insistently that several stopped, their drivers assuming that he wished to engage them. But M. de Charlus immediately sent them away.

"None of them will do," he said to me. "It's all a question of their lamps, the direction they're going home in. I hope, monsieur," he went on, "that you won't misinterpret the purely disinterested and charitable nature of the proposal I'm about to make to you."

I was struck, even more than I had been in Balbec, by the way his diction resembled Swann's.

"You are intelligent enough, I assume, not to imagine that it is inspired by a 'lack of connections,' by fear of solitude and boredom. There is no need for me to speak to you about my family, for it seems to me that a young man of your age who belongs to the lower middle class"—he emphasized the phrase with satisfaction—"must know his French history. It is the people of my world who read nothing and are as ignorant as lackeys. There was a time when the King's valets were recruited among the nobility, and now the nobility are scarcely better than valets themselves. But young middle-class people like you do read, and I'm sure you know Michelet's fine words about my family: 'I see them as very great, these powerful Guermantes. And what is the poor little King of France, shut up in his palace in Paris, compared with them?'[88] As for what I am personally, that, monsieur, is a subject I do not much care to talk about, but you may have heard—it was alluded to in an article in *The Times* that caused a considerable stir—that the Emperor of Austria, who has always honored me with his kind attention and is good enough to maintain cousinly relations with me, declared recently in an interview that was made public that if the Comte de Chambord had had the services of a man as thoroughly apprised of the undercurrents of European politics as myself, he would today be King of France. I have often thought, monsieur, that there was in me, thanks not to my humble gifts but to circumstances that you may one day have occasion to learn, a wealth of experience, a kind of secret dossier of inestimable worth, which I have not felt it proper to use for my own purposes, but which would be of priceless benefit to a young man to whom I would hand over, in a matter of months, what it has taken me more than thirty years to acquire, and which I am perhaps alone in possessing. I do not speak of the intellectual enjoyment you would gain in learning certain secrets that a present-day Michelet would give years of his life to discover, and in the light of which certain events would assume an entirely different aspect. And I do not speak only of events that have already occurred, but of the chain of circumstances." (This was a favorite expression of M. de Charlus's, and often when he used it he joined his hands in prayer, but with his fingers out straight, as though this complexus were there to illustrate the circumstances in question, which he did not specify, and the links between them.) "I could give you an explanation no one has ever dreamed of, not only of the past but of the future."

M. de Charlus broke off to question me about Bloch, whom he had heard discussed, but without appearing to be listening, at Mme de Villeparisis's salon. And in that tone which he was so artful at detaching from what he was saying that he seemed to be thinking of something completely different, and to be speaking automatically, simply out of politeness, he asked if my school friend was young, good-looking, and so forth. Had he heard him, Bloch would have had an even harder time than he did with M. de Norpois, but for very different reasons, deciding whether M. de Charlus was for or against Dreyfus. "It's no bad thing, if you wish to learn about life," said M. de Charlus when he had finished questioning me about Bloch, "to have a few foreigners among your friends." I told him that Bloch was French. "Is that so?" said M. de Charlus. "I took him to be Jewish." His assertion of such an incompatibility led me to believe that M. de Charlus was more anti-Dreyfusard than anyone I had met. And yet he went on to protest against the charge of treason leveled against Dreyfus. But he did so in these terms: "I believe that, according to the newspapers, Dreyfus has committed a crime against his country—that is what I understand, but I pay no attention to newspapers; I read them the way I wash my hands, and I don't think they deserve any more interest than that. In any case, the crime is nonexistent. This compatriot of your friend would have committed a crime against his country if he had betrayed Judaea, but what has that got to do with France?" I pointed out that if there were to be a war the Jews would be mobilized just like everyone else. "That may be, and I am not sure that it would not be imprudent. If we bring over Senegalese or Malagasies, I can't really see that their hearts will be set on defending France, and that's natural enough. It might be as well to convict your Dreyfus of a breach in the laws of hospitality. But enough of that. Perhaps you could ask your friend to get me invited to some attractive festival in the temple, a circumcision, or some Hebrew chants. He might perhaps hire a hall and provide me with some Biblical entertainment, like the young ladies of Saint-Cyr[89] who performed scenes taken from Racine's *Psaumes* to amuse Louis XIV. You might even arrange some comic turns. For instance, a contest between your friend and his father, in which he would smite him as David smote Goliath. That would make quite an amusing farce. He might even, while he was about it, give his mother a good thrashing, the old hag, or, as my old nurse would say, 'the old bag.' It would make an excellent spectacle, the sort of thing we like, eh, my young friend, with our taste for the exotic, and to thrash that non-European bitch would be giving the old cow what she deserves." As he made these dreadful, almost deranged remarks, M. de Charlus squeezed my arm until it hurt. I reminded myself of all that the Baron's family had told me about his wonderful kindness to this old nurse of his, whose Molièresque turns of phrase he had just recalled, and reflected that the connections, scantily investigated to date, I felt, between goodness and evil in the same heart, various as they might be, would be an interesting area of study.

I drew his attention to the fact that, in any case, Mme Bloch was no longer living, and in M. Bloch's case, I questioned to what extent he would enjoy an activity that might easily result in having his eyes put out. M. de Charlus seemed annoyed. "That," he said, "is a woman who made a big mistake by dying. As for blinding the husband, surely the synagogue itself is blind: it does not perceive the truth of the Gospel. Besides, just think, at this time when all those unfortunate Jews are trembling before the stupid fury of the Christians, what an honor it would be for them to see a man like myself stooping to enjoy their little games!" At this point I caught sight of M. Bloch *père* passing by, probably on the way to meet his son. He did not notice us, but I offered M. de Charlus the opportunity to make his acquaintance. I little suspected the fury this was to unleash in my companion: "Make his acquaintance! But you must have very little idea of social values! People do not make my acquaintance as easily as that. In the present instance, there would be two reasons for impropriety: the youth of the person making the introduction, and the unworthiness of the person introduced. At the very most, if I am ever to enjoy the Asiatic entertainment I outlined to you, I might spare this dreadful fellow a few kind-sounding words. But on condition that he would have allowed himself to be thoroughly thrashed by his son. I might go so far as to express my satisfaction." But as it happened, M. Bloch was paying no attention to us. He was busy greeting Mme Sazerat effusively, to her great delight. This startled me, for previously, in Combray, she was so anti-Semitic that she had been indignant with my parents for allowing young Bloch into the house. But Dreyfusism, like a strong gust of wind, had blown M. Bloch right up against her a few days before this. My friend's father had found Mme Sazerat charming and was particularly gratified by the lady's anti-Semitism, which he saw as a proof of the sincerity of her faith and the authenticity of her Dreyfusard views, and which also enhanced the value of the call she had authorized him to pay her. He had not even been wounded when she had said to him without thinking, "M. Drumont⁹⁰ has the nerve to put the Revisionists in the same bag as the Protestants and the Jews! A delightful hodgepodge!" "Bernard," he had said proudly to M. Nissim Bernard when he got home, "there's a woman with prejudice for you!" But M. Nissim Bernard had said nothing and had raised his eyes to heaven angelically. Saddened by the misfortune of the Jews, remembering his friendship with Christians, increasingly mannered and affected as time went on, for reasons to be revealed in due course, he now looked like a Pre-Raphaelite worm onto which hairs had been indecently grafted, like threads in the depths of an opal.

"This whole Dreyfus business," the Baron continued, still clasping my arm, "has only one drawback. It is destroying society (I don't mean polite society—society has long ceased to deserve such a laudatory epithet) by the influx of Mr. and Mrs. Cow, Cowshed, and Cow Dung, insignificant people whom I find even in the houses of my own cousins, because they belong to the Patriotic League, the Anti-Jewish League, or some other such league, as if a political opinion entitled them to social standing."

This frivolous attitude of M. de Charlus accentuated his family likeness to the Duchesse de Guermantes. I pointed out the resemblance to him. Since he was under the impression that I did not know her, I reminded him of the evening at the Opéra when he had seemed to be trying to avoid me. He assured me so forcefully that he had never seen me there that I should have ended up believing it had not a trifling incident presently occurred and led me to think that M. de Charlus, in his overweening pride perhaps, preferred not to be seen in my company.

"To get back to yourself," he said, "and my plans for you. Monsieur, there exists among certain men a Freemasonry which I can't describe to you now, but which numbers in its ranks four of the present sovereigns in Europe. Now, the entourage of one of them, the Emperor of Germany, is trying to cure him of his whims. This is a very serious matter and may lead to war. Yes, monsieur, I mean what I say. You know the story of the man who believed he had the Princess of China shut up in a bottle. It was a mad belief. He was cured of it. But as soon as he ceased to be mad, he became stupid. There are some sicknesses we must not seek to cure, because they are our only protection from others that are more serious. One of my cousins had a stomach complaint. He could digest nothing. The most experienced stomach specialists treated him with no effect. I took him to a certain doctor (another extremely interesting man, incidentally, about whom there is a lot I could tell you). He guessed at once that it was a nervous ailment, advised him to eat whatever he wanted without misgivings and that it would be easily digested. But my cousin also had nephritis. What the stomach digested perfectly well, the kidneys could no longer eliminate after a time, and my cousin, instead of living to a ripe old age with an imaginary stomach ailment that obliged him to stick to a diet, died at forty with his stomach cured but his kidneys ruined. Given an exceptional lead over your fellow beings, who knows, you may perhaps become what some eminent man of the past might have been if a beneficent spirit had revealed to him, among men who knew nothing of them, the secrets of steam and electricity. Don't be foolish and refuse out of a sense of tact. I want you to understand that, if I do you a great service, I do not consider you to be doing me any less a one. Society people have long ceased to interest me. I have only one passion left, to attempt to redeem the mistakes of my life by giving the benefit of my knowledge to a soul that is still innocent and capable of being fired by virtue. I have experienced great sorrow, monsieur, and I'll perhaps tell you about it one day; I lost my wife, the loveliest, noblest, most perfect creature imaginable. I have young relatives who are not—I won't say worthy, but capable of accepting the spiritual heritage I have been speaking of. Who knows but that you may be the person into whose hands it is to pass, the one whose life I shall be able to guide and raise to so high a plane? My own would gain in the bargain. Perhaps by teaching you the great secrets of diplomacy I might rekindle a taste for them in myself, and finally begin to do important things, in which you would have an equal share. But before I can decide this, I need to see you often, very often, every day."

I was thinking of taking advantage of these unexpectedly kind inclinations on M. de Charlus's part to ask him whether he could not arrange for me to meet his sister-in-law when, suddenly, my arm was violently jerked by something like an electric shock. M. de Charlus had hurriedly withdrawn his arm from mine. Although as he talked his eyes traveled everywhere, he had only just seen M. d'Argencourt emerging from a side street. As he caught sight of us, M. d'Argencourt appeared annoyed, cast a look of distrust in my direction—almost the same look, intended for a creature of another race, that Mme de Guermantes had reserved for Bloch—and tried to avoid us. But it seemed as if M. de Charlus was determined to show him that he was not at all anxious not to be seen by him, for he called over to him, merely to make an utterly insignificant remark. And, fearing perhaps that M. d'Argencourt did not recognize me, M. de Charlus informed him that I was a great friend of Mme de Villeparisis, of the Duchesse de Guermantes, of Robert de Saint-Loup, and that he, Charlus, was an old friend of my grandmother, and happy to show her grandson a little of the affection he felt for her. Nevertheless, I noted that M. d'Argencourt, to whom I had barely been introduced at Mme de Villeparisis's, and to whom M. de Charlus had now spoken at length about my family, was appreciably colder to me than he had been an hour ago, and subsequently, for a long time, he behaved with the same reserve whenever we met. On this occasion, he examined me with a curiosity in which there was no hint of friendliness, and it was even as if he had to overcome a sense of distaste when, on leaving us, after some hesitation, he held out a hand to me, which he immediately withdrew.

"An unfortunate encounter," said M. de Charlus. "That fellow Argencourt is well born but ill bred, a worse-than-second-rate diplomat, a loathsome husband and a womanizer, a double-faced stage character. He's one of those men who are incapable of understanding but perfectly capable of destroying the high things in life. I hope that our friendship will be one of them, if it is ever to establish itself, and I hope, too, that you will do me the honor of protecting it, as I shall, from the heels of those donkeys who, for lack of anything better to do, from clumsiness or spite, trample on what seemed made to endure. Unfortunately, most society people have been cast into that mold."

"The Duchesse de Guermantes appears to be a very intelligent woman. We were talking earlier about the possibility of war. It seems she is especially knowledgeable on the subject."

"She is nothing of the sort," replied M. de Charlus sharply. "Women, and many men for that matter, understand nothing about the things I wished to speak to you of. My sister-in-law is a charming woman who imagines she is still living in the days of Balzac's fiction, when women had political influence. Her society could at present only have an unfortunate effect on you, like for that matter all association with high society. That is precisely what I was about to say when that fool interrupted me. The first sacrifice you must make for me—I shall demand them in proportion to the gifts I bestow on you—is to give up society life. It pained me earlier to see you at that ridiculous gathering. You will tell me I was there myself, but for me it was not a social occasion, merely a family visit. Later on, when your position is established, if it amuses you to stoop to that sort of social activity, there may be no harm in it. And, then, I have no need to tell you how invaluable my services can be. The 'Open Sesame' to the Guermantes mansion, and any others worthy of throwing open their doors to you, lies with me. I shall be the judge of that, and I intend to remain in control of the situation. For the time being, you are a novice. There was something scandalous about your presence up there. You must avoid impropriety at all costs."

Since M. de Charlus was on the subject of this visit to Mme de Villeparisis's, I wanted to ask him about his exact relationship to the Marquise, about her birth, but formulated my question in a manner that deflected my intention, and I asked him instead what the Villeparisis family was.

"Oh dear, that's not a very easy question to answer," M. de Charlus replied in a voice that seemed to skate over his words. "It's as if you'd asked me to tell you what nothing was. My aunt, who does exactly what she pleases, took it into her head to get remarried to some little man, a certain M. Thirion, and so plunge the greatest name in France into oblivion. This Thirion thought that he could adopt some defunct aristocratic name with impunity, as people do in novels. History doesn't tell us whether he was tempted by La Tour d'Auvergne, whether he hesitated between Toulouse and Montmorency. Anyway, he made a different choice and became M. de Villeparisis. Since there have been no Villeparisis since 1702, I imagined that he meant to indicate modestly that he was a gentleman from Villeparisis, a tiny locality near Paris, that he had a solicitor's practice or a barbershop in Villeparisis. But my aunt had other ideas in mind–though these days she's reaching an age when she has scarcely an idea left in her head. She made the claim that this marquisate already existed in the family, wrote to us all, and wanted to put things on a proper footing, for some reason or other. If one lays claim to a name to which one is not entitled, then it's better not to make a song and dance about it, like our very good friend the so-called Comtesse de M——, who, against the advice of Mme Alphonse de Rothschild, refused to pay the price of religious conversion for a title that it would have done nothing further to authenticate in any case. The funny side of it is that ever since then my aunt has claimed monopoly of all the paintings connected with the real Villeparisis family, to whom the late Thirion was in no way related. Her country house has become something like an exclusive repository for their portraits, genuine or not, and the rising tide of them has meant that some of the Guermantes and Condé portraits–by no means small potatoes–have been swamped. The picture dealers manufacture new ones for her every year. And in the dining room of her country house there is even a portrait of Saint-Simon, because of his niece's first marriage to a M. de Villeparisis, as if the author of the *Mémoires* might not have other claims on the interest of visitors than not to have been the great-grandfather of M. Thirion."

The fact that Mme de Villeparisis was merely Mme Thirion completed her downfall in my estimation, which had begun when I saw the uneven gathering of people in her salon. I found it unfair that a woman whose very title and name were of relatively recent origin should be able to delude her contemporaries and might delude posterity by virtue of her friendships with royalty. Now that she had been restored to what she had seemed to me in my childhood, someone with nothing aristocratic about her, the distinguished relatives by whom she was surrounded seemed suddenly foreign to her world. She did not cease to charm us as a result of this. I continued to visit her occasionally, and from time to time she sent me tokens of remembrance. But in no way did it seem to me that she was part of the Faubourg Saint-Germain, and if I had needed any information about it, she was one of the last people I should have asked.

"At present," M. de Charlus continued, "by going into society you will only damage your position, warp your mind and character. And while we're about it, you must be particularly careful in your choice of friends. Take mistresses if your family raise no objection; it's none of my business, and I would go so far as to encourage it, you young rascal, a young rascal who will soon have to start shaving," he added, fingering my chin. "But your choice of men friends is particularly important. Eight out of ten young men are real scoundrels, little wretches capable of doing you irreparable harm. My nephew Saint-Loup, now, he might be the right sort of friend for you in a pinch. As far as your future is concerned, he can be of no conceivable use to you, but I can look after that. Yes, now that I come to think about it, as a person to go about with at times when you've had enough of me, he presents no serious drawbacks as far as I can see. At least he's a proper man, not one of those effeminate creatures one comes across everywhere nowadays, who look just like rent boys capable of bringing their innocent victims to a sorry end at the drop of a hat." (I did not know the meaning of this slang expression, "rent boy." Anyone who had known it would have shared my astonishment. Society people are only too pleased to talk slang, and people who may be suspected of certain things like to show that they are not afraid to mention them—a proof of innocence in their eyes. But they have lost their sense of proportion and no longer realize the point at which a particular joking remark will become too specific, too outrageous, and turn into evidence of corruption rather than of ingenuousness.) "He's not one of that sort. He's very nice, very serious."

I could not repress a smile at this epithet "serious," to which the intonation that M. de Charlus gave it seemed to imply the sense of "virtuous," of "orderly," in the way we call a young shopgirl "serious." At that moment a cab passed by, careering all over the place; a young cabman, who had deserted his box, was driving it from inside, seated on the cushions in what looked like a half-tipsy state. M. de Charlus hailed him immediately. The driver negotiated with him briefly.

"Which way are you going?"

"The same way as you." (This astonished me, because M. de Charlus had already refused several cabs with similarly colored lamps.)

"But I don't want to get up on the box. Does it bother you if I stay inside?"

"No, but lower the hood. So—think over my proposal," said M. de Charlus as he prepared to leave me. "I give you a few days to reflect on it. Write to me. But remember, I shall need to see you every day, and to have from you a guarantee of loyalty and discretion, though I do admit that that is what you seem to be offering. But I have been so deceived by appearances in the course of my life that I no longer care to trust in them. Damn it, it's the least I can expect, before giving up a priceless gift, that I should know into whose hands it is going. So make sure you bear in mind what I'm offering you. You're like Hercules at the parting of the ways—though, unfortunately for you, you don't seem to me to have the same muscular development. Try to avoid having to regret for the rest of your life that you didn't choose the path that leads to virtue. I say," he said, addressing the cabman, "haven't you put the hood down yet? I'll see to it myself. And I think I'd better drive, given the state you seem to be in."

He jumped in beside the driver at the back of the cab, and off they set at a brisk trot.

I, for my part, returned home, and no sooner had I done so than I came across the pendant to the conversation that had taken place a little earlier between Bloch and M. de Norpois, but in another form, brief, inverted, and nasty: this was a dispute between our butler, a Dreyfusard, and the Guermantes butler, an anti-Dreyfusard. The truths and counter-truths that clashed together on high among the intellectuals of the two leagues, the Patrie Française and the Droits de l'Homme,[91] were in fact spreading downward into popular opinion. M. Reinach's influence was having its effect on the feelings of people he had never set eyes on, even though for him the Dreyfus case presented itself to his reason merely as an irrefutable theorem, which he went on to "demonstrate" by the most astonishing victory for rational politics (a victory at France's expense, according to some) that has ever been seen. In two years he replaced a Billot ministry[92] with a Clemenceau ministry,[93] brought about a complete change in public opinion, got Picquart out of prison to appoint him, for no thanks, to the Ministry of War. Perhaps this rationalist manipulator of crowds was himself manipulated by his ances-try. When the most truthful philosophical systems are dictated to their originators, in the last analysis, by emotional causes, how are we to sup-pose that, in a simple case of politics like the Dreyfus Affair, similar causes may not, unbeknown to the reasoner, have governed his reason? Bloch believed that he had become a Dreyfusard for logical reasons, yet he knew that his nose, his skin, and his hair had been imposed upon him by his race. No doubt reason has a certain freedom; yet it obeys some laws that it has not chosen itself. The case of the Guermantes butler and our own was peculiar. The waves from the two currents of Dreyfusism and anti-Dreyfusism now splitting the country from top to bottom were largely silent, but the occasional echoes they sent out were genuine. When, in the middle of some talk that was deliberately avoid-ing mention of the Affair, you heard someone furtively announce an item of political news, generally false but always indicative of wish ful-fillment, you could induce from the nature of his predictions where his sympathies lay. Thus, on certain points, there came into conflict, on the one side a timid apostolate, on the other a righteous indignation. The two butlers I heard arguing on my way in were an exception to the rule. Ours insinuated that Dreyfus was guilty, the Guermantes' that he was innocent. They behaved in this manner not to hide their convictions, but out of shrewd, hardheaded competition. Our butler, who was not sure that there would be a retrial, wanted to compensate in advance for not winning the argument by denying the Guermantes' butler the satis-faction of seeing a just cause crushed. The Guermantes' butler thought that if a retrial was refused ours would be more incensed by the contin-ued detention of an innocent man on Devil's Island. The concierge was there as an observer. I had the impression that it was not he who was the cause of friction in the Guermantes household.

I went up and found my grandmother far from well, more so than previously. For some time now, without knowing quite what was wrong, she had been complaining about her health. It is illness that makes us recognize that we do not live in isolation but are chained to a being from a different realm, worlds apart from us, with no knowledge of us, and by whom it is impossible to make ourselves understood: our body.

Were we to meet a brigand on the road, we might manage to make him conscious of his own personal interest, if not of our plight. But to ask pity of our body is like talking to an octopus, for which our words can have no more meaning than the sound of the sea, and with which we should be terrified to find ourselves condemned to live. My grandmother's bouts of feeling unwell often escaped her attention, which was always directed at us. When they really troubled her, in the hope of curing them she tried in vain to understand them. If the morbid phenomena acted out in her body remained obscure and elusive to her own mind, they were clearly intelligible to certain beings belonging to the same natural realm as themselves, the ones whom the human mind has gradually learned to address in order to understand what the body is saying to it, just as we deal with a foreigner's words by seeking out someone from his country who will act as interpreter. These beings can talk to our body, can tell us if its anger is serious or will soon die down. Cottard, who had been called in to examine my grandmother—and who had tried our patience by asking with a wry smile, the moment we told him she was ill, "Ill? You're sure it's not what they call a diplomatic illness?"—put his patient on a milk diet in an attempt to soothe her feverishness. But the endless bowls of milky soup brought no relief, because my grandmother was liberal with the salt, the dangerous effects of which were then unknown (Widal[94] not yet having made his discoveries). For, medicine being a compendium of the successive and contradictory mistakes of doctors, even when we call in the best of them the chances are that we may be staking our hopes on some medical theory that will be proved false in a few years. So that to believe in medicine would be utter madness, were it not still a greater madness not to believe in it, for from this accumulation of errors a few valid theories have emerged in the long run. Cottard had suggested that we take her temperature. A thermometer was brought. Almost the whole length of the tube was empty of mercury. It was almost impossible to detect the silver salamander lurking at the bottom of the tiny reservoir. It seemed dead. The little glass pipe was placed in my grandmother's mouth. We had no need to leave it there long; the little sorceress did not take long to cast her horoscope. We found her motionless, perched halfway up her tower and sticking there, showing us with precision the reading for which we had consulted her, a figure that all the attention that my grandmother's mind could have focused on itself would not have been remotely capable of providing: 101°. For the first time we felt some anxiety. We shook the thermometer vigorously to blot out the fateful sign, as if by so doing it were possible to reduce the fever along with the temperature reading. Alas, it was more than obvious that the little sibyl, though devoid of reason, had not made an arbitrary forecast, because, the next day, scarcely had the thermometer been replaced between my grandmother's lips when almost at once, as though in a single bound, with proud certainty and intuition of a fact that was hidden from us, the little prophetess came to a halt at the same point, with implacable immobility, and indicated once again that reading of 101° with her glistening wand. She had nothing else to tell us, and in vain would it have been to long, wish, pray: she turned a deaf ear to us, and it seemed as though this were her final threatening word of warning. Then, in an attempt to constrain her to alter her pronouncement, we turned to another creature of the same kingdom, but a more powerful one, which is not content with questioning the body but capable of commanding it, a febrifuge of the same order as aspirin, which had not yet come into use at the time. We had not brought the thermometer down below 99.5°, in the hope that it would not have to rise from there. We got my grandmother to take this febrifuge, then inserted the thermometer again. Like an implacable warden presented with a permit from a higher authority whose protection one has secured, who finds it in order and replies, "Very well, there's no problem. With that you may pass," this time the vigilant wardress of the mercury column did not move. But she seemed to be saying, sullenly: "What good will this do you? Since you're friends of quinine, she'll give me the order not to move up once, ten times, twenty times. Then, if I know anything about it, she'll grow tired of telling me. It won't last forever. And where will that have got you?" And so my grandmother felt the presence within her of a creature who knew the human body better than she, the presence of a contemporary of vanished races, the presence of earth's first inhabitant—far earlier than the creation of thinking man; she could feel that age-old ally probing into her, a little roughly even, into her brain, her heart, her elbow, reconnoitering the ground, preparing everything for the prehistoric combat that took place immediately afterward. In a very short time, like a crushed Python,[95] the fever was conquered by the powerful force of a chemical, and my grandmother, across the kingdoms, passing beyond all vegetable and animal life, would have liked to be able to show it her gratitude. And she remained deeply affected by this encounter she had just had, across so many centuries, with something anterior to the creation even of plants. Meanwhile, the thermometer, like one of the Fates momentarily subdued by a more ancient god, held its silver spindle motionless. Alas, other, inferior creatures, trained by man to hunt the mysterious prey that he himself is unable to pursue in the depths of his being, were unkind enough to bring us a daily albumin count, not a large one, but steady enough so that it also seemed connected to some persistent, undetectable illness. Bergotte had jolted my instinctive and scrupulous refusal to grant my intellect pride of place when he spoke to me of Dr. du Boulbon as a practitioner who would not bore me, who would discover methods of treatment that, however strange they might appear, would adjust themselves to my particular way of thinking. But ideas transform themselves in us, they overcome our initial resistance to them, and feed upon rich reserves of intellect that existed ready-made for them without our knowing. So, as happens whenever remarks we have heard about someone we do not know have managed to awaken in us the idea of a great talent, of some kind of genius, in my inmost thoughts I now conferred upon Dr. du Boulbon that unbounded confidence inspired in us by a man who, with greater acuity than his fellows, perceives the truth. It is true that I knew him to be more of a specialist in nervous diseases, the man to whom Charcot[96] before his death had predicted that he would be the foremost authority in neurology and psychiatry. "Ah, I don't know about that. It's more than likely," remarked Françoise, who happened to be in the room and was hearing Charcot's name, and du Boulbon's, for the first time. Not that this prevented her in the least from remarking, "It's likely." Her "likely"s, "perhaps"es, and "I don't know"s were extremely irritating at such moments. One felt like retorting, "Of course you don't know, since you don't have a clue what we're talking about. How can you even say whether it's likely or not, when you know nothing about it? Anyhow, you can't go on saying you don't know what Charcot said to du Boulbon and the rest of it. You know now because we've told you, and your 'perhaps'es and 'likely's are out of place, because it's a fact."

In spite of his more specialized competence in the cerebral and nervous fields, since I knew that du Boulbon was a great doctor, a superior man of inventive and penetrating intellect, I entreated my mother to send for him, and the hope that, by a clear perception of what was wrong, he might cure the malady, finally prevailed over our fear that by calling in a consultant we would alarm my grandmother. What finally decided my mother was the fact that, unconsciously encouraged by Cottard, my grandmother no longer went out, scarcely left her bed. It was no use her answering us by quoting Mme de Sévigné's letter about Mme de La Fayette: "People said she was mad not to want to go out. I said to these persons of hasty judgment, 'Mme de La Fayette is not mad,' and confined myself to that. It has taken her death to make it plain that she was quite right not to go out."97 When du Boulbon was called in, he disagreed, if not with Mme de Sévigné, whom we did not quote to him, then at least with my grandmother. Instead of taking out his stethoscope, he fixed his wonderful eyes upon her, perhaps creating the illusion that he was making a thorough examination of his patient, or expressing the desire to give her that illusion (it seemed spontaneous but must have been something he had automatically developed), or else the desire not to let her see that he had something completely different on his mind, or to exert his authority over her—and he began to talk about Bergotte.

"Ah yes, madame, he's wonderful, and how right you are to admire him! But which of his books is your favorite? Oh, really? Well, well, perhaps that *is* the best one in the end. It's certainly his best-constructed novel. Claire is a charming character. Which of the male characters do you find most appealing?"

I thought at first that he was getting her to talk about literature in this way because he himself found medicine boring, perhaps also to parade his wide interests, and even, with a more therapeutic intention, to restore confidence to his patient, show her he was not alarmed, take her mind off her illness. But I realized afterward that, as a doctor who was chiefly distinguished as a specialist in mental illness and for his work on the brain, he had been using these questions to see if my grandmother's memory was functioning properly. He asked her a few apparently reluctant questions about her daily routine, his eyes unflinching and stern. Then, suddenly, as though he had glimpsed the truth and was determined to reach it at all costs, with a preliminary nod of the head, which seemed to be shaking off with some difficulty the flood of lingering hesitations that might have occurred to him and any objections we might have raised, looking my grandmother in the eye with his mind made up, as though he were at last on solid ground, punctuating his words in a quietly convincing tone with every inflection finely shaded by intelligence (and his voice, throughout his visit, remained what it naturally was, caressing, while under his bushy eyebrows his ironic eyes brimmed with kindness), he said:

"You will get well, madame, on whatever day you realize—and it is entirely up to you whether it is today or not—that there is nothing wrong with you and resume your normal life. You say you have not been eating, not going out?"

"But, Doctor, I have a temperature."

He felt her hand.

"You certainly don't at this moment. Besides, what a convenient excuse! Didn't you know that we make sufferers from tuberculosis with temperatures up to a hundred and two degrees eat hearty meals and expose them to the open air?"

"But I have a little albumin as well."

"That's not for you to decide. You have what I call 'mental albumin.' We've all of us suffered from our little albumin problems when we've been ill, and had them prolonged by our doctor fussing around and drawing our attention to them. For every one disorder that doctors cure with medication (it does happen occasionally, I'm told), there are ten others they provoke in healthy patients by inoculating them with a pathogenic agent a thousand times more virulent than all the germs you can name: the idea that one is ill. That conviction has a powerful effect on anyone, but particularly on neurotic people. Tell them that a closed window is open behind them and they'll begin to sneeze; pretend you've put magnesia in their soup and they'll have a bout of colic; or that their coffee was stronger than usual and they won't sleep a wink all night. Do you suppose, madame, that I needed to do more than look into your eyes, listen to the way you express yourself, and, if I may say so, observe your daughter and your grandson, who are so like you, to know what was the matter with you?"

"Your grandmother might perhaps go and sit, with the doctor's permission, along one of the quieter walks of the Champs-Élysées, near that clump of laurels where you used to play when you were small," my mother suggested to me, thus indirectly consulting du Boulbon, and therefore assuming a tone of shy deference, which would have been absent had she been addressing me alone. The doctor turned to my grandmother and, being a man of letters no less than a man of science, addressed her in this way:

"Go to the Champs-Élysées, madame, and the clump of laurels your grandson likes so much. Laurel will be healthy for you. It purifies. When Apollo rid the world of the serpent Python, it was with a laurel branch in his hand that he made his entry into Delphi. He used it to ward off the deadly germs of the venomous creature. So you see that the laurel is the most ancient, the most venerable, and, I may add—as something of therapeutic as well as prophylactic value—the most excellent of antiseptics."

Insofar as a great part of what doctors know is taught them by their patients, they are apt to believe that such knowledge is common to every patient they see; thus they delude themselves when they think that they can impress any patient of the moment with some remark they have gleaned from a previous one. And so it was with the shrewd smile of a Parisian in conversation with a country person, and hoping to impress by using a piece of rustic lore, that Dr. du Boulbon said to my grandmother, "Probably windy weather will help you sleep, whereas the strongest sleeping drugs have no effect." "Quite the opposite: the wind completely stops me from sleeping." But doctors have their sensitive points. "Ach!" muttered du Boulbon with a frown, as if someone had trodden on his toe and my grandmother's sleeplessness on blustery nights were a personal insult to himself. All the same, he was not unduly self-opinionated, and since, as a "superior" person, he felt himself bound not to put all his faith in medicine, he quickly regained his philosophic serenity.

My mother, desperately anxious to be reassured by Bergotte's friend, added her support to his diagnosis by telling him that a first cousin of my grandmother's, who suffered from a nervous complaint, had stayed shut up in her bedroom in Combray for seven years, without getting up more than once or twice a week.

"There we are, madame; I didn't know that, yet I could have told you as much."

"But, Doctor, I'm not at all like her. On the contrary, my doctor can't get me to stay in bed," said my grandmother, either because she was slightly irritated by du Boulbon's theories, or because she was anxious to lay before him possible objections to them, in the hope that he would refute these and that, once he had gone, she would no longer have any doubts about his heartening diagnosis.

"But of course you're not, madame. It isn't possible to have every single form of mental disturbance, if you'll forgive the expression. Yours are different, not like hers. Yesterday I visited a home for neurasthenics. I saw a man standing on a bench, motionless as a fakir, his neck bent down in a position that must have been really painful. When I asked him what he was doing there, he replied, without moving a muscle or turning his head: 'Well, Doctor, I get very bad rheumatism and I catch cold very easily. I've been taking too much exercise and stupidly getting myself too hot, with my neck touching my flannels. If I move it away from my flannels now, before I cool down, I'm bound to get a stiff neck and even catch bronchitis.' Which he would have done, in fact. 'A real neurotic, that's what you are,' I told him. And do you know the reason he gave to prove me wrong? It went like this: All the other patients in the home were obsessed with weighing themselves, to the point where the scale had to be padlocked to stop them from spending all day on it, whereas he had to be forced onto the machine, given his aversion to being weighed. He prided himself on not being obsessed like the others, oblivious of the fact that he had his own obsession and that it was this that protected him from one of a different kind. Please don't be offended by the comparison, madame, for that man who dared not turn his neck for fear of catching a cold is the greatest poet of our time. That poor maniac is the highest intellect that I know. Feel comfortable to be called a neurotic. You belong to the splendid, pitiable family that is the salt of the earth. Everything we think of as great has come to us from neurotics. They and they alone are the ones who have founded religions and created great works of art. The world will never realize how much it is indebted to them, particularly how much they have suffered in order to present it with their gifts. We appreciate good music, fine paintings, a thousand exquisite things, without knowing what they cost those who created them in terms of insomnia, tears, fitful laughter, nettle rash, asthma, epilepsy, and, worse still, a fear of dying, which you perhaps have experienced yourself, madame," he added with a smile at my grandmother, "for, when I came—admit it, now—you were not at your most self-assured. You thought you were ill, dangerously ill perhaps. Heaven only knows what you thought you had the symptoms of. You were not mistaken, you did have them. Nervous disorders have a genius for mimicry. There is no illness they can't counterfeit to perfection. They will produce lifelike imitations of dyspeptic swelling, morning sickness, irregular heartbeat, tubercular fever. If this can deceive the doctor, how much the more so the patient? Please don't think I'm pooh-poohing your sufferings. I wouldn't undertake to treat them unless I understood them properly. And let me say this: all real confessions are reciprocal ones. I said that without nervous disorder there can be no great artist. But," he added, raising a solemn index finger, "there can be no great man of science, either. I will go even further and say that, unless he himself is prone to nervous trouble, there is no—I won't say good doctor—but I do say the right doctor to treat nervous disorders. In the pathology of nervous diseases, a doctor who doesn't talk too much nonsense is a half-cured patient, just as a critic is a poet who has stopped writing poems and a policeman a burglar who has left his thieving behind. I, madame, do not, like you, fancy myself to be suffering from albuminuria, nor do I have your neurotic fear of food and fresh air, but I can never get to sleep at night without getting out of bed at least twenty times to see if the door is locked. And yesterday I went to that nursing home where I discovered a poet who wouldn't move his neck because I wanted to reserve a room; just between you and me, I spend my holidays there, getting treatment, at times when I have made my own troubles worse by wearing myself out curing other people's."

"But, Doctor, should I take the same sort of cure?" asked my grand-mother, horrified.

"There is absolutely no need for that, madame. The symptoms you show will disappear at my command. Besides, you have the company of a very effective person, whom I appoint as your doctor from now on. I mean your illness itself, your nervous hyperactivity. If I knew how to cure it, I'd take good care not to. All I need to do is to keep it under control. I can see one of Bergotte's books on your table there. Cured of your nervous complaint, you would no longer have any taste for it. Now, what right have I to supplant the pleasure it gives you with a nervous stability that would be quite incapable of giving you such pleasure? The pleasure itself is a powerful remedy, the most powerful of all perhaps. No, I have no quarrel with your nervous energy. All I ask is that it should hear what I have to say; I leave you in its charge. It needs to reverse its drive. The power it has been using to prevent you from leaving the house and eating properly needs to be used to make you eat, make you read, go out, and take as much pleasure in life as you can. Don't tell me that you feel tired. Tiredness is the body's reaction to a preconceived idea. Begin by removing it from your thoughts. And if ever you are slightly unwell, as everyone is at times, you won't feel as if you are, because your nervous energy will have provided you with what M. de Talleyrand shrewdly called 'imaginary good health.' See, it's begun to cure you already. You've been sitting up in bed listening to me without once lying back, your eyes are bright, and there's color in your cheeks. I've been talking to you for a good half-hour and you haven't even noticed the time. So, madame, I shall now take my leave of you."

When I had seen Dr. du Boulbon to the door and returned to the bedroom, where I found my mother alone, the distress that had been weighing upon me for several weeks suddenly lifted; I sensed that my mother was going to give vent to her own joy and would be able to see mine, too, and I felt that incapacity to bear the suspense of knowing someone is on the point of giving way to emotion in our presence; this, though different, is not unlike the fear of knowing that someone is about to come in through a closed door and give us a fright; I tried to speak to Mama, but my voice faltered, and, bursting into tears, I stayed there a long time with my head on her shoulder, bewailing, savoring, accepting, cherishing my grief, now that I knew it had gone out of my life, in the same way that we like to get carried away by good intentions that circumstances do not permit us to put into execution. Françoise annoyed me by not sharing in our joy. She was in a state of great excitement because a terrible scene had exploded between the footman and the telltale concierge. The Duchesse had had to intervene benevolently, restore a semblance of goodwill, and forgive the footman. For she was a kind woman, and her role as mistress would have been ideal had she not listened to idle chitchat.

For several days now, people had begun to learn of my grandmother's illness and to ask after her. Saint-Loup had written to me: "It is not my wish to intrude on this time when your dear grandmother is unwell by writing to reproach you, more than reproach you in fact, for something that has nothing to do with her. But I would be lying were I to say to you, if only obliquely, that I shall ever forget your perfidious conduct, or that I can ever forgive your letting me down so treacherously." But some other friends, who were under the impression that my grandmother was not seriously ill, or unaware that she was ill at all, had asked me to meet up with them the next day in the Champs-Élysées, to go on from there to visit someone, and then to a dinner party in the country, an idea that appealed to me. There was no longer any reason to forgo these two pleasures. When my grandmother had been told that she should now go out as much as possible, in accordance with Dr. du Boulbon's orders, she had herself at once suggested the Champs-Élysées. It would be easy for me to accompany her and, while she sat reading, to arrange with my friends where to meet them later; and there would still be time, if I hurried, to catch the train to Ville-d'Avray with them. When the time came, my grandmother did not want to go out, because she felt tired. But my mother, acting on du Boulbon's instructions, had the strength of mind to be firm and not to take no for an answer. The thought that my grandmother might relapse into her nervous debility and never recover from it brought her near to tears. The fine, warm weather that day could not have been more suitable for going out. As it moved through the sky, the sun dispersed its flimsy muslins here and there through the broken solidity of the balcony and coated the freestone ledge in warmth, in a blurred halo of gold. As Françoise had not had time to send a wire to her daughter, she went off immediately after lunch. She found she had done quite enough as it was by going to Jupien's earlier on to get a stitch put in the cape my grandmother was going to wear to go out. I was returning from my morning walk at the time and accompanied her into the waistcoat-maker's shop. "Has the young master brought you here," Jupien asked Françoise, "have you brought him to see me, or is it a fair wind and Dame Fortune that bring you both?" For all his lack of schooling, Jupien respected the rules of syntax as instinctively as M. de Guermantes, in spite of much effort, broke them. With Françoise gone and the cape mended, it was time for my grandmother to go and get ready. After obstinately refusing to let Mama stay and help her, left on her own, she took an endless time to dress, and now that I knew she was not ill, with that strange indifference we show toward our family during their lifetime, which makes them the last people to be taken into consideration, I thought it very selfish of her to take so long and risk making me late, when she knew that I had to meet my friends and was going off to dinner in Ville-d'Avray. In my impatience, I finally went down ahead of her, after being told twice that she was nearly ready. She joined me at last, without her usual apology for keeping me waiting like this, red-faced and confused, like someone in a hurry who has left half her things behind, just as I was reaching the half-open glass door that let in the liquid, chirping warmth from outside, as though a supply of heat had been released between the glacial walls of the house, without bringing any warmth to them at all.

"Oh dear, I could have worn another cape if you're going to meet your friends. This one's rather drab."

I was startled to see her so flushed, and took it that her lateness had put her into a great rush. Soon after we left the cab at the corner of the Avenue Gabriel on the Champs-Élysées, I watched my grandmother turn away without a word and make for the little old-fashioned pavilion with the green metal trellis-work where I had once waited for Françoise. The same park-keeper who had been there then was still there, talking to the "Marquise," as I followed my grandmother, who, doubtless because she was feeling sick, was holding her hand to her mouth, and went up the steps of this little rustic theater that had been erected in the middle of the gardens. At the entrance, as in those traveling circuses where the clown, dressed for the ring and with his face caked in white powder, takes the ticket money at the door himself, the "Marquise" was still there, taking the money, her huge, irregular snout of a face smeared with cheap makeup, and the little bonnet of red flowers and black lace propped on her ginger wig. But I do not think she recognized me. The park-keeper had abandoned his supervision of the green surroundings, which matched the color of his uniform, and was sitting beside her chatting.

"So," he was saying, "you're still here. You haven't thought of retirement?"

"And why would I want to do that, monsieur? Can you tell me where I'd be better off than here, where I'd be more nice and cozy? And, then, there're all the comings and goings, all the enjoyment of it. My little Paris is what I call it. My customers keep me in touch with what's going on. I mean, there's one of them went out just now, can't have been more than five minutes ago; he's a judge, and a high-up one, I can tell you. Well!" she broke out heatedly, as though she would have driven home her assertion with violence had any agent of authority shown signs of challenging its accuracy. "He's been coming here for the last eight years, I'm telling you, every single day God made, on the dot of three, always polite, never raising his voice, never dirtying a thing. He stays half an hour or so reading his papers while he spends a penny. Then, one day, he didn't come. I didn't notice it at the time, but that evening I suddenly thought, 'That gentleman didn't come today, did he? Perhaps he's dead.' I get attached to people when they behave nicely, and it gave me quite a turn. So I was really glad to see him come back the day after. I said to him, 'Monsieur, nothing bad happened to you yesterday, I hope?' And he told me straight that nothing had happened to *him,* it was his wife that had died, and it had upset him so much he hadn't been able to come. Of course he looked sad—well, you know, people who've been married twenty-five years—but even so, he seemed pleased to be back. You could tell that his little routine had been quite upset. I tried to cheer him up. I told him: 'Monsieur, you mustn't let yourself go. You keep coming here like you did before. It'll take your mind off things a bit, in the sad state you're in.' "

The "Marquise" resumed a gentler tone, for she had noticed that the guardian of shrubs and lawns was listening to her benignly, with no thought of crossing her, keeping his sword, which looked more like a gardening implement or some horticultural token, harmlessly in its sheath.

"And I'm choosy about my customers, you know," she went on. "I don't let just anyone into my parlors, as I call them. Don't you think it looks like a parlor, with my flowers there? I've got some really nice customers; there's always somebody bringing me a nice little spray of lilac or jasmine, or roses—my favorites, roses."

The thought that this lady held us in low esteem because we never brought her lilac or fine roses brought a blush to my cheeks, and in the hope of escaping physically from an adverse judgment, or of being judged only in my absence, I moved toward the exit. But it is not always life's givers of fine roses who receive our friendliest attention; the "Marquise," thinking that I was bored, turned to me:

"You wouldn't like me to open up one of the little stalls for you?"

And when I declined:

"No? You're quite sure?" she added with a smile. "You're very welcome to it, but I know how it is; it takes more than not having to pay to make you want to spend a penny."

At this point, a shabbily dressed woman rushed in who seemed to be in need of doing just that. But she did not belong to the right world for the "Marquise," who said to her curtly, with a snobbish bite in her voice:

"There's nothing vacant, madame."

"Will I have to wait long?" asked the poor lady, red-faced beneath the yellow flowers in her hat.

"Madame, I'd try somewhere else if I were you. You can see that these two gentlemen are still waiting," she replied, pointing to the park-keeper and myself. "I've only got one stall. The others are out of order. . . . She looked like a bad payer to me," she said to us afterward. "Not the sort we want here. They're not clean, no respect for the place. I'd have been the one who had to spend the next hour cleaning up after her ladyship. She can keep her small change."

At last my grandmother came out, and the thought that she might not give a generous enough tip to draw attention away from her indiscretion at taking so long made me beat a retreat to avoid any exposure to the scorn the "Marquise" would no doubt greet her with; I started to stroll down one of the paths, but slowly, so that my grandmother could catch up to me without difficulty. And it was not long before she did so. I was expecting her to say, "I'm afraid I've kept you waiting. I hope you'll still be in time for your friends," but she didn't say a word, and since I found this slightly hurtful, I was reluctant to be the first to speak. When I finally looked up at her, I noticed that as she walked beside me she kept her face turned the other way. I was afraid she might be feeling sick again. On closer inspection, I was taken aback by the uneven way she was walking. Her hat was crooked, her cape dirty; she had the disheveled and dejected appearance, the flushed, dazed look of someone who has just been knocked over by a carriage or pulled out of a ditch.

"I was afraid you were feeling sick, Grandmama. Are you feeling any better now?" I asked.

No doubt she thought it would be impossible for her not to answer without causing me alarm.

"I heard the whole of that conversation between the 'Marquise' and the park-keeper," she said. "She couldn't have been more like the Guermantes or that little Verdurin clan if she tried. What a genteel way of putting such things!" And she went on to add an apposite remark from her own special Marquise, Mme de Sévigné: "As I listened to them I thought they were preparing to bid me a delightful farewell."

This was her answer to me, and into it she had put all her refinement, her taste for quotations, her memory of classical literature, more deliberately even than she would normally have done, as if to prove that she was still very much in possession of all these faculties. But I guessed rather than heard what she said, so mumbled were her words as she clenched her teeth more than could be accounted for by the fear of vomiting.

"Come!" I said, lightly enough not to seem to be making too much of her illness, "since you're feeling a bit sick, we'll go home if you like. I don't want to make a grandmother with indigestion have to walk around the Champs-Élysées."

"I didn't like to suggest it because of your friends," she replied. "Poor boy! But since you don't mind, I think it would be wiser."

I was suddenly afraid that she might notice the odd way in which she was uttering her words.

"Come," I said briskly, "you're not to tire yourself out talking when you're feeling sick, it's silly. Let's get home first."

She smiled at me sadly and gripped my hand. She had realized she had no need to hide from me what I had guessed straightaway: that she had had a slight stroke.

PART II

CHAPTER I

My grandmother's illness—Bergotte's illness—The Duc and the doctor—
My grandmother's decline—Her death

WE MADE OUR WAY back along the Avenue Gabriel through the crowd of people out walking. I installed my grandmother on a bench and went off to look for a cab. I had always been accustomed to placing myself in her heart in order to form an opinion of the most insignificant person, but now she was a closed book to me, a part of the external world, and I was obliged to hide from her, more than from any casual passerby, what I thought about her state of health, and to betray no sign of my anxiety. I could not have mentioned it to her with any more confidence than to a stranger. She had suddenly restored to my keeping the thoughts, the sorrows that I had entrusted to her forever, since I was a child. She was not yet dead. But I was already alone. And even those references she had made to the Guermantes, to Molière, to our conversations about the little clan, now seemed baseless, random, outlandish, because they arose from the nonreality of this same being, who tomorrow perhaps would no longer exist, for whom they would cease to have any meaning, from the nonbeing—incapable of making such references—that my grandmother would soon be.

"Monsieur, I am not saying no, but you have no appointment, no number. And this is not my day for seeing patients. You must have a doctor of your own. I cannot stand in for him, unless he asks me to act as a consultant. It's a question of professional ethics. . . ."

Just as I was hailing a cab, I had run into the famous Professor E—, not quite a friend of my father and grandfather, but certainly acquainted with them, at all events, who lived on the Avenue Gabriel, and a sudden stroke of inspiration had made me stop him just as he was entering his house, thinking that he would perhaps be the very person for my grandmother to consult. But he was in a hurry, and after collecting his mail he clearly wanted to be rid of me, so the only way I could speak to him was by accompanying him up in the elevator, with him begging me to be allowed to press the buttons himself, a little quirk of his.

"But, Doctor, I'm not asking you to see my grandmother here and now, as you will realize when I've explained to you that she isn't in a fit state to come. I'm asking you to call at our house in half an hour, when I've taken her home."

"Call at your house? Monsieur, that is unthinkable. I'm dining with the minister of commerce. Before that I have a call to make. I must dress at once, and, to make matters worse, one of my tailcoats is torn and the other has no buttonhole for my decorations. I beg you, please don't touch the elevator buttons. You don't know how the elevator works. One should always proceed with caution. This buttonhole is going to delay me still further. But, out of friendship for your family, if your grandmother comes at once, I'll see her. I warn you, though, I won't be able to give her a minute more than a quarter of an hour."

I was on my way at once, without even getting out of the elevator, which Professor E— had himself set in motion to take me down, eyeing me distrustfully as he pushed the button.

We make a point of telling ourselves that death can come at any moment, but when we do so we think of that moment as something vague and distant, not as something that can have anything to do with the day that has already begun or might mean that death—or the first signs of its partial possession of us, after which it will never loosen its hold again—will occur this very afternoon, the almost inevitable afternoon, with its hourly activities prescribed in advance. We look forward to our daily outing as a means of getting our month's supply of fresh air; we have hesitated over which coat to wear, which cabman to hail; we are in the cab, the whole day is spread before us—a short one, because we need to get back home early enough for the visit of a friend—we hope that it will be as fine again tomorrow; and we have no suspicion that death, accompanying us in some obscure way, has chosen this very day to make its appearance, in a few minutes, roughly at the moment when the carriage reaches the Champs-Élysées. Perhaps people who are normally haunted by the fear of the utter strangeness of death will find something reassuring about this kind of death—about this kind of initial contact with death—in that it assumes a known, familiar, everyday character. It has been preceded by a good lunch and the same sort of outing that is made by perfectly healthy people. A drive home in an open carriage covers up its first attack; ill as my grandmother was, there were still several people who could bear witness to the fact that at six o'clock, as we returned from the Champs-Élysées, they had raised their hats to her as she drove by in an open carriage, on a beautiful day. Legrandin, making his way toward the Place de la Concorde, doffed his hat to us, and stopped with a surprised look on his face. I, who was not yet removed from life, asked my grandmother if she had acknowledged him, reminding her how touchy he was. My grandmother, finding my question no doubt very trivial, raised her hand in a gesture that seemed to convey, "What does it matter? It's of no importance whatsoever."

Yes, people could have borne witness to the fact that a little earlier, while I was looking for a cab, my grandmother was seated on a bench on the Avenue Gabriel, that a little later she had driven past in an open carriage. But would it have been really true? For a bench to stand there on an avenue—although it, too, may be subject to certain conditions of equilibrium—there is no need for energy. But for a living being to be stable, even when supported by a bench or in a carriage, there must be a taut balance of forces we do not usually perceive, any more than we perceive (because it acts ubiquitously) atmospheric pressure. Perhaps, if a vacuum were created inside us and we were left to bear the pressure of the air, we should feel, for a split second before our extinction, the terrible weight that now had nothing else to neutralize its effect. Similarly, when the dreadful depths of sickness and death open up inside us and we have nothing left to defy the havoc into which the world and our own bodies hurl us, to sustain even the weight of our muscles, even the shudder that strikes us to the very marrow, and even to keep still, in what we would normally regard as no more than a strained posture, all this demands, if we want our head to remain erect and our expression to keep its composure, a good deal of vital energy, and so turns into an exhausting struggle.

And if Legrandin had looked at us with astonishment on his face, it was because to him, as to others who passed us at the time, in the cab in which my grandmother was apparently sitting back, she had seemed to be sinking down, slithering into the abyss, desperately clinging to the cushions, which could scarcely hold back the impetus of her falling body, her hair disheveled, a distraught look in her eyes, which were no longer capable of focusing on the onrush of images their pupils could bear no more. She had seemed, even with me sitting beside her, to be plunged into that unknown world in which she had already received the blows whose marks I had noticed earlier in the Champs-Élysées, when I saw her hat, her face, her coat thrown into disarray by the hand of the invisible angel with whom she had wrestled.

It has occurred to me subsequently that this moment of her stroke cannot have come as a complete surprise to my grandmother, that she had possibly even foreseen it well before it occurred, lived with the thought that it would happen. She had not known, of course, when this fatal moment would come—of that she was unsure, as lovers are when a similar sense of uncertainty leads them to base unreasonable hopes and, in turn, unjustified suspicions on the fidelity of their mistresses. But these serious illnesses, like the one that had at last just struck her full in the face, seldom take up residence in a sick person for long before they kill him, and during this time, like "friendly" neighbors, they are quick to make themselves known to him. It is a terrible acquaintance, less for the suffering involved than for the novel strangeness of the terminal restrictions it imposes on life. We see ourselves dying, in this instance, when death has come to inhabit us as a hideous presence, not at the actual moment of death, but for months, or sometimes years before that. The sick woman makes her acquaintance with this stranger, whose comings and goings she hears in her brain. She does not know what he looks like, of course, but from the regular sounds she hears him make she gains an idea of his habits. Is he up to no good? One morning, she can no longer hear him. He has gone. Ah, if only he were gone for good! By evening, he is back. What are his plans? The consultant, questioned on the matter like an adored mistress, replies with assurances that are believed one day, mistrusted the next. Indeed, it is not so much the mistress's role as the role of questioned servants that the doctors play. They are only third parties. The person we press for an answer, the one we suspect of being about to betray us, is life itself, and although we feel it to be no longer the same, we still believe in it, or at least we remain uncertain about it, until the day it finally abandons us.

I got my grandmother into Professor E——'s elevator, and a moment later he came to take us into his consulting room. And there, pressed for time though he was, his haughty manner dropped, such is the force of habit, and with his patients his habit was to be friendly, not to say jovial. Knowing that my grandmother was a great reader, and being one himself, he devoted two or three minutes to quoting various lines of poetry appropriate to the glorious summer weather. He had placed her in an armchair and seated himself with his back to the light, so that he could see her properly. He gave her a thorough examination, during which I was obliged to leave the room for a moment. He went on with it when I returned, and when he had finished, he started to ply my grandmother with further quotations, even though the quarter of an hour was almost at an end. He even made a few rather subtle jokes, which I would have preferred to hear on some other occasion, but the tone of amusement in which he uttered them completely set my mind at rest. At this point I remembered that M. Fallières, the president of the Senate, had had a false stroke a number of years ago, and that, to the dismay of his rivals, he had resumed his duties again three days later and, it was said, had even started to make preparations to stand–in the more or less distant future–for president of the Republic. My confidence in my grandmother's prompt recovery was further boosted by the fact that, as I was recalling the case of M. Fallières, I was distracted from pursuing the parallel by a hearty burst of laughter at the end of one of Professor E——'s jokes. At which point he took out his watch, frowned frantically when he saw he was five minutes late, and, as he bade us farewell, rang for his dress clothes to be brought immediately. I waited for my grandmother to leave the room, closed the door, and asked the specialist to tell me the truth.

"There is no hope for your grandmother," he told me. "The stroke was brought on by uremia. Uremia in itself is not inevitably fatal, but this seems a hopeless case to me. I don't need to tell you that I hope I am mistaken. And with Cottard, you're in excellent hands. Now, if you'll excuse me," he added as he saw the maid come into the room with his tailcoat over her arm. "As I said earlier, I'm dining with the minister of commerce, and I have a call to pay before that. Ah, life is not a just a bed of roses, as people of your age are inclined to think."

And he graciously offered me his hand. I had shut the door behind me, and a footman was seeing us to the hall, when my grandmother and I heard angry shouting. The maid had forgotten to see to the buttonhole for the decorations. This would take another ten minutes. The professor raged away as I stood on the landing gazing at my grandmother, for whom there was no hope left. Each of us is very much alone. We set off back home.

The sun was going down; its glare lit up a never-ending wall along which our cab had to pass before it reached the street where we lived, a wall against which the shadow of horse and carriage cast by the setting sun stood out in black on a reddish background, like a funeral chariot on a piece of terra-cotta from Pompeii. We finally arrived home. I sat the sick woman down in the hall at the bottom of the staircase and went up to warn my mother. I told her that my grandmother had come home feeling slightly unwell, after a spell of dizziness. No sooner had I started to speak than my mother's face was stricken with a paroxysm of despair, yet a despair already so resigned that I realized she had been holding it in readiness for years against an uncertain but decisive day. She asked me no questions; it seemed as if, with the same passion malice expends on intensifying the suffering of others, her love did not want to admit that her mother was seriously ill, especially with a disease that might affect her mind. Mama was shuddering, weeping with a tearless face, and she ran to ask for the doctor to be fetched; but when Françoise asked who was ill, she could not answer; the words stuck in her throat. She hurried downstairs with me, erasing from her face the sob that creased it up. My grandmother was waiting below, on the sofa in the hall, but as soon as she heard us coming, she straightened her posture, stood up, and waved cheerfully to Mama. I had wrapped part of her head in a white lace shawl and told her it was to prevent her from catching cold on the stairs: I did not want my mother's attention too obviously drawn to the changed face, the distortion of the mouth. My precaution proved unnecessary: my mother went up to my grandmother, kissed her hand as though it were the hand of her God, supported her upright as far as the elevator, with infinite care which revealed, together with the fear of being clumsy and hurting her, the humility of someone who felt unworthy to touch what was for her the most precious thing she knew; but not once did she raise her eyes to the sick woman's face. Perhaps this was to prevent my grandmother from being saddened by the thought that her daughter had been alarmed by the sight of her face. Perhaps from fear of pain so excessive that she did not dare to confront it. Perhaps out of respect, because she felt it unacceptably impious to take note of any trace of mental debilitation on that revered face. Perhaps to be better able to preserve intact in her memory the true face of her mother, beaming with intelligence and kindness. So they went up side by side, my grandmother half hidden in her shawl, my mother averting her gaze.

All this time, there was one person who could not avert hers from what could be glimpsed of my grandmother's altered features, at which her daughter dared not look, someone whose eyes were fixed upon them dumbfoundedly, indiscreetly, and with an ominous stare: this was Françoise. Not that she was not genuinely fond of my grandmother (indeed, she had been disappointed and almost scandalized by Mama's coldness and would have preferred to see her throw herself weeping into her mother's arms), but she had this tendency to see only the worst side of things and had retained from her childhood two characteristics that would seem to be mutually exclusive: the impulsive reactions of uneducated people who make no attempt to hide the impression, or even the painful alarm, aroused in them by the sight of a physical change it would be more discreet to appear not to have noticed, and the insensitive brutishness of the peasant woman who tears the wings off dragonflies until she gets the chance to wring the necks of chickens, and lacks the sense of modesty to make her conceal the interest she feels at the sight of suffering flesh.

When my grandmother had been put to bed, thanks to Françoise's perfect care, she discovered she could speak more easily, the slight bursting or obstruction of a blood vessel brought on by the uremia having apparently been very minor. And at once she was concerned to be there for Mama, to help her through the most cruel moments she had yet experienced.

"Well, well, my dear," she said, taking her daughter's hand in her own, and keeping the other in front of her mouth as a means of accounting for the slight difficulty she still had in pronouncing certain words, "so this is the sort of pity you show your mother! You look as if you thought indigestion was something rather enjoyable!"

At this, for the first time, my mother's eyes fixed themselves passionately on my grandmother's, not wishing to see the rest of her face, and she replied with the first in the list of those false solemn promises we are unable to keep:

"Mama, you'll soon be well again, your daughter will make sure of that."

And, enveloping her strongest love, her utter determination that her mother should get well, in the kiss to which she entrusted them, accompanying it with her thoughts and her whole being until it reached her lips, she bent to bestow it humbly, reverently, on the treasured forehead.

My grandmother complained that she could feel something like an alluvial deposit of bedclothes constantly gathering on the side of the bed over her left leg, which she could not manage to shift. But she did not realize that she was herself responsible for it (which meant that every day she unjustly accused Françoise of not "making" her bed properly). With a jerky movement, she kept throwing to that side of the bed the whole frothy flood of the fine woolen blankets, which accumulated there like sand in a bay very soon transformed into a beach (unless a seawall is built) by the successive deposits of the waves.

My mother and I (our lies exposed before we uttered them by the unwelcome shrewdness of Françoise) would not even admit that my grandmother was seriously ill, as though to do so would give pleasure to her enemies (not that she had any), as if it were kinder to pretend that she was not really that ill; in short, we followed the same instinctive feeling that had led me to suppose that Andrée pitied Albertine too much to be really fond of her. You see the same phenomenon reproduced on a large scale in situations of crisis. In a war, a man who does not love his country says nothing against it, but regards it as doomed, pities it, sees everything in the blackest terms.

Françoise was a precious boon to us in that she could do without sleep and perform the most arduous tasks. And if, when she had gone to bed after several nights spent on duty, we were obliged to call her a quarter of an hour after she had fallen asleep, she was so happy to be able to carry out the most ungrateful tasks, as if they had been the simplest things in the world, that, far from doing them with bad grace, she expressed signs of modest satisfaction. It was only when it was time for mass, or breakfast, that Françoise would have slipped away to be there on time, even if my grandmother had been in her death throes. She neither could nor would let her place be taken by her young footman. It was true that she brought with her from Combray a very elevated idea of everyone's duty toward our family: she would not have tolerated any of our servants' "failing" us. This had made her into such a noble, imperious, and efficient instructress that we had never had a servant, however corrupt, who had not quickly modified and purged his conception of life to the point of shunning the customary tips from tradesmen and of running—however unobliging the servant had been previously—to relieve me of the smallest parcel and not to let me tire myself by carrying it. But in Combray, Françoise had also contracted the habit, which she had imported to Paris, of not being able to bear having anyone help her in her work. To be seen with a helper seemed like humiliation, and servants spent weeks without any response to the morning greeting they gave her, had even gone off on their holidays without her saying goodbye or their guessing why this was, when it was simply because they had offered to do part of her work on a day she had felt poorly. And particularly now, when my grandmother was so ill, Françoise saw her duties as hers and no one else's. She had no desire, in her official position, to be done out of her role during these gala days. And so her young footman, pushed to one side, did not know what to do with himself, and, not content with having followed Victor's example and supplied himself with writing paper from my desk, he had gone further and started to borrow volumes of poetry from my bookcase. He spent a good half of the day reading them, out of admiration for the poets who had written them, but also so that, during the rest of his time, he could embellish the letters he wrote to his friends in his native village with a sprinkling of quotations. Indeed, he thought this would dazzle them. But since his train of thought was rather muddled, he somehow got it into his head that these poems, randomly selected from my shelves, were common currency and everyday points of reference. So much so that, in writing to these village people he hoped to stun, he interspersed his own remarks with lines from Lamartine as if they were the equivalent of expressions like "What will be will be" or merely "Hello."

Because of the pain she was suffering, my grandmother was put on morphine. The trouble was that, although this relieved the pain, it also increased her albumin count. The blows we aimed at the evil disease that had settled inside her always fell wide of the mark; it was she, it was her poor body standing in the way, that became the target, yet she never uttered more than a faint groan by way of complaint. And we were unable to compensate for the pain we caused her by doing anything beneficial. The ferocious disease we would have liked to exterminate we were barely able to get anywhere near; we merely increased its virulence, and perhaps hastened the moment when its captive would be devoured by it. On days when the albumin count rose too high, Cottard, after some hesitation, stopped the morphine. In the brief moments of deliberation, when the relative dangers of various possible courses of treatment fought it out in his mind until he settled on one of them, this unprepossessing, commonplace man assumed something of the impressiveness of a general who, though unexceptional in all other respects, is a gifted strategist and, at a time of crisis, after a moment's reflection, can decide upon the wisest course of action in military terms and issue the order: "Advance eastward." In medical terms, however little hope there was of putting an end to this attack of uremia, it was important not to put a strain on the kidneys. But, on the other hand, when my grandmother was taken off morphine, the pain became intolerable; she would constantly attempt to move in a particular way, which it was difficult for her to do without groaning. Pain is largely a kind of need felt by the organism to acquaint itself with an unfamiliar state that is troubling it, to adjust its responses to that state. This origin of pain can be seen in the case of the sort of discomfort that affects only certain people. Two men come into a room filled with acrid smoke and go about their business, impervious to it; a third, with a more sensitive constitution, betrays constant discomfort. His nostrils never stop anxiously sniffing the smell, which he ought, it seems, to try not to notice, and which he will keep on seeking to assimilate, through closer acquaintance, to his troubled sense of smell. Hence the fact no doubt that deep preoccupation will prevent people from complaining of toothache. When my grandmother was in this sort of pain, the sweat trickled down her high mauve forehead, sticking strands of her white hair to it, and if she thought that there was no one in the room she would cry out, "Oh, this is dreadful!"; but if she caught sight of my mother, she would immediately devote all her energy to removing any sign of pain from her face, or, conversely, go on repeating the same words of complaint but adding explanations that altered, in retrospect, the meaning of the words my mother had overheard:

"Oh, my dear, it's dreadful to have to stay in bed on a fine, sunny day like this, when it would be good to be outside. Your instructions are making me weep with frustration."

But she could not hide the groaning pain in her eyes, the sweat on her forehead, the jerky spasm, repressed the minute it began, of her limbs.

"I'm not in pain. I'm complaining because I'm not lying comfortably, I feel my hair is a mess, I feel sick, I knocked my head against the wall."

And my mother, at the foot of the bed—riveted to this suffering as though, by piercing through with her gaze the pained forehead, the body where the disease lay hidden, she must eventually reach and remove it—my mother said:

"No, dear Mama, we won't let you suffer like this, we'll find something to help you, just be patient for a moment. Let me give you a kiss; but you're not to move."

And, stooping over the bed, with her knees bent, almost kneeling, as if the humility of her posture would facilitate the acceptability of this passionate gift of herself, she bent her face down toward my grandmother with the whole of her life contained in it, like a ciborium she was holding out to her, decorated with folds and dimples so enamored, so sorrowful, and so sweet that there was no way of telling whether they had been engraved on it by a kiss, a sob, or a smile. My grandmother, too, tried to lift up her face to Mama's. It was so changed that, had she been strong enough to go out, she would probably have been recognized only by the feather in her hat. Her features, as in a modeling session, seemed to be straining, in one undivided effort of concentration, to conform to a particular pattern that bore no resemblance to anything we recognized. The sculptor's work was nearing its end, and if my grandmother's face had grown smaller, it had also hardened. The veins that crossed it were not like veins of marble, but of some rougher stone. Constantly bent forward in an attempt to breathe properly, but also shrinking into itself through exhaustion, her face, eroded, diminished, terrifyingly expressive, seemed like the rough, purplish, ruddy, desperate face of some fierce guardian of a tomb in a primitive, almost prehistoric sculpture. But the work was not yet completed. Later, the sculpture would have to be smashed, then lowered into the tomb that had been so painfully guarded by those harshly contracted features.

At one point when, as the saying goes, we did not know which way to turn, because my grandmother was coughing and sneezing a lot, we took the advice of a relative who assured us that if we brought in the specialist X the trouble would be over in a matter of days. This is the sort of thing society people say about their doctors, and we believe them, just as Françoise believed newspaper advertisements. The specialist arrived, his bag packed with all the coughs and sneezes of his other patients, like Aeolus with his goatskin.[1] My grandmother bluntly refused to be examined. And we, in our embarrassment at having called out this doctor for nothing, deferred to his desire to examine our respective noses, although there was nothing wrong with them. He was of a contrary opinion; migraine and colic, heart disease and diabetes were all diseases of the nose that had been wrongly diagnosed. He said to each of us in turn: "I would like to take another look at that little hooter of yours. Don't put it off too long. A little ignipuncture and I'll soon get rid of it for you." We had other things on our minds, yet we still asked ourselves, "Get rid of what?" In a word, all our noses were infected; his only mistake was to have used the present tense. For, by the next day, his examination and provisional treatment had taken effect. We all got catarrh. And when he ran into my father having a coughing fit in the street, the thought that an ignorant person might attribute the attack to his intervention brought a smile to his lips. He had examined us at a moment when we were already ill.

My grandmother's illness occasioned excessive or inadequate expressions of sympathy from a number of people, which surprised us quite as much as the sort of chance discovery, made through one or another of them, of connecting links of circumstance, or even friendship, which we would never have suspected. And the signs of interest shown by the constant stream of callers who came to the house to inquire made us aware of the gravity of an illness that, until then, we had not sufficiently seen for what it was, or detached from the countless painful impressions we now experienced in my grandmother's presence. When informed by telegram, her sisters stayed in Combray. They had discovered a musician there who provided them with excellent chamber recitals, and they felt that, by listening to these instead of sitting at their sick sister's bedside, they were better able to achieve a sense of contemplation and exalted grief, which did nothing to alter the highly unusual form this assumed. Mme Sazerat wrote to Mama, but in the tone of someone whose abruptly broken engagement (the rupture being Dreyfusism, in this case) has alienated from one forever. By contrast, Bergotte came every day and spent several hours with me.

He had always liked to come regularly and spend a few hours in a house where he had no need to stand on ceremony. But in the past he had come in order to talk without being interrupted; now he came to sit in silence for long periods without being asked to say anything. For he was very ill—with albuminuria, like my grandmother, some people said. According to others, he had a tumor. He was growing weaker by the day; he found it difficult to climb our staircase, and even more difficult to go down. Although he clung to the banisters, he often stumbled, and I believe he would have stayed at home had he not been afraid of losing completely the habit of going out and the possibility of doing so, he, the "man with the goatee" I remembered as so alert not so very long ago. His eyesight had completely gone, and he often had difficulty with his speech.

But at the same time, in stark contrast to this, his books, once known only in literary milieux at a time when Mme Swann used to support various feeble efforts to disseminate them, but now grown in stature and strength in the eyes of all, had become increasingly popular with the general public, and to an impressive extent. No doubt it is often only after his death that a writer achieves fame. But in this case it was while he was still alive, and slowly crawling toward the death that awaited him still, that the writer watched the progress of his work toward Fame. A dead author can at least enjoy fame without fatigue. The celebrity of his name stops short at his tombstone. In the deafness of eternal sleep, he is not importuned by Glory. But for Bergotte this antithesis was not yet the case. He was still alive enough to suffer from the uproar. He still moved about, however painfully, while his books, bouncing around the place like daughters who are loved but whose impetuous youth and noisy pleasures are exhausting, brought a daily succession of fresh admirers somewhat too close to his bedside.

The visits he now paid us came several years too late for me, for I no longer had the same admiration for his work. This was not incompatible with the growth of his reputation. A writer's work is seldom completely understood and established before the work of another writer, still relatively unknown, has begun to replace it, among a handful of exacting minds, with a new cult, different from the one that has almost ceased to command allegiance. In Bergotte's books, which I constantly reread, the sentences were as clear to me as my own thoughts, I perceived them as distinctly as the furniture in my room and the carriages in the streets. Everything was easily visible—if not as one had always seen it, then certainly as one was accustomed to see it now. But a new writer had just started to publish work in which the relations between things were so different from those that connected them for me, that I could understand almost nothing in his writing. For instance, he would write, "The hoses admired the careful upkeep of the roads"—this was easy to grasp, I followed smoothly along these roads—"which set out every five minutes from Briand and Claudel." At this point I failed to understand, because I had expected the name of a town and been given the name of a person instead. Only I felt not that it was the sentence that was badly constructed, but that I myself lacked the energy and agility to see it through to the end. I would make a fresh start, working really hard to reach the point where I could see the new connections between things. At each attempt, about halfway through the sentence, I would fall back defeated, as I did later, in the army, in horizontal-bar exercises. Yet I still felt for the new writer the same admiration experienced by a clumsy boy at the bottom of the class in gymnastics when he watches another, more agile than himself. From then on I felt less admiration for Bergotte, whose transparency struck me as a shortcoming. There was a time when people recognized things easily when they were depicted by Fromentin² and failed to recognize them at all when they were painted by Renoir.

Today people of taste tell us that Renoir is a great eighteenth-century painter. But when they say this they forget Time, and that it took a great deal of time, even in the middle of the nineteenth century, for Renoir to be hailed as a great artist. To gain this sort of recognition, an original painter or an original writer follows the path of the occultist. His painting or his prose acts upon us like a course of treatment that is not always agreeable. When it is over, the practitioner says to us, "Now look." And at this point the world (which was not created once and for all, but as often as an original artist is born) appears utterly different from the one we knew, but perfectly clear. Women pass in the street, different from those we used to see, because they are Renoirs, the same Renoirs we once refused to see as women. The carriages are also Renoirs, and the water, and the sky: we want to go for a walk in a forest like the one that, when we first saw it, was anything but a forest—more like a tapestry, for instance, with innumerable shades of color but lacking precisely the colors appropriate to forests. Such is the new and perishable universe that has just been created. It will last until the next geological catastrophe unleashed by a new painter or writer with an original view of the world.

The writer who had supplanted Bergotte in my estimation sapped my energy not by the incoherence but by the novelty—perfectly coherent—of associations I was not used to making. Because I always felt myself falter in the same place, it was clear that I needed to perform the same feat of endeavor each time. And when I did, very occasionally, manage to follow the author to the end of his sentence, what I discovered was always a humor, a truthfulness, a charm similar to those I had once found reading Bergotte, only more delightful. I reflected that it was not so long ago that a renewal of the world, similar to the one I expected from his successor, had been brought about for me by Bergotte. And I started to wonder whether there was some truth in the distinction we are always making between art, which is no more advanced now than it was in Homer's time, and science, with its continuous progress. Perhaps, on the contrary, art was now like science in this respect; each new writer of originality seemed to me to have progressed beyond his predecessors; and who was to say whether, in twenty years, when I could follow today's newcomer effortlessly, another might not emerge and leave the present newcomer to go the way of Bergotte? I spoke to the latter about the new writer. He dampened my enthusiasm not so much by assuring me that his art was unpolished, facile, and hollow, as by telling me that he had seen him and very nearly mistaken him for Bloch. The image of Bloch then started to loom over the pages I read, and I no longer felt any compulsion to take the trouble to understand them. If Bergotte had denigrated his work to me, it was less, I think, through jealousy of his success than through lack of familiarity with his work. He read almost nothing any more. The bulk of his thought had already passed from his brain into his books. He had grown thin, as if they had been removed from him by surgery. His reproductive instinct no longer stirred him to any activity now that he had created an autonomous existence for the greater part of his thought. He led the vegetative life of a convalescent, of a woman after childbirth; his striking eyes now remained motionless, vaguely dazed, like the eyes of a man lying by the seashore and watching, in a vague daydream, only each tiny wave. And if I was now less interested in talking to him than I used to be, I felt no twinge of conscience about it. He was such a creature of habit that an inclination toward simplicity, or toward utter extravagance, would become indispensable to him for a certain time. I do not know what made him come to our house that first time, but subsequently he came every day simply because he had been there the day before. He would turn up as he might have entered a café, in order that no one should talk to him, or—very rarely—so that he might talk himself, and there was no way of telling in the end whether he was moved by our grief or whether he just enjoyed my company, had we wanted to find a reason for these assiduous visits of his. My mother was not indifferent to them, sensitive as she was to anything that might be seen as an act of homage to her sick mother. And every day she reminded me, "Make sure you don't forget to thank him properly."

We had the pleasure of a visit—a discreet feminine touch like the tea and cake offered us, between sittings, by a painter's mistress—a courtesy extra, over and above the calls paid by her husband, from Mme Cottard. She came to offer us her "lady-in-waiting," or if we preferred the services of a man, she would "scour the field" for one; and when we declined, she said she did hope that this was not some "setback" on our part, a word that in her terms signified a false excuse for not accepting an invitation. She assured us that the professor, who never mentioned his patients at home, was as distressed as if it had been she herself who was ill. It will be clear in due course that, even if this had been true, it would have meant very little and at the same time a great deal, coming as it did from one of the most unfaithful and most appreciative of husbands.

Equally helpful offers, and infinitely more touching ones in the way they were expressed (a blend of the highest intelligence, the warmest sympathy, and a rare gift for putting them into words), were addressed to me by the heir to the Grand Duchy of Luxembourg. I had met him in Balbec when he had come to visit one of his aunts, the Princess of Luxembourg, at a time when he himself was merely the Comte de Nassau. A few months later, he had married the beautiful daughter of another Luxembourg princess, who, as the only daughter of a prince who owned a huge flour-manufacturing business, was inordinately wealthy. At this juncture, the Grand Duke of Luxembourg, who had no children of his own and was devoted to his nephew Nassau, had obtained parliamentary approval for making him his heir. As with all marriages of this kind, the source of the bride's fortune was the problem, just as it was the motivating cause. I recalled the Comte de Nassau as one of the most striking young men I had ever met, already consumed at the time by a darkly blazing passion for his fiancée. I was deeply touched by the regular flow of letters he wrote me during my grandmother's illness, and Mama herself, equally moved, would sadly voice one of her mother's expressions: "Sévigné could not have put it better."

On the sixth day, Mama, in response to my grandmother's entreaties, left her for a while and pretended to go and rest. I should have liked Françoise to stay quietly at her bedside, so that my grandmother could go to sleep. In spite of my pleas, she left the room; she was fond of my grandmother; with her perceptiveness and her sense of pessimism, she regarded her as a doomed woman. This made her anxious to provide her with every possible care and attention. But she had just learned that the electrician had arrived, a man who was long established with his firm, which was run by his brother-in-law, and who was highly esteemed throughout our building, where he had been coming for years, particularly by Jupien. We had sent for this workman before my grandmother fell ill. It seemed to me that he could have been sent away or asked to wait. But Françoise's sense of protocol did not permit this: it would have been to show a lack of consideration for the excellent man; my grandmother's state of health was suddenly irrelevant. When, after a quarter of an hour, I lost patience and went to look for her in the kitchen, I found her chatting with the electrician on the landing of the back stairs with the door open, a precaution that had the advantage, should any of us arrive on the scene, of allowing them to pretend they were saying goodbye, but the drawback of letting in a terrible draft. So Françoise parted with the workman, but not before she had shouted after him to convey various greetings to his wife and brother-in-law that she had overlooked. This concern, characteristic of Combray, not to be found lacking in good manners was something Françoise extended even to foreign policy. People foolishly imagine that the large-scale dimen-

sions of social phenomena provide an excellent opportunity to penetrate further into the human soul; they ought, on the contrary, to realize
that it is by sounding the depths of a single individual that they might
have a chance of understanding those phenomena. Françoise had told
the gardener in Combray a thousand times that war was the most sense-
less of crimes, that life was the only thing that mattered. Yet, when the
Russo-Japanese conflict broke out, she felt ashamed, in relation to the
Tsar, that we had not gone to war to help "the poor Russians," because,
as she said, "we're allianced to them." She thought it discourteous to
Nicholas II, who had always "said such nice things about us"; as a token
of the same code, she would not have allowed herself to refuse a quick
drink with Jupien, even though she knew it would "upset her diges-
tion," and all of this meant that, by not going in person to make her
apologies to this worthy electrician who had been put to so much trouble, even with my grandmother at death's door, she would have felt she
was committing the same sort of discourtesy she imputed to France's
neutrality toward Japan.

Luckily, we were very soon rid of Françoise's daughter, who had to
spend several weeks away. To the habitual pieces of advice Combray
people give to the family of an invalid—"Have you thought of going
away for a while . . . a change of air . . . getting your appetite back . . ."
and so forth—she had added the almost unique idea, which she had
thought up specially and which she repeated doggedly every time we
saw her, as though she needed to drive it into people's heads, "She
ought to have taken *radical* care of herself from the start." She did not
recommend one sort of treatment over another, provided it was *radical*.
As for Françoise herself, she observed that my grandmother was being
given very little medication. Since, in her view, medicines only ruined
the stomach, she was glad about this, but more obviously humiliated by
it. She had some cousins in the south of France—people who were quite
well off—whose daughter, after falling ill in mid-adolescence, died when
she was twenty-three; for several years before her decease, the father and
mother had spent a fortune on drugs and doctors, on pilgrimages from
one thermal spa to another. Now, for Françoise, for the parents concerned, all this seemed somehow luxurious, as if they had owned race-
horses or a country manor house. The parents, however afflicted they

felt, derived a certain pride from the amount of money they had spent. They were left with nothing, least of all their most treasured possession, their child, but they were fond of repeating how they had done as much for her, more than as much, as the wealthiest people in existence. The ultraviolet rays to which the poor girl had been subjected several times a day for months on end were a particular source of pride. At times the father, his vanity flattered by some sense of glorious sacrifice surrounding his grief, would even reach the point of speaking of his daughter as though she had been a famous opera singer for whose sake he had been brought to ruin. Françoise was not unmoved by such theatricality; the staging of my grandmother's illness seemed to her to be rather thin in comparison, better suited to the boards of a minor provincial theater.

There came a moment when my grandmother's eyes were affected by her uremic disorders. For a few days, she could not see at all. Her eyes were in no way like those of a blind person and remained unchanged. And I realized that she could not see only from the strangeness of a certain smile of welcome she adopted the moment any of us came into the room, a smile that lasted until one had taken her hand in greeting, begun too soon and remaining stereotyped on her lips, fixed, but always face-on and endeavoring to be visible to everyone, because it could no longer rely on the eyes to control it, to indicate the right moment and direction, to focus it, to enable it to adjust itself to the change of position or facial expression of whoever had come in; because it existed in isolation, unaccompanied by a smile in her eyes, which would have diverted the visitor's attention from it for a second, its awkwardness drew undue attention to it and gave the impression of forced amiability. Then her eyesight returned completely, and from her eyes the nomadic illness passed to her ears. For a few days, my grandmother was deaf. And because she was afraid of being startled by the sudden appearance of someone she might not have heard enter, although she was lying with her face to the wall, she would keep turning her head sharply to the door. But her neck movements were awkward, for it takes more than a few days to adapt to such a change of reflex and, if not exactly to see sounds, then to listen with one's eyes. Finally, the pain diminished, but her difficulty in speaking increased. We were obliged to ask my grandmother to repeat almost everything she said.

And now that she sensed we could no longer understand her, she stopped speaking altogether and lay there motionless. When she caught sight of me she gave a sort of start, like someone who is suddenly unable to breathe, but her desire to speak to me resulted only in unintelligible sounds. Then, overcome by sheer helplessness, she would let her head fall back, lie stretched out on the bed, grave and stony-faced, her hands motionless on the sheet or engaged in some purely physical action, like wiping her fingers on her handkerchief. She had no desire to think. This would be followed by a state of constant restlessness. She would incessantly want to get up. But we dissuaded her as far as we could, for fear she would realize how paralyzed she was. One day when she had been left alone for a moment, I discovered her on her feet, in her nightdress, trying to open the window. In Balbec once, when a widow who had flung herself into the sea had been rescued against her will, my grandmother had said to me (moved perhaps by one of those forebodings we sometimes sense in the otherwise highly obscure mystery of our organic life, where the future is nonetheless reflected, it seems) that she could think of nothing so cruel as to snatch a desperate woman from the death she had deliberately sought and to bring her back to a life of torture.

We were only just in time to grab hold of my grandmother; she put up an almost violent struggle against my mother; then, overpowered, forcibly made to sit in an armchair, she ceased to will, to regret, her face became impassive once more, and she began meticulously to pick off the hairs left on her nightdress by the fur coat we had thrown over her shoulders.

The look in her eyes changed completely: often anxious, doleful, wild, it was no longer the look we knew, but the sullen expression of a driveling old woman.

By repeatedly asking her whether my grandmother would like her to see to her hair, Françoise ended up by persuading herself that the request had come from my grandmother herself. She brought brushes, combs, eau de cologne, a gown, and remarked: "It can't do Mme Amédée any harm if I comb her hair. No one's too weak to have their hair combed." Which meant, no one is ever too weak for someone else to be able, for that someone else's own comfort, to comb their hair. But when I came into the room, I saw in the cruel hands of Françoise, as delighted as if she were restoring my grandmother to health, beneath the grief-stricken strands of aged hair, which lacked the strength to bear contact with a comb, a head that was incapable of maintaining the position demanded of it and was falling about in a constant whirl in which exhaustion alternated with pain. I could feel that Françoise was coming to the end of her task, and I dared not hasten it by saying, "That's enough," in case she disobeyed me. But I did rush forward when Françoise, who wanted my grandmother to see whether her hair had been done properly, was about to hand her, in callous innocence, a mirror. I was initially glad that I had managed to snatch it away from her in time, before my grandmother, whom we had carefully kept away from mirrors, caught even a stray glimpse of a reflection she would have been unable to recognize. But, alas, when, a moment later, I bent to kiss the handsome forehead which had undergone such exhausting treatment, she looked up at me in astonishment, distrustful and deeply shocked: she had failed to recognize me.

In the opinion of our doctor, this was a symptom that the congestion of her brain was increasing. It must be relieved. Cottard was of two minds. Françoise hoped for a second that they were going to use "clarified" cupping glasses. She looked up the effects of this treatment in my dictionary but could find no reference to it. Had she said "scarified" instead of "clarified," she would still not have found any reference to this adjective, since she did not look it up under "c" any more than under "s"; in fact, she said "clarified" but wrote (and therefore assumed that the written form was) "esclarified." Cottard, to her disappointment, decided, without much hope, to use leeches. A few hours later, when I went into my grandmother's room, fastened to her neck, her temples, her ears, the tiny black reptiles were writhing in her blood-stained hair, Medusa-like. But in her pale face, now pacified and utterly motionless, I saw her beautiful eyes, wide open, luminous, and calm as they once used to be (perhaps even more brimming with intelligence than they had been before her illness, since, being unable to speak and forbidden to move, she entrusted to her eyes alone her thought, the thought that holds such immense sway inside us and offers us unexpected treasures, or which can seem reduced to nothing and then be reborn, as if by spontaneous generation, thanks to the removal of a few drops of blood), her eyes, soft and liquid as oil, in which the rekindled fire which was now burning, lit up for the sick woman the recaptured universe. Her calm was no longer the wisdom of despair but of hope. She realized she was feeling better, was anxious to be prudent and not to move, did no more than to bestow a lovely smile on me so that I should know she was feeling better, and gently pressed my hand.

I knew the disgust my grandmother felt at the sight of certain creatures, not to mention being touched by them. I knew it was out of respect for the advantageous relief they would bring that she endured the leeches. And so it infuriated me to hear Françoise chuckling at her as to a child who has to be humored, and repeating, "Oh, look at the little beasties crawling all over Madame!" Furthermore, this was to treat our invalid with a lack of respect, as though she had in fact slipped into her second childhood. But my grandmother, whose face now wore the calm forbearance of a stoic, did not even seem to hear.

Alas, no sooner had the leeches been removed than the congestion returned and grew steadily worse. At this critical stage of my grandmother's illness, it amazed me that Françoise was constantly going off somewhere. And why? She had ordered herself a mourning outfit and did not want to keep the dressmaker waiting. In most women's lives, everything, even the greatest sorrow, comes down to a question of "I haven't got a thing to wear."

A few days later, while I was asleep, my mother came to call me in the middle of the night. With the tender concern of the grief-stricken, for the petty comforts of others, evident even in extremity, she said:

"Forgive me for disturbing your sleep."

"I wasn't asleep," I answered as I awoke.

I said this quite genuinely. The great modification brought about by awakening is not so much our entry into the clear life of consciousness as the loss of all memory of the slightly more subdued light in which our mind had been resting, as in the opaline depths of the sea. The half-veiled thoughts on which we were still drifting a moment ago involved us in quite enough motion for us to refer to them as wakefulness. But, then, our awakenings themselves involve an interruption of memory. A short time later, we describe what preceded them as sleep because we no longer remember it. And when the bright star that, at the moment of waking, lights up behind the sleeper the whole expanse of his sleep, begins to shine, it creates the momentary illusion that he was not sleeping but awake—a shooting star in reality, which dispels along with its fading light both the illusory existence and the contours of the dream and merely enables the waking man to say, "I've been asleep."

In a voice so gentle that it seemed to be afraid of doing me harm, my mother asked whether it would tire me too much to get up, and, stroking my hands, she added:

"Poor boy, you have only your papa and mama to rely on now."

We went into the bedroom. Bent in a semicircle on the bed, a creature other than my grandmother, a sort of beast who had donned the same hair and nestled among the same bedclothes, lay panting, whimpering, making the blankets heave with its convulsions. The eyelids were closed, and it was because they did not shut properly rather than because they opened that they revealed a small corner of eyeball, misted, rheumy, reflecting dimness of organic vision and inner pain. All this agitation was not intended for our benefit; she neither saw nor knew us. But if it was only a beast that was stirring there, where was my grandmother? And yet the shape of her nose was still recognizable, bearing no relation now to the rest of her face, but with its beauty spot still there in one corner, and so was her hand as it pushed aside the bedclothes with a gesture that would have once meant that those bedclothes bothered her but now meant nothing.

Mama asked me to fetch a little water and vinegar to bathe my grandmother's forehead. It was the only thing that refreshed her, thought Mama, who could see that she was trying to push back her hair from her face. But I was being beckoned from the doorway. The news that my grandmother was close to death had spread through the house at once. One of those "extra pairs of hands," employed at exceptional times to take the burden off the regular servants (which means that deathbeds start resembling parties), had just opened the door to the Duc de Guermantes, who was now waiting in the hall asking for me; I had no alternative.

"My dear sir, I have just heard your macabre news. As a mark of sympathy, I should like to shake your father by the hand."

I replied that I was very sorry but it was a difficult moment for him to be disturbed. M. de Guermantes was like a caller who turns up just as one is about to go off somewhere. But he was so conscious of the importance of the courtesy he was showing us that it blinded him to everything else, and he insisted on being shown into the drawing room. As a rule, he tended to make a point of carrying out punctiliously the formalities with which he had decided to honor a person and took little heed of things like packed trunks or coffins standing in readiness.

"Have you sent for Dieulafoy? No? That was a serious oversight. Had you asked me, he would have come on my behalf. He never refuses me anything, although he has been known to refuse the Duchesse de Chartres. I clearly take precedence over a princess of the blood, it would seem. But we are all equals in the face of death," he added, not to assure me that my grandmother was becoming his equal, but possibly because he felt that a prolonged conversation about his power over Dieulafoy and his precedence over the Duchesse de Chartres would not be in very good taste. His advice did not in the least surprise me. I knew that among the Guermantes Dieulafoy's name was always referred to (only with slightly more respect) in exactly the same way as any other top-quality caterer or supplier. And the old Duchesse de Mortemart, a Guermantes by birth (I never could understand why a duchess is invariably referred to as "the old duchess X," or, conversely, if the duchess is young, in delicate Watteau-like tones, as "the little duchess Y"), could almost always be relied on, in serious cases, to give a wink of recommendation and come out with "Dieulafoy, Dieulafoy!" in the same way that for ice cream she would say "Poiré Blanche" or for high-class confectionery "Rebattet, Rebattet!" But what I did not know was that my father had in fact just sent for Dieulafoy.

At this juncture my mother, who was waiting impatiently for the arrival of oxygen cylinders which would help my grandmother breathe more easily, came out herself into the hall, where she little expected to find M. de Guermantes. I would have done anything to make him disappear. But, convinced that nothing was more important, could be more flattering to her or more indispensable to maintaining his reputation as a perfect gentleman, he seized me violently by the arm and, despite my repeated protestations of "Sir, sir, sir" in the face of this near assault, dragged me across to Mama with the words, "Would you do me the great honor of presenting me to your lady mother?," his voice wavering slightly on the word "mother." And it was so obvious to him that the honor was hers that he could not hide a smile even while he was adopting a suitably serious expression. I had no alternative but to effect an introduction, which immediately set him hopping about in a series of low bows, ready to begin the whole ritual of salutation. He even seemed inclined to enter into conversation, but my mother, beside herself with grief, told me to come quickly and did not even reply to the remarks made by M. de Guermantes, who, expecting to be received as a visitor and finding himself left alone in the hall instead, would have departed had he not at that moment caught sight of Saint-Loup, who had arrived in Paris that morning and come rushing to see us when he heard the news. "Well, what a pleasant surprise!" cried the Duc joyfully, grabbing his nephew by the sleeve and nearly tearing it off, heedless of the presence of my mother, who was again crossing through the hall. Saint-Loup was not altogether sorry, I think, despite his genuine sympathy, to avoid seeing me, given his attitude toward me. He was dragged off by his uncle, who had something important to say to him that he had been on the point of going to Doncières to impart, and was absolutely delighted to have saved himself the expense and trouble. "Now, if anyone had told me I had only to cross the courtyard to find you, I'd have thought they were taking me for a ride. As your friend M. Bloch would put it, it's a rather 'droll' coincidence." And as he disappeared with his arm round Robert's shoulder, "All the same," he went on, "I've obviously touched the hangman's rope or whatever; I do have the devil's own luck." It was not that the Duc de Guermantes was bad-mannered. Far from it. But he was one of those men who are incapable of putting themselves in the place of others, similar in this respect to undertakers and the majority of doctors, who, after composing their faces and saying, "This is a very painful time for you," perhaps even embracing you and recommending rest, then revert to treating a deathbed or a funeral just like some social gathering of a more or less restricted kind, at which, with the joviality they have just momentarily repressed, they scan the room for someone they can talk to about their humdrum affairs or ask to introduce them to someone else or offer a lift home in their carriage. The Duc de Guermantes, while congratulating himself on the "favorable wind" that had blown him to his nephew, was still so taken aback by the reception he had been given by my mother, quite understandable though that had been, that he later declared her to be as disagreeable as my father was civil, subject to "blanks" during which she seemed not to hear a single word you said to her, and, in his opinion, out of sorts and perhaps even not quite in her right mind. At the same time, from what I was told, he was willing to put it down partly to "the circumstances" and to admit that my mother had been greatly "affected" by the sad event. But his limbs were still twitching with a whole residue of gestures of greeting and backward bows he had been prevented from fully accomplishing, and he was so impervious to the real nature of my mother's grief that he asked me, the day before the funeral, if I was doing anything to take her mind off things.

A brother-in-law of my grandmother's, a monk whom I had never met, had telegraphed the head of his order in Austria and, having obtained special dispensation to come, arrived that day. Weighed down by grief, he sat by the bedside reading prayers and meditations yet never once shifting his penetrating gaze from the invalid. At one point when my grandmother had fallen unconscious, the sight of this priest's grief pained me, and my eyes came to rest on him. He seemed startled by my pity, and then an odd thing happened. He covered his face with his hands like a man absorbed in doleful meditation, but, taking it for granted that I would look away, he had left a small gap between his fingers, and I noticed it. And just as I was looking away, I glimpsed his sharp eye, which had been taking advantage of his sheltering hands to observe whether my sympathy was sincere. He was lying there in wait, like a priest in the shadow of a confession box. He saw that I had noticed and instantly shut tight the grille he had not quite closed. I met him again later, but never did we mention what had happened in that minute. It was tacitly agreed that I had not noticed him spying on me. Priests, like specialists in mental disorders, always have something of the examining magistrate about them. Besides, what friend is there, how-ever dear, in whose past, as in ours, there has not been some similar in-cident we find it more convenient to believe he has forgotten?

The doctor gave a morphine injection and, to make her breath-ing less painful, ordered oxygen cylinders. My mother, the doctor, the nurse held these in their hands; as soon as one was empty they were handed another. I had left the room briefly. When I returned I found myself in the presence of something like a miracle. Accompanied by a subdued incessant murmur, my grandmother seemed to be singing us a long, happy song, which filled the room, rapid and musical. I soon real-ized that it was scarcely less unconscious than, as purely mechanical as, the hoarse rattle I had heard earlier. Perhaps it faintly reflected some im-provement induced by the morphine. It was mainly the result, since the air was not passing in quite the same way through the bronchial tubes, of a change of register in her breathing. Released by the twofold effect of oxygen and morphine, my grandmother's breath was no longer a la-bored groan but, swift and light, it was gliding like a skater toward the delicious fluid. Perhaps the breath, imperceptibly, like the wind breath-ing into the stem of a reed, was mingled in this song with some of those more human sighs that, released at the approach of death, suggest im-pressions of pain or pleasure in those who can no longer feel, and which came now to give a more melodious stress, but without changing its rhythm, to the long phrase, which rose higher and higher, then descended, before issuing forth again from the lightened chest in its search for oxygen. And after reaching such a pitch, sustaining itself so vigorously, this song, mingled in its voluptuousness with a murmur of supplication, seemed at times to stop completely, like a spring run dry.

When she experienced great grief, Françoise felt the need (so futile) to express it but lacked the art (so simple) to do so. Having made up her mind that my grandmother was doomed, what she was most anxious to impart to us was what she, Françoise, felt. And all she could do was to repeat, "It's had a nasty effect on me," in the same tone in which she would say, when she had had too much cabbage soup, "There's some-thing weighing on my stomach," which, in both cases, was more natural than she seemed to think. However feebly expressed it was, her grief was nonetheless considerable, and it was made even worse by the fact that her daughter was detained in Combray (which this young Parisienne now referred to as "the back of beyond," where she felt herself becoming "a country bumpkin") and unlikely to be able to return in time for the funeral ceremony, which, Françoise felt certain, would be a grand occasion. Knowing that we were not in the habit of showing our emotions, she had taken the precaution of summoning Jupien in advance to spend every evening that week in her company. She knew he would not be free at the time of the funeral. She wanted at least to have the opportunity to "tell him all about it" when he got back.

For several nights now, my father, my grandfather, and one of our cousins had been keeping watch at the bedside and no longer left the house. Their continuous devotion eventually assumed a mask of indifference, and the interminable whiling away of time around this deathbed led them to indulge in the sort of small talk that inevitably accompanies prolonged confinement in a railway carriage. The cousin in question (a nephew of my great-aunt) aroused in me a degree of antipathy equal to the esteem he deserved and generally enjoyed.

He was always somewhere in the background on important occasions and was so assiduous in his solicitude for the dying that the families concerned, on the pretext that he was delicate, despite his robust appearance, bass voice, and flourishing beard, invariably begged him, with customary evasiveness of expression, not to come to the cemetery. I knew already that Mama, thoughtful for others despite her immense grief, would soon be telling him in different terms what he was accustomed to hear said on all such occasions:

"Promise me you won't come 'tomorrow.' Do it for 'her sake.' If not, then there's no need for you to attend 'the last part.' It's what she would have wanted."

It was no use; he was always the first to arrive "at the house," and for this reason he had been given, in another circle and unbeknown to us, the nickname "No Flowers by Request." And before attending "everything" he had always "looked after everything," which earned him this reaction from people: "We don't even have to thank *you*."

"What was that?" asked my grandfather loudly. He had grown rather deaf and had not managed to catch something my cousin had just said to my father.

"Oh, nothing," answered the cousin. "I was just saying that I'd had a letter from Combray this morning. They're having dreadful weather there, and here it's almost too hot."

"And yet the barometer is very low," said my father.

"Where did you say they're having bad weather?" asked my grandfather.

"In Combray."

"Ah! I'm not surprised. Whenever the weather's bad here, it's fine in Combray, and vice versa. Oh Lord! Speaking of Combray, has anyone remembered to tell Legrandin?"

"Yes, there's no need to worry, it's been done," said my cousin, whose cheeks, bronzed by a heavy growth of beard, gave the merest hint of a satisfied smile at having thought of it.

At this point my father rushed from the room. My immediate reaction was that there had been a change for better or worse. In fact, it was merely that Dr. Dieulafoy had just arrived. My father went off to the adjoining drawing room to receive him, the latest actor to step into the drama. He had been sent for not to tend the patient but to certify, almost like a lawyer. Dr. Dieulafoy may indeed have been a great physician, a wonderful professor of medicine; to these roles, in which he excelled, he added another, in which he remained for forty years unchallenged, a role as original as that of the actor representing the voice of reason—Scaramouche or the noble father—which consisted in coming to certify that a patient was on the point of death, or dead. His very name hinted at the dignity with which he would fulfill his role, and when the maid announced, "M. Dieulafoy," it was like something out of a play by Molière. The dignity of his bearing was bolstered, unobtrusively, by his lithe and attractive build. The overhandsome face was redeemed by a decorum appropriate to distressing circumstances. With unaffected gravity, the professor would enter the room in his distinguished black frock coat, utter not one word of condolence, which could have been construed as insincere, and do nothing that breached the rules of tact in the slightest way. At the foot of a deathbed it was he, not the Duc de Guermantes, who was the great nobleman. After examining my grandmother without fatiguing her, and with more than enough restraint to show respect to the acting doctor, he murmured a few words to my father and bowed respectfully to my mother, to whom I felt it was all my father could do not to say, "Professor Dieulafoy." But already the professor had turned away, not wishing to seem intrusive, and made a perfect exit, simply accepting the sealed envelope that was slipped into his hand. He did not seem to have seen it, and even we were left wondering for a moment whether we had really given it to him, so dextrously had he made it disappear, like a conjurer, yet without losing a single trace of the gravity—if anything, it was accentuated—of the eminent consultant in his long frock coat with its silk lapels, his handsome face weighed down with the most dignified commiseration. Both his poise and his deftness indicated that, however many other calls he had to make, he had no wish to appear to be in a hurry. For he was the embodiment of tact, intelligence, and kindness. This eminent man is no longer. Other doctors, other professors may have equaled or even surpassed him. But the "function" in which his knowledge, his physical endowments, and his excellent manners made him supreme no longer exists, for want of successors capable of performing it. Mama had not even noticed M. Dieulafoy: everything apart from my grandmother had ceased to exist. I remember (I am anticipating here) that at the cemetery, where we saw her, like a supernatural apparition, edge diffidently toward the grave, her eyes seemingly gazing after a being who had flown off and was already far away, my father said, "Old Norpois came to the house, to the church, and he's now here at the cemetery. He missed a very important meeting to get here. You ought to say a word to him, he'd be very touched," and all that my mother could do, when the ambassador bowed to her, was gently to incline her face, on which there was no sign of tears. Two days earlier—to anticipate again, before I return to the bedside of my dying grandmother—while we were watching over her dead body, Françoise, who half believed in ghosts and was terrified by the least sound, had said, "I think that's her." Yet it was not fear but, rather, an infinite sweetness that these words aroused in my mother, who would have longed for the dead to return and to have her mother with her sometimes still.

To return to those hours of dying:

"You heard about the telegram her sisters sent?" my grandfather asked my cousin.

"Yes, that Beethoven business. I was told about it. It ought to be framed. But I'm not surprised."

"And my poor wife was so fond of them," said my grandfather, wiping away a tear. "We mustn't hold it against them, though. They're stark raving mad, the pair of them. I've always said so. What's the matter? Aren't you continuing with the oxygen?"

My mother said:

"But won't Mama start having difficulty with her breathing again?"

The doctor reassured her:

"Don't worry. The effect of the oxygen will last a good while yet. We can go on with it again presently."

It seemed to me that he would not have said this of a dying woman, that if the good effect was going to last it meant that it was possible to do something to keep her alive. The hiss of the oxygen stopped for a few minutes. But the happy lament of her breathing still issued from her, light, disquieted, incomplete, beginning over and over again. At times it seemed as if it were all over: her breath stopped, either because of one of those shifts of octave that occur in the respiration of a sleeper or because of some natural interruption, an effect of anesthesia, developing asphyxia, a failure of the heart. The doctor took my grandmother's pulse once more, but already, as if a tributary had come to irrigate the dried-up riverbed, a new tune had taken up the interrupted phrase. It took over in another key with the same inexhaustible impetus. Who knows whether, without my grandmother's even being conscious of them, a host of happy and tender experiences constricted by suffering were not escaping from her now, like lighter gases that have been kept under pressure for a long time? It seemed that everything she had to tell us was pouring out, that it was us she was addressing with this prolixity, this eagerness, this effusion. At the foot of the bed, convulsed by every gasp of the dying woman, not weeping but at moments drowned in tears, my mother stood with the heedless desolation of leaves lashed by the rain and torn back by the wind. I was made to dry my eyes before I went to kiss my grandmother.

"But I thought she could no longer see," said my father.

"One can never tell," replied the doctor.

When my lips touched her face, my grandmother's hands quivered and a long shudder ran through her whole body—possibly an automatic reflex, or perhaps it is that certain forms of affection are hypersensitive enough to recognize through the veil of unconsciousness what they scarcely need the senses to enable them to love. Suddenly my grandmother started up, made a violent effort, like someone struggling to hold on to her life. Françoise was unable to offer any resistance to the sight of this and burst out sobbing. Remembering what the doctor had said, I tried to make her leave the room. At that moment my grandmother opened her eyes. I hurriedly thrust myself in front of Françoise to hide her tears while my parents were speaking to the dying woman. The hissing drone of oxygen had stopped; the doctor moved away from the bedside. My grandmother was dead.

A few hours later, Françoise was able for the last time, and without causing pain, to comb that beautiful hair, which was only slightly graying and had thus far seemed much younger than my grandmother herself. But this was now reversed: the hair was the only feature to set the crown of age on a face grown young again, free of the wrinkles, the shrinkage, the puffiness, the tensions, the sagging flesh which pain had brought to it for so long. As in the distant days when her parents had chosen a husband for her, her features were delicately traced by purity and submission, her cheeks glowed with a chaste expectation, a dream of happiness, an innocent gaiety even, which the years had gradually destroyed. As it ebbed from her, life had borne away its disillusions. A smile seemed to hover on my grandmother's lips. On that funeral couch, death, like a sculptor of the Middle Ages, had laid her to rest with the face of a young girl.

CHAPTER 2

A visit from Albertine—The prospect of a wealthy marriage for some
of Saint-Loup's friends—Guermantes wit and the Princess of Parma—
A curious visit to M. de Charlus—I fail increasingly to understand
his character—The Duchesse's red shoes

ALTHOUGH IT WAS SIMPLY a Sunday in autumn, I had just been reborn; life stretched out uninterruptedly before me, for that morning, after a series of mild days, there had been a chilly fog that had not cleared until around midday. And a change in the weather is enough to create the world and ourselves afresh. In the past, when the wind swept down my chimney I would listen to the blows it struck on the flue trap with as much emotion as if, like the famous motif on the strings that opens the Fifth Symphony,[3] they had been the irresistible calls of a mysterious destiny. Every change in the natural scene offers us a similar transformation by adapting our desires to harmonize with the fresh shape of things. The mist, from the moment I woke up, had turned me, not into the centrifugal being of fine days, but into a man of reclusion, hankering after the fireside corner and the shared bed, an Adam sensitive to cold in quest of a sedentary Eve, in this changed world.

Between the soft gray light of a morning landscape and the taste of a cup of chocolate, I instated all that was distinctive about the physical, intellectual, and moral life that I had taken with me to Doncières about a year earlier, which, blazoned with the oblong shape of a bare hillside—always present even when it was invisible—represented a series of pleasures that were utterly distinct from any others, incommunicable to friends in the sense that the impressions, richly interwoven with one another, that orchestrated them were more typical of them for me, in an unconscious way, than any facts about them I could have related to others. From this point of view, the new world into which I had been plunged by the morning mist was a world already known to me (which only made it more real) and forgotten for some time (which restored all its freshness). And I was able to study several of the pictures of misty landscapes acquired by my memory, notably a series of *Mornings in Doncières*, including my first morning in the barracks there and another in a nearby country house where I had gone with Saint-Loup to spend the night: from the windows of both, when I had drawn back the curtains at dawn before getting back into bed, in the first a cavalryman, in the second (at the narrow margin of a pond and a wood, all the rest of which was engulfed in the uniform and liquid softness of the mist) a coachman polishing a harness strap, had appeared like those rare figures, scarcely visible to the eye—forced to adapt itself to the mysterious blur of the half-light—that emerge from a worn fresco.

It was from my bed that I was now contemplating these memories, for I had returned to it to wait until evening, when, taking advantage of the absence of my parents, who had gone to Combray for a few days, I proposed to attend a little play that was being put on at Mme de Villeparisis's house. Had they returned, I should not have dared to do this: my mother, in the niceties of her respect for my grandmother's memory, wished any token of regret paid to it to be spontaneous and genuine; she would not have forbidden me to go, but she would have disapproved. From Combray, on the contrary, had I consulted her about this, she would not have replied with a doleful, "Do what you wish, you're old enough now to know your own mind," but, reproaching herself for having left me alone in Paris and gauging my grief by her own, she would have wished it could have been distracted by pleasures that she would not have allowed herself and which she convinced herself that my grandmother, in her overriding concern for my health and nervous stability, would have been the first to recommend.

That morning, the newly installed heating boiler had been lit. The disagreeable noise it made—a sort of spasmodic hiccup—was in no way connected to my memories of Doncières, but its prolonged encounter with them inside me that afternoon was to force it into such an affinity with them that, after I thought I had more or less forgotten it, whenever I heard the central heating it would bring them back to me.

I was alone in the house with Françoise. The gray daylight, falling like fine rain, wove an endless succession of transparent webs, through which the Sunday strollers appeared in a silvery haze. I had cast the *Figaro* to the foot of the bed; I had been having it delivered punctiliously ever since I had sent in an article, which had not yet appeared; despite the absence of sun, it was clear from the amount of daylight that we were still only halfway through the afternoon. The tulle window curtains, misted and friable as they would not have been on a fine day, had that same mixture of softness and brittleness as a dragonfly's wing and Venetian glass. I was all the more downcast to be spending this Sunday alone because that morning I had sent a note to Mlle de Stermaria. Robert de Saint-Loup, whose mother had at last managed—after various painful and abortive attempts—to get him to leave his mistress, and who had straightaway been sent to Morocco to forget the woman he had in fact ceased to love for some time, had sent me a line, which I had received the day before, announcing his imminent arrival in France for a short spell of leave. Since he would only be passing through Paris (where his family were doubtless afraid of his taking up again with Rachel), to show that he had been thinking of me, his letter informed me that in Tangiers he had met Mlle—or, rather, Mme de Stermaria, given that she had divorced her husband after three months of marriage. Remembering what I had said to him in Balbec, Robert had asked for an assignation with the young woman on my behalf. She would be delighted to dine with me, she had told him, on one of the days she was spending in Paris before returning to Brittany. He told me to lose no time writing to Mme de Stermaria, since she had almost certainly arrived. Saint-Loup's letter had come as no surprise, even though I had had no news from him since his letter accusing me of perfidy and treachery, written at the time of my grandmother's illness. I had immediately grasped what must have happened. Rachel, who liked to provoke his jealousy—she also had other causes for resentment against me—had persuaded her lover that I had made sly attempts to have relations with her in his absence. It was likely that he still believed this to be true, but he had ceased to be smitten with her, which meant that, true or not, it had become a matter of utter indifference to him, and our friendship alone was what continued to be important. On one occasion when I saw him afterward, I tried to broach the question of his accusations, and he merely smiled with benign affection in what seemed to be an apology, then changed the subject. None of this means that, a little later, he did not sometimes see Rachel when he was in Paris. The creatures who have played an important part in one's life rarely drop out of it for good, just like that. They come back into it from time to time (so much so that people start believing in the renewal of former love) before leaving it forever. Saint-Loup's breakup with Rachel had very soon become less painful to him, thanks to the soothing pleasure her constant demands for money provided. Jealousy, which protracts the experience of love, is not capable of containing many more elements than any other form of imagination. If, at the start of a journey, we set off with three or four images, which in any case will be lost on the way (the lilies and anemones on the Ponte Vecchio, the Persian church seen through the mist, and so forth), our trunk is already pretty full. When we leave our mistress, we would prefer her, until we have begun to forget, not to become the property of the three or four potential lovers we picture keeping her, in other words, of whom we are jealous: all those we do not picture count for nothing. Now, frequent demands for money from a former mistress give no more idea of her life in its entirety than high figures on a temperature chart would give of her illness. But the latter would at least indicate that she was ill and the former create the presumption—a vague enough one, it is true—that the woman in question—forsaken or forsaker—cannot have found much in the way of a rich protector. And so each demand is greeted with the joy that arises from a lull in the jealous man's torment, and is met with an immediate dispatch of money, for we would not like to think of her being in want of anything except lovers (one of the three we picture), until such time as we have been able to regain some composure and to discover our successor's name without flinching. Sometimes Rachel got back so late that it was possible for her to ask her former lover's permission to sleep beside him until morning. This was a great solace to Robert, for a simple fact like her not in the least disturbing his sleep when he himself occupied the greater part of the bed would make him realize just how intimately they had lived together. He could see that she was more comfortable close to his body than she would have been elsewhere, that, lying there beside him, she felt, even in a hotel, as if she were in a bedroom known from way back, a familiar setting in which one sleeps more soundly. He felt that his shoulders, his legs, his whole body, even when insomnia or preoccupation with work made him inordinately restless, were for her so entirely usual that they could not disturb her, and that her awareness of them added still further to her own sense of repose.

To go back a little. I had been all the more aroused by Saint-Loup's letter from Morocco in that I could read between the lines the things he had not dared to write more explicitly. "You need have no qualms about asking her to dine in private," he wrote. "She is a charming young woman with a delightful nature. You will get along splendidly with her, and I feel sure you will spend an enjoyable evening in her company." Since my parents were coming back at the end of the week, on Saturday or Sunday, and I should be obliged after that to dine at home every evening, I had written at once to Mme de Stermaria to propose any evening that would suit her up to Friday. A message was brought back to say that I should get a written reply from her at about eight o'clock that very evening. The time would have passed quickly enough had it been made easier by a visit from someone else during the course of the intervening afternoon. When the hours are enveloped in conversation, we become oblivious of the clock, do not even notice the time, and it slips away until suddenly, way beyond the point at which it escaped our attention, the nimble runaway reappears. But if we are alone, the thing on which our mind is set, by placing before us its still-distant and ever-awaited occurrence with tick-tock regularity, divides, or, rather, multiplies, the hours by all the minutes we would have left uncounted in the company of friends. And, pointed as it was by the never-ending return of my desire, toward the throbbing pleasure I would enjoy (not for some days, though, alas!) in Mme de Stermaria's company, this afternoon, which I was going to have to spend alone, seemed to me very empty and very melancholy.

Every now and then I heard the sound of the elevator coming up, but it was followed by another sound, not the one I was hoping for (its stopping on our floor) but a quite different one, which it made in its journey up to the floors above, and which, because it invariably meant the desertion of my landing when I was expecting a visit, stayed with me subsequently, even at a time when I no longer wanted any visitors, as a sound that was in itself painful, resounding with something like a sentence to solitary confinement. Weary, resigned, with several hours still of its immemorial task to do, the gray day stitched away at its pearly braidwork, and I was filled with the gloomy thought that I was to remain alone in close contact with it, and with no more degree of acquaintance between us than I would have had with a seamstress sitting by the window to work in a better light and taking absolutely no notice of the person there with her in the room. Suddenly, without my having heard the bell, Françoise opened the door to show Albertine into the room; she came in smiling, silent, plump, containing in the plenitude of her body, in readiness for me to continue living them, come to find out where I was, the days spent in that Balbec to which I had never since returned. No doubt, whenever we re-encounter someone with whom our relations—however trivial they may be—have now changed, it is like two distinct periods in time coming together. It does not take the visit of a former mistress who is now a friend to effect this, but simply the arrival in Paris of someone we have known on a daily basis in a certain kind of life, and the fact that this life has now ceased, if only a week ago. On each of Albertine's smiling, questioning, hesitant features I could spell out the questions: "And what about Mme de Villeparisis? And the dancing teacher? And the confectioner?" When she sat down, her back seemed to be saying, "There are no cliffs here, I know, but you don't mind if I sit beside you, as I used to in Balbec, do you?" She was like an enchantress representing a mirror of time. In this, she was like all the people we now only rarely see but with whom we once lived on more intimate terms. Yet with Albertine there was something more. True, even in our daily encounters in Balbec, I was always surprised when I caught sight of her: she changed so much from day to day. But now she was hardly recognizable. No longer bathed in a pink haze, her features now stood out like those of a statue. She had another face, or, rather, she had a real face at last; her body had developed. There was almost nothing left of the sheath in which she had been enclosed, and which in Balbec had almost completely masked her future figure.

This year, Albertine was back in Paris earlier than usual. Normally she did not arrive until spring, so that, already disturbed for some weeks by the storms that were crushing the first flowers, I could not distinguish, in my pleasure, between Albertine's return and that of the fine weather. It was enough to hear that she was in Paris and that she had called on me, for me to see her again like a rose by the sea. I am not quite sure whether it was the desire for Balbec or for her that took hold of me then; perhaps my desire for her was itself a lazy, cowardly, incomplete way of possessing Balbec, as if to possess a thing materially, to take up residence in a town, were equivalent to possessing it spiritually. And even materially, when she was not being swayed in my imagination before a horizon of sea but sitting there motionless beside me, she seemed to me often to be a very poor sort of rose, and I would have preferred to shut my eyes to avoid seeing the various blemishes on its petals and to imagine instead that I was breathing sea air.

I can say all this here, although I was not aware at the time of what was to happen later. Certainly, it is more reasonable to devote one's life to women than to postage stamps, old snuffboxes, or even paintings and statues. Yet these examples of collectors' pieces should alert us to variety, to having not a single woman but many. The charming associations between a young girl and the seashore or the braided hair of a church statue, an old print, or anything that makes one love her, become rather unstable the moment she steps into the room like a delightful picture. Establish your life with this woman and you will cease to see anything of what made you love her; yet it is true that the two dissociated elements can be reunited by jealousy. If, after a long period of living together, I was to end up seeing Albertine as no more than an ordinary woman, an intrigue between her and someone she had loved in Balbec would possibly have been enough to reincorporate within her the amalgamation of seashore and breaking waves. But such secondary associations no longer captivate the eye; it is to the heart that they speak in their deadly way. It is not possible, in so dangerous a guise, to regard the renewal of the miracle as a thing to be desired. But I am anticipating the course of events. And here I need only voice my regret that I did not have the sense simply to keep my collection of women as someone might keep a collection of antique opera glasses—never so complete, behind the glass of their cabinet, that there is not always room for another pair, rarer still.

Breaking with the normal pattern of her holiday arrangements, this year she had come straight from Balbec and had not stayed on there nearly as long as usual. I had not seen her for a long time. And since I did not know, even by name, the people she mixed with in Paris, I knew nothing of her life during the periods when she did not come to see me. They were often quite long. Then, one fine day, in would burst Albertine, a pink apparition on one of those silent visits who gave me little or no idea of what she had been doing in the interval, which remained plunged in the darkness of a life my eyes felt little interest in penetrating.

On this visit, however, certain signs seemed to indicate that some new experience must have taken place in that life. But perhaps the only thing one was entitled to conclude from them was that girls of Albertine's age change very quickly. For instance, her intelligence was more noticeable, and when I reminded her of the day she had insisted so heatedly that her idea of making Sophocles write "My dear Racine" was best, she was the first to laugh quite genuinely. "Andrée got it right. I was the stupid one," she admitted. "Sophocles ought to have written 'Sir.'" I replied that Andrée's "Sir" and "Dear Sir" were no less comic than her own "My dear Racine" or Gisèle's "My dear friend," but that in the end the really stupid people were the teachers who assigned letters from Sophocles to Racine. Here Albertine lost track. She was unable to see what was stupid about it; her intelligence was opening up but not fully developed. There were other, more attractive new changes in her; I sensed, in this same pretty girl who had just sat down by my bed, something that was different, and, in the lines that, in the gaze and the facial features, express someone's familiar purposes, a change of approach, a partial conversion, as if there had been something to break down those resistances I had met with in Balbec one now distant evening when we had formed a couple symmetrical with but the converse of the one we now formed this afternoon, for then it had been she who was lying down and I by her bedside. Wanting and not daring to find out whether she would now let herself be kissed, each time she rose to leave I asked her to stay a little longer. This was rather difficult, for although she had nothing to do (if she had, she would have rushed off to do it), she was set in her ways and in fact not very obliging toward me, as if she no longer took much pleasure in my company. Yet, each time, after consulting her watch, she sat down again at my request, so that in the end she had spent several hours with me without my having demanded anything of her; the things I said to her were related to those I had said during the preceding hours, were totally unconnected with what I was thinking about, what I desired, and remained doggedly parallel to all this. There is nothing like desire for obstructing any resemblance between what one says and what one has on one's mind. Time presses, and yet it seems as though we were trying to gain time by speaking about things that are utterly alien to the one thing that preoccupies us. We chatter away, whereas the words we should like to utter would by now have been accompanied by a gesture, if indeed we have not—to give ourselves the pleasure of immediate action, and to slake the curiosity we feel about the ensuing reactions to it—without a word, without so much as a by-your-leave, already made this gesture. It is true that I was not in the least in love with Albertine: born from the mist outside, she could do no more than satisfy the fanciful desire awakened in me by the change in the weather, poised midway between the desires that are satisfied by culinary arts and by monumental sculpture respectively, because it made me dream both of mingling my flesh with a substance that was different and warm, and of attaching to some point of my recumbent body a divergent body, as Eve's body is barely attached by the feet to the side of Adam, to whose body hers is almost perpendicular in the Romanesque bas-reliefs in the Balbec cathedral, representing in so noble and so placid a fashion, still almost like a classical frieze, the creation of woman; in them God is followed everywhere, as by two ministers, by two little angels recalling—like the winged, swirling creatures of the summer that winter has caught by surprise and spared—cupids from Herculaneum still surviving well into the thirteenth century, flagging now in their last flight, weary, but never relinquishing the grace we might expect of them, over the whole front of the porch.

In regard to the pleasure that would have released me from fantasies like these by fulfilling my desire, and which I would have sought quite as readily from any other pretty woman, had I been asked upon what—in the course of this endless chatter I used to hide from Albertine the one thing that was on my mind—my optimistic assumption about the likelihood of her obliging me was based, I should probably have replied that this assumption was provoked (as the forgotten elements of Albertine's voice retraced for me the contour of her personality) by the emergence of certain words that had not previously formed part of her vocabulary, at least not in the sense she now gave them. When, for instance, she said that Elstir was stupid and I protested:

"You don't understand," she answered with a smile, "I mean that he was stupid in this one case, but I'm perfectly well aware that he is a very distinguished man in reality."

Likewise, to indicate how smart the Fontainebleau golf club was, she declared:

"It's quite a selection, in fact."

In relation to a duel I had fought, she said of my seconds, "What choice seconds," and, looking at my face, confessed that she would like to see me "sport a mustache." She even went so far—and here my chances seemed to me to be considerable—as to use an expression that I would have sworn was unknown to her the year before and to say that a certain "lapse of time" had gone by since she last saw Gisèle. This was not to say that Albertine had not possessed, when I was in Balbec, a fairly respectable batch of expressions that immediately reveal a well-to-do family background, and which, from year to year, a mother passes on to her daughter just as she makes her a present on important occasions, as the girl grows up, of her own jewelry. It was apparent that Albertine had ceased to be a little girl when one day, to express her thanks for a present given her by a lady she did not know, she had said, "I really don't know how to thank you." Mme Bontemps had been unable to stop herself from exchanging glances with her husband, whose response had been:

"My word, and she's only about to turn fourteen."

Her more pronounced nubility came to the fore when Albertine, speaking of another girl, who had no idea how to behave, remarked, "You can't even tell whether she's pretty, she cakes her face in so much makeup." Finally, though still only a girl, she was already adopting the manner of a grown woman of her background and class when she responded to someone who was making faces with the words, "I can't bear to look at him, because it makes me want to do the same thing," or, to someone who was doing funny imitations, "What really amuses me is that when you imitate her you start to look exactly like her." All this is drawn from the social treasury. But what struck me was that Albertine's background was not likely to have provided her with the word "distinguished" in the sense that my father used it, of the odd colleague he had not yet met but whose great intelligence he had heard praised, to say, "He's said to be a very distinguished person." "Selection," too, even when used of a golf club, seemed as out of place in the Simonet family as it would be preceded by the adjective "natural" in a text published centuries before Darwin's researches. "Lapse of time" seemed more promising still. Finally came evidence of upheavals whose nature was unknown to me but sufficient to justify all my hopes, as Albertine said, with the confidence of a person whose opinion is not to be disregarded:

"*To my mind,* it is the best thing that could possibly happen. . . . I see it as the best way out, the stylish solution."

This was so novel, so clearly an alluvial deposit hinting at such capricious explorations on territory hitherto unknown to her, that no sooner were the words "to my mind" out of her mouth than I drew Albertine toward me, and at "I see it as" sat her down on my bed. It is no doubt the case that women with a smattering of culture, marrying well-read men, receive such expressions as part of their dowry. And shortly after the metamorphosis that follows the wedding night, when they start paying calls and becoming distant with their old friends, they have only to emphasize the two "l"s in the word when they denote someone as "intelligent" to impress upon their astonished audience that they have become married women; but this is precisely the sign of a changed state, and it seemed to me that just such a thing had happened with Albertine's vocabulary, a vocabulary in which the most daring expressions I had previously heard were to say of any rather odd person, "He's a bit of a character," or, if you suggested a game of cards, "I don't have money to throw away," or else, if any of her friends reproached her with something she felt to be unjustified, "That's a fine thing for *you* to say!," expressions dictated in such cases by a middle-class tradition almost as old as the *Magnificat* itself, which a girl who is slightly miffed and sure she is in the right uses "quite naturally," as they say—in other words, because she has learned them from her mother, just as she has learned to say her prayers or how to greet people politely. All these expressions she had learned from Mme Bontemps, along with a hatred of Jews and a respect for the color black because it is always suitable and never out of place, without any formal instruction on Mme Bontemps's part, but in the way that baby goldfinches model their twitter on that of their parents and so turn into true goldfinches themselves. Despite all this, "selection" struck me as foreign, and "I see it as" seemed inviting. Albertine was no longer the same and perhaps might not act, or react, in the same way.

Not only did I no longer feel any love for her, but I no longer ran the risk, as I might have done in Balbec, of wrecking her affection for me, since it no longer existed. There could be no doubt that she had long become quite indifferent to me. I realized that for her I was no longer in any way a member of the "little gang" into which I had once been so keen to seek admission and then so happy to have done so. And since she had not even retained the openness and good nature she had shown in Balbec, I felt no major scruples; but I think it was one last philological discovery that settled matters. As I continued to add further links to the chain of irrelevant remarks beneath which I hid my inner desire, with Albertine now secure on the corner of my bed, I talked about one of the girls from the little gang, who was less prominent than the others but whom I nonetheless thought quite pretty: "Yes," said Albertine, "she's like a little *mousmé*."[4] Obviously, when I first knew Albertine, the word *mousmé* was unknown to her. It was likely that in the normal course of events she would never have learned it, and as far as I was concerned that would have been fine, for there is no word that rankles more. The very sound of it sets your teeth on edge, like too large a piece of ice in the mouth. But, coming from Albertine, pretty as she was, not even *mousmé* could displease me. On the contrary, it seemed like a revelation, if not of an external initiation, then of some internal development. Unfortunately, it was now time to say goodbye to her if I wanted her to get home in time for dinner and myself to be up in time for mine. Françoise was preparing it; she did not like it to be delayed and must already have been thinking that one of the articles of her code had been contravened, in that Albertine, in the absence of my parents, should be paying me so long a visit, and one that was going to make everything late. But in the face of *mousmé* all these arguments fell away, and I hastened to say:

"You know, I'm not in the least ticklish. You could tickle me for a whole hour and I wouldn't feel a thing."

"Is that so?"

"I promise you."

She no doubt understood that this was the clumsy expression of a desire, for, like someone who offers to give you an introduction you have not dared to solicit but to whom your words have indicated that it could be useful to you, she said with womanly meekness:

"Would you like me to try?"

"If you'd like to, but it would be easier if you lay down properly on the bed."

"Like this?"

"No, farther in."

"Are you sure I'm not too heavy?"

As she said this, the door opened and Françoise walked in carrying a lamp. Albertine just had time to regain her chair. Perhaps Françoise had chosen this moment to startle us, after listening at the door or even peeping through the keyhole. But I had no need to suppose anything of the sort: she might well have disdained the use of her eyes to ascertain what her instinct must have adequately enough detected, for, throughout her service with me and my parents, fear, prudence, alertness, and cunning had finally taught her that instinctive and almost divinatory knowledge of us that the sailor has of the sea, the quarry of the hunter, and if not the doctor then often the patient of the disease. All the knowledge she was in the habit of acquiring would have astounded anyone, for as good a reason as the advanced state of certain areas of knowledge among the ancients, given the almost negligible means of information at their disposal (hers were no less so: a handful of chance remarks forming barely a twentieth part of our conversation at dinner, gleaned in passing by the butler and inaccurately transmitted to the staff quarters). Even her mistakes resulted, like theirs, like the fables in which Plato believed, from a false conception of the world and from preconceived ideas rather than from an inadequacy of material resources. Similarly, even today, the most important discoveries about insect behavior have been made by a scientist with no laboratory, no apparatus at his disposal. But if the drawbacks of her position as a servant had not prevented her from acquiring the learning indispensable to the art that was its ultimate goal—the art of confounding us by communicating the results of her discoveries—the constraints on her time had been even more effective; here hindrance had not merely been content not to paralyze her enthusiasm, it had powerfully fired it. And of course Françoise neglected no auxiliary stimulant, such as diction and attitude. As she never believed anything we said to her when we wanted her to believe it, and since she accepted beyond a shadow of doubt the absurdest things anyone of her own status told her that might at the same time offend our views, in the same way that her manner of listening to our assertions pointed to her incredulity, so the tone she used to report (indirection enabling her to fling the most offensive insults at us with impunity) a cook's account of threatening her employers and forcing any number of concessions out of them by treating them like dirt in public, indicated that she treated the story as gospel truth. Françoise even went so far as to add, "If *I'd* been the mistress, I'd have been very put out, I can tell you." However much, despite our initial dislike of the lady on the fourth floor, we might shrug our shoulders at this unedifying tale as if it were an unlikely fable, its teller knew just how to invest her tone with all the trenchant punch of the most unshakable and infuriating confidence in what she was saying.

But above all, just as writers, when their hands are tied by the tyranny of a monarch or of poetic convention, by the strict rules of prosody or state religion, often achieve a power of concentration they would not have had under a system of political freedom or literary anarchy, so Françoise, by not being free to respond to us in an explicit manner, spoke like Tiresias and would have written like Tacitus.[5] She knew how to contain everything she could not directly express in a sentence we could not denounce without casting aspersions on ourselves—in less than a sentence, in fact, in a silence, in the way she placed an object.

For instance, whenever I inadvertently left on my table, among other letters, one that should have been kept from her eyes, because, say, it spoke about her in a malevolent way which suggested that the malevolence was shared by the recipient as well as the writer, the same evening, if I returned home with a feeling of uneasiness and went straight to my room, there on top of my letters, arranged in the right order in a neat pile, the compromising document would be the first thing to catch my eye, as it could not have failed to catch the eye of Françoise, placed by her right on the top, almost separately, with an obviousness that was a form of speech with an eloquence all of its own, which, as soon as I came into the room, startled me like a sudden shout. She excelled in setting up these stage effects, intended to provide the spectator, in her absence, with sufficient information to realize that she knew everything by the time she made her entry. Her art of making inanimate objects speak in this way had all the inspired diligence of Irving and Frédérick Lemaître.[6] In the present instance, holding over Albertine and myself the lighted lamp, which missed none of the still-visible dents in the quilt left by the girl's body, Françoise looked like *Justice Shedding Light on Crime*.[7] Albertine's face lost nothing in the lamplight. It revealed on her cheeks the same sun-glazed surface I had found so attractive in Balbec. In the light of the lamp, this face of hers, which sometimes, out of doors, looked pallid and wan, now showed surfaces so glowingly and evenly colored, so firm and so smooth, that they might have been compared to the sustained flesh tints of certain flowers. But Françoise's unexpected entry had startled me, and I cried out:

"What, the lamp already? Goodness, it's very bright!"

My intention might well have been, in the second of these remarks, to cover my confusion, and in the first, to excuse the fact that I was late. Françoise replied with barbed ambiguity:

"Am I to snuff it 'orf' then, sir?"

" 'Orf'? 'Off,' surely? She's the one who's 'off,' if you ask me . . ." Albertine whispered in my ear, leaving me charmed by the familiar quickness of mind with which, taking me at once for master and accomplice, she insinuated this psychological affirmation in the interrogative mood of a grammatical question.[8]

When Françoise had left the room and Albertine was seated once again on my bed, I said to her:

"What really worries me is that if we go on like this I may have to kiss you."

"What a lucky misfortune that would be."

I did not respond at once to this invitation. Another person might even have found it superfluous, for Albertine's way of pronouncing her words was so carnal and so soft that her speech alone was like a kiss. A word from her lips was a favor, and her conversation smothered you in kisses. And yet her invitation was very gratifying. It would have been so coming from any pretty girl of the same age; but that Albertine should now be so easily accessible to me gave me more than pleasure, it presented me with a series of images instilled with beauty. I remembered Albertine first of all against the seashore, almost painted upon a background of sea, no more real for me than those theatrical tableaux where it is not clear whether one is looking at the actress billed to appear, at an understudy who is standing in for her, or simply at a projection. Then the real woman had detached herself from the beam of light, come toward me, but only for me to perceive that in the real world she had none of the amorous accessibility she had seemed to possess in the magic tableau. I had learned that it was not possible to touch her, to kiss her, that all one could do was to talk to her, that for me she was no more a woman than a cluster of jade grapes, that inedible table decoration so fashionable at one time, are really grapes at all. And now she was appearing to me on a third level, real as in my second experience of

her, but available as she had been in the first—available in a way that
was all the more delicious for my having imagined for so long that she
was not. My surplus of knowledge about life (life less uniform, less
simple than I had first imagined) inclined me provisionally toward ag-
nosticism. What can one claim with any certainty, when the thing one
thought probable at first has then turned out to be false and, in a third
instance, to be true? (And, alas, I was far from finished with my discoveries about Albertine.) In any case, even if there had not been the romantic attraction of this discovery of a greater wealth of planes revealed
one after another by life (an attraction the opposite of the one experienced by Saint-Loup during the dinners in Rivebelle when he recognized, beneath the masks life had superimposed on a calm face, features
to which his lips had once been pressed), the knowledge that to kiss Albertine's cheeks was something possible gave me perhaps greater pleasure than the fact of kissing them. What a difference there is between
possessing a woman with one's body alone, because she is no more
than a piece of flesh, and possessing the girl one used to see on the
beach with her friends on certain days, without even knowing why it
was on those days and not on others, so that one trembled to think one
might not see her again. Life had been so kind as to reveal the whole extent of this young girl's life, had lent first one optical instrument, then
another, to see her with, and then added to carnal desire the accompaniment, multiplying and diversifying it, of other desires, more spiritual
and less easily satisfied, which lie inert and unaffected when it is merely
a question of the conquest of a piece of flesh, but which, when they
want to gain possession of a whole field of memories from which they
have felt nostalgically exiled, surge up wildly around carnal desire, extend it, are unable to follow it to the fulfillment, the assimilation, impossible in the form in which it is sought, of an immaterial reality, but
wait for this desire halfway and, the moment the memory of it returns,
are there to escort it once more; to kiss, not the cheeks of the first
woman who comes along—anonymous, devoid of mystery and glamour,
however cool and fresh those cheeks may be—but those of which I had
so long been dreaming, would be to know the taste, the savor, of a color
I had so often contemplated. One sees a woman, a mere image in life's

scene, like Albertine silhouetted against the sea, and then it becomes possible to detach that image, bring it close, and gradually observe its volume, its colors, as though it had been placed behind the lenses of a stereoscope. For this reason, women who tend to be resistant and cannot be possessed at once, of whom indeed it is not immediately clear that they can ever be possessed at all, are the only interesting ones. For to know them, to approach them, to conquer them is to make the human image vary in shape, in size, in relief, a lesson in relativity in the appreciation of a woman's body, a joy to see anew when it has regained its slender outline against the backdrop of reality. Women who are first encountered in a brothel are of no interest, because they remain static.

There was also the fact that Albertine held in an unbroken ring around her all the impressions of a series of seascapes that were particularly dear to me. I felt that, kissing this girl's cheeks, I should be kissing the whole Balbec seashore.

"If you're really going to let me kiss you, I'd rather reserve it for the right moment. Only you mustn't forget that you've said I may. I want a voucher: 'Valid for one kiss.' "

"Do I have to sign it?"

"But if I took it now, should I have another one for later?"

"You do make me laugh with your vouchers. I shall issue a new one every now and then."

"One more thing. You know, in Balbec, before I got to know you, you used to have a hard, canny look. You couldn't tell me what you were thinking about when you looked like that?"

"No, I don't remember at all."

"Well, this may remind you. One day your friend Gisèle jumped with her feet together over the chair an old gentleman was sitting in. Can you remember what was in your mind at that moment?"

"Gisèle was the one we saw least of. She was part of the gang in a way, but not really. I was probably thinking how common and bad-mannered she was."

"Oh, is that all?"

I should really have liked, before kissing her, to have been able to re-create in her the mystery she had held for me on the beach before I knew her, to discover in her the place where she had lived before that; in default of such mystery, I could at least insinuate all the memories of the time we had spent in Balbec, the sound of the waves breaking beneath my window, the shouts of the children. But as I let my gaze wander over the lovely pink globe of her cheeks, whose gently curving surfaces merged into the first low folds of her beautiful black hair, which ran in animated ridges, rose into steep foothills, and molded the hollows and slopes of its valleys, I could not help saying to myself: "Now, at last, after failing in Balbec, I am going to discover the taste of the unknown rose in Albertine's cheeks. And since the circles through which we are able to make things and people pass in the course of our existence are not that numerous, perhaps I shall be able to consider my own in some sense fulfilled when I have taken the blossoming face to which I had given pride of place out of its distant setting, brought it on to this new plane, and at last have knowledge of it through the lips." I told myself this because I believed there was such a thing as knowledge through the lips; I told myself that I was going to know the taste of this bodily rose because it had not occurred to me that man, a creature clearly less rudimentary than the sea urchin or even the whale, nevertheless lacks a certain number of essential organs, and notably possesses none that will serve for kissing. For this absent organ he substitutes his lips, and thus perhaps manages to achieve a more satisfactory result than if he were reduced to caressing the beloved with a horny tusk. But the lips, designed to bring to the palate the taste that lures them, have to be content, without understanding their mistake or admitting their disappointment, with drifting over the surface and coming up against the barrier of the cheek's desirable impenetrability. And at the moment of actual contact with the flesh, the lips, even supposing they might become more expert and talented, would doubtless be unable to enjoy any more fully the flavor that nature prevents them from grasping spontaneously, for in the desolate zone in which they are unable to find their rightful nourishment they are alone, long since abandoned by the eyes and then the nose in turn. For a start, as my mouth began to move toward the cheeks my eyes had led it to want to kiss, my eyes changed position and saw different cheeks; the neck, observed at closer range and as if through a magnifying glass, became coarse-grained and showed a sturdiness which altered the character of the face.

Apart from the latest developments in photography—which lay down at the foot of a cathedral all the houses that so often, from close up, seemed to us to be as high as towers, which deploy like a regiment, in file, in organized dispersion, in serried masses, the same monuments, bring together on the *piazzetta* the two columns that were so far apart a while back, distance the nearby Salute, and, on a pale and lifeless background, manage to contain an immense horizon beneath the arch of a bridge, in a single window frame, between the leaves of a tree in the foreground that is more vigorous in tone, frame a single church successively in the arcades of all the others—I know of nothing that is able, to the same degree as a kiss, to conjure up from what we believed to be something with one definite aspect, the hundred other things it may equally well be, since each is related to a no less valid perspective. In short, just as in Balbec Albertine had often seemed different to me, now—as if, by magically accelerating the speed of the changes of perspective and coloring a person offers us in the course of our various encounters, I had tried to contain them all within the space of a few seconds in order to re-create experimentally the phenomenon that diversifies a person's individuality and to draw out separately, as from a slipcase, all the possibilities it contains—now what I saw, in the brief trajectory of my lips toward her cheek, was ten Albertines; because this one girl was like a many-headed goddess, the head I had seen last, when I tried to draw near, gave way to another. As long as I had not touched it, I could at least see this head, and a faint perfume came to me from it. But, alas—for, when we kiss, our nostrils and eyes are as ill placed as our lips are ill made—suddenly my eyes ceased to see, and my nose, in turn, crushed against her cheek, no longer smelled anything, so, without my efforts' bringing me any clearer notion of the taste of the rose I desired, I discovered, from these abominable signs, that I was finally in the process of kissing Albertine's cheek.

Was it because we were playing out a reversal of our scene together in Balbec (figured by the rotation of a solid body), because I was the one lying in bed and she the one who was not, and thus in a good position to evade a rough pass and to control how far things went, that she now allowed me to take so easily what she had formerly refused with such a stern look? (Doubtless, from that earlier look the voluptuous expression her face assumed now, as my lips approached it, differed only by an infinitesimal deviation of its lines, but one that can accommodate all the difference there is between putting an end to a wounded man's life or nursing his wounds, between a sublime portrait and a grotesque one.) Not knowing whether I had to give credit and owed gratitude for this change of attitude to some benefactor who, in these last months, in Paris or in Balbec, had been unwittingly working on my behalf, I mainly attributed it to the present positioning of our bodies. But Albertine provided me with another explanation, precisely this: "Oh well, when we were in Balbec, I didn't really know you. For all I could tell, you might have had wicked designs on me." This explanation left me perplexed. No doubt Albertine was being sincere. It is by no means easy for a woman to recognize in the movements of her limbs, in the sensations experienced by her body, during a close conversation with a male friend, the unknown sin she trembled to think a stranger might be planning for her downfall!

At all events, whatever changes might have occurred recently in Albertine's life (and might possibly have explained why she should have so easily granted to my momentary and purely physical desire what she had refused with horror to my love when we were in Balbec), an even more startling one became apparent that very evening, as soon as her caresses had satisfied me in a way that she could not have failed to notice, and which I had even feared might provoke her to the slight gesture of revulsion and offended modesty Gilberte had made in similar circumstances behind the laurel bushes in the Champs-Élysées.

The exact opposite happened. Already, when I had made her lie on my bed and begun to fondle her, Albertine had adopted an expression, unfamiliar to me on her part, of docile compliance, of almost childish simplicity. By effacing all her customary preoccupations and pretensions, the moment preceding sexual pleasure, similar in this respect to the moment that follows death, had restored her rejuvenated features to something like the innocence of earliest childhood. And perhaps everyone whose particular talent is brought into play becomes modest, intent, and charming—especially if such talent gives us great pleasure, makes the giver happy and anxious that we should enjoy it to the full. But this new expression on Albertine's face contained more than disinterestedness, professional diligence, and generosity; there was a kind of onrush of anticipated involvement; and she had gone back further than to her own childhood; she had returned to the early days of her race. Whereas I had looked for nothing more than physical relief, and finally secured it, Albertine seemed to feel that it would be somehow coarse of her to think that this physical pleasure could be devoid of moral sense or conclusive in itself. And when I reminded her of her dinner, she, who had been in so great a hurry earlier on, now, doubtless because she felt that kissing implied love and that love was the most important commitment there is, remarked:

"Oh, it really doesn't matter. I've got plenty of time."

She seemed embarrassed by the idea of getting up and going after what had just happened, embarrassed out of a sense of acceptable behavior, just as Françoise, without feeling thirsty, had felt bound to accept with polite cheerfulness the glass of wine that Jupien offered her and would never have dared just to drink up and go, however urgent the call of duty. Albertine—and this was perhaps, with another, which will be clear in due course, one of the reasons that had made me unconsciously desire her—was one of the incarnations of the charming little French country girl typified in stone in Saint-André-des-Champs. I recognized in her, as I did in Françoise, who was soon nonetheless to become her deadly enemy, a courtesy toward host and stranger, a sense of propriety, a respectful bedside manner.

In the months preceding her daughter's marriage, Françoise, who after the death of my aunt felt obliged to speak only in tones of lamentation, would have felt shocked if the young woman had not taken her fiancé's arm when the two of them walked out together. Albertine, lying motionless beside me, said:

"What nice hair you have, what nice eyes. You're sweet."

I pointed out to her that it was getting late, and when I added, "You don't believe me?," she replied, in words that were perhaps true, but only since a couple of minutes ago and for the next few hours:

"I always believe you."

She spoke about myself, my family, my social background. "Oh, I know your parents know some very nice people," she said. "You're a friend of Robert Forestier and Suzanne Delage." For a minute these names meant absolutely nothing to me. Then, suddenly, I remembered that I did once use to play with Robert Forestier in the Champs-Élysées and had never seen him since. As for Suzanne Delage, she was the great-niece of Mme Blandais, and I had once been meant to go to a dancing lesson and even to play a small part in theatricals at her parents' house. But the fear of having a giggling bout or a nosebleed had prevented me, so that in fact I had never set eyes on her. At the very most I had some notion that I had once heard that the Swanns' feather-hatted governess had been with the Delages at one time, but perhaps it was her sister or some friend. I protested to Albertine that Robert Forestier and Suzanne Delage occupied a very small place in my life. "That may well be, but your mothers are close friends and that helps to place you. I often run into Suzanne Delage on the Avenue de Messine. She has a lot of style." Our mothers were acquainted only in the imagination of Mme Bontemps, who had learned that I had once been a playmate of Robert Forestier, to whom, it appeared, I used to recite poetry, and had concluded from this that we were bound by family ties. I have been told that the mere mention of my mother's name was enough for her to come out with, "Oh yes, she moves with people like the Delages, the Forestiers . . . ," awarding my parents high marks they had done nothing to deserve.

Quite apart from all this, Albertine entertained some extremely silly social notions. She classed the Simonnets with a double "n" as inferior not only to those with a single "n" but to everyone else in the world. That someone else should be called by the same name as yourself and not belong to your family is ample reason for despising him. Of course there are exceptions. It may happen that two Simonnets (introduced to each other on the sort of social occasion when people experience the urge to talk, about no matter what, and feel particularly well disposed toward one another—for instance, in a funeral procession on its way to the cemetery), finding they have the same name, will seek, with mutual goodwill and to no effect, to discover some evidence of kinship. But that is only an exception. There are plenty of dishonorable men in the world, but we neither know nor care. Yet, if a similarity of names causes letters addressed to them to be dropped through our mail slot, or vice versa, we start to feel mistrust, often justified, as to their moral worth. We are afraid of being confused with them and forestall possible confusion with a scowl of disgust when anyone mentions them to us. When we read our own name, as borne by them, in the newspaper, they seem to have usurped it. The misdemeanors of other members of the social body are a matter of indifference to us. It is our namesakes we make to bear the brunt for them. The hatred we channel toward the other Simonnets is all the more intense for not being personal but hereditarily transmitted. Two generations pass, and we remember only the scowl of disgust our grandparents kept for the other Simonnets; we know nothing of the reason behind it; it would come as no surprise to learn that the whole thing had begun with a murder. Until the day comes—and it is by no means unheard of—when a male Simonnet and a female Simonnet who are in no way related bring matters to a close by getting married.

Not only did Albertine speak to me about Robert Forestier and Suzanne Delage, but quite spontaneously, with the urge to confide induced by the proximity of two bodies, initially at least, during a first phase before it has engendered a special duplicity and secrecy in one party toward the other, she told me a story about her family and one of Andrée's uncles, which in Balbec she had refused to divulge at all; but now she felt she ought not to appear to have any secrets from me. At present, had her dearest friend said anything against me, she would have felt duty-bound to repeat it to me. I insisted she go home, and she eventually did so, but she was so discomfited on my account by my lack of courtesy that she laughed almost as though she were apologizing for me, like a hostess who has admitted an improperly dressed guest but has her qualms about it.

"Why are you laughing?" I asked.

"I'm not laughing, I'm smiling at you," she replied affectionately. "When shall I see you again?" she added in a way that suggested she did not regard what we had just done (generally the crowning moment) as even the prelude to a great affection, a pre-existent affection we owed it to ourselves to discover, to confess, and which alone could account for what we had just indulged in.

"Since you give your permission, I'll send word for you to come when I can."

I dared not let her know that I was putting the chance of seeing Mme de Stermaria before everything else.

"It will have to be on the spur of the moment, I'm afraid. I never know beforehand. Would it be possible to send round for you on the evenings I'm free?"

"It will be quite possible shortly, because I shall have my own entrance at my aunt's. But for the moment it's not. Anyway, I'll just come round on the off chance tomorrow or the day after, in the afternoon. You needn't see me if you're busy."

When she got to the door, surprised that I had not gone to open it for her, she offered me her cheek, now that she felt there was no need for any gross physical desire to make us kiss. Since our brief pass a while back was the sort of thing that is sometimes induced by deep intimacy and heartfelt choice, Albertine had felt it her duty to improvise and add temporarily to the kisses we had exchanged on my bed the emotion that such kisses would symbolize for a knight and his lady in the songs of a Gothic jongleur.

After the departure of this young Picarde, who might have been a figurine carved on the porch of Saint-André-des-Champs by its sculptor, Françoise came and handed me a letter that filled me with joy, for it was from Mme de Stermaria, agreeing to dine with me on Wednesday. From Mme de Stermaria, that is, for me, not so much from the real Mme de Stermaria as from the one who had been on my mind all day before Albertine's arrival. It is the wicked deception of love that it begins by making us dwell not upon a woman in the outside world but upon a doll inside our head, the only woman who is always available in fact, the only one we shall ever possess, whom the arbitrary nature of memory, almost as absolute as that of the imagination, may have made as different from the real woman as the real Balbec had been from the Balbec I imagined—a dummy creation that little by little, to our own detriment, we shall force the real woman to resemble.

Albertine had made me so late that the play had just finished when I arrived at Mme de Villeparisis's; and since I had little desire to get caught up in the stream of guests who were pouring out of the room discussing what was on everyone's mind—the separation, said to be already effected, between the Duc de Guermantes and the Duchesse—I had occupied a vacant wing chair in the outer room to wait for an opportunity to greet my hostess, when from the main salon, where she had doubtless been sitting in the front row, I saw emerging, majestic, fully swathed, and drawn to her full height in a long gown of yellow satin with huge black poppies stitched onto it in relief, no less a person than the Duchesse herself. To catch sight of her no longer disturbed me in the least. There had been a day when, placing her hands on my forehead (as she did when she was afraid of hurting my feelings) and saying, "These outings you make in the hope of meeting Mme de Guermantes have to stop. You're getting quite a reputation for yourself. Besides, you can see how ill your grandmother is. You have more serious things to think about than hanging around after a woman who couldn't care less about you anyway," instantaneously, like a hypnotist returning you from the distant country you thought you were in and opening your eyes, or like a doctor recalling you to a sense of duty and reality and curing you of the imaginary disease in which you had been wallowing, my mother had woken me up from a dream that had gone on for too long. The rest of the day had been devoted to a final farewell to this disease I was renouncing; I had sung the words of Schubert's "Lebewohl" for hours on end and with tears in my eyes:

> Farewell, strange voices call thee,
> Sweet sister of the angels, far from me.

And then it was over. I had given up my morning walks, and with so little effort that my prognosis, which we shall see was to turn out to be false, led me to believe that it would be easy for me, in the course of my life, to give up seeing a woman. And then, after Françoise had told me that Jupien, who was eager to find larger premises, was looking out for a shop in the neighborhood, anxious to try to find one for him (and quite happy, too—while ambling along the street I had already heard from my bed in luminous clamor like a beach—to see behind the raised iron shutters of their shops the young dairy women in their white sleeves), I had reason to start taking these morning walks again. And quite uninhibitedly this time, for I was aware that I was no longer going out to catch a glimpse of Mme de Guermantes; I was rather like a woman who takes infinite precautions as long as she has a lover and, from the day she breaks with him, leaves his letters lying about the place, at the risk of disclosing to her husband a guilty secret that ceased to alarm her the minute she ceased to harbor it.

What it hurt me to see was that there were unhappy people in almost every house I passed. In one the wife was always in tears because her husband was unfaithful. In the next it was the reverse. In another a hardworking mother, beaten up by her drunkard son, tried to conceal her misery from the eyes of the neighbors. Half of humanity spent its life in tears. And when I was better acquainted with it, so exasperating did I find it that I wondered whether the people in the right might not be the adulterous husband and wife, who were unfaithful only because their rightful happiness had been denied them, and who behaved in a charming and loyal way to everyone but their own partners. After a while, I no longer even had the excuse of helping Jupien to take me on my morning peregrinations. For news circulated that the cabinetmaker in our courtyard, whose workrooms were separated from Jupien's shop only by the thinnest of partitions, was about to be given notice by the agent because his hammering made too much noise. Jupien could have hoped for nothing better; the workrooms had a basement for storing lumber, which adjoined our cellars. He would keep his coal there and knock down the partition to make one big shop. One further related detail: since Jupien, who found that M. de Guermantes was asking an exorbitant rent, let people be shown over the premises in the hope that the Duc, discouraged by his failure to find a tenant, would come round to reducing the rental for him, Françoise, after noticing that the concierge left the door of the shop with the "For Rent" sign on the latch well past the usual hours for showing people around, scented a trap laid by him to lure the fiancée of the Guermantes footman (the couple would find a lovers' hideaway there) and to catch the pair out.

However that might be, and although I no longer had any need to search for premises for Jupien, I continued to go out for walks before lunch. In the course of them, I would often encounter M. de Norpois. And he was often quite capable, as he conversed with a colleague, of inspecting me from top to toe and then looking back toward his interlocutor without so much as a smile in my direction or any more sign of acknowledgment than if he had never set eyes on me before. For, as far as these important diplomats are concerned, to look at you in a certain way is intended to convey to you not that they have seen you but that they have not, and that they have some serious matter to discuss with their colleague. A tall woman I often ran into near the house was less discreet. For, although I did not know her, she would turn round after me, linger—to no avail—at shopwindows, smile as though she were going to kiss me, make suggestive gestures of availability. All this turned to ice the moment she encountered anyone she knew. For a long time now on these morning errands, depending on what I had to do, even if it was merely buying a newspaper, I had taken the most direct route, with no regret if it lay outside the usual ambit of the Duchesse's walks, and if on the contrary our paths coincided, I felt no sense of misgiving or dissimulation, because this no longer seemed to me to be the forbidden path on which I wrenched from an unwelcoming woman the favor of setting eyes on her against her will. But it had never entered my mind that my recovery, by restoring me to a normal attitude toward Mme de Guermantes, would effect a similar change in her and open up the possibility of a friendliness, even a friendship, which I no longer cared about. Up to this point, the joint efforts of the whole world to bring me into contact with her would have come to nothing in the face of the evil fate projected by unrequited love. Fairies more powerful than humans have decreed that in such cases there is nothing to be done until the day our hearts sincerely utter the magic words: "I am no longer in love." I had resented the fact that Saint-Loup had not taken me to see his aunt, but he was no more capable than anyone else of breaking a spell. As long as I was in love with Mme de Guermantes, I was pained by the marks of affection, the compliments I received from others, not just because they did not come from her but because they never reached her ears. And had she known of them, it would not have made an ounce of difference. Yet, if attachment is involved, even the slightest details—an absence, declining a dinner invitation, an unintentional, unconscious stiffening of behavior—make more difference than all the cosmetics and fine clothes in the world. More people would climb the social ladder if these things were taught as part of the art of social success.

As she crossed the room in which I was sitting, her mind intent on memories of friends I did not know whom she would perhaps be seeing again in a while at another party, Mme de Guermantes caught sight of me in my wing chair, truly indifferent, and seeking only to be polite, whereas before, while I was in love, I had tried so hard, and without success, to appear indifferent; she left the stream of guests, came over to address me with the same smile she had worn that evening at the Opéra, which the painful feeling of being the object of a love she did not return was no longer there to efface:

"No, don't move. You don't mind if I sit down with you for a moment?" she said as she gracefully gathered up the folds of her immense skirt, which would otherwise have occupied the whole chair.

She was taller than I, and made even bigger by the bulk of her dress, and I found myself almost touching her lovely bare arm, on which an almost invisible ubiquitous down seemed to create a perpetual golden rising haze, and the blond coils of her hair as I caught their scent. With scarcely any room to sit down, she could not easily turn to face me, and, obliged to look straight in front of her rather than at me, she assumed the dreamy, soft expression you see in portraits.

"Have you any news of Robert?" she asked.

At that moment Mme de Villeparisis passed by us.

"Well, what a fine time to arrive when for once we do see you here!"

And, noticing that I was in conversation with her niece, and imagining perhaps that we were more intimate than she had realized:

"But don't let me interrupt your conversation with Oriane," she added (for the good offices of a procuress are among the duties of a hostess). "You wouldn't care to dine with her here on Wednesday?"

This was the day on which I was to dine with Mme de Stermaria, and I declined.

"Saturday, then?"

Since my mother was returning on Saturday or Sunday, it would have been rather tactless not to stay at home and dine with her in the evening. So I declined again.

"Ah, you're not an easy person to invite."

"Why do you never come and see me?" said Mme de Guermantes when Mme de Villeparisis had moved off to congratulate the performers and present the leading lady with a bouquet of roses whose value lay entirely in the hand that offered it, given that it had cost only twenty francs. (This, by the way, was as high as she was prepared to go when an artist had performed only once. Those who gave their services at all her afternoon and evening receptions received roses painted by the Marquise.) "It's so tedious never to meet except in other people's houses. Since you won't dine with me at my aunt's, why don't you come and dine with me at home?"

Various people who had lingered to the last possible moment on some pretext or other but were now on their way out, seeing that the Duchesse had sat down to talk to a young man on a seat so narrow that there was only room for two people, thought they had been misinformed, and that it was not the Duchesse but the Duc who was seeking a separation, on my account, at which point they lost no time in making the fact known. I was in a better position than anyone to know how false it was. But it nonetheless surprised me that, in one of those awkward periods when a separation is in process but not yet finalized, the Duchesse, instead of withdrawing from social life, should actually choose to invite someone who was a comparative stranger. It crossed my mind that it was the Duc alone who had resisted her having me in the house and that, now that he was leaving her, she saw no further reason why she should not surround herself with the people she liked.

Two minutes earlier, I should have been dumbfounded had anyone told me that Mme de Guermantes was going to invite me to visit her, let alone dine with her. It was one thing to realize that the Guermantes salon was incapable of providing the special qualities I had extracted from the name, but the fact that I had been forbidden entry, by obliging me to see it as we see the salons described in a novel or pictured in a dream, made me imagine it, even when I felt sure it was just like any other, as something quite different; between myself and it stood the dividing line at which reality ends. To dine with the Guermantes was to undertake a journey long hoped for, to make a desire pass from my head and appear before my eyes, and to become acquainted with a dream. It might well have occurred to me to think that the dinner in question was one of those dinners to which the hosts invite someone with the words, "Do come. There'll be absolutely no one but ourselves, I promise you," thus deceitfully attributing to the pariah their own fear of his mixing with their friends, and even seeking to transform into an enviable privilege, exclusively reserved for their closest friends, the quarantine they have imposed on the ostracized man, who becomes both unfit for society and favored without any choice in the matter. I felt, on the contrary, that Mme de Guermantes was anxious for me to sample the choicest she had to offer when she went on to ask me, presenting me with something like the prospect of the purplish delight of a visit to Fabrice's aunt and the miracle of an introduction to Count Mosca:9

"Do you happen to be free on Friday, for a small dinner party? It would be so nice. There'll be the Princess of Parma, such a charming person. Not that I'd invite you to meet people who were anything other than agreeable."

Cast off by the intermediate social world in its perpetual rise to betterment, the family still plays an important part in more static milieux like the lower middle classes or the princely aristocracy, incapable of rising higher because above it, from its own special point of view, there is nothing more. The friendship shown me by her "aunt Villeparisis" and by Robert had perhaps made me, for Mme de Guermantes and her friends, who fed on their own company and frequented the same little circle, an object of their curious scrutiny, quite unbeknown to myself.

Her relations with these two relatives had a homely familiarity about them, daily and down-to-earth, very different from the sort of thing we imagine, relations in which, if we happen to be included, our actions, far from being ejected from the picture like a speck of dust from the eye or a drop of water from the windpipe, may remain engraved, and will still be recounted and commented upon years after we ourselves have forgotten them, in the palace in which we are amazed to find them preserved like a letter in our own hand among a priceless collection of autographs.

Merely fashionable people may have to defend their doors from excessive invasion. But the Guermantes door had no need of that. Hardly ever did an outsider have occasion to present himself at it. On the rare occasions when the Duchesse had one pointed out to her, she would never have dreamed of bothering about the social credit he might bring, since this was something she conferred and could not receive. She thought only of his real qualities. Mme de Villeparisis and Saint-Loup had assured her of mine. And no doubt she would not have believed them had she not also observed that they could never manage to secure my presence when they wanted it, that I therefore attached no importance to society, which seemed to the Duchesse a sign that an outsider was to be ranked with people she thought of as "agreeable."

It was quite a picture, in the course of conversation about women for whom she did not care, to see the way her face changed at the mention, in connection with one of these, of, say, her sister-in-law. "Oh, *she's* charming," she would say with discriminating assurance. The only reason she advanced this statement was that the lady in question had refused to be introduced to the Marquise de Chaussegros and the Princesse de Silistrie. What she did not add was that the lady had refused to be introduced to herself, the Duchesse de Guermantes. This was nevertheless what had happened, and ever since, the Duchesse's mind had been busy trying to fathom the motives of this lady who was so choosy about her acquaintances. She was dying to be invited to her house. Society people are so used to being sought after that anyone who shuns them becomes a rare bird and monopolizes their attention.

Was Mme de Guermantes's true motive for inviting me (now that I was no longer in love with her) that I did not seek out the society of her relatives, however much they sought after my own? I have no idea. At all events, once she had decided to invite me, she was anxious to do me the full honors of her establishment and to keep away any of her friends whose company might have discouraged me from further visits, the friends she knew to be boring. I had been at a loss to account for the

Duchesse's change of direction when I had seen her deviate from her path among the stars, come to sit down beside me, and invite me to dinner; it was swayed by causes unknown to me. For want of any special sense of guidance in these matters, we imagine that the people we know only slightly—as I knew the Duchesse—think of us only on the rare occasions they see us. Yet this mental oblivion in which we deem ourselves to be held is purely arbitrary. So much so, in fact, that, while we inhabit the silence of solitude, which is like the silence of a clear night sky, imagining the various queens of society pursuing their course in the heavens at an infinite distance from us, we are unable to resist a sudden start of alarm or delight if there falls upon us from on high, like an aerolite engraved with our name, which we thought was unknown on Venus or Cassiopeia, an invitation to dinner or a snippet of wicked gossip.

Perhaps there had been times when, following the example of the Persian princes who, according to the book of Esther, had the books of records read out to them in which were inscribed the names of certain subjects who had shown zeal in their service, Mme de Guermantes had consulted her list of worthy people and stopped at my name with the words, "He's someone we ought to ask to dine with us at some point." But other thoughts had distracted her ("Beset by seething cares, a prince's mind is constantly dragged on by fresh concerns"), until the moment she had caught sight of me sitting there alone like Mordecai at the palace gate; and once the sight of me had refreshed her memory, she wished, like Ahasuerus, to lavish her gifts upon me.[10]

But I have to say that an utterly different sort of surprise was in store for me after the one I had experienced when Mme de Guermantes issued her invitation. Since I had felt it would be more modest of me, and more grateful also, not to conceal this initial surprise but, rather, to exaggerate the joy it gave me, Mme de Guermantes, who was getting ready to move on to her last party of the evening, had said to me, almost as a justification, and for fear that I might not be altogether certain who she was, given my apparent astonishment at her invitation: "You know I'm the aunt of Robert de Saint-Loup, who is so fond of you, and we've already met each other here, of course." Replying to this in the affirmative, I added that I also knew M. de Charlus, "who was very kind to me in Balbec and in Paris." Mme de Guermantes reacted with great surprise, and her eyes seemed to revert, for verification of my words, to some much earlier page of her internal register. "I see, so you know Palamède, do you?" This name sounded very sweet coming from the lips of Mme de Guermantes, because of the instinctive simplicity with which she spoke of a man who was so brilliant a figure in the eyes of the world, but for her was no more than her brother-in-law and the cousin with whom she had grown up. Into the indistinct grayness which the life of the Duchesse de Guermantes represented for me, the name Palamède introduced something like the brightness of the long summer days she had spent playing with him as a girl in the garden at Guermantes. Moreover, in this long-distant period of their lives, Oriane de Guermantes and her cousin Palamède had been very different from what they had since become; particularly M. de Charlus, who had indulged to the full in the artistic tastes he had so carefully curbed in later life that I was amazed to learn that it was he who had painted the huge fan decorated with black-and-yellow irises the Duchesse was now unfolding. She could also have shown me a little sonatina he had once composed for her. I was completely unaware of all these talents, which the Baron never mentioned. Let it be said in passing that M. de Charlus did not at all relish being called Palamède by his family. One could certainly understand why its short form "Mémé" might displease him. Such silly abbreviations are a sign of the aristocracy's inability to appreciate its own poetry (and the same thing is true of Jewry: Lady Rufus Israels's nephew Moses was commonly referred to as "Momo") as well as its concern not to be seen attaching importance to anything aristocratic. Now, in this matter of poetry, M. de Charlus had more imagination and a more blatant sense of pride. But this was not the reason he so disliked "Mémé," since he also disliked the handsome name Palamède. The truth was that, considering himself, knowing himself, to be from a princely family, he would have liked his brother and sister-in-law to address him as "Charlus," just as Queen Marie-Amélie or the Duc d'Orléans might speak of their sons and grandsons, nephews and brothers as "Joinville, Nemours, Chartres, Paris."

"What a dark horse that Mémé is!" she exclaimed. "We spent hours talking to him about you, and he told us that he would be delighted to make your acquaintance, as if he'd never met you in his life. You must admit he's odd, and—though it's not very nice of me to say such a thing about a brother-in-law I'm very fond of and admire immensely—a little bit mad at times."

I was particularly struck with the word "mad" used of M. de Charlus, and it occurred to me that this semi-madness might perhaps account for certain things, like his apparent delight at the idea of asking Bloch to beat his own mother. I came to the conclusion, not only from the things he said but from the way he said them, that M. de Charlus must be a trifle mad. The first experience of hearing a lawyer or an actor speaking is striking because the tone is so different from conversation. But because everyone else seems to find this quite natural, you say nothing about it, to them or to yourself, and concentrate instead on the degree of skill involved. The very most one might think, of an actor at the Théâtre-Français, is, "Why, instead of letting his raised arm fall naturally, did he take ten minutes to bring it down in a staccato movement broken by pauses?" or of a Labori,[II] "Why, the minute he opened his mouth, did he use those tragic, unexpected sounds to say the simplest things?" But since everyone takes these things for granted, they come as no shock. In the same way, on reflection, M. de Charlus spoke of himself very grandiloquently, in a tone that had nothing to do with ordinary speech. It felt as if he constantly needed to be told, "But why are you shouting so loud? Why are you so brazen about yourself?" Yet everyone seemed to be in tacit agreement that things were perfectly all right as they were. So you got caught up in a circle of people who danced to the tune of his inflated manner of speaking. But certainly there were moments when a stranger might have thought he was listening to a raving lunatic.

"But," the Duchesse continued, with the hint of effrontery that stemmed from her characteristic directness, "are you absolutely sure you're not thinking of someone else? Can you really be talking about my brother-in-law Palamède? I know he loves mystery, but this seems to be taking things a bit far, I must say! . . ."

I replied that I was absolutely sure and that M. de Charlus must have misheard my name.

"Oh well, I must be leaving you," said Mme de Guermantes with what sounded like regret. "I have to look in on the Princesse de Ligne for a moment. You're not going on there? No? You don't care for society? You're quite right, it's too tedious for words. I wish I didn't have to go! But she's my cousin, it would be rude. I'm sorry for my own sake, quite selfishly, because I could have taken you and even brought you back afterward. Well, goodbye, then. I can't tell you how much I'm looking forward to Friday."

That M. de Charlus should have blushed to be seen in my company by M. d'Argencourt was one thing. But that to his own sister-in-law, and a woman who had such a high opinion of him, he should deny all acquaintance with me, acquaintance that would have been quite natural since I knew both his aunt and his nephew, was beyond my comprehension.

I shall close this episode by remarking that from one point of view there was something of true grandeur about Mme de Guermantes, in that she had the capacity to efface utterly from her memory the things that other people would have only partially forgotten. Even if she had never experienced me pestering her, following her, tracking her down on her morning walks, if she had never had to acknowledge my daily greeting with riled impatience, or to send Saint-Loup packing when he begged her to invite me, she could not have behaved toward me with more gracious and natural charm. Not only did she waste no time on postmortems, hints, meaningful smiles, and innuendos, not only did her present affability, by not dwelling on the past or showing the least reticence, have something as proudly upright about it as her own majestic stature, but the grudges she might have borne anyone in the past were so completely reduced to ashes, and the ashes were themselves cast so far from her memory or at least from her behavior, that to look at her face, whenever she needed to treat with the most admirable simplicity what for so many people would have been a pretext for rekindling smoldering resentments and recriminations, was to experience something like a process of purification.

But if I was surprised by the change that had occurred in her attitude toward me, how much more did it surprise me to discover the even greater change in my feeling toward her! Had there not been a time when I could remuster life and strength only if, in my endless invention of new strategies, I could find someone to secure me an invitation from her and, after this initial boon, to procure many others for my increasingly demanding emotions? It was the impossibility of any advance in this direction that had made me leave for Doncières to visit Saint-Loup. And now, strangely enough, it was through the effects of a letter from him that I was agitated, but this time on account not of Mme de Guermantes but of Mme de Stermaria.

Let me add, as a final word in my account of this evening, that something happened in the course of it that was denied a few days later but which really startled me at the time, caused a short rift between myself and Bloch, and in itself constitutes one of those curious anomalies that will be explained at the end of this volume (*Sodome I*[12]). At this evening party at Mme de Villeparisis's, Bloch kept on boasting to me about the friendly manner shown him by M. de Charlus, who, when he passed him in the street, looked him straight in the face as though he recognized him, was anxious to make his acquaintance, knew very well who he was. This made me smile at first, because Bloch had expressed himself so vehemently in Balbec on the subject of the very same M. de Charlus. And I merely concluded that Bloch, like his father in regard to Bergotte, knew the Baron "without actually knowing him." What he had taken for a friendly glance was in fact an absentminded one. But in the end Bloch gave so many precise details and seemed so sure that on two or three occasions M. de Charlus had wished to address him that, remembering I had spoken about my friend to the Baron, who had in fact asked me various questions about him as we were walking away together from Mme de Villeparisis's, I assumed that Bloch was not lying, that M. de Charlus had heard his name, realized that he was my friend, and so on. And so, some time later, at the theater, I asked M. de Charlus if I might introduce Bloch to him, and when he assented, I went off in search of my friend. But the minute M. de Charlus set eyes on him, a look of astonishment appeared on his face, where it was instantly repressed to become one of blazing fury. Not only did he not offer Bloch his hand, but whenever Bloch addressed him he replied in the most insolent manner, in a peevish and hurtful tone of voice. So that Bloch, to whom, from what he had said, the Baron had been all smiles until then, was under the impression that I had spoken ill of him rather than recommended him during the brief conversation that, knowing M. de Charlus's appreciation for etiquette, I had had with him about my friend before I introduced the two of them. Bloch left us, worn down by his efforts, like someone who has been trying to mount a horse that is constantly on the point of taking the bit between its teeth, or to swim against waves that continually fling him back on the beach, and did not speak to me again for six months.

There was nothing delightful about the days preceding my dinner engagement with Mme de Stermaria; I found them unbearable. For, as a general rule, the shorter the time that separates us from the project we have in mind, the longer it seems, because we measure it on a more re-duced scale, or simply because of the fact that we even bother to mea-sure it. The papacy, we are told, measures time by the century and may in fact not think to measure it at all, since its goal is eternity. My own being no more than three days in front of me, I counted the seconds, I indulged in the fantasies that are the mere beginnings of caresses, ca-resses filled with the frustration of not being able to have the woman herself there to respond (precisely those caresses, and no others). And in the end, if it is true that in general the difficulty of attaining the ob-ject of desire increases that desire (the difficulty, not the impossibility, for that suppresses it entirely), then, with a desire that is purely physical, the certainty that it will be realized at a definite point on the horizon is hardly less of a stimulant than uncertainty—almost as much as the anxi-ety of doubt, the absence of doubt makes waiting for inevitable pleasure intolerable, because it turns the period of waiting into an endless series of imagined fulfillments and, by the frequency of our anticipated repre-sentations of them, divides time into as many tiny sections as any that could be devised by the anguish of doubt itself.

What I needed was to possess Mme de Stermaria: for several days now, my desires had been unflaggingly active rehearsing this pleasure in my imagination, to the exclusion of any other; any other sort of grati-fication (pleasure with another woman) would not have been suffi-ciently prepared for, since pleasure is merely the realization of a prior urge, which is not always the same and changes in accordance with the multiple variations of one's fantasies, the random functions of memory, one's sexual needs at the time, the particular desires available, since the most recently fulfilled of them lie dormant until the disappointment they brought has been more or less forgotten; I had already left the high road of general desires and turned off along the path of a more specific one; had I wanted to change my mind in favor of another assignation, I should have had to retrace my steps too far to get back to the high road and take another path. To possess Mme de Stermaria on the island in the Bois de Boulogne where I had asked her to dine with me, this was the pleasure that constantly occupied my imagination. It would have been destroyed, of course, if I had dined there without her; but perhaps equally diminished had I dined, even with her, somewhere else. And, indeed, the attitudes involved in our way of envisaging any sexual pleasure come before the woman herself, the type of woman who is suitable for the purpose. They dictate the pleasure, and the setting, too; and for this reason they give alternate prominence in our capricious minds to this or that woman, this or that place, this or that bedroom, which in other weeks we should have spurned with disdain. Born from our attitude at the time, certain women are incomplete without the double bed in which we find appeasement at their side, whereas others, to be caressed with a more secret intention, need leaves blown by the wind, the sound of water in the dark, things as light and evasive as they are.

There had been a time, long before I received Saint-Loup's letter and before any Mme de Stermaria had appeared in my life, when the island in the Bois had seemed to be the perfect setting for pleasure, probably because I found myself going there to bewail the fact that I had no pleasure to conceal in its shelter. The edges of the lake from which you get to the island, and along which, in the last weeks of summer, Parisian ladies who have not yet left the city go to stroll, are where you wander about, not knowing how to find her or whether indeed she has not already left Paris, in the hope of seeing the girl you fell in love with at the last ball of the season and will not have the opportunity of seeing again at any evening party before next spring. Sensing it to be the day before, if not the day after, the beloved's departure, you follow the beautiful paths beside the shimmering water and see a first red leaf already blooming like a last rose; you scan that horizon where, through some artifice the opposite of that used in the panoramas beneath whose rotundas wax figures in the foreground create on the painted canvas behind the illusory impression of depth and volume, your eyes travel uninterruptedly from the cultivated park to the natural heights of Meudon and Mont Valérien without knowing where to draw the boundary, and make the real countryside intrude upon the creation of the gardener, whose artificial charm they project well beyond its own limits—like those rare birds reared to roam free in a botanical garden, which, every day, wherever they happen to alight on their winged journeys, lend an exotic note to the surroundings, even as far as the outlying woods. Between the last of the summer parties and winter exile, you roam anxiously through this romantic domain of chance encounters and lovers' melancholy, and it would come as no surprise to discover that it was situated outside charted territory, any more than if, looking down from the terrace at Versailles, an observatory around which the clouds gather against the blue sky as they do in a Van der Meulen painting,[13] after leaving nature behind by standing up there above it, you were to be told that, at the point where the natural scene begins again, at the end of the great canal, the villages hidden in the distance, on a horizon as dazzling as the sea, are called Fleurus and Nijmegen.

Then, once the last carriage has gone by and you have the painful feeling that she will not come now, you go to dine on the island; above the quivering poplars, reminding you endlessly of the mysteries of evening rather than responding to them, a pink cloud adds a last patch of living color to the now tranquil sky. A few drops of rain fall noiselessly on the ancient water, which, in its divine infancy, still changes constantly with the conditions of the moment, and continually forgets the reflections of clouds and flowers. And after the geraniums, by intensifying their brilliant color, have put up a vain struggle against the gathering twilight, a mist comes to envelop the island as it falls into slumber; you walk in the moist darkness along the water's edge, where the only thing likely to startle you is the silent passage of a swan, like the briefly wide-open eyes and smile of a child in bed at night who you thought was asleep. And because you feel alone and the world can seem far away, you long all the more to have a lover walking beside you.

But to this island, where even in summer there was often a mist, how much happier I would have been to bring Mme de Stermaria now that the cold season, the end of autumn, had come! If the weather since Sunday had not in itself made the places in which my imagination was living grayish and maritime—as other seasons made them balmy, luminous, Italian—the hope of possessing Mme de Stermaria in a few days would have been enough to raise, twenty times an hour, the curtain of mist in my monotonously pining imagination. In any case, the fog, which had extended even to Paris since the previous day, not only made me think incessantly about the native province of the young woman I had invited, but, since it was likely that it would invade the Bois by evening, especially the edges of the lake, far more thickly than the center of the city, I felt that it would turn the Île des Cygnes into something of the Breton island whose marine and misty atmosphere had always clung like a garment to the pale silhouette of Mme de Stermaria in the mental picture I had of her. Of course, when we are young, at the age I was at the time of my walks along the Méséglise way, our desires and convictions confer on a woman's clothing a unique character, an irreducible essence. We chase after the reality of a thing. But by the very fact of constantly letting it elude us, we end up noticing that, after all the vain attempts that have led to nothing, there is something solid there after all, which is what we have been pursuing. We begin to distinguish, to identify what it is we love, we try to procure it for ourselves, if only by artificial means. Then, in the absence of any convincing reality, costume comes to replace that reality by creating a deliberate illusion. I was perfectly aware that within half an hour's distance from home I should not be in Brittany. But by walking arm in arm with Mme de Stermaria in the dusk of the island, by the water's edge, I should be behaving in the same way as other men who, unable actually to penetrate a convent, do at least, before possessing a woman, dress her up as a nun.

I was even able to entertain the hope of listening to something like the lapping of the waves with the young woman, for, the day before our dinner engagement, the weather turned stormy. I was starting to shave before going to the island to reserve a private dining room (although at this time of year the island was empty and the restaurant deserted) and set the menu for our dinner next day, when Françoise announced the arrival of Albertine. I had her shown in at once, unconcerned that she would see the unsightly dark stubble on my chin, whereas in Balbec I had never felt smart enough for her, and there she had cost me as much agitation and worry as Mme de Stermaria did now. I was anxious that the latter should retain the best possible impression from the evening we were to spend together. And so I asked Albertine to come with me to the island straightaway to help me select the menu. The woman to whom one devotes oneself entirely is so rapidly replaced by another that it comes as a surprise to discover one is devoting oneself all over again, all the time, without any hope it will come to anything. In response to my proposal, Albertine's smiling pink face—beneath the flat toque she was wearing, which came down very low above her eyes—seemed to hesitate. She must have had other plans in mind; but if so, she found no difficulty in abandoning them for me, to my great satisfaction, for I attached a great deal of importance to the presence of a young housewife who would be able to order dinner far better than I could.

It is certain that she had represented something quite different for me in Balbec. But even when we consider it insufficient at the time, our intimacy with the woman we love creates between her and us, despite its painful shortcomings, social ties that outlast our love and even the memory of that love. Then, in the woman who is now no more to us than a means, a path toward others, we are just as astonished and amused to discover in our memory the original special appeal of her name for the other being we once were, as if, after giving a cabman an address on the Boulevard des Capucines or on the rue du Bac, thinking only of the person we are going to see there, we were to remind ourselves that these names were once those of the Capuchin nuns whose convent stood there and of the ferry across the Seine.

All the same, my Balbec desires had brought Albertine's body to such a degree of maturity, accumulated such fresh sweet savors in it, that during our excursion to the Bois, while the wind like a careful gardener shook the trees, brought down the fruit, swept up the dead leaves, I told myself that, had there been any risk of Saint-Loup's being mistaken or of my having misunderstood his letter, so that my dinner with Mme de Stermaria might lead to nothing, I should have made an assignation for very late the same evening with Albertine, in order to forget during an hour of purely sensual indulgence—by holding in my arms a body whose now abundant charms my curiosity had once calculated and weighed up in detail—the emotions and possible disappointments of this incipient love for Mme de Stermaria. And, of course, had I imagined that Mme de Stermaria would grant me none of her favors at this first meeting, my picture of an evening spent in her company would have been a rather disappointing one. I knew only too well from experience how strangely the two successive stages of our incipient love for a woman we have desired without knowing her, loving her for the particular world she inhabits rather than for her still-unfamiliar self—how strangely these two stages are reflected in the domain of reality, that is to say, no longer in ourselves but in our meetings with her. Without ever having spoken with her, we have hesitated, tempted as we were by the poetic fantasy she represented for us. Will it be this woman or some other? And at once our dreams focus upon her, become an integral part of her. The first meeting with her, shortly to follow, ought to reflect this onset of love. Far from it. As if material reality also needed its first stage, loving her already, we talk to her in the most inconsequential fashion: "I invited you to dine on this island because I thought you would like the setting. It's not because there's anything particular I want to say to you. But I'm afraid it's rather damp, and you may be rather cold." "But not at all." "You're saying that out of politeness. Rather than annoying you by dwelling on the subject, I shall allow you, madame, to carry on braving the cold for another quarter of an hour, but then I shall oblige you to leave with me. I don't want to be responsible for your catching a chill." And, without really having talked to her at all, we take her home, remembering nothing of her except perhaps a certain look in her eyes, but thinking only of seeing her again. Then, at the second meeting (when even that look in her eyes, our sole memory of her, has vanished, but, for all that, we are still thinking only about seeing her again), the first stage is left behind. Nothing has happened in the interval. And yet, instead of talking about the suitability of the surroundings, we say, without causing surprise to the new person, whom we find unattractive but to whom we should like to have our name mentioned at every moment of the day: "It's going to be hard for us to deal with all the obstacles that stand in the way of our feelings. Do you think we shall be able to do that? Shall we be able to show our friends they were wrong and live happily together in the future?" But these contrasting conversations, the first inconsequential, the second alluding to love, would not take place; Saint-Loup's letter was sufficient assurance of that. Mme de Stermaria would give herself on the very first evening, so I should have no need to summon Albertine to the house as a last resort at the end of the evening. It would be unnecessary; Robert never exaggerated, and his letter was clear!

Albertine spoke very little, sensing that I had things on my mind. We went a little way on foot into the greenish, almost submarine grotto of a cluster of tall trees, on the dome of which we heard the wind lashing and the rain splashing. I trod down dead leaves, which sank into the soil like seashells, and poked with my stick at chestnuts, prickly as sea urchins.

The remaining leaves on the trees, convulsed in the wind, followed it only as far as their stems would permit, but sometimes these broke and the leaves fell to the ground, where they then rushed to catch up with the wind again. I had the joyous thought that, if this weather lasted, the island would feel that much more remote the following day, and in any case completely deserted. We returned to our carriage, and since the gusting wind had died down, Albertine asked me to go on as far as Saint-Cloud. Like the dead leaves on the ground, the clouds in the sky were following the wind. And a flock of migrant evenings, their various layers—pink, blue, green—made visible by a sort of conic section cut into the sky, were stationed there in readiness for departure to warmer climes. To get a closer view of a marble goddess in the posture of springing from her pedestal and, alone in a great wood that seemed to be consecrated to her, filling it with the mythological terror, half animal, half sacred, of her frenzied leaps, Albertine climbed up onto a mound while I waited for her on the road. Seen from below in this way, she herself—no longer coarse and fleshy, as she had been a few days earlier, on my bed, when the texture of her neck was seen close up under the magnifying glass of my eyes, but finely chiseled—seemed like a small statue on which the happy days in Balbec had left their patina. When I found myself alone again at home, reminding myself that I had spent the afternoon on an excursion with Albertine, that I was dining in two days with Mme de Guermantes, and that I needed to answer a letter from Gilberte, three women I had loved, it occurred to me that our social life, like an artist's studio, is filled with abandoned sketches depicting our momentary attempts to capture our need for a great love, but what did not occur to me was that sometimes, if the sketch is not too old, we may return to it and transform it into a completely different work, possibly more important than the one we had originally planned.

The next day, the weather was cold and fine: winter was in the air (and in fact autumn was so far advanced that it was a miracle we had been able to find a few domes of green-gold in the already ravaged Bois). As I awoke, I saw, as I had from the window of the Doncières barracks, a carpet of dull white mist hanging gaily in the sunlight, thick and soft as spun sugar. Then the sun disappeared, and the mist became denser in the afternoon. Darkness fell early, and I dressed for the evening, but it was still too soon to leave the house; I decided to send a carriage for Mme de Stermaria. I was reluctant to accompany the carriage myself, not wishing to force my company upon her during the journey, but I sent a note with the driver to ask her whether I might come and collect her. In the meantime, I lay down on my bed, closed my eyes for a second, then opened them again. Above the curtains there was now only a thin strip of daylight, growing steadily dimmer. This idle time of the day was familiar, the long hallway to pleasure, whose dark, delicious emptiness I had become acquainted with in Balbec, when, alone in my room as I was now, while everyone else was at dinner, I felt no sadness as I saw the daylight fade above the curtains, knowing that in a while, after a night of polar brevity, it would be resuscitated in the more dazzling brightness of the blazing lights at Rivebelle. I sprang from my bed, put on my black tie, gave my hair a brush, the final gestures of last-minute presentability, performed in Balbec not for myself but for the women I would see in Rivebelle, as I smiled at them in anticipation in the corner mirror of my room, and for this reason gestures that had remained in my mind as signs of a forthcoming entertainment involving lights and music. They conjured it up like magic signs, even brought it into being already, and thanks to them I had as clear an idea of its reality, as complete an enjoyment of its heady, frivolous charm, as I used to have in July at Combray, when I heard the packer's hammer blows and enjoyed the warmth and sunlight in the cool darkness of my room.

And so it was no longer just Mme de Stermaria I wished to see. Forced now to spend my evening with her, I would have preferred, since this was my last evening before my parents returned, to have it free and to be able to seek out some of the women I had seen in Rivebelle. I washed my hands one last time, and, moving round the apartment propelled by my sense of pleasure, I went to dry them in the dim light of the dining room. I thought it was open onto the lighted hall, but what I had taken to be the bright space of the doorway (the door was in fact closed) turned out to be the reflection of my white towel in a mirror placed against the wall, waiting to be mounted before Mama's return. I thought back to all the other illusions like this that I had discovered in the apartment, not exclusively optical ones, for when we first arrived I thought that our neighbor had a dog on account of the prolonged, almost human yapping that came from a kitchen pipe whenever the tap was turned on. And the door to the landing never closed by itself, very slowly, against the drafts on the staircase without giving a performance of the voluptuous, doleful broken phrases played above the Pilgrims' Chorus toward the end of the overture to *Tannhäuser*. As it happened, just after I had put my towel back in its place, I had the opportunity to hear a fresh performance of this dazzling piece of symphonic composition, for the bell rang, and I rushed to open the entrance door to the driver who was bringing me the answer to my note. I expected the message to be "The lady is downstairs," or "The lady is awaiting you." Instead, he had a letter in his hand. I wavered for a moment before reading to see what Mme de Stermaria had written, which, as long as she held the pen in her hand, might have been different, but was now, once she had sent it away, a force of destiny pursuing its course alone, and which she could do nothing further to change. I asked the driver to wait downstairs for a moment, despite the fact that he grumbled about the fog. As soon as he was gone, I opened the envelope. The printed card inside read "Vicomtesse Alix de Stermaria," and on it my guest had written: "My deepest apologies. Something has come up that means I am unable to dine with you this evening on the Île du Bois. I was so looking forward to it. I will write to you properly from Stermaria. I'm so very sorry. Kindest regards." I stood there motionless, stunned by the shock. At my feet lay the card and envelope, discarded like the wad in a firearm after the shot has been fired. I picked them up and scrutinized her message. "She says she is unable to dine with me on the Île du Bois. Perhaps that means she might be able to dine with me somewhere else. It would be too indiscreet of me to go and collect her, but at least that is one possible interpretation of her message." And the Île du Bois, where my thoughts had been installed in advance with Mme de Stermaria for the last four days, was where they obstinately remained. My desire automatically returned to the path it had been bent on following for so many hours now, and in spite of this message, which was too recent to override the force of desire, I went on instinctively preparing to leave the house, like a student who tries to answer just one more question even after the examiners have failed him. I eventually decided to tell Françoise to go down and pay the driver. I went down the passage and, failing to find her, passed through the dining room; suddenly my footsteps ceased to resound on the wooden floor, as they had been doing up to this point, and were muffled in a silence that, even before I had realized its cause, made me feel stifled and confined. It was the carpets that, in preparation for my parents' return, were in the process of being relaid, carpets that look so good on bright mornings, when the sun awaits you amid their disorder like a friend come to take you out to lunch in the country and shines down on them in a forest light, but which now, on the contrary, represented the first stage of preparation for the prison of winter, which, as one who was shortly to be obliged to take his meals at home, I would no longer be free to leave when I chose.

"Take care you don't trip, Monsieur. They're not tacked down properly yet," Françoise called out. "I ought to have lit the rooms. It's the end of 'September' already. The fine days are over."

Winter on its way; at the corner of the window, as in a piece of Gallé glass, an encrusted vein of snow; and even in the Champs-Élysées, instead of the girls one expects to find there, nothing but solitary sparrows.

What added to my despair at not seeing Mme de Stermaria was that her answer led me to believe that, while I, hour after hour since Sunday, had been living for this dinner alone, she had probably never given it a second thought. I learned later on that she had married, an absurd love match with a young man she must already have been seeing at this time, who had probably made her forget my invitation. For, had she remembered it, she would presumably not have waited for the carriage, which I had not sent through any previous arrangement, before sending me word that she was otherwise engaged. My fantasies of a young feudal maiden on a misty island had paved the way to a love that did not yet exist. Now my disappointment, my anger, my desperate desire to recapture the woman who had just refused me, enabled me, by bringing my sensibility into the picture, actually to focus upon the possible love that up to this point my imagination alone had conjured up, though rather more lamely.

How many of them there are in our memories, how many more have we forgotten—those faces of girls and young women, all of them different, which we have endowed with charm and the frenzied desire to see them again, simply because they eluded us at the last minute! In the case of Mme de Stermaria much more was involved, and all I needed now, in order to love her, was to see her again and renew those impressions, so vivid but far too short-lived, which my memory would otherwise be powerless to sustain in her absence. Circumstances were not in my favor; I did not see her again. It was not she that I loved, but it could well have been. And possibly one of the most painful things about the great love affair I was shortly to have was remembering the present evening and telling myself that, had circumstances been very slightly different, my love might have directed itself elsewhere, to Mme de Stermaria in fact; and that, directed to the woman who was to inspire it so soon afterward, it was therefore not—as I was so anxious, so needed to believe—absolutely inevitable and predestined.

Françoise had left me on my own in the dining room, after telling me how unwise of me it was to stay there before she had lit the fire. She was on her way to prepare something for dinner, for from this very evening, even before my parents returned, my seclusion was beginning. My attention turned to a huge bundle of carpets, still rolled up, propped against a corner of the sideboard, and, burying my head in it, swallowing the dust together with my own tears, as the Jews once covered their heads with ashes in times of mourning, I started to sob. I was shivering, not only because the room was cold, but because a clear drop in temperature (against the danger of being discovered and, it has to be said, the even slightly agreeable feeling we make no attempt to resist) is brought about by certain kinds of tears that fall from our eyes, drop by drop, like a fine, penetrating, icy rain, and seem as if they will never cease. Suddenly I heard a voice:

"May I come in? Françoise told me you were likely to be in the dining room. I came by to see whether you would like to come and have dinner somewhere, if you're up to it. There's a fog outside you could cut with a knife."

It was Robert de Saint-Loup, who had arrived in town that morning, when I thought he was in Morocco or on his way back by sea.

I have already said (and it was precisely Robert de Saint-Loup who had, quite unbeknown to himself, helped me to clarify my thoughts on the matter) what I think about friendship: namely, that it adds up to so little that I find it hard to understand how men with some claim to genius—like Nietzsche, for instance—can have been naïve enough to credit it with a certain intellectual value and as a result to deny themselves friendships in which no intellectual esteem was involved. Yes, it has never failed to surprise me that a man whose degree of self-honesty even led him to cut himself off from Wagner's music out of scruples of conscience could have imagined that truth can be attained by the mode of expression, intrinsically vague and inadequate, represented by actions in general and friendships in particular, or that there can be any sort of sense in an act like putting one's work aside to go and see a friend in order to share one's grief at the false report that the Louvre has gone up in flames. I had reached the point, in Balbec, of thinking that the pleasure of playing with a group of girls has a less pernicious effect on the life of the mind, to which at least it remains foreign, than friendship, which is totally bent on making us sacrifice the only part of ourselves that is real and incommunicable (except through art) to a superficial self that, unlike the other, finds no joy on its own; what it finds instead is a vague, sentimental satisfaction at being cherished by external support, hospitalized in the individuality of another person, where, in gratitude for the protection afforded by this, it radiates approval of its well-being and marvels at qualities it would castigate as failings and seek to correct in itself. Moreover, the denigrators of friendship can, without any illusions and with some remorse, be the finest friends in the world, in the same way that an artist who is nurturing a masterpiece and feels it his duty to devote his life to his work, can nevertheless, in order not to appear or to run the risk of being selfish, give his life over to a futile cause, and give it all the more courageously in that the reasons for which he would have preferred to do the opposite were disinterested ones. But, whatever my view of friendship, to mention only the pleasure it procured me, so mediocre in quality that it seemed to fall halfway between fatigue and boredom, there is no potion so deadly that it cannot in certain circumstances become precious and restorative by providing us with just the boost we needed and the warmth we are unable to muster of our own accord.

The desire to ask Saint-Loup to take me to see some of the Rivebelle women, as I had wanted to do an hour ago, was of course far from my mind; the aftermath of my disappointment about Mme de Stermaria was there to stay, but Saint-Loup's presence, at a moment when any reason for happiness had left my heart, was like the arrival of kindness, gaiety, life—external to me, no doubt, but offered to me, asking only to be made mine. He did not himself grasp the significance of my cry of gratitude and my tears of affection. And what can be more paradoxically affectionate than one of those friends—a diplomat, an explorer, an airman, or a soldier like Saint-Loup—who, obliged to leave again the next day for the country and from there for God knows where, seem to derive from a single evening in our company, and to our great surprise, given the rare and fleeting nature of such evenings, an impression of such enjoyment and yet (also to our surprise, since they have enjoyed themselves so much) do not seek to prolong the experience or to repeat it more often? Something as ordinary as a meal with us provides these travelers with the same exotic and exquisite pleasure as our boulevards provide for someone from Asia. We left together to go dine, and as I went downstairs I thought back to Doncières, where every evening I used to join Robert at a restaurant, and the little dining rooms there I had forgotten. I remembered one I had utterly forgotten, not in the hotel where Saint-Loup dined but in a more modest one, half inn, half boardinghouse, where the landlady and one of her servants waited at table. The snow had forced me to stop there. Robert was not dining at the hotel that evening in any case, and I had not wanted to walk on any farther. My meal was served in a little paneled room upstairs. The lamp went out during dinner, and the serving maid lit two candles. Pretending that I could not see very well as I held out my plate while she helped me to potatoes, I took her bare forearm in my hand as if I were guiding it. Seeing that she made no attempt to withdraw it, I began to fondle it; then, without a word, I drew her whole body close, blew out the candles, and told her to grope about me for some money. For the next few days, the adequate enjoyment of physical pleasure seemed to me to require not only this serving maid but the paneled dining room and its conducive seclusion. Yet, out of habit and from friendship, and until I left Doncières, I went back every evening to the other restaurant, where Saint-Loup and his friends dined. But even this hotel, where he boarded with his friends, had been absent from my thoughts for a long time. We put our experience to very little use and fail to make the most of those hours on long summer evenings or unseasonal wintry nights when it nevertheless seemed to us that they might contain some grain of peace or pleasure. But such time is not entirely wasted. When new moments of pleasure announce themselves in their turn, ones that could pass by in the same way, similarly tenuous and linear, former moments return and bring with them the well-grounded basis for rich orchestration. They develop in this way into one of those typical instances of happiness that we recapture only occasionally but which continue to exist; in the present instance, it was the abandonment of everything else to go and dine in comfortable surroundings, whose physical reality memory helps to endow with the enticements of travel, in the company of a friend who is going to rouse our dormant life with all his energy, all his affection, to communicate to us a glow of pleasure, quite different from anything we might owe to our own efforts or to social distractions; we are going to devote ourselves entirely to him, to make professions of friendship that, born within the confines of the hour and remaining enclosed within it, will perhaps be forgotten the following day; but these were professions I could make without misgivings to Saint-Loup, since, with a courage that embodied a great deal of wise experience and the hunch that friendship cannot be probed in detail, the following day he would be gone.

If, as I came downstairs, I relived those evenings in Doncières, suddenly, when we reached the street, the almost total darkness, in which the fog seemed to have extinguished the streetlamps (they were visible, and even then very faintly, only from close up), took me back to some dim memory of arrival in Combray by night, when the town was lit only at distant intervals and you groped your way through a humid, warm, holy criblike darkness in which the lamps flickered here and there with no more light than from a candle. Between that year (whichever year it was) and the evenings in Rivebelle, reflected a while back above the curtains in my bedroom, what a world of difference! As I took note of this, I felt a sense of inspired exhilaration, which might have resulted in something had I remained alone and so avoided the detour of the many futile years I was yet to spend before discovering the invisible vocation which is the subject of this book. Had this discovery been made that evening, the carriage I found myself in would have deserved to rank as more memorable than Dr. Percepied's, in which I had composed the little descriptive piece about the Martinville steeples, recently unearthed, as it happened, which I had reworked and offered without success to the *Figaro*. Is it because we relive past years not in their continuous sequence, day by day, but by fixing our memory on the coolness or sunshine of one particular morning or evening spent in the shade of some isolated setting, enclosed, static, arrested, lost, remote from everything else, and because the changes gradually effected not only in the world outside but in our dreams and in our developing personality, changes that have carried us along through life from one phase to a wholly different one without our noticing, are therefore nullified, that, if we relive another memory taken from a different year, the gaps, the immense stretches of oblivion between the two, make us feel something like a huge gulf of difference in altitude or the incompatibility of two utterly dissimilar qualities of breathed atmosphere and surrounding coloration? But between the successive memories of Combray, Doncières, and Rivebelle which had recently occurred, I now felt that, much more than a distance in time, there was the sort of distance there would be between different universes whose substance was not the same. Had I wanted to reproduce in writing the material in which my slightest memories of Rivebelle were carved, I would have had to take the substance that had up until now resembled the somber, rugged sandstone of Combray, vein it in pink, and suddenly transform it into something translucent, dense, cool, and resonant. But Robert had finished giving his instructions to the driver and now joined me in the carriage. The ideas that had been passing through my mind were dispelled. They are goddesses who sometimes deign to make themselves visible to a solitary mortal, at a crossroads, or even in his bedroom while he sleeps, and they stand in the doorway to bring him their annunciation. But as soon as he is no longer alone, they vanish in a refusal to appear to more than one person at a time. So instead I found myself thrown back on friendship.

Robert had warned me when he arrived that it was very foggy outside, but as we were talking the fog had grown steadily thicker. It was now no longer merely the light mist that I had been hoping to see rise from the island and envelop Mme de Stermaria and myself. Once you moved a foot or two away from them, the streetlamps were invisible, and it became as dark as night in an open field, in a forest, or preferably on the mellow Breton island where I should have liked to be; I was as lost as if I were on the coast of some Northern sea, risking my life a score of times before reaching the safety of the solitary inn; no longer a mirage that is sought after, the fog was becoming one of those dangers to be fought off, so that finding our way safely to our destination meant that we experienced the difficulties, the anxiety, and finally the delight that the sense of safety—so much taken for granted by those who are not threatened by the loss if it—confers upon the perplexed and disoriented traveler. Only one thing threatened to mar my pleasure during our adventurous carriage journey, by throwing me into a momentary spell of angry amazement. "You know," said Saint-Loup, "I told Bloch you weren't that fond of him, that you found him rather vulgar. You know me, I like things to be clear-cut," he concluded smugly, in a tone of voice that brooked no argument. I was dumbfounded. Not only did I have the most absolute confidence in Saint-Loup, in the loyalty of his friendship, which he had betrayed by what he had said to Bloch, but it also seemed to me that he ought to have been held back from doing this by his defects as much as by his good qualities, by that extraordinary fund of good breeding which could carry politeness to the point of unwarranted reticence. Was the triumphant manner he adopted the sort of manner we assume to conceal a sense of embarrassment when we have admitted something we know we ought not to have done? Was it simply heedlessness? Or stupidity, making a virtue out of a defect of his of which I was unaware? Or a passing bout of ill-humor toward me, prompting him to try to end our friendship? Or else a passing bout of ill-humor directed at Bloch, to whom he had wanted to say something hurtful even if it meant compromising me? At all events, his face was marred, while he uttered these vulgar words, by a horribly twisted expression, which I encountered only once or twice in all the time I knew him, and which began by running more or less down the middle of his face before it reached his lips and contorted them into a hideous low smirk, almost bestial for a second, and no doubt inherited. Such moments, which probably occurred only once or twice a year, must have represented a partial eclipse of his true self, due to the passage across it of the personality of some ancestor reflecting itself upon him. Like the smug expression on Robert's face, the words "I like things to be clear-cut" fed equally into my misgivings and should have incurred a similar condemnation. I felt like telling him that a liking for clear-cut situations ought to entail restricting outbursts of plain speaking to one's own affairs and not making a cheap virtue out of them at the expense of other people's feelings. But the carriage had already drawn up outside the huge, brightly lit glass front of the restaurant, the sole point of light in the murky darkness. The fog itself, in the brightness cast by the comfortably lit interior, seemed to be standing there on the pavement to usher you in, like footmen whose faces reflect the joyful hospitality of their master; it was shot through with the most delicate glints of light and pointed the way in like the pillar of fire that guided the Hebrews.[14] As a matter of fact, there were many of these among the evening's diners. For this was the restaurant to which Bloch and his friends had been coming for a long time to meet up in the evening, intoxicated by their fast of coffee and political curiosity, more famished than they are after their ritual fast, which occurs only once a year. Because all mental excitement creates some dominant cause of attachment, something superior to the habits involved in it, there is no taste at all enthusiastically pursued that does not thus gather around it a group of people which it unites and in which the general esteem is what each member devotes most of his life to seeking. In one place, be it only some little provincial town, you will find a group of enthusiastic music-lovers; the greater part of their time and money is spent on chamber-music sessions, on meetings devoted to musical discussion, in cafés where they find themselves surrounded by music-lovers and rub shoulders with musicians. Another group, keen on flying, devote their attentions to being well in with the old waiter in the glass bar perched above the airport; sheltered from the wind in this glass lighthouse cage, they can follow, in the company of an airman who is not flying that day, the moves of a pilot looping the loop, or another, who was invisible a moment ago, suddenly coming in to land and hitting the runway with the great roaring wings of the Roc.[15] The little group that met to try to perpetuate and delve into the swift turn of emotions involved in the Zola trial attached a similar importance to the café we were in. But they were not well received by the young aristocrats who composed the other half of the clientele and had taken to frequenting a second room in the café, separated from the other by a narrow parapet supporting a row of plants. They viewed Dreyfus and his supporters as traitors, although, twenty-five years later, when people's ideas had had time to sort themselves out and Dreyfusism to acquire a certain glamour in the light of history, the Bolshevistic and dance-obsessed sons of these same young aristocrats would declare to the "intellectuals" who questioned them that, had they been alive at the time, they would have undoubtedly been pro-Dreyfus, despite the fact that they had no more clue about the significance of the affair than Comtesse Edmond de Pourtalès or the Marquise de Galliffet,[16] further shining examples of glamour already extinct by the time these noble sons were born. For, on the night of the fog, the aristocrats of the café, who were later to become the fathers of these retrospectively Dreyfusard young intellectuals, were still bachelors. Clearly a rich marriage was envisaged for them by all their families, but none of them had so far achieved it. Still only a virtual reality, this rich marriage, which was a common goal several of them shared (there were indeed several "suitable matches" in view, but when it came down to it the number of big dowries available was considerably lower than the number of aspirants involved), merely served to create a certain amount of rivalry between these young men.

Since Saint-Loup stayed outside for a few minutes to give the driver instructions to collect us after dinner, it was my misfortune to have to enter the place on my own. And, to begin with, once I had engaged myself with the unfamiliar workings of the turning door, I became alarmed that I should never get out of it. (Let me add, for the lovers of precise vocabulary, that the drum-shaped entrance in question, despite its harmless appearance, is known as a "revolver," from the English term "revolving door.") That evening, the proprietor, unwilling either to brave the damp fog outside or to abandon his customers, nevertheless remained posted by the entrance so that he could enjoy the joyful grievances of new arrivals, their faces positively glowing with the satisfaction of people who had had difficulty getting there and been afraid of getting lost. But the smiling cordiality of his welcome vanished at the sight of a stranger trying to disengage himself from the revolving glass panels of the door. This flagrant sign of ignorance made him frown like an examiner who is totally disinclined to utter the words *"Dignus est intrare."*[17] To cap it all, I went and sat down in the room reserved for the young aristocrats, from which he made no bones about coming to oust me, pointing me, with a rudeness from which all the other waiters immediately took their cue, to a place in the other room. This was still less to my liking because I found myself sitting on an already crowded wall seat staring straight at the door reserved for the Hebrews, which did not revolve, but opened and closed continuously, exposing me to a horrible draft. But the proprietor refused my request for another seat with the words, "Monsieur, I really can't disturb other people just on your account." Yet he soon forgot me, his late and troublesome client, in his fascination with the arrival of each newcomer, who, before ordering his beer, his cold chicken wing, or his hot toddy (it was long past the hour for dining), was first obliged, as in old tales, to pay his dues by recounting his adventure as soon as he entered this sanctuary of warmth and safety, where the contrast with perils just escaped created the mood of gaiety and comradeship you find in cheerful partnership around a campfire.

One of the arrivals reported that his carriage, thinking it had reached the Pont de la Concorde, had managed to circle the Invalides three times; another that his, as it tried to make its way down the Avenue des Champs-Élysées, had driven into a clump of trees at the Rond-Point and taken three-quarters of an hour to find its way back to the road. There then followed various lamentations about the fog, the cold, the deathly silence of the streets, all delivered and received with the same unexpected joviality that was connected with the pleasant atmosphere of the room, which, except for where I was sitting, was warm; the bright lights, which dazzled people's eyes to life again after their experience of foggy blindness; and the buzz of talk, which brought back sound to muffled ears.

New arrivals were hard put to it to keep silent. Their unusual adventures, which each of them thought unique, set their tongues on fire, and their eyes scoured the place in search of someone to engage in conversation. The proprietor himself lost all sense of social distinctions: "M. le Prince de Foix got lost three times on his way from the Porte Saint-Martin," he said, laughing unabashedly and actually pointing out the famous aristocrat, as if he were about to effect an introduction, to a Jewish lawyer who on any other evening would have been separated from him by a barrier far harder to surmount than the parapet and its row of plants. "Three times! Well, I never!" said the lawyer, touching his hat. These words of friendly interest were not something the Prince appreciated. He belonged to an aristocratic group that seemed to be solely preoccupied with the overstepping of social boundaries, even in regard to nobles who were not of the very highest rank. Not to respond to a greeting; if the polite person in question repeated the offense, to snigger contemptuously or fling back their heads in fury; to affect not to know an elderly man who had done them a favor in the past; to reserve their handshakes and greetings for dukes and the really intimate friends to whom these dukes introduced them: such was the attitude of these young men, and more particularly of the Prince de Foix. This attitude was fostered by the muddled conduct of early manhood (a stage of life, even for the middle class, when someone's behavior can come across as ungrateful and loutish because he has long put off writing to a benefactor who had just lost his wife and, to simplify matters, decides to ignore him when they meet), but what really lay behind it was an acute caste snobbery. It is true that, like the manifestations of certain nervous disorders that become less pronounced in later life, this snobbery would usually lose some of its offensive manner in these men who had been so intolerable when they were young. Once he has outgrown his youth, a man will rarely remain a prisoner to his insolence. He had thought it was the only way to behave; then he suddenly discovers that, even for a prince, there are such things as music, literature, not to speak of standing for the post of deputy. And so his scale of human values changes and he starts talking to people who were once the target of his dismissive gaze. And good luck to such spurned people if they have had the patience to wait until their forties and are mature enough—if "mature" is the word—to enjoy the civility and polite acknowledgment so cuttingly refused them when they were twenty!

And since we are on the subject of the Prince de Foix, it is worth mentioning that he belonged to a set of a dozen or fifteen young men and to a more intimate group of four. The dozen or fifteen shared the characteristic, from which the Prince was, I think, exempt, that each of them presented a dual aspect to the world. Riddled with debt, they were regarded as complete nobodies by their tradesmen, despite the pleasure these took in addressing them as "M. le Comte," "M. le Marquis," "M. le Duc," and so forth. They hoped to solve their problems by means of the famous "rich marriage" ("a fat windfall," as the expression still was), and since only four or five of the large dowries they coveted existed, several of them were secretly setting their sights on the same marriage partner. The secret was so well kept that when one of them arrived at the café and announced, "My dear fellows, I'm too fond of you all to hold back the news of my engagement to Mlle d'Ambresac," there would be an outburst of exclamation, several of the group being under the impression that their chances of marriage to Mlle d'Ambresac were as good as settled, and therefore lacking the necessary composure to stifle at source their cries of rage and stupefaction: "So it's marriage you're after, is it, Bibi?" the Prince de Châtellerault could not help exploding, dropping his fork in surprise and despair, for he had been fully expecting the engagement of this same Mlle d'Ambresac to be made public, but with himself, Châtellerault, named as the future husband. And yet God only knows all that his father had been slyly implying to the Ambresacs about Bibi's mother. He could not keep himself from repeating the same sort of remark again, "So you think it will be fun to get married, do you?," but Bibi, better prepared now that he had had plenty of time to adopt an appropriate attitude since the semi-official stage of the engagement, replied with a smile, "I'm pleased, not to be getting married, which I didn't particularly want to do, but to be marrying Daisy d'Ambresac, who is utterly delightful." It took no more time than the duration of this sentence for M. de Châtellerault to regain his composure, but he was already thinking that he must immediately change his tactics and set his sights on Mlle de la Canourgue or Miss Foster, numbers two and three on the dowry list, pacify the creditors who were setting store by the Ambresac marriage, and, finally, explain to the people to whom he had sung Mlle d'Ambresac's praises that this marriage was all very well for Bibi, but that if he himself had married her he would have set his entire family at odds with him. Mme Soléon, he would claim, had in fact gone so far as to say that she would close her doors to the couple.

But if, in the eyes of tradesmen, restaurant proprietors, and so forth, they seemed of little account, by contrast, as men of dual personality, as soon as they appeared in society they were no longer judged by the dilapidated state of their fortunes and the pathetic way they worked to repair them. They were once more M. le Prince X, M. le Duc de Y, and were esteemed only by their quarterings. They would take precedence over a nobleman who was almost a multimillionaire, and seemingly a man who lacked nothing, because, as heads of their house, they were by descent sovereign princes of small territories where they were entitled to do things like minting money and so forth. Often, in the café, one of them would lower his eyes when another entered, in order to avoid exchanging the usual statutory greetings. This was because his imaginative pursuit of riches had involved inviting a banker to dine with him. Every time a society gentleman gets involved with a banker in such circumstances, it leaves him poorer by a hundred thousand francs, which does nothing to keep him from repeating the process with another. Nothing keeps us from continuing to light candles in church or to consult doctors.

But the Prince de Foix, himself a rich man, belonged not only to this fashionable set of fifteen or so young men, but to a more exclusive and closely knit group of four, which included Saint-Loup. Known as the four gigolos, they were never invited to anything separately, were always to be seen riding together at the country houses where their hostesses provided them with adjoining bedrooms; as a result, especially since the four of them were extremely good-looking, rumors circulated about the nature of their intimacy. As far as Saint-Loup was concerned, I was in a position to denounce such rumors categorically. But the curious thing is that, if it eventually came to light that the rumors were true of all four of them, then each one had been utterly unaware of the facts in relation to the other three. Yet each had done his utmost to inform himself about the others, either to gratify a desire or, more likely, a grudge, to prevent a marriage, or to have the upper hand over the friend whose secret he had uncovered. A fifth member (for in groups of four there are always more than four) had joined this Platonic quartet, a man far more suspect than the others. But religious scruple had held him back until long after the group had broken up and he himself was a married man, the father of a family, one minute rushing off to Lourdes to pray that the next baby might be a boy or a girl, and the next flinging himself at soldiers.

Despite the Prince's character, the fact that the lawyer had made his remark without really addressing him directly made him less angry than he would have been otherwise. There was also the fact that this evening was a rather exceptional one. And, indeed, the lawyer was no more likely to become acquainted with the Prince de Foix than was the driver who had taken His Lordship to the café. And so the Prince felt that he might even permit himself to reply—contemptuously, of course, and as if to no one in particular—to this man who had addressed him and who, thanks to the fog, was somewhat like a fellow traveler encountered on some beach at the ends of the earth, a place battered by wind or shrouded in mist: "Losing one's way is nothing; the problem is finding it again." These words of wisdom impressed the proprietor, for he had heard them several times already that evening.

In fact, he had the constant habit of comparing what he had heard or read with things that were already familiar to him, and if he could detect no difference between the two, he felt a stir of admiration. This sort of mental response is not to be ignored, for, applied to political conversation, to the reading of newspapers, it shapes public opinion and thus contributes to the greatest events in the world. Many German café-owners, simply through being impressed by a customer or a newspaper informing them that France, England, and Russia were "on the warpath" against Germany, made war possible, at the time of Agadir, even if no war actually happened.[18] If historians have not been wrong to renounce their method of approaching the actions of nations as determined by the will of kings, they ought to substitute for the latter the psychology of the individual—and the humblest individual at that.

In the matter of politics, the proprietor of the café into which I had

just walked had for some time been applying his learning-by-rote mentality exclusively to a number of set pieces on the Dreyfus case. If the
terms he had committed to memory did not figure in the remarks of a
customer or the columns of a newspaper, then he would declare that
the article bored him to tears or that the customer was not giving a true
picture. But the Prince de Foix's words aroused such admiration in him
that he barely gave the Prince time to finish his sentence. "Well said,
Prince, well said"–which effectively meant "faultlessly recited"–"how
true, how very true," he exclaimed, "swelling into ecstasies of satisfaction," as the *Arabian Nights* puts it. But the Prince had already departed
into the smaller room. And since life returns to normal even after the
most singular events, those who had emerged from the sea of fog began
to order their drinks or their food; among them were a party of young
men from the Jockey Club who, in view of the exceptional circumstances, made no bones about installing themselves at a couple of tables
in the larger room and were therefore quite close to me. Thus the cata-
clysm had established, even between the smaller room and the larger
one, among all these people stimulated by the comfort of the restaurant
after their long wanderings through the ocean of fog, a familiarity from
which I alone was excluded, and which must have been something
like the spirit that prevailed in Noah's Ark. I suddenly caught sight
of the proprietor bowing and scraping, and the full complement of
waiters rushed forward to do likewise, with the eyes of the whole restaurant turned upon this scene. "Quick, send Cyprien to me, a table for
M. le Marquis de Saint-Loup," cried the proprietor, for whom Robert
was not only a great nobleman, highly esteemed even by the Prince de
Foix, but a customer of wildly lavish tastes who spent a good deal of
money in this restaurant. Those dining in the big room looked on with
curiosity, while those in the smaller one all tried to be the first to hail
their friend as he finished wiping his shoes. But just as he was about to
enter the smaller room, he caught sight of me in the big one. "Good
God!" he exclaimed. "What *are* you doing in there in front of a wide-
open door?" As he said this, he cast a furious glance at the proprietor,
who ran to shut the door, deflecting the blame onto his waiters: "I'm always telling them to keep it closed."

In order to join Saint-Loup, I had had to disturb the people sitting at the same table and those sitting at the tables in front of mine. "Why did you move? Would you prefer to dine here, rather than in the small room? You'll be freezing, you poor fellow. You'll be good enough to keep that door permanently out of use," he said to the proprietor. "I'll see to it at once, M. le Marquis. Any new customers will simply have to pass through the smaller room." And, to emphasize his eagerness to dance attendance, he commandeered the services of a headwaiter and several others for the purpose, issuing vociferous threats about the consequences of neglecting his orders. To make me forget that marks of respect toward me had not been forthcoming until Saint-Loup's arrival on the scene, he became excessively attentive, and just in case I should think that this was prompted by the fact that his rich and noble client was clearly my friend, he smuggled in a series of private little smiles in an attempt to convey a truly personal liking for me.

A remark made by one of the diners behind me made me turn my head for a second. Instead of the words, "Yes, I'll have the chicken wing and a little champagne, too, but not too dry," I thought I had heard, "I would prefer glycerine. Yes, hot, that's right." I was anxious to take a look at the ascetic who was inflicting such a diet upon himself, but I quickly turned back to Saint-Loup to avoid being recognized by the man with the strange appetite. It was simply a doctor I knew whose advice was being asked by another customer, who had taken advantage of the fog to pin him down in this café. Like stockbrokers, doctors use the first person singular.

Meanwhile, I looked at Robert and various thoughts passed through my mind. There were in this café, and I had come across them elsewhere, a large number of foreigners, intellectuals, would-be artists, who were resigned to the laughter aroused by their pretentious capes, their 1830s neckties, and even more by their clumsy way of carrying themselves, and often deliberately provoked that laughter in order to show that it meant nothing to them; yet they were men of real intellectual and moral worth, profoundly conscious of the world. To people who could not endure any oddity or eccentricity of appearance they were unacceptable (as Bloch was to Albertine), the Jews among them in particular—the unassimilated ones, of course; the others are not relevant here. With hindsight, it was generally realized that, even if their hair was too long, their noses and eyes were too big, their gestures theatrical and jerky, and this did nothing to endear them to people, it was infantile to judge them on this account, for they were highly intelligent and goodhearted men who, in the long run, could become profoundly endearing. Among the Jews especially, there were few whose parents did not have a kindness of heart, a broad-mindedness, an honesty, in comparison with which Saint-Loup's mother and the Duc de Guermantes came across as the sorriest of moral figures in their desiccated emotions, the surface religiosity they cultivated only to condemn scandal, and their clannish apology for a Christianity which never failed to lead (through the unexpected channels of the intellect at the expense of all else) to colossally wealthy marriages. But, for all this, Saint-Loup, in whatever way the faults of his parents had combined to create a new set of qualities, was governed by a delightful openness of mind and heart. And whenever—to the undying glory of France, let it be said—such qualities are found in a pure-blooded Frenchman, whether he belongs to the aristocracy or to the people, they flower—"flourish" would be too strong a word for something so persistently controlled and contained— with a grace that even the most admired foreigner cannot offer to us. Of course, others have their intellectual and moral qualities, too, and if to appreciate them we have first to put behind us what we see as unacceptable, shocking, and risible, they remain no less precious. But it is nonetheless a pleasant thing, and perhaps something exclusively French, that what is spontaneously judged to be fine, what carries conviction to the mind and the heart, should be first of all pleasing to the eye, delicately colored, perfectly chiseled, and should embody its inner perfection in substance and shape. I looked at Saint-Loup and thought what a pleasant thing it is when there is no physical impediment to hinder a person's inner grace, and when the curves of the nostrils are as delicate and as perfectly formed as the wings of the tiny butterflies that settle on flowers in the fields around Combray; I thought, too, that the true *opus francigenum*,[19] the secret of which was not lost in the thirteenth century and would not perish along with our churches, is not to be found so much in the stone angels of Saint-André-des-Champs as in those young

Frenchmen—nobles, bourgeois, or peasants—whose faces are sculpted with the same delicacy and boldness as those on the famous porch, traditional and still alive.

After leaving us for a moment to bestow his personal supervision upon the closing of the door and our orders for dinner (he laid great stress on our choosing "butcher's meat," which presumably meant that the poultry was rather indifferent), the proprietor came back to inform us that the Prince de Foix would be honored to be allowed to dine at a table next to M. le Marquis. "But they are all taken," said Robert, as he inspected the tables that were blocking the way to mine. "There is really no problem," the proprietor announced. "If M. le Marquis is agreeable, I can easily ask these people to move. It is always such an honor to oblige M. le Marquis!" "You're the one who has to decide," said Saint-Loup to me. "Foix is a good fellow. I don't know whether he'd bore you, but he's less of a fool than most of them." I told Robert that of course I should be happy with such company but that, now that I was having the rare pleasure of dining with him at all, I should be just as pleased to dine with him on my own. "That's a very fine cloak the Prince has," the proprietor interjected as the two of us deliberated. "Yes, I know," said Saint-Loup. I wanted to tell Robert that M. de Charlus had concealed from his sister-in-law that he knew me and to ask him what the reason might be, but the arrival of M. de Foix put paid to this. He had come over to see whether his request had been welcomed, and we saw him standing a few feet away. Robert introduced us, but made it quite clear that the two of us had things to talk about and would prefer to be left alone. As the Prince moved away, he added to the farewell bow he made me a smile in Saint-Loup's direction, which seemed to express regret that my friend had wished to curtail a meeting that the Prince himself would have liked to see prolonged. But at this point Robert suddenly seemed gripped by some idea he had, moved away with his friend, left me with the words, "Do sit down and start your dinner, I'll be back in a moment," and disappeared into the smaller room. I, meanwhile, as a stranger, endured the painful experience of hearing the smart young men around me telling the most improbable and nasty stories about the adoptive Grand Duke of Luxembourg (the former

Comte de Nassau), whom I had met in Balbec and who had expressed such delicate proofs of sympathy during my grandmother's illness. One of these young men was claiming that the Grand Duke had said to the Duchesse de Guermantes, "I expect everyone to rise to their feet when my wife arrives," and that she had returned the remark, "So we are to stand for your wife, are we? A bit different from her grandmother, I must say—men were expected to lie down for her," a remark that, had it been made at all, would have been lacking not only in wit but in truth, since the grandmother of the young Princess had always been a paragon of propriety. Then someone told a story about the Grand Duke's once going to Balbec to visit his aunt the Princess of Luxembourg, staying at the Grand-Hôtel, and complaining to the manager (my friend) that the Luxembourg standard was not being flown on the front; and because this standard was less familiar and less in use than the British or Italian flag, it had taken several days to find one, much to the Grand Duke's annoyance. I did not believe a word of this, but I was determined, once I went to Balbec, to ask the manager and to satisfy myself that it was pure invention.

While I was waiting for Saint-Loup, I asked the restaurant proprietor to bring me some bread. "But of course, M. le Baron, at once," came the obsequious reply. "I'm not M. le Baron," I returned with mock regret. "I do beg your pardon, M. le Comte!" I had no time to launch a second protest, which would almost certainly have promoted me to the rank of marquis: Saint-Loup, as he had promised, had returned promptly and appeared in the doorway holding the big vicuña cloak belonging to the Prince de Foix, from whom he had clearly borrowed it to keep me warm. He signaled to me not to move and started to come toward me; but either my table would have to be moved again or I would need to change my seat if he was going to sit down. No sooner had he entered the big room than he sprang lightly onto one of the red plush benches running round its walls, on which, apart from myself, three or four young Jockey Club members were sitting, friends of his, who had not been able to find places in the smaller room. Between the tables there were electric wires, placed fairly high; Saint-Loup jumped nimbly and safely over them like a steeplechaser clearing a fence;

embarrassed though I was that it was being done wholly for my benefit and to save me from a trifling inconvenience, the surefootedness of my friend's acrobatic feat nonetheless amazed me; and I was not alone in this: although they would probably have been only mildly appreciative of a similar feat on the part of a less distinguished and less generous client, the proprietor and his staff stood by in fascination, like racing enthusiasts at the enclosure; one of the assistant waiters stood rooted to the spot, holding a dish that was awaited at a table nearby; and when Saint-Loup, who needed to pass behind his friends, climbed onto the back of their bench and moved along it in a balancing act, muffled applause broke out from the body of the room. When he reached my seat, he brought himself to a halt with the precision of a chieftain paying tribute before the throne of a sovereign and, stooping down, he courteously and submissively handed me the vicuña cloak, which, a moment later, when he had sat down beside me, he arranged around my shoulders as a light, warm shawl, without my having to lift a finger.

"Oh yes, while I'm thinking of it," said Robert, "my uncle Charlus has something to say to you. I promised I'd get you to go and see him tomorrow evening."

"Funny, I was just going to mention him to you. But tomorrow evening I'm dining with your aunt Guermantes."

"Ah yes, there's a fabulous blowout at Oriane's tomorrow. I'm not invited. But my uncle Palamède doesn't want you to go. Can't you get out of it? Anyway, go and see my uncle afterward. He seems anxious to see you. You could get there by eleven, don't you think? Eleven o'clock, don't forget. I'll tell him that. He's very touchy about these things. If you don't turn up he'll be really insulted. Oriane's do's never finish very late. Actually, I need to go and see Oriane about getting a transfer from Morocco. She's so good about that sort of thing, and she can twist Général de Saint-Joseph round her little finger. He's the man in charge of these things. But don't say anything about it to her. I've mentioned it to the Princess of Parma, and there should be no problem. Interesting place, Morocco. I could tell you a lot about it. Some very decent fellows out there. Mental equals and all that."

"You don't think the Germans are going to go to war over it?"

"No, not really. They're annoyed with us, and they've got every right to be. But the Kaiser wants a state of peace. They're always making us think they want war, to force us to give in. It's like a game of poker. The Prince of Monaco, one of Wilhelm II's agents, comes and tells us in confidence that Germany will attack if we don't give in. So we give in. But even if we were to refuse, there would be no war of any description. You need only to think what a cosmic thing a war would be today. It would be more catastrophic than the Flood and the *Götterdämmerung*[20] put together. Only it wouldn't last so long."

He talked to me about friendship, special affinities with people, about missing them (even though, like all travelers of his kind, he was going away again the next day to spend some months in the country and returning to Paris for only a couple of days on his way back to Morocco, or elsewhere); but the words he let fall that evening kindled a pleasant glow of thoughts in the warmth of my heart. Our rare conversations alone together, and this one in particular, have assumed, in retrospect, the status of important turning points. For him, as for me, this was the evening of friendship. And yet the friendship I felt for him at this moment was scarcely, I feared (with some remorse), what he would have liked to inspire. Still in the throes of the pleasure it had given me to see him come cantering toward me and gracefully reaching his goal, I felt that this pleasure arose from the fact that each of his movements as he had moved along the wall bench possibly derived its meaning from, was motivated by, something very personal to Saint-Loup himself, but that what really lay behind it was something he had inherited, by birth and upbringing, from his race.

Certainty of taste (with regard not to aesthetics but to personal behavior) in a man of refinement, allowing him, when faced with a novel set of circumstances, to adopt instinctively—like a musician who is asked to perform a piece he has never seen—the appropriate attitude and action and to apply the right mechanism and technique, then enabling him to exercise his taste without the inhibitions that would have paralyzed so many young middle-class men with the fear both of making themselves ridiculous in the eyes of strangers through their unconventional behavior and of appearing too ready to show off in the eyes of

their friends—a fear that, in Robert's case, was replaced by a disdain he
had certainly never felt in his heart but had received by inheritance in
his body (it had molded the attitudes of his ancestors into a familiarity
which, as they saw it, could only flatter and enchant those to whom it
was addressed)—along with this went a noble liberality which, instead of
flaunting his considerable material advantages (lavish expenditure in
this restaurant had succeeded in making him, here as elsewhere, its
most fashionable and favored customer, as was made quite evident by
the deference shown him not only by the waiters but by all its most distinguished young patrons), led him in fact to trample them underfoot,
just as he had trampled, physically and symbolically, upon those plush
benches, which seemed to this friend of mine to represent some sumptuous processional path, important to him only because it enabled him
to join me with more grace and speed. These, then, were the inherently
aristocratic qualities that shone through his body—not opaque and dim,
as mine would have been, but meaningful and limpid—as the industri-
ous energy and power that created it shines through a work of art, and
translated the movements of the light-footed acrobatics Robert had
conducted along the wall into movements as intelligible and charming as those of horsemen on a marble frieze. Robert's response to this
might have been: "Was it really worth it to have grown up despising
birth, honoring only justice and intellect, choosing companions, outside the friends imposed upon me, who were awkward and ill dressed
but eloquent, only to discover that I come across solely, and am fondly
remembered, not as the person the worthy efforts of my will have modeled to my likeness, but as a person not of my making, not even myself,
the one I've always despised and striven to overcome? Was it worthwhile to love my best friend as I have done, only to find that his greatest pleasure when he is with me is to discover something far more
general than myself, a pleasure that has nothing to do with friendship
(as he says himself, but cannot seriously believe), but something intellectual and detached, a kind of artistic appreciation?" This is what I now
fear Saint-Loup may have thought at times. In which case, he was mistaken. If he had not (although he in fact had) loved something more
exalted than the innate suppleness of his body, if he had not been de-

tached for so long from aristocratic arrogance, then there would have been something more self-conscious, more heavy-handed about his very agility, and a vulgar self-advertisement in his behavior. In the same way that Mme de Villeparisis, on an intellectual level, had needed a great deal of serious thought in order to convey a sense of the frivolous in her conversation and in her memoirs, so, in order for Saint-Loup's body to carry so much nobility, all ideas of nobility had first to leave his mind, which was intent on higher things, before returning to his body to re-establish themselves there as noble attributes of an utterly unstudied kind. In this way, his distinction of mind went largely hand in hand with a physical distinction that would not have been complete without it. An artist has no need to express his thought directly in a work for the work to reflect its quality; it has even been said that the highest praise of God is to be found in the denial of Him by the atheist, who considers creation to be perfect enough to dispense with a Creator. And I was more than aware, too, that it was not merely a work of art I was admiring in this young horseman unfolding along the wall the frieze of his cantering path; the young Prince (a descendant of Catherine de Foix, Queen of Navarre and granddaughter of Charles VII) he had just left to be alone with me, the privileges of birth and fortune he was putting second to me, the proud and nimble ancestry which lay behind the assurance, agility, and courtesy with which he had wrapped the warm vicuña cloak around my shivering body—were not all these things like friends of longer standing in his life, on account of whom I might have expected that we should always be kept apart, but whom he was nonetheless sacrificing to me out of choice, the sort of choice that can be made only by a lofty mind, with that supreme liberty reflected in Robert's impulses and in which perfect friendship thrives?

The crass arrogance that was to be detected behind the familiarity of the Guermantes manner—in contrast to the distinction it assumed in Robert's code of conduct, in which hereditary disdain was merely the outward manifestation, transformed in his case into an unconscious grace, of a genuine moral humility—had been impressed upon me, not by M. de Charlus, in whom certain defects of character that I still found rather impenetrable were superimposed on his aristocratic habits, but by the Duc de Guermantes. Yet he, too, despite the overall impression of vulgarity my grandmother had found so distasteful when she had encountered him years earlier at Mme de Villeparisis's, showed traces of ancient grandeur, as I was to discover when I went to dine at his house the day after my evening with Saint-Loup.

These were not the traces I had noticed, either in himself or the Duchesse, when I first met them at their aunt's, any more than I had noticed the differences that set La Berma apart from her colleagues when I saw her for the first time, although in her case any distinctive qualities were infinitely more striking than those of society people, since, the more focused they are, the more evident such qualities become, the more accessible to the mind. And yet, however subtle shades of social distinction may be (subtle enough for an acute observer like Sainte-Beuve, in his attempt to portray the shades of difference between the salons of Mme Geoffrin, Mme Récamier, and Mme de Boigne, to make them appear so alike that the essential point to emerge from his inquiry, unintentionally, is that salon life is vacuous[21]), for the same reason as with La Berma, by the time the glamour of the Guermantes had worn off for me and my imagination no longer busied itself distilling the droplet of whatever originality they had, I was able to ponder that droplet in all its incomprehensible mystery.

Since the Duchesse had made no mention of her husband at her aunt's evening party, I wondered whether, given the flurry of rumors about divorce, he would be present at the dinner. But I did not have to wait long to find out, for, through the bevy of footmen who were standing about in the hall and who (since they must until then have regarded me much in the same way as they did the children of the cabinetmaker—that is, in a kindlier light than their master, but as someone he could not possibly receive in his house) must have been asking themselves what had brought about this revolutionary change in the order of things, I saw M. de Guermantes threading his way toward me; he had been watching out for my arrival so that he could greet me on his own threshold and take my coat himself.

"Mme de Guermantes will be overjoyed," he said to me in an artfully persuasive tone. "Please let me help you off with your clobber." He felt it both chummy and comic to use popular expressions. "My wife was just a wee bit afraid you might opt out, even though you had fixed a date. We've been saying to each other all day, 'You'll see, he won't come.' I have to say that Mme de Guermantes had more faith in you than I did. You're not an easy person to pin down, and I was sure you were going to run out on us."

And the Duc was such a bad husband, even a brutal one according to some, that you felt grateful to him, as you do toward nasty people for any sign of kindness they show, for referring to her as "Mme de Guermantes," words that seemed to spread a protective wing over the Duchesse and to create the impression that they were inseparable. Meanwhile, taking me familiarly by the hand, he made it his duty to guide me around the reception rooms. A common expression from the lips of a peasant may seem attractive to us if it points to the survival of some local custom or bears the trace of some historic event, unknown perhaps to the speaker; likewise, the politeness shown me by M. de Guermantes—and it was to be sustained throughout the evening—charmed me as a survival of habits that were many centuries old, seventeenth-century habits in particular. People of past centuries seem infinitely remote from us. We cannot venture to assign to them any underlying motives beyond the ones they formally express; it amazes us to discover some sentiment that is roughly akin to our own feelings in a Homeric hero, or some skillful tactical feint by Hannibal during the Battle of Cannae, where he let his flank retreat in order to encircle his enemy by surprise; it is as if we imagined these two figures, the epic poet and the general, to be as remote as animals at the zoo. Even with some of the courtiers of Louis XIV, when we find signs of courtesy in letters written by them to some man of inferior rank who could be of no service to them at all, their letters leave us astonished because they come as a sudden revelation that these great noblemen believed in a whole host of things that they never express directly but which govern their conduct, in particular the belief that they are honor-bound to feign certain sentiments and to fulfill with the utmost punctiliousness certain codes of polite behavior.

This imagined remoteness of the past perhaps partially explains how even great writers have prized the works of mediocre mystifiers like

Ossian as examples of inspired beauty.²² We are so astonished that bards from the distant past should have modern ideas that if, in what we assume to be an old Gaelic poem, we come across an idea we should have thought of as highly ingenious in a contemporary, we fall back in amazement. A gifted translator has only to introduce into an ancient text he is reconstructing more or less faithfully, a few passages that, signed with a contemporary name and published separately, would seem no more than agreeable, and the immediate effect is to assign a moving grandeur to his poet, who is thus made to perform on the keyboards of several centuries at once. The translator himself could have written only a mediocre book, had that book been published as his original work. Offered as a translation, it seems a masterpiece. Not only is the past not so elusive, it actually stays put. It is not only months after the outbreak of a war that laws passed without haste can effectively influence its course, it is not only fifteen years after an unexplained crime that a magistrate can still find the evidence that will throw light on it; after hundreds and hundreds of years, the scholarly study of the place-names and customs of some remote region can still unearth from them some legend that long predates Christianity, already unintelligible, perhaps even forgotten at the time of Herodotus, which, in the name given to a rock, in a religious ritual, still lives on in the present, like an emanation now charged with even greater meaning, stretching far, far back into the past, unflinching. There was an emanation, too, far less ancient, of court life, if not in the manners of M. de Guermantes (they were often vulgar), then in the mind that controlled them. I was to experience it again, like a scent of the past, when I rejoined him a little later in the drawing room. For I did not go there at once.

As we were leaving the hall, I had mentioned to M. de Guermantes that I was very keen to see his Elstirs. "Then I shall be pleased to show you them. Is M. Elstir one of your friends, then? How untoward of me not to have known. I do have some slight acquaintance with him. He's an amiable man, what our fathers used to call a 'gentleman.' I could even have asked him to honor us with his presence at dinner tonight. He would have been most flattered to spend an evening in your company, I'm sure." When the Duc tried to force the manner of the Ancien

Régime in this way, he was unconvincing; but, the next minute, he had slipped back into it persuasively without conscious effort. After asking whether I should like him to show me the pictures, he conducted me to them, graciously standing aside at each door, full of apologies when he was obliged to precede me in order to show me the way—a little scene that, since the occasion described by Saint-Simon on which an ancestor of the Guermantes did him the honors of his house with the same punctilious performance of a gentleman's frivolous duties, and, before it filtered through to the present day, must have been enacted by many another Guermantes for many another visitor. And as I had told the Duc that I would very much like to be left alone for a while with the pictures, he discreetly withdrew, telling me that I would find him in the drawing room when I was ready.

But the moment I was left alone with the Elstirs, I completely forgot about time and dinner; once again, as in Balbec, I had before me fragments of that world of strange new colors, the projection of the great painter's particular vision, which his speech in no way conveyed. The parts of the walls that were covered by his paintings, each of them part of a homogeneous whole, were like the luminous images of a magic lantern, which, in this instance, was the mind of the artist, the strangeness of which one would never have suspected from simply knowing the man—in other words, as long as one had seen only the lantern shielding the lamp before any colored slide had been inserted. Among these pictures, several of the ones that society people found most absurd interested me more than the rest, because they re-created the optical illusions that make it clear that we should never be able to identify objects if we did not have recourse to some process of reasoning. On just how many occasions, as we are moving along in a carriage, have we not seen a bright street opening up a few meters away, when what our eyes are really confronting is merely a patch of wall in the full glare of sunlight creating the mirage of depth. Bearing this in mind, it surely makes sense—not from any artifice of symbolism but from a sincere desire to return to the root of our impression—to represent one thing by the other for which, in an initial flash of illusion, we mistook it. Surfaces and volumes are in reality independent of the names our memory imposes on things once we have recognized them. Elstir was trying to wrench the immediacy of his impression away from what he already knew; he had often struggled to undo the various mental assumptions we impose upon the visual process.

The people who detested these "horrors" were startled to discover that Elstir admired Chardin, Perronneau,[23] and many other painters whom they themselves, with their feet firmly on the ground, liked. They had no conception of the fact that Elstir's effort to reproduce reality (along with his own distinctive taste for certain experiments) was the same as the effort made by Chardin and Perronneau, and that consequently, when he was not absorbed in his own work, he admired theirs as an attempt similar to his own, as something like a collection of fragments anticipating his own achievement. But it did not occur to society people to bring to Elstir's work the temporal perspective that enabled them to like, or at least to look painlessly at, the paintings of Chardin. And yet the older ones among them might have reminded themselves that in the course of their lives they had gradually seen, as the years distanced them from it, the unbridgeable gap between what they regarded as a masterpiece by Ingres and something they supposed must forever remain a horror (Manet's *Olympia*, for example) diminish to the point where the two canvases seemed like twins.[24] But in our inability to move back from the particular to the general, we never learn, and are always imagining ourselves to be faced with some experience that has no precedents in the past.

In two of the pictures (more realistic in manner and from an earlier period), I was touched to discover the same person, portrayed in one of them in evening dress in his drawing room, and in the other wearing a coat and top hat at a working-class festivity by the riverside, where he was clearly out of place, which proved that for Elstir he was not only a regular sitter but a friend, even a patron, whom he liked to introduce into his paintings, as Carpaccio once introduced—with the most perfect likeness—Venetian noblemen into his, or as Beethoven liked to inscribe at the head of a favorite work the beloved name of the Archduke Rudolph. There was something magical about this waterside carnival. The river, the women's dresses, the sails of the boats, the numerous reflections between the various elements in the painting all fitted together on the square of canvas Elstir had cut out of a wonderful afternoon. The marvelous shimmer on the dress of a woman who had stopped dancing for a moment because she was hot and out of breath was reflected, too, in the same way, in the cloth of a motionless sail, in the water of the little port, in the wooden landing stage, in the leaves on trees and in the sky. In one of the pictures I had seen in Balbec, the hospital, as beautiful beneath its lapis-lazuli sky as the cathedral itself, with a daring that surpassed Elstir the theorist, Elstir the man of taste, the lover of medieval culture, seemed to be singing out, "There is no such thing as Gothic, as a masterpiece; a humdrum hospital is every bit as good as an illustrious porch"; what I now heard was: "The slightly vulgar lady whom the man with an eye for women wouldn't bother to look at as he passed by, and would exclude from the poetic scene nature presents to his eyes, is beautiful, too; the light on her dress is the same light that falls on the sail of that boat; everything is equally precious; the tawdry dress and the sail that is beautiful in itself are both mirrors of the same light. All the worth they have is conferred upon them by the painter's eye." And this eye had been able to arrest the passage of the hours for all time in this luminous moment when the lady had felt hot and stopped dancing, when the tree was encircled by a ring of shade, when the sails seemed to be gliding over a glaze of gold. But precisely because that moment had such a forceful impact, the fixity of the canvas conveyed the impression of something highly elusive: you felt that the lady would soon return home, the boats vanish from the scene, the shadow shift, night begin to fall; that pleasure fades away, that life passes, and that the instant, illuminated by multiple and simultaneous plays of light, cannot be recaptured. I recognized yet another, admittedly different aspect of the Instant in a collection of watercolors on mythological themes, early works of Elstir, which also hung on the walls of this room. Society people with "advanced" views went "as far as" these early works, but no further. They were certainly not his finest achievement, but already the honesty with which the subject matter had been thought out took away its chill. So the Muses, for example, were depicted as though they were creatures belonging to a now fossilized species but also as figures who could easily have been encountered, in mythological times, in groups of two or three, along some mountain path in the evening. In some of the pictures a poet, depicted as the sort of specimen who would also have been of particular interest to a zoologist (on account of a rather sexless appearance), strolled with a Muse, like those creatures of different but kindred species in the natural world that move about together. In one of these watercolors, a poet, exhausted by a long journey in the mountains, has encountered a centaur, who, pitying his exhaustion, is carrying him home on his back. In others, the vast landscape (in which the mythical scene, the legendary heroes occupy a tiny place and seem almost lost) is rendered, from the mountaintops to the sea, with an exactitude that conveys the time of day not to the hour but to the very minute, by depicting the precise angle of the setting sun and the fleeting fidelity of the shadows. And by making the symbolic world of legend instantaneous in this way, the artist gives it a sort of lived historical reality, painting and relating it as a vivid instance of the past.

While I was examining Elstir's paintings, the arrival of the other guests had been signaled by repeated rings at the doorbell, which had lulled me into a sweet oblivion. But the silence that followed the rings at the door and had already lasted for some time finally succeeded—less rapidly, it is true—in rousing me from my musings, as the silence following Lindor's music wakes Bartholo from his sleep.[25] Fearing I might have been forgotten and that they had already passed to the table, I hurried to the drawing room. At the door of the Elstir collection I found a servant waiting for me—white-haired or powdered, I could not tell, and looking like a Spanish minister, though he treated me with the same respect he would have shown to a king. His manner gave me the impression that he would have waited for me for another hour, and I felt alarm at the thought that I had delayed dinner, especially since I had promised to be with M. de Charlus by eleven.

The Spanish minister conducted me to the drawing room (not before I had encountered, on the way, the footman plagued by our concierge; he was radiant with delight when I inquired after his fiancée, told me that, as it happened, they both had the day off tomorrow and would be able to spend the whole of it together, and sang the praises of Mme de Guermantes). I feared that I should find M. de Guermantes in a bad mood. On the contrary, he welcomed me with a delight that was obviously partly assumed and dictated by politeness, but was otherwise sincere, prompted both by his stomach, famished by the long delay, and by his awareness that his impatience was shared by the rest of his guests, who completely filled the room. I learned later that I had kept them waiting for nearly three-quarters of an hour. The Duc de Guermantes probably thought that it would do no harm to prolong the general torment for a couple of minutes, and that, since his politeness had driven him to postpone moving to the table for so long, it would be more consummate still if, by not having dinner announced immediately, he could persuade me that I was not late and had not kept people waiting. And so he asked me, as if we had an hour to kill before dinner and some of the guests had not yet arrived, what I thought of the Elstirs. But in the same breath, taking care not to let his hunger pangs become too obvious, and in order not to lose another second, he began, in concert with the Duchesse, to start introducing me to the guests. It was only then that I became aware (I, who until this evening—apart from my introductory spell in Mme Swann's salon—had been accustomed, in my mother's drawing room in Combray or Paris, to the patronizing or defensive gaze of straitlaced bourgeois ladies who treated me as a child) of a change of surroundings comparable to Parsifal's sudden introduction to the world of the flower-maidens.[26] The flower-maidens who surrounded me now, in extremely low-cut gowns (their naked flesh appearing on either side of a twisting spray of mimosa or the broad petals of a rose), greeted me only with long, caressing glances, as though shyness alone held them back from kissing me. Which is not to say that the majority of them were not highly respectable, morally speaking; the majority, but not all, for even the more virtuous among them did not share the revulsion my mother would have felt toward those of easier virtue. In the Guermantes world, vagary of conduct, denied by saintly friends in the face of the evidence, seemed to matter much less than the maintenance of social relations. People feigned ignorance of their hostess's sexual availability, provided that there were no embarrassing omissions on her guest list. Since the Duc paid little attention to his other guests (from whom he had long had no more to learn, and vice versa) but a great deal to me, whose particular brand of superiority was unfamiliar to him and inspired the sort of respect the great noblemen at the court of Louis XIV used to feel for bourgeois ministers, he clearly considered that my not knowing the people present was a matter of no importance—to me, if not to them—and although I was worried, on his account, about the impression I might make on them, he was thinking only of the impression they would make on me.

And the very first thing that happened was a miniature twofold imbroglio. Indeed, no sooner had I entered the drawing room than M. de Guermantes, without even giving me the opportunity to pay my respects to the Duchesse, led me—as though he wanted to give a pleasant surprise to the person in question, to whom he seemed to be saying, "Here's your friend; you see, I'm bringing him along by the scruff of his neck"—toward a lady of rather diminutive proportions. Well before the Duc had propelled me toward her, the large, soft, dark eyes of this lady had been turned in my direction, fixed upon me with the sort of knowing smile we address to an old friend who has perhaps not recognized us. Given that this was indeed the case with me and I could not remember for the life of me who she was, I averted my gaze as I moved toward her, in order not to have to respond until our introduction released me from the awkward situation. Meanwhile, the lady continued to maintain in precarious balance the smile she was fixing upon me. She seemed eager to be relieved of it, and to hear me say, "Ah, madame, of course! How happy Mama will be to hear that we've met again!" I was as impatient to know her name as she was to see that I did greet her with every sign of recognition, so that her smile, after being indefinitely prolonged like some sustained musical note, might finally drop. But M. de Guermantes so mismanaged our introduction (or so it seemed to me) that I ended up with the impression that he had named only me, and I was still left in ignorance as to the identity of this unknown friend I was supposed to know; nor did she have the good sense to name herself, so obvious did the grounds of our intimacy seem to her, however obscure they were to me. Indeed, when I drew close, she did not offer me her hand but clasped mine as if she had known me all her life, and spoke to me as if the happy memories to which her mind reverted were as much mine as hers. She told me how sorry Albert (her son, it seemed) would be not to have been present. I racked my brains for a school friend named Albert and could think only of Bloch, but this could not be Bloch's mother, since she had been dead for many years. I struggled in vain to imagine the past experience common to her and to me to which her thoughts were taking her back. But I could no more identify it through the jet-black translucence of the wide, soft pupils, which allowed only her smile to pierce the surface, than one can distinguish a landscape from behind a pane of blackened glass, even when the sun is blazing on it. She asked me whether my father was not working too hard, if I would like to go with Albert to the theater sometime, if I was in better health, and as my replies fumbled through the mental darkness I found myself in, and became distinct only when I explained that I was not feeling very well that evening, she drew up a chair for me herself, putting herself out in ways I had never known in other friends of my parents. The clue to my puzzlement was finally supplied by the Duc: "She thinks you're charming," he murmured in my ear. I somehow felt I had heard these words before. They were the words Mme de Villeparisis had spoken to my grandmother and me after we had made the acquaintance of the Princess of Luxembourg. The situation was now clear to me: the present lady had nothing in common with Mme de Luxembourg, but from the words uttered by the man who had served her up to me, I recognized what sort of species of creature I was dealing with. Someone of royal blood. She had never once heard of my family or myself, but, as a daughter of the noblest race and someone with the greatest fortune in the world (she was the daughter of the Prince of Parma and had married an equally princely cousin), she was always anxious, out of gratitude to her Creator, to prove to her neighbor, however poor or humble he might be, that she did not look down on him. And, indeed, I ought to have guessed this from her way of smiling, for I had already observed this sort of behavior when I saw the Princess of Luxembourg buying rye-bread rolls on the beach in Balbec to give to my grandmother, as though to a deer at the zoo. But this was only the second princess of royal blood to whom I had been presented, and I might have been excused for my failure to recognize in her the characteristic affability of the great. Besides, had not the great themselves gone out of their way to warn me not to overestimate this affability, since the Duchesse de Guermantes, who had gestured such lavish greetings to me at the Opéra, had looked so much askance when I acknowledged her in the street subsequently, like someone who has given a person a gold piece and feels that this releases her from any further obligation? As for M. de Charlus, his changes of mood were even more sharply contrasted. And as the reader will learn, I was later to know highnesses and majesties of a quite different sort, queens who play at being queens and speak not after the conventions of their kind, but like queens in Sardou's plays.[27]

If M. de Guermantes had been in so much haste to present me, it was because the presence of anyone not personally known to a royal personage is an intolerable state of affairs and must not continue for a second more than it has to. It was the same haste Saint-Loup had shown to be introduced to my grandmother. A further point: in a fragmentary survival of court life known as social etiquette, which, far from being superficial, operates an inside-out reversal through which it is the surface that becomes essential and profound, the Duc and Duchesse de Guermantes saw it as their duty (more incumbent upon them, more inflexible than the duties of charity, chastity, pity, and justice, which at least one of them all too often neglected) to make sure that when they addressed the Princess of Parma they hardly ever did so other than in the third person.

As a compensation for the visit to Parma that I had never made (and which I had wanted to make ever since certain Easter holidays well in the past now), meeting its Princess—who, I knew, owned the finest palazzo in that unique city, where in fact everything must be homogeneous, isolated as it was from the rest of the world within its polished walls, in the atmosphere, stifling as an airless summer evening on the piazza of a small Italian town, of its dense and cloying name—ought to have brought about a sudden revelation, in place of what I had tried so long to imagine, of all that was real about Parma, in a sort of fragmentary arrival there without ever having made the journey; it was, in terms of the algebra of my journey to the city of Giorgione,[28] something like a simple equation, with Parma as the unknown factor. But if, for years now, like a perfumer adding fragrance to a solid block of fat, I had been drenching this name, Princess of Parma, with the scent of thousands of violets, my efforts were merely rewarded, when I set eyes on the Princess, who until then I would have sworn must be no less than La Sanseverina herself,[29] by the onset of a further process (not completed, let me say, until a few months later), which consisted in expelling, by means of fresh chemical additives, all the essential oil of violets and all the Stendhalian perfume from her name, and replacing them with the image of a little dark lady, bent on good works, and so humbly amiable that it did not take more than a moment to sense the lofty pride from which such amiability stemmed. And though she was essentially similar to any other great lady, she was no more Stendhalian than, say, the rue de Parme in the Quartier de l'Europe,[30] which bears far less resemblance to the name of Parma than it does to the other, neighboring streets and reminds one less of the Charterhouse in which Fabrice dies than of the concourse in the Gare Saint-Lazare.

There were two explanations for her amiability. The first and more general one had to do with the way this daughter of kings had been brought up. Her mother (not merely related to all the royal families of Europe but also—in contrast to the ducal house of Parma—richer than any reigning princess) had instilled into her from her earliest childhood the arrogantly humble precepts of an evangelical snobbery; with the result that every line of her daughter's face, the curve of her shoulders, the movements of her arms seemed to repeat those precepts: "Never forget that if God has caused you to be born on the steps of a throne you must not make that an excuse for looking down upon those to whom Divine Providence has willed (praise the Lord) that you should be superior by birth and fortune. On the contrary, you must be kind to those of humble station. Your ancestors were Princes of Cleves and Juliers from the year 647; God in His bounty has decreed that you should hold the vast majority of the shares in the Suez Canal and three times as many Royal Dutch as Edmond de Rothschild; your pedigree, in a direct line, had been established by genealogists from the year 63 of the Christian Era; you have two empresses as sisters-in-law. So never speak to anyone as if you were mindful of these great privileges, not that they are unstable (for nothing can alter the antiquity of blood, and the world will always need oil), but because it is unnecessary to draw attention to the fact that you are of nobler birth than others, or that your investments are gilt-edged, since everyone knows this already. Support the needy. Give to all those whom the bounty of heaven has been gracious enough to put beneath you all that you can afford to give without debasing your rank—that is to say, help in the form of money, even tending to the sick, but of course never any invitations to your receptions, which would do them no good and, by diminishing your prestige, would detract from the effectiveness of your good deeds."

And so, even at times when she could not do good, the Princess endeavored to make it plain, or, rather, to let it be thought, by a whole external play of sign language, that she did not consider herself superior to the people she was with. She treated each of them with the charming politeness with which well-bred people treat their inferiors and was continually trying to oblige by pushing back her chair to make more room, holding my gloves, offering me all the helpful attention that a middle-class person would frown upon but which is willingly bestowed by sovereign ladies or, instinctively and out of professional habit, by trusty servants.

The other reason for the amiability shown me by the Princess of Parma was more specific, yet in no way dictated by some mysterious affection for me. But I did not have the opportunity to dwell on it at the time. For already the Duc, who seemed to be in a hurry to complete the round of introductions, had whisked me off to another of the flower-maidens. When I heard her name I mentioned that I had passed by her château, not far from Balbec. "Oh, I would have been so delighted to show you around," she replied, almost in a whisper, as though to emphasize her modesty, yet in a tone deliberately chosen to express her deep regret at the loss of an opportunity to enjoy so exceptional a pleasure, and she added, with a meaningful look: "I do so hope that another visit is not entirely out of the question. But I have to say that what would interest you even more is my aunt Brancas's château. It was built by Mansard,[31] and it's the jewel of the area." Not only would she herself have been happy to show me her place, but her aunt Brancas would have been no less delighted to do me the honors of hers, or so I was assured by this lady, who was evidently of the opinion that, especially at a time when the land looked as if it would pass into the hands of financiers with their vulgar habits, it was important that the great should maintain the lofty traditions of lordly hospitality, by issuing promises that did not commit them to anything. It was also because she was anxious, like everyone else in her world, to say the things that would give most pleasure to the person she was addressing, to give him the highest idea of himself, to make him think that he flattered people by writing to them, that his hosts were honored by his presence, that he was a most sought-after guest. The desire to give people this comforting picture of themselves does, it is true, sometimes exist even among the middle classes. They, too, can have the same amiable disposition, in the form of an individual quality compensating for some defect, if not, alas, in the case of the most reliable male friends among them, then at least in the most agreeable of the female ones. But with the middle classes, such a disposition flourishes only in isolated cases. In an important section of the aristocracy, on the contrary, this characteristic has ceased to be individual; cultivated by upbringing, sustained by the idea of a personal grandeur that need fear no humiliation, that knows no rival, that realizes that affability can put people at their ease and is happy to be affable, it has become the generic feature of a class. And even those whose personal shortcomings are too contrary for them to feel it in their hearts bear the unconscious trace of it in their words or gestures.

"She's a very goodhearted woman," said the Duc de Guermantes of the Princess of Parma, "and she knows how to play the *grande dame* better than anyone."

While I was being introduced to the ladies in the room, one of the gentlemen there had been showing constant signs of agitation: this was Comte Hannibal de Bréauté-Consalvi. Arriving late, he had not had time to find out who the other guests were, and when I entered the room, recognizing me as a guest who was not one of the Duchesse's regular circle and who must therefore have some extraordinary claim to admission, he settled his monocle beneath the vaulted arch of his eyebrow, in the firm belief that this would enable him to see what manner of man I was. He was aware that Mme de Guermantes had a "salon" (the invaluable prerogative of really superior women), which meant that from time to time she added to the people of her own set some celebrity who had lately come into the public eye after discovering a new cure or producing a masterpiece. The Faubourg Saint-Germain had not yet recovered from the shock of learning that the Duchesse had not been afraid to invite M. Detaille[32] to the reception given for the King and Queen of England. The more intelligent women of the Faubourg were not easily consolable for not having been invited, so deliciously exciting would it have been to come into contact with that strange genius. Mme de Courvoisier claimed that M. Ribot[33] had also been of the party, but this was mere invention, designed to make people believe that Oriane was plotting an embassy for her husband. And to top it all, M. de Guermantes, with a gallantry that put him in the same league as the Maréchal de Saxe,[34] had presented himself at the stage door of the Comédie-Française and begged Mlle de Reichenberg[35] to come and recite before the King, something she had duly done, which constituted an event without precedent in the long tradition of society receptions. As he recalled all these unexpected turns of event (and they had his entire approval, since he himself was an ornament to any salon and, in the same way as the Duchesse de Guermantes, but with the difference of gender, a figure who set the seal of distinction upon it) M. de Bréauté, when he asked himself who I could be, felt that the field of possibility was very wide. For an instant the name of M. Widor[36] passed through his mind, but he concluded that I was too young to be an organist, and M. Widor not sufficiently acclaimed to be received. It seemed more plausible to regard me simply as the new attaché at the Swedish Legation, who had been mentioned to him, and he was preparing to inquire about King Oscar, by whom he had several times been very hospitably received; but by the time the Duc introduced me and gave my name, M. de Bréauté, even though the name was completely unknown to him, had decided that since I was there I must be some sort of celebrity. It

was utterly typical of Oriane, who had the knack of attracting to her salon men who were in the public eye—one of them to a hundred of her
own, of course, otherwise the tone would have been lowered. Satisfied
on this point, M. de Bréauté began to lick his chops and to sniff the
air hungrily, his appetite whetted not only by the certainty of a good
dinner but by the character of the party, which my presence could not
fail to make interesting, and which would add spice to his table talk
next day, when he went to luncheon at the Duc de Chartres's. He had
not quite decided whether I was the man who had been making those
experiments with a serum against cancer, or the author of the new
"curtain raiser" currently in rehearsal at the Théâtre-Français, but, as a
great intellectual, a great collector of "travelers' tales," he kept constantly
bowing in my direction, sending me signs of mutual understanding,
smiles filtered through his monocle; either he had the mistaken notion
that someone of distinction would esteem him more highly if he could
manage to convey the illusion that for him, the Comte de Bréauté-
Consalvi, the privileges of the mind were no less worthy of respect than
those of birth, or he simply needed to express his satisfaction and
found it difficult to do so, in his ignorance of the language in which he
ought to address me; the overall impression was of someone who found
himself face-to-face with one of the "natives" of an undiscovered country on which his raft had landed, from whom, in the hope of gain, he
would endeavor, as he observed their customs with interest and made
sure he maintained demonstrations of friendship by uttering loud cries
of benevolence like themselves, to obtain ostrich eggs and spices in exchange for glass beads. Having responded as best I could to his joyous
satisfaction, I went on to shake hands with the Duc de Châtellerault,
whom I had already met at Mme de Villeparisis's, and who remarked
that she was a shrewd old bird. He was a Guermantes through and
through with his fair hair, his aquiline profile, the skin blemishes on his
cheeks, all of these traits of the Guermantes family portraits that have
come down to us from the sixteenth and seventeenth centuries. But
since I was no longer in love with the Duchesse, her reincarnation in
the features of a young man offered me no attraction. I read the hook
in the Duc de Châtellerault's nose as the signature of a painter whose

work I had long studied but who no longer interested me at all. I then said good evening also to the Prince de Foix and was rash enough to submit my knuckles to the viselike grip of the Prince von Faffenheim's German handshake, accompanied by an ironic or good-natured smile, from which they emerged the worse for wear; this was M. de Norpois's friend, who, thanks to the craze for nicknames dominant in this circle, was known so universally as Prince Von that he himself would sign his letters "Prince Von" or, when he was writing to his intimates, "Von." The abbreviation at least had the merit of being understandable, given his triple-barreled name. It was less easy to understand the reasons for replacing "Elizabeth" with "Lili" or "Bebeth," like the swarm of "Kiki"s that flourished in a very different social world. One can understand how people, idle and frivolous though they are in general, might have adopted "Quiou" in order not to waste the time it would have taken to say "Montesquiou." But it is less easy to see what they gained by nick-naming one of their cousins "Dinand" instead of "Ferdinand." It would nonetheless be wrong to suppose that, in the invention of nicknames, the Guermantes invariably proceeded by syllabic cuckooing. For instance, two sisters, the Comtesse de Montpeyroux and the Vicomtesse de Vélude, both of them enormously fat women, were never known to be addressed—without the least trace of annoyance on their part or of amusement on anyone else's, so ingrained was the habit—as anything other than "Petite" and "Mignonne" respectively. Mme de Guermantes, who adored Mme de Montpeyroux, would, if the latter had been seriously ill, have asked her sister with tears in her eyes if "Petite" was feeling horrible. Mme de l'Éclin, who parted her hair in the middle and brought it down to cover her ears entirely, was always known as "Starving Belly."[37] Sometimes an "a" was simply added to the surname or first name of the husband to designate the wife. For instance, the most miserly, most sordid, most inhuman man in the Faubourg was named Raphael; his charming lady, his flower springing also from the rock, always signed herself "Raphaela." But these are just a few specimens of many, many name-games to which we can always return if need be, and explain some of them.

I then asked the Duc to introduce me to the Prince d'Agrigente. "You mean to tell me that you haven't met our wonderful Gri-Gri!"

he exclaimed and gave M. d'Agrigente my name. The Prince's own, so often dropped by Françoise, had always seemed to me like a transparent sheet of glass, through which I could see, struck by the slanting rays of a golden sun on the shore of the violet sea, the pink cubes of an ancient city of which I did not doubt that the Prince—who happened by some brief miracle to be passing through Paris—was himself the actual sovereign, as luminously Sicilian and shiny with age as the city itself. Alas, the vulgar bumbler to whom I was introduced, and who wheeled around to bid me good evening with a heavy-handed nonchalance he mistook for elegance, was as remote from his name as he was from a work of art he might have owned without betraying any reflection of it, or without ever having looked at it. The Prince d'Agrigente was so entirely devoid of anything princely, anything remotely reminiscent of Agrigento, that one began to imagine that it was his name alone, utterly distinct from himself, bound in no way to his person, that had been able to draw into itself anything vaguely poetic there might have been about this man, as about any other, and then to have imprisoned it in its magic syllables. If such a process had occurred, then it had done so most successfully, for there remained not an atom of charm to be elicited from this kinsman of the Guermantes. With the result that he found himself at one and the same time the only man in the world who was the Prince d'Agrigente and, of all the men in the world, the one who was perhaps least so. For all that, he was very happy to be what he was, but as a banker is happy to hold a number of shares in a mine, without caring whether the mine answers to the charming name of Ivanhoe or Primrose or is simply called Mine Number One. These introductions have taken so long to recount, but in fact they only lasted a few moments after my entry into the room; as they were drawing to a close—and Mme de Guermantes was saying to me in an almost imploring voice, "I'm sure Basin is tiring you out, dragging you around from person to person; we want you to meet our friends, but we are particularly anxious not to tire you. We so much want you to come again often"—the Duc, with a somewhat awkward and timorous gesture, gave the signal (which he would gladly have given at any point during the hour I had spent with the Elstirs) for dinner to be served.

I should mention that one of the guests was still missing, M. de

Grouchy, whose wife, née Guermantes, had arrived on her own, her husband being due to come straight from the country, where he had been shooting all day. This M. de Grouchy, a descendant of the First Empire Grouchy, of whom it has been falsely said that his absence at the start of the Battle of Waterloo was the principal cause of Napoleon's defeat, came from an excellent family, though not excellent enough for those obsessed with blue blood. Thus the Duc de Guermantes, who was to prove less fastidious about such matters in later life in regard to himself, was in the habit of saying to his nieces, "What a misfortune for that poor Mme de Guermantes"—the Vicomtesse de Guermantes, Mme de Grouchy's mother—"that she has never succeeded in marrying off any of her children." "But, Uncle, the eldest girl married M. de Grouchy." "I don't call that a husband! But it seems that your uncle François has proposed to the youngest one, so perhaps they won't all be left to live as old maids."

No sooner had the order to serve dinner been given than, with a vast gyratory swish, multiple and simultaneous, the double doors of the dining room swung open; a butler who looked like a court chamberlain bowed before the Princess of Parma to announce, *"Madame est servie,"* in the same tone of voice he would have used to say, "Madame is in her death throes"; this, however, did nothing to cast gloom over the party, for it was with the sprightly air of summer frolics at Robinson[38] that the couples advanced behind one another toward the dining room, separating only when they reached their places and the footmen settled them in their seats; last of all, Mme de Guermantes advanced toward me to be taken in to dinner, without my feeling the least shadow of possible timidity, for, like a huntress whose great muscular dexterity has given her a natural grace of movement, and no doubt observing that I had placed myself on the wrong side of her, she pivoted round me so skillfully that I found her arm resting on my own and fell quite naturally into her rhythm of precise and noble deportment. I yielded to this all the more readily because the Guermantes attached no more importance to it than a truly learned man does to his learning, with the result that one is less intimidated in his company than in that of an ignoramus; other doors swung open to admit the steaming soup, as though the dinner were taking place in an artfully contrived puppet theater, where, at a signal from the puppet master, the late arrival of the young guest set all the machinery in motion.

The signal from the Duc that had set in motion this vast, ingenious, obedient, and sumptuous human clockwork had been timid, not majestically imposing. As far as I was concerned, the indecisiveness of the gesture did not detract from the effect of the spectacle it commanded. For I sensed that what had made it hesitant and uneasy was the fear of letting me see that they had been waiting only for me to begin dinner, and that they had been waiting for a long time, in the same way that Mme de Guermantes was afraid that, after I had looked at so many pictures, a continuous flow of introductions would tire me out and prevent me from relaxing in their company. So that it was the absence of grandeur in this gesture that disclosed the Duc's true grandeur and his indifference to the splendor of his surroundings, his consideration for a guest, however insignificant, whom he wished to honor. It was not that there was anything particularly extraordinary about M. de Guermantes in many ways, nor was he exempt from the absurd foibles of a man with too much money or from the arrogance one would expect from an upstart, which he certainly was not. But just as a public official or a priest sees his own humble talents multiplied to infinity (as a wave is by the whole mass of sea behind it) by the forces that stand behind him, the machinery of the French government or the Catholic church, so M. de Guermantes was carried along by that other force, the genteel manners of the aristocracy in their truest form. This courteous gentility excluded a great many people. Mme de Guermantes would not have admitted Mme de Cambremer or M. de Forcheville to her society. But the moment anyone appeared eligible for admission to the Guermantes circle (as was the case with me), this courtesy disclosed a wealth of hospitable simplicity even more splendid, if such a thing is possible, than those historic rooms and their marvelous furniture.

When he wished to give pleasure to someone, by skillfully turning to advantage the particular circumstances and place, M. de Guermantes saw to it that the person in question felt he was the center of attention. No doubt at Guermantes his "distinctions" and "favors" would have assumed another form. He would have ordered his carriage to take me for a drive alone with himself before dinner. Such as they were, there was something touching about his attentions, as there is, when one reads the memoirs of the period, about the courtesy of Louis XIV when he responds in a kindly manner, with a smile and slight bow, to someone who has come to solicit his favor. At the same time, we need to bear in mind that, in both instances, such politeness did not extend beyond the strict sense of the word.

Louis XIV (much as he is reproached for his scant regard for etiquette by those of his contemporaries who were obsessed with true nobility, so much so that, according to Saint-Simon, he ranked very low as a king, compared with Philippe de Valois, Charles V, and the like) had the most meticulous instructions drawn up in order that princes of the blood and ambassadors should know to what sovereigns they ought to give precedence. In certain cases, when agreement cannot be reached, a compromise solution is provided: the son of Louis XIV, Monseigneur, will receive such-and-such a sovereign out of doors, in the open, so that it may not be said that in entering the palace one of them had preceded the other; and the Elector Palatine, entertaining the Duc de Chevreuse at dinner, in order not to let his guest take precedence, pretends to be taken ill and dines with him lying down, thus solving the difficulty. When M. le Duc avoids the occasions on which he must wait upon Monsieur, the latter, on the advice of the King, his brother, who is deeply attached to him, finds some excuse for making his cousin attend his levee and forcing him to put on the royal shirt. But as soon as deeper feelings are involved, matters of the heart, this sort of duty, so inflexible when etiquette alone prevails, changes entirely. A few hours after the death of this brother, one of the people he loved most dearly, when Monsieur was "still warm" (as the Duc de Montfort puts it), Louis XIV is to be found singing tunes from operas, amazed that the Duchesse de Bourgogne, who can scarcely conceal her grief, should be looking so melancholy, and, in an attempt to restore gaiety to his court at once, ordering the Duc de Bourgogne to start a game of *brelan* in order to get his courtiers back to the card tables. Now, M. de Guermantes showed a similar contrast, not only in his social and more public activities, but in his most spontaneous utterances, his preoccupations, his daily routine: the Guermantes were no more prone to grief than other mortals, and it could even be said that they were really less sensitive to it; yet one saw their names every day in the social columns of the *Gaulois* on account of the incredible number of funerals at which they would have felt it culpable not to have their presence recorded. Like a traveler discovering the almost identical turf-roofed houses and the terraces that may have greeted the eyes of Xenophon or Saint Paul, I discovered still intact after two centuries in the manners of M. de Guermantes, a man of touching kindness and unspeakable inflexibility, a slave to the most petty obligations yet not to the most sacred commitments, the same aberration that typified court life under Louis XIV, which removes scruples of conscience from the domain of the affections and morality and transforms them into questions of pure form.

Another reason for the friendliness shown me by the Princess of Parma, a more specific one again, was that she was convinced beforehand that everything she saw at the Duchesse de Guermantes's, people and things alike, was superior to anything she had herself. It is true that she behaved in the same way at everyone else's house: the simplest dish, the most ordinary flowers sent her into raptures, and she would ask if she might send round her head cook or head gardener the next morning to copy out the recipe or to examine the species of flower in question, to the chagrin of both cook and gardener, who were highly paid, kept their own carriages, and, more important, jealously guarded their professional reputations; they found it deeply humiliating to have to come and inquire about a dish they despised, or to adopt a variety of carnation that was not half so fine or so variegated, did not produce so large a blossom as the ones they had long been growing for the Princess. But if, on the one hand, her astonishment at the sight of the most ordinary things was contrived and intended to show that her superior rank and riches did not spur her to the arrogant pride forbidden by her early instructors—masked by her mother and intolerable in the eyes of her Creator—on the other, she regarded the Duchesse de Guermantes's drawing-room, in all sincerity, as a privileged place in which she could move only from surprise to delight. The Guermantes were certainly different from the rest of society (they were more precious and rare), but not enough to justify such a reaction. My first impression of them had been quite the opposite: I had found them very ordinary, just like anyone else, but this was because, before actually meeting them, I had seen them, as I saw Balbec, Florence, and Parma, as magical names. And of course all the women in this drawing room, whom I had imagined as Dresden figures, turned out to be like the great majority of women. But, in the same way as Balbec or Florence, the Guermantes, after initially disappointing the imagination by having more in common with the rest of humanity than with their name, were subsequently capable, though to a lesser degree, of presenting various distinctive characteristics as food for thought. Their actual physique, the color (a peculiar pink blending at times into purple) of their skin, a particular sort of almost luminous, fine blond hair, even in the men, massed in soft, golden tufts, halfway between wall lichen and cat fur (a strikingly bright feature, which went hand in hand with a certain intellectual brightness, for, if people spoke of a Guermantes complexion, Guermantes hair, they also spoke of Guermantes wit, as of the wit of the Mortemart family—a certain social quality of superior refinement dating back well before Louis XIV and all the more widely recognized in that they promulgated it themselves), all this meant that, in the very core material, however precious it might be, of the aristocratic society in which they were to be found embedded here and there, the Guermantes remained recognizable, easy to detect and to follow, like the streaks of paleness in jasper and onyx, or, better still, like the supple waves of the tresses of light whose unbraided hairs run like flexible rays inside moss agate.

The Guermantes—those, at least, who were worthy of the name— were not only graced with an exquisite quality of flesh, of hair, of limpid gaze, but had a way of holding themselves, of walking, of bowing, of looking at you before shaking your hand, which made them as different in all these respects from any ordinary member of fashionable society as he himself was from a peasant in a smock. And despite their affability one was apt to think: "Is it not true that they have the right, though they do not show it, when they see us walk, bow, leave a room, or do any of the things that, when done by them, become as graceful as the flight of a swallow or a swaying rose, to think, 'These people are of a different breed from us, and we are the princes of the universe'?" Later on, I realized that the Guermantes did indeed think of me as belonging to a different breed, but one that aroused their envy, because I possessed merits of which I was unaware, and which they professed to regard as the only things that mattered. Later still, I came to feel that this profession of faith was only half sincere, and that in their responses to things admiration and envy went hand in hand with scorn and astonishment. The bodily flexibility peculiar to the Guermantes was twofold: on the one hand, it was always in action, at every moment, so that if, for example, a male of the Guermantes species was about to bow to a lady, he offered a silhouette of himself in which there was a precarious balance between asymmetry of movement and a nervous attempt to compensate for it, one leg dragging a little, either deliberately or because it had been broken so often in the hunting field that, in its effort to keep pace with the other leg, it caused a slump in the trunk of the body, which was counterpoised by the upward thrust of one shoulder, while the monocle was inserted in the eye to raise the eyebrow just as the tuft of hair on the forehead fell forward in the bowing movement; on the other hand, like the shape that wave, wind, and wake have permanently bequeathed to a shell or a boat, the other manifestation of this flexibility was, so to speak, stylized into a sort of fixed mobility, curving the arched nose, which—beneath the blue, protruding eyes, above the overly thin lips, from which, in the women, there emerged a husky voice—recalled the legendary origin fawningly attributed in the sixteenth century by parasitic and Hellenizing genealogists to this family, ancient beyond question, but not to the extent they claimed when they gave as its source the mythological coupling of a nymph and a divine bird.

The Guermantes were no less odd from the intellectual than from the physical point of view. Apart from Prince Gilbert (the husband of "Marie-Gilbert," a man of antiquated ideas, who made his wife sit on his left when they went out in their carriage because her blood, though royal, was inferior to his own, and who was in any case an exception, a laughingstock to the rest of his family when he was not present, and the butt of endlessly invented anecdotes), the Guermantes, though they moved among the cream of the aristocracy, affected to set no store by nobility. The theories of the Duchesse de Guermantes, who, admittedly, by virtue of being a Guermantes, had become something rather different and more appealing, set intelligence so far above everything else, and were so socialist politically, that one wondered where in her mansion the genie in charge of the aristocratic way of life had room to hide; always invisible, yet clearly lurking about the place, in the entrance hall, in the drawing room, in her dressing room, this genie reminded the servants of this woman who did not believe in titles to address her as "Madame la Duchesse," and reminded the woman herself, who cared only for reading and was no respecter of persons, to go out to dinner with her sister-in-law when the clock struck eight, and to put on a low-cut dress for the occasion.

The same family genie presented Mme de Guermantes with a picture of the social duties of duchesses (or at least of the grandest among them, who, like herself, were also multimillionaires), of hours sacrificed to boring tea parties, society dinners, and festivities, when they might have been spent reading interesting books, as tiresome necessities comparable to rainy days, and to which Mme de Guermantes acquiesced with a sparkle of rebellious humor, but without going so far as to examine the reasons for her acquiescence. Yet the curious coincidence by which Mme de Guermantes's butler addressed her always as "Mme la Duchesse" did not appear to shock this woman who believed only in the intellect. It never occurred to her to ask him to address her simply as "madame." Giving her the utmost benefit of the doubt, it was just credible that absentmindedness caused her to catch only the word "madame" and that the other words appended to it passed unheard. But though she might feign deafness, she was not dumb. And of course, whenever she had a message to give to her husband, she would say to the butler, "Remind M. le Duc . . ."

The family genie had other functions as well, one of which was to prompt them to hold forth on morality. It is true that there were Guermantes who cultivated intellect and Guermantes who cultivated morals, and the two tendencies were usually distinct. But the former—including a Guermantes who had forged checks, had cheated at cards, and was the most delightful of them all, open to every new and plausible idea–had more intelligent things to say about morals than the latter, and in the same mode as Mme de Villeparisis, when the family genie chose to express itself through the lips of the old lady. When it expressed itself through them, you would suddenly find the Guermantes adopting a tone almost as antiquated as, as good-natured as, and (because of their superior charm) more touching than that of the Marquise, to say of a servant, "One feels that she is basically very sound, not at all a common girl; she must come from a decent family, a girl who's never got into trouble, certainly." At such moments, the family genie displayed itself as a tone of voice. But at times it manifested itself in a person's bearing, too, in facial expression, the same in the Duchesse as in her grandfather the Maréchal, a sort of mercurial convulsion (like that of the Serpent, the genius of the Carthaginian Barca family)[39] which had more than once made my heart jump on those morning walks of mine when, before I had recognized Mme de Guermantes, I could feel her eyes fixed upon me from inside a small cheese shop. This genie had intervened in a situation that was far from insignificant not merely for the Guermantes but for the Courvoisiers, a rival branch of the family and, though from as noble stock as the Guermantes (it was in fact to his Courvoisier grandmother that the Guermantes attributed the strong bias shown by the Prince de Guermantes to speak of birth and titles as the only things that mattered), their opposite in every sense. Not only did the Courvoisiers not assign to intelligence the same importance as the Guermantes, they had a different notion of what it was. For a Guermantes (even a stupid one), to be intelligent meant to have a scathing tongue, to be capable of making tart comments, of not taking no for an answer; it also meant the ability to hold one's own in painting, music, and architecture alike, and to speak English. The Courvoisiers had a less exalted notion of intelligence, and unless one belonged to their world, being intelligent came close to meaning "having probably murdered one's parents." For them, intelligence was the sort of burglar's jimmy by means of which people one did not know from Adam forced their way into the most distinguished salons, and the Courvoisiers knew to their cost that you always ended up ruing the day you allowed people of "that sort" into your circle. The most trivial statements made by intelligent people outside the "society" world met with the Courvoisiers' systematic distrust. When someone once happened to remark, "But Swann is younger than Palamède," Mme de Gallardon had retorted, "That's what *he* told you, and, coming from him, you may be sure it's in his interest to have said so." Better still, when someone remarked, in relation to two highly distinguished foreign ladies whom the Guermantes were entertaining, that one of them had been received first because she was the elder, Mme de Gallardon had inquired, "But is she really the elder?," not in a positive manner, indicating that such persons did not have an age, but as if they were in all likelihood devoid of any civil or religious status, any familiar mold, and were therefore more or less of an age, like two kittens from the same litter that only a veterinarian would be able to distinguish from each other. Yet, in a sense, the Courvoisiers, more than the Guermantes, preserved the integrity of the titled class, through both the narrowness of their minds and the malevolence of their hearts. Just as the Guermantes (for whom, below the royal families and a few others like the Lignes, the La Trémoïlles, and their kind, all the others were a vague jumble of small fry) were insolent toward people of ancient stock who lived in the vicinity of Guermantes, precisely because they paid no attention to the second-rate qualities so prized by the Courvoisiers, the absence of such qualities was of little matter in their eyes. Certain women who did not enjoy a particularly exalted rank in their native provinces but had made brilliant marriages and were rich, pretty, the darlings of duchesses, became highly desirable, elegant imports in Paris, where people are never particularly awake to who one's "father and mother" were. It might even happen, though this was rare, that such women were received, through the good offices of the Princess of Parma, or by virtue of their own attractions, by certain members of the Guermantes family. But the indignation with which the Courvoisiers regarded them was relentless. To meet with such people between five and six in the afternoon at their cousin's, people with whose relatives their own did not care to be seen associating at home in the Perche, became a growing source of rage and endless ranting. For instance, the minute the charming Comtesse G— entered the Guermantes drawing room, Mme de Villebon's face assumed exactly the expression required of it had she been compelled to recite the line

And if one alone is left, then that one will be me,[40]

a line that, as it happened, was unknown to her. Almost every Monday, this Courvoisier had tucked into cream-stuffed éclairs within a few feet of the Comtesse G—, but to no consequence. And Mme de Villebon confessed in secret that she was at a loss to understand how her cousin Guermantes could receive into her society a woman who, in Châteaudun, did not belong even to the ranks of the second-best. "Why my cousin should be so particular about whom she knows, I really can't imagine—what *does* she think she's about!" was Mme de Villebon's conclusion, accompanied by a change of facial expression, this time smilingly sardonic in its exasperation, which, in a game of charades, would have merited another line of verse, no more familiar to her than the first:

Thanks to the gods! My misfortune exceeds my hopes.[41]

And let us anticipate events to comment that the *persévérance* (which rhymes with *espérance* in the following line) shown by Mme de Villebon in snubbing Mme G— was not entirely without its effect. In the eyes of Mme G— it endowed Mme de Villebon with a distinction so exalted (and so imaginary) that, when the time came for Mme G—'s daughter— the prettiest girl, and the wealthiest one, too, in the ballrooms of that season—to marry, people were astonished to see her turn down a whole string of dukes. And this was because her mother, remembering the weekly humiliations she had to endure on the rue de Grenelle in memory of Châteaudun, could conceive of only one possible husband for her daughter—a Villebon son.

A single point at which the Guermantes and the Courvoisiers converged was the art—and such a diverse art it is—of keeping one's distance. The Guermantes way of doing this was not entirely uniform throughout the family. And yet, to take an example, all of them—all those who were true Guermantes, that is—when you were introduced to them, indulged in a kind of ceremony, almost as though by holding out their hands to you they were performing an act as weighty as conferring a knighthood upon you. The moment he heard your name uttered by the person introducing you, a Guermantes, even a twenty-year-old Guermantes, but treading already in the footsteps of his elders, let fall upon you, as though he had not made up his mind to acknowledge you, a gaze that was generally blue and always as cold as a steel blade, seemingly destined to plunge into the deepest recesses of your heart. And this is just what the Guermantes imagined themselves to be doing, since they all regarded themselves as first-class psychologists. They also felt that this inspection intensified the affability of the greeting that was to follow it, which would not be delivered without a shrewd idea of your worth. All this occurred at a distance from yourself that would have been too close for a passage of arms, but seemed immense for a handshake, and was as chilling in the latter case as it would have been in the former, so that when the Guermantes in question, after a lightning tour of the last hiding places of your soul and your integrity, had deemed you worthy to consort with him in future, his hand, directed toward you at the end of an arm stretched out to its full length, seemed to be presenting a rapier for single combat, and the hand was in fact placed so far in front of the Guermantes himself at that moment that when he proceeded to bow his head it was difficult to distinguish whether it was yourself or his own hand he was acknowledging. Some of the Guermantes, who lacked any sense of moderation or were incapable of refraining from repeating themselves incessantly, went even further and repeated this ceremony every time they met you. Given that they no longer needed to proceed with the preliminary psychological scrutiny for which the "family genie" had delegated its powers to them, and whose findings they had presumably kept in mind, the persistence of the delving gaze preceding the handshake could be explained only in terms of an automatic reflex the gaze had acquired, or by some hypnotic power they believed themselves to possess. The Courvoisiers, whose physique was different, had tried in vain to adopt the same penetrating gaze and had been forced to fall back upon a haughty starchiness or a hurried offhandedness. On the other hand, it was from the Courvoisiers that a rare handful of Guermantes women seemed to have borrowed the feminine form of greeting. So that, when you were presented to one of them, she made you a sweeping bow in which she carried toward you, almost at an angle of forty-five degrees, her head and bust, while the rest of her body (which was very tall) up to the pivot point of her belt remained stationary. But no sooner had she projected the upper part of her person toward you in this way than she thrust it backward, beyond the vertical, in a brusque withdrawal of roughly equal length. This subsequent reversal neutralized what seemed to have been conceded to you; the ground you believed yourself to have gained did not even remain with you, as in a duel; the original positions were retained. The same annulment of affability through retreat into distance (originating with the Courvoisiers and intended to show that the initial advances made were no more than a momentary feint) was equally evident in the letters you received from ladies of both the Courvoisier and Guermantes families, and particularly in the early days of acquaintance with them. The "body" of the letter might contain the sort of things you would be likely to write only to a friend, but you would have been hard put to it to see yourself as a friend of the lady in question, since the letter would open with *"Monsieur"* and end with *"Croyez, monsieur, à mes sentiments distingués."* Yet, between this cold opening and the icy formula of conclusion, which altered the meaning of everything else, there might (if it was in answer to a letter of condolence) be a series of the most touching accounts of the grief experienced by the Guermantes lady at the loss of her sister, of the closeness that had existed between them, of the beauty of the place where she was staying, of the consolation she derived from her delightful grandchildren—in short, it was simply a letter such as one finds in printed collections, the intimate character of which implied no more intimacy between yourself and the writer than if she had been Pliny the Younger or Mme de Simiane.[42]

It is true that certain Guermantes ladies wrote to you from the first as "My dear friend," or "Dear friend"—and these were not inevitably the most unaffected of them, but, rather, those who, living among kings and being at the same time women of "easy virtue," assumed in their pride the certainty that everything that came from them gave pleasure, and in their corruption the habit of not grudging you any of the satisfactions they had to offer. Yet, since to have had a common great-great-grandmother in the reign of Louis XIII was enough for a young Guermantes to be able to refer to the Marquise de Guermantes as "Aunt Adam," the Guermantes were so numerous that even in simple rituals, like the form of salutation given to a newcomer, for example, they had a whole repertory of different forms. Each subgroup of any refinement had its own ritual, and it was handed down from parents to children like a recipe for a healing poultice or a special way of making jam. Thus we have seen Saint-Loup ready to unleash his handshake in an almost involuntary gesture as soon as he heard one's name, without any concomitant eye movement, without any additional form of greeting. Any unfortunate commoner who happened to be presented to a member of the Saint-Loup subgroup for some particular reason—though this rarely occurred—would scratch his head over this abrupt and minimal greeting, with its deliberately adopted stance of nonrecognition, wondering what it was that this Guermantes (male or female) had against him. And he would be mightily surprised to learn that the Guermantes in question had thought fit to make a special point of writing to the person responsible for introducing them, in order to tell him how delighted he or she had been with the stranger and what a pleasure it would be to meet him again. As idiosyncratic as this mechanical gesture of Saint-Loup was the rush of complicated hopping and skipping practiced by the Marquis de Fierbois (condemned as ludicrous by M. de Charlus), or the gravely measured paces of the Prince de Guermantes. But, given the sheer size of the corps de ballet involved, it is not possible to describe here the richness of this Guermantes choreography.

To return to the lively antipathy which set the Courvoisiers against the Duchesse de Guermantes, the former might have had the consolation of feeling sorry for her as long as she was still unmarried, for at that stage of her life she was by no means wealthy. Unfortunately, a sort of smoky haze of its own peculiar kind had always enveloped and concealed from view the wealth of the Courvoisiers, which, however great it might be, remained obscure. If an extremely wealthy daughter of the Courvoisier family married very advantageously, it did her little good; it was invariably the case that the young couple had no house of their own in Paris, would "descend on" their in-laws there, and spend the rest of the year in the provinces, in the midst of a society that was unadulterated but dull. Whereas Saint-Loup, who had almost nothing to his name but debts, dazzled Doncières with his carriages and horses, a Courvoisier who was rolling in money always took the tram. And (though many years earlier, of course) a Guermantes of the opposite sex, Mlle de Guermantes (Oriane), who had hardly a penny, created more of a stir by the way she dressed than all the Courvoisiers put together. The very outrageousness of her remarks was a sort of advertisement for her style of dressing and doing her hair. She had had the audacity to say to the Russian Grand Duke, "Well, sir, it seems that you would like to have Tolstoy assassinated?" at a dinner party to which none of the Courvoisiers, who knew next to nothing about Tolstoy, had been invited. They knew even less about the Greek authors, if we may judge by the example of the Dowager Duchesse de Gallardon (mother-in-law of the Princesse de Gallardon, herself a young girl at the time), whom Oriane had not honored with a single visit in all of five years, who replied to someone who had asked why Oriane failed to put in an appearance, "It seems that she recites Aristotle"—meaning Aristophanes—"in society. I won't have that sort of thing in my house!"

One can imagine how greatly this "sally" by Mme de Guermantes on the subject of Tolstoy, if it infuriated the Courvoisiers, commanded the admiration of the Guermantes and, beyond them, everyone who was not merely closely but even remotely attached to them. The Dowager Comtesse d'Argencourt, née Seineport, who received almost everyone because she was a bluestocking, and, in the face of her son's terrible snobbery, passed on the remark to her literary friends with the comment, "You know, Oriane de Guermantes is as sharp as a needle and clever as a monkey, a widely gifted woman who produces watercolors worthy of a great painter and better poetry than most great poets; and she couldn't come from a better family: her grandmother was Mlle de Montpensier, and she's the eighteenth Oriane de Guermantes, without any misalliance; it's the purest, the oldest blood in the whole of France." And so the bogus men of letters, the half-baked intellectuals entertained by Mme d'Argencourt, picturing Oriane de Guermantes, whom they would never have the opportunity to know personally, as something more wonderful and more extraordinary than the Princess Bedr-el-Budur,[43] not only felt ready to die for her when they learned that so noble a person worshipped Tolstoy above all others, but also felt their minds renewed with fresh strength in their love of Tolstoy, in their will to resist tsarism. These liberal ideas of theirs might well have become enfeebled, they might have begun to doubt the superiority of them, no longer daring to confess to them, when, suddenly, along came Mme de Guermantes herself—that is to say, a girl of such unmistakable culture and authority, who wore her hair flat on her forehead (something no Courvoisier would ever have dreamed of doing)—and gave them this strong boost. A certain number of things, good or bad in themselves, gain enormously in this way by receiving the support of people who have authority over us. For instance, among the Courvoisiers, the rituals of civil behavior in the street consisted in a certain manner of greeting people, very unbecoming and far from civil in itself, which was nevertheless recognized as the distinguished way of bidding someone good day, with the result that everyone else, effacing their natural smiles of greeting, forced themselves to imitate these frigid gymnastics. But the Guermantes in general and Oriane in particular, even though they were thoroughly conversant with these rituals, did not hesitate, if they caught sight of you from a carriage, to greet you with a friendly wave, and in a drawing room, leaving the Courvoisiers to give their stiff, self-conscious bows, they themselves bowed in the most charming way, held out their hands as though to an old friend with a smile in their blue eyes, so that suddenly, thanks to the Guermantes, the substance of stylish manners, previously rather dry and empty, was enhanced by everything that people would have naturally wished it to be but had forced themselves to shut out, a true welcome, an expression of genuine friendliness, something spontaneous. In a similar fashion, but by a process of rehabilitation which in this case is less easy to justify, people who are most prone to an instinctive taste for bad music and for tunes, however trite, that have something easy and alluring about them, manage to stifle this penchant of theirs by schooling themselves in symphonic music. But once they have arrived at this point, when they find a musician like Richard Strauss, whose dazzling orchestral palette they quite rightly admire, adopting the most vulgar motifs with an indulgence worthy of Auber, the original preferences of these people in the hands of so high an authority suddenly find a justification that delights them, and when they listen to *Salome* they have no qualms about going into ecstasies, and with a twofold gratitude, about the sort of thing it would now be inadmissible for them to enjoy in *Les Diamants de la couronne*.[44]

Whether it was authentic or not, Mlle de Guermantes's heckling remark to the Grand Duke, peddled from house to house, provided an opportunity to talk about the excessive elegance of Oriane's style of dress at the dinner party in question. But if such splendor (and this is precisely what made it inaccessible to the Courvoisiers) springs not from wealth but from extravagance, then the latter nevertheless lasts longer if it is supported by the former, which allows it to come fully into its own with all lights ablaze. Now, given the principles openly paraded not only by Oriane but by Mme de Villeparisis—namely, that nobility is of no importance, that it is ridiculous to concern oneself with rank, that money does not mean happiness, that intellect, feeling, talent are the only things that matter—the Courvoisiers were justified in hoping that, as a result of the formative influence of the Marquise, Oriane would marry someone who was not a society figure, an artist, a former criminal, a tramp, a freethinker, and that she would join the ranks, for good and all, of people the Courvoisiers referred to as having gone "wildly astray." Their expectation was all the more justified because Mme de Villeparisis, who was at that time experiencing an awkward crisis socially (none of the brilliant personalities I was to meet in her salon had at that point started to frequent it again), made no bones about displaying her intense horror of the society that excluded her. Even when she spoke of her nephew the Prince de Guermantes, whom she did still see, she could not taunt him enough for his infatuation with his noble birth. But the moment it became a matter of finding a husband for

Oriane, the operation was no longer guided by the principles paraded by aunt and niece, but by the mysterious "family genie." As unerringly as if Mme de Villeparisis and Oriane had never discussed anything but sources of income and family pedigrees as opposed to matters of literary quality and evaluation of character, and as if for a few days the Marquise had been—as she would be in the end—dead and lying in her coffin in the Combray church, where each member of the family became simply a Guermantes, devoid of individuality or first names (as attested by the single "G" in purple surmounted by the ducal coronet on the extensive black pall), it was on the wealthiest and the most nobly born, on the most eligible man in the Faubourg Saint-Germain, on the eldest son of the Duc de Guermantes, the Prince des Laumes, that the family genie had directed the sights of the intellectual, the defiant, the evangelical Mme de Villeparisis. And for two hours, on the day of the wedding, Mme de Villeparisis was at home to all the noble persons she was accustomed to pour scorn upon and whom she did scorn in the company of the few close middle-class friends she had invited and among whom the Prince des Laumes immediately left his visiting card, only to sever connections with them the following year. And as a final disaster as far as the Courvoisiers were concerned, the same maxims about intellect and talent as the sole markers of social superiority began to be trotted out once again in the household of the Princesse des Laumes immediately after her marriage. And in this respect, incidentally, the attitude maintained by Saint-Loup when he was living with Rachel, frequenting friends of Rachel, and hoping to marry Rachel, whatever horror it provoked in the family, was less fraught with falsehood than that of the Guermantes young misses in general, in the way they sang the praises of the intellect, barely allowing the possibility that anyone could cast doubt upon the equality of mankind, all of which led, when it came to the point, to the same result as if they had clung to the opposite principles—which is to say, to marrying an extremely wealthy duke. Saint-Loup, on the contrary, acted on what he believed, which led people to say that he was heading for a sorry downfall. Certainly, from a moral standpoint, Rachel left a lot to be desired. But it is by no means certain, had she been no better than what she was but had ranked as a duchess or a millionairess, that Mme de Marsantes would not have been in favor of the match.

However, to return to Mme de Laumes (shortly afterward, on the death of her father-in-law, to become the Duchesse de Guermantes), it was an added disaster for the Courvoisiers that the theories of the young Princesse, by remaining confined to her speech, should in no way have guided her conduct; for this philosophy (if that is what we are to call it) did absolutely nothing to detract from the elegance of the Guermantes salon. No doubt, all those who were not received by Mme de Guermantes imagined that it was because they were not clever enough, and there was a rich American lady who had never owned a single book apart from an ancient little copy, never opened, of Parny's poems,[45] set in place on one of the tables in her small drawing room because it belonged to the same period as the furniture, whose way of showing what store she set by the things of the mind was to rivet her gaze on the Duchesse when the latter made her appearance at the Opéra. And, again, no doubt Mme de Guermantes was sincere when she singled out someone on account of his or her intelligence. When she said of a woman, "It seems she's quite charming," or of a man that he was "one of the cleverest people alive," she imagined herself to have no other reason for admitting the individual to her circle than the charm or the intelligence in question, unless the family genie intervened at the last moment; deeper under the surface, at the dark entrance to the domain where the Guermantes exercised their judgment, this vigilant genie debarred them from finding this man clever or that woman charming if he or she was without social merit, actual or potential. The man was pronounced learned, but in the sense that a dictionary is learned, or, on the contrary, as common, with the mind of a traveling salesman; the woman pretty, but with an appalling sense of style or too talkative. As for the people of indeterminate social status, they were just too dreadful—and what snobs they were! M. de Bréauté, whose country house was very near Guermantes, consorted with no one below the rank of Highness. But he was utterly unaffected by all that and longed only to spend his time in museums. And so, when anyone described M. de Bréauté as a snob, Mme de Guermantes became indignant. "Babal a snob! But, my dear man, you must have taken leave of your senses; he's just the opposite. He loathes smart people. He won't let himself be introduced to any of them. Even in my house! If I invite him along with someone he doesn't know, he'll come, but he never stops grumbling about it."

This is not to say that, even in practice, the Guermantes did not attribute a great deal more value to intelligence than did the Courvoisiers. In a positive sense, the difference between the Guermantes and the Courvoisiers in this respect had already begun to bear very promising fruit. For example, the Duchesse de Guermantes, enveloped moreover in a mystery that had set so many poets dreaming from afar, had given the ball I have already mentioned, at which the King of England had never enjoyed himself so much ever before, for she had had the idea, which would never have occurred to any Courvoisier, and the audacity, which would have daunted the courage of all the Courvoisiers put together, of inviting, apart from the personages referred to earlier, the musician Gaston Lemaire and the dramatist Grandmougin.[46] But these intellectual leanings came across chiefly in a negative light. If the necessary quota of intelligence and charm declined steadily as the rank of the person who was anxious to be received by the Duchesse de Guermantes became more exalted—descending to zero when significant crowned heads of royalty were involved—by contrast, the further it fell below this royal level the more demanding the quota became. For instance, when the Princess of Parma received, there were a number of people whom Her Royal Highness would receive because she had known them since childhood, or because they were related to some duchess or other, or part of the entourage of some sovereign, regardless of whether these people were unattractive or boring; now, as far as a Courvoisier hostess was concerned, reasons such as "a favorite of the Princess of Parma," or "a half-sister of the Duchesse d'Arpajon on the mother's side," or "spends three months every year with the Queen of Spain" would have been sufficient to make her invite such people, but Mme de Guermantes, who had politely acknowledged their greetings at the Princess of Parma's for ten years, had never once allowed them to cross her threshold, since she was of the view that the same rule applied to a drawing room in a social as in a physical sense: it would take only a few pieces of furniture that were not particularly pleasing but had been put there to fill the room, and as a sign of the owner's wealth, to turn it into something dreadful. A drawing room of this sort is like a book in which the author cannot refrain from using language to parade his own learning, brilliance, fluent ease. Like a book, like a house, the quality of a salon, Mme de Guermantes quite rightly thought, depended essentially on what you excluded.

Many of the friends of the Princess of Parma whom the Duchesse de Guermantes had acknowledged for years with no more than the same conventional greeting or an exchange of calling cards, without ever receiving them at her house or going to their receptions, complained about this in undertones to Her Highness, who, on days when M. de Guermantes came to visit her on his own, would drop a hint in his direction. But the wily nobleman, a bad husband to the Duchesse in that he kept mistresses, but her most reliable accomplice when it came to the proper functioning of her salon (and of Oriane's own witty sense of humor, which was the salon's chief attraction), would come out with: "But does my wife know her? Oh, well, I suppose she ought to. But the truth is, madame, that Oriane doesn't care for female conversation. She is surrounded by a court of superior minds—I'm not her husband, I'm only the senior valet. Apart from a handful of really witty women, the female sex bores her. And, madame, Your Highness, with all her shrewd judgment, is surely not going to tell me that the Marquise de Souvré is a witty woman. Yes, I quite understand, Your Highness receives her out of the goodness of her heart. And, then, Your Highness knows her. You tell me that Oriane has met her. It's quite possible, but only once or twice, I assure you. And, then, I must explain to Your Highness, I'm rather to blame for all this. My wife is very easily tired, and she's always so very anxious to be friendly that if I let her have her way she would never stop calling on people. Only yesterday evening, despite the fact that she was running a temperature, she was afraid of offending the Duchesse de Bourbon by not paying her a visit. I had to put my foot down and forbid them to send the carriage round. Do you know, madame, I have a very good mind not to tell Oriane that you've mentioned Mme de Souvré to me. Oriane is so devoted to Your Highness that she'll go at once to invite Mme de Souvré. That will mean another call to be made, it will oblige us to make ourselves known to the sister, whose husband I know well. I'd rather not mention it to Oriane at all, if Your Highness has no objection. We'll save her a great deal of fatigue and flurry. And I assure you, it will be no loss to Mme de Souvré. She has a wide acquaintance, moves in the most brilliant circles. We hardly entertain at all, really, just a few little dinner parties. Mme de Souvré would be bored to death." The Princess of Parma, naïvely convinced that the Duc de Guermantes would not pass along her request to the Duchesse and dismayed at her failure to procure the invitation solicited by Mme de Souvré, was all the more flattered to think that she was one of the habitués of such an exclusive salon. This flattering state of affairs was certainly not without its problems. Thus, whenever the Princess of Parma invited Mme de Guermantes, she had to rack her brains to be sure that there was no one among her other guests whose presence might offend the Duchesse and make her decline further invitations.

On ordinary weekdays (after dinner, to which she always invited a few people, very early, for she held on to old customs), the Princess of Parma's drawing room was open to her regular guests and, generally speaking, to the whole of the higher aristocracy, French and foreign. The order of her receptions was for her to leave the dining room, sit down on a sofa in front of a large round table, and chat with a couple of the most important ladies who had dined with her, or else to cast her eyes over a magazine, or to play cards (or pretend to play, in accordance with a German court custom), either a game of patience or a game with some prominent partner—real or imaginary—of her choice. Toward nine o'clock, the double doors of the big drawing room were constantly opening and closing and opening up again to admit the visitors who had bolted their dinner (or, if they had dined out, skipped coffee with a promise to return later, after intending only "to go in at one door and out through another") in order to accommodate themselves to the Princess's timetable. She, meanwhile, absorbed in her game or her conversation, pretended not to notice the new arrivals, and it was only when they were standing a few feet away that she rose graciously from the sofa with a benevolent smile for the women. The latter would then make a deep curtsy before Her Highness, who would stand there to receive what was tantamount to a genuflection, and this involved their bringing their lips down to the level of her handsome hand, held very low, and kissing it. At this point, the Princess, just as if she had been surprised each time by a formality with which she was in fact perfectly familiar, would raise the kneeling lady almost bodily, with incomparable grace and sweetness, and kiss her on both cheeks. A grace and sweetness that were conditional, one might say, upon the meekness with which the arriving guest bent her knee. This was probably the case; and it seems that in an egalitarian society social etiquette would disappear, not, as people imagine, through lack of breeding, but because the one side would lose the deference due to a prestige that must be imaginary to be effective, while, more important, the other would lose the affability that is generously dispensed and cultivated when it is felt to be infinitely precious to the recipient, a sense of the precious that, in a world based on equality, would suddenly die a death, like everything that has only a fiduciary value. But this disappearance of social etiquette in a transformed society is by no means a certainty, and we are occasionally too ready to believe that present circumstances are the only ones in which certain phenomena can thrive. People of great intelligence believed that there could not be any diplomacy or foreign alliances in a republic, and that the peasant class would not tolerate the separation of church and state. After all, the existence of social etiquette in an egalitarian society would be no more miraculous than the success of the railways, or the use of the airplane in war. And, then, if etiquette was to disappear, there is nothing to show that this would be a bad thing. And would not a society become secretly more hierarchical as it became ostensibly more democratic? Very possibly. The political power of the Popes has increased enormously since they ceased to possess either states or an army; cathedrals meant far less to a devout Catholic of the seventeenth century than they do for a twentieth-century atheist, and if the Princess of Parma had been the sovereign ruler of a state, no doubt it would have occurred to me to speak of her about as much as of a president of the Republic—which is to say, not at all.

Once the postulant had been raised up and embraced by the Princess, the latter sat down again to her game of patience, unless the newcomer was a lady of some importance, in which case she sat her down in an armchair and talked to her for a while.

When the drawing room became too crowded, the lady-in-waiting whose duty it was to act as a steward cleared some space by leading the guests into an immense hall onto which the room opened, a place filled with portraits and various trophies relating to the House of Bourbon. At this point the Princess's closest friends were quite willing to chaperone people around this hall and provide interesting commentaries, to which the younger guests had not the patience to listen, being more absorbed in the spectacle of living royalty (and the chance of getting themselves presented to it by the lady-in-waiting and her attendants) than in studying the relics of dead sovereigns. Too busy with the thought of meeting important people and angling for invitations, they had no idea, even after several years, of the contents of this priceless museum of the archives of the monarchy, and held only a blurred memory of it as a place decorated with cacti and giant palms, which made this center of social elegance look like the palmarium at the Paris Zoo.

Of course, the Duchesse de Guermantes, in a spirit of self-sacrifice, did occasionally appear on these evenings to pay an after-dinner call on the Princess, who kept her all to herself for the whole evening, while engaging in banter with the Duc. But when the Duchesse came to dine, the Princess took care not to invite her regular guests and closed her doors to the world after dinner, in the fear that too indiscriminate a choice of guests might incur the displeasure of the fastidious Duchesse. On such evenings, should any of the faithful who had not been warned present themselves at Her Highness's doors, the porter would inform them, "Her Royal Highness is not at home this evening," and they would turn away. But many of the Princess's friends would have known in advance that on that particular day they would not be invited to call. These were special social occasions, ones that were barred to many who must have longed for admission. Those who were excluded were fairly certain who figured in the ranks of the elect, and would murmur among themselves in a fit of pique: "You know, of course, that Oriane de Guermantes never goes anywhere without her entire general staff." With the help of this body, the Princess of Parma attempted to surround the Duchesse with a sort of protective rampart against those whose chances of impressing her were in any way slight. But there were several of the Duchesse's preferred friends, several members of this glamorous "general staff," toward whom the Princess of Parma found it difficult to be affable, seeing that they displayed scant affability toward herself. It is very likely that the Princess of Parma would have been the first to admit that people might derive more pleasure from the company of the Duchesse de Guermantes than from her own. She could not ignore the fact that there was always a dense throng of people at the Duchesse's "at homes," or that she herself would often encounter three or four members of royalty there who thought that she deserved no more than to receive their visiting cards. And, however much she might memorize Oriane's witticisms, copy her style of dress, serve identical strawberry tartlets at her own tea parties, there were still occasions when she was left by herself all day in the sole company of her lady-in-waiting or some counselor from a foreign legation. And so, if someone never let a day pass without going to spend a couple of hours at the Duchesse's (as Swann had done, for instance, at an earlier period) yet only set foot at the Princess of Parma's once every two years, the latter was not particularly inclined, even for the sake of humoring Oriane, to make "advances" to this Swann or whomever by inviting him to dinner. In short, inviting the Duchesse to her house was for the Princess of Parma a rather vexing business, so strongly was she beset by fear that Oriane would find fault with everything. But, by contrast, and for the same reason, when the Princess of Parma came to dine with Mme de Guermantes, she could be certain in advance that everything would be perfect, delightful, and she had only one misgiving, the fear of being unable to understand, remember, engage people, of being unable to assimilate ideas and personalities. On this score, my presence aroused her attention and stimulated her cupidity, in exactly the same way that a novel style of decorating a dinner table with garlands of fruit might have done, uncertain as she was which of the two—the table decoration or my presence—was more distinctive as one of those charms that were the secret of the success of Oriane's receptions, and, in her uncertainty, firmly resolved to try to have them both at the next dinner party she gave. In fact, what fully justified the ecstatic curiosity the Princess of Parma brought to the Duchesse's house was that element of the comical, the dangerous, the exciting into which the Princess would plunge in a kind of timidity, a thrill of shock and delight (as at the seaside when the waves are heavy and the bathing attendants warn people of the danger for the simple reason that none of them can swim), and from which she would emerge feeling braced, happy, rejuvenated—the element known as the Guermantes wit. This wit of the Guermantes—something as nonexistent as the squared circle in the eyes of the Duchesse, who regarded herself as the only Guermantes to possess it—had the same sort of repute as *rillettes de Tours* or biscuits made in Rheims. All the same, it is probable (since an intellectual characteristic does not propagate itself through the same channels as the color of someone's hair or complexion) that various close friends of the Duchesse who were not of her blood possessed the same wit, which, by contrast, had failed to inculcate itself into certain members of the Guermantes family who were all too impervious to wit of any kind. Generally speaking, those who were endowed with the Guermantes wit and not related to the Duchesse shared the characteristic feature of having been brilliant men, well equipped for a career either in the arts, diplomacy, parliamentary eloquence, or the army, to which they had preferred a clannish society life. Perhaps such a preference could be explained by a certain lack of originality, initiative, willpower, health, luck—or by snobbishness.

For some of them (though these, it must be said, were the exception), if the Guermantes salon had been the stumbling block in their careers, it had been against their will. So, for instance, a doctor, a painter, and a diplomat with a fine career before him had failed to achieve the sort of success for which they were nonetheless more brilliantly equipped than most, because their friendship with the Guermantes meant that the first two were regarded as men of fashion and the third as a reactionary, and this had prevented all three from earning the recognition of their peers. The old-fashioned gown and red cap still donned by the electoral bodies of the university faculties are—or at least were, until fairly recently—something more than a purely external survival from a narrow-minded past and an unyielding sectarianism. Beneath the cap with its golden tassels, like the high priests of the Jews in their conical headgear, the "professors" were still, in the years that preceded the Dreyfus case, deeply rooted in strictly pharisaical ideas. Du Boulbon was at heart an artist, but he was safe because he did not care for society. Cottard belonged to the Verdurin circle, but Mme Verdurin was one of his patients, then was further protected by his vulgarity, while at his own house he entertained no one outside the faculty, at banquets bathed in a whiff of carbolic acid. But in staunchly corporate bodies, where in fact rigid prejudice is simply the price to be paid for a spotless reputation, for the most lofty conceptions of morality, which falter in more tolerant, liberal (and ultimately more corrupt) milieux, a professor in his gown of scarlet faced with ermine, like that of a Doge of Venice (that is to say, the equivalent of a duke) shut away in the ducal palace, was as virtuous, as committed to noble principles, but as merciless toward any outside element as that other admirable but fearsome Duc, M. de Saint-Simon. The outsider here was the fashionable society doctor with his alien manner, his different social connections. To make good, the unfortunate man of whom we are now speaking, so as not to be accused by his colleagues of scorning them (who but a man of fashion would think of such a thing!) by keeping the Duchesse de Guermantes from them, would hope to disarm them by throwing mixed dinner parties at which the quota of medical guests was outnumbered by the fashionable ones. He was unaware that this was a way of signing his own death warrant, or, rather, he discovered as much when the Council of Ten[47] (a little larger in number) had to appoint to a vacant chair, when it was inevitably the name of another doctor, a more regular if more mediocre one that emerged from the fatal ballot, and the "Veto" echoed around the ancient faculty, as solemn, as absurd, and as terrible as the "Juro" that spelled the death of Molière.[48] The same was true of the painter who was permanently labeled a "society figure," when those members of fashionable society who dabbled in art had managed to get themselves labeled as artists; the same was true of the diplomat who had too many ties with reactionaries.

But such cases were extremely rare. The typical kind of distinguished man who formed the backbone of the Guermantes salon was someone who had voluntarily (as he saw it at least) renounced all else, everything that was incompatible with the Guermantes wit, the Guermantes code of manners, with the subtle charm that was odious to any "body" of people who were in the least "corporate."

And the people who were cognizant of the fact that one of the habitués of the Duchesse's drawing room had once been awarded the gold medal of the Salon, that another, secretary to the Bar Council, had made a brilliant debut in the Chamber, that a third had ably served France as chargé d'affaires, might well have found themselves regarding people who had now done nothing for twenty years as "failures." But few of them were apprised of such facts, and the persons concerned would have been the last to remind anyone, since, precisely by keeping step with the very spirit of the Guermantes wit, they considered these former claims to distinction as valueless: was it not just such wit that encouraged them to denounce as a toadying bore and as a shop boy, respectively, a couple of eminent ministers—one a trifle solemn, the other with a taste for puns—whose praises were sung by the newspapers, but in whose company Mme de Guermantes would begin to yawn and show signs of impatience if a hostess had unwisely sat them next to her at dinner? Since being a high-ranking statesman was in no sense a recommendation in the eyes of the Duchesse, those of her friends who had resigned from a "career" in the diplomatic services or the army, or who had never stood for Parliament, as they came day after day to lunch and talk with their great friend, or when they encountered her in the houses of royalty (held by them, as it happened, in low esteem—or so they said), felt that they had made the right choice, however much their melancholy air, amid all the gaiety, seemed to suggest that the reality of their feeling was slightly different.

And it must be said that the refinements of society life, the sparkle of conversation at the Guermantes', did have something real about it, however tenuously so. No official office was worth more than the personal charm of certain of Mme de Guermantes's favorites, whom the most powerful ministers would have failed to attract to their houses. If in this salon so many intellectual ambitions and even noble endeavors had been buried forever, then at least the rarest flowering of society so-phistication had blossomed from their dust. Indeed, witty men–like Swann, for instance–regarded themselves as superior to men of merit, whom they despised, but that was because what the Duchesse prized above all else was not intelligence but–intelligence in a superior form, in her view, rarer, more exquisite, elevating it to a verbal species of talent–wit. And in the past, at the Verdurins', when Swann branded Bri-chot and Elstir as a pedant and an oaf respectively, in the face of all the learning of the one and the genius of the other, it was the infiltration of the Guermantes spirit that had led him to classify them in these terms. Never would he have ventured to present either of them to the Duch-esse, in his instinctive awareness of the manner in which she would have received Brichot's verbal onslaughts and Elstir's "tosh," since to the Guermantes mind pretentious and prolix speech in a serious or farcical vein was consigned to the category of the most intolerable imbecility.

As for those Guermantes of the true flesh and blood, if the Guermantes spirit had not infected them so completely–in a way that is familiar in literary coteries, for example, where everyone has identical pronunciation, enunciation, and, as a consequence of this, the same way of thinking–it was certainly not because originality is more strongly ingrained in society circles and therefore inhibits imitation. But imita-tion requires not only the absence of any unsuppressible originality, but also a relatively skillful ear, enabling you first of all to discern what you will then go on to imitate. And there were Guermantes who lacked this musical sense just as completely as the Courvoisiers.

To take as an example the activity that is known (in another sense of the word "imitation") as "giving an imitation of someone" (the Guer-mantes called it "doing takeoffs"), Mme de Guermantes could do these to perfection until she dropped, and still the Courvoisiers were as inca-pable of realizing what was going on as if they had been a bunch of rab-bits instead of men and women, because they had never managed to observe the particular defect or accent the Duchesse was endeavoring to impersonate. When she "did a takeoff" of the Duc de Limoges, the Courvoisiers would protest, "Oh no, he doesn't really speak like that. I dined with him again at Bebeth's last night and he talked to me all evening. He didn't speak like that at all!" whereas any Guermantes who had a smattering of culture would exclaim: "My word, how droll Oriane is! The startling thing is that when she's mimicking him she actually looks like him! It's as if he's in the room. Oriane, do give us a little more Limoges!" Now, Guermantes like these (without even including those utterly remarkable members of the family who greeted the Duchesse's impersonations of the Duc de Limoges with admiring remarks: "Oh, you really have got him to a tee!" or "You do get him exactly right!") might well be devoid of wit in Mme de Guermantes's eyes (and she was right about this), but by dint of hearing and repeating the Duchesse's words they had managed, more or less, to end up imitating her way of expressing herself, of judging people, everything that Swann, like the Duchesse herself, would have called her way of "editing" what she said, so that in their conversation they presented something that seemed to the Courvoisiers to be uncomfortably close to Oriane's wit, and which they themselves regarded as Guermantes wit. Since such Guermantes were to her not only kinsfolk but admirers into the bargain, Oriane (who kept the rest of the family strictly at arm's length and now used her disdain to avenge the spitefulness they had shown her in her girlhood) went to call on them now and again, generally accompanied by the Duc, when she went for a drive with him in the summer months. These visits were quite something. As she entertained her guests in her large drawing room on the ground floor, the Princesse d'Épinay's heart would miss a beat when she saw from a distance, like the first glimmer of a harmless enough fire or the "scouting party" of an unexpected invasion, making her way slowly across the courtyard in a diagonal, the Duchesse, wearing a stunning hat and tilting a parasol that wafted summer fragrance. "Why, it's Oriane," she would remark, as if she were saying *En garde!*" as a prudent warning to her lady visitors, so that they would have time to retreat in an orderly manner and evacuate the drawing rooms without panic. Half the people present did not dare to stay and would rise to go. "But, please, why? Do sit down again, you really must do me the pleasure of staying a little longer," the Princesse would say in an offhand, easy manner (to show she was a *grande dame*) but in a voice that now rang false. "You may well have things to say to each other." "No? You're in a hurry? Oh, very well, I shall come and see you," the lady of the house would reply to those whom she would just as soon see take their departure. The Duc and the Duchesse would give a very courteous greeting to the people they had been seeing there for years though without ever coming to know them any better, while, for their part, the people concerned had the good sense scarcely to muster a "good day." Scarcely had they left the room when the Duc would begin to inquire benignly who they were, to give the impression that he was taking an interest in the intrinsic quality of people he never received on account of the malevolence of fate or the state of Oriane's nerves, on which the company of women had a harmful effect: "Tell me, who *was* that little woman in the pink hat?" "But, my dear cousin, you've seen her hundreds of times, she's the Vicomtesse de Tours, one of the Lamarzelles by birth." "But what I'm saying is, she was pretty and she has a lively look about her. If it weren't for a slight defect in her upper lip, I'd say she was quite stunning. If there's a Vicomte de Tours, the man can't have a dull moment. Oriane, do you know whom her eyebrows and hairline reminded me of? Your cousin Hedwige de Ligne." The Duchesse de Guermantes, who was apt to become listless whenever mention was made of any woman other than herself, let the subject drop. She had not reckoned with her husband's weakness for letting it be known that he knew all about the people he did not personally receive, a trait of his that convinced him that he showed himself to be more "serious" than his wife. "But," he would suddenly exclaim emphatically, "you mentioned the name Lamarzelle. I remember, when I was in the Chamber, hearing a remarkable speech made. . . ." "That was the uncle of the young woman you saw a moment ago." "Indeed! What talent! . . . No, my dear girl," he assured the Vicomtesse d'Égremont, whom Mme de Guermantes could not endure, but who, in her refusal to budge from the Princesse d'Épinay's drawing room, where she willingly demeaned herself in the role of parlormaid (even if this did not stop her from slapping her own when she returned home), stayed there, abashed and tearful, but stayed there all the same, when the ducal couple were present, taking their cloaks, trying to make herself useful, discreetly offering to retire to the next room. "You're not to make tea for us; let's just sit and talk together; we're unassuming people, no fuss. Besides," he went on, turning to the Princesse d'Épinay (leaving Mistress d'Égremont to her blushes, abasement, ambition, and zealous attentiveness), "we can only spare you a quarter of an hour." This quarter of an hour would be entirely devoted to a sort of exhibition of the witty remarks made by the Duchesse during the previous week, and which she herself would certainly have made no mention of had not her husband, by appearing, with great adroitness, to scold her by alluding to the incidents that had provoked them, obliged her to repeat them as though reluctantly.

The Princesse d'Épinay, who was fond of her cousin and knew that she had a weakness for compliments, would go into raptures over her hat, her parasol, her witty remarks. "You can talk to her as long as you like about her clothes," the Duc would say in the gruff tone he had assumed and then tempered with a wicked smile, so that his gruffness should not be taken seriously, "but for heaven's sake don't speak to her about her wit. I could do without having such a witty wife. You're probably thinking of the disgraceful pun she made about my brother Palamède," he added, knowing quite well that the Princesse and the rest of the family had not yet heard it, and delighted to have an excuse for showing off his wife. "In the first place, I find it quite disgraceful that someone who, I have to admit, has occasionally said some quite good things, should make bad puns, but especially about my brother, who is very touchy, and if it's going to lead to any unpleasantness between us, that would really be taking things too far!"

"But we have no idea! One of Oriane's puns? It's sure to be outstanding. Oh, do tell us?"

"No, no," rejoined the Duc, still gruff, but his face lighting up with a smile. "I'm more than glad you haven't heard it. Seriously, now, I'm very fond of my brother."

"Look here, Basin," the Duchesse would exclaim, the moment having come for her to take up her husband's cue, "I can't think why on earth you should say that it might annoy Palamède; you know quite well it would do nothing of the sort. He's far too intelligent to take umbrage at a stupid joke that has nothing offensive about it. You'll make people think I said something nasty, when I simply came out with something that wasn't in the least funny. You're the one who's making a mountain out of it by getting so indignant. I simply don't understand you."

"You're intriguing us horribly. What's it all about?"

"Oh, obviously, nothing serious!" exclaimed M. de Guermantes. "You may have heard that my brother wanted to give Brézé, the country house he got from his wife, to his sister Marsantes."

"Indeed, but we were told that she didn't want it, that she didn't care for that part of the country, that the climate didn't suit her."

"Exactly. Well, someone told my wife all about it and said that if my brother was giving this house to our sister it wasn't so much to please her as to tease her. What this person actually said was that Charlus was such a tease. Well, you know, Brézé is fit for a king. It must be worth millions. It used to be crown property, and it has one of the finest forests in France. There are plenty of people who'd be only too delighted to be teased about something like that. And so, when she heard the word 'tease' applied to Charlus because he was giving away such a marvelous property, Oriane couldn't stop herself from bursting out—quite involuntarily, I have to say—without any hint of malice—it came out like a flash of lightning—with the words, 'A tease? A teaser? Then he must be Teaser Augustus!' You understand," he went on, resuming his gruff tone, but not before he had cast a sweeping glance around the room to see how his wife's witticism had been taken—and in some doubt as to the extent of Mme d'Épinay's knowledge of ancient history—"you understand, it's an allusion to Augustus Caesar, the Roman Emperor. It's rather stupid, a bad play on words, quite unworthy of Oriane. But, then, I'm more circumspect than my wife. I may be less witty, but I think of the consequences. Should the remark reach my brother's ears by some ghastly misfortune, life won't be worth living. All the more so," he added, "because Palamède, as you know, is very high and mighty and a great stickler in these matters, very sensitive to gossip. You have to admit that, quite apart from this business of Brézé, 'Teaser Augustus' suits him really quite well. That's what redeems my wife's witticisms: even when she stoops to feeble puns, she's always witty and she really does describe people rather well."

And so, thanks on one occasion to "Teaser Augustus," on another to something else, the visits the Duc and Duchesse paid to their kinsfolk replenished the stock of anecdotes, and the excitement they caused lasted long after the witty lady and her impresario had left. The hostess in question would begin by lingering delightedly with the privileged guests who had been at the entertainment (those who had remained, that is) upon the clever things Oriane had come out with. "You hadn't heard 'Teaser Augustus'?" the Princesse d'Épinay would ask. "But of course," the Marquise de Bavano would reply with a blush, "the Princesse de Sarsina–La Rochefoucauld told me about it, but not in quite the same terms. But it must have been so much more interesting to hear it repeated like that in the company of my cousin," she added, as though she had been speaking of a song accompanied by the composer himself. "We were speaking about Oriane's latest sally–she was here just now," people would say to some recently arrived caller, who was bound to be extremely upset that she had not come an hour earlier.

"What! Has Oriane been here?"

"Yes indeed, if you'd come a little earlier . . ." the Princesse d'Épinay would reply, not exactly reproachfully, but making it clear how much the blunderer had missed. She had only herself to blame if she had not been present at the creation of the world or at Mme Carvalho's latest performance.[49] "What do you think of Oriane's latest? I must say I really like 'Teaser Augustus,' " and the witticism would be served up again cold at lunch the next day in the company of a few close friends invited for the purpose, and would reappear with different sauces throughout the rest of the week. Indeed, that very week Mme d'Épinay, in the course of her annual visit to the Princess of Parma, seized the opportunity to ask whether Her Royal Highness had heard the witticism, and repeated it to her. "Ah! 'Teaser Augustus,' " said the Princess of Parma, wide-eyed with admiration in advance, but begging for complementary glosses, which Mme d'Épinay was by no means loath to furnish. "I have to admit that I like 'Teaser Augustus' enormously as a piece of 'editing,' " the Princesse concluded. In fact, the word "editing" was not at all appropriate for the pun in question, but the Princesse d'Épinay, who had the temerity to believe that she had inherited part of the Guermantes wit, had borrowed the expressions "original edition" and "editing" from Oriane and used them rather indiscriminately. Now, the Princess of Parma—who was not overfond of Mme d'Épinay, whom she considered ill favored, knew to be penny-pinching, and believed, on the authority of the Courvoisiers, to be malicious—recognized the word "editing," which she had heard Mme de Guermantes use but would not herself have known how or when to apply. She came to the vague conclusion that it must indeed have been the "original editing" that formed the attraction of "Teaser Augustus" and, without quite forgetting her antipathy toward her plain and miserly guest, could not repress a hint of admiration for a person endowed to such a degree with the Guermantes wit, so much so that she was on the point of inviting the Princesse d'Épinay to the Opéra. She was held back by the thought that it would perhaps be wiser to consult Mme de Guermantes first. As for Mme d'Épinay, who, unlike the Courvoisiers, was forever going out of her way to be obliging to Oriane and was genuinely fond of her, though jealous of her fashionable friends and slightly irritated by the fun the Duchesse made of her in front of everyone on account of her meanness, she reported, when she returned home, how hard the Princess of Parma had found it to grasp the point of "Teaser Augustus" and declared what a snob Oriane must be to number such a cuckoo among her friends. "I should never have been able to call regularly on the Princess of Parma even if I'd wanted to," she told the friends who were dining with her, "because M. d'Épinay would have never allowed it, on account of her immorality," alluding to certain purely fictive excesses on the Princess's part. "But even if I had had a more lenient husband, I have to say that I could never have called on her on a regular basis. I don't know how Oriane can stand going to see her so frequently. I go there once a year, and it's all I can do to stay to the end of my visit." As for those of the Courvoisiers who happened to be at Victurnienne's[50] on the day of Mme de Guermantes's visit, the Duchesse's arrival put most of them to flight on account of their exasperation at the "highfalutin salaams" people directed at Oriane. One alone remained on the day of "Teaser Augustus." He did not quite see the point, but he half understood it, being an educated man. And the Courvoisiers went about repeating that Oriane had called Uncle Palamède "Caesar Augustus," which was, according to them, a good enough description of him. "But why all this endless fuss about Oriane?" they pursued. "People couldn't create more fuss if she were a queen. After all, what is Oriane? I'm not saying that the Guermantes aren't an old family, but the Courvoisiers are in no way inferior to them, either in illustriousness, antiquity, or marriage alliances. It must not be forgotten that on the Field of the Cloth of Gold,⁵¹ when the King of England asked François I who was the noblest of the lords there present, the King of France replied, 'Courvoisier, Sire.' " But even if all the Courvoisiers had stayed in the room to hear them, Oriane's words would have fallen on deaf ears, since the incidents that usually gave rise to them would have been regarded by them from a totally different point of view. If, for instance, a Courvoisier found herself running out of chairs in the middle of a reception she was giving, or if she mistook the name when she was talking to a guest whose face she did not recall, or if one of her servants said something stupid, the Courvoisier lady, extremely annoyed, flushed, quivering with agitation, would deplore so unfortunate an occurrence. And when she had a gentleman visitor in the room and Oriane was expected, she would ask in an anxious and imperious tone, "Do you know her?," fearing that if her visitor was not acquainted with her his presence might make a bad impression on Oriane. But, on the contrary, Mme de Guermantes used such incidents as opportunities to invent stories that would make the Guermantes laugh until the tears ran down their cheeks, so that one was forced to envy the lady in question for having run out of chairs, for having made a gaffe or allowing her servant to make one, for having received someone no one else knew, as one is forced to be thankful that famous authors have been kept at a distance and betrayed by women when their humiliations and sufferings have been, if not the actual goad to their genius, then at least the subject matter of their writings.

The Courvoisiers were equally incapable of rising to the spirit of innovation that the Duchesse de Guermantes introduced into society life, which, adapted by her with unerring instinct to the demands of the moment, made it into something artistic, when the purely mechanical application of hard and fast rules would have produced results as unfortunate as those faced by a man who, anxious to succeed in love or in politics, had in his own life followed the exploits of Bussy d'Amboise[52] to the letter. If the Courvoisiers gave a family dinner or a dinner party to meet some prince, the additional presence of some man of wit or some friend of their son seemed to them sufficiently anomalous to produce the direst consequences. A Courvoisier lady whose father had been a minister under the Empire and who had to give an afternoon reception in honor of the Princesse Mathilde, deduced with geometrical logic that she could invite only Bonapartists. She knew practically none. All the smart women of her acquaintance, all the presentable men she knew, were ruthlessly barred, because, with their Legitimist views or affiliations, they might, according to Courvoisier logic, have given offense to Her Imperial Highness. The latter, who in her own house was accustomed to receive the flower of the Faubourg Saint-Germain, was somewhat surprised when all she found at Mme de Courvoisier's was a notorious old sponger, a widow whose husband had been a *préfet* under the Empire, the widow of the postmaster general, and a handful of other people known for their loyalty to Napoleon III, their stupidity, and their dreariness. Yet the Princesse Mathilde was far from chary with her flow of sweetness and sovereign grace toward these disastrous plain Janes, whom the Duchesse de Guermantes, for her part, took good care not to invite when it was her turn to entertain the Princesse; she invited instead, without any *a priori* reasoning about Bonapartism, the choicest assembly of all the beautiful women, of every cast of mind, of every celebrity, whom, by some flair, some subtle sense of tact, she felt likely to be acceptable to the niece of the Emperor, even when they actually belonged to the Royal House. Even the Duc d'Aumale was present, and when, as she made her exit, the Princesse raised Mme de Guermantes from her deep curtsy and her attempt to kiss her hand, and kissed her on both cheeks, it was from the bottom of her heart that she was able to assure the Duchesse that she had never spent so agreeable an afternoon or attended so successful a party. The Princess of Parma was a Courvoisier in that she was incapable of innovation in social matters, but unlike the Courvoisiers in that the surprises the Duchesse de Guermantes perpetually held in store for her engendered in her not, as in them, antipathy, but a sense of wonder. This reaction was further intensified by the fact that the Princess's state of culture lagged enormously behind the times. Mme de Guermantes was herself a great deal less advanced than the Princess supposed. But she needed to be only the tiniest bit more advanced than Mme de Parme to astound the latter, and, as each generation of critics confines itself to maintaining a diametrically opposite view of the truths espoused by its predecessors, she had only to say that Flaubert, that enemy of the bourgeois, was a bourgeois to his fingertips, or that there was a great deal of Italian music in Wagner, to expose the Princess, at the cost of constantly renewed mental exhaustion, as the swimmer's eyes are exposed in a stormy sea, to horizons that seemed to her to be unimaginable and condemned to remain dim. Stupefaction was also caused by the paradoxes uttered not merely in connection with works of art but with persons of their acquaintance and with current goings-on in society. No doubt the incapacity that prevented Mme de Parme from distinguishing the genuine Guermantes wit from certain crudely acquired manifestations of it (this tended to make her believe in the high intellectual worth of certain Guermantes, especially certain female members of the family, whom she later found herself bewildered to hear described by the Duchesse as utter dimwits) was one of the causes of the astonishment the Princess invariably felt when she heard Mme de Guermantes pass judgment on other people. But there was also a further reason, one that I, who knew more about books than people at that time, more about literature than about life, explained to myself with the thought that the Duchesse, by thriving on this worldly life, the idleness and sterility of which are to real social activity what, in art, criticism is to creativity, extended to the members of her circle the instability of viewpoint, the unhealthy thirst, of the quibbler who, in order to slake a mind too desiccated, goes in search of any old paradox that is at all fresh and will not hesitate to uphold the thirst-quenching opinion that the great *Iphigénie* is Piccinni's and not Gluck's, and at a pinch that the true *Phèdre* is the one by Pradon.[53]

When an intelligent, educated, witty woman had married a diffident lout who was seldom seen and never heard, Mme de Guermantes would get it into her head one fine day to indulge in an intellectual thrill not only by decrying the wife but by "discovering" the husband. In regard to the Cambremer household, for instance, had she found herself living in such a section of society at the time, she would have decreed that Mme de Cambremer was stupid, and, by contrast, that the interesting party, misunderstood and delightful, condemned to silence by a prattling wife, but worth a thousand of her kind himself, was the Marquis, and by declaring this the Duchesse would have felt the same sense of refreshing relief as the critic who, after people had been admiring *Hernani* for seventy years, confesses to a preference for *Le Lion amoureux*.[54] From this same morbid need for arbitrary novelty, if there was a model wife, a saintly woman whom people had been pitying since her youth for being married to a scoundrel, a day would come when it would occur to Mme de Guermantes to assert that this scoundrel was perhaps a frivolous man but one with a heart of gold, and that he had been driven to utterly irresponsible behavior by the implacable harshness of his wife. I knew that in the long course of the centuries it was not only with the works of different artists but actually with the various works of one artist that critics had enjoyed pushing back into the shade what for too long had been radiant, and bringing into the light what had seemed doomed to permanent obscurity. Not only had I seen Bellini, Winterhalter,[55] the Jesuit architects, a Restoration cabinetmaker come to take the place of men of genius, who were described as tired simply because idle intellectuals had grown tired of them, in the same way that neurasthenics are tired and faddish. I had seen Sainte-Beuve preferred alternately as critic and poet, Musset rejected for his verse apart from a few insignificant pieces, and vaunted as a writer of stories. No doubt it is wrong of certain essayists to set above the most famous scenes of *Le Cid* or *Polyeucte* some speech from *Le Menteur*[56] that, like an old street map, gives us information about the Paris of the day, but their predilection, justified if not by aesthetic considerations then by documentary interest, is still too rational for the irrationality of critical taste. It will give away all of Molière for a single line of *L'Étourdi*,[57] and, even when it pronounces Wagner's *Tristan* to be deadly boring, will make an exception of "a charming note on the horns" at the point where the hunt goes by. This depravity of judgment helped me to understand the similar tendency in Mme de Guermantes, which led her to conclude that a man of their circle, who was recognized as a good fellow but a fool, was a monster of egotism, shrewder than people thought; that another, who was well known for his generosity, might be taken as the personification of avarice; that a good mother had no time for her children; and that a woman who was thought to be loose was really someone of the noblest sentiments. As though vitiated by the inanity of society life, Mme de Guermantes's intelligence and sensibility were too vacillating for disgust not to follow pretty swiftly in the wake of infatuation (even if it meant that she was still ready to be attracted once more by the kind of cleverness that she had alternately sought and abandoned), and for the charm she had seen in some kindhearted man not to change, if he came to see her too often or took too much for granted that she would be able to guide him in a way she could not, into an irritation that she believed came from her admirer but which was due in effect to the utter impossibility of finding pleasure when one spends all one's time looking for it. The Duchesse's vagaries of judgment spared no one, except her husband. He alone had never loved her; in him she had always sensed a soul of iron, indifferent to her caprices, disdainful of her beauty, violent, one of those unbendable wills under whose domination alone highstrung people can set themselves at rest. For his own part, M. de Guermantes, pursuing a single model of feminine beauty but seeking it in mistresses whom he regularly replaced, had as his accomplice in mocking them, once he had left them, one lasting and identical associate, whose chatter often irritated him, but whom he knew that everyone regarded as the most beautiful, the most virtuous, the cleverest, the most cultured woman among the aristocracy, as a wife whom he, M. de Guermantes, was only too lucky to have found, who covered up for all his carryings-on, entertained like no one else in the world, and sustained the reputation of their salon as the foremost one in the whole Faubourg Saint-Germain. This was a common opinion that he himself shared; often at odds with his wife, he was proud of her. If, being as tight with money as he was ostentatious, he refused her the pettiest sums for charities or for the servants, he insisted on her having the most sumptuous clothes and the finest equipages to be had. Finally, he was anxious to show off his wife's wit. Now, whenever Mme de Guermantes had just thought up some new and savory paradox suddenly setting askew the merits and defects of one of their friends, she would be dying to try it out on those who were capable of appreciating it, to bring out the full flavor of its psychological originality and the brilliance of its lapidary malice. These new opinions probably and usually contained no more truth than previous ones, often less; but this very element of the arbitrary and the unexpected gave them something intellectual that made them thrilling to communicate. Except that the patient on whom the Duchesse had exercised her psychological gifts was normally an intimate friend in regard to whom the people she was keen to present with her discovery were utterly unaware that he did not still figure at the center of her good books; and there was also the fact that Mme de Guermantes's reputation for being an incomparable friend, feeling, tender, and devoted, made it difficult for her to launch the attack herself; the most she could do was to intervene later, as though under constraint, by taking up her cue in order to appease and, to all effects and purposes, to contradict, but actually to support a partner who had taken it upon himself to provoke her; this was precisely the role in which M. de Guermantes excelled.

As for social behavior, Mme de Guermantes experienced yet another arbitrarily theatrical pleasure in expressing some views on the subject that whipped the Princess of Parma into a state of perpetual and delicious surprise. But the particular pleasure the Duchesse experienced in this area was something whose nature I tried to comprehend not so much with the help of literary criticism as with instances of political life and the reports of parliamentary debates. Since the flow of contradictory edicts by which Mme de Guermantes constantly reversed the scale of values among the people of her world was no longer enough to distract her, she also sought, in the way she conducted her own social behavior and accounted for her own most trifling decisions on society matters, to savor those artificial emotions, to fulfill those artificial duties that stir the feelings of parliaments and impress themselves on the minds of those who dabble in politics. We know that when a minister explains to the Chamber that he believed he was doing the right thing in following a line of conduct that actually seems quite straightforward to the commonsense person who sees the report of the sitting in his newspaper the next morning, nevertheless this commonsense reader feels suddenly stirred, and begins to doubt whether he was right to approve the minister's conduct, when he reads that the latter's speech was heard amid an uproar and punctuated with expressions of reprehension such as "It's a disgrace!" uttered by a deputy whose name and titles take up so much space in the report, and are followed by an account of such emphatic reactions on his part, that in the space devoted to describing this outburst the words "It's a disgrace!" occupy less room than a hemistich in an alexandrine. For instance, in the days when M. de Guermantes, the Prince des Laumes, sat in the Chamber, one would read the following sort of thing in the Paris newspapers, though what one was reading was intended primarily for the Méséglise constituency, to show the electorate there that they had not given their votes to an inactive or dumb representative:

MONSIEUR DE GUERMANTES-BOUILLON, PRINCE DES LAUMES: "This is a serious matter, gentlemen." (Hear, hear! from the center and from some of the benches on the right, loud exclamations from the extreme left.)

The commonsense reader still retains a glimmer of loyalty to the wise minister, but finds his heart stirred by fresh palpitations when he reads the first words of the speaker who rises to reply to this:

"The astonishment, or should one say stupor even" *(tangible stirrings on the right side of the House),* "caused me by the words of one who is still, I presume, a member of the Government . . ." *(Thunderous applause; several deputies then rush forward toward the ministerial bench; the undersecretary of state for postal and telegraphic services, without rising from his seat, gives a nod of approval.)*

This "thunderous applause" banishes the last vestige of resistance from the mind of the commonsense reader; he regards as an insult to the Chamber, a monstrous insult, what is in fact a way of proceeding that is intrinsically insignificant; it may be some quite predictable item, such as wanting to make the wealthy pay more than the poor, the exposure of some iniquity, the preference for peace over war, and he will find it scandalous and see it as going against certain principles to which he had actually never given a thought, principles not engraved in the heart of man, but ones that move him strongly on account of the acclamations they provoke and the close-knit majorities they rally together.

It must at the same time be recognized that this subtlety on the part of politicians, which served to explain the Guermantes circle to me and, at a later stage, other social groups, is no more than the perversion of a particular nicety of interpretation often described by the expression "reading between the lines." If representative assemblies contain elements of this absurdity, brought about by the perversion of such nicety of distinction, they also contain elements of stupidity, brought about by the lack of it, in the public, who take everything literally, who do not suspect dismissal when a high dignitary is relieved of his office "at his own request," and say, "He cannot have been dismissed, because he was the one who asked to go," or suspect defeat when, in the face of the Japanese advance, the Russians strategically fall back on stronger positions, prepared in advance, or a refusal when a province has demanded its independence from the German Emperor and he cedes it religious autonomy. But to revert to these sessions in the Chamber, it is also possible that when they commence the deputies themselves are like the commonsense person who will read the report in the newspapers. Informed that a group of workers on strike have sent their delegates to parley with a minister, they may ask themselves naïvely: "Well, well, I wonder what they've been talking about. Let's hope it's all settled," at the very moment the minister rises to address the Chamber in a solemn silence that is already setting the tone for artificial emotions. The minister's first words ("There is no need for me to inform the Chamber that I have too high a sense of government duty to have received a deputation that the authority invested in me is under no obligation to take into account") produce a dramatic effect, for this was the one hypothesis that the common sense of the deputies had failed to anticipate. But precisely because of its dramatic effect, it is greeted with such applause that it is several minutes before the minister can make himself heard again, and he will return to his bench to be congratulated by his colleagues. They are as deeply moved as they were on the day he failed to invite the chairman of the municipal council, a man who supported the Opposition, to a grand official reception, and his colleagues declare that on this occasion, as on the previous one, he has acted like a true statesman.

At this period of his life, M. de Guermantes had, to the great scandal of the Courvoisiers, often been among the crowd of colleagues who came forward to congratulate the minister. I later heard it said that, even at a time when he was playing a fairly important role in the Chamber and was being thought of as a likely candidate for ministerial office or for an embassy, when a friend came to ask him a favor he was infinitely less affected, and his political behavior a great deal less that of a person of importance, than anyone who did not happen to be the Duc de Guermantes. For, if he said that nobility was of little account, that he considered his colleagues to be his equals, he actually believed no such thing. He sought, pretended to value, but in fact despised political status, and since in his own eyes he remained M. de Guermantes, it did not cocoon his person in the sort of starchiness of high office that affects others and makes them unapproachable. And in this respect his pride was a protection against every assault not only on his behavior, which was ostentatiously familiar, but on any genuine simplicity he might actually possess. To return to the artificial, dramatic decisions of his wife, so like those of politicians, Mme de Guermantes was no less disconcerting to the Guermantes, the Courvoisiers, the Faubourg in general, and the Princess of Parma most especially, in her habit of issuing unexpected decrees behind which one sensed certain principles, all the more impressive the less one was aware of them. If the new Greek minister gave a fancy-dress ball, everyone chose a costume and everyone wondered what the Duchesse would wear. One lady imagined that she would appear as the Duchesse de Bourgogne, another suggested the likelihood of coming as the Princess of Deryabar,[8] a third as Psyche. Finally, a Courvoisier asked, "What are you going as, Oriane?" and received the tart rejoinder, "Why, nothing at all!," the only response no one had thought of, and one that set every tongue wagging about what was seen as something that revealed Oriane's opinion as to the true social position of the new Greek minister and the proper form to be adopted toward him—that is to say, the opinion that ought to have been anticipated, that a duchesse "was not obliged" to attend the fancy-dress ball given by this new minister. "I don't see that there's any necessity to go to the Greek minister's: I don't know him; I'm not Greek; so why should I go to his house? I have no cause for social intercourse in such a place," said the Duchesse.

"But everyone's going, it will be charming, from everything I hear," cried Mme de Gallardon.

"But it's also just as charming to stay at home by one's own fireside," rejoined Mme de Guermantes.

The Courvoisiers could not get over this, but the Guermantes, without following suit with their cousin, approved: "Of course, not everyone's in a position like Oriane to flout convention so utterly. But in a sense, you can't say she's wrong in her desire to show that we do rather overstep the mark in groveling before these foreigners, when we're not always sure quite where they come from."

Naturally, Mme de Guermantes, perfectly aware of the string of comments that either attitude would provoke, derived as much pleasure from appearing at a party at which the hostess dared not rely on her presence as she did by staying at home or spending the evening at the theater with her husband, on the night of a party to which "everyone was going," or else, when people imagined that she would put the finest diamonds to shame by wearing some antique historic tiara, by making her entrance without a single jewel and wearing a style of dress quite different from the one that people had wrongly supposed to be obligatory for the occasion in hand. Although she was anti-Dreyfusard (while believing Dreyfus to be innocent, just as she devoted her time to society life while believing only in the life of the mind), she had created a stunning sensation at a party given by the Princesse de Ligne, first of all by remaining seated when all the ladies present had risen to their feet as Général Mercier[59] entered the room, and then by getting up and asking for her carriage in a voice for all to hear when a Nationalist speaker had started to hold forth, thereby showing that in her opinion talking politics had no place in the world of society; all heads had turned in her direction at a Good Friday concert at which, although a Voltairean, she had felt it indecent to bring Christ onto the stage. We know how important, even for the great queens of society, is the time of year when the social calendar commences: so much so that the Marquise d'Amoncourt—who, with her burning need to say something (a psychological quirk, and a lack of sensitivity to boot), always ended up making a fool of herself—had even gone so far as to reply to someone who had called to offer condolences on the death of her father, M. de Montmorency, "I think what makes such grief more difficult to bear is that it should come at a time when one's mantelpiece is simply smothered in invitation cards." Well, at this point in the social calendar, when anyone invited the Duchesse de Guermantes to dine—with great urgency, in case she was already engaged—she would turn down the invitation with the one excuse that no society person would ever have thought of: she was about to set off on a cruise—"Quite fascinating, my dear!"—of the Norwegian fjords. Society people were thunderstruck by this, and, without any notion of following the Duchesse's example, nevertheless derived from her project the sense of relief you get when you read Kant, and when, after the most rigorous demonstration of determinism, it transpires that above the world of necessity there is the world of freedom. Every really original invention stirs the interest even of people who can derive no benefit from it. The invention of steam navigation was almost nothing when compared with the implementation of steam navigation at that sedentary time of the year known as "the season." The idea that anyone could turn down a hundred dinners or luncheon parties on purpose, twice as many tea parties, three times as many receptions, the most brilliant Mondays at the Opéra and Tuesdays at the Théâtre-Français to visit the Norwegian fjords was no more explicable to the Courvoisiers than the idea of *Twenty Thousand Leagues Under the Sea*, but it conveyed to them a similar impression of independence and charm. So that not a day passed without somebody's being heard to ask, not merely, "You've heard Oriane's latest quip?" but "You know Oriane's latest?" And following upon "Oriane's latest?" and "Oriane's latest quip," people would say, "How typical of Oriane!," "Isn't that vintage Oriane for you?" For instance, Oriane's latest might be that, finding herself obliged to write on behalf of some patriotic circle to Cardinal X, Bishop of Mâcon (normally referred to by M. de Guermantes as "M. de Mascon," because he thought this to be more "traditional"), when everybody was trying to figure out what form her letter would take, had no problem as to the opening address, the choice being between "Eminence" and "Monseigneur," but was in a quandary as to the rest, Oriane's letter, to the general astonishment, began, "M. le Cardinal," following an old Academic formula, or "My cousin," this term being in use among the princes of the church, the Guermantes, and crowned heads of state, who were accustomed to praying God to take each and all of them into "His fit and holy keeping." All that was needed to start people talking about "Oriane's latest" was to be in a theater at which everyone who was anyone in Paris was present for the performance of some charming play, to look for Mme de Guermantes in the Princess of Parma's box, in the box of the Princesse de Guermantes, or in those of countless others who might have invited her, and to discover her sitting by herself, dressed in black, wearing a diminutive hat, in an orchestra box in which she had taken her seat before the curtain went up. "You can hear better, when it's a play that's worth listening to," she would explain to the scandalized Courvoisiers, the admiringly bewildered Guermantes, and the Princess of Parma, who suddenly became convinced that the "fashion" for hearing the beginning of a play was more up-to-date, betokened more originality and intelligence (no surprise coming from Oriane) than late arrival for the last act after a grand dinner party and a look-in at some reception or other. These, then, were the various ways of astonishing people for which the Princess of Parma knew she ought to be prepared if she asked Mme de Guermantes about some literary or society matter, which meant that, during these dinner parties at the Duchesse's, Her Royal Highness never broached the slightest subject unless it was with the uneasy and titillating caution of the bather emerging from between two knife-edged breakers.

Among the elements that were absent from the two or three other roughly equivalent leading salons of the Faubourg Saint-Germain and differentiated the Duchesse's own from them, just as Leibniz allows that each monad reflects the whole universe and also adds to it something of its own, one of the least attractive was normally furnished by one or two extremely beautiful women who had no other claim to be there but their beauty and the use to which M. de Guermantes had put it, and whose presence revealed at once, as does the presence of otherwise unaccountable paintings in other salons, that in this one the husband was a passionate connoisseur of the feminine graces. These women were all more or less the same; for the Duc had a taste for tall women, at once statuesque and nonchalant, of a type halfway between the *Venus de Milo* and the *Winged Mercury*; often fair-haired, rarely dark, occasionally auburn, like the most recent addition, who was at this dinner, the very Vicomtesse d'Arpajon with whom he had been so enamored that for a long time he had obliged her to send him as many as ten telegrams a day (to the Duchesse's mild irritation) and corresponded with her by carrier pigeon when he was staying at Guermantes, and from whose company in fact he had long been so incapable of tearing himself away that, one winter he had been forced to spend in Parma, he traveled back to Paris every week, making a two-day journey in order to see her.

In the normal course of events, these bit-part beauties had once been his mistresses but no longer were (as in the case of Mme d'Arpajon), or were on the point of ceasing to be. It may well have been that the glamour the Duchesse held in their eyes, and the hope of being invited to her salon, though they themselves came from highly aristocratic backgrounds, however second-rank, had prompted them, even more than the good looks and generosity of the Duc, to yield to his desires. Not that the Duchesse would have imposed any insurmountable obstacle in the way of their being admitted to her society; she was aware that in more than one of them she had found an ally, thanks to whom she had obtained countless things that she wanted and which M. de Guermantes would pitilessly refuse to his wife as long as he was not in love with someone else. And so the reason they were not received by the Duchesse until a liaison was already far advanced had essentially to do with the fact that the Duc, each time he embarked on a full-scale love affair, had expected it to be no more than a brief fling, in exchange for which he considered an invitation from his wife to be excessive. And yet he found himself offering just this as the reward for far less–for a first kiss, for instance–because he had met with unexpected resistance, or, conversely, because there had been no resistance. In love, it often happens that gratitude, the desire to give pleasure, causes us to be generous beyond the limits of what hope and self-interest had envisaged. But then the implementation of this offer would become hindered by further complications. For a start, all the women who had responded to M. de Guermantes's love, and occasionally even when they had not yet yielded to it, he had kept cut off from the world one after another. He no longer allowed them to see anyone, spent almost all his time in their company, looked after the education of their children, to whom he sometimes, if one was to judge by certain glaring resemblances later on, had occasion to present a little brother or sister. And if, at the start of the liaison, the idea of an introduction to Mme de Guermantes, utterly absent from the Duc's intentions, had played a part in the mind of the mistress in question, in the course of the liaison the lady's views had altered: the Duc was no longer for her the husband of the most fashionable woman in Paris but a man whom the new mistress was in love with, and a man who had given her the means and the inclination for a more luxurious style of life and had turned upside down her notions of the relative importance of questions of social snobbery and material advantage; and occasionally these mistresses of the Duc were animated by a jealousy of Mme de Guermantes, in which all these factors played a part. But this was extremely rare; besides, when the day set aside for the introduction eventually came round (usually at a time when it had become a matter of more or less indifference to the Duc, whose behavior, like everyone else's, was more often dictated by previous behavior than by the original motive for the introduction, which had ceased to operate), it frequently happened that it was Mme de Guermantes who had sought the acquaintance of the mistress, in whom she hoped, and was so very anxious, to find a precious ally against her dreadful husband. None of this means that in their own house, except on rare occasions, when, if the Duchesse talked too much, he let fall a few words or, more dreadful still, maintained an excruciatingly meaningful silence, M. de Guermantes failed in the keeping up of "outward appearances" toward his wife. People who did not know them might easily be taken in. Sometimes, in the autumn, between the Deauville races, taking the waters, and departure for the hunting season in Guermantes, in the few weeks that people spend in Paris, since the Duchesse was fond of *café-concerts,* the Duc would accompany her to one in the evening. The audience noticed at once, in one of the little open boxes where there is just enough room for two people, this Hercules in his *"smoking"* (for in France anything that is the least bit British gets given the name it happens not to have in England),⁶⁰ his monocle scrunched into his eye, a fat cigar, from which he now and then took a puff, in his fleshy but finely shaped hand, on the ring finger of which a sapphire sparkled, keeping his eyes mostly turned toward the stage but, when he did let them fall upon the audience, in which there was absolutely no one he knew, softening them with a gentle look, reserved, polite, and respectful. When a refrain struck him as amusing and not too risqué, the Duc turned round to his wife with a smile and would share with her, with a twinkle of indulgent complicity, the innocent merriment the new song had aroused in him. And the spectators might well have believed that there was no better husband in the world, or anyone more enviable than the Duchesse—this woman who was excluded from all the real interests in the Duc's life, the woman he did not love, and to whom he had never once stopped being unfaithful. When the Duchesse felt tired, the audience would see M. de Guermantes rise to his feet, put on her wrap with his own hands, arranging her necklaces so that they did not catch in the lining, and clear the way for her to the exit with an attentive display of care which she received with the haughty chill of a woman of the world who takes such behavior for granted, simply as conventional good manners, at times even regards it with the slightly ironical bitterness of the disabused wife who has no illusions left to shatter. Despite these outward appearances—another of the aspects of the politeness that has transferred, at some remote point in time that has never come to an end for those who have survived it, a deep-seated sense of duty from the depths to the surface—the Duchesse did not have an easy life. M. de Guermantes reverted to humane behavior and generosity only when there was a new mistress, who would, as it happened, more often than not side with the Duchesse: the latter could then see opportunities opening up for her once more to be generous toward inferiors, charitable toward the poor, and even, later on, to buy herself a fabulous new motorcar. But the irritation that generally arose fairly rapidly in Mme de Guermantes in regard to persons she found too submissive did not spare the Duc's mistresses. The Duchesse very soon grew tired of them. As it happened, at that time, too, the Duc's liaison with Mme d'Arpajon was coming to an end. There was another mistress in the offing.

No doubt the love M. de Guermantes had borne each of them in turn would one day make itself felt anew: for a start, this love, as it faded away, bequeathed his mistresses to the surroundings like beautiful marble statues—beautiful to the Duc at least, since part of him became an artist in this respect, because he had loved them and was appreciative now of contours he would not have noticed without making love to them—that juxtaposed, in the Duchesse's drawing room, their various forms, which had long been hostile to one another, eaten up with jealousies and quarrels, but were finally reconciled in the peace of amity; and this amity was itself an effect of the love that had caused M. de Guermantes to observe, in the women who had been his mistresses, virtues shared by all human beings but perceptible only to the lover's sensuality, to the point where an ex-mistress who has become "a really close friend" and would do anything in the world for one has become a cliché, like the doctor or father who is not a doctor or a father but a friend. But during the initial stages of rupture, the woman whom M. de Guermantes was on the point of abandoning would make a fuss, create scenes, become demanding, appear indiscreet and pestering. The Duc would begin to take a sudden dislike to her. At this stage, Mme de Guermantes would have the opportunity to bring to light the real or imagined defects of a person who annoyed her. Known to be kind, Mme de Guermantes would take the constant telephone calls from the abandoned mistress, receive her confidences, offer a shoulder to cry on, without complaint. She would laugh about it with her husband, then with a few close friends. And, imagining that the sympathy she showed toward the unfortunate woman gave her the right to make fun of her, even to her face, whatever the lady in question might say, provided it could be kept within the bounds of the absurd behavior that the Duc and herself had recently decided to ascribe to her, Mme de Guermantes had no qualms about exchanging ironically knowing glances on the matter with her husband.

Meanwhile, as she took her place at table, the Princess of Parma suddenly remembered that she had thought of inviting Mme d'Heudicourt to the Opéra, and, seeking assurance about any offense to Mme de Guermantes that might be involved, she was looking for an opportunity to sound her out on the matter. At this point, M. de Grouchy came into the room, his train having been held up for an hour because of a derailment. He offered his apologies as best he could. Had she been a Courvoisier, his wife would have died of shame. But Mme de Grouchy was not a Guermantes for nothing. As her husband was offering his excuses, she broke in:

"I see that, even in small matters, arriving late is a tradition in your family."

"Sit down, Grouchy, and don't let them disparage you," said the Duc. "Though I move with the times, I have to admit that the Battle of Waterloo had its good side, since it brought about the Bourbon Restoration—and, better still, in a way that made them unpopular. But it seems to me that you're a real Nimrod!"[61]

"As it happens, I did get quite a good bag. You'll allow me, of course, to send six brace of pheasant to the Duchesse tomorrow?"

Some thought seemed to flicker in Mme de Guermantes's eyes. She insisted that M. de Grouchy must not put himself to the trouble of sending the pheasants. And, signaling to the footman with a fiancée with whom I had chatted on my way from the Elstir room, she said to him:

"You'll go and collect M. le Comte's pheasants tomorrow and bring them straight back. Grouchy, you won't mind if I give a few of them away, will you? Basin and I can't eat a dozen pheasants by ourselves."

"But the day after tomorrow will be soon enough," said M. de Grouchy.

"No, I'd rather it were tomorrow," the Duchesse insisted.

Poullein had turned pale: he would miss his meeting with his fiancée. This was adequate opportunity for the Duchesse to divert the conversation; she liked to cultivate the common touch with people.

"I know it's your day off," she said to Poullein. "All you need to do is to change with Georges. He can take tomorrow off and stay here on duty the day after."

But the day after, Poullein's fiancée would not be free. He had no interest at all in having the day off then. As soon as Poullein had left the room, everyone complimented the Duchesse on her kindness toward her servants.

"But I only treat them as I'd like people to treat me."

"But that's just it. They have every reason to say they've found a good position in this house."

"Nothing so special about that. But I think they all like me. That one is a trifle irritating because he's in love. He finds it appropriate to go about with a lovesick look on his face."

At this point Poullein re-entered the room.

"You're right," said M. de Grouchy, "he doesn't look very cheerful. One needs to be kind to these people, but not too kind."

"I realize that I'm not very good with servants. He'll have nothing to do all day but go and fetch your pheasants, sit around the house doing nothing, then eat his share of the treat."

"There are plenty of people who would be glad to be in his place," said M. de Grouchy. "Envy makes people blind."

"Oriane," said the Princess of Parma, "I had a visit from your cousin Heudicourt the other day. Of course, she's a highly intelligent woman. She's a Guermantes—need one say more?—but they tell me she has a wicked tongue. . . ."

The Duc's eyes met his wife's in a prolonged gaze of deliberate stupefaction. Mme de Guermantes began to laugh. The Princess took some time to become aware of this.

"But . . . do you mean . . . you don't agree with me?" she said with some misgiving.

"Really, madame, it's too good of you to pay any attention to the faces Basin makes. Now, Basin, you're not to insinuate anything nasty about our relatives."

"Does he think she's overly malicious?" the Princess asked pointedly.

"Oh, certainly not!" came the Duchesse's reply. "I don't know who told Your Highness she was malicious. Quite the contrary. She's an excellent creature who never spoke ill of or did any harm to a soul."

"Oh, I see," said Mme de Parme, much relieved. "It was not something I had noticed myself, either. But I know it's difficult not to be malicious when one has a great deal of wit. . . ."

"Ah! Now, wit is a quality of which she has even less."

"What, less wit?" asked the Princess, stupefied.

"Come, now, Oriane," broke in the Duc in a slightly sulky tone, as he darted amused glances about the table, "you heard the Princess tell you she was highly intelligent."

"But isn't she?"

"Highly wide around the waist, certainly."

"Don't listen to him, madame, he's not being truthful. She's as stupid as a . . . euh . . . goose," interposed Mme de Guermantes in a loud and husky voice (she had far more "old-world charm" than the Duc himself could sometimes muster when he was not deliberately trying, but her charm was quite different from the deliquescent, lace-jabot style of her husband, and far more subtle, in fact, with its almost countrified pronunciation and its delightfully rough, earthy tang). "But she's the finest woman in the world. And I'm not sure how far one can talk of stupidity in her case. I don't believe I know anyone like her; she's a case for medical treatment, there's something pathological about her, some sort of natural naïveté, or stupidity, or 'retarded development,' like the sort of thing you come across in melodramas or in *L'Arlésienne*.⁶² When she comes here, I'm always wondering whether the moment may not have arrived for her intelligence to show itself at last, which always makes me a little jumpy." These turns of phrase impressed the Princess wonderfully, but she remained flabbergasted by the Duchesse's verdict. "She told me your joke about 'Teaser Augustus'—Mme d'Épinay mentioned it as well. Quite delightful," she said by way of response.

M. de Guermantes explained the joke to me. I was wanting to tell him that his brother, who pretended not to know me, was expecting me that very evening at eleven. But I had not inquired of Robert whether I might mention this rendezvous, and, given that M. de Charlus had arranged it with me in a way that practically contradicted what he had told the Duchesse, I thought it more tactful not to mention it.

" 'Teaser Augustus' isn't bad," said M. de Guermantes, "but Mme d'Heudicourt probably didn't tell you about the far better remark Oriane made to her the other day in reply to a luncheon invitation?"

"Oh no! Do tell me!"

"Come, now, Basin, there's no need for that. In the first place, it was a stupid remark, and it will make the Princess think me even worse than my dopey cousin. Though I don't know why I call her my cousin. She's one of Basin's cousins. Still, I suppose she is related to me in a sense."

"Oh!" exclaimed the Princess of Parma as she confronted the idea that she could possibly think of Mme de Guermantes as stupid, protesting desperately that nothing could ever make the Duchesse fall from the place she held in her esteem.

"Besides, we've already deprived her of the qualities of the mind, and since the remark you're referring to tends to deny her certain qualities of the heart, it seems to me quite out of place to repeat it."

" 'Deny her'! 'Out of place'! How well she expresses herself!" said the Duc with a pretense of irony, to win admiration for the Duchesse.

"Come, come, Basin, you mustn't make fun of your wife."

"I should explain to Your Royal Highness," the Duc went on, "that Oriane's cousin may be superior, kind, on the stout side, anything you care to mention, but she isn't exactly—how shall I put it—open-handed."

"Oh, I know, she's terribly close-fisted," the Princess broke in.

"I would not have ventured to put it like that, but you have hit on exactly the right words. It comes across in the way she keeps house, especially the food she serves. It's excellent, but she does eke it out."

"That can give rise to some fairly amusing goings-on," M. de Bréauté broke in. "For instance, my dear Basin, I once went down to Heudicourt on a day when you were expected, Oriane and yourself. The most sumptuous preparations had been made, and then, in the afternoon, a footman brought in a telegram to say you weren't coming."

"That doesn't surprise me at all," said the Duchesse, who not only was difficult to pin down but liked people to know it.

"Your cousin read the telegram, was bitterly disappointed, then immediately, quick as a flash, telling herself that there was no point in going to unnecessary expense for unimportant nobility such as myself, she called the footman back. 'Tell the cook not to put on the chicken,' she shouted. And that evening I heard her asking the butler, 'And what about yesterday's leftover beef? Aren't you going to serve it up?' "

"All the same, one has to say that the fare one gets there is of the best," said the Duc, who imagined that the use of this word would show him to be very much of the old school. "I know of no establishment where one eats better."

"Or less," the Duchesse chipped in.

"The food is quite wholesome and quite adequate for what you would call an old Farmer Grimes like myself," the Duc went on. "One doesn't overindulge."

"Oh, if we are to understand it as taking a cure, then that's another matter; it's clearly more health-inspired than rich and copious. Not that it's *that* special," Mme de Guermantes added, as someone who was not too keen that the award of "best table in Paris" should go to any table but her own. "My cousin follows the same pattern as the constipated writers who present us with a one-act play or a sonnet every fifteen years. The sort of things people call little masterpieces, little jewels of nothing–the sort of thing I really hate, in fact. The food at Zénaïde's place isn't bad, but one would find it more humdrum if she were less parsimonious. There are things her cook does well, and others he makes a complete mess of. I've had some dreadful dinners there, as one does in most places, only they've done me less harm than elsewhere, because one's stomach is, after all, more sensitive to quantity than to quality."

"Well, to get to the end of the story," the Duc concluded, "Zénaïde was adamant that Oriane should go to luncheon with her, and since my wife is not very keen on going out anywhere, she resisted the invitation; she wanted to be sure that she was not being trapped into some great shindig, and tried in vain to find out who else would be there to luncheon. 'You must come,' insisted Zénaïde, as she boasted about all the good things there would be to eat. 'There'll be a chestnut purée, that's all I need to tell you, and there'll be seven little *bouchées à la reine.*' '*Seven!*' cried Oriane. 'Then there'll be at least eight of us to lunch!' "

After a few seconds, the Princess finally saw the point and let her laughter break forth like a clap of thunder. "Ah, 'there'll be at least eight of us'–it's a delightful one. How very charmingly you edit it!" she said, after making a supreme effort to recall the expression she had heard used by Mme d'Épinay, which was more appropriate in this instance.

"Oriane, that was very delightful of the Princess; she said your remark was 'well edited.' "

"But, my dear, there's nothing new in what you're saying. I know how witty the Princess is," replied Mme de Guermantes, who readily appreciated a remark when it was uttered by a royal personage and flattered her own wit at the same time. "I am very proud that Madame should appreciate my humble attempts at 'editing.' Though I don't remember saying such a thing. And if I did, it was to flatter my cousin, for, if she had provided seven 'mouthfuls,'[63] the mouths to feed, if I can put it like this, would have been a dozen if not more."

During this time, the Comtesse d'Arpajon, who had told me before dinner that her aunt would have been so happy to show me around her Normandy residence, was saying to me, over the Prince d'Agrigente's head, that where she would most like to invite me was to the Côte d'Or, because there, at Pont-le-Duc, she would be in her own home.

"The archives of the château would be of interest to you. There is some absolutely fascinating correspondence between all the most prominent figures in the seventeenth, eighteenth, and nineteenth centuries. I spend many very happy hours there, living in the past," the Comtesse assured me, and I was reminded of M. de Guermantes remarking that she was an extremely cultured woman as far as literature was concerned.

"She owns all M. de Bornier's[64] manuscripts," the Princess continued, alluding to Mme d'Heudicourt, and eager to make the most of any good cause she might have for cultivating the society of such a person.

"She must have dreamed it–I don't believe she ever even knew him," said the Duchesse.

"The really interesting thing about these correspondences is that they are between people of different countries," the Comtesse d'Arpajon continued, as someone who was allied to the principal ducal and even reigning families of Europe and was always happy to remind people of the fact.

"But surely, Oriane," said M. de Guermantes meaningfully, "you can't have forgotten that dinner party where you had M. de Bornier next to you at table!"

"Basin," the Duchesse broke in, "if you're trying to tell me that I knew M. de Bornier, why, of course I did, he even called on me on several occasions, but I could never bring myself to invite him, because it would have meant having the house disinfected with formol after every visit he made. As for the dinner you're referring to, how could I ever forget it? But it was certainly not at Zénaïde's place. She never set eyes on Bornier in her life and would probably think, if you mentioned *La Fille de Roland* to her, that you were talking about a Bonaparte princess who was thought to be engaged to the son of the King of Greece. No, it was at the Austrian Embassy. That dear man Hoyos imagined he was doing me a favor by plunking that evil-smelling Academician right next to me. It was like sitting next to a whole platoon of gendarmes. I was obliged to hold my nose as best I could all through dinner. I didn't dare breathe until they brought on the Gruyère!"

M. de Guermantes had obtained his hidden objective and conducted a furtive inspection of his guests' faces to gauge the effect produced by the Duchesse's witticisms.

"And I find there is a peculiar charm in old exchanges of letters," continued the lady of impressive literary culture, who had such fascinating letters in her château, quite undeterred by the intervening head of the Prince d'Agrigente.

"Have you noticed that an author's letters are often superior to the rest of his work? Who was the man who wrote *Salammbô*?"

I would have preferred not to have to reply and to curtail this conversation, but I felt it would be rather unkind to the Prince d'Agrigente; he was pretending to know perfectly well whom *Salammbô* was by and to be leaving it to me to say, whereas he was actually in a painful quandary.

"Flaubert," I ended up saying, but the assenting nods performed by the Prince's head smothered the sound of my remark, with the result that the lady I was talking to was not exactly sure whether I had said Paul Bert or Fulbert, names that did not ring quite right in her ears.

"At all events," she went on, "how fascinating his correspondence is, and how superior to his books! It explains him, in fact, because one sees from everything he says about the difficulty he has writing a book that he wasn't a true writer, not a talented man."

"Speaking of correspondences, I find Gambetta's quite wonderful," said the Duchesse de Guermantes, to show that she was not afraid to display her interest in a proletarian and a radical. M. de Bréauté, who fully grasped the witty effect of her audaciousness, looked around him with a gaze at once tipsy and affectionate before wiping his monocle.

"By God, it was devilishly dull, that *Fille de Roland*," said M. de Guermantes, with the satisfaction he derived from the sense of his own superiority over a work that had bored him to tears, and perhaps also from the *suave mari magno*[65] sensation one has in the middle of a good dinner when one recalls such terrible evenings at the theater. "Still, it had some good lines, and a patriotic spirit."

I said something that implied my utter lack of enthusiasm for M. de Bornier.

"Ah! You've got something against him?" the Duc asked with curiosity, for he always supposed, when anyone spoke ill of a man, that it must be on account of a private resentment, just as to speak well of a woman indicated an incipient infatuation.

"You clearly bear him some sort of grudge. What did he do to you? Do tell us! Come on, there must be some skeleton in the closet or you wouldn't sound so disparaging. It goes on too long, *La Fille de Roland*, but there is a whiff of feeling to it."

" 'Whiff' is exactly the right word for an author with such a smell about him," broke in an ironic Mme de Guermantes. "If this poor child has ever been in the man's company, one can quite understand that he got up his nose!"

"I have to say, though, madame," the Duc went on, addressing the Princess of Parma, "that, quite apart from *La Fille de Roland*, I'm terribly old-fashioned in my literary and even in my musical tastes. There's no old junk too rubbishy for my palate. You won't believe this, perhaps, but in the evenings, when my wife sits down at the piano, I find myself asking for some old tune by Auber or Boieldieu, or even Beethoven! That's what I like. But as for Wagner, it sends me to sleep immediately."

"You're wrong there," said Mme de Guermantes. "Even with his insufferable long-windedness, Wagner had elements of genius. *Lohengrin* is a masterpiece. Even in *Tristan* there are occasionally intriguing passages. And the Spinning Chorus in *The Flying Dutchman* is perfect heaven."

"But I'm right, aren't I, Babal?" said M. de Guermantes, turning to M. de Bréauté. "What we like is, 'The gatherings of noble companions are all held in this charming haunt.'[66] That's delightful. And *Fra Diavolo*, and *The Magic Flute*, and *Le Chalet*, and *The Marriage of Figaro*, and *Les Diamants de la couronne*—that's what we call music! It's the same thing in literature. For instance, I love Balzac—*Le Bal de Sceaux*, *Les Mohicans de Paris*."[67]

"Oh, my dear, if you're off on the subject of Balzac, we'll be here forever. Save it up for one of Mémé's visits. He's even worse—he knows Balzac by heart."

Irritated by his wife's interruption, the Duc shot her a momentary look of menacing silence. In the meantime, Mme d'Arpajon had been involved in an exchange with the Princess of Parma about poetry, tragic and otherwise, the words of which did not reach me distinctly until I caught the following remark from the lips of Mme d'Arpajon: "Oh, Madame is quite right. I admit that he paints us an ugly picture of the world, because he can't distinguish between ugliness and beauty, or, rather, because his insufferable vanity leads him to believe that everything he says is beautiful. I agree with Your Highness that, in the piece we're talking about, there are some ludicrous things, quite unintelligible, and some errors of taste, and that it's difficult to understand, as much trouble to read as if it were written in Russian or Chinese, because quite clearly it's simply *not* what we'd call French; but, still, when one has taken the trouble, how rewarding a work it is, how truly imaginative!" I had missed the opening sentences of this little lecture. I eventually gathered not only that the poet who was incapable of making the distinction between beauty and ugliness was Victor Hugo, but, furthermore, that the poetry that was as hard to understand as Russian or Chinese was "When the child appears, the family circle cheers loudly . . . ," a piece dating from the poet's earliest period, and perhaps even nearer to Mme Deshoulières than the Victor Hugo of *La Légende des siècles*.[68]

Far from thinking Mme d'Arpajon ridiculous, I saw her (the first person at this table—such an ordinary, humdrum table—at which I had sat down with such disappointment), I saw her in my mind's eye, beneath that lace cap of hers with the long spiral ringlets falling remorsefully from either side, a cap worn by Mme de Rémusat, Mme de Broglie, Mme de Saint-Aulaire,[69] all those distinguished ladies whose delightful letters quote so learnedly and so aptly from Sophocles, Schiller, and the *Imitation of Christ*, but whose reactions to the earliest poetry of the Romantics provoked the alarm and exhaustion that were inseparable, in my grandmother's eyes, from Mallarmé's late poetry.[70]

"Mme d'Arpajon is very fond of poetry," the Princess of Parma remarked to Mme de Guermantes, impressed by the tone of the former's lecture.

"No, she doesn't understand a thing about it," returned Mme de Guermantes in an undertone, taking advantage of the fact that Mme d'Arpajon, who was countering an objection raised by Général de Beautreillis, was too intent on what she was saying to hear what the Duchesse was whispering. "She's become very bookish since she was abandoned. I don't mind telling Your Highness that I'm the one who has to bear the brunt of it all, because it's to me she comes running whenever Basin hasn't been to see her, which is practically every day. But it really isn't my fault if she bores him, and I can't force him to go and see her, though I'd prefer him to be a little more loyal to her, because it would mean I saw somewhat less of her myself. But she drives him mad, and no wonder. She's not a dreadful person, but, believe me, she's unimaginably boring. She gives me such a headache each day that I'm forever having to take painkillers. And it's all because Basin took it into his head to go to bed with her behind my back for a year or so. And as if that wasn't enough, I've got a footman who's in love with a little slut and goes about sulking if I don't ask the young lady to quit her streetwalking profits for half an hour to come and have tea with me! It's enough to drive one mad!" the Duchesse concluded languidly. The main reason why Mme d'Arpajon was driving M. de Guermantes to distraction was that he had recently become the lover of another woman, the Marquise de Surgis-le-Duc, as I discovered.

As it happened, the footman who had been deprived of his day off was at that moment waiting at table. And it struck me that he had not recovered from his disappointment and was doing his job with all this on his mind, for I noticed that, as he was offering the various dishes to M. de Châtellerault, he performed his task so awkwardly that the young Duc's elbow was constantly coming into contact with his own. The young Duc showed no sign of annoyance with the blushing footman, but, on the contrary, looked up at him with a smile in his clear blue eyes. I saw this good humor as a token of kindness on the guest's part. But the insistent smiling eyes led me to think that he was aware of the servant's disappointed hopes and that what he was in fact feeling was perhaps a malicious amusement.

"But, my dear, you're revealing nothing new, you know, in what you're telling us about Victor Hugo," the Duchesse went on, turning this time to Mme d'Arpajon, whose worried turn of the head she had just intercepted. "You mustn't expect to launch his early work. We all know it is talented. It's the later Victor Hugo that's so dreadful—*La Légende des siècles*, and the other titles I can't remember. But *Les Feuilles d'automne*, *Les Chants du crépuscule* are often the work of a poet, a true poet. Even *Les Contemplations* still has some fine things in it," added the Duchesse, with whom her listeners dared not disagree, and with good reason. "But I confess that I prefer to venture no further than the *Crépuscule*! It's certainly true that in Victor Hugo's better poems, and they do exist, one frequently stumbles upon an idea, even a profound one."

And with just the right shade of feeling, bringing out the melancholic thought with the full force of her intonation, projecting it to a world beyond the sound of her voice, and gazing steadily ahead of her in a dreamy, charming manner, the Duchesse said, "Listen to this," and started to recite slowly: " 'Suffering is a fruit God lets not grow on any branch too frail to bear it.'[71] Or this," she continued: " 'The dead don't linger on. . . . Alas, they fall to dust less quickly in their graves than in our hearts!' "[72]

And while a smile of disillusionment puckered her sorrowful lips with an elegant twist, the Duchesse rested the dreamy gaze of her lovely, clear blue eyes upon Mme d'Arpajon. I was getting to know those eyes, and that voice, with its heavy drawl, its rasping flavor. In this voice and those eyes, I recognized much of the natural world around Combray. It is true that in the affected way the voice sporadically betrayed the earthiness of the soil there were many elements involved: the wholly countrified origins of one branch of the Guermantes family, longer-rooted, sturdier, wilder, more pugnacious than others; and then that automatic reflex characteristic of genuinely refined people and people of intelligence who know that refinement has nothing to do with mincing one's words, the reflex of nobles who fraternize more readily with their farmers than with the middle classes—all of these being particularities that Mme de Guermantes's regal status enabled her to show off more freely, with no holds barred. It appears that some of her sisters shared the same voice; she detested them, and they—less intelligent than she and married to men somewhat below their station (if one can use such an expression to refer to unions with obscure noblemen, burrowed away in the provinces or in one of the lackluster circles of the Faubourg Saint-Germain in Paris)—possessed this voice themselves but had curbed it, corrected it, toned it down as far as they were able to do so, just as any one of us seldom has the nerve to be himself, as opposed to putting his efforts into aping the most fashionable models of the done thing. But Oriane was far more intelligent, far wealthier, and, most important, so much more fashionable than her sisters; as the Princesse des Laumes, she had commanded such an impressive élan in the company of the Prince of Wales that she came to realize that her discordant voice was an attraction, and, with audacious confidence in her own idiosyncrasy, she had used it to create, in the world of society, what in the theatrical world a Réjane or a Jeanne Granier[73] (and of course no comparison is implied here between the respective merits and talents of these two actresses) created with theirs, something admirable and distinctive that certain sisters of Réjane and Granier, utterly unknown to the world, possibly tried to conceal as a defect.

In support of all these reasons for cultivating her native idiosyncrasies, Mme de Guermantes's favorite writers—Mérimée, Meilhac, and Halévy—had contributed, together with a respect for "naturalness," an inclination toward the prosaic, through which she attained to poetry, and a purely society cast of mind, which called up various landscapes before my eyes. Besides, the Duchesse was quite capable, by bringing an artful refinement of her own to these various influences, of having selected for most of her words the pronunciation she thought of as most "Île-de-France," most "Champenoise," since, if not to the same degree as her sister-in-law Marsantes, she rarely strayed beyond the pure choice of words that might have been used by an old, established French writer. And when one was tired of the composite hodgepodge of modern speech, it was very restful to listen to Mme de Guermantes's talk, even with the knowledge that it could express far fewer things—almost as restful, if one was alone in her company and she restrained and clarified the flow of her speech still further, as listening to an old song. Then, as I looked and listened to Mme de Guermantes, I could see, calmly imprisoned in the unending afternoon of her eyes, an expanse of sky of the Île-de-France or of Champagne, bluish, slanting, at the same angle of incline as in the eyes of Saint-Loup.

And so, in these various influences, Mme de Guermantes expressed at once the most ancient period of aristocratic France, then, much later, the manner in which the Duchesse de Broglie might have enjoyed and found fault with Victor Hugo under the July Monarchy, and, finally, a keen appreciation for the literature that sprang from Mérimée and Meilhac. I found the first of these influences more to my taste than the second, and it did more to alleviate the disappointment of my journey to and arrival at the Faubourg Saint-Germain, so different from what I had imagined it to be; but I found the second preferable to the last. For, while Mme de Guermantes was a Guermantes almost to her fingertips, her à-la-Pailleron[74] preferences, her taste for Dumas *fils*[75] were calculated and deliberate. Since such tastes were the opposite of my own, she fed me with literature when she spoke to me about the Faubourg Saint-Germain, and never seemed so stupidly Faubourg Saint-Germain as when she talked about literature.

Moved by the last lines recited, Mme d'Arpajon burst forth with, " 'These relics of the heart, they also have their dust!'[76] Monsieur, you must write that down for me on my fan," she said to M. de Guermantes.

"The poor woman, I feel sorry for her!" the Princess of Parma remarked to Mme de Guermantes.

"No, please, madame, spare your feelings. She has only got what was coming to her."

"But—you'll forgive me for saying this—she does really love him, doesn't she?"

"Oh, not in the least. She isn't capable of it. She thinks she loves him, just as, at this very moment, she thinks she has been quoting Victor Hugo, when in fact she was reciting a line from Musset. Look," said the Duchesse in a melancholic voice, "nobody could be more moved by true feeling than I. But let me tell you something. Only yesterday she made a terrible scene with Basin. Your Highness is perhaps inclined to think that it was because he's in love with other women, because he no longer loves her. Far from it. It was because he won't put her sons forward for the Jockey! Is that the behavior of a woman in love, madame? No! I will go further," Mme de Guermantes added sharply. "She is a creature of unusual insensitivity."

Meanwhile, it was with an eye sparkling with satisfaction that M. de Guermantes had been listening to his wife talking "point-blank" about Victor Hugo and quoting those few lines. The Duchesse might often be irritating, but at moments such as this he was proud of her. "Oriane is really extraordinary. She can talk about anything, she's read everything. She couldn't possibly have guessed that the conversation this evening would turn to Victor Hugo. Whatever the subject, she's ready for it. She can hold her own with the most learned people. This young man here must be quite enthralled."

"But shall we change the subject?" Mme de Guermantes continued. "She's a very high-strung woman. You must think me very old-fashioned," she continued, turning to me. "I know that nowadays it's seen as a weakness to favor ideas in poetry, poetry with some thought to it."

"It's old-fashioned?" the Princess of Parma asked, slightly a-tremble at the effect upon her of this new wave she had not expected, although she knew that the Duchesse de Guermantes's conversation was always apt to offer a succession of delightful thrills, the breathtaking panic, the healthy fatigue, after which her thoughts instinctively turned to the necessity of taking a footbath in a bath cubicle and a brisk walk in order to "adjust herself" to the experience.

"Personally speaking, Oriane," said Mme de Brissac, "I don't have any objection to Victor Hugo's having ideas—quite the contrary—but I do object to the way he seeks them in hideous things. It was he, in the end, who accustomed us to ugliness in literature. There's already quite enough ugliness in life as it is. Why can't we just be allowed to forget it while we're reading? A painful sight from which we would turn away in real life—that's what attracts Victor Hugo."

"Victor Hugo is not as realistic as Zola, surely?" inquired the Princess of Parma.

At the name Zola, not a single muscle stirred on the face of M. de Beautreillis. The General's anti-Dreyfusism lay too deep for him even to attempt to give expression to it. And his benign silence when such topics were broached touched the hearts of the uninitiated as the sign of the same delicacy that a priest shows in avoiding any reference to one's religious obligations, a financial adviser in making sure that he does not recommend the companies he himself controls, a strong man in behaving like a lamb and refraining from fisticuffs.

"I know you're related to Admiral Jurien de La Gravière," Mme de Varambon, the Princess of Parma's lady-in-waiting, said to me with a knowing look. An excellent woman within her limits, she had been procured for the Princess a long time ago by the Duc's mother. She had not so far addressed me, and subsequently I could never rid her, despite the admonitions of the Princess of Parma and my own protestations, of the idea that I was in some way connected with the admiral-Academician, who was a complete stranger to me. The utter refusal of the Princess of Parma's lady-in-waiting to see me as anything other than the nephew of Admiral Jurien de La Gravière was in itself quite a common and laughable phenomenon. But the mistake she made was only an extreme and desiccated instance of the countless mistakes, more trivial, more pointed, unintentional, or deliberate, that accompany our names on the particular index card the world allots us. I remember a friend of the Guermantes who had expressed a keen desire to make my acquaintance and alleged as the reason for this that I was a great friend of his cousin Mme de Chaussegros, "a charming woman, so very fond of you." I was punctilious enough to insist—in vain—that there was some mistake, that I was not acquainted with Mme de Chaussegros. "Then it's her sister you know; it amounts to the same thing. She met you in Scotland." I have never been to Scotland, and in my honesty I went to the trouble—a complete waste of time—of pointing this out to the person I was addressing. It was Mme de Chaussegros herself who had said that she knew me (and no doubt she sincerely believed it), as the result of some initial confusion, for from then on she never failed to greet me whenever she caught sight of me. And since, after all, the milieu in which I moved was identical to that of Mme de Chaussegros, there was no rhyme or reason in the way I played the situation down. To say that I was a close friend of the Chaussegros family was, quite literally, a mistake, but from the social point of view it gave some idea of my actual position, if one can speak of social position in regard to the young man I was at the time. It mattered little that this friend of the Guermantes should tell me things about myself that were untrue, and the idea of me he continued to hold neither underestimated nor overestimated me in society terms. After all, for those of us who are not in the acting profession, when another person forms a false idea of us, imagines we are friends with a lady who is unknown to us but whom we have reputedly met in the course of a delightful journey we have never made, the tedium of constantly inhabiting the same skin becomes dispelled for a moment, as if we were actually going onstage. Mistakes that proliferate harmlessly enough when they are without the unbending rigidity of the one that had been made, and would continue to be made for the rest of her life, in spite of my denials, by Mme de Parme's fool of a lady-in-waiting, stuck for all time in the belief that I was related to that boring man Admiral Jurien de La Gravière. "She's got no head for these things," the Duc told me, "and she really ought not overdo the alcohol. I think she's somewhat under the influence of Bacchus at the moment." As it happened, Mme de Varambon had been drinking only water, but the Duc liked an opportunity to pop up with his favorite expressions.

"But Zola's not a realist, he's a poet, madame!" said Mme de Guermantes, drawing her inspiration from the critical articles she had read over the last few years and converting them to her individual brilliance. Agreeably jostled, up to this point, by the experience of bathing in wit,

a bath stirred up especially for her, which she was taking this evening, and which, in her view, must be particularly beneficial for her
health, allowing herself to be borne along by the successive waves of
paradox as they broke, the Princess of Parma now gave a sudden start
for fear of being knocked to her feet. And it was with a catch in her
voice, as though her breath had been taken away, that she gasped out:

"Zola a poet!"

"Why, certainly," answered the Duchesse, laughing, delighted by
this suffocated reaction. "Your Highness has surely observed how he ele-
vates everything he touches. I can see you're about to tell me that he
only touches the things that bring us . . . pleasure. But he makes that
into something colossal. He's master of the epic dungheap! The Homer
of the sewers! He can't write Cambronne's expletive[77] in big enough
letters."

Despite the intense exhaustion she was beginning to feel, the Princess was enchanted; never had she felt in better humor. She would not
have exchanged the highly invigorating salts of these divine dinner parties at Mme de Guermantes's for an invitation to Schönbrunn,[78] which
was the one thing that really flattered her.

"He writes that word with a big 'C,' " Mme d'Arpajon burst forth.

"Surely with a big 'M,' I think, my dear," replied the Duchesse de
Guermantes, but not until she and her husband had looked at each
other with a twinkle in their eyes that implied, "How stupid can you
get?" "And while I think of it . . ." said Mme de Guermantes, turning to
me with a smiling, tender gaze that lingered on my face, because, as an
accomplished hostess, she was anxious to display her knowledge of an
artist who was of particular interest to me and to provide me with the
opportunity to exhibit mine if I wanted, "while I think of it," she said,
gently waving her feather fan, utterly conscious of the fact that she was
at that moment exercising the full duties of hospitality, and simultaneously, in order not to be found wanting in any of them, signaling for
me to be served with more asparagus *sauce mousseline,* "while I think of
it, I do believe that Zola has actually written a study on the work of Elstir, the painter whose pictures you were looking at a while ago. The
only ones of his that I like, as it happens," she added. In fact, she hated

Elstir's painting, but found something special in anything that was in her own house. I asked M. de Guermantes if he knew the name of the gentleman in the top hat who featured in the picture of the crowd, and whom I recognized as the same person whose formal portrait was next to this picture in the Guermantes collection, both paintings dating roughly from the same period of Elstir's work, when his individuality had not yet fully emerged and he modeled himself slightly on Manet. "Heavens!" he replied. "I know it's someone who is neither unknown nor a fool in his line of business, but I have no head for names. It's on the tip of my tongue—M. . . . M. . . . Oh well, never mind, I've forgotten. Swann would be able to tell you. He's the one who made Mme de Guermantes buy all that stuff. She's always too good-natured, always afraid of hurting people's feelings if she says no. Between you and me, I think he's landed us with a lot of old doodles. What I *can* tell you is that the gentleman you mean is a sort of Maecenas for M. Elstir. He launched him and has often helped him out of difficulties by commissioning paintings from him. As a token of gratitude to this man—if gratitude is what you call it, it's a matter of taste—Elstir painted him among that crowd. He stands out rather oddly, all dressed up to the nines like that. He may be one of your real pundits, but he's obviously got no idea where and when one wears a top hat. With that thing on his head, among all those hatless girls, he looks like a small-time provincial lawyer out on the town. But, tell me, you seem really keen on his paintings. Had I known that, I'd have had all the answers ready for you. Not that there's much need to rack one's brains to say all there is to be said about M. Elstir's paintings, as there would be if we were talking about Ingres's *La Source* or *The Princes in the Tower* by Paul Delaroche.[79] The thing one appreciates in Elstir is the shrewd observation, the humor, the Parisian aspect, and after that one moves on to the next thing. You need no special knowledge to look at that sort of thing. I realize, of course, they're only sketches, but I don't find that they're worked enough. Swann had the nerve to try and make us buy a painting called *A Bundle of Asparagus*. It was in the house for several days, in fact. That was all there was in the picture, a bundle of asparagus just like the ones you're eating now. But I have to say I refused to swallow M. Elstir's asparagus. He was asking three hundred francs for it. Three hundred francs for a bunch of asparagus! A louis is as much as they're worth, even early in the season. I thought it was a bit stiff. And when his things have people in them as well, I find it all rather sordid and depressing, not nice at all. It surprises me that someone with a discriminating mind like yourself, someone with a superior mind, actually likes that sort of thing."

"I really don't know why you say that, Basin," said the Duchesse, who did not take kindly to any aspersions cast on the contents of her reception rooms. "I am rather disinclined to dismiss every aspect of Elstir's work as undistinguished. There are things one takes to, others one doesn't. But you can't say there's a consistent lack of talent. And you have to admit that the paintings I purchased are unusually beautiful ones."

"As far as that sort of painting is concerned, Oriane, I infinitely prefer that little sketch by M. Vibert[80] we saw at the watercolor exhibition. There's nothing much in it, if you like, you could hold it in the palm of your hand, but you can see that there's a sense of wit written all over it: that unkempt scarecrow of a missionary standing in front of the snug prelate who is making his little dog do tricks, it's a perfect little poem of shrewdness and even profundity."

"I believe you are acquainted with M. Elstir," the Duchesse said to me. "As a man, he's very nice."

"He's intelligent enough," said the Duc. "After talking to him, one finds it quite a surprise that his paintings should be so run-of-the-mill."

"He's more than intelligent, he's really quite witty," said the Duchesse with that look of unequivocal appreciation of someone who knew what she was talking about.

"Didn't he start doing a portrait of you, Oriane?" inquired the Princess of Parma.

"Indeed he did. He painted me as red as a beet. It's not the sort of thing that's going to set him down for posterity. It's ghastly. Basin wanted to destroy it."

This last statement was one that Mme de Guermantes was always making. But at other times she chose to judge differently: "I don't care for his work, but he did once do a good portrait of me." The first of these judgments was usually addressed to people who asked the Duchesse about her portrait, the second to those who did not mention it and whom she was anxious to apprise of its existence. The first was inspired by concern with her appearance, the second by vanity.

"Make a portrait of you look ghastly! In that case, it wouldn't be a portrait, it would be a travesty. I don't even know how to hold a paintbrush, but I'm sure if I were to paint you by merely setting you down as I see you I'd produce a masterpiece," said the Princess of Parma ingenuously.

"He probably sees me as I see myself, without the frills," said Mme de Guermantes with a look that was at once melancholic, modest, and winsome, the one that she saw as best calculated to make her appear different from what Elstir had portrayed.

"That portrait cannot be without its appeal for Mme de Gallardon," said the Duc.

"Because she knows nothing about pictures?" asked the Princess of Parma, in the knowledge that Mme de Guermantes had unbounded contempt for her cousin. "But she's a very kindhearted woman, is she not?" The Duc assumed a look of deep astonishment.

"Why, Basin, can't you see that the Princess is making fun of you?" (Nothing was further from the Princess's mind.) "She knows as well as you do that Little Miss Gallardon is a venomous serpent," continued Mme de Guermantes, whose vocabulary was confined by habit to all these antiquated expressions and as richly flavored as the dishes that you can come across in the delicious books of Pampille,[81] but which have become so rare in real life, food in which the jellies, the butter, the juices, the quenelles are all unadulterated, in which even the salt comes specially from the salt marshes of Brittany: from her accent, her choice of words, one felt that the basis of the Duchesse's conversation came directly from Guermantes. In this respect, the Duchesse was very different from her nephew Saint-Loup, who was steeped in countless new ideas and expressions; it is hard, when the mind is murky with Kantian ideas and Baudelairean longings, to write the exquisite French of Henri IV, and so the very purity of the Duchesse's language was a sign of limitations, and that, in her, intelligence and sensitivity alike had remained closed to any new departures. Here again, Mme de Guermantes's mind attracted me just because of what it excluded (which was precisely what constituted the substance of my own mind) and everything that, on account of this exclusion, it had been able to preserve, the seductive vigor of supple bodies which no exhausting reflection, moral anxiety, or nervous disorder has distorted. Her mind, shaped so long before my own, was for me the equivalent of what had been offered me by the behavior of the girls of the little gang along the seashore. Mme de Guermantes offered me, tamed and subdued by good manners, by respect for intellectual values, the energy and charm of a cruel little girl from one of the noble families around Combray, who from her childhood had ridden horses, sadistically tormented cats, gouged out the eyes of rabbits, and, though remaining a paragon of virtue, might equally well have been, some years back now, and so much did she share his dashing style, the most glamorous mistress of the Prince de Sagan. The only thing was that she was incapable of understanding what I had sought for in her—the magic surrounding the name Guermantes—and the tiny speck of it I had actually found, a countrified vestige from Guermantes. Our contact was based on a misunderstanding that could not fail to become apparent the moment my homage, instead of being addressed to the relatively superior being she believed herself to be, was diverted to some other woman of similar mediocrity and exuding the same unconscious charm. A misunderstanding so natural, and one that will always exist between a young dreamer and the society woman he elects, but one that disturbs him profoundly for as long as he remains ignorant of the nature of his imaginative bent and has not yet resigned himself to the inevitable disappointments he is bound to discover with people, as is the case with the theater, with travel, with love.

After M. de Guermantes had declared (following upon Elstir's asparagus and the asparagus that had just been served after the *poulet financière*) that green asparagus grown in the open and, as the charming writer who signs herself E. de Clermont-Tonnerre[82] so quaintly puts it, "without the impressive rigidity of their sisters," ought to be eaten with eggs, M. de Bréauté came out with the reply: "One man's meat is another man's poison. In the province of Canton, in China, the greatest delicacy that can be offered to someone is a dish of ortolan eggs in a state of advanced putrefaction." M. de Bréauté, the author of an essay on the Mormons that had appeared in the *Revue des deux mondes*,[83] moved only in the most aristocratic circles, but even then only in such as boasted a certain reputation for intellect. The result of this was that his presence, if it was at all regular, in a lady's house indicated that she had a "salon." He claimed to loathe society, and assured each one of his duchesses in turn that it was for her wit and beauty that he sought out her society. They all believed him. Whenever he resigned himself, with a heavy heart, to attending an important function at the Princess of Parma's, he collected all his ladies around him to bolster himself up, and thus appeared to be moving only in the midst of a close circle of acquaintances. So that his reputation as an intellectual might not be eclipsed by his society interests, he put into practice certain maxims from the Guermantes repertory, and would set out with fashionable women on long scientific expeditions during the season of society balls; when some snobbish character—in other words, some person who had not yet "arrived" socially—began to make his presence felt socially, he would become ferociously obstinate in his refusal to make that person's acquaintance, to allow himself to be introduced. His hatred of snobs derived from his own snobbishness, but it led the simple-minded (in other words, everyone) to believe that he was untainted by it.

"Babal always knows everything!" the Duchesse de Guermantes exclaimed. "I find it quite charming that there's such a thing as a country where your dairyman will supply you with really rotten eggs dating back to the year one. I can just picture myself dipping my fingers of buttered toast into them. And I must say that it's not unknown for such things to happen at Aunt Madeleine's"—Mme de Villeparisis—"things served up in a state of putrefaction, even eggs." Then, at signs of protest from Mme d'Arpajon, she added: "Come, now, Phili, you know it as well as I do. You can see the chicken in the egg. I can't for the life of me think how they're well behaved enough to stay inside the shell. It's not an omelette she serves, it's a whole chicken coop, but at least it's not written on the menu. It was just as well you didn't come there to dinner the day before yesterday; we had brill poached in carbolic acid! Not exactly a hospitable table—more like a hospital for contagious diseases. I must say that Norpois pushes loyalty to the heights of heroics: he had a second helping!"

"I think I saw you there the day she said her piece to that man Bloch"—M. de Guermantes, in a possible attempt to give a Jewish name a more foreign lilt, did not pronounce the "ch" in Bloch like a "k" but as the "ch" in the German *hoch*—"when he described some *pow ut*"— poet—"or other as sublime. Châtellerault made a brave attempt to break M. Bloch's shins, but the fellow didn't understand and thought that my nephew's kicks were aimed at a young woman sitting right next to him." At this juncture M. de Guermantes colored slightly. "He didn't realize that he was irritating our aunt by overdoing all those 'sublime's of his. Anyway, Aunt Madeleine, who's never short of words, came out with, 'In that case, monsieur, what adjective are you going to keep for M. de Bossuet?' " M. de Guermantes was of the opinion that when you mentioned a famous name the use of "M." and the nobiliary particle was a must for anyone of the "old school." "It was worth waiting for."

"And what did M. Bloch have to say to that?" asked Mme de Guermantes in an offhand sort of way, copying her husband's Teutonic pronunciation to compensate for a momentary lapse in her own original contribution to the subject.

"Ah! I can assure you that M. Bloch didn't wait for any more. He's still running."

"And, indeed, I have a distinct memory of seeing you there that evening," Mme de Guermantes said to me with some insistence, as if a recollection of this sort on her part must be something deeply flattering to me. "It's always so interesting at my aunt's. At that last evening do— where we met, in fact—I meant to ask you whether the old gentleman who was passing us wasn't François Coppée.[84] You must know who everybody is," she continued, genuinely envious of my contacts with poets and their kind, and also in an attempt to be nice to me and to emphasize the standing, in the eyes of her other guests, of a young man so well versed in literature. I assured the Duchesse that I had not been aware of any celebrities at Mme de Villeparisis's reception. "What!" exclaimed Mme de Guermantes unthinkingly, thus betraying the fact that her respect for men of letters and her contempt for society were more superficial than she said—or even thought, perhaps. "What! No famous authors present! You astonish me! I saw quite a number of impossible-looking people!"

I remembered the evening in question perfectly well, on account of an utterly trivial incident. Mme de Villeparisis had introduced Bloch to Mme Alphonse de Rothschild, but my old school friend had not caught the name and, under the impression that he had been introduced to a slightly mad old English lady, had replied only in monosyllables to the garrulous remarks of this former beauty, until Mme de Villeparisis, introducing her to someone else, had pronounced the words "Baronne Alphonse de Rothschild," quite clearly this time. At this point, in one fell swoop, so many ideas of millions and glamour, which it would have been wiser to distinguish separately, had suddenly coursed through Bloch's mind, that he had had something like a heart attack and a brain-storm combined, and had burst out in the dear old lady's presence, "If only I'd known!," an outburst of such stupidity that it had prevented him from sleeping a wink for a whole week. There was nothing particularly interesting in this remark of Bloch's, but I retained it as proof that sometimes in life, in moments of exceptional emotion, people do say what they think.

"I do believe that Mme de Villeparisis is not exactly what one would call a . . . 'moral' person," said the Princess of Parma, who knew that people did not call on the Duchesse's aunt and, following the remarks just made by the Duchesse herself, thought it permissible to speak her mind quite freely on the subject. But, catching a look of disapproval on the Duchesse's face, she immediately added, "But of course an intellect of such a high order excuses everything."

"You take the same view of my aunt as the rest of the world," replied the Duchesse. "On the whole, it is quite mistaken. It's just what Mémé was saying to me only yesterday." She blushed, and some memory that was hidden from me clouded her eyes. I formed the conjecture that M. de Charlus had asked her to cancel my engagement with him, given that he had sent Robert to ask me not to go to her dinner. I sensed that the blush—equally incomprehensible to me—I had noticed on the Duc's face when he made some brief reference to his brother was possibly there for the same reason. "My poor aunt! She will always have a reputation as a lady of the old school, a woman of sparkling wit and the loosest morals. And yet one couldn't conceive of a more middle-class, serious-minded, and lackluster person. She will go down as a patroness of the arts, which is tantamount to saying that she was the mistress of a famous painter, though he was never able to make her understand what a painting was. And as for her personal life, far from being a depraved woman, she was so much cast in the mold of marriage, so conjugal from the very start, that her lack of success in keeping a husband—and in any case he was a scoundrel—that she has never had a liaison without taking it as seriously as a regular marriage, with the same upsets, the same quarrels, the same fidelity. Mind you, such relationships are often the most genuine ones. Generally speaking, there are more inconsolable lovers than there are husbands."

"And yet, Oriane, if you take the case of your brother-in-law Palamède, whom you were speaking of a moment ago, no mistress in the world could ever dream of being grieved for as that poor Mme de Charlus has been."

"Ah!" replied the Duchesse. "Your Highness must allow me a slight difference of opinion on that matter. People don't all like to be mourned for in the same way. We all have our preferences."

"Still, he has made a regular cult of her since she died. It's true that people sometimes behave toward the dead in a way they would not have done toward the living."

"For a start," rejoined Mme de Guermantes in a dreamy voice which masked her facetious intent, "we go to their funerals, which we never do for the living!" M. de Guermantes gave M. de Bréauté a sly glance, as though he was trying to incite him to laughter at the Duchesse's wit. "At the same time, I admit quite frankly," Mme de Guermantes continued, "that the manner in which I should like to be mourned for by a man I loved is not the one followed by my brother-in-law."

A shadow passed over the Duc's face. He did not like to hear his wife pronounce random judgments, particularly about M. de Charlus.

"You're not easy to please. His grief was edifying for everyone," was his curt rejoinder. But in dealing with her husband the Duchesse had the boldness of an animal-tamer, or of people who live with a madman and have no fear of provoking him:

"Well, if you want to put it like that, I suppose you're right: it is edifying. He goes every day to the cemetery to tell her how many luncheon guests he had, he misses her enormously, but it's as if he's mourning a cousin, a grandmother, a sister. It's not the grief of a husband. It's true that the two of them were real saints, which makes the whole thing rather out of the ordinary." Incensed by his wife's chatter, M. de Guermantes glared at her with frightening fixity; his look was explosive. "I'm not trying to say anything against poor Mémé," the Duchesse continued. "By the way, he was unable to be here this evening. I know that there's no one as kind as he is. He's delightful, he has delicacy, and a sense of feeling that you don't usually find in men. He's as soft as a woman, Mémé is!"

"Don't talk rubbish," M. de Guermantes broke in sharply. "There's nothing effeminate about Mémé. I can't think of anyone more manly than he is."

"But I'm not suggesting for a moment that he's the least bit effeminate. Do at least try and follow what I'm saying," the Duchesse continued. "He's always like this when he thinks anyone is getting at his brother," she added, turning to the Princess of Parma.

"It's very nice of him, a delight to hear him. There's nothing so fine as two brothers who are fond of each other," said the Princess of Parma, as many humbler folk might have replied, for it is possible to belong to a princely family by blood and to a very plebeian one by intellect.

"While we're on the subject of your family, Oriane," said the Princess, "I saw your nephew Saint-Loup yesterday. I suspect he wants to ask you a favor." The Duc de Guermantes knitted his Olympian brow. When he was unwilling to do someone a favor, he did not care for his wife to take charge of it, knowing that it would come down to the same thing in the end and that the people to whom she would be obliged to address herself would put it down to the joint account of the household, just as much as if it had been requested by the husband alone.

"Why didn't he ask me himself?" said the Duchesse. "He spent two hours here yesterday and, good heavens, I can't tell you how tiresome he was. He would be no more stupid than anyone else if he had only had the good sense, like many people of our acquaintance, to remain a fool. It's that intellectual façade of his that gets in the way. He wants to be receptive . . . but receptive to all the things he doesn't have a clue about. The way he carries on about Morocco, it's dreadful."

"He can't go back there, because of Rachel," said the Prince de Foix.

"But I thought they'd split up," broke in M. de Bréauté.

"I don't know about splitting up, but I came across her two days ago in Robert's bachelor apartment and they didn't look like two people who'd quarreled, believe me," replied the Prince de Foix, who liked to spread every bit of gossip that might possibly damage Robert's chances of marrying, and who might have been misled by the intermittent resumptions of an affair that was to all intents and purposes at an end.

"Your Rachel was speaking to me about you. I run into her occasionally in the morning in the Champs-Élysées. She's rather flighty, as you put it, what you call *loose*, a kind of 'Dame aux Camélias'[85]—figuratively speaking of course." These words were addressed to me by Prince Von, with that desire of his to appear conversant with French literature and the refinements of Paris.

"But of course, that's what it was! Morocco . . ." the Princess burst forth, flinging herself into this opening.

"What can he want with Morocco?" M. de Guermantes inquired sternly. "Oriane can do nothing for him in that department, as he is perfectly well aware."

"He thinks he invented strategy," said Mme de Guermantes, pursuing her theme, "and then he uses impossible words for the simplest thing, which doesn't stop him from making smudges all over his letters. The other day he told us he'd been served some *sublime* potatoes, and that he'd taken a *sublime* stage box."

"He speaks Latin," said the Duc, going one better.

"What! Latin?" queried the Princess.

"On my word of honor, Your Highness can ask Oriane whether I'm not telling the truth."

"Why, yes, madame. The other day, just like that, in a single sentence, he came out with: 'I can think of no more moving example of *sic transit gloria mundi.*' I can repeat the sentence to Your Highness, because, after scores of inquiries and by having recourse to *linguists,* we managed to reconstruct it, but Robert just flung it out without pausing for breath, and we could barely perceive that there was Latin in it. He was like a character out of *Le Malade imaginaire*! And it all had to do with the death of the Empress of Austria!"[86]

"The poor woman!" exclaimed the Princess. "What a delightful creature she was!"

"Yes," said the Duchesse, "a wee bit mad, a tiny bit insane, but a thoroughly good sort, a nice, kindly lunatic. The only thing I could never understand was why she never managed to get herself a set of false teeth that fitted properly. They always came loose before she'd finished a sentence, and she had to stop short in case she swallowed them."

"That Rachel was telling me about you. She said that our friend Saint-Loup idolized you, that he was even fonder of you than he was of her," said Prince Von, addressing me and devouring his food like a red-faced ogre as he spoke, all his teeth exposed by his perpetual grin.

"In which case she must be jealous of me and hate me," I replied.

"Not in the least; she said all sorts of nice things about you. Now, the Prince de Foix's mistress would perhaps be jealous if he preferred you to her. You don't know what I mean? Come home with me and I'll explain it all to you."

"I'm afraid that's not possible: I have an appointment with M. de Charlus at eleven."

"Well, now, he sent me an invitation yesterday to dine with him this evening, but asked me not to come after a quarter to eleven. But if you really must go and see him, at least come with me as far as the Théâtre-Français, you'll be in the periphery," said the Prince, who was doubtless under the impression that his last word meant "neighborhood" or possibly "centrally placed."

But the wide-eyed gaze on his coarse, handsome red face alarmed me, and I declined his offer by telling him that a friend was coming to collect me. There was nothing offensive about this response as far as I could see. But the Prince apparently thought differently and did not address another word to me.

"I really must pay a visit to the Queen of Naples—she must be grieving terribly," the Princess of Parma said, or at least appeared to me to have said. For her words had reached me only indistinctly through Prince Von's remarks, closer to my ear yet spoken in an undertone. No doubt he had been afraid, if he spoke any louder, that the Prince de Foix might hear him.

"Oh, I don't really think that's the case," said the Duchesse. "I don't believe she feels any grief at all."

"None at all? You always go to extremes, Oriane," said M. de Guermantes, reverting to his role as the cliff that, by resisting the wave, forces it to fling its crest of foam even higher.

"Basin knows as well as I do, if not better, that I'm telling the truth," replied the Duchesse, "but he feels he has to behave sternly because you're here and is frightened that I might shock you."

"Oh, please, not in the least!" exclaimed the Princess of Parma, fearing that some detail of these delicious evenings at the Duchesse de Guermantes's might get altered on her account and that she would lose this forbidden fruit, which even the Queen of Sweden had not yet acquired the right to taste.

"Why, Basin himself had it from her own lips. When he asked her with the usual expression of condolence—'I see the Queen is in mourning. May I ask for whom? Your Majesty must be greatly grieved?'—she said, 'No, it's not full mourning but rather, a light mourning, a very light mourning in fact. It's my sister.' The truth is, she's delighted by it, as Basin knows perfectly well. She invited us to a party that very evening and presented me with two pearls. Would that she could lose a sister every day! She's not mourning for her sister's death—she's as pleased as can be about it. She probably says to herself, like Robert, '*sic transit . . .*' or whatever it is," she added modestly, perfectly well aware of how to complete the tag.

All this was in fact merely Mme de Guermantes showing off her witty mind, and in the most mendacious manner: the Queen of Naples, like the Duchesse d'Alençon, also tragically departed, was a warmhearted woman and mourned her relations with sincerity. Mme de Guermantes knew these noble Bavarian sisters, her cousins, too well not to be aware of this.

"He is anxious not to return to Morocco," said the Princess of Parma, seizing once more upon the name Robert, which Mme de Guermantes had held out to her, quite unintentionally, like a lifeline. "I believe you know Général de Monserfeuil."

"Only very slightly," replied the Duchesse, who was a close friend of the officer in question. The Princess explained what it was that Saint-Loup wanted.

"Heavens, well, yes, if I see him . . . It's possible I may run into him," replied the Duchesse, trying to avoid seeming unhelpful—her relations with Général de Monserfeuil appeared to have grown rapidly more remote the minute there had been any question of her asking him for some favor. This hesitancy was still not good enough for the Duc, who interrupted his wife:

"You know perfectly well you won't be seeing him, Oriane," he said, "and, besides, you've already asked him to do a couple of things that he hasn't done. My wife is obsessed with pleasing people," he added, getting increasingly testy in order to force the Princess to withdraw her request without making her doubt his wife's good nature, and so that Mme de Parme should put the whole thing down to his own fundamentally curmudgeonly nature. "Robert could get anything he wanted out of Monserfeuil himself. Only, as he happens not to know what it is he wants, he gets us to do it, because he knows there's no better way of making the whole thing fall through—Oriane has already asked too many favors of Monserfeuil. A request from her at this point would be a reason for him to refuse."

"Oh, in that case, it would be better for the Duchesse to do nothing," said Mme de Parme.

"Quite so," came the Duc's final word on the matter.

"That poor general, he's been defeated again at the elections," said the Princess of Parma, to change the subject.

"Oh, it's nothing serious, it's only the seventh time," said the Duc, who, after being forced to quit politics himself, quite enjoyed hearing about other people's failures at the polls. "He consoled himself by deciding to give his wife another baby."

"What! Is that poor Mme de Monserfeuil pregnant again?" exclaimed the Princess.

"But of course," replied the Duchesse, "it's the only sort of *campaign* the poor general has never lost."

In the time that followed, I was continually to be invited, however small the party, to the dinners and luncheons whose guests I had at one time imagined to resemble the Apostles in the Sainte-Chapelle. And in fact they did assemble there like the early Christians, not to partake of merely material nourishment, which was in fact exquisite, but in a sort of social Eucharist; and very soon, in the course of a few dinner parties, I took in the acquaintance of all the friends of my hosts, friends to whom they introduced me with such a distinct hint of benevolent condescension (as to someone for whom they had always had a sort of parental affection) that there was not a single one of them who would not have felt he was failing the Duc and Duchesse if he had given a ball without including my name on the list, and along with all this, as I savored one of the Yquems from the recesses of the Guermantes cellars, I enjoyed ortolans prepared in accordance with various recipes tastefully devised and modified by the Duc himself. However, for one who had already sat down more than once at the mystic board, the manducation of the ortolan was not obligatory. Old friends of M. and Mme de Guermantes would come in to see them after dinner—"at toothpick time," as Mme Swann would have said—as casual visitors, and would be offered *tilleul* in winter in the lighted drawing room or, in summer, a glass of orangeade in the darkness of the tiny rectangular garden outside. No one could remember the Guermantes' serving anything other than orangeade at these after-dinner evenings in the garden. There was something ritualistic about it. The introduction of other refreshments would have seemed to be perverting the tradition, just as a grand reception in the Faubourg Saint-Germain is no longer such if it includes a play or music. It must be assumed that you had come along simply—even if there were five hundred people present—to pay a call on, let us say, the Princesse de Guermantes. Because I managed to procure, in addition to the orangeade, a carafe of stewed cherry or pear juice, people marveled at the weight I carried. It was because of this that I took a dislike to the Prince d'Agrigente, who, like all people lacking in imagination but not in acquisitiveness, show great surprise at what you happen to be drinking and ask if they may taste a little of it themselves. The result of this was that, on all of these occasions, M. d'Agrigente, by reducing my ration, spoiled my enjoyment. For this fruit juice is never served in sufficient quantities to quench the thirst. There is nothing so easy to drink as this color of fruit, transmuted into a flavor, and the fruit, when stewed in this way, seems to have reverted to the time when it was blossom. With its crimson flush like an orchard in springtime, or else colorless and cool like the breeze beneath the fruit trees, the juice can be sniffed, its every drop admired, and M. d'Agrigente prevented me, regularly, from enjoying it to the full. Despite these fruit-juice concoctions, the time-honored orangeade persisted, as did the *tilleul*. In these modest beverages, the social communion service still took place. In this respect, no doubt, the friends of M. and Mme de Guermantes were still, as I had originally imagined them, more out of the ordinary than their disappointing appearance might have suggested to me. A great many elderly men came to call and to receive from the Duchesse, together with the invariable drink, a welcome that was often almost frosty. Now, snobbishness could not have accounted for this, since the men in question were of the highest rank, nor could love of luxury: they may well have had a taste for it, but they could have enjoyed glittering luxury in less exalted social surroundings, for on those very same evenings the charming wife of a colossally wealthy financier would have moved heaven and earth to have them join the brilliant two-day shooting party she was to put on for the King of Spain. They had nevertheless declined her invitation and had stopped by completely on the off chance that Mme de Guermantes was at home. They were not even certain of finding absolutely like-minded people at her house, or feelings that were particularly cordial; Mme de Guermantes would throw out occasional comments—on the Dreyfus case, on the Republic, on the anticlerical laws, or even muted innuendos about themselves, their weaknesses, their boring conversation—which they were obliged to pretend they had not heard. No doubt, if they chose to keep on coming it was because of their polished training as epicures of refined society and their distinct awareness of the perfect, prime quality of the social platter, the reassuring familiarity and bite of what was to be tasted there, free from hybridity or adulteration, something with an origin and history they recognized as well as she who served it to them, so that they remained more "noble" in this respect than they themselves realized. Now, among the visitors to whom I was introduced after dinner on this occasion, it turned out that there was Général de Monserfeuil, to whom the Princess of Parma had alluded, and whom Mme de Guermantes, whose salon he frequented regularly, had not expected that evening. On hearing my name, he made a bow, as though I had been the president of the Supreme War Council. I had imagined it to be simply through some deepseated reluctance to oblige, in which the Duc, as in wit if not in love, was his wife's accomplice, that the Duchesse had all but refused to speak to M. de Monserfeuil on her nephew's behalf. And I saw in all this an indifference all the more reprehensible in that I got the impression, from a few words the Princess of Parma had let slip, that Robert's post was a perilous one, and that it would be wise to have him assigned to something else. What really revolted me was the genuine malice on Mme de Guermantes's part when, after the Princess of Parma had made the timid suggestion that she herself might have a word with the general on her own initiative, the Duchesse did all she could to dissuade Her Highness.

"But, madame," she burst out, "Monserfeuil has no standing or influence whatsoever with the new government. It would be an utter waste of effort."

"I think he can hear what we're saying," murmured the Princess, as a way of inviting the Duchesse to lower her voice.

"Your Highness has nothing to fear, he's as deaf as a post," said the Duchesse, making no attempt to speak more quietly. The general could hear her every word.

"What I find worrying is that I believe M. de Saint-Loup to be in a rather unsafe place," said the Princess.

"It can't be helped," the Duchesse replied, "he's in the same situation as everyone else. The only difference is that he was the one who asked to be sent there. And, then, it's not really unsafe, not really. If it were, you know me, I would do something about it. I'd have spoken to Saint-Joseph about it during dinner. He carries far more influence, and he gets on with the job! As you can see for yourself, he's already left. In fact, it would be less awkward than speaking to this one, who just happens to have three of his sons in Morocco at present and is unwilling to ask for their transfer; he might well object on those grounds. Since Your Highness insists, I shall talk with Saint-Joseph—if I see him, that is—or to Beautreillis. They explained to us the other day where Robert is. I don't think he could be anywhere better."

"What a pretty flower; I've never seen one like that. There's no one like you, Oriane, for finding such marvelous things!" said the Princess of Parma, fearing that Général de Monserfeuil might have overheard the Duchesse and seeking to change the subject. I recognized the plant as one of those I had watched Elstir painting.

"I'm delighted you like it; these flowers are ravishing; just look at the little mauve velvet collars on them; the unfortunate thing is that—as sometimes happens with people who are very pretty and very nicely dressed—they have an ugly name and a dreadful smell. All the same, I'm very fond of them. But what is rather sad is that they're going to die."

"But they're growing in a pot; they aren't cut flowers?" asked the Princess.

"No," the Duchesse answered with a smile, "but it amounts to the same thing, since they're all ladies. It's a species of plant where the ladies and the gentlemen don't grow on the same stalk. I'm like the people who keep a lady dog. I need a husband for my flowers. Otherwise I won't have any young ones!"

"How very strange. Are you saying that in nature . . . ?"

"Yes, there are some insects who take it upon themselves to bring about the marriage, as with royalty, by proxy, without the partners concerned ever having set eyes on each other. And let me assure you, I always tell the servant to put the plant near the window as often as possible, on the courtyard side and the garden side in turn, in the hope that the right insect will arrive. The odds are almost impossible. Just think, that insect would have to have just come from one of the same species and the opposite sex, and would then have had to take it into his head to come and leave his card at the house. He hasn't appeared so far; I think my plant still merits the status of virgin, but I must say that a little more loose behavior would please me better. It's the same thing, you know, with that fine tree of ours in the courtyard: it will die childless, because it belongs to a species that's very rare here. In its case, the wind is responsible for bringing about the union, but the wall is a bit too high."

"That's true," said M. de Bréauté, "you ought to have knocked a few centimeters off the top—that would have done it. You need to know about these things. The vanilla flavoring of that excellent ice cream you gave us this evening, Duchesse, comes from a plant of the same name. It produces flowers that are both male and female, but there is a kind of tough partition between them which means that they are shut off from each other. So no one could get any fruit from them until a young Negro, a native of Réunion called Albius—rather a comic name for a black man, given that his name means 'white'—took it into his head to bring the separate organs into contact by using the point of a needle."

"Babal, you're divine, you know everything," cried the Duchesse.

"But you yourself, Oriane, have taught me things I knew nothing about," said the Princess.

"I am bound to explain to Your Highness that it is Swann who has always told me a great deal about botany. Sometimes, when we thought it would be too tiresome to go off to some tea party or an afternoon reception, we used to set off for the country, and he would show me extraordinary marriages between flowers, far more amusing than marriages between people—and it all takes place without luncheon parties or gatherings in the sacristy. We never had time to go very far. Now that there are motorcars, it would be delightful. Unfortunately, since then there has been the business of his own marriage, an even more astonishing affair, which makes everything rather difficult. Ah, madame, life is a dreadful thing: we spend our entire time doing things that bore us, and then, when we happen to come across someone with whom we could go and look at something really interesting, he has to go and get in-

volved in a marriage like Swann's. Faced with the alternatives of giving
up my botanical excursions and having to frequent a person of disre-
pute, I have chosen the first of these two disasters. But in the end
there's no need to go so far afield. It seems that even here, in my tiny
piece of garden, more improper activities take place in broad daylight
than at nighttime . . . in the Bois de Boulogne! It's simply that they attract no attention, because between flowers that sort of thing takes
place very unobtrusively—you see a little orange shower, or else a very
dusty fly coming to wipe its feet or take a bath before it penetrates a
flower. And that's all there is to it!"

"That's a splendid chest of drawers, too, that the plant is standing
on; it's Empire, I think," said the Princess, whose lack of familiarity
with the works of Darwin and his flowers made it difficult for her to
grasp the Duchesse's jokes.

"It's lovely, isn't it? I'm delighted that Your Highness likes it," replied the Duchesse. "It's a very fine piece. I have to tell you that I've always adored Empire style, even when it wasn't in fashion. I remember
that at Guermantes I got into terrible trouble with my mother-in-law for
asking to have all the splendid furniture Basin had inherited from the
Montesquious brought down from the attic, and using it to furnish the
wing we lived in."

M. de Guermantes smiled, though he must have remembered that
things had happened very differently. But the witticisms of the Princesse
des Laumes on the subject of her mother-in-law's bad taste had been
traditional during the short period the Prince had been in love with his
wife, and his love for the latter had been outlived by a certain amount
of contempt for the intellectual inferiority of the former, a contempt
that nonetheless went hand in hand with a great deal of attachment and
respect for her.

"The Iénas have the same armchair with Wedgwood medallions. It's
a fine chair, but I prefer mine," said the Duchesse, taking the same im-
partial stance she would have had she owned neither of these two pieces
of furniture. "I do admit, though, that they have some wonderful things
that I don't."

The Princess of Parma said nothing.

"But it's true. Your Highness hasn't seen their collection. Oh, you really ought to accompany me to their place one day. It's one of the most magnificent things in Paris. Like a museum come to life."

And since this suggestion was one of the most "Guermantes" of the Duchesse's audacious ploys (the Iénas ranking as mere usurpers in the eyes of the Princess of Parma, their son, like her own, bearing the title of Duc de Guastalla), in launching it thus Mme de Guermantes could not refrain (so much did her love of her own originality still prevail over the deference she owed to the Princess of Parma) from darting amused smiles at her other guests. They, too, forced themselves to smile in response, at once alarmed, amazed, and above all delighted to think that they were witnessing Oriane's "latest" and would be able to retail it "hot off the press." They were only half astounded, knowing as they did that the Duchesse was capable of throwing all the Courvoisier prejudices to the winds in favor of some more conspicuous and enjoyable achievement. Had she not, in the course of the last few years, brought together the Princesse Mathilde and the Duc d'Aumale, who had written that famous letter to the Princesse's own brother, "In my family all the men are brave and all the women chaste"? Now, since princes remain princely even at times when they appear to want to forget the fact, the Duc d'Aumale and the Princesse Mathilde had enjoyed themselves so much at Mme de Guermantes's that they had subsequently exchanged visits, with the same ability to forget the past that was shown by Louis XVIII when he appointed Fouché as minister, the very man who had voted for the death of his brother. Mme de Guermantes was now nursing a similar plan to effect a reconciliation between the Princesse Murat and the Queen of Naples. To return to the circumstances at hand, the Princess of Parma appeared to show the sort of embarrassment that might have been felt by the heirs apparent to the thrones of the Netherlands and Belgium, the Prince d'Orange and the Duc de Brabant respectively, had anyone offered to present to them M. de Mailly-Nesle, Prince d'Orange, or M. de Charlus, Duc de Brabant. But before anything further could happen, the Duchesse, whom Swann and M. de Charlus between them (although the latter was utterly set on ignoring the Iénas' existence) had finally, and with great difficulty, persuaded to appreciate Empire style, broke forth with this:

"Honestly, madame, I can't tell you how beautiful you'll find it! I have to admit that Empire style has always exerted a fascination for me. But, believe me, the Iénas' collection is almost hallucinatory. The sort of–what shall I call it?–backwash from the Egyptian expedition, and then, too, the returning tide of antiquity into our own times, all those things invading our houses, the sphinxes couching at the foot of our armchairs, the snakes coiled around candelabras, a huge Muse holding out a little torch for you to play card games under, or who has quietly perched on your mantelpiece and is leaning against the clock; and then all the Pompeiian lamps, the little boat-shaped beds, looking as if they had been found floating on the Nile, so that you expect to see Moses climb out of them, the Roman chariots galloping along the bedside tables. . . ."

"They're not very comfortable, those Empire chairs," ventured the Princess.

"True," the Duchesse agreed, "but," she added with an insistent smile, "I love being uncomfortable on those mahogany seats covered with dark-red velvet or green silk. I love that discomfort of warriors who have only ever known the curule chair and cross-stack their fasces and pile up their laurels in the middle of the great room. I can assure you that at the Iénas' one doesn't for a moment stop to think about how comfortable one is when one sees that strapping minx of a Victory painted in fresco on the wall. My husband will say that I make a very poor Royalist, but I think all the wrong things, you know; I can assure you that, in those people's house, one comes round to loving all the capital 'N's, all those Napoleonic bees. Good lord, we haven't exactly wallowed in monarchist glory for a good many years, and those warriors who brought back so many crowns that they stuck them on the arms of chairs–well, I find it all rather stylish! Your Highness ought to come."

"Good gracious me, if you think so," said the Princess, "but I don't think it will be easy."

"But Your Highness will find that it will all go very smoothly. They are kind people, and they're no fools. We took Mme de Chevreuse there," added the Duchesse, fully aware of the force of this example, "and she was enchanted. The son is really rather pleasant. . . . I shouldn't really say this," she went on, "but he has a bedroom, and more particularly a bed, in which I should love to sleep—alone, of course! More improper still is the fact that I went to see him once when he was ill and lying in this bed. At his side, along the bed frame, there was a carved Siren, stretched out at length, a ravishing creature with a mother-of-pearl tail, holding some sort of lotus flowers. I do assure you," continued Mme de Guermantes, slowing her pace to bring into even bolder relief the words she seemed to be modeling with her beautiful pouting lips, the tapering of her long expressive hands, and, as she spoke, fastening on to the Princess a gentle, intent, deep gaze, "that, with the palm fronds and the golden crown on one side, it was deeply moving, exactly the same layout as Gustave Moreau's *Young Man and Death*.[87] Your Highness is of course acquainted with that masterpiece."

The Princess of Parma, who had never even heard of Moreau, nodded in vigorous assent and smiled warmly in order to demonstrate her admiration for this painting. But the intensity of her charade did not manage to compensate for the light that fails to shine in our eyes when we do not know what it is that people are talking to us about.

"A good-looking boy, I believe?" she asked.

"No, he looks just like a tapir. His eyes are rather like those of Queen Hortense[88] painted on a lampshade. But he probably decided that it would be rather ridiculous for a man to go on looking like that, and so the look fades into the cheeks, which have been scrubbed until they shine, and this makes him look rather Mameluke. You get the impression that the scrubber must come round every morning. It was Swann," she continued, reverting to the young Duc's bed, "who was struck by the resemblance between that Siren and Gustave Moreau's *Death*. But anyway," she added, in a more rapid yet still-serious tone, calculated to provoke a more humorous effect, "there was nothing really to cause alarm; it was only a headcold, and the young man is now back in fine fettle."

"I'm told he's a snob?" opined M. de Bréauté with a malicious spurt of interest, expecting the same sort of precise reply he would have received from asking, "I'm told he has only four fingers on his right hand; is that so?"

"Go-o-o-od hea-ea-ea-ea-vens, no-o-o-o," replied Mme de Guer-mantes with a sweet smile of indulgence. "He *seems* a tiny bit snobbish perhaps, because he's so very young, but I would be surprised to hear that was really the case, because he's intelligent," she added, as though to her mind there were some utter incompatibility between snobbish-ness and intelligence. "He has subtlety, and I've known him to be quite amusing," she continued, smiling once again, like one who had an expert appreciation and appetite for such things, as though judging someone to be amusing required a certain amount of gaiety from the speaker, or as though the Duc de Guastalla's witty thrusts were present in her mind as she spoke. "Anyway, since he's never received anywhere, he can't have much opportunity for his snobbishness," she went on to say, ob-livious of the fact that none of this was doing very much to encourage the Princess of Parma.

"I cannot help wondering what the Prince de Guermantes will say if he hears I've been to see her. He calls her Mme Iéna."

"What!" exclaimed the Duchesse with extraordinary promptitude. "Don't you know that we were the ones who let Gilbert have a whole set of games-room furniture in the Empire style!" (She now bitterly re-gretted relinquishing it.) "It came to us from Quiou-Quiou. It's a prize collection! We didn't have room for it, though I think it looked better here than it does in his place. It's utterly beautiful, half Etruscan, half Egyptian. . . ."

"Egyptian?" inquired the Princess, to whom "Etruscan" conveyed very little.

"Well, you know, a bit of both. It was Swann who told us; he ex-plained it all to me, only you know what a poor, ignorant creature I am. And then, madame, what one has to bear in mind is that the Egypt of Empire style has nothing to do with the real Egypt, any more than its Romans with the real Romans, or its Etruscan . . ."

"I see!" said the Princess.

"No, it's like what they used to call a Louis XV costume during the Second Empire, when Anna de Mouchy and our dear Brigode's mother were girls. Basin was talking to you just now about Beethoven. We heard something of his played the other day that was really rather fine, though rather cold, with a Russian theme. It's somewhat pathetic that he thought it to be Russian. It's like those Chinese painters who thought they were copying Bellini. And even in the same country, whenever anyone looks at things in a slightly new way, ninety-nine people out of a hundred are utterly incapable of seeing what is put in front of them. It takes them at least forty years to manage to see it."

"Forty years!" cried the Princess, alarmed at the thought.

"Why, yes," the Duchesse went on, giving more and more weight to her words (practically my own, in fact, for I had just come out with a similar idea within her earshot) by pronouncing them in a certain manner, the equivalent of the use of italics on the printed page, "it's something like the first isolated individual of a species that does not yet exist but will multiply in time, an individual endowed with some kind of *sense* not available to the human species around him. I can hardly cite myself as an example, because I, on the contrary, have always loved any interesting artistic development from the very start, however innovatory. But, anyway, the other day I was with the Grand Duchess in the Louvre and we went past Manet's *Olympia*. Nowadays it shocks no one. It looks like something by Ingres! And yet heaven knows how I had to go to war on behalf of that painting, which I don't altogether like, though it's unquestionably not just any old thing. Perhaps the Louvre isn't quite the place for it."

"The Grand Duchess is well?" inquired the Princess of Parma, to whom the Tsar's aunt was infinitely more familiar than Manet's model.

"Yes, indeed so. We talked about you. After all," continued the Duchesse, holding to her theme, "the truth of the matter is, as my brother-in-law Palamède is always telling us, that there is a strange language barrier between oneself and other people. Though I admit there's no one it's truer of than Gilbert. If you'd find it entertaining to go the Iénas', you have too much sense to let your actions be governed by what the poor fellow might think; he's a sweet, innocent creature, but he really does live in another world. I feel closer, more akin to my coachman, even to my horses, than to a man who keeps harking back to what people might have thought in the reign of Philip the Bold or Louis the Fat. Can you imagine, when he goes for a walk in the country, he waves the peasants out of his way with his stick, affably enough, and says things like, 'Get along with you, you peasant rogues!' It really does amaze me when I find him addressing me as if he were one of those recumbent figures on an old Gothic tomb. This living gravestone may be my cousin, but he frightens me, and the only thing I can think of is to let him stay in his medieval world. Having said that, I do admit that he's never assassinated anyone."

"It just so happens that I've been dining with him at Mme de Villeparisis's," said the general, but without so much as a smile on his face, or any sign that he endorsed the Duchesse's joking banter.

"Was M. de Norpois present?" asked Prince Von, whose mind was still bent on the Academy of Moral Sciences.

"He was," said the general. "He was talking about your Emperor, as it happens."

"It seems that Kaiser Wilhelm is highly intelligent, but he doesn't like Elstir's work. I don't say that to disparage him," said the Duchesse, "I happen to share his point of view. Although Elstir has done a fine portrait of me. You haven't seen it? It's not a good likeness, but it's intriguing. He's interesting to sit for. He's portrayed me like some old woman. It's modeled on Hals's *The Women Regents of the Old Men's Almshouse.* I imagine you know those 'sublimities,' to borrow one of my nephew's favorite expressions," she said, turning to me with a delicate flutter of her black feather fan. Rather than sitting erect on her chair, she threw her head nobly backward, for, though she was always the *grande dame,* she was somewhat given to acting the part as well. I told her that I had once been in Amsterdam and The Hague, but that, since my time there was limited and I wanted to avoid muddling everything up, I had left out Haarlem.

"Ah, The Hague! What a gallery!" exclaimed M. de Guermantes. I remarked that he had doubtless admired Vermeer's *View of Delft.* But the Duc was less informed than arrogant. And so he made do with a complacent reply, as he did every time anyone spoke to him about a picture in a gallery, or in the Salon, of which he had no recollection: "If it's to be seen, I've seen it!"

"What? You went all the way to Holland and you never visited

Haarlem!" exclaimed the Duchesse. "Why, even if you had only a quarter of an hour in the place, they're an extraordinary thing to have seen, those Hals pictures. I'd go so far as to say that even catching a glimpse of them from the top of a moving tram, supposing they were on view in the street, would be an eye-opener." I was taken aback by this remark as indicative of a misconception about the way in which artistic impressions are formed in our minds, and because it seemed to imply that our eye in this instance is simply a piece of recording apparatus that takes snapshots.

M. de Guermantes, delighted that she should be talking to me with such competence about things that interested me, stood gazing at the impressive posture his wife was famous for, listening to what she was saying about Frans Hals and thinking: "She's an ornament of erudition on every subject. Our young guest can boast that he's stood in front of a great lady of the old school in every sense of the term, the likes of whom couldn't be found today." This is how I beheld the two of them, removed from the name Guermantes, in which, back in the past, I had imagined them to be leading an unimaginable life, but today just like other men and other women, merely lagging a little behind their contemporaries, but unevenly so, like so many households of the Faubourg Saint-Germain in which the wife has been clever enough to stop at the golden age of the past, the husband misfortunate enough to descend to its distasteful aspects, she remaining Louis XV while her husband is pompously Louis-Philippe. That Mme de Guermantes should be like other women had been a disappointment for me at first; I reacted to it now, with the help of so much fine wine, as something almost wondrous. A Don John of Austria, an Isabella d'Este, catalogued for us in the world of names, have as little connection with the great moments of history as the Méséglise way had with the Guermantes one. Isabella d'Este, in real life, was no doubt a very minor princess, similar to those who under Louis XIV achieved no special rank at court. But because we feel her to be of a unique and thus incomparable essence, we are unable to conceive of her as being any less great than he, so that a supper party with Louis XIV would appear to us as merely rather interesting, whereas with Isabella d'Este we would find ourselves miraculously transported into the presence of a heroine of romance. But after studying Isabella d'Este and patiently transplanting her out of that magic world into the world of history, after ascertaining that her life, her thoughts, contained nothing of the mysterious strangeness suggested to us by her name, once we have recovered from our disappointment, we are eternally grateful to that Princess for having had a knowledge of Mantegna's paintings almost equal to that of M. de Lafenestre,[89] hitherto despised by us as "lower than dirt," to use one of Françoise's expressions. After scaling the inaccessible heights of the name Guermantes, as I descended the inner slope of the Duchesse's life and discovered the already familiar names of Victor Hugo, Frans Hals, and, regrettably, Vibert, I felt the same astonishment that an explorer does after he has taken into account, in order to visualize the singularity of the native customs in some wild valley of Central America or North Africa, its geographical remoteness, the strange names of its flora, and then discovers, once he has made his way through a screen of giant aloes or manchineels, inhabitants who (sometimes indeed among the ruins of a Roman theater and beneath a column dedicated to Venus) are engaged in reading *Mérope* or *Alzire*.[90] And in its remoteness and difference from, its superiority to, the educated middle-class women I had known, the corresponding culture by which Mme de Guermantes had forced herself, with no ulterior motive, no ambitious aim, to descend to the level of women she would never know, had the praiseworthy merit, almost touching in its uselessness, of a knowledge of Phoenician antiquities in a politician or in a doctor.

"I might have been able to show you a very fine one," Mme de Guermantes said to me amiably, referring still to Hals, "the finest one of all, according to some people, which was left to me by a German cousin. Unfortunately, it turned out to be 'enfeoffed' in the castle. You don't know the expression? Neither do I," she added, with her fondness for witticisms (which, as she saw it, made her seem modern) about old customs to which she was nonetheless unconsciously and fiercely attached. "I'm glad you've seen my Elstirs, but I have to say that I would have been a great deal gladder to have done you the honors of my Hals, my 'enfeoffed' painting."

"I've seen that one," said Prince Von, "it belongs to the Grand Duke of Hesse."

"Quite so; his brother married my sister," said M. de Guermantes, "and it so happens that his mother and Oriane's were first cousins."

"But to return to M. Elstir," the Prince went on, "I shall make so bold as to say, without having any opinion of his work, which is unknown to me, that the persistent hatred the Kaiser shows him ought not to be held against him in my view. The Kaiser is a wonderfully intelligent man."

"Yes, I've met him at dinner twice, once at my aunt Sagan's and then at my aunt Radziwill's, and I must say I found him somewhat unusual. I certainly didn't think he was simple! But there's something slightly funny about him, something *forced*"—she emphasized the word— "like a green carnation, I mean something that surprises me and makes me feel rather uncomfortable, a thing that it's surprising that anyone should have been able to create but which would have been just as well left uncreated, it seems to me. I do hope I'm not offending you?"

"The Kaiser is man of quite exceptional intelligence," Prince Von proceeded. "He is passionately devoted to the arts; his sense of taste in works of art is all but infallible; he never makes an error of judgment; if something is good he recognizes it at once and takes a dislike to it. If he detests something, there can be no doubt about it, the thing is excellent." Everyone smiled.

"How very reassuring," said the Duchesse.

"I'm rather inclined to compare the Kaiser," continued the Prince, whose inability to pronounce the word "archaeologist" (that is, as though it were spelled with a "k") did nothing to stop him from taking every opportunity to use it, "to an old archaeologist"—which the Prince pronounced as "arsheologist"—"we have in Berlin. If you set him in front of a genuine piece of Assyrian antiquity, this old arsheologist weeps. But if it is a modern fake, if it is something that is not really old, he fails to weep. And so, when they want to know whether an arsheological piece is really old, they take it to the old arsheologist. If he weeps, they buy the piece for the museum. If there are no tears, they send it back to the dealer and prosecute him for fraud. Well, every time

I dine at Potsdam, if the Kaiser says to me of a play, 'Prince, you must see it, it's a work of genius,' I remind myself not to go to it, and when I hear him railing against an exhibition, I rush to see it at the earliest opportunity."

"Isn't it true that Norpois is in favor of an Anglo-French understanding?" said M. de Guermantes.

"What good would that do you?" asked Prince Von, who could not endure the English, in a manner that was at once irritated and wily. "The English are so *schtubid.* I realize they would not be of use to you as soldiers. But one can nonetheless judge them on the *schtubidity* of their generals. A friend of mine was talking to Botha the other day—you know, the Boer leader. This leader told him: 'It's terrible, an army like that. I'm rather fond of the English, as it happens, but just imagine that I, a mere *peassant,* have thrashed them in every battle. And in the last one, when I was overpowered by a force twenty times the strength of my own, even when I was surrendering because I had to, I still managed to take two thousand prisoners! That was all right because I was only a leader of an army of *peassants,* but if those poor fools ever have to stand up to a real European army, one trembles to think what might happen to them!' Besides, you have only to see how their king, whom you know as well as I do, passes for a great man in England."

I scarcely listened to those anecdotes, something like the ones M. de Norpois used to tell my father; they afforded no food for my preferred patterns of thought; and, besides, even had they possessed the elements they lacked, they would have needed to be of a highly exciting nature for my inner life to be aroused during those hours spent in society when I lived on the surface, my hair well groomed, my shirtfront starched—that is to say, hours in which I could feel nothing of what I personally regarded as pleasure.

"Oh, I don't agree with you there," said Mme de Guermantes, who felt that the German Prince was wanting in tact. "I find King Edward a charming man, so simple, and much shrewder than people think. And the Queen is, even now, the most beautiful thing I've ever seen."

"But, *Matame* la Duchesse," said the Prince, who was losing his temper and unable to see that he was causing offense, "the fact remains that if the Prince of Wales had been an ordinary person there isn't a club that wouldn't have blackballed him, and nobody would have been willing to shake hands with him. The Queen is delightful, excessively sweet, and of limited intelligence. But, still, there's something shocking about a royal couple who are literally kept by their subjects, who get the big Jewish financiers to pay all the bills they ought to pay themselves, and make them baronets in exchange. It's like the Prince of Bulgaria. . . ."

"He's our cousin," said the Duchesse, "a man of wit."

"He's mine, too," said the Prince, "but that is no reason for us to have a high opinion of him. No, it's us you ought to make friends with, it's the Kaiser's dearest wish, but he wants it to come from the heart. He puts it this way: 'What I want to see is a hand clasped in my own, not someone touching their hat to me!' With that you would be invincible. It would be a more practical solution than the Anglo-French rapprochement preached by M. de Norpois."

"You know him, of course," said the Duchesse, turning to me so as not to leave me out of the conversation. Remembering that M. de Norpois had had occasion to remark that I had looked as though I had wanted to kiss his hand, thinking that he had almost certainly repeated this story to Mme de Guermantes and could, in any event, only have spoken of me to her with malice, since, in spite of his friendship with my father, he had had no qualms about making me appear so ridiculous, I did not respond to this as a man of the world would have done. Such a man would have said that he detested M. de Norpois and had made it quite clear to him; he would have said this to give the impression that he was the deliberate cause of the ambassador's slanders, which would then have been seen as no more than lying, calculated instances of retaliation. But instead I answered that, to my deep regret, I was afraid that M. de Norpois did not like me. "You're quite wrong," replied Mme de Guermantes, "he likes you very much indeed. You can ask Basin. If I have a reputation for telling people only what they want to hear, Basin certainly doesn't. He'll tell you that we've never heard Norpois speak about anyone so kindly as he speaks about you. And only the other day, he was talking about creating a fine post for you at the ministry. Since he knew that you weren't in the best of health and would not be able to accept it, he had the delicacy not to mention a word about this kind thought to your father, for whom he has unbounded respect." M. de Norpois was the very last person I should have expected to do me a service. The truth was that, since his was a mocking and even somewhat malicious nature, those who, like me, had let themselves be taken in by his outward appearance of a Saint Louis dispensing justice under an oak tree, by the glib tones of commiseration that emerged from his slightly too harmonious way of speaking, suspected real treachery when they learned of some slander directed toward them by a man whose words had always seemed so heartfelt. These slanders were a frequent enough occurrence. But they did not prevent him from taking a liking to people, from praising those he liked, and taking pleasure in showing willingness to help them.

"Not that I'm at all surprised at his appreciating you," said Mme de Guermantes. "He's an intelligent man. And I can quite understand," she added for the benefit of those present, alluding to a plan of marriage of which I knew nothing, "that my aunt, who has long ceased to amuse him as an old mistress, may not seem of very much use to him as a new wife. Especially since I understand that even as a mistress she hasn't performed for years now. Her only relations, if I can put it like that, are with the good Lord above. You can't believe how churchy she is, and Boaz-Norpois could well take Victor Hugo's lines to heart: 'How long it is since she with whom I slept, O Lord, forsook my bed for yours.'⁹¹ Really, my poor aunt is like those avant-garde artists who have ranted against the Academy all their lives and end up starting a little academy of their own, or those unfrocked priests who then fabricate a religion of their own. They might as well stick to the cloth, or not hang around in a group. But who knows," the Duchesse continued meditatively, "it may be in anticipation of widowhood. There's nothing sadder than weeds one's not entitled to wear."

"Ah! If Mme de Villeparisis were to become Mme de Norpois, I think our cousin Gilbert would have a fit," said Général de Saint-Joseph.

"The Prince de Guermantes is a charming man, but he really is a stickler for matters of birth and etiquette," said the Princess of Parma. "I went to spend a couple of days with him in the country, when the Princesse had the misfortune to be ill in bed. I went there with Petite." This was a nickname given to Mme d'Hunolstein because she was an enormous woman. "The Prince came to meet me at the foot of the steps, offered me his arm, and pretended not to see Petite. We went up to the reception rooms, and it was only then, as he stepped back to let me pass, that he brought himself to say: 'Oh, good day to you, Mme d'Hunolstein'—he always calls her that now, since her separation—pretending that he had only just noticed Petite, in order to indicate that he had had no reason to come down to receive her at the foot of the steps."

"That doesn't surprise me in the least. I don't need to point out," said the Duc, who regarded himself as extremely up-to-date, more contemptuous than anyone in the world of matters of birth, and even Republican in spirit, "that I don't have a lot in common with my cousin. As Your Highness can imagine, our opinions on most subjects are about as distinct as day and night. But I must say that if my aunt were to marry Norpois, for once I should share Gilbert's view of the matter. To be the daughter of Florimont de Guise and to make such a marriage would be enough to send the cat into stitches, as they say—how else can I put it?" This last phrase, which the Duc usually used in the middle of a sentence, was utterly superfluous in the context. But he felt a constant need to utter it, which made him shift it to the end of a sentence if he could not get it in elsewhere. It functioned for him, among other things, as an element of prosody. "Mind you," he added, "the Norpois are excellent folk; they hail from a fine place, from good stock."

"Look here, Basin, it's no good you poking fun at Gilbert if you're going to speak the same language he does," said Mme de Guermantes, for whom, like the Prince and the Duc de Guermantes, the "goodness" of a family, no less than that of a wine, consisted precisely in its age. But, less outspoken than her cousin and more subtle than her husband, she made a point of never letting her words play false to the Guermantes spirit, and despised rank in what she said while she was ready to honor it in the way she behaved.

"But isn't there some sort of cousinly connection between you?"

asked Général de Saint-Joseph. "I have an idea that Norpois married a La Rochefoucauld."

"But not at all in the way you are thinking. She belonged to the branch of the Duc de La Rochefoucauld, and my grandmother comes from the Ducs de Doudeauville. She was the actual grandmother of Édouard Coco, the wisest man in the family," replied the Duc, whose conception of wisdom was rather superficial. "The two branches of the family haven't intermarried since Louis XIV's time. The connection would be rather remote."

"Really, how interesting. I never knew that," said the general.

"And if I'm right," the Duc went on, "his mother was the sister of the Duc de Montmorency and had originally been married to a La Tour d'Auvergne. But since those Montmorencys are barely Montmorencys, and those Tour d'Auvergnes aren't Tour d'Auvergnes at all, I can't see that it gives him any great station. He says—and this is more to the point—that he's descended from Saintrailles, and since we ourselves are in a direct line of descent . . ."

There was in Combray a rue de Saintrailles to which I had never given a second thought. It led from the rue de la Bretonnerie to the rue de l'Oiseau. And since Saintrailles, the companion of Joan of Arc, had married a Guermantes and brought into that family the county of Combray, his arms were quartered with those of the Guermantes at the base of one of the windows in Saint-Hilaire. I recalled the darkish sandstone steps, while a modulation of sound brought back that name Guermantes in the forgotten tone in which I once used to hear it, so different from the tone in which it merely indicated the genial hosts with whom I was dining that evening. If the name Duchesse de Guermantes was a collective noun in my mind, it was not so merely in history, as the accumulation of all the women who had borne it in turn, but also in the course of my own short early life, which had already seen, in this single Duchesse de Guermantes, so many women superimpose themselves, each one vanishing as soon as the next had sufficiently materialized. Words do not change their meaning over the centuries as much as names do for us in the space of a few years. Our memories and our hearts are not large enough to remain faithful. We do not have enough room, in our present mental space, to keep the dead alongside the living. We are obliged to build on top of what has gone before and is unearthed only by a chance excavation, like the one just opened up by the name Saintrailles. I felt it would be pointless to explain all this, and a little earlier in the evening I had even implicitly lied by not replying to M. de Guermantes's question, "You don't know our little patch of the woods?" Perhaps he was quite well aware of the fact that I did know it, and had refused to press his question only out of good breeding. Mme de Guermantes drew me out of my daydream.

"Personally, I find all this sort of thing makes me die of boredom. It's really not always as boring as this in this house. I do hope you'll dine with us again soon as a compensation, and with no pedigrees next time," the Duchesse said to me in an undertone, unable to appreciate the charm I might find in her house, and without the humility to be content to let it appeal to me simply as a herbarium filled with outmoded specimens.

What Mme de Guermantes believed to be disappointing my expectations was on the contrary what in the end—for the Duc and the general went on relentlessly with their discussion of pedigree—saved my evening from being a complete disappointment. How could I have felt other than disappointed until now? All of the dinner guests, cloaking the mysterious names under which I had merely known and imagined them at a distance in bodies and minds similar or inferior to those of everyone else I knew, had given me the impression of a commonplace dullness which the initial view of the Danish port of Elsinore would give to any passionate admirer of *Hamlet*. No doubt these geographical regions and the historic past that injected forest glades and Gothic steeples into their names had to a certain extent shaped their faces, their minds, and their prejudices, but had survived in them only as does the cause in the effect—that is, as something that can be unearthed by the intelligence but in no way perceived by the imagination.

And these prejudices from the historical past instantly restored to the friends of M. and Mme de Guermantes their lost poetry. It is true that the notions possessed by the nobility that make them the scholars, the etymologists of the language not of words but of names (and even then only in comparison with the ignorant majority of the middle classes, for, if, on the same level of mediocrity, a devout Catholic would be better able to answer questions on the liturgy than a freethinker, by contrast, an anticlerical archaeologist can often teach his parish priest a thing or two about everything connected even with that priest's own church), those notions, if we are to stick to the truth—that is to say, to the spirit—had none of the charm for these noblemen that they had for a middle-class person. Possibly they knew better than I did that the Duchesse de Guise was Princess of Cleves, of Orléans, of Porcien, and so forth, but long before they knew all these names, they had known the Duchesse de Guise's face, which was subsequently what this name reflected back to them. I had begun with the fairy, even if she was soon fated to perish; they had begun with the woman herself.

In middle-class families you sometimes see jealousies starting up when the younger sister marries before the elder. Similarly, the aristocratic world (the Courvoisiers in particular, but the Guermantes, too) reduced its nobiliary greatness to mere levels of domestic superiority out of a childishness I had originally come across in books (the only place I found any charm in it). Does not Tallemant des Réaux[92] seem to be speaking about the Guermantes, as opposed to the Rohans, when he relates with evident satisfaction that M. de Guéménée shouted to his brother, "You can step inside! This is not the Louvre!" and said of the Chevalier de Rohan himself (because he was the natural son of the Duc de Clermont), "At least he's a prince!" The only thing that distressed me during the evening's conversation was to discover that the absurd gossip about the charming adopted Grand Duke of Luxembourg found as much credence in this salon as it did among Saint-Loup's friends. It was plainly an epidemic that would last perhaps for no longer than a year or so, but it had infected everyone. People repeated the same false gossip, or created more. I gathered that the Princess of Luxembourg herself, while ostensibly defending her nephew, was supplying weapons to attack him with. "You are wrong to stand up for him," M. de Guermantes told me, just as Saint-Loup had done. "Look, even leaving aside the views of our family, which are unanimous on the subject, you have only to talk to his servants, and they, after all, are the people who know us best.

Mme de Luxembourg gave her little Negro page to her nephew. The page came back in tears: 'Grand Duke beat me, me no bad boy, Grand Duke bad man, real bad.' And I have this on good authority, from Oriane's cousin."

I cannot say, now that I come to think about it, how many times I heard the word "cousin" used in the course of the evening. On the one hand, M. de Guermantes, at almost every name mentioned, would exclaim, "But he's Oriane's cousin!" with the same delight as a man lost in a forest who sees a signpost with two arrows pointing in opposite directions, each followed by a very low number of kilometers, reads the words "Belvédère Casimir-Perier" and "Croix du Grand-Veneur," and recognizes from them that he is on the right road. On the other hand, the word "cousin" was being used for a wholly different purpose (an exception to the rule prevailing at this gathering) by the Turkish ambassadress, who had joined the party after dinner. Devoured by social ambition and endowed with a real gift for assimilating knowledge, she would ingest with equal facility Xenophon's account of the Ten Thousand[93] or the details of sexual perversion among birds. It would have been impossible to fault her on any of the most recent German publications, whether they dealt with political economy, mental illness, the various forms of onanism, or the philosophy of Epicurus. She was a dangerous woman to listen to into the bargain, since she was perpetually getting things wrong and would point out ladies of irreproachable virtue as women of the loosest morals, would put you on your guard against a man of the most honorable intentions, and would tell you anecdotes that seemed to come out of a book, not because they were serious, but because they were utterly improbable.

Very few people opened their doors to her at this period. For a few weeks she would frequent socially brilliant women like the Duchesse de Guermantes, but as far as the noblest families were concerned, she had mostly confined herself, of necessity, to obscure branches of the family the Guermantes no longer frequented. She attempted to persuade people of her social standing by quoting the most distinguished names of little-known people who were her friends. The immediate reaction to this on the part of M. de Guermantes, who thought that she was referring to people with whom he frequently dined, was to quiver with delight at finding himself in familiar territory and to utter the rallying cry: "But he's Oriane's cousin! I know him like the back of my hand. He lives on the rue Vaneau. His mother was Mlle d'Uzès."

The ambassadress was forced to admit that her specimen had been drawn from a smaller stable. She tried to connect her friends with those of M. de Guermantes by means of a detour: "I know very well who you mean. No, it's not them, it's their cousins." But these words of partial withdrawal launched by the unfortunate ambassadress soon lost any momentum they had. For M. de Guermantes, losing interest, answered, "Oh, then I don't know whom you're talking about." The ambassadress made no reply, for, if she never knew anyone other than "the cousins" of the people she ought to have known, very often these "cousins" bore no relation to them at all. Then M. de Guermantes would offer a fresh wave of "But she's Oriane's cousin," words that seemed, in his eyes, to have the same practical value in each of his sentences as certain adjectives the Roman poets found convenient because they provided them with dactyls or spondees for their hexameters. At any event, the explosion "But she's Oriane's cousin!" seemed to me quite natural applied to the Princesse de Guermantes, who was indeed very closely related to the Duchesse. The ambassadress did not appear to care for the Princesse. She said in an undertone: "The woman is stupid. And, no, she's not *that* beautiful. That reputation is usurped. Anyway," she added with a look that was at once studied, dismissive, and conclusive, "I find her deeply antipathetic." But often the question of tenuous relationships extended a great deal further, Mme de Guermantes making it a point of honor to address as "Aunt" ladies with whom it would have been difficult to find a common ancestress without going back at least to Louis XV, just as, whenever "hard times" brought about the marriage of a multimillionairess to a prince whose great-great-grandfather had married, like Oriane's, a daughter of Louvois, one of the joys of the rich American lady, after a first visit to the Hôtel de Guermantes, where she was, incidentally, rather coolly received and more or less gone over with a fine-tooth comb, was to be able to use the term "Aunt" to Mme de Guermantes, who allowed her to do so with a maternal smile. But I little cared what "birth" meant for M. de Guermantes and M. de Monserfeuil; in the conversations they held on the subject, the only pleasure I sought was a poetic one. Without being conscious of it themselves, they procured me this pleasure in the same way that farmers or seamen would have done talking about the soil or the tides, realities too ingrained in their lives for them to be able to enjoy the beauty that I myself undertook to extract from them.

Sometimes a name would remind me not so much of a pedigree as of a particular fact or date. As I heard M. de Guermantes recall that M. de Bréauté's mother had been a Choiseul and his grandmother a Lucinge, I would imagine that beneath the ordinary shirtfront with its plain pearl studs I could see bleeding in two crystal globes those august relics, the hearts of Mme de Praslin and of the Duc de Berry.[94] Other associations were more voluptuous: the fine and abundant hair of Mme Tallien or Mme de Sabran.[95]

Occasionally I saw more than a simple relic. Better informed than his wife about the nature of their ancestors, M. de Guermantes had a command of memories that gave his conversation the fine feel of an ancient mansion, lacking in real masterpieces but still full of authentic pictures, of middling interest and imposing, giving an overall impression of grandeur. When the Prince d'Agrigente inquired why Prince Von had referred to the Duc d'Aumale as "my uncle," M. de Guermantes replied, "Because his mother's brother, the Duke of Württemberg, married one of Louis-Philippe's daughters." I was immediately deep in contemplation of a reliquary, similar to those painted by Carpaccio or Memling, from its first panel, in which the Princesse was figured, at the wedding festivities of her brother the Duc d'Orléans, wearing a simple garden dress as a sign of her ill-humor at seeing her ambassadors return empty-handed after being sent to sue on her behalf for the hand of the Prince of Syracuse, to the last panel, in which she has just given birth to a son, the Duke of Württemberg (the very uncle of the Prince with whom I had just dined), in the castle known as Fantaisie, one of those places that are themselves as aristocratic as certain families. For such places, too, outlasting a single generation, become associated with more than one historical personage; this one in particular contains alongside one another the memories of the Margravine of Bayreuth; of that other, rather unpredictable Princesse (the sister of the Duc d'Orléans), who was said to have found a certain appeal in the name of her husband's castle; of the King of Bavaria; and, finally, of Prince Von, who was the present inhabitant, and who had just asked the Duc de Guermantes to write to him there, since he had succeeded to it and rented it only during the Wagner festival performances, to the Prince de Polignac, another delightful "fantasist." When M. de Guermantes, to explain how he was connected to Mme d'Arpajon, was obliged to go back, so far and so simply, along the chain of linked hands formed by three or five ancestresses, to Marie-Louise or to Colbert, the same thing happened again: in each of these cases, an important historical event appeared only in passing, masked, distorted, curtailed, in the name of a property, in the first names of a woman, chosen for her because she was the granddaughter of Louis-Philippe and Marie-Amélie, considered no longer as King and Queen of France, but only in their capacity as grandparents for bequeathing a heritage. (For different reasons, in a glossary to the works of Balzac, where the most illustrious names figure only in terms of their connection with *La Comédie humaine*, you can find Napoleon occupying far less space than Rastignac, and occupying it only because he once spoke to the Saint-Cygne ladies.) Thus does the heavy structure of the aristocracy, with its rare windows, admitting a scant amount of daylight, showing the same incapacity to soar, but also the same massive, blind force as Romanesque architecture, enclose all our history within its sullen walls.

Thus did the blank spaces of my memory gradually fill with names that, as they arranged and composed themselves in relation to one another, and as the connections between them became more and more numerous, resembled those perfected works of art in which there is not a single brush stroke that does not contribute to the whole, and in which every element in turn receives from the rest a justification it confers on them in its turn.

After M. de Luxembourg's name had been brought up again, the Turkish ambassadress told us how, when the young bride's grandfather (the man who had made a vast amount of money out of flour and pasta) had invited M. de Luxembourg to lunch, the latter had written to decline and addressed the envelope to "M. de ——, miller"; the grandfather had written back, "I am all the more disappointed that you were unable to come, my dear friend, in that I should have been able to enjoy your company in privacy, for we were only a small party and there would have only been the miller, his son, and yourself." This anecdote was not only utterly distasteful to me, but inconceivable, as I knew it to be morally impossible that my dear M. de Nassau should write to his wife's grandfather (and a man whose fortune he was likely to inherit) addressing him as "miller"; but there was the further point that its stupidity was glaringly apparent from the start, the word "miller" having been so obviously dragged in only to lead up to the title of the La Fontaine fable.[96] But there is a kind of silliness in the Faubourg Saint-Germain, especially when it is aggravated by malice, which led everyone to applaud the words of this anecdote as "inspired" and to see the grandfather, whom they all suddenly confidently declared to be a remarkable man, as a wittier one than his grandson-in-law. The Duc de Châtellerault wanted to take advantage of this story to recount one I had already heard in the café—"Everyone was made to lie down!"—but no sooner had he begun with an account of M. de Luxembourg's claim that M. de Guermantes ought to stand up in his wife's presence than the Duchesse stopped him and protested, "No, he's absurd to a degree, but he certainly wouldn't go that far." My private conviction was that all this gossip at M. de Luxembourg's expense was equally untrue, and that whenever I found myself face-to-face with one of the participants or onlookers in the story I would hear the same denial. The only thing I wondered about was whether the denial I had just heard from Mme de Guermantes had arisen from a concern with the truth or from pride. In any event, pride succumbed to malice, for she went on to say with a laugh: "Not that I haven't had my little snub, too. He invited me to tea to introduce me to the Grand Duchess of Luxembourg, which is how he has the good taste to describe his wife when he's writing to his aunt. I wrote back to say I was sorry I couldn't come and I added, 'Do tell the "Grand Duchess of Luxembourg" (in quotation marks) that if she wants to come and see me I'm at home every Thursday after five.' I was even snubbed twice. I happened to be in Luxembourg and telephoned to ask to speak to him. His Highness was going to luncheon, had just finished luncheon, two hours went by, and there was no reply. So I employed another method: 'Would you tell the Comte de Nassau to come to the phone?' Cut to the quick, he was there at once." Everyone laughed at the Duchesse's story and at further stories in the same vein—that is to say, untrue ones (I am convinced of it), for a kinder, more intelligent, more refined, in a word more exquisite man than this Luxembourg-Nassau I had never met. The sequel will show that it was I who was right. Yet I must admit that, among the spate of her nasty remarks, Mme de Guermantes did have a kind word to say about him.

"He wasn't always like that," she remarked. "Before he went off his head, like the man in the storybook who thinks he's become king, he was far from stupid, and, indeed, in the early days of his engagement, he used to speak of it in a rather charming way, as an undreamed-of happiness: 'It's just like a fairy tale; I shall have to make my entry into Luxembourg in a fairy coach,' he told his uncle d'Ornesson, who said in turn—for you know that Luxembourg is not a very big place—'A fairy coach, eh? I'm afraid you'd never get in with that. I'd suggest a goat cart myself.' Not only did this not annoy Nassau, but he was the first to tell us the story, and to laugh at it."

"Ornesson is full of witticisms. He has every reason to be: his mother was a Montjeu. He's in a bad way these days, poor Ornesson."

This name had the merit of interrupting the stale, malicious gossip that would otherwise have gone on forever. For M. de Guermantes went on to explain that the M. d'Ornesson's great-grandmother had been the sister of Marie de Castille Montjeu, the wife of Timoléon de Lorraine, and therefore Oriane's aunt. This meant that the conversation reverted to genealogies, and I had the imbecile Turkish ambassadress murmuring in my ear, "You appear to be very much in the Duc de Guermantes's good books. Be careful." And when I asked for an explanation: "I mean—and I think you'll understand what I mean—that he's a man to whom one could safely entrust one's daughter, but not one's son." Now, if ever, on the contrary, there was a man who was a passionate and exclusive lover of women, that man was the Duc de Guermantes. But error, gullibly credited untruth were for the ambassadress like a life-sustaining element without which she could not function. "His brother Mémé, whom, for other reasons, I happen to dislike deeply"—the fact was that he refused to acknowledge her—"is genuinely distressed at the Duc's morals. So is their aunt Villeparisis. Ah, how I adore that woman. She's a real saint, a perfect example of the way great ladies used to be. She's not only a living image of virtue, but of reserve as well. She still addresses Ambassador Norpois as 'monsieur,' even though she sees him every day. And he, by the way, made an excellent impression in Turkey."

I did not even bother to reply to the ambassadress, because I was anxious to listen to the genealogies. Not all of them were important. It so happened that one of the unexpected alliances about which I learned from M. de Guermantes in the course of the conversation was a misalliance, but not without its charm, since it united, under the July Monarchy, the Duc de Guermantes and the Duc de Fezensac with two beauties, the daughters of a famous navigator, and graced these two duchesses with the unexpected piquancy of a bourgeois exoticism, an element of India à la Louis-Philippe. Otherwise, under Louis XIV, there was a Norpois who had married a daughter of the Duc de Mortemart, whose illustrious title, in those far-off times, struck the name Norpois, which to me sounded humdrum and of possibly recent origin, and engraved it deeply with the beauty of an old medal. And again in these cases, it was not solely the less well-known name that benefited by the association: the other, turned into a cliché by its glitter, struck me more forcibly in its novel, less illustrious form, just as among the portraits painted by a brilliant colorist the most striking is sometimes the one that is all in black. The fresh mobility that seemed to me to animate all these names, as they came to join others from which I should have supposed them to be remote, was not due to my ignorance alone; the to-ings and fro-ings they were performing in my mind had been performed no less freely in those periods when a title, always attached to a given territory, would always follow it from one family to another, to the point, for example, where I could successively discern, in the fine feudal structure constituted by the title Duc de Nemours or Duc de Chevreuse, nestling as in the hospitable abode of a hermit crab, a Guise, a Prince of Savoy, an Orléans, a Luynes. In some instances, several remained in competition for a single shell: for the Principality of Orange, the royal house of the Netherlands and MM. de Mailly-Nesle; for the Duchy of Brabant, the Baron de Charlus and the royal house of Belgium; various others for the titles of Prince of Naples, Duke of Parma, Duke of Reggio. In others it was the other way round: the shell had been so long uninhabited by proprietors long since dead that it had never occurred to me that this or that name of a castle could have been, at a period that was after all comparatively recent, the name of a family. And so, when M. de Guermantes replied to a question put to him by M. de Monserfeuil, "No, my cousin was a fanatical royalist. She was the daughter of the Marquis de Féterne, who had some part in the Chouan uprising," when I saw this name Féterne, which to me, ever since my stay in Balbec, had been the name of a castle, become something I had never dreamed it could possibly be, the name of a family, I felt the same sense of astonishment I would have done reading a fairy tale in which turrets and flights of steps come to life and turn into people. In this sense, it could be said that history, even mere family history, restores old stones to life. There have been men in Parisian society who played as considerable a part in it, who were more sought after for their distinction or their wit, who were just as well born as the Duc de Guermantes or the Duc de La Trémoïlle. Today they have fallen into oblivion, because, since they left no descendants, their name, which is no longer heard, echoes with an unfamiliar ring; at the very most, like the name of a thing in which we never expect to discover the name of a person, it survives in some castle, in some remote village. There will soon be a day when the traveler who stops in the heart of Burgundy, in the tiny village of Charlus, to look at its church, if he is not studious enough or in too much of a hurry to examine its tombstones, will go away ignorant of the fact that the name Charlus was the name of a man who ranked with the greatest. This thought reminded me that it was time for me to leave, and that, while I was standing there listening to M. de Guermantes talking genealogy, the time I had promised to call on his brother was fast approaching. Who knows, I went on thinking, whether one day "Guermantes" itself may survive as anything other than a place-name, except to archaeologists who stop briefly in Combray, stand before the window of Gilbert the Bad, and have the patience to hear out the account given them by Théodore's successor or to read the *curé*'s guide? But as long as a great name is not extinct, it keeps the men and women who bore it in the limelight; and no doubt part of the interest the illustriousness of these families assumed for me lay in the fact that it is possible, starting from the present, to follow them back step by step to well before the fourteenth century, and to find the memoirs and correspondence of all the forebears of M. de Charlus, of the Prince d'Agrigente, of the Princess of Parma, in a past that would shroud the origins of a middle-class family in impenetrable darkness, documents in which we can ascertain, in the luminous backward projection of a name, the origin and persistence of various nervous characteristics, vices, and disorders of one or another of the Guermantes. Almost pathologically identical with their namesakes of the present day, from century to century they arouse the startled interest of their correspondents, whether these predate the Princess Palatine and Mme de Motteville, or follow on from the Prince de Ligne.

Yet my historical curiosity paled before my aesthetic pleasure. The names I had heard uttered had a disembodying effect on the Duchesse's guests—in spite of the fact that they might be called the Prince d'Agrigente or the Prince de Cystria—whose masks of flesh and absent or vulgar intelligence had transformed them into rather ordinary specimens, to the point where I ended up feeling that I had landed on the Guermantes doormat not as upon the supposed threshold but at the terminus of the magic world of names. The Prince d'Agrigente himself, the moment I heard that his mother had been a Damas, a granddaughter of the Duke of Modena, was set free, as from an unstable chemical alloy, from the face and speech that prevented one from recognizing him, and joined up with Damas and Modena, themselves mere titles, to form an infinitely more seductive combination. Each name displaced by the attraction of another, with which I had never suspected it of having any affinity, left the static position it had occupied in my brain, where familiarity had dulled it, and, going off to join the Mortemarts, the Stuarts, and the Bourbons, linked up with them to form branches of the most graceful pattern and changing color. The name Guermantes received from all those fine names—extinct and so all the more glowingly rekindled, with which I learned only now that it was connected—a new and purely poetic sense. At the very most, on the tip of each spray that burgeoned forth from the proud stem, I could see it flower into the face of some wise monarch or illustrious princess, like the father of Henri IV or the Duchesse de Longueville. But since these faces, different in this respect from those of the guests in the room, were in no way overlaid by the residue of physical experience or social mediocrity, they remained, in their handsome outlines and shifting reflections, homogeneous with the names that, at regular intervals, each with its own coloring, detached themselves from the Guermantes genealogical tree, and disturbed with no foreign or opaque matter the translucent, alternating, multicolored buds that, like the ancestors of Jesus in windows figuring the tree of Jesse, blossomed on either side of the glass tree.

I had already made several attempts to take my leave, for various reasons, but principally because of the insignificance that my presence was imposing on the party, although it was one of those I had long imagined as being so glamorous, as it doubtless would have been had there been no awkward witness present. At least my departure would allow the guests, once the trespasser had disappeared, to form themselves into a closed circle. They would be free to celebrate the mysteries for which they had gathered there, and they had certainly not gathered to discuss Frans Hals or miserliness, and to discuss such matters in the same way as people do in bourgeois society. The talk was trivial, no doubt because I was present, and, seeing all these pretty women kept apart, it pained me to think that my presence was preventing them from proceeding, in the most precious of its salons, with the mysterious life of the Faubourg Saint-Germain. But every attempt I made to leave was being foiled by M. and Mme de Guermantes, who carried the spirit of self-sacrifice to the point of constantly detaining me. More curious still, several of the ladies who had come running with delight, in all their finery, glittering with jewels, only to attend a party that, because of me, differed from parties given elsewhere than in the Faubourg Saint-Germain really no more than one feels oneself, in Balbec, to be in a town that differs from what one usually sees—several of these ladies took their leave, not in a state of disappointment, as they had every reason to be, but thanking Mme de Guermantes effusively for the delightful evening they had spent, as though on other days, the days on which I was not present, nothing different happened.

Was it really for dinner parties like the present one that all these people dressed up and refused middle-class women admittance to their exclusive drawing rooms? For dinner parties like this, which would have been no different even in my absence? For a second I suspected as much, but the suspicion was too absurd. Plain common sense enabled me to brush it aside. And had I embraced it, what would have been left of the name Guermantes, already so demoted since the Combray days?

Besides, these flower-maidens were, to a strange extent, easily pleased with another person, or anxious to please that person, for more than one of them, with whom I had exchanged, in the course of the entire evening, no more than a handful of casual remarks, the stupidity of which had left me blushing, made a point, before she left the drawing room, of coming to tell me, as she held me in a fond look from her lovely eyes and straightened as she spoke the spray of orchids that followed the curves of her bosom, what a deep pleasure it had been to make my acquaintance, and to speak to me—a veiled allusion to a dinner invitation—of her desire to "arrange something" after she had "fixed a day" with Mme de Guermantes. None of these flower-ladies left the room before the Princess of Parma. The presence of the latter—one must never leave before royalty—was one of the two reasons, neither of which I had suspected, why the Duchesse had been so insistent on my remaining. The minute Mme de Parme rose to her feet, there was the feeling that everyone had been set free. Each of the ladies, after making a genuflection before the Princess, received from her in a kiss, and like a benediction they had begged for on their knees, permission to ask for their cloaks and their attendants. With the result that, at the main door, there was something like a vociferous recital of great names from the history of France. The Princess of Parma had forbidden Mme de Guermantes to accompany her down to the hall for fear of her catching cold, and the Duc had added, "Come, now, Oriane, since Madame gives you leave to stay here, remember what the doctor told you."

"I think that the Princess of Parma was *very pleased* to dine with you." I knew the formula. The Duc had come from the other end of the drawing room to utter it to me, in an obliging, fulsome manner, as though he were awarding me a diploma or offering me a plate of petits fours. The pleasure that he appeared to be feeling at that moment, which brought such a gentle expression to his face for that instant, led me to sense that the order of attentiveness to which his gesture belonged was of the kind that would be with him until the very end of his life, like those honorific sinecures that are retained even by the senile.

Just as I was about to leave, the Princess's lady-in-waiting reappeared in the drawing room, in search of some flowers she had forgotten, marvelous pinks, from the Guermantes estate, which the Duchesse had offered Mme de Parme. This lady-in-waiting was rather flushed, and one felt that she had just been put roundly in her place, for the Princess, so kind toward everyone else, could not conceal her impatience at the stupidity of her attendant. And so the latter picked up the bunch of pinks and moved off in a hurry, but, to preserve some element of unflustered behavior and willful independence, she blurted out to me as she passed, "The Princess tells me I'm keeping her waiting; she is impatient to be gone *and* she wants to take the pinks. Heavens! I'm not some little bird, I can't be all over the place at once."

Alas! The rule about not leaving before royalty was not the only thing that detained me. I was unable to leave immediately for another reason: that the lavishness (unknown to the Courvoisiers) for which the Guermantes, whether opulent or practically ruined, were famous when they entertained their friends, was not only lavishness in material terms but also, as I had often experienced with Robert de Saint-Loup, a lavishness of charming words, courteous gestures, a whole gamut of verbal elegance nourished by real intensity of feeling. But as this last, in the idleness of fashionable existence, finds no outlet, it poured forth at times, seeking some channel of expression in a kind of fleeting effusiveness, which was all the more anxiously solicitous, and which might, on the part of Mme de Guermantes, have been mistaken for affection. She did in fact feel it at the moment she let it overflow, for she discovered then, in the company of the friend, man or woman, she was with at the time, a sense of intoxication, in no way sensual, similar to that which music induces in certain people; she would find herself picking a flower from her bodice, or a medallion, and giving it to someone with whom she would have liked to prolong the evening, yet with the melancholy feeling that to prolong it would have led to nothing but idle chatter, which would have absorbed nothing of the nervous pleasure, the fleeting emotion of the experience, and which would have been reminiscent in this respect of the impression of lassitude and regret that follow the first warm days of spring. And as far as the friend was concerned, it was important that he not be too taken in by the promises, more thrilling than any he had ever heard, proffered by these women, who, because they are particularly susceptible to the sweetness of a moment, turn it, with a delicacy, a nobility not granted to ordinary creatures, into a masterpiece of endearment and kindness, and no longer have anything of themselves left to give in the moment that follows. Their affection does not outlive the moment of elation that dictated it; and the subtlety of mind that had led them at that point to intuit all the things that you wished to hear, and to say them to you, will enable them, a few days later, to pinpoint your foibles and use them to entertain another of their guests, with whom they will in turn be enjoying one of these *moments musicaux* which are so short-lived.

In the hall, I asked a footman for my snowboots, which I had brought as a precaution against the snow (a few flakes had fallen and already turned to slush), and, not realizing how unfashionable they were, I started to feel, because of the contemptuous smiles I was getting, a sense of shame, which reached its peak when I realized that Mme de Parme had not in fact left and was watching me put on my American rubbers. The Princess came across to me. "Oh, what a good idea!" she exclaimed. "It's so practical! What a very sensible man. Madame, we shall have to buy some of those," she said to her lady-in-waiting, as the ironic reception of the footmen turned to respect and the other guests crowded around to ask where I had managed to find these wonderful things. "With those on your feet, you'll have nothing to fear, even if it snows again and you've got far to go. You're not at the mercy of the weather," the Princess said to me.

"Oh, as far as the weather's concerned, Your Royal Highness can set her mind at rest," broke in the lady-in-waiting knowingly. "It won't snow again."

"And how could you possibly know that?" questioned the peerless Princess of Parma in a withering tone provoked by the one thing that could manage to ruffle her, the stupidity of her lady-in-waiting.

"I can assure Your Royal Highness that it can't snow again. It's a physical impossibility."

"But why?"

"It can't snow again because they've taken the necessary steps to prevent it. They've put salt on the roads!"

The simple-minded lady did not notice the Princess's anger or other people's mirth, for, instead of remaining silent, she said to me with a bland smile, disregarding utterly the denials I had made of any connection with Admiral Jurien de La Gravière, "Not that it matters, in any case. Monsieur must have strong sea legs. It runs in the family!"

After escorting the Princess of Parma to her carriage, M. de Guermantes picked up my greatcoat with the words, "Let me help you into your skin." And he no longer used this expression with an apologetic smile, for, given the way the Guermantes affected simplicity, the most low-class expressions, just because they were low-class, had become aristocratic.

An exhilaration that, because it was artificial, tailed off into melancholy was what I also felt, though quite differently from Mme de Guermantes, once I finally left her house in the carriage that was to take me to M. de Charlus. We are free to abandon ourselves to one or the other of two forces, one arising in ourselves, emanating from our deepest impressions, the other affecting us from without. The natural accompaniment of the first is a joy, the joy that springs from the life of creative people. The other current, the one that aims to introduce into us the impulses by which people external to ourselves are stirred, is not accompanied by pleasurable feeling; but we can add pleasure to it through a vicarious reaction, adopting an intoxication so artificial that it quickly turns into melancholy, into boredom: whence the gloomy faces of so many society people and their pronounced tendency toward nervous conditions that may even lead to suicide. Now, in the carriage that was taking me to M. de Charlus, I was prey to this second sort of exhilaration, very different from that afforded by a personal impression, like those I had received in other carriages: once in Combray, in Dr. Percepied's gig, from which I had seen the Martinville steeples against the setting sun; another day in Balbec, in Mme de Villeparisis's barouche, when I tried hard to work out what it was I was reminded of by an avenue of trees. But in this third carriage, what I had before my mind's eye was those conversations that had seemed so tedious at Mme de Guermantes's dinner party—for example, Prince Von's stories about the Kaiser, General Botha, and the British Army. I had just slid these into the inner stereoscope we use, as soon as we are no longer ourselves, as soon as we adopt a society spirit and wish to receive our life only from others, to bring into solid relief what they have said and done. Like a man who has had too much to drink and feels full of kindness and consideration for the waiter who has been serving him, I marveled at my good fortune—something I had not felt, for sure, at the actual moment—in having dined with someone who knew Wilhelm II so well and had told stories about him that were, upon my word, extremely witty. And as I recalled, together with the Prince's German accent, his story about General Botha, I laughed out loud, as if my laughter, like certain kinds of applause which bolster one's inner admiration, was a necessary corroboration of the story's comic qualities. Through the magnifying lenses, even those of Mme de Guermantes's pronouncements that had struck me as stupid (such as her remarks about seeing Frans Hals paintings from a tram car) assumed an extraordinary life and depth. And I have to say that, even if this sense of elation was quick to subside, it was not completely nonsensical. Just as there may come a day when we are happy to know the person whom we despise most because he happens to be connected with a girl with whom we are in love, to whom he can introduce us, and thus becomes useful and agreeable, something we would never have dreamed he could be, so there is no conversation, any more than there are personal relations, from which we can be certain that we shall not one day derive some benefit. What Mme de Guermantes had said to me about paintings it would be interesting to see, even from a tram car, was untrue, but it contained a grain of truth that was valuable to me at a later stage.

Similarly, the lines from Victor Hugo she had quoted in my presence were admittedly from an earlier period of his work than the one in which he became something more than a new man, in which he evolved a literary species that was previously unknown, endowed with more complex organs. In these early poems, Victor Hugo is still a thinker, rather than a natural force content with providing food for thought. His "thoughts" he expressed at this period in the most direct form, almost in the sense in which the Duc understood the word when he found it old-fashioned and cumbersome of his guests at big parties at Guermantes to append to their signatures in the visitors' book some philosophic-poetical reflection, and would warn newcomers in a pleading voice, "Your name, my dear fellow, but no 'thoughts,' I beg you!" Now, it was these "thoughts" of Victor Hugo (almost as absent from *La Légende des siècles* as "tunes" and "melodies" are from Wagner's later manner) that Mme de Guermantes was so fond of in his early work. Nor was she altogether wrong here. They were moving, and already around them, before their form had yet achieved the depth it was to acquire only later on, the flooding tide of words and richly articulated rhymes made them very different from the lines you find in Corneille, for example, in which Romantic feeling, sporadic and restrained, and therefore all the more moving, has nevertheless not managed to penetrate to the physical sources of life, or modified the unconscious and generalizable organism in which the idea is implicit. And so I had been wrong to confine myself up to this point to Hugo's later collections. It is true that Mme de Guermantes had used only a fractional part of the earlier ones to embellish her conversation. But the point is that, by quoting an isolated line in this way, you increase its power of attraction tenfold. The lines that had entered or returned to my mind in the course of this dinner party acted as magnets in their turn, powerfully called up the poems within which they were normally embedded, so that my magnetized hands were unable to put up more than forty-eight hours' resistance to the force that drew them toward the volume in which *Les Orientales* or *Les Chants du crépuscule* were bound. I cursed Françoise's footman for having made a gift of my copy of the *Feuilles d'automne* to his native village, and lost no time sending him out to buy me another. I reread these volumes from cover to cover and found respite only when

I suddenly stumbled, waiting there for me in the light in which she had bathed them, on the lines that Mme de Guermantes had quoted. For all these reasons, talk with the Duchesse was like the discoveries we make in the library of a country house, outdated, incomplete, incapable of forming a mind, devoid of almost everything we value, but occasionally offering us some curious piece of information, or even a quotation from a fine passage that was unknown to us and which subsequently we are happy to remember as something we were introduced to because of a stay in a splendid stately home. And because we have discovered Balzac's preface to the *Chartreuse* or some unpublished letters of Joubert, we are then tempted to exaggerate the value of our stay there, the barren frivolity of which we forget in the light of a single evening's happy discovery.

From this point of view, if this social world had been unable to respond initially to what my imagination expected, and was consequently to strike me first of all by what it had in common with every other world rather than the ways it differed from them, it nonetheless revealed itself to me as something quite distinct. Noblemen are almost the only people who can teach you as much as peasants; their conversation is adorned with everything that concerns the land, dwellings as people used to live in them in the past, old customs, everything about which the moneyed world is profoundly ignorant. Even supposing that an aristocrat of the most moderate aspirations has finally caught up with the times in which he lives, his mother, his uncles, his great-aunts keep him in touch, when he recalls his childhood, with a style of life that is almost unknown today. In the death chamber of a deceased contemporary, Mme de Guermantes would not have pointed out, but would have been the first to notice, all the lapses from traditional practice. It shocked her to see women mingling with the men at a funeral, when there was a special ceremony that ought to be celebrated for the women themselves. As for the pall, which Bloch would doubtless have seen as reserved for funerals, on account of the pallbearers mentioned in reports of funeral ceremonies, M. de Guermantes could remember the time when, still a child, he had seen it borne at the wedding of M. de Mailly-Nesle. Whereas Saint-Loup had sold his priceless "genealogical tree," together with old portraits of the Bouillons and letters of Louis XIII, in order to buy Carrière paintings[97] and Art Nouveau furniture, M. and Mme de Guermantes, inspired by a sentiment in which a fervent love of art may have played less part and made them appear more commonplace, had kept their marvelous Boulle furniture,[98] which presented a quite different overall appeal to an artistic mind. A literary mind would similarly have been enchanted by the conversation, which for him—for a hungry man has no need of another to keep him company—would have been a living dictionary of all the expressions that are passing out of the language by the day (Saint-Joseph neckties, children pledged to wear blue, and so on), and which survive today only among people who have taken it upon themselves to act as the obliging and benevolent custodians of the past. The pleasure that a writer experiences in their company, far more than in that of other writers, is not without its risks, for he is in danger of believing that the things of the past have a charm in themselves, of transporting them raw into his work, which, if he does, becomes stillborn and smacks of staleness, for which he consoles himself with the thought, "It's appealing because it's authentic, that's how people talk." These aristocratic conversations had the further charm, in Mme de Guermantes's case, of being conducted in excellent French. For this reason, they made it permissible for the Duchesse to react hilariously to the words "vatic," "cosmic," "Pythian," "supereminent," which formed part of Saint-Loup's vocabulary—in the same way as she did to his Bing furniture.[99]

But in the end, the stories I had heard at the Duchesse's house, very different in this respect from the feelings aroused in me by the hawthorns or the taste of a *madeleine,* left me cold. Entering me for a moment and possessing me only physically, it was as though, being of a social, not an individual, nature, they were anxious to escape. I writhed as I sat in the carriage like a prophetess in a trance. I envisaged another dinner party at which I myself might become a sort of Prince X, or a Mme de Guermantes, and tell the same sort of stories. In the meantime, I stammered them out through my trembling lips and tried in vain to restore order to a mind that was carried away by a centrifugal force. And so it was with a feverish impatience not to have to bear the weight of all this any longer on my own, in a carriage where I made up for the lack of conversation by talking aloud to myself, that I rang at M. de Charlus's door, and it was in long monologues with myself, in which I rehearsed everything I was going to tell him with scarcely a thought of what he might have to say to me, that I spent the whole of the time awaiting him in a drawing room into which I had been shown by a footman, and which I was too wound up to take in. I was so anxious for M. de Charlus to listen to the stories I was dying to tell him that I was bitterly disappointed to think that the master of the house had perhaps gone to bed, and that I would have to go back home to work off my verbal intoxication. I had just noticed, in fact, that I had spent twenty-five minutes, that they had perhaps forgotten about me, in this room about which, despite the long wait, the most I could have said was that it was huge, greenish in color, and contained a handful of portraits. The need to talk prevents one not only from listening but from noticing anything, and in this case the absence of any description of external surroundings is description enough of an internal state. I was on the point of leaving the room to try to summon someone and, if I found no one, to make my way back to the entrance lobby and have myself let out, when, just as I had risen and taken a few steps across the mosaic parquet, a footman came in and said with a worried expression on his face: "M. le Baron has been engaged all evening. There are still several people waiting to see him. I shall do my utmost to get him to receive Monsieur. I've already telephoned twice to his secretary."

"No, please don't trouble yourself further. I did have an appointment with M. le Baron, but it's now very late, and if he's busy this evening I can come back another day."

"Oh no, monsieur, you mustn't leave," exclaimed the footman. "M. le Baron might be annoyed. I'll try again."

I recalled what I had heard about M. de Charlus's servants and their devotion to their master. It could not quite be said of him, as it could of the Prince de Conti, that he sought to please a valet as much as a minister, but he had been so skillful in presenting the least thing he demanded of them as a sort of favor that at night, when his personal valets were assembled around him at a respectful distance, and after running his eye over them, he would say, "Coignet, the candlestick!" or "Ducret, my nightshirt!," it was with an envious grumble that the others withdrew, jealous of the servant who had been singled out by the master. Two of them, in fact, who loathed each other, would each try to snatch the favor from the other by using the flimsiest of pretexts to take some message to the Baron, if he had gone upstairs earlier than usual, in the hope of being entrusted that evening with the duty of candlestick or nightshirt. If he spoke to one or another of them directly about something outside their duties, or, even more, if in winter, in the garden, knowing that one of his coachmen had caught cold, he said to him after ten minutes, "Wrap yourself up properly," the others would not speak to the man with a cold for a fortnight, out of jealousy for the favor conferred on him.

I waited ten minutes more; then, after I was requested not to stay too long because M. le Baron was tired and had had to send away several most important people who had made appointments with him many days ago, I was ushered into his presence. This theatrical to-ing and fro-ing around M. de Charlus was beginning to strike me as a great deal less impressive than the down-to-earthness of his brother Guermantes, but already the door stood open to reveal a glimpse of the Baron in a Chinese dressing gown, with his throat bare, stretched out on a sofa. My eye was arrested in the same instant by the mirrorlike nap of a top hat, abandoned on a chair with a cape, suggesting that the Baron had only just arrived back home. The footman withdrew. I imagined that M. de Charlus would come over to greet me. Without stirring an inch, he fixed me with the harshest of looks. I went over to him and said good evening. He did not hold out his hand, made no reply to my greeting, did not ask me to take a chair. After a moment's pause, I asked him, as one would ask an ill-mannered doctor, whether I needed to remain standing. There was nothing nasty about the way I said this, but the cold fury on M. de Charlus's face seemed to intensify. Nor was I aware that at home, in the country, at the Château de Charlus, he was in the habit—so much did he love to play the king—of sprawling in an armchair in the smoking room, leaving his guests to stand around him. He would ask one of them for a light, offer another a cigar, before saying, after a few moments had elapsed, "But, Argencourt, why don't you sit down? Take a chair, my dear man," or something of the sort, having made a point of keeping them standing simply to remind them that permission to be seated came from him. "Sit in the Louis XIV chair," he answered me imperiously, as though he was forcing me to keep my distance rather than inviting me to sit down. I occupied an armchair that was fairly close. "Ah, so that is what you call a Louis XIV chair! I can see that you're a well-educated young man," he broke out in derision. I was so astonished that I stayed in my seat, neither getting up to leave, as I ought to have done, nor moving to another chair, as he wished me to do. "Monsieur," he said, weighing each of his words in turn and prefixing the more insolent of them with a double consonant, "the interview I have condescended to grant you, at the behest of a person who desires to remain nameless, will put a period to our relations. I will make no secret of the fact that I had hoped for better things. I should perhaps be putting too great a strain on the meaning of the words, which one ought not to do, even with people who are ignorant of their value, simply out of respect for oneself, were I to tell you that I had felt a certain liking for you. But I think that the word 'benevolence,' in its most effectively tutelary sense, would exceed neither what I felt nor what I was proposing to offer. I had given you to understand, as soon as I returned to Paris, while you were still at Balbec, that you could count upon me." Remembering the unexpected outburst with which M. de Charlus had parted from me in Balbec, I made a vague gesture of denial. "What!" he burst out angrily (and, indeed, his white, convulsed face differed as much from his ordinary face as the sea on a stormy morning, when, instead of its usual smiling surface, you see a seething mass of snakelike spray and foam). "Are you suggesting that you did not receive my message—almost a declaration—that you were to remember me? How was the cover of the book I sent you decorated?"

"With some very pretty intertwined figures," I told him.

"Ah!" came the scornful reply. "Young Frenchmen know little of the treasures of our land. What would you have to say about a young Berliner who was ignorant of the *Walküre*? In fact, you must have eyes that are blind, since you yourself told me that you spent two hours in front of that particular treasure. I can see that you know no more about flowers than you do about styles. Don't start protesting about styles," he exploded in a shrill scream of rage, "you don't even know what you're sitting on. You present your backside with a Directory fireside chair and tell it it's sitting on a Louis XIV wing chair. One of these days you'll mistake Mme de Villeparisis's lap for the toilet seat, and one begins to wonder what you'd leave in it. It's just like your not even noticing the lintel of myosotis over the Balbec church door on the binding of that book by Bergotte. Could there have been a more obvious way of saying to you, 'Forget me not'?"

My eyes were upon M. de Charlus. It was true that his magnificent head, repugnant though it was, far surpassed the heads of all his relatives; he was like an aging Apollo; but it was as if an olive-greenish, bilious juice was about to seep out of his malevolent mouth. Intellectually, there was no denying that the vast compass of his mind embraced a great many things that would forever remain unknown to the Duc de Guermantes. But, however fine the language in which he cloaked all his hatreds, you had the feeling that, even if his words were motivated by hurt pride or disappointment in love, by rancor, sadism, a need to tease or obsession, this man was capable of murder, and of proving by dint of logic and eloquence that he had been right to commit murder and was still head and shoulders above his brother, his sister-in-law, and all the rest of them.

"As in Velázquez's *Surrender of Breda*," he continued, "the victor advances toward the man who is humblest in rank, and as is the duty of every noble soul, since I was everything and you were nothing, it was I who took the first steps toward you. You have responded stupidly to what it is not for me to describe as an act of grandeur. But I refused to be discouraged. Our religion exhorts us to be patient. The patience I have shown toward you will be counted, I hope, to my credit, as will the mere smile brought to my lips by what might be decried as impertinence, were it within your power to be impertinent to one who is head and shoulders above you. But all that, monsieur, is now neither here nor there. I have submitted you to the test that the one eminent man among us has appositely called the test of too much kindness, which he rightly declares to be the most terrible test of all, the only one that can separate the wheat from the chaff. I can scarcely reproach you for your lack of success in it, for those who emerge triumphant are very few. But, and this is the conclusion I feel myself entitled to draw from these last words we shall exchange on earth, at least I mean to protect myself from your slanderous attempts upon me."

Thus far, it had never occurred to me that M. de Charlus's rage could have been caused by an unflattering remark that someone had repeated to him; I racked my brains; I had not spoken about him to anyone. Some malicious person had invented the whole thing. I protested to M. de Charlus that I had said absolutely nothing about him. "I don't think I can have offended you by mentioning to Mme de Guermantes that we were on friendly terms with each other." He smiled disdainfully, raised his voice to its highest pitch, then, softly attacking the shrillest and most injurious note:

"Oh, monsieur," he said, as he reverted extremely slowly to a natural intonation, seeming to revel as he went in the oddities of this descending scale, "I think you do yourself an injustice to accuse yourself of having said that we were *friends*. I don't expect much verbal accuracy from someone who can barely tell the difference between a piece of Chippendale furniture and a rococo chair, but I really can't believe," he went on, in a series of vocal caresses that became increasingly sardonic to the point of causing a charming smile to play across his lips, "I really can't believe that you can ever have said—or thought, for that matter—that we were *friends*. Had you boasted of being *presented* to me, of having *talked* to me, of *knowing* me slightly, of having been offered, almost unasked, the possibility of becoming an eventual *protégé* of mine, *that* I would have found, on the contrary, quite natural and intelligent on your part. The extreme difference in age between us makes it possible for me to recognize without absurdity that such a *presentation*, such *talks*, the vague glimmer of any *relationship* between us would have been for you, it is not for me to say an honor, but, still, all things considered, an advantage, in regard to which, it seems to me, you were silly enough not to divulge it, but to have had no idea how to hold on to it. I will even go as far as to say," he added, switching abruptly for a second from haughty anger to a gentleness so tinged with regret that I thought he was going to burst into tears, "that, when you failed to reply to the proposal I made to you from Paris, it seemed to me so utterly unlikely on your part, since you had struck me as well brought up and from a good *middle-class* family"—it was only on this adjective that his voice gave a slight hiss of impertinence—"that I was foolhardy enough to credit all the false excuses people make, letters gone astray, wrong addresses. I realize that it was very gullible of me, but Saint Bonaventure chose to believe that oxen could fly rather than that his brother monk was capable of lying. But all that is over. The idea didn't appeal to you, and that's that. Only it seems to me that you might have taken the trouble"—and here there were genuine tears in his voice—"were it only out of consideration for my age, to write to me. I had planned some infinitely attractive possibilities for you, though I had taken good care not to let you know what they were. You chose to refuse before you knew. That was up to you. But, as I say, one can always *write*. In your position—indeed, even in my own—I would have done so. That is why I prefer mine to yours—I say this because I believe all our positions are equal, and I am more sympathetically disposed toward an intelligent laborer than I am toward a great many dukes. But I can say that I prefer to be in my position, because, in the whole course of my life, which is beginning to be a pretty long one, I know that I have never done what you did." He had his head turned away from the light, and I could not see if tears were falling from his eyes, as his voice led me to suppose. "I said I had come well out of my way to meet you. The effect of that was to make you withdraw twice as far. Now it is my turn to withdraw, and we shall know each other no longer. I shall put your name from my mind, but not your behavior, so that, on occasions when I might be tempted to believe that men have feelings, good manners, or merely the intelligence not to let slip an unrivaled opportunity, I can remind myself that that is to ask too much of them. No, that you should have said you knew me when such a thing was true—and from now on it will no longer be the case—I see that as only natural, and take it as an act of homage, I mean as something agreeable. Unfortunately, in other places and circumstances, you have made remarks of a very different kind."

"Believe me, monsieur, I have said nothing that could offend you."

"And who says that I'm offended?" he burst out furiously, starting up with a jerk on the sofa on which he had so far been reclining motionless, while, as the pallid, frothing snakes in his face stiffened tensely, his voice became alternately shrill and deep, like the deafening uproar unleashed by a storm. (His normally forceful voice, which tended to make people turn in the street, was a hundred times more forceful, as a forte is when played by an orchestra rather than on the piano, and changed to a fortissimo at the same time. M. de Charlus roared.) "Do you imagine you have the power to offend me? Have you no idea to whom you are speaking? Do you imagine that the poisonous spittle of five hundred little men of your sort, hoisted onto one another's shoulders, could even drool down on to the tips of my august toes?"

For the last few minutes, my desire to persuade M. de Charlus that I had never spoken or heard anyone speak ill of him had given way to a wild rage, provoked by the words that, to my mind, were dictated to him solely by his colossal pride. And perhaps they stemmed, in part at least, from this pride. Almost everything else was the result of a feeling that was as yet unknown to me, and which I could not therefore be blamed for underestimating. In the absence of my familiarity with this feeling, I could at least, had I remembered Mme de Guermantes's words, assumed an element of madness in this pride of his. But at the time, the idea of madness did not cross my mind. As I saw it, he was filled merely with pride, I merely with fury. This fury (at the point when M. de Charlus ceased to shout, in reference to his august toes, with an irked majesty, a vomit of disgust at his unnamed blasphemers) was no longer able to contain itself. I was seized with a compulsion to hit something, and with the little discernment I had left, not wanting to show bodily disrespect to a man so much older than myself, or even, in view of their artistic worth, to the pieces of German porcelain surrounding him, I grabbed hold of the Baron's new top hat, threw it to the ground, trampled on it, and, bent on pulling it to pieces, I ripped out the lining, tore the crown in two, heedless of the continuing vociferations of M. de Charlus, then, crossing the room to make my exit, opened the door. I was dumbfounded to discover two footmen standing on either side of it, slowly moving away in an attempt to create the impression that they had only been casually passing in the course of their duty. (I subsequently learned their names: one was called Burnier, the other Charmel.) I was not taken in for a moment by the explanation their leisurely movement seemed to offer. It was utterly unconvincing. Three other explanations seemed more likely: one was that the Baron occasionally received guests against whom, if he happened to need assistance (but why?), he found it necessary to have reinforcements at hand; a second was that, drawn by curiosity, they had been listening at the keyhole, not expecting me to come out so quickly; the third, that the whole drama M. de Charlus had performed in front of me had been rehearsed in advance and that he himself had instructed them to listen, out of a love for spectacle combined perhaps with a *nunc erudimini*[100] from which each one of them would learn a lesson.

My anger had done nothing to calm the Baron's own, and my departure from the room seemed to be causing him sharp distress; he called me back, had his servants call me back, and finally, forgetting that a moment ago, when he had mentioned his "august toes," he had imagined he was making me a witness to his own deification, he came running after me at top speed, caught up with me in the hall, and stood barring the door. "Come, now," he said, "don't be childish; come back for a minute; he that loveth well chasteneth well, and if I have chastened you well it is because I love you well." My anger had abated. I chose to ignore the word "chasten" and followed the Baron, who called a footman and, as if nothing had happened, had him remove the remains of the ruined hat, which was replaced by another.

"If you will be good enough to tell me who it is has treacherously maligned me," I said to M. de Charlus, "I will stay here to hear his name and to confute the impostor."

"Who? You mean you don't know? Do you retain no memory of the things you say? Do you imagine that the people who are good enough to tell me about such things do not swear me to secrecy in the first place? And do you think I am going to break such a promise?"

"Monsieur, is it really impossible for you to tell me?" I asked, unsuccessfully racking my brains in one last effort to discover to whom I could have spoken about M. de Charlus.

"Have I not made it clear that I have promised my informant to keep his name secret?" he said in a categorical tone. "I see that your taste for abject remarks is matched only by your taste for futile persistence. You ought at least to have the intelligence to benefit from this last encounter with me, and to use your words to better effect than to talk nonsense."

"Monsieur," I replied as I made a move to leave, "you are insulting me. I am defenseless, because you are far older than I, and we are not equally matched. Moreover, I am unable to convince you. I have already sworn to you that I have said nothing."

"So you're calling me a liar!" he shouted in a terrible voice, leaping forward to within a foot or so of me.

"You have been misinformed."

At which, in a gentle, affectionate, melancholy tone, as in those symphonies that are performed without any break between the various movements, and in which a graceful scherzo, pleasing and idyllic, follows the thunderclaps of the opening movement, he said, "That is very possible. As a rule, a remark repeated at second hand is rarely true. You have only yourself to blame if you have failed to benefit from the opportunities for seeing me I offered you and thus not furnished me, through the confidence which frank exchange of daily conversation promotes, with the unique and sovereign antidote against a remark that branded you as a traitor. In any event, true or false, the remark has had its effect. I can never erase the impression it made upon me. I cannot even say that he who loveth well chasteneth well, for I have certainly chastened you but I no longer love you." In the course of these remarks, he had forced me to sit down once more and had rung the bell. A different footman came into the room. "Bring something to drink and order the brougham." I said I was not thirsty and that I had my own carriage. "They have probably paid the driver and sent him away," he said. "You needn't worry about that. I'm ordering a carriage to take you home. . . . If you're anxious about the lateness of the hour . . . I could have given you a room here. . . ." I told him that my mother would be worried. "Ah! Of course. Well, true or false, the remark has had its effect. My liking for you was rather premature, and it had flowered too soon. Like those apple trees of which you spoke so poetically in Balbec, it has been unable to resist the first frost." If M. de Charlus's liking for me had been destroyed, his behavior could not have been more at variance with the fact, since, while assuring me that we had fallen out, he was making me stay and drink, offering to put me up for the night, and now arranging for me to be sent home. He looked as if he was dreading the moment he must leave me and find himself on his own again, the same sort of slightly anxious fear his sister-in-law and cousin Guermantes had seemed to me to be feeling an hour ago, when she had tried to force me to stay a little longer, with something of the same momentary fondness for me, the same effort to prolong the minute.

"Unfortunately," he continued, "the gift of making something that has been destroyed rebloom is not one I have. My affection for you is quite dead. Nothing can revive it. I don't think it would be unworthy of me to confess that I regret it. I always feel myself to be rather like Victor Hugo's Boaz: 'I am widowed and alone, and darkness falls upon me.' "[101]

I walked back through the big greenish drawing room with him. I let drop a chance remark about how beautiful I thought it was. "Isn't it?" he replied. "One needs to have something to love. The paneling is by Bagard.[102] The rather charming thing about it, you know, is that it was made to go with the Beauvais chairs and the consoles. Notice that it takes up the same decorative design. There used to be only two places where you could see this, the Louvre and M. d'Hinnisdal's house. But, naturally, as soon as I decided to come and live in this street, an old family house of the Chimays' came on the market that no one had ever seen before because it was destined just for *me*. On the whole, it's really rather good. It might be better, but really it's not bad. Some pretty things, are there not? Mignard's portrait of my uncles the King of Poland and the King of England, for example. But why am I telling you all this? You know it as well as I do, since you were waiting in this room. No? Ah, then they must have shown you into the blue drawing room," he said with what could have been taken for rudeness directed at my lack of curiosity, or personal superiority, and lack of interest in where I had been kept waiting. "Have you seen what's in this cabinet? These are all the hats worn by Mme Élisabeth, the Princesse de Lamballe, and Marie-Antoinette. You're not interested, are you? You appear not to see them. Perhaps there's something wrong with your optic nerve. If this sort of beauty appeals to you more, here is a rainbow by Turner beginning to shine out between these two Rembrandts, as a sign of our reconciliation. Can you hear? Beethoven has come to join him." And, indeed, the first chords of the third movement of the *Pastoral* Symphony, "Joy After the Storm," could be heard, performed somewhere close by, on the first floor perhaps, by a group of musicians. "There you are, one never knows. One really never knows. Invisible music. It's pretty, is it not?" he said to me in a slightly impudent tone, somehow reminiscent of Swann's influence and accent. "But you don't care two hoots about it. You want to go home, even if it means showing disrespect for Beethoven and for me. You're carrying out your own sentence," he added with affectionate regret when the moment had come for me to leave. "You'll forgive me for forgetting my good manners and not accompanying you home," he said. "Since I have no desire to see you again, there would be very little point in spending five more minutes in your company. But I'm tired, and I have a great deal to do." Then, noticing it was a fine night, he changed tack: "Ah well, perhaps I will come in the carriage after all. There's a superb moon, which I'll go and inspect in the Bois after I've taken you back. Why, you don't know how to shave! Even on a night when you've been out to dinner, there are still a few hairs left on your face," he said, taking my chin between two fingers, drawn there, it seemed, as if by a magnet, and, after a moment's resistance, running up to my ears like the fingers of a barber. "Ah, how pleasant it would be to look at 'the blue moonlight' in the Bois with someone like yourself," he said with sudden and almost involuntary gentleness, then added sadly: "For you're nice, really. You could be nicer than anyone," he added, laying his hand paternally on my shoulder. "I have to say that at first I hardly thought you were worth noticing." I ought to have reflected that this was still the case. I had only to remind myself of the rage with which he had spoken to me barely half an hour previously. In spite of this, I had the impression that he was, for the moment, sincere, that his kindness of heart was getting the better of what I regarded as an almost delirious condition of touchiness and pride. The carriage was there waiting for us, and still he prolonged the conversation. "Come," he said abruptly, "get in. You'll be home in five minutes, and I shall then bid you a good night that will sever our relations for all time. It is better, since we must part forever, that we should do so, as in music, on a tonic chord." Despite these solemn affirmations that we should never meet again, I could have sworn that M. de Charlus, irked at his loss of temper earlier and afraid that he had hurt my feelings, would not have been averse to seeing me once more. Nor was I mistaken, for a moment later he said: "There, now, I've actually forgotten the most important thing. In memory of your grandmother, I have had a rare edition of Mme de Sévigné bound for you. Which means that this will not be our last meeting. One must console oneself with the thought that complicated affairs are rarely settled in a day. Just look how long it took to negotiate the Congress of Vienna."

"But I could send someone round for it without disturbing you," I said to oblige him.

"Will you learn to hold your tongue, you little fool," he replied angrily, "and not push your grotesque behavior to the point of assuming that the likelihood of being received by me—I don't say the certainty, for perhaps one of my servants will hand you the volumes—is some trifling honor." He regained control of himself: "I do not wish to part from you on these words. No dissonance; before the eternal silence, a chord on the dominant!" It was for his own nerves that he seemed to dread a return home immediately after harsh words of discord. "You would not like to come to the Bois," he said in a tone that was not interrogative but affirmative, not, it seemed to me, that he did not want to make the offer, but because he was afraid that his pride would be injured by a refusal. "Well, there we are," he continued, still marking time, "it is the hour, as Whistler says, when the bourgeois go to bed"—perhaps he wished now to exploit my own sense of pride—"the moment to start taking a look at the world. But you don't even know who Whistler is."[103] I changed the subject and asked him whether the Princesse d'Iéna was an intelligent woman. M. de Charlus stopped me and replied, in the most contemptuous tone I had yet heard him adopt:

"Ah! There, monsieur, you are alluding to an order of nomenclature that means nothing to me. There is perhaps an aristocracy among the Tahitians, but I have to confess I know nothing about it. But, strangely enough, the name you have just pronounced did ring in my ears a few days ago. I was asked if I'd be willing for the young Duc de Guastalla to be presented to me. The request astonished me, for the Duc de Guastalla has no need of an introduction to me, for the simple reason that he is my cousin and has known me all his life; he's the son of the Princess of Parma, and, like a dutiful young relative, he never fails to come and pay his respects to me on New Year's Day. But, after informing myself, I discovered that the person in question was not a relative of mine but the son of the person you are interested in. Since there is no princess with that name, I imagined that the person concerned must be some poor creature sleeping under the Pont d'Iéna, who had assumed the picturesque title of Princesse d'Iéna, in the same way that people talk of the Panther of the Batignolles[104] or the Steel King.[105] But no, it was the name of a rich person whose handsome furniture I had admired at an exhibition, and, unlike the owner's title, the furniture had the merit of being genuine. As for this alleged Duc de Guastalla, I thought he must be my secretary's stockbroker, given that you can buy almost anything with money. But no. It was the Emperor, it appears, who amused himself by conferring on these people a title that was simply not his to confer. I don't know whether he did it as a sign of power, ignorance, or malice, but to me it was a very nasty trick to play on these unwitting usurpers. But I can't really enlighten you much on the matter; I'm competent only to discuss the Faubourg Saint-Germain, and there, if you can manage to secure an introduction, you'll find plenty of old harpies to amuse you, straight out of Balzac. All that is of course a far cry from the prestige of the Princesse de Guermantes, but without me and my 'open Sesame,' access to her is impossible."

"The Princesse de Guermantes has a very fine house, monsieur."

"Oh, it's not just very fine. It's the finest thing in the world. After the Princesse herself, that is."

"Is the Princesse de Guermantes superior to the Duchesse de Guermantes?"

"Oh, there's no comparison." It should be observed that, whenever people in society have the least spark of imagination, they will crown or dethrone, as their likings and quarrels dictate, the people whose position seemed most solid and entrenched. "The Duchesse de Guermantes"—by not referring to her as "Oriane," he was perhaps emphasizing the distance between her and me—"is delightful, far superior to anything you can have imagined. But there is really no comparison between her and her cousin. The Princesse is exactly what people in the marketplace might imagine Princess Metternich to have been. But La Metternich was a woman who thought she had launched Wagner because she knew Victor Maurel.[106] The Princesse de Guermantes, or, rather, her mother, actually *knew* Wagner. That is something prestigious in itself, not to mention the woman's extraordinary beauty. And those Esther gardens!"

"Is it possible to visit them?"

"No, not unless you are invited, but they never invite *anyone* unless I ask them to." But, having enticed me with the bait of this offer, he immediately withdrew it and held out his hand, for we had arrived at my door. "My role is over, monsieur. I will simply add these few words. Another will perhaps offer you his affection one day as I have done. May you learn something from this present instance. Remember it well. Affection is always precious. What we cannot do alone in life, because there are things we cannot ask, or do, or wish, or learn by ourselves, we can do together, without there needing to be thirteen of us, as in the Balzac novel,[107] or four, as in *The Three Musketeers*. I bid you farewell."

He must have been feeling tired and have abandoned the idea of going to look at the moonlight, for he asked me to tell the coachman to drive home. But then he made a brusque movement, as if he was about to change his mind. But I had already given the instruction, and, so as not to lose any more time, I went and rang at my doorbell, oblivious now of the fact that I had been dying to tell M. de Charlus the stories about the Kaiser and General Botha, which had obsessed me a while earlier, but which his unexpectedly thunderous reception had chased far from my mind.

When I got in, I saw on my desk a letter that Françoise's young footman had written to one of his friends and had left lying there. Ever since my mother had been away, there was no liberty he shrank from

taking; I was even more at fault for taking the liberty of reading the letter lying there without an envelope for all to see and—this was my sole
excuse—almost asking to be read.

Dear Friend and Cousin,

I hope this finds you in good health and the same with all the young
family particularly my young godson Joseph what I have not yet had the
pleasure of meeting but prefer to you all as being my godson, these relics of
the heart has also their dust, upon their blest remains let us not lay our
hands. Besides dear friend and cousin who is to say that tomorrow you and
your dear wife my cousin Marie, will not be both hurled headlong to the
bottom of the sea like the sailor clinging to the mast on high, for this life is
but a dark valley. Dear friend I must tell you that my principal occupation
to your astonishment I feel sure, is now poetry which enraptures me, for we
must do something. And so dear friend do not be too surprised that your
last letter is unresponded, for lack of pardon let oblivion come. As you
know, Madame's mother has passed away amid unspeakable sufferings which
fairly exhausted her for she saw as many as three doctors. The day of her funeral was a big day for all Monsieur's relations came in crowds as well as
several Ministers. It took them more than two hours to get to the cemetery
which will make you all open your eyes wide in your village for they certainly wont do as much for Mère Michu. So all my life will be but one long
sob. I am greatly enjoying the motorcycle what I recently learned. What
would you say my dear friends if I arrived suddenly like that at full speed at
Les Écorres. But on that score I shall no longer keep silence for I feel that
the frenzy of grief sweeps its reason away. I am associating with the
Duchesse de Guermantes, people as what you have never even heard in our
ignorant part of the world. So it is with pleasure that Im going to send the
works of Racine, Victor Hugo, the Selected works of Chenedollé, of Alfred
de Musset, for I want to cure the land which give me birth of ignorance
which leads inevitably to crime. I cant think of anything more to say to you
and send you like the pelican wearied by a long flight my best regards as
well as to your wife my godson and your sister Rose. May it not be said of
her: And rose she has lived only as roses live, as has been said by Victor
Hugo, the sonnet of Arvers, Alfred de Musset all those great geniuses who
because of that were sent to die at the stake like Joan of Arc. Am looking
forward to your next missive, yours with a brother's love Périgot Joseph

Any life that represents something mysterious, like some last illusion to be shattered, exerts a pull on us. This said, the mysterious description of the Princesse de Guermantes provided by M. de Charlus, which had led me to conceive of her as an extraordinary being quite different from anyone I knew, was not enough to explain my amazement, shortly followed by my fear of being the target of a bad joke engineered by someone who wanted to see me expelled from a house to which I had not been invited, when, about two months after my dinner with the Duchesse and after her departure to Cannes, I opened an envelope that suggested nothing out of the ordinary to me, and read the following words on a printed card: "The Princesse de Guermantes, née Duchesse en Bavière, At Home, the —th." No doubt an invitation from the Princesse de Guermantes was really no more difficult to obtain, from a society point of view, than a dinner invitation from the Duchesse, and my smattering of heraldic knowledge told me that the title of prince is not superior to that of duc. I also told myself that the intelligence of a society woman could not be so radically dissimilar from that of the rest of her kind, as M. de Charlus claimed, or so radically dissimilar from that of any other woman. But my imagination, like Elstir in the process of creating some effect of perspective independently of the notions of physics he might use in other circumstances, depicted for me not what I knew but what it saw: what it saw, that is to say, what the name showed it. Now, even before I knew the Duchesse, the name Guermantes preceded by the title Princesse, like a note or a color or a quantity sharply modified by the values surrounding it, by the mathematical or aesthetic "sign" governing it, had always called up something quite different to my mind. With the title of princesse, it is to be found mainly in the memoirs from the periods of Louis XIII and Louis XIV, and in those of the English court, the Queen of Scotland and the Duchesse d'Aumale; and I pictured the house of the Princesse de Guermantes as a place quite regularly frequented by the Duchesse de Longueville and the great Condé, whose presence there made it unlikely that I should ever enter it.

Much of what M. de Charlus had told me had whipped my imagination into vigorous activity and, by causing it to forget how much it had been disappointed by reality at Mme de Guermantes's (people's names and place-names are similar in this respect), had steered it toward Oriane's cousin. It was also the case that I was misled by M. de Charlus about the imaginary value and variety of society people only because he was himself misled. Perhaps this was because he did nothing, did not write, did not paint, did not even read anything in a serious and thorough manner. But, superior as he was by several degrees to society people when it came to drawing his conversational matter from them and the spectacle they represented, this did not mean that he was understood by them. Speaking as an artist, he could at the most bring out the deceptive charm of society people. But he could do this for artists only, and in relation to them he might be said to have been playing the part of the reindeer among the Eskimos: this prized creature plucks for them from barren rocks lichens and mosses that they themselves could neither discover nor put to use, but which, once they have been digested by the reindeer, become a form of food the inhabitants of the Far North can assimilate.

To which I may add that M. de Charlus's depiction of society was animated in the most lively way by the blend of his ferocious hatreds and his devoted affections, the hatreds directed mainly toward young men, the adoration aroused principally by various women.

If among these the Princesse de Guermantes had been enthroned in pride of place by M. de Charlus, his mysterious remarks about the "inaccessible Aladdin's palace" in which his cousin lived did not sufficiently account for my feeling of stupefaction.

Despite the contribution from various subjective points of view in these artificial magnifications—and this is something I shall discuss at a later stage—the fact remains that there is a degree of objective reality in all these people, and consequently a difference between them.

And how could it be otherwise? The world of people we associate with, bearing so little resemblance to the way we imagine it, is still the same world we have seen described in the memoirs and letters of eminent people and have felt a desire to know. The completely nondescript old man we meet at a dinner party is the same man who wrote the proud letter to Prince Friedrich Karl, which we read with such enthusiasm in a book about the 1870 war. Dinner parties bore us because our imagination is absent, and reading interests us because it is keeping us company. But the people in question are the same. We would have liked to know Mme de Pompadour, who was so stalwart a patron of the arts, and we would have been as bored in her company as we are among all the modern Egerias[108] at whose houses we cannot bring ourselves to pay a second call, so mediocre is their company. The fact remains that these discrepancies do exist. People are never completely alike, their way of behaving toward us, even, one might say, at the same level of friendship, reveals differences that offset one another in the end. When I knew Mme de Montmorency, she took pleasure in saying disagreeable things to me, but if I asked her a favor, she would oblige me in the most generous way by effectively using all the influence she had to obtain it. Whereas another woman—Mme de Guermantes, for instance—would never have wished to hurt my feelings, never said anything about me except what might give me pleasure, lavished upon me all the gestures of friendliness that for the Guermantes constituted the richness of moral life, but, had I asked her for the least thing beyond that, would not have budged an inch to procure it for me, as in those country houses where the guest is provided with a chauffeur and a valet but where it is impossible to obtain a glass of cider for which no provision has been made in the entertainment arrangements. Which was for me the true friend—Mme de Montmorency, so happy to ruffle my feelings and always so willing to oblige, or Mme de Guermantes, distressed at the least offense toward me and incapable of the least effort to be helpful? Again, it was said the Duchesse de Guermantes spoke only about frivolous matters, and her cousin, who was intellectually very drab, invariably about interesting things. Types of mind are so various, so conflicting, not only in literature but in society, that Baudelaire and Mérimée are not the only people with the right to mutual scorn. These distinctive characteristics produce in every person a system of looks, words, and actions so coherent, so despotic, that it seems superior to any other when we are in the presence of any given individual. In the presence of Mme de Guermantes, her words, deduced like a theorem from her cast of mind, seemed to me to be both inevitable and appropriate. And at heart I agreed with the Duchesse when she told me that Mme de

Montmorency was stupid and kept an open mind toward anything she did not understand, or when she said, after hearing about some malicious remark made by the latter, "So that's what you call a kind woman. I call her a monster." But this tyranny of immediate presence, this self-evident lamplight which makes the already distant dawn pale to the faintness of something barely remembered, disappeared once I was out of Mme de Guermantes's presence and some other lady said to me, putting herself on my level and placing the Duchesse far below either of us, "Oriane is not really interested in anything or anybody," or even (something that it would have seemed impossible to believe in Mme de Guermantes's presence, so loudly did she deny it), "Oriane is a snob." Since there is no mathematical formula that would enable us to convert Mme d'Arpajon and Mme de Montpensier into uniform quantities, it would have been impossible for me to answer had anyone asked me which of the two seemed superior to the other.

Now, among the characteristics peculiar to the Princesse de Guermantes's salon, the one most usually mentioned was an exclusiveness due in part to the Princesse's royal birth, but more particularly to the almost fossilized rigidity of the Prince's aristocratic prejudices, prejudices that, incidentally, the Duc and Duchesse had not blushed to deride in my presence, and of course such exclusiveness inevitably made me feel it even more unlikely that I should have been invited by this man, who dealt only in royal personages and dukes and was given to making a scene at every dinner party because he had not been seated as he would have been by right under Louis XIV, an entitlement that, thanks to his immense erudition in matters of history and genealogy, he was the only person to recognize. On this account, in the matter of the differences that distinguished them from their cousins, many people settled in favor of the Duc and Duchesse. "The Duc and Duchesse are far more up-to-date, far more intelligent; *they've* got better things to interest them than the number of quarterings a person has; their salon is three hundred years in advance of their cousins'," were the customary remarks, and with these in mind I trembled as I looked at the invitation card, since they made it all the more likely that it had been sent to me as a hoax.

If the Duc and Duchesse had not still been in Cannes, I could have tried to find out from them whether the invitation I had received was genuine. My state of uncertainty is in fact by no means something that would be unknown to a man of the world, as I flattered myself into believing for a moment, and consequently a writer, even if he belonged to the world of society, ought to reproduce it in order to be thoroughly "objective" in his portrayal of class distinctions. In fact, only a few days ago, in a charming volume of memoirs, I came across an account of uncertainties analogous to those induced in me by the Princesse de Guermantes's invitation. "Georges and I"—or "Hély and I"; I don't have the book at hand to check—"were so itching to be invited to Mme Delessert's salon that when we actually received an invitation from her we thought it prudent, quite independently, to make sure that we were not the victims of some April Fool's joke." Now, the writer is none other than the Comte d'Haussonville (the man who married the Duc de Broglie's daughter), and the other young man who will ascertain "independently" whether he is being hoaxed or not is, according to whether he is called Georges or Hély, one or the other of the two inseparable friends of M. d'Haussonville, either M. d'Harcourt or the Prince de Chalais.

On the day of the Princesse de Guermantes's reception, I learned that the Duc and Duchesse had returned to Paris the previous day. They would not have come back specially for the Princesse's ball, but one of their cousins was seriously ill, and there was also the fact that the Duc was very anxious to attend a fancy-dress event that evening, to which he was to go as Louis XI and his wife as Isabeau de Bavière. I made up my mind to call on her that morning. But they had gone out early and not yet returned; I kept watch for their carriage at first from a little room that seemed to me to be a good lookout post. As it turned out, I had chosen my observation point very badly, for I could scarcely see into our courtyard, though I caught a glimpse of several others, and this, while of no practical use, diverted me for a time. It is not only in Venice that there are these views onto several houses at once that have drawn painters. The same is true of Paris. The reference to Venice is not random. The poor quarters of that city are what spring to mind when you see the poor quarters of Paris in the morning, with their tall, widening

chimneys turned to the most vivid pinks, the brightest reds by the sunlight, a whole garden flowering above the houses, and flowering in such
a variety of shades of color as to suggest the garden of a tulip-fancier in
Delft or Haarlem planted above the city. And then the close proximity of the houses, with their windows facing one another across a common courtyard, makes each window into a frame in which a cook stares
dreamily down outside, or, farther off, a girl is having her hair combed
by an old woman whose witchlike face is barely distinguishable in the
shadow; and so for the neighbors in the adjoining houses each courtyard, suppressing sound through distance and revealing silent gestures
in a rectangle placed under the glass of closed windows, contributes to
an exhibition of a hundred Dutch paintings placed side by side. It is
true that from the Hôtel de Guermantes there was not the same sort of
view, but there were interesting ones all the same, particularly from
the odd trigonometric point where I had taken up position, and from
which there was an uninterrupted view, across the relatively featureless
and steeply sloping area in between, as far as the distant heights formed
by the mansion of the Princesse de Silistrie and the Marquise de Plassac,
extremely noble cousins of M. de Guermantes whom I did not know. Between me and this mansion (the home of their father, M. de Bréquigny)
nothing but blocks of fairly low buildings, facing in every possible direction, which, without obstructing the view, emphasized the distance
with their oblique planes. The red-tiled turret of the outhouse in which
the Marquis de Frécourt kept his carriages was in fact topped by a
pointed roof that rose higher, but it was so narrow that it did not hide
the view, and reminded me of those charming old buildings in Switzer-
land that rear up in isolation at the foot of a mountain. All these vague
and divergent points of focus on which my eyes came to rest made
Mme de Plassac's mansion, which was in fact quite near but looked de-
ceptively distant as in an Alpine landscape, seem as though it were separated from us by several streets or by numerous foothills. When its wide
square windows, dazzling in the sunlight like flakes of rock crystal, were
thrown open while the housework was being done, as the eye followed
from one floor to the next the various footmen whom it was impossible to see clearly but who were obviously beating carpets or wielding

feather dusters, there was the same sense of pleasure as seeing a land-scape by Turner or Elstir with a traveler in a stagecoach, or a guide, at different heights on the Saint-Gothard. But from the vantage point where I had taken up position, I should have run the risk of missing M. or Mme de Guermantes, so that when, in the afternoon, I found time to resume my watch I simply went and waited on the staircase, from which the opening of the carriage gate could not pass unnoticed, and it was on this staircase that I posted myself, even though the Alpine de-lights of the Hôtel de Bréquigny and Tresmes, so dazzling to the eye with their footmen made minute by distance as they did the house-work, were not on view from where I was. Now, this wait on the stair-case was to entail such considerable discoveries and to reveal to me so important a landscape, no longer Turneresque but moral, that it is pref-erable to delay my account of it for a moment and turn first to my visit to the Guermantes, once I knew they had returned home. I was received by the Duc alone, in his library. As I was walking toward the door, out came a little man with the whitest hair and of shabby appearance, wear-ing a little black tie like the one worn by the Combray lawyer and by several of my grandfather's friends, but more diffident-looking than they were, and, bowing to me effusively, he utterly refused to pass downstairs until I had walked in. The Duc shouted after him from the library something I did not catch, while he responded with a further se-ries of bows, addressed this time to the wall, for the Duc could not see him, though the bows were repeated endlessly, like the redundant smiles of people talking to each other on the telephone; he had a falsetto voice, and he bowed to me once more with the humility of a trades-man. And he might indeed have been a tradesman from Combray, so provincial was his manner, the old-fashioned, mild manner of the ordi-nary people and the modest old folk of that part of the world.

"Oriane will be with us in a while," the Duc said to me when I had joined him in the library. "Since Swann is coming around a bit later with the proofs of his study of the coinage of the Order of Malta and, worse still, some huge photograph he has had taken showing both sides of the coins, Oriane thought it better to get dressed first, so that she can keep him company until it's time to go out to dinner. We've already got so much clutter around the place we don't know what to do with, and I'm wondering where we're going to stick this photograph. But my wife is too good-natured, incapable of saying no to people. She thought it would be nice to ask Swann to provide some means of seeing all those Grand Masters of the Order whose medals he found in Rhodes all together, side by side. I said Malta, but I meant Rhodes; in any case, it's the same Order of Saint John of Jerusalem. In fact, she's interested in all that only because Swann is. Our family is very much mixed up in the whole thing; even today, my brother, whom you've met, is one of the highest dignitaries in the Order of Malta. But if I'd mentioned it all to Oriane, she wouldn't have listened to me for a moment. Yet it only took the fact that Swann's researches into the Templars (amazing the passion people of one religion have for studying others) led him on to the history of the Knights of Rhodes, who succeeded the Templars, for Oriane to insist on seeing the heads of these knights. They were very small fry compared to the Lusignans, Kings of Cyprus, from whom we descend in a direct line. But so far Swann hasn't shown any interest in them, so Oriane couldn't care less about the Lusignans." I had no immediate chance to explain to the Duc why I had come. As it happened, several relatives or friends, including Mme de Silistrie and the Duchesse de Montrose, came to call on the Duchesse, who often received people before dinner, and, not finding her there, stayed for a time with the Duc. The first of these ladies (the Princesse de Silistrie), unostentatiously dressed, curt but friendly in manner, was holding a walking stick. I was concerned at first that she had injured herself or was disabled in some way. On the contrary, she was very sprightly. She spoke sadly to the Duc about a first cousin of his—not on the Guermantes side, but more distinguished still, were such a thing possible—whose health, which had been in a very serious condition for some time, had suddenly deteriorated. But it was obvious that the Duc, though he was sympathetic to the state of his cousin's health and kept on repeating, "Poor Mama! He's such a fine chap," was being optimistic about his case. The truth of the matter was that he was looking forward to the dinner party he was to attend, was not at all bored by the thought of the big reception at the Princesse de Guermantes's, but, above all, he was to go on at one o'clock in the morning with his wife to a grand supper party and fancy-dress ball, he as Louis XI and the Duchesse as Isabeau de Bavière, and the costumes were ready and waiting. So the Duc had a mind not to be disturbed amid all these revelries by the sufferings of his good cousin Amanien d'Osmond. Then two other ladies carrying walking sticks, Mme de Plassac and Mme de Tresmes, both daughters of the Comte de Bréquigny, came in to pay Basin a visit, and declared that Cousin Mama's state was now beyond hope. The Duc shrugged his shoulders and changed the subject by asking them whether they were going to Marie-Gilbert's that evening. They replied that they were not, in view of the extreme nature of Amanien's condition, and in fact they had excused themselves from the dinner to which the Duc was going, and then proceeded to spell out the guest list to him: the brother of King Theodosius, the Infanta Maria Concepción, and so on. Since the Marquis d'Osmond was less closely related to them than he was to Basin, their "defection" struck the Duc as some kind of indirect reproach for his conduct, and he was barely civil to them. And so, although they had come down from the heights of the Hôtel de Bréquigny to visit the Duchesse (or, rather, to announce to her the alarming character, incompatible for his relatives with their attendance at society events, of their cousin's illness), they did not stay long, but, armed with their alpenstocks, Walpurge and Dorothée (such were the names of the two sisters) retraced the craggy path to their mountain home. I never thought to ask the Guermantes what was the meaning of these sticks, such a common sight in a certain quarter of the Faubourg Saint-Germain. It is possible that, regarding the whole parish as their domain and averse to taking cabs, these ladies were in the habit of walking about a great deal, and that, owing to some old fracture caused by immoderate devotion to hunting and to the falls from the saddle often attendant upon it, or simply rheumatism caused by the dampness of the Left Bank and of old country houses, a stick was necessary. Perhaps they had not set out on any long expedition in the area and had merely come down to their garden (very close to the Duchesse's own) to pick fruit for their compotes, and stopped by on their way home to say good evening to Mme de Guermantes, though without going so far as to bring secateurs or watering cans into the house. The Duc seemed touched that I should have come to see them the very day of their return home. But his expression darkened when I told him that I had come to ask his wife to find out whether her cousin had really invited me. I had touched upon one of those forms of help that neither M. nor Mme de Guermantes was keen to give. The Duc explained to me that it was too late, that if the Princesse had not sent me an invitation it would make him appear to be asking for one, that his cousins had refused him one on a previous occasion, and that he did not wish now to create the remotest impression that he was interfering with their guest lists, "meddling" with their arrangements, and, finally, that he could not be sure that he and his wife, who were dining out that evening, would not come home straight afterward, in which case their best excuse for not having gone to the Princesse's reception would be to conceal the fact that they were back in Paris, instead of rushing to inform her of the fact, which would be inevitable if they sent her a message or telephoned her about me, and certainly too late to be of any use, since it was more than likely that the Princesse's guest list would be finally drawn up by now. "You're not in her bad books, are you?" he asked suspiciously, with that constant anxiety the Guermantes had of not being abreast of the latest society quarrels and of people's possible attempts to patch them up by using them as intermediaries. Then, at last, since the Duc was in the habit of assuming responsibility for any decision that might seem unwelcome, he said to me suddenly, as though the idea had just occurred to him: "Look here, my boy, I'd really prefer to say nothing to Oriane about what you've said. You know how kindhearted she is, and, besides, she's enormously fond of you; she'd want to send word to her cousin, whatever I said to dissuade her, and if she's tired after dinner, there won't be any option, she will be forced to go to the reception. I've made up my mind; I shall say nothing to her about it. Anyhow, you'll be seeing her in a while. Not a word about all this, I beg you. If you decide to accept our cousins' invitation, I've no need to tell you what pleasure it will give us to spend the evening with you." Humane motives are too sacred for the person they are used to appeal to not to bow before them, whether he believes them to be sincere or not; I did not wish for a mo-

ment to appear to be weighing up the relative importance of my invitation and the possible fatigue of Mme de Guermantes, and I promised to
say nothing to her about the object of my visit, acting as though I had
been completely taken in by this rigmarole M. de Guermantes had
staged for my benefit. I asked him if there was any chance of my meeting Mme de Stermaria at the Princesse's.

"Indeed not," he replied with an air of expert assurance. "The name
you mention is known to me from club directories—it's not at all the
type of person who goes to Gilbert's. You'll meet no one there who is
not excessively genteel and extremely boring, duchesses with titles that
one thought were extinct who have been trotted out for the occasion,
all the ambassadors, large numbers of Coburgs and foreign royalties,
but don't expect the least hint of a Stermaria. Gilbert would have a fit at
the mere thought. Oh, by the way, you like painting, don't you? I must
show you a superb picture I bought from my cousin, partly in exchange
for the Elstirs, which we didn't really care for in the end. It was sold to
me as a Philippe de Champagne, but personally I think it's by someone
even more famous. Do you want to know what I think? I think it's a
Velázquez, and of his finest period," said the Duc, looking me straight
in the eye, either to gauge my reaction or to accentuate it. A footman
came in.

"Mme la Duchesse wishes to know if M. le Duc will be good enough
to see M. Swann, since Madame is not quite ready."

"Show M. Swann in," said the Duc after consulting his watch and
seeing that he himself still had a little time left before he need go and
dress. "As ever, my wife, who told him to come, isn't ready. No point in
saying anything in front of Swann about Marie-Gilbert's reception,"
said the Duc. "I don't know whether he's been invited. Gilbert is very
fond of him, because he thinks that he's the natural grandson of the
Duc de Berry, there's a whole story involved there. (Otherwise—you can
imagine!—my cousin, who nearly has a stroke if he sees a Jew a mile off.)
But now, of course, the Dreyfus case has made matters worse. Swann of
all people ought to have realized that he must drop all connection with
those people, instead of which he comes out with the most unfortunate
views."

The Duc called the footman back in to find out whether the man he had sent to Cousin d'Osmond's for news had returned. His plan was as follows: Since he rightly believed his cousin to be dying, he was anxious to obtain news of him before his actual death—that is, before he was obliged to go into mourning. Once he was covered by the official certainty that Amanien was still alive, he would push off to his dinner, to the Prince's reception, to the fancy-dress party he was to attend as Louis XI and where he had a most titillating assignation with a new mistress, and put off any further inquiries until the next day, when his pleasure was over. Then he would don mourning if his cousin had passed away in the course of the evening. "No, M. le Duc, he is not back yet." "Damn and blast it! Nothing is ever done in this house until the last minute," shouted the Duc, thinking that Amanien might have "snuffed it" in time to be in the evening paper and to make him miss his party. He sent for *Le Temps*, in which there was nothing.

I had not seen Swann for a very long time, and I wondered for a moment whether he used formerly to clip his mustache or not to wear his hair *en brosse,* for there was something different about him. It was simply that he was very "different" because he was very ill, and illness alters the face as much as growing a beard or changing the part in one's hair. (Swann's illness was the same one that carried off his mother, who had been struck down by it at exactly the age he now was. In fact, heredity makes our lives as full of cabalistic ciphers and horoscopic forecasts as if sorcerers really existed. And just as there is a given life expectancy for humanity in general, so there is one for families in particular—that is, in any one family, for those members of it who resemble one another.) Swann was dressed with an elegance that, like his wife's, connected what he now was with what he had once been. In a very fitted pearl-gray frock coat that did justice to his tall, slim figure, and white gloves with black stitching, he was wearing a gray topper of a flared shape that Delion now made only for him, for the Prince de Sagan, M. de Charlus, the Marquis de Modène, M. Charles Haas, and Comte Louis de Turenne. I was surprised at the charming smile and affectionate handclasp with which he returned my greeting, for I thought that after so long he would not recognize me so quickly; I gave voice to my astonishment;

he responded to this with peals of laughter, a hint of indignation, and a further squeeze of my hand, as if it were to cast doubt on his soundness of mind or the sincerity of his affection to imagine that he did not recognize me. And yet this was in fact the case; as I learned long afterward, he did not realize who I was until several minutes later, when he heard my name mentioned. But no change in expression, in his words, in his conversation with me, betrayed the realization that something M. de Guermantes let drop enabled him to make, so confident a master was he of the social game. In fact, he brought to it the same spontaneity of behavior and the same individual initiative, even in matters of dress, that typified the Guermantes style. And so the greeting the old clubman had given me without recognizing me was not the cold, stiff greeting of a man of the world merely going through the motions, but a greeting full of real friendliness, of genuine charm, similar to those, say, of the Duchesse de Guermantes (who, if she ran into you, even made a point of smiling at you first, before you had greeted her), in contrast to the more automatic greetings practiced by the ladies of the Faubourg Saint-Germain. Similarly, the hat he placed on the floor beside him, in conformity with a custom that was beginning to disappear, was lined, unconventionally, in green leather, because (as he would have us believe) it showed the dirt far less, but in fact because it was extremely chic.

"I say, Charles, you're a great expert, I've got something to show you. And then, my boys, I'm going to ask your permission to leave you together for a moment while I go and dress for dinner. I don't imagine Oriane will be very long now, in any case." He then showed Swann his "Velázquez." "But this seems familiar," said Swann with the pained expression of a sick man for whom even speaking is an effort.

"Yes," said the Duc, in a tone rather flattened by the time the expert was taking to express his admiration. "You've probably seen it at Gilbert's."

"Yes, of course, I remember."

"What do you think it is?"

"Well, if it was at Gilbert's, it's probably one of your *ancestors*," said Swann with a mixture of irony and deference toward a grandeur that he would have felt it impolite and absurd to ignore, but which, for reasons of good taste, he chose to refer to only in a playful manner.

"Of course it is," said the Duc bluffly. "It's Boson, the umpteenth member of the Guermantes family. But I don't give a damn about all that. You know I'm not as feudal as my cousin. Rigaud, Mignard, even Velázquez are some of the names I've heard mentioned," he went on, scrutinizing Swann like an inquisitor or a torturer in a dual attempt to read his thoughts and to influence his response. "Well, now," he concluded (for, when he was led to bludgeon someone into delivering the opinion he wanted to hear, it took only a few seconds for him to start believing that it had been spontaneously uttered), "come on, none of your flattery. Do you think it's by one of the big names I've just mentioned?"

"N-n-n-o," Swann replied.

"So what, then? I know nothing about these things, it's not for me to judge who painted this old fossil. But you're a lover of these things, a master of the subject—who do you think did it?"

Swann hesitated for a moment in front of this canvas; it was quite clear he thought it dreadful. "It was done by malicious intent, I should say," came his amused reply to the Duc, who could not repress a start of rage. This subsided, and he said: "Be good fellows, both of you, and wait a minute for Oriane. I'll be back as soon as I've put on my tails. I'll send word to my good lady that you're both waiting for her."

I chatted with Swann briefly about the Dreyfus case and asked him how it was that all the Guermantes were anti-Dreyfusards. "In the first place, because all these people are anti-Semitic at heart," replied Swann, although his experience made him perfectly well aware that some of them were not, but, like everyone who holds deep convictions, he preferred to explain the fact that other people did not share them by assuming that they had incurable preconceptions and prejudices rather than reasons that were more open to discussion. Also, as a man who had reached the premature end of his life, like a weary animal that is being tormented, he was loathing these persecutions and turning back to the spiritual fold of his fathers.

"I've certainly been told the Prince de Guermantes is anti-Semitic," I remarked.

"Oh, *him*! He's unmentionable. Do you know that, when he was in the army and had an excruciating toothache, he preferred to sit it out in agony rather than go to the only dentist in the area, who happened to be Jewish, and that later on, when a wing of his country house caught fire, he let it burn to the ground rather than send to the neighboring property—it belongs to the Rothschilds—for hoses?"

"Are you going to the reception at his place this evening, by any chance?"

"Yes," he replied, "although I really don't feel up to it. But he sent me a wire to tell me he has something to say to me. I can feel that I'm soon unlikely to be well enough to go and see him or to receive him myself—I'd find it too stressful—so I'd rather get it over with at once."

"Yet the Duc de Guermantes isn't anti-Semitic, is he?"

"But you can see for yourself he is, since he's an anti-Dreyfusard," replied Swann, not realizing that he was begging the question. "Nonetheless, I'm upset I disappointed the fellow—sorry! the Duc—by not admiring his Mignard or whatever he thinks it is."

"But at least," I continued, reverting to the Dreyfus case, "the Duchesse is a woman with intelligent views."

"Yes, she is charming. But for me she was even more charming when she was still the Princesse des Laumes. Her mind has become more sharp-edged somehow—it was all much softer in her younger days as a *grande dame*. But, anyway, what do you expect, younger or older, men or women, these people belong to a different race, they can't help it with a thousand years of feudalism in their blood. And, of course, they are under the impression that all that has absolutely no bearing on the views they hold."

"All the same, Robert de Saint-Loup is a Dreyfusard."

"Ah! So much the better, given that his mother is so anti. I'd heard he was, but I wasn't certain. That delights me. Nor does it surprise me—he's highly intelligent. That certainly counts for a lot."

Swann's Dreyfusism had made him extraordinarily naïve and shifted his way of looking at the world toward an impulsiveness, an instability of judgment more pronounced even than the similar effects of his marriage to Odette in the past; this recent class demotion was more like a reassessment of class and something entirely to his credit, since it made him return to the paths trodden by his own people from which he had been led astray by the aristocratic company he kept. But precisely at the moment when his clearsightedness enabled him, thanks to the principles inherited from his ancestors, to perceive a truth that was still hidden from society people, Swann nevertheless showed a comic capacity to hoodwink himself. He put everything he admired or disdained to the test of a new criterion, Dreyfusism. That the anti-Dreyfusism of Mme Bontemps should make him dismiss her as a fool was no more astonishing than that he should have thought her intelligent at the time of his marriage. Nor was it particularly serious that this new tide of opinion should affect his political judgments and make him forget that he had once branded Clemenceau as a man with mercenary motives, a British spy (an absurdity originating from the Guermantes circles), while he now declared that he had always regarded him as a voice of conscience, a man of steel like Cornély.[109] "No, I've never expressed a different view to you. You're thinking of someone else." But the tide washed beyond his political judgments and overturned Swann's literary judgments, too, even his way of expressing them. Barrès had lost any talent he once had, and even his early works were on the feeble side and scarcely the sort of thing you would want to reread. "Just try it, you won't be able to get to the end. How different from Clemenceau! Personally, I'm not anticlerical, but put them side by side and it's pretty clear that Barrès lacks any backbone. He's a very great man, our Clemenceau. He really knows the language!" Yet the anti-Dreyfusards were in no position themselves to criticize such madness. According to them, one was a Dreyfusard only because one was of Jewish origin. If a practicing Catholic like Saniette was also in favor of reviewing the case, it was only because he was cornered into it by Mme Verdurin, who conducted herself like a wild radical. Her foremost grudge was against "the cloth." Saniette was more foolish than malicious, and had no idea of the harm the Patronne was doing him. And if you pointed out that Brichot was equally a friend of Mme Verdurin but was also a member of the Patrie Française, that was because he was more intelligent.

"You see him occasionally?" I asked Swann, in reference to Saint-Loup.

"No, never. He wrote to me the other day asking me to persuade the Duc de Mouchy and various other members to vote for him at the Jockey—where he was accepted, for that matter, as smoothly as posting a letter."

"In spite of the Affair!"

"The question never came up. And let me tell you that since all this business began I never set foot in the place."

M. de Guermantes rejoined us and was shortly followed by his wife, now attired for the evening, tall and proud in a red satin gown, the skirt bordered with sequins. She wore in her hair a long ostrich feather dyed bright red, and over her shoulders a tulle wrap of the same color. "How smart to have one's hat lined in green," said the Duchesse, who missed nothing. "But with you, Charles, everything is so tasteful—what you wear, what you say, what you read, and what you do." Swann, meanwhile, without seeming to have caught these remarks, was contemplating the Duchesse as he might have studied the canvas of a master, and then sought her eyes, pulling his face into an expression that conveyed the word "Gosh!" Mme de Guermantes burst into laughter. "So you like the way I'm dressed. I'm delighted. To be honest, I can't say I'm very pleased with it myself," she continued with a sullen look. "God, what a bore it is to dress up and go out when it would be so much nicer to spend the evening at home!"

"What magnificent rubies!"

"Ah, my dear Charles, at least it's clear you know what you're talking about, not like that oaf Monserfeuil, who asked me if they were real. I have to admit I've never seen finer ones myself. They were a present from the Grand Duchess. They're a little on the large side for my liking, rather too much like claret glasses filled to the brim, but I'm wearing them because we shall see the Grand Duchess this evening at Marie-Gilbert's," added Mme de Guermantes, in no way suspecting that her last remark nullified what the Duc had previously told me.

"What's taking place at the Princesse's?" Swann asked.

"Oh, almost nothing," the Duc hastened to reply, thinking that this question meant that Swann had not been invited.

"What are you talking about, Basin? The world and his wife have been invited. We'll be crushed to death by tiresome people. What will be lovely, though," she added, looking discriminatingly at Swann, "if this storm in the air now doesn't break, will be those marvelous gardens. You know them, of course. I was there a month ago, when the lilacs were in flower. You can't imagine how lovely they were. And then the fountain—it's really like having Versailles in Paris."

"What sort of person is the Princesse?" I asked.

"Why, you know quite well, since you've seen her here, that she's as beautiful as the daylight, and also a touch stupid, but very nice, for all her Germanic haughtiness, full of kindness and blunders."

Swann was too shrewd not to realize that the Duchesse was trying to show off the "Guermantes wit," and in a rather cheap manner, since she was merely serving up a rather debased version of a few of her old quips. Nevertheless, to indicate to the Duchesse that he appreciated her intention to be amusing, and as though she really had been, he gave a rather forced smile, a particular form of insincerity that made me feel the same embarrassment I had experienced in the past when I heard my parents discussing the corruption of certain sections of society with M. Vinteuil (when they knew only too well that far greater corruption reigned at Montjouvain), or Legrandin coloring his speech for the benefit of fools, selecting subtle adjectives when he was perfectly well aware that they would be incomprehensible to his rich or smart yet illiterate audience.

"Come, now, Oriane, what are you saying?" said M. de Guermantes. "Marie stupid? Why, she's read everything, and she's musical to the tips of her fingers."

"But, my poor dear Basin, you're like a babe in arms. As if one couldn't be all that and rather stupid at the same time! 'Stupid' is too strong a word. No, she's fuzzy-minded, she's Hesse-Darmstadt, Holy Roman Empire, wa-wa-wa. Even her pronunciation sets me on edge. But I have to say she has a charming way of being batty. In the first place, the very idea of stepping down from her German throne to go marry a private individual, as if she were the most middle-class woman alive. It's true that she chose *him*! Ah, but of course," she added, turning to me, "you don't know Gilbert. To give you some idea, he's the man who once took to his bed because I left my calling card at Mme Carnot's.[110] . . . But, my dear Charles," said the Duchesse, changing the subject, since she could see that the story of the card and Mme Carnot seemed to anger M. de Guermantes, "you know, you've not sent me the photograph of those Knights of Rhodes you've taught me to love, and with whom I'm so keen to become acquainted."

During all this, the Duc's eyes had not left his wife's face. "Oriane, you might at least tell the whole story instead of keeping half of it back. I ought to explain," he said in rectification of her omission and addressing himself to Swann, "that the British ambassadress at the time, a very worthy woman, but one who tended to live on the moon and was apt to mismatch her guests, conceived the rather outlandish idea of inviting us with the president and his wife. Even Oriane was rather taken aback by this, especially as the ambassadress was familiar enough with people of our kind not to invite us to such an incongruous gathering. There was a minister present who's a known swindler . . . but the less said about that the better—we simply hadn't been warned, we were caught in a trap, though I have to say that all these people behaved very decently. And it would have been better left at that. But Mme de Guermantes, who rarely does me the honor of asking my opinion, thought fit to leave her card at the Élysée the following week. It was perhaps a bit extreme of Gilbert to regard that as a stain upon our name. But one simply has to bear in mind that, politics apart, M. Carnot, who as it happens held his position very respectably, was the grandson of a member of the revolutionary tribunal that saw eleven members of our family to their deaths in a single day."

"In that case, Basin, why did you use to go and dine at Chantilly every week? The Duc d'Aumale, too, was the grandson of a member of the revolutionary tribunal, but with this difference: Carnot was a decent man and Philippe-Égalité a dreadful villain."

"I'm sorry to interrupt, but I did send that photograph," said Swann. "I can't understand why it hasn't reached you."

"That doesn't altogether surprise me," said the Duchesse. "My servants tell me only what they want me to know. They probably have an aversion to the Order of Saint John." And she rang the bell.

"I was never very enthusiastic about those dinners at Chantilly, you know, Oriane."

"Not enthusiastic? That's why you took your nightshirt in case the Prince asked you to stay the night–which he rarely did, of course, being a complete lout, like all the Orléans family. Do you happen to know whom we're dining with at Mme de Saint-Euverte's?" Mme de Guermantes asked her husband.

"Apart from the guests already known to you, there'll be the brother of King Theodosius. He was invited at the last moment."

At this piece of news, the Duchesse's features were a picture of contentment, while her speech exuded boredom: "Oh God, more princes!"

"But this one is agreeable and intelligent," said Swann.

"Not entirely so, however," replied the Duchesse, who seemed to be seeking words that would convey her thought with more novelty. "Have you ever noticed with princes that the nicest of them are never entirely nice? No, I'm not joking. They always have to have an opinion about everything. And since they have no opinions of their own, they spend the first half of their lives asking us ours and the second serving them back up to us. They're not happy unless they can say that this has been well played and that not so well. Even when there's no difference. That little Theodosius Jr., now–I forget his name–once asked me what an orchestral motif was called. I told him," said the Duchesse, her eyes sparkling, and laughter bursting from her lovely red lips, " 'An orchestral motif, of course.' And, oh dear, he was none too pleased with that, really. Oh, my dear Charles," Mme de Guermantes continued listlessly, "how tiresome these dinners can be. There are evenings when one would sooner die! But of course dying is perhaps just as tiresome, since we don't know what it's like."

A servant appeared. It was the young fiancé who had come to grief with the concierge until the Duchesse, out of kindness, had restored a semblance of peace between them.

"Am I to inquire after M. le Marquis d'Osmond this evening?" he asked.

"Most certainly not; do nothing until tomorrow morning! There's not even any need for you to remain here tonight. His footman, who's a friend of yours, might well come round with news and send you out after us. Go out somewhere, anywhere, go and live it up, sleep out, but I don't want to see your face here before tomorrow morning."

The young footman's face was overjoyed. At last he would be able to spend long hours with his betrothed, whom it had become practically impossible for him to see since yet another scene with the concierge when the Duchesse had considerately explained to him that, to avoid further conflict, it would be better if he did not go out at all. The thought of finally having a free evening bore him on a tide of happiness that the Duchesse saw and understood. She felt something like a pang and an itching in her whole body as she imagined this happiness being enjoyed behind her back, concealed from her, and it made her irritated and jealous. "No, Basin, he's to remain here. He's not to stir out of the house."

"But, Oriane, that's absurd. You have all your servants here, and then, at midnight, there'll be the costumer and the dresser for the fancy-dress ball. There's absolutely nothing to keep him here, and since he's the only one who is friendly with Mama's footman, I'd much rather he be well out of the house."

"Look, Basin, will you just listen to me for a moment. It so happens I shall have a message for him in the course of the evening, I'm not sure at what time. You're not to stir from here for a second," she said to the despairing footman.

If there were constant quarrels, and if servants did not remain long with the Duchesse, the person responsible for this continual state of warfare was certainly there to stay, but that person was not the concierge. No doubt for the meatier tasks, for the tortures it was more strenuous to inflict, for the quarrels that ended in blows, the Duchesse entrusted the heavy tools to him; and these were roles he played without suspecting that he had been cast for them. Like her servants, he admired the Duchesse's kindness; even the less clearsighted of her footmen who had left her service and came back to visit Françoise were of the opinion that to be employed by the Duc would have been the best position in Paris if it had not been for the concierge's lodge. The Duchesse made use of the lodge in the same way as people have long made use of clericalism, Freemasonry, the Jewish peril, and so forth. A footman came into the room.

"Why has the package M. Swann sent not been brought up? And since you're here, has Jules come back yet? He went for news of M. le Marquis d'Osmond. You probably know that Mama is very ill, Charles."

"He's just arrived back, M. le Duc. They're expecting M. le Marquis to pass away at any moment."

"Ah, he's alive!" exclaimed the Duc with a sigh of relief. "So they're expecting, are they? To the devil with your expecting! While there's life there's hope," said the Duc cheerfully, turning to us. "They've already been talking about him as though he were dead and buried. In a week, he'll be chipperer than me."

"It's the doctors who said he wouldn't last the evening. One of them wanted to call again during the night. The head doctor told them it was pointless: M. le Marquis would be dead by then. They've only kept him alive by giving him enemas of camphorated oil."

"Shut up, you stupid fool!" shouted the Duc in a furious rage. "Who asked for your opinion? You haven't understood a word they told you."

"It wasn't me they told, it was Jules."

"I asked you to shut up!" roared the Duc, and he turned toward Swann: "How wonderful he's still alive! He's bound to regain his strength in due course. Still alive after such a critical turn—that in itself is really quite something. One can't expect miracles. It can't be too dreadful having a little enema with camphorated oil," he added, rubbing his hands. "He's alive. What more could one want? After all he's gone through, that's really quite impressive. To have a constitution like that is even something to be envied. Ah, these invalids, their every need is attended to in a way that ours aren't. At lunch today some blasted chef presented me with a leg of lamb and *sauce béarnaise*—done to a turn, I admit, but for that very reason I ate so much of it that it's still lying on my stomach. But that doesn't mean that people will come inquiring after me as they do after my dear cousin Amanien. There's too much inquiring going on. It's wearying for him. He needs breathing space. They're killing the poor man with their endless sending around for news."

"Just wait a moment," said the Duchesse to the footman as he was leaving the room. "I asked for the package with the photograph M. Swann sent to be brought up."

"It's so large, Mme la Duchesse, that I wasn't sure if it would get through the door. We've left it in the hall. Does Madame wish me to bring it up?"

"In that case, no. They should have told me, but if it's so big I shall see it later, when I come downstairs."

"I also forgot to tell Mme la Duchesse that Mme la Comtesse Molé left a card this morning for Madame."

"What, this morning?" said the Duchesse disapprovingly, being of the opinion that so young a woman ought not to take the liberty of leaving cards at that time of day.

"About ten o'clock, Mme la Duchesse."

"Bring me the cards."

"In any case, Oriane, when you say that it was a funny idea of Marie's to marry Gilbert," said the Duc, reverting to his earlier topic of conversation, "it's you who have a peculiar way of writing history. If anyone was a fool in that marriage, it was Gilbert, for choosing, of all people, a woman so closely related to the King of the Belgians, who has usurped the name of Brabant from us. In a word, we are of the same blood as the Hesse family, and of the elder branch. It's always stupid to talk about oneself," he said, addressing himself to me, "but it is true that whenever we've been to Darmstadt, and not only Darmstadt but even to Cassel and all over electoral Hesse, all the landgraves have invariably been courteous enough to yield us right of precedence as members of the elder branch."

"Oh, now, Basin, you're not trying to tell me that a person who was honorary commandant of every regiment in her country, who was to be engaged to the King of Sweden . . ."

"Really, Oriane, that's a bit much. Anyone would think you didn't know that the King of Sweden's grandfather was tilling the soil in Pau at a time when we had been holding pride of place all over Europe for nine hundred years."

"Which doesn't alter the fact that if someone were to say in the street, 'Look, there's the King of Sweden,' everyone would rush as far as the Place de la Concorde to see him, whereas if he said, 'There's M. de Guermantes,' no one would know who he was talking about."

"What sort of argument is that?"

"Nor can I understand how, once the title of Duc de Brabant has passed into the Belgian royal family, you can make any claim to it."

The footman returned with the Comtesse Molé's card, or, rather, what she had left to pass for a card. Claiming that she did not have one with her, she had produced from her pocket a letter addressed to herself, removed the contents of the envelope that bore the name "La Comtesse Molé," and folded down the corner to present it. Since the envelope was rather large, in accordance with that year's fashion in notepaper, this handwritten "card" was almost twice the size of an ordinary visiting card.

"This is an example of what people call Mme Molé's 'simple ways,'" said the Duchesse ironically. "She would have us believe she had no cards on her, so that she can show off her inventiveness. But we know all about that, don't we, my dear Charles? We're a bit too grown-up and inventive ourselves not to see into the mind of this little lady of four years' social experience. She's charming, but, for all that, it doesn't seem to me that she carries enough weight to imagine that she can amaze the world with the tiny effort it takes to leave an envelope instead of a card—and to leave it at ten in the morning. Her old mother mouse will show her that she knows a thing or two about those sorts of tricks."

Swann could not hold back his laughter at the thought that the Duchesse, who happened to be rather jealous of Mme Molé's success, would draw on her stock of "Guermantes wit" to find some insolent response to her visitor.

"As for the title of Duc de Brabant, I've told you a hundred times, Oriane . . ." the Duc resumed, but the Duchesse cut him short without listening.

"But, my dear Charles, I'm dying to see your photograph."

"Ah! *Extinctor draconis latrator Anubis*,"[III] said Swann.

"Yes, it was so charming, what you told me about that in connection with the San Giorgio in Venice. But why Anubis? I don't follow."

"What's the one like who was an ancestor of Babal?" M. de Guermantes asked.

"You want to see his Babby Babal, do you?" said Mme de Guermantes dryly, to show that she herself despised the wordplay. "I want to see them all," she added.

"Listen, Charles, let's go downstairs until the carriage comes," said the Duc. "You can pay your call on us in the hall, because my wife won't give us a moment's peace until she's seen your photograph. I'm less impatient, if the truth be told," he added complacently. "I can bide my time, but she would see us all dead first."

"What an excellent suggestion, Basin," said the Duchesse. "Let's go into the hall. At least we'll know why we've come down from your study, though we'll never know how we have come down from the counts of Brabant."

"I've told you a hundred times how the title came into the House of Hesse," said the Duc (as we moved off to see the photograph, and I thought of the ones that Swann used to bring me in Combray), "through the marriage of a Brabant in 1241 with the daughter of the last Landgrave of Thuringia and Hesse, so that really it's the title of Prince of Hesse that came to the House of Brabant, rather than that of Duc de Brabant to the House of Hesse. You'll remember that our battle cry was that of the Ducs de Brabant—'Limbourg to her conqueror!'—until we exchanged the arms of Brabant for those of Guermantes, something we were wrong to do in my opinion, and the example of the Gramonts will do nothing to make me change it."

"But," replied Mme de Guermantes, "since it's the King of the Belgians who conquered it . . . Besides, the Belgian Crown Prince is known as Duc de Brabant."

"But, my dear, what you're saying is unsound, it doesn't hold water. You know as well as I do that there are assumed titles that can perfectly well survive even if the territory is occupied by a usurper. For example, the King of Spain is yet another who describes himself as Duc de Brabant, on the grounds of rights to possession less ancient than ours, but more ancient than those of the King of the Belgians. He also calls himself Duke of Burgundy, King of the West and East Indies, Duke of

Milan. Yet he's no more in possession of Burgundy, the Indies, or Brabant than I am of Brabant myself—or the Prince of Hesse, if it comes to that. The King of Spain likewise proclaims himself King of Jerusalem, as does the Emperor of Austria, and Jerusalem belongs to neither."

He broke off for a moment, uneasy that the mention of Jerusalem might have embarrassed Swann, in view of "current events," only to resume at a faster pace:

"What you have just said could be applicable to anyone. In the past we were Ducs d'Aumale, a duchy that has passed as regularly to the House of France as Joinville and Chevreuse have to the House of Albert. We make no more claim to those titles than to that of Marquis de Noirmoutiers, which was at one time ours and became very regularly monopolized by the House of La Trémoïlle, but because certain transfers of titles are valid, it does not follow that they all are. For instance," he continued, turning to me, "my sister-in-law's son bears the title of Prince d'Agrigente, which comes to us from Joan the Mad, as the title of Prince de Tarente comes to the La Trémoïlles. Now, this title of Tarente was given by Napoleon to a soldier, who may well have done his job excellently, but by doing this Napoleon was giving away something that was not his to give, even less so than Napoleon III when he created a Duc de Montmorency, since Périgord at least had a mother who was a Montmorency, whereas the Tarente of Napoleon I had no more of a Tarente about him than Napoleon's wish that he should be created one. That didn't prevent Chaix d'Est-Ange, in some mention of your uncle Condé, from asking the imperial attorney if he had fished up the title of Duc de Montmorency from the moat at Vincennes."

"Look, Basin, I'd like nothing better than to follow you to the moat at Vincennes, or even to Taranto. Which reminds me, dear Charles, of something I wanted to say to you when you were telling me about your San Giorgio of Venice. Basin and I were thinking of spending next spring in Italy and Sicily. If you were to accompany us, think what a difference it would make! I'm not thinking only of the pleasure of having you with us, but imagine, after all you've so often told me about the remains of the Norman Conquest and of the classical world, just imagine what a trip like that would be like, with you as company! I mean, even Basin—what am I saying! I mean Gilbert—would benefit from it, because

I feel that even his claims to the throne of Naples and all that sort of thing would begin to interest me if they were explained by you in old Romanesque churches or in little villages perched on hills, as they are in primitive paintings. But we're going to look at your photograph. Unwrap it," said the Duchesse to a footman.

"Please, Oriane, not this evening! You can look at it tomorrow," begged the Duc, who had already been shooting me signs of alarm at the vast size of the photograph.

"But I need to look at it with Charles," said the Duchesse with a smile that was both misleadingly concupiscent and psychologically calculated, for, in her desire to please Swann, she spoke of the enjoyment this photograph would give her as of the benefit an invalid feels he would derive from eating an orange, or as though she had simultaneously planned to run off with several lovers and informed a biographer of tastes that were to her credit.

"In that case, he can make you a special visit," declared the Duc, to whom his wife was obliged to yield. "You can spend three hours together in front of it, if that's what you want," he added ironically. "But where are you going to put a toy as big as that?"

"In my bedroom, of course. I want to have it somewhere I can look at it properly."

"Well, just as you please. If it's in your room, there's little chance of my ever seeing it," said the Duc, heedless of the revelation he was so unthinkingly making about the negative character of his conjugal relations.

"Just make sure you undo it very carefully," Mme de Guermantes told the servant (she was being liberal with her instructions out of consideration for Swann). "And don't ruin the envelope, either."

"Even the envelope has to be treated with care!" the Duc whispered in my ear, raising his hands to the ceiling. "Say, Swann," he added, "what amazes me—dull, unimaginative husband that I am—is, how did you manage to find an envelope that size? Where of all places did you dig it up?"

"Oh, the photographers are always sending things like that. But the man's an oaf; I see he's written on it 'La Duchesse de Guermantes' and omitted 'Mme.' "

"I forgive him," said the Duchesse, her mind elsewhere; she seemed struck by a sudden idea of an amusing kind, but repressed a faint smile and returned her attention to Swann: "Come, now, you haven't told us—are you're coming to Italy with us?"

"I really don't think, madame, that it will be possible."

"Oh well, Mme de Montmorency is the luckier woman. You went with her to Venice and Vicenza. She told me that with you one saw things one would never see otherwise, things no one has ever mentioned before, that you'd shown her unheard-of marvels, and that even among the familiar things she learned to appreciate details that without you she would have passed by a score of times without ever noticing. She was clearly more privileged than we are to be. . . ." She turned to the servant: "You will take the huge envelope that contained M. Swann's photograph, and you will leave it with the corner turned down, as a calling card from me at Mme la Comtesse Molé's, at half past ten this evening."

Swann burst out laughing.

"I should like to know all the same," Mme de Guermantes asked him, "how you can tell ten months beforehand that it will be impossible to come with us."

"My dear Duchesse, I can tell you if you really want me to, but, first of all, you can see that I'm not at all well."

"True, my dear Charles, I don't think you look at all well, and it pains me to see you so out of sorts, but I'm not asking you to accompany us next week, I'm asking you come with us in ten months. Ten months is surely enough time to get oneself treated?"

At this point a footman came to announce that the carriage was at the door. "Come, Oriane, time to saddle up," said the Duc, who had been champing at the bit for some time now, just as if he had been one of the horses that stood waiting.

"Very well. Will you tell me in one word why you can't come to Italy?" the Duchesse challenged Swann as she rose to take leave of us.

"But, my dear friend, it's because I shall have been dead for several months by then. According to the doctors I've consulted, by the end of the year my present illness—and as far as that goes it could carry me off at any time—will leave me three or four months to live at the most, and even that is an optimistic estimate," replied Swann with a smile, as the footman opened the glass door of the hall for the Duchesse to leave.

"What on earth are you telling me?" the Duchesse burst out, stopping short for a second on her way to the carriage and raising her handsome, melancholy blue eyes, her gaze now fraught with uncertainty. Poised for the first time in her life between two duties as far removed from each other as getting into her carriage to go to a dinner party and showing compassion for a man who was about to die, she could find no appropriate precedent to follow in the code of conventions, and, not knowing which duty to honor, she felt she had no choice but to pretend to believe that the second alternative did not need to be raised, thus enabling her to comply with the first, which at that moment required less effort, and thought that the best way of settling the conflict would be to deny that there was one. "You must be joking," she said to Swann.

"It would be a joke in charming taste," replied Swann ironically. "I don't know why I'm telling you this. I've never mentioned my illness to you before. But since you asked me, and since now I may die at any moment . . . But, please, the last thing I want to do is to hold you up, and you've got a dinner party to go to," he added, because he knew that for other people their own social obligations mattered more than the death of a friend, and as a man of considerate politeness he put himself in their place. But the Duchesse's own sense of manners afforded her, too, a confused glimpse of the fact that for Swann her dinner party must count for less than his own death. And so, while still moving toward her carriage, she said with a droop of her shoulders, "Don't worry about the dinner party. It's of no importance!" But her words put the Duc in a bad mood, and he burst out: "Come along, Oriane, don't just stand there with your chatter, whining away to Swann, when you know very well that Mme de Saint-Euverte makes a point of having her guests sit down at the table at eight o'clock sharp. We need you to make up your mind. The horses have been waiting for a good five minutes now. Forgive me, Charles," he said, turning to Swann, "but it's ten minutes to eight. Oriane is always late, and it will take us more than five minutes to get to old Mother Saint-Euverte."

Mme de Guermantes made a decisive move toward the carriage and said a last farewell to Swann. "Look, we'll talk about this some other time. I don't believe a word you've been saying, but we need to discuss it, just the two of us. I'm sure they've given you unnecessary cause for alarm. Come and have lunch, any day you like"—for Mme de Guermantes, lunch was the answer to all problems—"you need only to let me know the day and the time." And, lifting her skirt, she set her foot on the carriage step. She was about to get in when the Duc caught sight of her foot and thundered out: "Oriane, you wretched woman, what are you thinking of? You're still wearing your black shoes! With a red dress! Go up quickly and change into your red ones. No, wait," he said, turning to the footman, "go and tell Madame's maid to bring down a pair of red shoes at once."

"But, my dear," said the Duchesse softly, embarrassed to see that Swann, who was leaving the house with me but had stepped back to let the carriage pass out in front of us, had heard this, "given that we're late . . ."

"No, no, we have plenty of time. It's only ten to. It won't take us ten minutes to get to the Parc Monceau. And anyway, what does it matter? Even if we arrive at half past eight, they'll still wait for us, but you simply can't go there in a red dress and black shoes. Besides, we won't be the last to arrive, believe me. The Sassensages are coming. You know that they never turn up before twenty to nine."

The Duchesse went up to her room.

"Huh!" said M. de Guermantes to Swann and me. "People laugh at us poor husbands, but we're not completely useless. If it weren't for me, Oriane would have gone out to dinner in black shoes."

"They were by no means a disaster," said Swann. "I noticed the black shoes and I didn't find them remotely offensive."

"You may be right," replied the Duc, "but it looks more elegant to have them matching the dress. Anyway, you can set your mind at rest. No sooner had she got there than she would have noticed, and I would have been the one who had to come back and fetch the others, which means I wouldn't have eaten till nine o'clock. Goodbye, my dear boys," he said, thrusting us gently away, "off you go, now, before Oriane comes down. It's not that she doesn't like seeing you both. On the contrary, she's too fond of seeing you. If she finds you still here, she'll start talking again. She's already very tired, and she'll be dead by the time she gets to that dinner. And, quite frankly, I have to tell you that I'm dying of hunger. I had a miserable lunch this morning, when I came from the train. That *sauce béarnaise* was damn good, certainly, but in spite of that I won't be sorry, no two ways about it, to sit down to dinner. Five to eight! That's women for you! She'll give us both indigestion before the night's out. She's far less robust than people think."

The Duc had absolutely no qualms in speaking in this way about his wife's petty discomforts and his own to a dying man, for, because they were what was uppermost in his mind, they seemed more important to him. And so, after he had gently steered us to the door, it was merely his jocund sense of good manners that led him to boom out after Swann, who was already in the courtyard, in a voice for all to hear:

"Now, mind you don't let all this damned doctors' nonsense get to you. They're fools. You're in strapping shape. You'll live to see us all in our graves!"

Notes

1. **Léon Daudet:** Daudet (1867–1942), prolific French novelist, essayist, journalist, and polemicist, was the son of the novelist Alphonse Daudet. This dedication is a mark of gratitude for the part Daudet played in the award of the Prix Goncourt to Proust in 1919.

PART I

1. **the Lusignan family:** in medieval romance, the fairy Mélusine is reputed to have founded the House of Lusignan, from which the Duc de Guermantes will later affirm that the Guermantes are descended.
2. **those musical instruments:** more sophisticated developments of the pianola (introduced into France in 1904), which could reproduce the characteristic style of a particular performer.
3. **the Ark of the Flood . . . Mount Ararat:** Genesis 8:4.
4. **Childebert:** Childebert, c. 495–558, son of Frankish King Clovis I.
5. **Boucher:** François Boucher (1703–70), French painter.
6. **"have money," "fetch water":** the bad grammar is noticeable only in French: Françoise says *"avoir d'argent"* instead of *"avoir de l'argent,"* etc.
7. **Mme de Sévigné:** the Marquise de Sévigné (1626–96), famous for her letters, particularly those to her daughter, Mme de Grignan. She figures importantly as a literary model for the narrator's grandmother.
8. **La Bruyère:** Jean de La Bruyère (1645–96), moralist, author of shrewd character portraits. The verb in question is *plaindre*.
9. **Whistler:** James Whistler (1843–1903), American painter who created a series of landscapes entitled *Harmonies*.
10. **Mérimée:** Prosper Mérimée (1803–70), author of short stories, novels, plays, known for playful and ironic treatment of Romantic themes.

11. Meilhac: Henri Meilhac (1831–97), best known for his collaborations with Ludovic Halévy (1834–1908) in producing the witty and irreverent libretti for most of Offenbach's operettas. The pair were reponsible for the comedy *Le Mari de la débutante* as well as the libretto for Bizet's *Carmen*.

12. Zaïre or possibly Orosmane: Orosmane is the Turkish Sultan in love with his Christian captive Zaïre, whom he kills in a fit of jealousy, in Voltaire's tragedy *Zaïre* (1732).

13. "Proudhon": Pierre-Joseph Proudhon (1809–65), anarchist and socialist theorist.

14. " 'Joy! . . . happiness!' ": Saint-Loup's words here are an (inaccurate) quotation from Pascal's *Mémorial*, the document he wore sewn into his clothing, recording his second, "mystical" conversion in 1654.

15. the Dreyfus case: cause célèbre that gave rise to *l'affaire Dreyfus* or the Dreyfus Affair, and which dominated French public life at the end of the nineteenth and beginning of the twentieth centuries.

In December 1894, Captain Alfred Dreyfus was convicted of spying for the Germans and sent to Devil's Island; Dreyfus was an officer in the French military intelligence; he was also Jewish. In 1896, however, new evidence came to light that suggested Dreyfus was innocent and implicated another figure, Commandant Esterhazy. Concern that Dreyfus's conviction might have been unsound was aired in public in late 1897, precipitating a controversy that was to divide French politicians and intellectuals deeply for over a decade, with ramifications that were to be felt for decades to come. The French military hierarchy closed ranks around Esterhazy (who, according to discoveries made by Lieutenant Colonel Georges Picquart, was very probably guilty) in order to conceal irregularities in Dreyfus's original trial. Dreyfus himself was returned to France in 1899 for a show trial that led to his conviction for a second time. He was finally pardoned, however, in 1906.

The Dreyfus Affair became the focal point for divisions that had been endemic in Third Republic France from the outset. The army's honor, Catholicism, and the identity of France as a nation-state were pitted against the universalist ideals of the Republic and its uncompromisingly secular framework. The Affair also brought into the open the widespread, but controversial, anti-Semitism that was so prevalent in some classes of French society (as we in fact see in Proust). Public figures could scarcely avoid taking sides as Dreyfusards or anti-Dreyfusards, but allegiances were not always predictable along straightforward political lines. Prominent Dreyfusards included Jaurès, Clemenceau, Péguy, Mirbeau, Anatole France, Joseph Reinach, Proust himself, and, of course, Zola, whose famous article "J'accuse" ("I Accuse," published in January 1898) became a rallying call for left-leaning intellectuals.

Important anti-Dreyfusards included Barrès, Rochefort, Maurras, Claudel, Valéry, and Drumont. The Dreyfus Affair placed writers and intellectuals center stage in French political debates; through the affair they claimed a position in French public life and ethical debates that they were to retain throughout much of the twentieth century.

It is not entirely clear from references in *Guermantes* exactly when this portion of the novel is set, but, broadly speaking, Proust depicts the late 1890s. I have indicated further precise details of the Affair in notes only where they are relevant to understanding the drift of the text. The Affair is notoriously complex, and my account here offers only the barest outline. For a more thoroughgoing account of the Affair and its ramifications, readers may consult Jeffrey Mehlman, "The Dreyfus Affair," in *A New History of French Literature*, ed. Denis Hollier (Cambridge, Mass., 1989), pp. 824–30.

16. Palissy's ceramics: Bernard Palissy (1510–90), French craftsman known for his ceramics and enamels.

17. Sedan: after his defeat at Sedan (September 1870), Napoleon III was imprisoned in a castle near Kassel; hence the question of Bismarck's permission.

18. a Fould or a Rouher: Achille Fould (1800–1867), a French banker who became minister of finance under Napoleon III. Eugène Rouher (1814–84), another figure of bourgeois origins, who became minister of commerce and agriculture under the Second Empire, and eventually prime minister in 1867.

19. Berthier or Masséna: Louis-Alexandre Berthier (1753–1815) and André Masséna (1756–1817) were famous marshals who collaborated closely with Napoleon.

20. the Danaids: in Greek mythology, the Danaids, the daughters of King Danaus, murdered their husbands on their marriage night and were subsequently condemned to fill up a leaky jar with water eternally in Hades.

21. Gutenberg and Wagram: the code names of two of the earliest Paris telephone exchanges. Proust here exploits their significance as proper names: the first of the inventor of printing, the second of the Prince de Wagram (1883–1918), who was known for his passion for motorcars and his collection of modern painting.

22. the *"Intran":* an abbreviation for *L'Intransigeant*, a daily newspaper founded in 1880.

23. the Institut: this is the Institut de France, which is made up of five academies (including the Académie Française). The academy in question here is the Académie des Sciences Morales et Politiques, as indicated by the name of one of its members, the economist Paul Leroy-Beaulieu (1843–1916), later in the paragraph.

24. M. Méline: Jules Méline (1838–1925), prime minister for two years during the Dreyfus case.

25. "a peasant of the Danube": an allusion to a fable by La Fontaine (*Fables*, XI, vii). The expression "peasant of the Danube" came to be used of unprepossessing people whose frank words expressed forgotten truths.

26. "Boucheron": a Parisian jeweler's on the Place Vendôme, founded in 1858.

27. "Rachel, when of the Lord": the tag attached to Rachel's name comes from an aria in Halévy's opera *La Juive*, first perfomed at the Paris Opéra in 1835.

28. a louis: twenty francs.

29. Taverne de l'Olympia: a much-frequented Parisian nightspot on the Boulevard des Capucines, near the famous theater of the same name, which had opened in 1893.

30. Prince Eugène: probably Eugène de Beauharnais (1781–1824), the son of Alexandre and Joséphine de Beauharnais, and Napoleon's stepson.

31. M. de Jussieu: probably Bernard de Jussieu (1699–1777), the most famous member of a whole family of botanists.

32. the Jardin de Paris: an open-air concert park.

33. *Wilhelm Meister:* the first part of *Wilhelm Meister* is almost entirely devoted to Meister's theatrical vocation and lingers upon the fascination of the theater wings and stage sets.

34. Watteau: Antoine Watteau (1684–1721), artist, well known for studies of actors, who left many red chalk sketches. The dancer described here is probably inspired by Nijinksi.

35. Mascarille: a comic character (the impudent valet) created by Molière.

36. Decamps: Alexandre-Gabriel Decamps (1803–60), French painter who specialized in Oriental subjects.

37. Darius: Darius I (550–486 B.C.), the Persian King who built Susa and Persepolis. Fragments of a frieze from Susa, depicting archers in long robes, are to be found in the Louvre.

38. "Decazes": minister of the interior in 1819, forced to resign after the assassination of the Duc de Berry in 1820.

39. "M. Molé": Louis-Mathieu, Comte Molé (1781–1855), prime minister under Louis-Philippe. He made the reception speech for the poet Alfred de Vigny at the Académie Française in 1845.

40. a story by Wells: Proust seems to have in mind H. G. Wells's *The Invisible Man* (1897).

41. Thiers: Adolphe Thiers (1797–1877), journalist and politician. President of the Republic 1871–73.

42. Messalinas: Messalina was the wife of the Roman Emperor Claudius, renowned for her debauchery.

43. **"Golden Rose"**: a jewel offered by the Pope to a Catholic princess on the fourth Sunday in Lent.

44. **Mme Ristori**: Adélaïde Ristori (1822–1906), Italian tragic actress with a great success in France.

45. **Coysevox**: Antoine Coysevox (1640–1720), whose sculptures adorn Versailles.

46. **abbess of . . . eastern France**: the Duchesse de Montmorency (1601–66) retired to the convent in Moulins after her husband was beheaded for conspiracy against Richelieu.

47. **"Joubert"**: Joseph Joubert (1754–1824), author of *pensées*, maxims, and letters.

48. **"Sylva"**: Carmen Sylva was the pen name of Elizabeth, Queen of Romania (1843–1916), who wrote stories and poems in German and French.

49. **Augier**: Émile Augier (1820–89), successful French dramatist of the Second Empire.

50. **"a frog . . . an ox"**: the allusion is to La Fontaine's fable (I, iii) about the frog who wanted to be as big as the ox.

51. **"M. de Borelli . . . Rostand"**: Raymond de Borelli (1837–1906), minor dramatist; Léon-Gustave Schlumberger (1844–1929) and Georges d'Avenel (1855–1939), historians; Pierre Loti, pseudonym for Louis-Marie-Julien Viaud (1850–1923), novelist; Edmond Rostand (1868–1918), dramatist.

52. **"M. Deschanel"**: Paul Deschanel (1855–1922), politician who became president of the Republic in 1920 for a brief time.

53. **"Pisanello and van Huysum"**: Antonio Pisanello (1395–1455), Italian painter; Jan van Huysum (1682–1749), Dutch landscape painter, specializing in still lifes and floral compositions.

54. **"M. Cherbuliez"**: Victor Cherbuliez (1829–99), a French novelist of Swiss origin, given to adventure novels with broad historical panoramas.

55. **"Hébert's *Virgin* or Dagnan-Bouveret"**: Ernest Hébert (1817–1908), painter of historical subjects and portraits; Jean Dagnan-Bouveret (1852–1929), a portrait painter much favored by the Parisian aristocracy.

56. **"*Farà da sé*"**: *l'Italia farà da sé* ("Italy will act on her own") was the slogan of nineteenth-century Italian nationalists who sought unification of their country without foreign intervention.

57. **"*Principiis obsta*"**: "Resist from the start," a quotation from Ovid, *Remedia amoris*, 91–92.

58. **"*Arcades ambo*"**: "Arcadians both of us": Virgil, *Eclogues*, VII, 4.

59. **" 'Does the bottle . . . drunk' "**: the line is in fact from the Romantic poet Alfred de Musset, not Augier.

60. **"*The Seven Princesses*"**: a play (*Les Sept Princesses*) written in 1891 by the Belgian poet and dramatist Maurice Maeterlinck (1862–1949). In one act, it concentrates essentially on decor and atmosphere rather than on action.

61. **"Sar Péladan"**: the French Decadent writer Joseph Péladan (1858–1918),

novelist, essayist, and author of "occultist" dramas. He claimed to be a Rosicrucian magus (Sar).

62. swan-drawn bark: a reference to the hero's appearance at the end of Act I of Wagner's *Lohengrin*.

63. the Zola trial: Zola was brought to trial in 1898, after the publication of his famous letter to the president of the Republic, published in *L'Aurore* of January 13 of the same year and entitled "J'accuse," proclaiming the innocence of Dreyfus after Esterhazy's acquittal.

64. "M. de Miribel": Miribel (1831–93) had been chief of staff of the French army.

65. "Henry": Colonel Hubert-Joseph Henry, an ardent anti-Dreyfusard, forged a crucial incriminating document against Dreyfus. This was exposed in 1898, and he was imprisoned. He committed suicide the day after his imprisonment.

66. "Moira": a divinity personifying destiny in Greek mythology.

67. "Patrie Française": an anti-Dreyfus league founded in 1898 by various literary figures, soon joined by a great many academics, opposed to a retrial.

68. the "Syndicate": during the Dreyfus Affair, French anti-Semites chose to imagine that the country was the victim of a conspiracy led by a Jewish "Syndicate."

69. "M. Émile Ollivier's": Émile Ollivier (1825–1913), minister of justice under Napoleon III, a somewhat discredited figure after his support for declaring war in 1870.

70. Paty de Clam: in charge of the first Dreyfus inquiry, and one of the witnesses in the Zola trial.

71. Cavaignac and Cuignet: Godefroy Cavaignac (1853–1905), war minister in 1898, continued to see Dreyfus as guilty and to oppose retrial, even after Cuignet, who was attached to his department in the War Ministry, had communicated Henry's forgery to him and Henry had been found guilty.

72. Reinach: Joseph Reinach (1856–1921) was a fervent supporter of retrial, and author of a monumental study of the Dreyfus Affair.

73. *"in petto"*: "deep down."

74. *"inter pocula"*: "in his cups"—i.e., to a close circle of friends.

75. Prince Henri d'Orléans: great-grandson of Louis-Philippe who publicly congratulated Esterhazy after his acquittal in February 1898.

76. "Chartres": the Duc de Chartres was father of the Prince d'Orléans.

77. "Princesse Clémentine": Clémentine d'Orléans, daughter of Louis-Philippe and mother to Ferdinand de Bulgarie.

78. "Caudine Forks . . . company": this alludes to a conference in September 1898, presided over by the newspaper editor Gérault-Richard, in which the Socialists were to discuss the Dreyfus Affair and at which Jaurès was to speak.

The Caudine Forks were the narrow pass where the Roman army was trapped by the Samnites in 321 B.C. and made to pass under the yoke.

79. **Japhetics:** the descendants of Japheth, the third son of Noah and father of the white race.

80. **M. Judet's ...** *Journal:* Judet adopted a Nationalist line in this newspaper.

81. **Brunetière's course of lectures:** Ferdinand Brunetière (1849–1906), French critic. Taught at the École Normale Supérieure and was director of the *Revue des deux mondes.*

82. **"Well, talk of ... himself":** a pun is involved here: in French, *quand on parle du loup* means "speak of the devil."

83. **Bernard:** Samuel Bernard (1651–1739), a French financier.

84. **Vaulabelle:** Achille Tenaille de Vaulabelle (1799–1879), journalist, politician, and historian.

85. **Voisenon or a Crébillon** *fils:* eighteenth-century authors of licentious fiction.

86. **"M. de Schlegel":** Wilhelm von Schlegel (1767–1845), German Romanticist, critic, philologist, and translator.

87. **"Diogenes":** legend has it that the Greek philosopher Diogenes (413–327 B.C.) lived in a tub in protest against wealth and superfluity and was to be found one day walking the streets of Athens in broad daylight with a lighted lamp in his hand. When asked why he was doing this, he replied, "I am looking for an honest man."

88. **" 'I see them ... with them' ":** the quotation is a pastiche of the French historian Jules Michelet (1798–1874).

89. **"Saint-Cyr":** convent school near Versailles, founded by Madame de Maintenon in 1686 for young ladies from impoverished noble families. Several of Racine's works were performed there by the pupils.

90. **"M. Drumont":** Édouard Drumont (1844–1917), pamphleteer and journalist, responsible for the dissemination of anti-Semitic and xenophobic ideas, who led a campaign against Dreyfus based on despicable arguments.

91. **the Droits de l'Homme:** this second league was founded in February 1898 and represented Dreyfusard intellectuals.

92. **Billot:** Jean-Baptiste Billot (1828–1907) was minister of war from 1896 to 1898.

93. **Clemenceau:** Georges Clemenceau (1841–1929) came to the political forefront thanks to the Dreyfus Affair. Proust is being fanciful about Reinach's influence in these two cases.

94. **Widal:** Fernand Widal (1862–1929), French doctor and bacteriologist.

95. **Python:** the oracular serpent Python was killed by Apollo.

96. **Charcot:** Jean-Martin Charcot (1825–93) was the founder of modern neurology. Freud was his most famous pupil.

97. **"People said . . . go out"**: an incomplete quotation from Mme de Sévi-gné's letter to the Comtesse de Guitaut, June 3, 1693.

PART II

1. **Aeolus with his goatskin:** in classical mythology, Aeolus is the ruler of the winds, which he can keep tied up in a sack to prevent them from blowing.
2. **Fromentin:** Eugène Fromentin (1820–76), painter, novelist, and art critic.
3. **Fifth Symphony:** of Beethoven.
4. *mousmé:* the French transliteration of a Japanese word *(musume)* meaning "girl" or "young woman," introduced into France in Pierre Loti's novel *Madame Chrysanthème* (1887).
5. **like Tiresias:** i.e., enigmatically, like the prophet in Greek mythology; **like Tacitus:** i.e., with the concision characteristic of this Roman historian.
6. **Irving and Frédérick Lemaître:** both famous nineteenth-century actors.
7. *Justice Shedding Light on Crime:* the slightly misquoted title of an allegorical painting by Pierre-Paul Prud'hon (1758–1823) in the Louvre.
8. **" 'Off' ":** the French plays with a pun occasioned by a grammatical mistake on Françoise's part. Albertine's correction of the grammar carries the implication (phonically) that Françoise is an old shrew.
9. **Fabrice's aunt . . . Count Mosca:** these are characters from Stendhal's novel *The Charterhouse of Parma.*
10. **Mordecai . . . Ahasuerus:** in the Old Testament book of Esther, Mordecai exposes a plot against the Persian King Ahasuerus (Xerxes), who learns, as his book of records is read aloud to him, that Mordecai, the cousin of his wife, Esther, has not been rewarded for this exposure, and hastens to redeem the situation. This material inspired Racine's tragedy *Esther,* from which the quotation here is taken. The lines are spoken by Ahasuerus as he deplores his failure to reward Mordecai earlier and offers as excuse (Act II, scene iii, lines 543–44): *"De soins tumultueux un prince environné / Vers de nouveaux objets est sans cesse entraîné."*
11. **Labori:** Fernand Labori (1860–1917), one of the most brilliant lawyers of his day. He defended Dreyfus and Zola.
12. *Sodome I:* the first part of *Sodom and Gomorrah* was originally published together with the second part of *Guermantes* in 1921.
13. **Van der Meulen:** Antoine Van der Meulen (1634–90), painter in the service of Louis XIV.
14. **the pillar of fire:** Exodus 13:21–22.
15. **the Roc:** the huge bird from the *Arabian Nights,* described in "The Story of Sindbad the Sailor."
16. **Comtesse Edmond de Pourtalès or the Marquise de Galliffet:** the former

(c. 1832–1914) was lady-in-waiting to the Empress Eugénie, wife of Napoleon III; the latter (1842?–1901) was the daughter of the financier Jacques Laffitte, and was renowned for her elegance.

17. *Dignus est intrare:* "He is worthy to enter" (i.e., "to qualify").

18. Agadir: the French presence in Morocco (supported by Britain and Russia) was challenged by Germany, notably in 1911, when a German gunboat was sent to Agadir.

19. *opus francigenum:* i.e., French Gothic art.

20. *Götterdämmerung: The Twilight of the Gods,* the fourth and final opera in Wagner's *Ring* cycle.

21. Mme Geoffrin (1699–1777), **Mme Récamier** (1777–1849), **and Mme de Boigne** (1781–1866): distinguished salon hostesses described by the nineteenth-century critic Sainte-Beuve. Proust used the *Mémoires* of Mme de Boigne to shape his portrait of Mme de Villeparisis.

22. Ossian: Between 1760 and 1763, the Scottish writer James Macpherson (1736–96) published poems purporting to be the work of a third-century Gaelic bard, Ossian. These had a marked influence on the development of Romantic poetry in France and Europe.

23. Chardin, Perronneau: Jean-Baptiste Chardin (1699–1779) and Jean-Baptiste Perronneau (1715–83), French painters.

24. Manet's *Olympia:* this canvas (1863) created a scandal when it was first exhibited in 1865 and remained controversial until it was eventually admitted to the Louvre in 1907 and hung near the "accepted" masterpiece, *La Grande Odalisque* (1814) of Ingres.

25. the silence . . . sleep: see Beaumarchais, *The Barber of Seville*, Act III, scene v: "The lack of noise that had sent Bartholo to sleep awakens him."

26. Parsifal's . . . flower-maidens: in the second act of Wagner's *Parsifal*, the hero finds himself in a field of flower-maidens sent to tempt him and to deflect him from his quest for the Holy Grail.

27. queens in Sardou's plays: the historical improbability of characters in the plays of Victorien Sardou (1831–1908) was a subject of mockery.

28. city of Giorgione: i.e., Venice.

29. La Sanseverina: the aunt of the hero, Fabrice del Dongo, in Stendhal's *The Charterhouse of Parma.*

30. Quartier de l'Europe: the district behind the Gare Saint-Lazare in Paris, where each street bears the name of a European city.

31. Mansard: François Mansard or Mansart (1598–1666), one of the creators of the classical style in French architecture.

32. Detaille: Édouard Detaille (1848–1912), French painter, particularly of military or historical subjects.

33. Ribot: Alexandre Ribot, minister of foreign affairs from 1890 to 1893.

34. Saxe: Maréchal de Saxe (1696–1750), celebrated for his military prowess and for a colorful private life.

35. Mlle de Reichenberg: French actress (1853–1924).

36. Widor: Charles-Marie Widor (1844–1937), French organist and composer.

37. "Starving Belly": the nickname arises from the fact that Mme de l'Éclin's ears are covered and relates to the French expression *Ventre affamé n'a pas d'oreilles* ("Words are wasted on a starving person" or, more literally, "A starving belly has no ears").

38. Robinson: a favorite pleasure ground and walking place for Parisians just to the south of the city.

39. the Serpent … family: the serpent is the emblem of the Barca family (Hamilcar and his daughter) in Flaubert's novel *Salammbô*.

40. "And if one alone …": the last line of the poem "Ultima verba" from Victor Hugo's collection *Les Châtiments* (1853). In French, *"Et s'il n'en reste qu'un, je serai celui-là."*

41. "Thanks to the gods! …": Racine, *Andromaque*, V, v, 1613. In French, *"Grâce aux dieux! Mon malheur passe mon espérance."*

42. Pliny the Younger or Mme de Simiane: both authors of literary correspondence. Pliny the Younger (c. A.D. 61–c. 112), Roman author known principally for his letters. Mme de Simiane (1674–1739), the granddaughter of Mme de Sévigné, with whom she corresponded, and whose letters she published.

43. the Princess Bedr-el-Budur: a character from the *Arabian Nights* with whom Aladdin fell in love.

44. *Les Diamants de la couronne*: a comic opera (1841) to music by Auber.

45. Parny's poems: Évariste-Désiré De Forges, Vicomte de Parny (1753–1814), pre-Romantic poet published in luxury editions.

46. Lemaire … Grandmougin: Gaston Lemaire (1854–1928), composer of light operas. Charles Grandmougin (1850–1930), patriotic poet and dramatist much favored by high society.

47. Council of Ten: this takes up the previous allusion to the Venetian Doges. The Council of Ten was created in Venice in 1310 to control the power of the Doges.

48. "Juro" that spelled the death of Molière: Molière, acting in his own play—*Le Malade imaginaire*, in 1673—was seized by convulsions and spat blood at a point in the play when he was about to utter the word "Juro" ("I swear"). He died a few hours later.

49. Mme Carvalho: a French singer (1827–95) who made her debut at the Opéra-Comique in 1850 and was particularly associated with the operas of Gounod.

50. Victurnienne: i.e., Mme d'Épinay.

51. the Field of the Cloth of Gold: the name of the plain in the Pas-de-Calais where François I and Henry VIII of England met in a vain attempt to form a joint alliance against Holy Roman Emperor Charles V.

52. Bussy d'Amboise: Louis Bussy d'Amboise (1549–79), governor of Anjou, whose duels and love conquests became legendary.

53. the great . . . Pradon: Gluck's opera *Iphigénie en Tauride* (1779) is generally thought superior to Piccinni's (1781), though both are inspired by the same subject. Similarly, Racine's *Phèdre* (1677) is recognized as superior to the tragedy *Phèdre et Hippolyte* written two years later by Pradon (1632–98) and set up to eclipse the Racine play.

54. people . . . Le Lion amoureux: Victor Hugo's *Hernani* (1830) established him as the leading Romantic dramatist in France. *Le Lion amoureux* (1866) is a historical comedy by François Ponsard (1814–67), whose work represented a reaction against Romantic drama.

55. Bellini, Winterhalter: it is not clear which of the three Venetian painters from the Bellini family Proust has in mind here. François-Xavier Winterhalter (1805–73), German painter who came to France in 1834 and became the official court portrait painter under the Second Empire.

56. *Le Cid . . . Le Menteur:* all three plays by Corneille (1606–84), the first two tragedies, the third a comedy.

57. *L'Étourdi:* an early comedy of Molière.

58. the Princess of Deryabar: a heroine from the *Arabian Nights*.

59. Général Mercier: Auguste Mercier (1833–1921), war minister between 1893 and 1895 (Dreyfus was arrested in 1894).

60. *"smoking":* in French, a dinner jacket is known as *"un smoking."*

61. Nimrod: a mighty hunter; see Genesis 10:9.

62. *L'Arlésienne:* Alphonse Daudet's 1872 drama, taken from one of his stories, in which the brother of the hero is simple-minded.

63. " 'mouthfuls' ": *une bouchée à la reine* is a kind of vol-au-vent. The words mean "a mouthful fit for a queen" and enable Mme de Guermantes to pun on the word *bouchée* here.

64. M. de Bornier: Henri de Bornier (1825–1901), French dramatist, author of the historical drama *La Fille de Roland* (1875).

65. *suave mari magno:* the opening words of a passage in Lucretius (*De natura rerum*, II, 1–2). The relevant passage translates as follows: "It is pleasant, when a vast sea is troubled by the winds, to gaze from the shore upon another's great tribulation."

66. " 'The gatherings . . .' ": from a duet in a comic opera by Louis-Joseph-Ferdinand Hérold (1791–1833), popular in the Romantic period. In French, *"Les rendez-vous de noble compagnie / Se donnent tous en ce charmant séjour."*

67. *"Les Mohicans de . . . Paris":* the list here represents a wild scramble of indiscriminate musical tastes and a half-baked literary awareness (*Les Mohicans de Paris* is by Alexandre Dumas, not Balzac).

68. **"When the child appears . . .":** the first lines of a poem from Hugo's *Feuilles d'automne* (1831), seen here as closer in spirit to the idyllic lyricism of the poetry of Mme Deshoulières (1638–94) than to the epic, visionary manner of Hugo's later collection, *La Légende des siècles* (poems written between 1840 and 1877). In French, *"Lorsque l'enfant paraît, le cercle de famille / Applaudit à grands cris."*

69. **Rémusat . . . Saint-Aulaire:** all three women were literary hostesses in the first half of the nineteenth century.

70. **Mallarmé's late poetry:** the late poetry of Stéphane Mallarmé (1842–98) is notorious for its demands on the reader.

71. **" 'Suffering is a fruit . . .' ":** the last lines of the poem "L'Enfance" from Hugo's collection *Les Contemplations* (1856). In French, *"La douleur est un fruit, Dieu ne le fait pas croître / Sur la branche trop faible encor pour le porter."*

72. **" 'The dead don't linger on . . .' ":** lines of another Hugo poem ("À un voyageur") from the collection *Les Feuilles d'automne* (1831). In French, *"Les morts durent bien peu. . . . / Hélas, dans le cercueil ils tombent en poussière, / Moins vite qu'en nos coeurs!"*

73. **a Réjane or a Jeanne Granier:** Gabrielle Réju, known as Réjane (1856–1920), and Jeanne Granier (1852–1939), both famous French actresses of the period.

74. **Pailleron:** Édouard-Jules-Henri Pailleron (1834–99), French dramatist, author of superficially witty comedies.

75. **Dumas *fils*:** Alexandre Dumas (1824–95), son of the famous novelist, who ranked as an important dramatist of the Second Empire.

76. **" 'These relics of the heart . . .' ":** a line from *La Nuit d'octobre* (1837) by the French Romantic poet Alfred de Musset. In French, *"Ces reliques du coeur ont aussi leur poussière!"*

77. **"Cambronne's expletive":** this is a euphemism for the word *merde* ("shit"). Thus the joke about "big M" and "big C" that follows.

78. **Schönbrunn:** the summer residence of the Habsburgs, close to Vienna.

79. **"Delaroche":** Paul Delaroche (1797–1856), Academic painter specializing in historical subjects.

80. **"M. Vibert":** Jehan G. Vibert (1848–1902), French painter who specialized in comic scenes.

81. **"Pampille":** the pseudonym of Mme Léon Daudet, a cooking-and-fashion journalist for the right-wing *L'Action française*. She published a regional cookbook in 1913.

82. E. de Clermont-Tonnerre: Élisabeth de Gramont, duchesse de Clermont-Tonnerre (1875–1954). The quote comes from her *Almanach des bonnes choses de France* (1920).

83. *Revue des deux mondes:* widely read bimonthly review founded in 1829. It covered the arts and culture, politics and economics.

84. "Coppée": François Coppée (1842–1908), French poet. His poetry drew upon descriptive realism to create an idealized representation of working-class Parisian life.

85. "Dame aux Camélias": Dumas *fils*'s play, *La Dame aux camélias* (1852), concerns the doomed passion of a courtesan and the son of an honourable family. It has achieved legendary status as the basis for Verdi's opera *La Traviata*.

86. "the Empress of Austria": assassinated in Geneva in September 1898. She was sister to the Queen of Naples, mentioned later in this conversation.

87. Moreau: Gustave Moreau (1826–98), French painter much admired by Symbolist and Decadent writers.

88. Queen Hortense: Hortense de Beauharnais (1783–1837), married against her wishes to Louis Bonaparte in 1802.

89. M. de Lafenestre: George Lafenestre (1837–1919), art critic who taught at the École du Louvre.

90. *Mérope* or *Alzire:* tragedies by Voltaire, 1743 and 1736 respectively.

91. " 'How long it is . . .' ": lines from Hugo's poem "Boaz endormi." In French, *"Voilà longtemps que celle avec qui j'ai dormi, / Ô Seigneur, a quitté ma couche pour la vôtre!"*

92. Tallemant des Réaux: Gédéon Tallemant des Réaux (1619–92), French memorialist.

93. the Ten Thousand: the expedition of ten thousand Greeks led to conquer the Persian Empire, recounted in Xenophon's *Anabasis*.

94. beneath the . . . Duc de Berry: Proust is alluding here to two murders. The first connects the names Choiseul and Praslin: in 1847, Charles de Choiseul, Duc de Praslin, murdered his wife and then poisoned himself. The second links the names Lucinge and Berry: the Duc de Berry was murdered by a workman in 1820; the Princesse de Lucinge was his daughter.

95. Mme Tallien or Mme de Sabran: Mme Tallien (1773–1835), a beauty of the Directory period. Mme de Sabran (1693–1768), one of the mistresses of the Regent Philippe d'Orléans.

96. the La Fontaine fable: "The Miller, His Son, and the Donkey" (*Fables*, III, i).

97. Carrière: Eugène Carrière (1849–1906), painter of portraits and family scenes.

98. Boulle: André-Charles Boulle (1642–1732), French cabinetmaker. His work represents the height of Louis XIV style.

99. Bing: Siegfried Bing (1838–1905), French collector who introduced an Art Nouveau style of furnishing.

100. *nunc erudimini:* "now . . . be instructed" (Psalms 2:10).

101. "I am widowed . . . ' ": *"Je suis veuf, je suis seul, et sur moi le soir tombe."*

102. Bagard: César Bagard (1639–1709), woodcarver and decorator.

103. Whistler: Charlus seems to be referring to remarks made in Whistler's piece "Ten o'Clock," collected in his *The Gentle Art of Making Enemies* (1890).

104. the Panther of the Batignolles: the name of a Parisian anarchist circle around 1880.

105. the Steel King: the American industrialist Andrew Carnegie (1835–1919).

106. Maurel: Victor Maurel (1848–1923), famous French baritone who had sung Wagner.

107. the Balzac novel: in fact, three pieces of fiction, which Balzac published between 1833 and 1835 under the title *L'Histoire des Treize* (*The History of the Thirteen*). The Thirteen of the title refers to thirteen select men recruited to form a "special world."

108. Egerias: counselor, adviser. From the name of the nymph who instructed Numa Pompilius (753–673 B.C.), second king of Rome.

109. Cornély: Jean-Joseph Cornély (1845–1907), French journalist whose initial sympathies were Royalist but who came out in support of Dreyfus in 1897 and subsequently worked for the radical press.

110. Mme Carnot: the wife of French President Sadi Carnot (1837–94). He was president from 1887 until his death by assassination.

111. *"Extinctor . . . Anubis":* "Barking Anubis, slayer of the dragon." Swann's words read obscurely here, but Proust's rough draft would suggest that this is a Latin motto struck on the medallion of one of the knights of the Order of Saint John of Jerusalem in the series of photographs sent to Mme de Guermantes.

Synopsis

La Berma compared to Elstir (45). The arrival of the Duchesse de Guermantes in the box of the Princesse de Guermantes (46). The style of the two women compared (47). Mme de Cambremer and her social aspirations (48–51). The Duchesse de Guermantes acknowledges my presence with a smile (52).

My daily attempts to run into Mme de Guermantes in the street (52). My successive images of her (53–57). Françoise's silent disapproval and perplexing attitude toward me (57–61). My obsession with Mme de Guermantes prevents me from working (61). Her apparent displeasure at my attempts to run into her leads me to a different tactic (62–63): I decide to visit her nephew Saint-Loup in his garrison, in an attempt to approach the Duchesse through him (63–64).

Doncières
Arrival at the cavalry barracks and Saint-Loup's welcome (64–67). His room (67–68). Different qualities of noise and silence (68–71). My first night, spent in Saint-Loup's room (72). I study the photograph of Mme de Guermantes (73–74). Morning view of the surrounding countryside (74–75). My hotel in Doncières (75–78). The world of sleep (78–82). Field maneuvers (84–85). My visits to the barracks (85–86). Saint-Loup's popularity (86–88). The streets of Doncières at nighttime (88–91). Dinner with Saint-Loup and his friends (91–93). I ask him to mention me to his aunt and ask him for her photograph (93–96). His desire to show me off to his friends (97–98). His denial of the rumors of his engagement to Mlle d'Ambresac (98). The army and the Dreyfus case (99). Major Duroc (99). Discussions of military strategy (103–11). Battles and ideas (105–7). Is there an aesthetics of military art (107)? The general and the particular (111). The pleasure these dinners provide (111). Yet I am still oppressed at times by the memory of Mme de Guermantes (113–15). The rift between Saint-Loup and his mistress (115). Silence as a powerful weapon and the pains of uncertainty (116–17). Saint-Loup's dream (117). Rupture with his mistress avoided (118). Elstir's paintings as a pretext for a visit to Mme de Guermantes (119–20). The Prince de Borodino and his barber (121). The merits of the various officers (121). The Prince de Borodino and Saint-Loup: a confrontation of two types of nobility (122–27). My grandmother's telephone call (126–30). The Young Ladies of the Telephone and the miracle of the voice heard across distance (127–28). The distress caused by this telephone call and my decision to return to Paris (129–31). Strange salute from Saint-Loup, to whom I fail to say goodbye (132–34).

Paris
I return to discover my grandmother aged and changed by illness (134–35). Mme de Guermantes does not invite me to see her Elstir paintings (135). The end of winter (136–37). Resumption of my morning walks and meetings with

the Duchesse (137–39). My afternoon dreams (139–40). A brief visit from Saint-Loup (140–41). Speech habits of Françoise and her daughter (141–42). Memory of plans for an Italian journey (142). My father is resigned to the idea of my becoming a writer, but I am unable to start writing (143). His changed opinion of the Duc de Guermantes (144); he advises me to frequent the salon of Mme de Villeparisis (144–45). His strange encounter with Mme Sazerat (145); her Dreyfusard sympathies (146).

Saint-Loup comes to Paris on leave (147). On my way to meet him, I encounter Legrandin, who professes to despise the world of society (147–48). I accompany Saint-Loup to meet his mistress in the suburban village where she lives (148–49); his devotion to her (149–50); the Boucheron necklace (150). Blossoming pear trees (150–51). I recognize Saint-Loup's mistress as "Rachel, when of the Lord" (152). The power of the imagination (152–54). Return to Paris by train; Rachel's encounter with two tarts at the station and the possible effect of this on Saint-Loup (155–57).

Rachel's conversation at lunch: her reaction to Dreyfus (158). Saint-Loup's jealousy (158–59). Rachel and Aimé, the headwaiter from Balbec (159–60). Literary conversation with Rachel (160–61). Her maliciousness (161). M. de Charlus comes looking for his nephew (162). Rachel and Saint-Loup quarrel, and he moves to a private room, to which we are later summoned in turn (163–64). The quarrel is made up (164). The effects of champagne (165).

At the theater; my new views about actors (166–67). Rachel's cruelty to a young actress (166–67). Rachel's transformation onstage (168–69). Backstage (170–71). Robert's explanation of his strange salute the day I left Doncières (170). The strange dancer, who provokes another fit of jealousy in Saint-Loup (171–72). A further quarrel and Rachel's cruelty (172–74). Saint-Loup slaps an onlooking journalist (175). Street incident: Saint-Loup attacks the loiterer who accosts him (176–77). I leave Robert and agree to meet him later at Mme de Villeparisis's (177).

An afternoon reception at Mme de Villeparisis's; her social decline; her literary gifts (178–80). Her desire to set up a brilliant salon and to attract Mme Leroi (182). Furnishings and portraits in her drawing room (182–83). Her distance from the Dreyfus Affair (183). My old school friend Bloch (183–85). The Fronde historian (186). The Duc de Guermantes's joke about the Queen of Sweden (187). Mme de Villeparisis's memoirs (187–88). Arrival of the old lady with Marie-Antoinette hair (189); the "three Fates" of the Faubourg Saint-Germain (189–92). The portrait of the Duchesse de Montmorency (192). Arrival of the Duchesse de Guermantes (193). Arrival of Legrandin and his social behavior (194–96). Mme de Guermantes and Madame de Cambremer (197). Mme de Guermantes's face and presence devoid of the glamour of her name (198–99). Her luncheons with distinguished men (200–202). Her Mérimée/

Meilhac/Halévy cast of mind (201). Her influence on writers (201–2). Her views on Bergotte (205–6). Arrival of the Comte d'Argencourt, the Baron de Guermantes, and the Duc de Châtellerault; the fashion of hats on the floor (206–7). Reactions to Mme de Villeparisis's flower painting (207–8). The overturned vase and Bloch's bad manners (209). The peremptory behavior of Mme de Villeparisis toward her princely relatives (209–10). Sir Rufus Israels and Bloch's lack of breeding (212–13). M. de Norpois joins the party and is introduced to Bloch (214–15). Norpois's tastes in literature and painting (216–17). Arrival of M. de Guermantes (217). Norpois and my father's candidacy for the Academy (218–19). Mme de Guermantes on love, on Rachel, on Odette Swann, on Maeterlinck, on Mme de Cambremer (221–26). Norpois and Bloch discuss the Dreyfus Affair (226–29). The laws of imagination and of speech (229–30). Saint-Loup's Dreyfusism offends the Faubourg Saint-Germain (230–32). Further conversation between Norpois and Bloch on Dreyfus (233–40). Bloch's subsequent exchanges with Argencourt, Châtellerault, and the archivist (240–41). Bloch's departure and Mme de Villeparisis's feigned sleep (242). Further ironic responses to Maeterlinck from Mme de Guermantes (243). Arrival of Mme de Marsantes, Robert's mother (243). Mme Swann and Dreyfus (246). Saint-Loup arrives (248). Mme de Guermantes in conversation with me (248). Norpois and the Prince de Faffenheim (249–57). The arrival of Mme Swann, and Mme de Guermantes's prompt departure (257). Arrival of Charlus ("my uncle Palamède") (257). In connection with Mme Swann, I remember a recent visit from Charles Morel, the son of my uncle's old valet (257–60). Mme Swann, and the "lady in pink" (260–61). Charlus and Mme Swann (261). Charlus, Mme de Villeparisis, and the money order (261–63). Charlus's coldness toward me (264). Mme Swann reveals Norpois's opinion of me (265). Mme de Villeparisis's affected disdain for Mme Leroi (267). I discover that Charlus and the Duc de Guermantes are brothers (271–72). The Boucheron necklace and Saint-Loup's departure (272–73). His mother's distress (275–77). Mme de Villeparisis tries to dissuade me from leaving with Charlus (277–78).

Charlus offers to guide my life (279–81). His dreadful, almost deranged remarks about Bloch's family (281–84). He renews his offer to guide me (284–85). A frosty encounter with M. d'Argencourt (285–86). Charlus advises me to avoid society (287). His views on Mme de Villeparisis's family (287–88). His advice on my choice of friends (289). His strange choice of a cab (289–90).

I return home to an argument about the Dreyfus Affair between two butlers (290–91). I find my grandmother's health has worsened (291).

My grandmother's illness (292). Cottard's visit (292). The thermometer (292–94). Dr. du Boulbon's visit and diagnosis (295–300). He reassures us (300). A letter from Saint-Loup (301). An outing to the Champs-Élysées with my grandmother (301–3). The "Marquise" of the little pavilion and the park-keeper (303–5). My realization that my grandmother has had a slight stroke (305–6).

PART II: CHAPTER 1

On the Avenue Gabriel, encounter with Professor E—, who agrees to examine my grandmother (309–10). The approaching presence of death (310–12). "There is no hope for your grandmother" (314). We return home; my mother's silent distress (314). Françoise's scrutiny (315). False reassurance (316). Françoise's devotion (317). Cottard prescribes morphine (318). My grandmother hides her pain (319). Sickness as a sculptor (320). The specialist X (320–21). My grandmother's sisters remain in Combray (321). Daily visits from Bergotte, a sick man himself (321–22). The growing success of his books; I admire him less now (322–23). Time and the work of art (323–24). Visit from Mme Cottard (325). Kind attention from the heir to the Grand Duchy of Luxembourg (325–26). Françoise's odd code of priorities (326–28). My grandmother's condition worsens (328–29). She attempts suicide (329). Françoise combs her hair (330). The leeches (330–31). My mother wakes me in the middle of the night (331). My grandmother seems transformed into a beast (332). The Duc de Guermantes calls (332–33). My mother fails to reply to his greeting (334). Saint-Loup arrives (334). My grandmother's brother-in-law, the monk (335). The oxygen cylinders (336). Françoise and grief (336–37). Our "dutiful" cousin (337–38). Dieulafoy's visit (338–39). My grandmother's death (340–41).

PART II: CHAPTER 2

A Sunday morning in autumn (342). The mist and memories of Doncières (342–43). My parents away in Combray: my plans for the evening (343). The water heater (343). Mme de Stermaria's divorce (344). Saint-Loup breaks with Rachel but sees her from time to time (344–45). A letter from him encouraged me to contact Mme de Stermaria, to whom I send a letter suggesting a rendezvous (346). A visit from Albertine (347). The Balbec Albertine and Albertine now (347–48). She has matured (349). I find her physically attractive (350). Changes in her vocabulary (351–54). Tickling on the bed (354). Françoise interrupts (354). Françoise's powers of divination and her language of disapproval (354–56). Françoise leaves (357). Albertine's kiss and the successive images it provokes (357–63). Her social ideas (364–65). Albertine leaves, and I am brought a note from Mme de Stermaria, agreeing to dine with me the following Wednesday (366). I arrive late at Mme de Villparisis's, where I encounter

Mme de Guermantes, no longer infatuated with her, thanks to my mother's intervention (367). My morning walks now have a different purpose: I am looking for new premises for Jupien (367–68). My observations on these walks (369–70). Encounters with Norpois and a tall woman [later disclosed as the Princesse d'Orvillers in *Sodom and Gomorrah*] (369). Mme de Guermantes sits with me and invites me to dinner (370). The motivation behind such an invitation (371–74). Our conversation about M. de Charlus (374–77). Mme de Guermantes leaves (377). Her capacity for not bearing grudges (377). A brief rift between Bloch and myself: Charlus refuses to acknowledge him (378–79).

Mme de Stermaria: days of waiting (379–80). Evocation of previous excursions to the Bois de Boulogne (380–82). Mme de Stermaria associated with the mists of Brittany (382). I go to the Bois with Albertine to make reservations for my dinner with Mme de Stermaria: excursion to Saint-Cloud (383–86). The following day: preparation for my dinner appointment (386–87). Mme de Stermaria calls off the engagement (388). My despairing reactions (389). Arrival of Saint-Loup (390).

Saint-Loup invites me to dine with him at a restaurant (390). Reflections on friendship (391–92). Memories of Doncières (392–93). We leave for the restaurant: the fog in the streets; writing and the need for solitude; the "invisible vocation . . . subject of this book" (393–94). Saint-Loup's remarks to Bloch about me (395). At the restaurant: two rooms, two coteries—Dreyfusard intellectuals and young aristocrats (396–97). I negotiate the revolving door; frosty reception from the proprietor (397–98). Other arrivals out of the fog; the Prince de Foix (398–99). Marriage prospects and the Prince de Foix's friends (400–402). The restaurant proprietor (402–4). The Jews (404–5). The pure Frenchman (405). I am introduced to the Prince de Foix (406). Malicious gossip about the Duke of Luxembourg (406–7). Saint-Loup's acrobatics and the vicuña cloak (407–8). An invitation from M. de Charlus (408). Saint-Loup's distinction, the nobility of his race, a work of art (409–11).

Dinner with the Guermantes; the Duc's welcome (412). His language and manners and the survival of the past (412–14). I visit the Guermantes Elstirs (414–18). I join the other dinner guests (418–19). The flower-maidens (419–20). My meeting with the Princess of Parma (420–23). Reasons for her amiability (423–24). Comte Hannibal de Bréauté-Consalvi (425–27). The Duc de Châtellerault, the Prince de Foix, Prince Von (427–28). The Guermantes' craze for nicknames (428). The Prince d'Agrigente (428–29). The absence of M. de Grouchy (429–30). We proceed to the table (430). M. de Guermantes's manner and the court of Louis XIV (431–33). The Princess of Parma and Guermantes superiority (433–34). The Guermantes physique (434–36). The family genie (436–37). The Guermantes and the Courvoisiers (437–39). The art of keeping one's distance

(439–42). The antipathy of the Courvoisiers toward Mme de Guermantes (442–43). Intelligence and talent as social values for the Guermantes (443–48). The Duc a bad husband but a valuable social accomplice to his wife (449). The salon of the Princess of Parma (450–53). Wit and the Guermantes salon (454–58). The "imitations" of Mme de Guermantes (457). Her intimidating presence on her visits to relatives (458). The Princesse d'Épinay (458). Witty remarks and puns of Mme de Guermantes (460–61). "Teaser Augustus" (461). The Courvoisiers incapable of appreciating the Duchesse's wit or rising to her social innovations (463). Mme de Guermantes's artistic tastes (466). Her morbid need for arbitrary novelty (467). M. de Guermantes acts as a foil to his wife's wit (468–69). The Guermantes and politics: social conduct and political conduct (470–73). "Oriane's latest" (474). The Duc's mistresses; Mme de Guermantes's relation to them (476–80). Late arrival of M. de Grouchy (480). The Duchesse's unkindness to her footman Poullein (481). Her sarcasm about her cousin Mme d'Heudicourt (483–85), about the dramatist Bornier (485–86). Various views of literary correspondence (487). The musical and literary tastes of M. de Guermantes (487–88). Mme d'Arpajon and poetry (488). The Duc de Châtellerault and the footman (489–90). The literary tastes of the Duchesse de Guermantes; her views on Hugo (490–93). My exchange with the Princess of Parma's lady-in-waiting: mistaken identities (494–95). Mme de Guermantes on Zola (495–96). The Guermantes on Elstir: *A Bundle of Asparagus*; the portrait of the Duchesse (496–99). The purity of the Duchesse's speech and her closed mind (499–500); the magic of her name absent from her presence (500). M. de Bréauté's particular brand of snobbery (500–1). Mme de Guermantes on her aunt (Mme de Villeparisis) (501). An exchange between Mme de Villeparisis and Bloch (501–2). The Duc and Duchesse differ over Charlus's mourning for his wife (504–5). Saint-Loup needs to ask a favor of Mme de Guermantes about his posting in Morocco (505–6). Her exasperation with her nephew's way of speaking (506). Prince Von's remarks to me about Saint-Loup, Rachel, and Charlus (506–7). The Queen of Naples in mourning (508). Général de Monserfeuil, and Saint-Loup's desire not to return to Morocco (509). After-dinner rituals of *tilleul* and orangeade (510–11). The Duchesse's refusal to help Saint-Loup through Monserfeuil (511–12). The pollination of flowers by insects (513). Marriages between flowers and marriages between people: Swann (514). Mme de Guermantes and the Empire style (515). The Iénas, the Princess of Parma, and the Duc de Guastalla (516–19). The Duchesse de Guermantes on innovation in art (520). Manet's *Olympia* (520). Remarks on Dutch painting: Hals and Vermeer (521). My depreciated view of the Guermantes (522–23). The Hals of the Grand Duke of Hesse (524). The intelligence of the Kaiser (524–25). Opinions of English royalty (525). I learn from Mme de Guermantes that I am liked by M. de Norpois (526). She gives her views on an anticipated marriage between Norpois and Mme de Villeparisis (527). Genealogies from the Duc de Guermantes (528–29). The name Saintrailles provokes a memory of Combray (529). The poetry of genealogy saves my evening from disappointment (530). Further gossip about the Grand Duke of Luxembourg distresses me (531). "But he's Oriane's cousin!": a rallying cry during the evening (532–33). The Turkish ambassadress (533). Further effects of genealogies: names and facts (534). More malicious gossip about the Duke of Luxembourg (535). The Turkish ambassadress makes unsavory insinuations about M. de Guermantes (537–38). Further genealogies: the mobility of names; my historical curiosity and aesthetic pleasure (538). The Guermantes doormat no longer a threshold to the magic world of names (540). My attempts to leave (541). The "flower-maidens" leave after the Princess of Parma (542). I am detained by the verbal elegance of my hosts (543). My snowboots and my departure (544).

In the carriage taking me to my appointment with M. de Charlus, my exhilaration and melancholy as I review the evening's events (545–46). Reflections on Victor Hugo provoked by hearing his work quoted by Mme de Guermantes (547). What the social world can teach us (548).

My visit to M. de Charlus after the Guermantes dinner party: a long wait in a drawing room (550). M. de Charlus and his servants (550–51). He receives me in his dressing gown with haughty condescension and anger (551). The cover decoration of the book by Bergotte (552). The test to which he has submitted me; his angry reproaches; my disclaimers and his mounting fury (552–56). In a fit of anger, I trample on his top hat and start to leave (556). He calls me back but refuses to say who has maligned me to him (557). He calms down and eventually decides to drive me home (558). Description of his green drawing room (559). Despite his affirmations that we shall never see each other again, he finds a pretext for a further meeting (560). His contempt for the Princesse d'Iéna (561–63). His admiration for the Princesse de Guermantes, to whose society he holds the key (562–63). I arrive back home to discover a letter from Françoise's footman to his cousin (563–64).

About two months later, I receive an invitation from the Princesse de Guermantes (565). The imaginary value and variety of society people (565–66). The reality and diversity of people despite the "tyranny" of their immediate presence: Mme de Montmorency and Mme de Guermantes (566–68). The exclusive salon of the Princesse de Guermantes (568). Needing reassurance that the Princesse's invitation is genuine, I decide to call on the Duc and Duchesse de Guermantes, who have gone out (569). I keep watch for their return from a vantage point in our apartment (569). The view of surrounding courtyards and houses (569–71). I resume my watch in the afternoon and make a discovery to be described later [see the opening section of *Sodom and Gomorrah*] (571). The Duc receives me in his library (571). Various visitors announce the critical illness of Amanien d'Osmond, the Duc's cousin; the Duc's self-interested response (572–73). The Duc's unhelpful attitude toward my inquiries about the invitation from the Princesse de Guermantes (574). Swann arrives, greatly changed (575). His opinion of the Duc's "Velázquez" (577). Swann's Dreyfusism and altered sense of judgment (578–81). Mme de Guermantes joins us; her attempts to be witty at the expense of the Prince and Princesse (581–82). Her unkindness to her young footman (584–85). Further self-interested reactions from the Duc at the news of his dying cousin (586). Mme Molé's visiting card (588). Swann's illness and Mme de Guermantes's reaction (592–95). The red shoes (594).